Book Three
January 1978 – December 1978

Also by LK Hunsaker

Finishing Touches
Off The Moon
Protect The Heart
Moondrops & Thistles

The Rehearsal Series

A Different Drummer
The Highest Aim
Of Chaotic Currents

For Children

Stanley: A Raindrop's Story

Rehearsal
Of Chaotic Currents

a novel

LK Hunsaker

*"Nobody, as long as he moves about among the chaotic
currents of life, is without trouble."*
Carl Jung

Elucidate Publishing
PO Box 1262, Hermitage PA 16137

United States of America

This novel is also available in electronic format.

Dedication

To the America of my youth and all of its huge potential through good and bad, celebration and devastation. May that light always shine in the harbor and upon us all.

Acknowledgements

My biggest thanks must go to my family. I get fully obsessed while working on this series and they often don't see me for days other than on a brief clip to the kitchen for more coffee where sometimes I hear them speak to me and sometimes I respond. I appreciate their unending patience and the times when they insist I reappear in the "real" world.

Also, and again, to Liz, my first reader for every book. Every book is better because of her input.

Thank you to Annette McRoberts for catching my typos and for questioning sentence structures.

Thanks to those along the way who have been influential in making me a better writer: Dorothy Murphy, my mom who has a nice way with words and passed it along; Kathi, Richard, & Kelli, my siblings who let me practice on them by correcting their grammar (they didn't even smack me for it, which probably would have been deserved); my fellow authors from Writing.com and the BookSpa, too many to name; and every author I've ever read, also far too many to name.

To the musicians who inspire and uplift me every day, in particular Phillip Hartsock who let me use his lyrics and the rest of the Mandolin Whiskey gang for letting me stalk them.

Finally, a huge thanks to the fans of the series who keep asking for the next one, and to every one of my readers. It's an amazing thing to put so much love into creating these characters and to have them so loved by others in return.

Rehearsal

Of Chaotic Currents

Exposition

5 January 1978

Evan swallowed his nerves by focusing on his friend. Most often, it was Duncan's calm, unruffled demeanor that helped maintain his own fake appearance of certainty. He absorbed it, meshed with it to an extent. Never, when he was out on stage, did he feel he was there alone. He and Duncan were partners, fueled by each others' passion for music, calmed by each others' presence. He had never admitted it to anyone, but before meeting the guitarist in that little dark nowhere bar, Evan never expected he could allow himself to go as far into music as he'd always wanted to go.

They were there now. Together.

And better, they were there in his friend's homeland, his beginnings.

In the four years since Duncan had joined Raucous, it was the first time they got overseas. Edinburgh. Duncan's home. Raucous was only there because of him, not only there overseas but there in the big venues playing to nearly full stadiums with hundreds of screaming fans sporting the band's logo, holding signs with their names, grabbing at them, following them from town to town, seeking out their hotel, offering more than they should offer.

Not that Evan never took advantage of the offers. It was hard not to when he was single and they were everywhere. He did try to be discreet, more than two of his band mates were. More than Susie realized. At least, he thought she didn't.

Sobered by the unwanted intrusion of his thought, Evan returned focus to his friend. Odd. He felt much calmer himself than Duncan looked. The man was nearly unflappable, even with hundreds screaming. Normally. Not tonight. Tonight he paced, head down. Also odd. Their sixth tour and Duncan chose this one to worry.

Evan moved into his path. "It's strange to see you so nervous."

Duncan raised an eyebrow. "An' who says I am?" He looked over at something dropped by a roadie, turned back with a shrug. "Maybe I am. I canno' imagine why they are making such a scene. It is no' like many of them knew I existed when I was livin' here. Or would have wanted t' know."

"They want to know now. Of course you have your brother to blame for some of this."

"Yeah and I will be talking t' him about making a big deal out of me playin' here, about too much damn focus on me. I told him I didnae want that. It should have stayed about the band as a whole."

Evan set a hand on his shoulder. "You deserve this. You've earned it. Go out there and enjoy the hell out of it."

"You are awful calm tonight." He flicked his gaze to behind Evan, only for a second.

"Well. With all the attention on you, no one's going to pay much attention to me." He laughed when his friend shoved him away.

The commotion that began at the airport as the band arrived in Edinburgh had continued outside Duncan's parents' house, on the outskirts of the property. Fans were there when they arrived; many stayed through the night as though the band might try to escape and nearly blocked their way as they left for the night's venue. Evan figured it wouldn't bother Duncan if it had been for Raucous in general, as was normal. It was the flood of white cardboard signs with his name and 'Welcome Home' and several offers of marriage and lots of 'I Love You's directly aimed at their lead guitarist that did it. The crowd was heavily there for Duncan: the Scotland native who had finally emerged after five years of hiding in the States and made such a huge splash in America that he could hardly be in public anymore. At least not without plenty of guards. Evan could tell he hadn't expected the same in his hometown.

It was well-deserved, though, as he'd told his friend. Regardless of what their record company thought, all Raucous members and a ton of fans agreed with the music reviewer who insisted Duncan McGuire would go down as one of rock's greatest guitarists.

Nervous excitement bounced all around her and it was all Susie could do to keep her cool and act the part of assistant manager. She wanted to run over to her husband before he went out into public view and smother him with her incredulity at where they were and what they were doing. They'd come so far, all of them. They'd worked so hard for this, sacrificed so much through the years: social time, jobs, girlfriends, tempers, money for equipment. When other single guys went to bars or hung out with friends after work, they had returned from work, eaten quick meals, and gone to practice. They'd done it since they were teens, all of them. Even many weekends when they didn't have shows, they practiced. They wrote and recorded and eventually gave up their jobs, their security nets, and plunged in. They all deserved this: the coveted UK tour they thought was only a dream for so many years. Duncan joining them helped make it possible with his guitar work, his songs, and his brother promoting them. The band didn't dare resent him for it. She supposed they would if he let it get to his head, if he acted like he had any part of it. He didn't.

He was the one who got them there, though, along with Adam's planning and Danny's help. Adam Zeger, the independent producer becoming a name in his own right for the way he propelled Raucous up and out, had encouraged Duncan's brother to focus on him as he tagged along on their last tour and wrote tour memoirs to send back to Edinburgh's *Scotsman* newspaper. Susie knew Duncan didn't realize he had. She had known, as the band's assistant manager, but she decided it was best to let that bit of information alone. With Danny still using his last name of O'Neil and Duncan now using McGuire, it wasn't horribly obvious Danny was promoting his own brother. Some knew. Many did by now. But only in some circles.

While waiting for the stage manager to send them out, the band joked with each other. Doug set a hand on Duncan's shoulder, smiled about something he'd said, got a nod...

And she realized he was right. Her husband had been right when he said she was getting more distant from them, more part of management than part of the band. Before, she was always right there in the middle of the jokes, always a part of what was said. More and more often now, she wasn't. She was with Adam and Roy making arrangements, planning, learning the job, or with Paula talking about what they wanted as far as publicity and what they didn't, how far they were willing to go. Susie had become their go-between, balancing their conservativism with their publicist's need to do her job as effectively as possible, with whatever means she could use. Although Roy Mason was technically still their manager, Susie had picked up a lot of his duties since he didn't always jump as fast as the band wanted. She felt more like Adam's assistant than Roy's. Adam called himself their liaison with Axis Records, but he was much more. Their newest album, *Intoxication*, held a thank you note to their friend and mentor, Adam Zeger.

Of course it wasn't only management business that separated her from the band. There was Danielle. Her daughter was nearly two already. She was such an incredible handful, and Susie still didn't want her in the public light. She wanted to maintain as much normalcy for her baby as possible.

Since they'd arrived in Duncan's beloved Scotland from snow-covered Massachusetts, Laura had claimed her niece as much as Nella allowed. Duncan's sister was an incredible help, as was her daughter's willingness to socialize with most anyone.

Little hands pulled at her shirt and Susie picked Nella up with some effort. She wouldn't be able to hold her much longer. As Susie hoped the whole time she was expecting, Danielle had inherited at least some of Duncan's sturdiness. She was getting too big for Susie's 5'2" frame to handle well, even if she had been working with her husband on building her strength.

Nella threw an exaggerated pout from beneath dark curls and Susie brushed the unruly hair back from her face. "What's wrong, sweetie?"

Laura rolled her eyes. "She wanted t' go ou' with 'er daddy and go' mad at me when I said she couldnae."

"Oh Danielle. You know you can't go on stage."

"*My* da'yee." She reached a chubby hand toward where the guys grabbed their instruments amid rounds of loud applause.

"Daddy's working."

She shook her head. "My da'yee play 'tar. I play too."

"You can play '*tar* with him when he's not working. Look. They're about to start." Susie put her finger to her lips in a hush motion and thanked Beau with a grin when he pulled chairs over for her and Laura. Danny was floating around somewhere, still taking notes as an ongoing tour memoir. Gene and Linda and Aunt Loretta were out in the front row. Most of Gene's coworkers and acquaintances and relatives were scattered around behind them.

Susie knew how tall Duncan's father had to be sitting. Part of her wished she could be out in the audience beside them, watching her in-laws' expressions, pretending to ignore her husband's flirtation with girls close to the front, and catching her band from the best angle. She could see some of the flirting and she chuckled when he teased a girl who reached for him. He walked up to where she could almost touch him and looked directly at her with that charming, devilish grin.

"I wasnae sure he would do tha' with Mum and Dad ou' there." Laura had her eyes on him, too.

"I wasn't, either. I imagine he's not thinking about it." She cringed when he moved a step closer. Too close. "I'm glad he is, though. It looks better for him."

"He worries abou' upsetting you."

Susie turned her eyes to Duncan's sister. Her sister. With the noise, she wasn't sure she'd heard Laura right.

"Or more about the fans upsettin' you."

"No. He knows I don't worry about them."

"Bu' y' hide Danielle."

"Oh. Just because I don't want them to bother her as she gets older and they will if they recognize her. Or maybe they won't, but I want to be sure."

"She is friendly, Suse. She doesnae mind being talked to."

"She's a little friendlier than I appreciate. It's good. I know it is. But it's scary." Susie stroked her daughter's head. Danielle took no notice. Her eyes were glued to the stage. "People can be cruel. I don't want them to say stupid things to her. Repeating the lies that are going around."

"Ach, well, as she gets older, I cannae see her puttin' up with it. She will likely knock them ou' like her daddy would. I think y' wouldnae have t' worry so."

"Maybe." She hugged Danielle as though able to protect her from the cruelty of the future. She would as well as possible. It was her job, wasn't it? To protect her child? Susie's dad seemed to think it was. So did Evan, as protective as he had always been toward her. And Duncan, although his was a different kind of protectiveness. He was watchful, wary. But he stayed out of anything he expected she could handle on her own. Susie appreciated that about him. He didn't treat her like a china doll or like a child. She would have to be careful to watch that line while she protected Danielle. She didn't want her daughter to think Susie believed she was incapable of taking care of herself. She wanted her daughter to be well able to take care of herself.

Beau handed her a ginger ale and Laura an Irn Bru. Susie smiled at her young bodyguard and thanked him. Danielle tried to grab it and Susie helped her take a drink. Beau learned fast. He knew she preferred to share her drink with her daughter instead of juggling two. He also knew that although she at times enjoyed an Irn Bru, the sweet orange-flavored Scottish soda, she preferred her ginger ale. And it had no caffeine to add to Danielle's energy level. The sugar was bad enough.

Nella got fidgety anyway and readily agreed to take Beau's hand to walk around backstage to watch the roadies who often talked with the girl as they worked. Their 6'4" large-muscled blonde bodyguard was wonderful with Danielle, and despite the sweetness in his face, he was not a young man to mess with, as well-trained as he was. He was also very loyal, enough Susie could let them wander together without worry.

With a breath of relief, she stretched her shoulders and moved to where she could get a glimpse of Duncan's family. Gene was, of course, sitting shoulders straight and chin up, enjoying every bit of the performance. Linda, also, with an extra touch of softness in her expression. She'd been through an incredible amount of worry about her son, before and after he left her home. Every time her eyes touched him, they showed both the past fear and the full appreciation of how well he was doing, of how proud she was.

Susie had to look away from them. She turned her attention to the people in the crowd she didn't know. Young and old and in between, they were all fully fixed on the band, on one member in particular or darting around the stage to watch them all. Of course most eyes were on Mike, their lead with the dark blonde hair and svelte build. Always. He always captivated his audience with his incredible voice and the way he put it out there with his pure love of the music.

From Mike, she moved her attention to Stu at his keyboards. The youngest, he was also the most energetic. The music flowed through his small frame out of every pore, just as his friendly, open personality did. Doug at the drums was as he was in everyday life: precise, technically skillful, and steady. On top of it, though, she saw what he didn't show off stage — a strong artistic quality that gave him a unique style. The tallest of the group, at 5'11 — or 5'10 and a half, as Stu always emphasized in order to make his friend only two inches taller than himself — was also the oldest and the band's most calming influence. He was built sturdier than Mike and Susie figured playing the drums for so long had helped that, but he was still less broad then Evan.

Her Evan looked every bit the school sports star he'd been. His brown hair was always neatly trimmed at his nape and behind his ears and he was always well-matched but understated, casual. A half inch shorter than Doug, Evan's build was substantial, yet he moved with a grace most wouldn't expect. And he was easing into his role as rock star as gracefully as he did everything. At times, Susie missed seeing him on lead guitar where he was before Duncan joined the band, but he had such a nice feel for his bass that no one else would be able to play the parts quite the same way he did. She studied his fingers, his stature, the tilt of his head, the grace of his movements. He flirted with fans also, but subtly. A light grin, a glance, a quick nod. It was enough to provoke screams and smiles. He was getting horribly good at it. Susie was more proud of him for overcoming his stage fright, as well as for leading the band from the back, than she could ever tell him.

Her husband may have been the catalyst that led to their UK tour, but Evan was the backbone that held them together long enough to get there. And he was the one who found Duncan and pulled him in. The band owed him a lot, and they all knew they did. So did she.

Glissando

7 January 1978

"Wake up, my luv. We need t' be goin' soon."

Susie opened her eyes to her husband's gentle sexy voice. Damp dark hair fell over his forehead and the top of his bare shoulders. She reached up to stroke the curling ends and allowed her fingers to trace down his smooth, muscular chest. After three years and four months of marriage, she was still absolutely enamored of him, physically and otherwise, all the way around. She slid her hand around behind his arm and tugged lightly. "Come back to bed."

He leaned down and gave her a soft kiss. "An' I would, bu' we would miss our ride t' Stirling."

"Tell them we'll catch up. Your tech can do sound check for you." Susie moved her other hand up behind his head and pulled him in. He'd just showered. His skin was still moist and he smelled of the lavender soap Linda McGuire always made sure to leave in their bathroom during their visits ever since Susie had mentioned how she liked it.

After marrying Linda's son without her knowledge and pulling him to stay in the States with her, Susie knew her mother-in-law could easily not like her much. She'd expected her not to. But if she couldn't have her own mom around, Susie was terribly glad Duncan's mother decided to be a real mom to her, as well as she could with the ocean between them most of the year.

She pushed the thought aside. As much as she liked Linda, Susie didn't want her in mind while she had Duncan locked in against her body, only the sheet between them. Not that it was between them much anymore with his hand sliding down to her hip and up again. And she didn't want it between them. "Is Nella still asleep?"

"Nae." Duncan kissed her neck. "She is down havin' breakfast. Y' need t' get up so y' have time t' eat, as well. Come, Suse." He tried to pull away.

She tightened her arms around his neck, caught his eyes, and reclaimed his mouth. He gave in to her. To an extent. She teased his lips as he pulled back.

"Y' are makin' this too hard t' refuse, Babe. Y' have t' stop now."

"Mm. I'm trying very hard not to let you refuse." She sat up when he did, merged in as close as possible, and trailed her lips across his shoulder while caressing his spine with her fingertips, down to the hem of his jeans.

Escaping, Duncan clasped her hands between his. "Y' are goin' t' be the death of me yet, my luv. Especially if I have t' tell my band mates I missed the bus because y' wouldnae let me ou' of bed after y' kept me up so late last night."

She leaned in to kiss his shoulder. "You tell them that. But I don't think *I* was the one keeping *you* up."

"Ah y' *were* keeping me up. No' that I am complaining." With a wink, he stood and moved back a step.

She noticed his bare feet. "Did you run into Marta while walking around the house like that? I can imagine how red she'd get if she saw you half naked." Susie chuckled at the thought of the McGuires' young maid who still blushed when Duncan joked with her.

He raised an eyebrow. "I havenae left the room. Ev knocked while I was gettin' Danielle dressed and took her down with 'im." He pulled lightly at her hands. "Areyae ge'in' up, Babe?"

"I suppose, since you're not coming back to bed." With the help of his strong arm, Susie forced herself up and wrapped around him, her head against his shoulder. She was too tired to travel and then support a show, even a small show at a Scottish castle.

"Tonigh' I will come back t' bed." He stroked her hair and held her close.

"With Nella in the room."

"Nae, Laura 'as offered t' keep Danielle in her room as long as she is travellin' with us. We 'ave our nights t' ourselves for some time yet."

"Mm." She kissed his neck, felt the stubble and the warmth. "Remind me to thank her."

"I 'ave already." He raised her face to his and met her lips.

Susie had every reason to believe he was more interested in going back to bed than to Stirling at the moment, even if he was more excited than he allowed anyone to know to be on tour in his beloved home country. Through the kiss she could feel it. The excitement. The passion. She wasn't sure how much of it was for her and how much for the coming tour. Either way, she'd accept as much of it as she could get whenever she could get it. There had been enough tours by now she knew the constant demands would drain him more the longer it went on and he would seek time alone while off duty. It was okay. Evan was opposite. The longer they were on the road, the more he sought her out to help calm him.

"Come." Duncan kissed her nose and backed away. "Y' need t' eat so y' can keep up your strength. For tonight, when I am hyped up from the show." He threw a grin and turned to find his shirt.

8 January

Duncan had to convince her it would be fine to let Danielle go with Mike, Doug, Stu, and his family to see Stirling Castle. Susie didn't want to go. After whatever she'd felt at Edinburgh Castle her first time in Scotland, she had no interest in seeing others. Danielle did. She insisted on going to see the big, big castle that Danny told her about. Ev was more interested in the Wallace Monument that he decided to take Susie to see instead of the castle. Duncan figured it would only be the two of them, him and his wife, but he wouldn't turn his friend down.

In truth, he was glad to share more of Scotland's history with him. Susie would have been more comfortable letting Danielle go to the castle if Ev had gone, as well, but his family would be there, including his parents, and she couldn't quite say it wasn't all right to leave Danielle in their care for a couple of hours.

He would like to take Ev to the castle, as well, if they had the time to do both. Adam hadn't allowed that much time, but Duncan was happy enough with a couple of hours in Stirling before they moved on to the night's show in Perth and then up into the Highlands the following day, to Aberdeen, and back south to Glasgow. Duncan had managed to persuade them not to bother with air travel within Scotland. There was no distance long enough a drive to be worth the hassle of it, and few places in the Highlands with ability to fly into. He wanted to be on the ground where he could see the land close up. With no one at Axis understanding how little time road travel would take, even jumping north and south, it allowed plenty of tour time where he could show off his country to his friends.

And to his wife. She didn't tire on their way up the narrow stone steps of the Wallace Monument, a tall narrow square stone building. He insisted she walk ahead of him. The stairs were steep; they allowed him a nice view of her backside as she treaded her way up. Ev shook his head at him but stayed quiet about it.

Susie was well energized today, despite her keeping him up again so late the night before. To be honest, it was more the other way around but she didn't seem to mind at all. At each floor, she stopped to read the history. Mainly Ev read the history; Duncan related it to Susie with Ev interspersing a few things he read. The sword that supposingly belonged to William Wallace himself grabbed her attention and rightly, since the thing was taller, shaft to tip, than she was.

"How big was he?"

Duncan slid a hand along her back. "I couldnae tell you but likely not a lot taller than his Claymore."

"Then how on earth did he use it?"

"With both hands, my luv, an' whole hearted, the way any real Scot does anything, y' ken."

She grinned and set a hand on his stomach.

"Come on up to the top. I will show you how close we are to where he won his first battle in the war for Scottish Independence, for all the good it did us." He glanced over at Ev and got the nod to say he'd follow.

Susie's hair was down, unbound, as he liked it, and the wind blowing through the openings at the top of the monument tossed it about, made her rope it in one hand. She didn't let it bother her as she wandered over to look out over Stirling. "This is amazing."

Ev agreed as he looked over her shoulder. "That's the Forth, isn't it?"

"Yeah, and if you come this way, you will see the bridge." He led them a couple of openings to the right. "And the castle." He pointed farther out.

"It's still standing. I guess that means Nella is being decently behaved."

He caressed her shoulder. "Stop worrying. She is fine."

Ev moved into talk about the wars and the September 11th Stirling Bridge victory that, even though it didn't lead to independence, at least fueled the thought of it, he guessed, and the importance of fighting to have their own king on the throne.

"Aye right, but it wasnae so much the thought of putting the Stuarts back on the throne that made the Highlanders fight. It was the thought of leaving their clans respected as clans and allowing them the right to make their own rules. Similar to your states that have their own rules, at least to an extent. That mattered to them more than near anything else, the independence of retaining their own individuality. Once you lose that..."

Ev nodded. "Right. And you're a admirer of Wallace. Didn't know you were."

"Yeah, I am. Not only because he stood up and fought for what he thought was right, but because even when they were about to hang him for treason, he said he couldnae be convicted of treason since he was never a subject of the English king. Again, it didnae help him not be hanged, but it left a message. It is one thing I adore about the US. You are not and have never been subjects of your government. From your beginning, you have been citizens in charge of your government."

"We were subjects of an English king, though, in the beginning."

"Before you were Americans. Not since then. And the Scots could have been independent if they didnae turn on each other. It was a Scot who turned Wallace in to the English. Many Scots turned on their freedom fighters instead of standing with them. I donae ever see us being what we could have been. But as I told Danny, as long as we are still allowed our individual freedoms, I amnae sure it would matter at this point to try again. Too many would still turn on those who tried, out of fear. Too many would rather be taken care of than to take care of themselves. It is sad. And it feels untrue to the Scottish spirit."

Ev rubbed his neck. "I don't know. I see a lot of that going on in the States, too."

"I think there are still too many true American spirits to let it go that far."

"Hope so."

Susie walked away, over to another opening on the other side. Duncan followed to point out the Ochil Hills. "The beginning of the Highlands."

She tilted her face up to his. "I love being here with you. It's been some time since you talked of Scotland. It's nice to hear it again."

"Is it? I thought maybe we had turned y' away."

"No. I just feel like..." She looked back out at the hills. "You belong here."

"Suse." He moved in front of her, took her face in his hands. "I belong where you are, you and Danielle. I am happy with that."

"Are you? You're ... different here, Duncan. More ... more you. Does that make sense? Whatever it is, I love seeing it."

"Then we will visit often, yes?" He grinned and gave her a soft kiss.

12 January

Evan kept an eye on the time through wishing it wouldn't go so fast. Susie was fully engrossed in their visit of the Hunterian Art Gallery and its section of Scottish artists. Nella had done well with Evan giving her piggy-back rides when she got tired of walking, but she was losing interest. Her mom wasn't.

Duncan had hesitated at Susie's idea of roaming the gallery. He didn't want to turn her down, but he had no interest in museums. Stu's idea of wandering Glasgow and popping into pubs here and there was of much more interest to him. Evan wouldn't have minded pub hopping, but he'd seen pubs, so he offered to go with Susie and Danielle. His friend gave him a grateful nod. It was only the three of them. Doug and Adam made other plans in the city. Mike agreed with Stu, as did Danny. Laura wavered, but at the end her brother's company won out.

They had only forty-five minutes before the car would be in front of the building to take them to the restaurant where they'd all meet up for dinner. He reminded Susie of the time. She still wanted to see the Whistler exhibit. By the time they got there, Nella was whining. She wanted food. And she wanted her daddy. Since her daddy wasn't right there, she hung on Susie.

"Look baby. This is paint. Like you do with your crayons." Susie picked Danielle up to show her the Sketch for Annabel Lee. "It's pretty, isn't it? Do you like the colors?"

"No." Nella shook her head and pulled back, her arms around Susie's shoulders, trying to urge her to move, to get out of the building.

"Nella, don't pull. Sit still if you want up." Susie adjusted her on her hip. "You don't like the colors?"

"No. I no' like it. Boring. Yes."

Evan chuckled at the term she'd picked up from Stu. Her new favorite word.

"It's not boring. Behave. We'll leave in a few minutes. I want to look." Susie adjusted her again, holding with both arms.

"No, I no' look more. I ge' Da'yee."

When she jerked at her mom again, Evan tried to take her. "Come on, little one. If you don't hold still for your mom, you have to come to me."

"No, I not." She wrapped her arms tighter around Susie's neck.

"It's fine." Susie gave him an exasperated look mixed with gratitude and moved on. She did her best to keep Nella interested but the girl got more whiny and jerked more.

Evan pried her arms away and took her, whether or not she wanted him. She threw a fit and he told her to hush but people gave them nasty glances and Susie said to forget it; it was time to go. She took Nella back again when she wouldn't hush for him and the girl cuddled into her shoulder. She was tired, but she was far too heavy for her mom. Susie wouldn't let him try again. She didn't want the attention.

Duncan paced in front of the restaurant. Ten minutes late. Danny told him to relax, girls were always late. Susie usually wasn't. Ev never was. He turned at a car approaching. Their car. As it stopped, Susie got out and shoved a hand through her hair then reached in to grab Danielle. The girl pushed to get down.

Susie held tight. "No. You're *not* running from me again. *Stop* it."

Evan took her as he got out and had to yank his head back before Danielle hit it with her own.

Duncan went to take her. "Stop this now."

"She's yours tonight." Susie rubbed her arm and explained that she'd let go of Danielle for two seconds to put her coat on and the girl ran off, through the front door to the sidewalk. Luckily, some guy caught her before she got far and held onto her. "Scared me to death. I slipped on the stairs, ice or something, and by the time I grabbed the rail and yanked my arm, she was ... she would have been in the road or..."

Duncan looked over at Ev. "Where were you?"

"He was in the restroom. It was my fault. I shouldn't have let her go even for two seconds the way she'd been pulling at me. I could have waited to put my coat on but I was ready to go. She was being so horrendous..."

"Are you alright?" She nodded and he gave Danielle to his brother. "Nae, donae fuss at me or at your uncle. Behave." The girl frowned but stayed silent. "Come inside, Babe. Let me look at your arm."

"No, it's fine. I just pulled it a bit. But she could have..."

"She is fine, and you are off duty tonight. It is my turn." He brushed a hand through her hair.

She hugged him and related how helpful Ev had been, that Nella had fussed most of the way through, wanting Susie to carry her, wanting to run through the hallways, refusing to look for more than a few minutes. She thanked Ev for the help, apologized that he couldn't see much with Nella acting that way, and for being stuck with them all day long.

"I wasn't stuck. And I'm sure I saw as much as you did."

Her response was cut off by Danny calling them to "get their arses inside" so they could eat. As though his brother hadn't been eating all day long.

Inside with her coat off, Susie wrapped around him. He gave her a kiss alongside her head. "Come, my luv. Sit and relax now and I will take care o' those muscles for y' later."

She caught his eyes. "I'm holding you to that. I missed you today."

He grinned, a teasing grin. "I think y' are taking it for more than I meant."

"Am I?"

"Hey, we can hear you."

Danny pushed at Stu. "Yea and we already know they are disgusting like that. Let them alone. Nella Bird, I will tie y' in that chair if you get up again. Sit still."

He chuckled as his brother again picked the girl up and settled her in the booster seat. He put her between himself and Laura, across the table. Their waitress gave most of her attention to Danielle and Danny played up the fact she thought Danielle was his. Stu gave him a hard time about using the child to flirt. Susie said it was fair enough if he was willing to deal with her during dinner. And she said someone at the museum complimented Evan on *his* beautiful daughter, and he hadn't corrected them, either.

Duncan raised his beer at his friend in salute. "Brave to claim her when she is acting that way. If she keeps it up, I can blame it on you."

Ev laughed. "Well I guess that would be fair, although anyone looking at the two of you would know better. Not to mention how she kept calling for her daddy when I wouldn't let her down to run. I was half afraid someone would accuse me of kidnapping the kid. We didn't get far from your wife, just in case."

"That would have made great headlines." He took the last swallow of his beer. "Come help me buy another round." At the bar as they waited on their drinks, he threw Ev an unamused look when he chuckled at an overtly flirting girl coming onto Duncan. He got away from her easily enough with mention of his wife and daughter across the room.

"You just destroyed her night. Poor girl."

"If y' laugh I will go tell her you are looking for company."

"Yeah, that's all I need. Bridgette may not wait me out for this tour as it is."

"Donae think she will?"

Ev shrugged. "She might. Said she would but I have my doubts. Guess we'll find out."

Duncan tried to pay for the drinks. His father had already covered the bill for the night. They knew who Ambassador McGuire was, even in Glasgow. They'd never cross him. He shrugged it off and leaned closer to his friend. "Adam said today talk is spreading in the States. There is a photo going around. I want t' know how y' want to handle it before I mention it to Susie."

"What photo?"

"Of the two of you. At the New Year's Eve show in town."

"Have I seen it?"

"I would guess not or y' would know. Some jackass grabbed a shot when y' were giving her greetings for the year, in the two seconds she was away from my side. It looks like something it is not and they are making the most of it."

Ev grimaced. "How bad?"

"Accusing you of an affair."

"With your wife?"

Duncan gave him a light nod and took a swallow of his beer. "I amnae worried about it, but y' might want to call Bridgette tonight and explain. And if y' decide to address it and want me to back you, say the word. If you want to ignore it as the garbage it is, we can do that."

Address it. No, he did not want to address questions about his relationship with her, even if nothing had happened. He sighed. "I don't know; the last time I tried to address that, I failed in the biggest way I could. Not sure I want her that mad at me again."

Duncan chuckled. "Ah well, she would get over it again, but if y' donae want to say anything, we will let it be."

He felt her hands slide up his back and over his shoulders as he tucked Danielle in for the night. He had to tell her, before she heard it elsewhere. With thanks to his sister for keeping their daughter in the adjoining room, he stood and moved so Susie could give Danielle a kiss and good night wishes.

She stood again and inched in against him, but addressed Laura. "She should sleep well as much as she wore herself out."

"Donae worry. Go on t' bed and let him make it up to y' for giving y' such a lively and stubborn little one t' deal with."

Susie chuckled. "I think the stubborn part is more my fault."

Duncan rubbed her back. "Night Laurie. Knock if she needs us."

"As if y' would hear me." With a teasing grin, she play-shoved him toward the door. "Just donae be too awful loud. The walls donae look too wide."

He shook his head and decided not to comment. Susie was well used to his brother and sister by now, and how open they were about everything. She didn't bother to get embarrassed. As soon as he closed the door, Susie slid her hands under his shirt. "I think I was promised a shoulder massage."

"I think y' are right." He leaned in to kiss her neck. "First, there is something y' should know."

"I heard. The walls aren't thick. I'll be good."

He pressed her up against the door. "Damn, I am in love with you."

"Gonna prove it?" She lowered her hands to grip the back of his thighs.

"Suse..." He forced himself to tell her about the photo and the suggestion she was having an affair with Ev.

"Hm. I'm not." She kissed his neck, and his jaw.

"It'd be damn hard for y' to do so, considering."

"Considering I save all my energy for you?" She pressed into his mouth, explored it with her tongue.

He hardened against her, pulled her away from the door, toward the bed. "Maybe I should say as much, tell them y' willnae let me sleep at all since y' insist on being with me night and morning and..."

She chuckled. "Uh huh, tell them that. Don't forget the times we find a hiding spot during the day."

Of course she knew he wouldn't. Their private life was private. It was tempting, though. He would love to brag about how affectionate she was, about how often she wanted him.

She tugged at his shirt and pulled it over his head, skimmed her fingers down his chest. "So maybe I haven't looked quite attached enough to you in public recently. May have to change that." She kissed his bare shoulder, cuddled in close.

"Y' donae have t' prove anything t' anyone." He felt her nails tease his back.

"No. I know. But it might be fun."

"G' ahead. Keep trying t' suffocate me, Babe. Y' havenae done it yet."

"Careful what you ask for."

He stepped back enough to set his hands alongside her face and meet her eyes. "G' ahead."

17 January

Susie sat beside Adam on the train half listening and half making notes of what she wanted to remember about Aberdeen and Wick. She'd decided to keep a tour journal for Danielle, to show her all the places she'd been and things she'd done. Now and then she added comments about things her dad said and...

"Did you hear me?"

"Sorry. No. Just a second." She finished the thought in her head about the Wallace statue in Aberdeen and the inscription urging people to live free. Liberty, it said. Live in liberty, not slavish. Something like that. She'd ask Duncan later if he knew it better. She should have written it earlier. "Okay." She gave Adam her attention. "I heard you say Stevie Wonder and Fleetwood Mac won big at the Music Awards. After that, I missed it." And the Sex Pistols had given their last concert a few days before. Not a band she would miss.

"Right. Well, I didn't necessarily want to say it once not to mention twice. But..." He lowered his voice. "Your plan to convince fans you and Evan haven't ... well, it's backfiring. It looks like you're trying to prove something, making a point, as though you have to."

She scratched the back of her hair where her ponytail tugged at her head. "Oh Adam, seriously, what's new? Why do we care about this stuff anymore?"

"I had a feeling you did."

"Well you know, some days I do, but I can't stop it." She looked over where Duncan and Evan were talking and playing cards. "It'll go away again. As close as they are, I can't imagine anyone would believe it for long."

"Or they believe he doesn't care."

She laughed, and her husband looked over. "Right. You know, it's not hurting anything. If they want to make an issue of me hanging all over my husband, just because I want to hang all over him and I'm not annoying him yet, so be it. If I don't, they make an issue of that. I can't win no matter which way I turn so I might as do whatever the hell I want, right?"

"Well. Within reason."

"Like you have to worry about that." With Duncan still glancing over, curious as to what had her so amused, Susie went to him, raised his face with her fingertips, and kissed him. "Smothering you yet?"

"Nae, keep trying, Babe."

She heard Nella laugh and tell someone mummy and daddy "kissing 'gain" and Evan suggested the game was over.

"No, you can have him back." She threw Evan a grin. "I'm going to go harass my daughter." She felt Duncan's hand skim her thigh as she moved out of his reach.

21 January

Duncan viewed the outskirts of Inverness noting every detail he could sink into his memory. It had been some time since he'd visited the city, although it was one of his favorite places: packed full of a mix of historic buildings and constant activity, with the river running through the middle and Loch Ness at its southern tip. They'd had time the day before to wander the city and travel down the loch a ways.

They stopped at the Caledonian Canal and had fish and chips. Duncan introduced them to black pudding, which only Stu would take more than a bite of and Mike wouldn't touch. They visited Urquhart Castle where the wind whipped through the openings of the still partially intact lookout tower and stood at its edge under open sky allowing the wind to toss their hair and clothing until it felt like it might knock them off. Susie had gripped his arm and let Ev keep a close eye on Danielle.

It was too cold for the visit, much too cold for Susie, and they cut it short, half jogging back up the paved path on the steep hill that led to the café where they grabbed coffee and scones. He would have stayed out longer and considered it. He could have caught up after they'd warmed themselves, but he didn't want to stand out there alone. He would have to take her back again in the summer. By themselves with Danielle.

His daughter didn't seem to mind the cold. She darted up and down the narrow stone steps and ran along the pathways, despite how bundled Susie had her. Stu spent the most time chasing her, warning Nessie would get her if she stopped. After Laura explained that Nessie was the infamous sea monster living in Loch Ness, Danielle continually asked to be picked up to peek over the castle walls and down at the loch to look for him. His daughter was less than half Scottish by blood, but by heart, she was a full hardy, bonny Scottish lass. And she looked it.

"Not glad to be leaving, right?"

He turned to Ev when his friend sat next to him on the little bus Stu and Mike joked about not being a real bus. Most drivers would have no interest in maneuvering an American sized bus on the narrow Scottish roads. His band mates continually found it interesting how 'small' everything in Scotland was, other than the vast expanses of dark green and brown hills that dominated the Highlands.

"You all right?"

Duncan nodded. "It would be nice t' have come when it was warmer. It is more beautiful in the summer."

"I'm sure it won't be hard to convince your wife to come back with you. She's pretty enamored with it."

"Yes. She fits well here, in the wild of the Highlands." He looked back out over the land. Duncan wasn't technically a Highlander since he was born near Edinburgh, but he'd spent as much time as he could in the northern hills whenever he'd saved just enough money to grab a train over a weekend or mid-week during school breaks. He couldn't count the times he'd been railed on for doing so. He refused to let it stop him. The freedom the hills of heather and broom and tumbling burns gave him was worth the hell of having to return home again. He'd known one day he wouldn't return home. He would keep going toward the hills, toward the freedom. He didn't ever plan to return to the place where he grew up that was supposed to have been home. Edinburgh was as close as he needed to be.

He turned back to his friend. "Are y' enjoying the overseas tour like y' expected? You have not said much about it."

Ev grinned. "More than I expected. I can see why your homeland pulls at you. It's magnificent. The whole atmosphere is incredible. And it's nice to finally see you within your roots."

His roots. Ev knew more about his roots than most anyone. He knew more than Duncan would ever tell his parents, or his siblings. Only Susie knew more. They did pull at him. Now, while sharing it with his wife and his band, it pulled at him more strongly than it had during the past eight years of being away. "Would you be able t' stay, to move from the States, if you ever had reason?"

"If she wanted... I mean, if I had what you have and it meant that much, with someone who felt so strongly about being here. Like you, I would have to go back and visit, but yes. Here, I could. I could be comfortable in Scotland."

If she wanted. Duncan knew it was a slip, as fast as Ev changed tracks. He decided to let it go. "Even if we do not tour here again, y' should come back. Mum would let y' stay at the house."

"Might have to do that."

At his daughter's sudden cry, Duncan found where she was. Susie had her, brushing fingers through her bangs. Another bump on the head, he supposed, but she calmed already. Danielle. His daughter needed to know her roots, also, regardless of whatever else ever happened. "Ev, if y' do get charge of Danielle some day, if it ever came t' that, I would want her t' come. I would want her to know Scotland, to feel she has a home here, as well."

"Of course, but I'm sure you and Susie will take care of that. Are you thinking of duel citizenship for her?"

"Possibly. I havenae brought it up with Susie yet, though. She might no' be so keen on the idea."

Ev shrugged. "I can't imagine why not. You do know she would still move here if you asked."

Duncan eyed him. "Trying t' get rid of us?"

"You know I'm not." He glanced over at them and returned his gaze. "But I know you're thinking about it. I can see you are."

A deep breath filled Duncan's body and soul. Scottish air. Yes, he couldn't help but think about it. He did fit here. More than anywhere else, except wherever his wife and daughter were. "I cannot do it to her."

Ev looked relieved. "I guess selfishly, I'll have to be glad you can't."

Duncan nodded and turned back to the window. He wanted to be out climbing one of the hills, sleeping under the sky.

If she wanted. The words echoed through his brain. Ev would move for her if she wanted. He didn't mean some girl he might find. He meant Susie. He still loved her. Not that it mattered. What *she* wanted mattered, and Duncan had no doubt about that.

1 February

"Le' me take 'er for y'."

Susie grinned at Duncan's cousin and then checked her daughter's face. "I don't know if she will. She's tired from all the activity."

"I think she will 'ave t', as much as it looks like y' are havin' trouble holdin' ont' her. She will outgrow y' soon, y' ken." Collin spoke to Nella and tried to urge her over to his arms. "Come, li'l dove."

Nella held tighter. Susie gave her cousin another grin. "Thanks anyway."

"Then y' should sit, in the least, if she has t' be as stubborn as her uncle. Y' maybe shoul' have named her after DJ instead. He was always the more reasonable one."

"Maybe it is the name." Susie grinned and stroked Nella's head. "I can't sit, though. She'll throw a fit. I'll give her to Duncan when he's done." Susie knew from Collin's face he thought she should insist, but they were backstage. She couldn't allow the commotion. Not that Nella would be heard over the music screaming through the huge amps or the fans yelling or singing along. Still, she didn't want the local roadies to see Duncan's daughter making trouble.

Nella would have gone to Danny, Susie knew, but Danny and Laura had decided to sit in the audience for the Dublin show, with their family. The McGuires had come to Ireland both for the show and to celebrate Danielle's birthday. They booked a hotel event room for the day and many of their acquaintances came by. Susie couldn't help think how proud her mom would have been to know they were spending her granddaughter's birthday in her native Ireland. Angela McKenna Brooks had never been able to visit although she'd talked of it often.

Susie managed not to let it show how much she wished her mom was there until her dad surprised her. Duncan's idea. He'd arranged with Adam to have the show in Dublin on Nella's birthday and asked John to schedule a visit. The next two days, they had free. No shows. No interviews. Only sight-seeing time.

"Collin says Danielle is wearin' y' out and willnae go t' anyone." Gene startled her with his sudden presence. "Are y' alright, luv?"

"Yes. And she's too tired, but it's okay. I'm getting used to it." Actually, her arms felt like they were about to fall off.

"Why do y' not go down in the audience and sit with her there? Would y' no' like to see them from the front?"

"Oh. I don't want her down there. People have cameras and there's so much noise and she's over-tired already."

"Give her t' me, then." Gene picked the half-sleeping girl out of her arms and brushed a hand over Nella's head at her protest. "Now then, li'l lass, donae be peely wally with me. It willnae ge' y' anywhere."

Susie considered asking Gene what he'd just said, but she supposed she could understand well enough. She stretched her arms and shoulders and watched Danielle settle in against her grandpa.

"Go on with Collin now." He glanced behind him. "G' and watch your band from where y' should be, right ou' front. Laura and I will take gud care of the tyke."

Susie nearly jumped at the offer. She wasn't hounded in the UK, or in southern Ireland, like she was in the States. If anyone recognized her, which she doubted, they didn't show they did. Maybe sitting in the audience would work.

"Go on." Laura pushed at her. "She will be fine. Y' know we will take care o' her weel. Collin, come an' take her ou' now."

Susie checked Nella. Her daughter didn't seem to notice. She'd be fine with her grandpa.

Taking the seat next to her dad, she gladly accepted his arm with a smile. He leaned over and kissed the side of her head. "They insisted I stay here and relax. I hope you didn't need me. I would have..."

"No, she's fine with Gene. And I think he's glad to have the excuse to hold onto her while she's too tired to want to get down and run. He missed all of that with Duncan when he was a baby." She hoped no one would overhear with as loud as she had to talk over the music. Not likely, she supposed.

"I can't imagine." He squeezed her shoulder. "You were the best thing to ever happen to me, along with your mother."

"I'm so glad you're here. Seeing Ireland wouldn't be the same without you." With a smile at her husband to acknowledge he'd seen her out in the audience, Susie leaned her head against her dad's shoulder. She was tired, too. Danielle had been at her most high-spirited with the commotion and the gifts. Between running after her and the early morning flight and the emotions of the day, Susie was hanging by the last bits of energy she could muster. She couldn't imagine how her guys were on stage giving such a vivid, explosive performance. But she found herself wishing it would go on all night.

Drying quickly, she slipped into her nightgown and looked forward to the lusciously plump bed. They had a suite, not only a room. Her husband had arranged that, as well, along with the following late morning before they were to meet the others for brunch.

Susie opened the door to near darkness. Was he asleep already? As she turned the corner into the main room of the suite, candles greeted her. And red roses on the table. He met her with a glass of wine in each hand, his body covered only by black boxers that sat low on his hips.

"What is all this? Aren't you exhausted?"

He handed her one of the glasses and leaned in for a light kiss. "Nae, I am turned on too much to be exhausted."

"Are you? Why? Is it the bags under my eyes or the way I yawn?"

A grin made his eyes sparkle. "I' is because the beautiful mother of my daughter is still here with me two years after her birth, and I am still grateful y' didnae break your promise on tha' day."

"I would never break a promise to you."

He touched her lips again, moving nearly against her. "Thank you."

"For what?" She traced fingers down his shoulder and rested them on his waist.

"For my daughter." He kissed her shoulder. "For still being here." Her neck. "For putting up with the craziness of my job and doing it so well." He teased her lips and took a sip of his wine, his gaze locked on hers. "Mostly, for choosing me as your mate. I am still grateful for that, as well. Every day, Suse."

A shiver ran up her spine. "Oh. And I'm grateful you didn't give up."

He closed the distance and claimed her mouth. Susie took him in, as deeply as she could manage, her fingers against the bare skin of his taut back. She had to focus on not spilling the wine. She wanted it out of her hand in order to use them both to caress him, to feel him, to keep him pulled in tight.

"Duncan." She kissed his neck.

"Mm. Yes, my luv?"

"I love you so. Let me put this glass down so I can show you how much."

3 February

Evan noticed Susie shiver and wandered over to where she leaned against the damp stone wall looking out over the Cliffs of Moher. Judging where the wind hit her, he positioned himself in between and stood close. Twice her girth, he easily blocked all but the swirls that brushed up around him.

She turned and gave him a grin.

"So what do you think of the land of the other half of your roots?"

"Other than freezing and wet?" She chuckled. "Beautiful. It's so ... earthy. Does that make sense? I mean it's so unpretentious, strong and ... just what it is, you know?" She ran her hand along the top edge of the jagged weather-worn stone. "It feels natural. Not only because their fences are stones found right here in the land, but ... I don't know how to describe it. There's a connection I feel. Like my ancestors know I'm here. It's nothing like when my grandparents actually visited and I just wanted them to leave again. It feels ... welcoming, like maybe my ancestors would be more accepting of who I am, my mixed roots, of my Scottish husband's rugged wanderlust that draws me in." She shrugged. "Ireland is part of your roots, too. What do you feel here?"

"Honestly?" He nudged closer when she shivered again and rubbed a hand down her arm. "I felt more home in Scotland than I do here, which I suppose doesn't make sense. This is magnificent, all of Ireland. Less Dublin than the rest..."

"Yes, it's too crowded and too ... something."

"College town and business center. As for the rest of it, I agree with you, and I love it, but it doesn't have the same draw that Scotland had. I suppose I won't tell Mom that."

She grinned and moved into him, accepting his arm, and his warmth. "Well you know the Scots and Irish are really so intermixed that maybe you only think your roots are Irish. A lot of Scots settled here after they were hired as warriors, you know. Maybe farther back, you're more Scottish."

"Could be. And I have every feeling your ancestors would be more than accepting of you. From what I've read, family is more sacred to them than anything else. They would easily see you feel the same. Have you thought of trying to look them up? The ones still here?"

"I thought about it, but not for long. I guess I was afraid they'd be too much like my grandparents and I'm not sure I want to know if they are. I'm kind of tired of being pushed away for how I was born, for others' choices I had nothing to do with."

Evan held tighter. "The people who matter won't ever push you away. The rest are not worth worrying about. And you know I never will."

"You better not. That, I couldn't deal with."

He kissed the side of her head. She knew better. She knew he never could. "I think everyone's about ready to go. Stu's in the bus trying to warm up. Maybe you should be, too."

"I guess. But this is so incredible. Did you see the puffin down by the water?"

"Yes. Laura says they're her favorite part of being here. You might have to come back again when it's warmer, although from what they say, it doesn't tend to get very warm even in summer."

"I heard. Guess I'll have to be sure to have a warm body with me, then." She tilted her face up in a smile.

Evan saw Laura's camera flash and she threw a wink before she turned to get more photos of Nella and John. He hoped she would send him a copy of it. "You know, I think it's going to be nearly as hard for you to leave Ireland as it will be for your husband to leave Scotland after tour. Something tells me you'll have to come back soon." And maybe he could find a girl by then who would be willing to do a double date overseas.

Duncan looked over at Collin's nudge, and then to where he nodded. He saw Laura get a photo of Susie and Evan at the cliff wall, a nice one of them. He'd have to tell her to send a copy of it.

"Mate, if I were you, I wouldnae be appreciatin' that."

He raised an eyebrow at his cousin. "And why would you not?"

"They are getting friendly up there, and close."

"I have told you, they are friends and have always been. She does not do well with cold. I would guess he is trying to make sure she stays at least a bit warm." Duncan called over to where John again lifted Danielle off a large rock. "Do you want me to take her?"

John shook his head. "We're fine."

"Daddy! *Look*!" She started to pull herself up again.

"Get down, Danielle. It is too slippery and you will fall."

She complained when John set her back on the ground.

"Man, you are too trusting." Collin kept his voice low. "He has designs on her, even if the rumors arenae true as of now. I wouldnae turn my back if I were you."

Duncan bristled. "Collin, you are nearly a brother to me, but be careful about what you say about either my wife or my friend. I donae worry because I donae have to worry. Donae speak to me of it again." He walked away and over to where Danny leaned back against the rock wall talking with Adam. "I am surprised you are still out here. Are you not cold?"

"Too fucking frozen to move. Although it isnae as bad as it was last year this time in your new homeland."

Duncan recognized the dig but chose to ignore it. "And I hear there is a hell of a snowstorm moving in. I am wishing it would wait till we are home."

Adam rolled his eyes. "I'm just as glad we'll miss it. I hate snow. I hate ice even worse. Some day I'm getting a winter house in Florida."

"Areyae now? Big music business down there?"

He shrugged. "I did say some day."

Danny shivered and wrapped his arms around himself. "Can we drag your wife away from here yet?"

"Yeah I think Ev is talking her down now."

Danny glanced over at them, but unlike Collin, he knew better than to express whatever crossed his mind. "I am grabbing Laura and heading to the bus, then, with Stu, the smart one of the bunch. You are going to have to lasso your daughter. Good luck."

With a chuckle, Duncan headed over to Danielle and scooped her into his arms as she complained to her grandpa about wanting to climb. "I think we will have to build you a jungle gym in the backyard, yes?"

She frowned and shook her head. "No. No big, big bears and wild jungle a'mals in Nella yard. No."

John scuffed her hair. "I think Stu should stop buying you all of those animal books. Your imagination is way too active."

"It is no' the books. It is the way he tells it." Duncan squeezed his daughter with a kiss on her head. "No animals, my sweet. A jungle gym is a bunch of things you can climb up on like a monkey would. Y' will be the only wild thing in the yard."

"Yes!" She set cold hands on each side of his face. "And rocks. *Big* rocks, and water, and ... and birdies. *Look.*" She pointed at a small flock of seagulls in the air.

"No big rocks. You would scare your mum half to death."

She shook her head. "I big, my daddy. I c'imb. Yes. I not hurt."

"We will talk about it later. Ready t' go back to the hotel?"

"No. I see birdies and wa'er. *Big* water."

"It is beautiful, yes, but it is getting too cold."

"Not cold. No."

John reclaimed her and set her on her feet. "How could you be with all that activity? But your mom is. Time to go. No fussing." He called to Susie as they approached. "I'm taking her to the bus. Get your last views in."

Susie left Ev's side to take his and slid her hands beneath his unzipped coat. The cold from her fingers penetrated his skin through his thick shirt and he pulled his coat over her sides.

She buried her face into his neck. "How can you be so warm?"

In a brief jealous moment, Duncan wished Collin and Danny were still close enough to see the way she snuggled against him. "I have been chasing Danielle."

"Hm. And maybe you do have a wood burner inside, as Laura said." She kissed his neck and snuggled her cold nose back in close.

He held her tight. She remembered it. From one of their early tours, when they'd been out on the beach, still unmarried, and she wondered how he was so warm. He'd repeated Laura's line. And she remembered. She had also said it would be handy on cold nights, blushing when he took it differently than she meant. Or maybe it was what she meant. He had never doubted her attraction for him, not since the day they met. She never tried to hide it. "Come, Suse. They are all ready t' go."

"I know. Sorry for holding everyone up, but I hate to leave this."

He leaned back to see her face. "I will bring y' back if you like. Just let me know."

"Careful. I'll hold you to that."

Duncan kissed her. Ev had caught up with John and Danielle, giving them privacy, and he decided to use it. He'd shared her well the past two days her dad had been with them. He deserved time on the Cliffs with just her, in the cold misty air, as she soaked heat from his body.

7 February

Susie settled Danielle at the hotel room table with her Crayons and sheets of blank paper. Her little legs were folded beneath her to help her be high enough to see what she was doing: drawing music, she said, as she listened to her dad write it.

Somehow, Danielle always knew when Duncan hit the point he needed alone time, quiet. And he had. He sat at the edge of their bed, faced away from them, and worked on a new song. The music, anyway. He wasn't singing. And he didn't take notes.

She wanted to go sit behind him and rest her head against his back as she often did when he wrote. But if their two year old could be mature enough to let him be when he wanted space, then she could. Instead, she picked up the book she'd been reading off and on and settled at the other end of the bed, leaned back against the headboard. The quiet time was nice after the commotion. It didn't happen often on tours, not with Danielle mostly unwilling to settle at all until she dropped from fatigue far too late at night.

One month. They'd now been in the UK for a month, at his parents' house, in hotels, on buses. She was ready to be home. And yet, she wasn't. Susie couldn't imagine why the silence, near silence other than the strum of the Mustang, bothered her this time. She wanted to talk. Adult talk. About nothing particular, but something other than band business or promotion. Other than two year old chatter.

Giving up on the book, she let herself reflect on the whirlwind sight-seeing in between shows. They were in England now, close to Winchester. She hoped to get over to see the Cathedral but wasn't sure it would fit in their plans. Actually, she was pretty sure it wouldn't. In the morning, they had an interview with a paper Danny set up through his connections. Then a meeting with a local band that would open for them, and sound check, and a quick dinner, and getting ready for the show.

If Danny and Laura were still there, Susie would ask if at least one of them would skip the morning band stuff and go with her. They were back home. Danielle was back to sharing their room. For the past five days and a few more to come.

At a knock, Duncan didn't even look up. Susie went to get it. She couldn't resist touching the back of his head as she passed him. Checking first, she opened it to Evan. Maybe she would have adult conversation tonight.

He was dressed nice, in jeans and a dark brown shirt. His hair combed and jaw shaved. "Hey Angel, I've come to steal your husband, if you don't mind."

"Oh. He's..."

"Writing." Evan looked in around her.

"Yeah, but come in and you can try." Susie half wished Duncan would say no and Evan would stay and talk with her. Before he got very far in, Nella jumped up from the table and ran over to grab his hand. "Look. I draw music. Come."

Duncan at least acknowledged him before he continued the section he was in the midst of perfecting. Evan let Nella drag him to the table and listened to her explain, complimented her on it, and kept an eye on his friend. Waiting for the right time to interrupt. Susie had seen him do it often enough, she knew he was.

The music stopped and Duncan went to the dresser where he had paper, wrote a few notes, and joined them at the table. He listened to Nella explain again as he picked up the three pages she'd done. "Can I have them?"

She bobbed her head. "Yes. For you, my da'yee. You have ever and ever."

"I will keep them forever." He kissed the top of her head.

"So Laura was telling me the other day about a pub nearby she said we should check out." Evan studied his friend. "Interested?"

"I am workin'."

"I know, but it'll wait. You can work on it at the next place just as well. Being here may be nothing much to you, but I'm taking advantage while I can. Put your shoes on and let's go."

Susie watched Duncan hesitate. He wanted alone time. But Evan so much wanted to hang out with his friend in the UK while he could. She asked who was going. Only the two of them, if Evan could get Duncan to go, but he invited her, to be polite. She refused.

"Are y' sure? Stu or Doug would watch her. Or Mike. He owes y' babysitting time."

She was sorely tempted to agree, to go out with her guys, only the three of them. But Evan would have invited her right away if he wanted her to go. "No, I think I'll enjoy the quiet while I can. Go ahead. Have fun. Be careful."

Evan gave her a grin. "Don't sit around and worry. I'll return him to you."

She wanted to go. She wanted to watch them hang out as they always used to, back before she met Duncan and partly took him away. Before she interfered. She wouldn't tonight.

At the click of the door, Susie turned from the television she could barely hear to find her husband. "Hey. Have fun?"

"Yeah." He motioned behind him, said it was safe, and stared at his daughter's bed as Evan came in with him.

Susie glanced over to where Stu was asleep beside Danielle. "He helped calm her down. She said she wouldn't sleep until you were here. Drove me crazy. I was afraid she'd wake up if I got him up and have to start all over again." She looked at Evan. "Brought him back the same as he left, I see."

"Maybe a touch more relaxed." He gave his friend a grin.

Duncan went to Stu and pushed at his shoulder. "Wake up n' ge' ou' of my room." A sleepy murmur drifted up at another push and Duncan took his arm and helped pull him to his feet. "Thank y' for the help; now ge' out."

"Damn." Stu shoved a hand over his face and through his hair. "Didn't mean to fall asleep. Sorry."

Susie wasn't sure if he was talking to her or her husband, but he had nothing to be sorry about. She'd enjoyed having him there as they talked and he entertained Nella. He assured Susie he wasn't doing anything with the girls floating around him although it looked like he was. Publicity, he said. To keep Roy from yelling. Kara knew he wasn't taking any of them to bed. She wasn't concerned. He wouldn't do anything to screw it up. He was "keeping this one."

Nella started to stir and Evan went to her.

"No, she'll settle again." Susie got up to interfere.

"Relax, Angel. I'm taking her with me. Already have the cot in my room." He talked to Nella as he lifted her into his arms, and she cuddled in against him. "Let's go, Stu. Awake enough to walk?"

"Yeah." He rubbed his hair again.

Susie gave Stu a hug and thanked him for his help. And Duncan pushed him out of their room. Evan chuckled, cuddled Danielle in after Duncan gave her a good night kiss, and closed the door behind him.

"He only stopped by because he knew you were both out."

Duncan turned to her. "Y' donae have t' explain."

"You seem upset he was here. Why?"

"Nae my luv, I am glad he helped y'. And y' know I donae care if he is here when I amnae." His accent was thick. His voice husky. "Was I rude t' him?"

"A little."

He frowned and drew closer, touched her face. "I will apologize in the mornin'. Is tha' alrigh'? Tonight I have y' to myself and I plan t' take full advantage o' that."

11 February

Evan looked over from his book, or more accurately from where he'd been staring out the window at the southern Scotland landscape from the train window in between reading, when his friend lowered beside him, guitar in hand.

"Need your thoughts. Busy?"

"Sight-seeing. We are back in Scotland now, am I right?"

Duncan glanced out the window. "Barely. No' a lot here t' see from the train. Want t' jump off and hike a while? I can show you something worth lookin' a' that way."

"Tempting. Doubt your wife would approve."

"She could come with. Would wear Danielle ou' good."

Evan grinned. The thought was horribly tempting.

"Would y' come back an' hike with me? Tread through the hills and camp a' night? Sometime it would work with the band schedule."

"Absolutely. Say when."

Duncan gave him a nod and turned back to the Mustang. He always wrote with the Mustang, though he most often used the Strat on stage, or the Telecaster. He played a few measures, syncopated, a touch discordant, and stopped. "I like it and I don't. Canno' figure out why I don't quite. Donae want t' throw it out but I canno' figure how t' fix it since I don't know why I donae like it. Wha' do y' think?"

Evan wondered if his friend realized his accent was wavering as much as the section he'd just played. Back and forth between American and Scottish, and more Scottish the longer he was home, or at least close to home. "Play it again." He focused on the individual notes, the rhythm, the key change. And he nodded. "I think the key change is wrong. Maybe ... G instead of...."

"Instead of E. Yeah, I think y' are right." He played it again, making the change. And again the same way, then the first way, his eyes closed, concentrating on the sound. He changed it again, to F. "That is it. F, no' E." He played it again with the F change and nodded. "Y' are right."

"But not G." Evan grinned.

"Better in G than E. Better yet in F. Do y' think?"

"Have more of it written than that? Hard to tell where you're trying to go without hearing the rest."

"Nearly all."

"Let me hear it."

With another nod, Duncan started at the beginning. Mike moved closer, as did Stu, beside where Susie was now fully tuned in, as well. At the chorus, he sang, his eyes on his wife. An incredible song. They all said as much when he stopped.

"Definitely better in F."

Duncan turned back to him. "So grab your bass and let's work on this."

15 February

She felt lazy sitting and letting Duncan refill her tea, but she was tired. Beyond tired. The one extra show this afternoon as a last minute addition to the tour was one more show than she wanted. It was a nice sign, though, due to demand from fans who couldn't get tickets for the first Edinburgh concert. It sold out. This one was close to it. Of course, she figured some had been to the first one, as well. It should make Axis happy, since their label had been so hesitant to send them.

Even with their sight-seeing time, Raucous had a large number of shows in only five weeks. Adam expected sales to prove it was well worth it. They'd jumped from Scotland to Ireland, to England, Wales, and back to Scotland, covering a lot of ground and building their fan base. Their songs were on the UK radio more often. They'd done a couple of quick interviews and three radio shows.

They were all exhausted.

Susie had hoped to take them into Edinburgh to really see the city. Possibly they could still fit it in after the next day's open house.

"Are y' alright, luv?" Aunt Loretta took the chair beside her. "You donae have t' stay up on our account, if y' would like to turn in."

"I'm okay. I'm pretty used to this by now. And Nella napped too long earlier. She'll never give in to bed yet."

"We can watch over her. And her father is gud with her, from wha' I 'ave seen. I am sure he can ge' her in bed when it is time."

"Oh, he's incredible with her. She goes to sleep for him much better than for me."

"He enjoys bein' a father."

"Yes." She caught Duncan's eyes across the room. He had her tea but was stopped by Collin's parents and Adam. Roy hadn't agreed to stay at the McGuire house, but Adam did with Susie's push.

"We werenae sure how he would feel about it, considerin' wha' he went through with Tom. Too often, it has such a bad effect when a child no' treated right gets t' be a parent."

"I suppose. But it was opposite for him. He wanted to be opposite everything Tom was."

Loretta gave her a light grin. "And he is. Bein' around his aunt and uncle so much helped that, I think, even if he didnae know Collin's parents were family a' the time."

"Maybe, but I think it's just his nature. He's one of the kindest hearted people I've ever known. He doesn't have it in him to be that way."

"Oh, luv. I think he could 'ave. Y' have seen his temper, yes? It has worried us often." She took Susie's hand. "Donae misunderstand. I luv him as my own and I would do anything in the world for 'im. Bu' it is there."

"But there's a difference between a temper that stems from seeing wrong and wanting to fix it, and just being mean. Even with the temper, he's opposite Tom in that way. He doesn't have a mean side anywhere within him. I never would have married him if he did. I would never risk putting my children through that."

"Children? Y' are still planning on another?"

"Oh. I meant ... just that I always... Well, I'd planned on two or three before I knew about my limitations. And I always knew I'd be careful with who I chose, because of them. A good father was up at the top of my had-to-have list for a husband. I did well with that. He is wonderful with her. She's so attached to him."

Susie listened to Loretta talk about Danielle and what a lively spirit she was, how much like Duncan when he was little but with less reserve. Yes, Susie would love to have more children with him. He was such a good father; he deserved more children. He caught her eyes, said something to Adam, and came to her. He always knew when she needed him.

Duncan handed her the cup and caressed her shoulder. "Why do I think I should ask what y' are talking about?"

Susie sipped her tea. It had just the right amount of sugar. "You, as a child."

He raised an eyebrow. "That cannae be gud. Donae listen t' anything she is tellin' you. I have already admitted I was a rotten child. We can leave out the details." His fingers moved up to her neck with a gentle caress.

"Y' were never rotten, luv. Y' were spirited and curious, but always y' were a gentlemen when it mattered."

"I think y' are being nice because y' donae see me often."

"Rubbish. I would take y' in as my own, and I often tried."

"Because y' are some kind of saint."

Susie started to call to Nella to get down off the piano bench, but Linda saw her and sat next to her. "Speaking of a rotten child. She's much too full of herself tonight."

"She is spirited and curious." Loretta threw Duncan a wink.

"She's exhausting."

"She is fine with Mum. Come and sit with me." Duncan helped her to her feet and led her to the love seat so he could sit next to her.

Susie cuddled into him, grateful for the contact and the warmth, as well as his fingers continuing their caress. She had to force her focus back on the conversation, on his aunt. "We have to be exhausting for you, too. We are grateful you're putting up with all of us a couple more days, but we could have gone to a hotel."

"We wouldnae hear of it. It is lovely havin' you all here and gettin' t' know your friends. I 'ave been annoyin' Evan much of the night with my chatter. I can see why he is important t' you both. He adores y' so. A charming lad."

"I'm sure he's not annoyed." Susie found where he was: nearby with Doug and Gene and Linda, with Laura at his side and Nella in his arms. "He enjoys being here. Still, there are a lot of us."

"An' there is a lo' of the house, as well. One o' the few times it 'as made sense t' have such a monstrous thing t' care for. Havin' y' stay is entirely selfish, y' ken. We ge' more time with y' this way."

Selfishly, Susie was glad, also. She loved the McGuire residence, although Duncan was still uncomfortable with how large and overdone it was. Susie ignored that. She focused on its warmth and welcome, how she felt so at home there with him. He'd been hesitant about letting the guys even see it, much less stay there. Except Evan who had already visited and never commented on the size or splendor of Ambassador McGuire's residence. Stu and Mike had of course joked with him about it, considering how Duncan had been barely making ends meet and sleeping wherever he could find somewhere halfway safe after moving to the States. Stu's "nice digs for a street rat's parents" comment brought him an unimpressed look from Duncan and a punch to the arm from Susie.

He was dealing with it well, though, other than when the house servants called him Mr. McGuire in front of his band mates instead of his name and acted as though he was part master of the house. Susie knew they considered him to be just that, regardless of how he insisted he wasn't. Gene apparently made it clear to them all that his son was as much an owner of the property as he was. He'd told Duncan he was. As Gene's only biological heir, responsibility would fall on him when the time came.

The groups chatting around the room soon joined all together, other than Mike, Stu, Danny, and Collin. Susie had seen Danny tap Stu on the chest as he talked with Marta and drag him off somewhere. She didn't even want to know where. Or why. She was pretty sure Danny had cleaned up his act for the most part, but she didn't think he had completely.

"I will be back in a minute." Duncan kissed the side of her head, told Nella to stay with her grandpa when she started to follow, and headed the direction his brother disappeared.

Laura took her side. "Dad 'as been practicing on the violin for y'."

"Laura." Gene gave her a look.

Susie grinned. "Have you? Do I get to hear it?"

"I am sure y' are too tired t' have me squeal bad notes in your ear."

"And I'm sure you won't squeal bad notes." She gave her father-in-law another smile. "Really, I'd love to hear it."

Linda rubbed her husband's arm. "How can y' say no t' that? They will be leavin' us in a couple of days and then y' will wish y' had."

Gene gave in and Susie grinned at Evan as he went to find his instrument.

She watched him tune, by ear as Duncan did, and hoped her husband would be back soon to hear his dad play. She considered going to find him, to help buffer if necessary, when movement at the far door pulled her eye. They were all there.

Duncan moved up behind her and set a hand on her shoulder. She grasped his fingers and looked up to see his face. He was impressed by his father's skill. There was also something more. Respect, maybe. The more Duncan got to know Gene McGuire, the more he came to appreciate being his son.

After a couple of songs, both Celtic, Gene set the violin on his lap.

"It was beautiful. Thank you." Susie didn't want to push but she wished he would keep going.

"DJ, go an' grab your guitar for a duet." Laura got up and pressed against her brother. "I 'ave been wanting to hear that."

He tried to refuse, said he'd played enough recently, and wouldn't back down until Gene asked if they could do just one song. Danny and Collin threw comments that Duncan was afraid he couldn't keep up with his father. Danielle frowned at them and Duncan scooped her up and took her with him.

"Canny wha' y' say about her dad." Laura focused on her cousin. "She doesnae think y' are funny an' she will hold it against y'."

"She will ge' over i'." Collin plopped down on the floor. "Wouldnae want his head t' ge' big only 'cause his face is everywhere now, would y'?"

"He willnae." Laura's frown looked so much like Nella's, Susie nearly laughed.

Collin did. "An' I think it is his baby sister who doesnae think we are funny, ne'ermind his daughter."

"Y' are right. I donae think y' are funny."

"Laurie luv, areyae nae too old t' still hero worship your big brother? I would've thought y'd've grown ou' of it by now."

"Nae, and I willnae, either." She raised her chin as Collin and Danny laughed. "So y' just watch wha' y' say around me, as well. I amnae afraid t' box your ears again as I used t' do."

They laughed harder and Stu and Mike joined in, not at Laura but just at their laughter. Susie looked over at Evan. He returned the gaze. They both knew darn well what the four of them had been doing.

The parents tried to turn the conversation and calm things down until Duncan returned with his Mustang. And with Evan's acoustic bass. "If I have t' get stuck playin', so do you."

Evan gave him a grin and waited for Duncan to tune, then tuned his own from his friend's guitar.

"Wha' did you want to hear that we would both know?" He asked Laura.

"Amazing Grace. Do y' still remember it?"

Duncan nodded and focused on his guitar, playing notes and chords here and there, as though reminding himself. Then he looked over at Gene and got a nod to start.

It was absolutely gorgeous. One she'd never heard him play, and with his father adding the violin ... she wished they could stay longer, do this every night. Evan didn't join them. He listened, as struck as she was by how well they played together, read each other.

"Sing it, DJ." Laura softly interrupted at the end of a verse.

He hesitated, but gave in. Susie closed her eyes part way through. Gorgeous. Soul-wrenching gorgeous. The lyrics, music, the way he sang them with emotion creeping in farther than he normally allowed. He knew more verses than she'd even heard. Danielle crawled onto her lap and cuddled in. Her soft pudgy little girl hands gripped Susie's thin long fingers. Delicate, Duncan called them. He was always so careful with her hands. Nella played with her rings as she often did when she was tired. They didn't twist as easily as usual. She'd gained some weight, enough to fill her out better, make her look healthier. And she was plenty warm at the moment.

Moisture tickled her eyes. It was so gorgeous. Duncan was so gorgeous, inside and out. Backward and forward. His looks, his voice. The way he moved his fingers on the strings. The way he held his head. Even his neck was gorgeous. She'd compared his neck to other men as soon as she'd started thinking how nice his was, and it was, more than most. And his eyes. His light blue eyes. The long lashes. The just-right tilt and arch of his eyebrows. As his eyes caught hers, she knew he realized she'd been studying him again. He often caught her just looking at him. It didn't bother him anymore.

Maybe she shouldn't have been thinking about her husband's looks during the song, still ... it was amazing that she'd been given someone so incredibly perfect for her. Maybe not perfect generally; his buddies might argue, but for her, he was. She still couldn't imagine how she'd been touched so deeply with the gift of him, of his daughter. Or how her prayers had been answered so well that Nella turned out so much like him as she'd repeatedly prayed.

As the song ended, she didn't dare speak. Collin called for something more upbeat and after some comparing notes, they pulled Evan in to join them. Nella became heavier against her and gave up playing with Susie's rings to just hold her hand. When the music slowed again, Nella's eyes closed. Susie leaned her head against her child's head, smelled traces of baby shampoo mixed with the sweetness of little girl scent. Nella still had that fresh baby smell after her bath. She would grow out of it soon, Susie supposed.

Duncan looked over. "I think it is time for bed."

"Hey, no way. It's early." Stu jumped up. "How 'bout a midnight swim. No way I'm gonna sleep yet."

"I amnae not sure y' should get into the water tonight."

"Hell, I have to do something to use this energy."

Susie cradled Nella in against her, a hand over her ear to try not to let the noise wake her, as Laura agreed to go swimming and Stu offered her an arm up to go with him.

"Y' donae plan t' take my sister swimmin' on your own."

"Aw, come on. You're seriously worried about me? Kara would never speak to me again."

"She wouldnae be the only one." Duncan took Danielle and adjusted her against his shoulder as the guys agreed to join the party.

"Go with them." Susie brushed the side of his leg as she stood. "I'll get her to bed."

Linda and Gene said they should both go with their friends. When Gene claimed Danielle, Susie considered arguing, but the thought of the warm indoor pool after a long five weeks, their insistence, and her husband's eyes made it too hard to resist.

Evan pushed himself up to sit at the edge of the pool. Stu was right. It was a nice way to relax and unwind, and he was relaxed and unwound enough to call it a night. While he sat and allowed the extra water to drip off his skin, he watched Laura harass her brothers and brush off Stu's flirting.

From the far end, Susie dove beneath the surface and gracefully made her way across the pool, emerging close to him. Her shoulders just above the water, she wiped her face and slid her hands over her hair. It was pulled back and wrapped into a messy bun to keep it out of her way. Moving the rest of the way to where Evan sat, she turned her back to the wall, propped her hands on each side, and raised herself up beside him.

"Tired?" She sat close, her gaze on where the others still splashed.

"Getting there."

"I'm well past there. Think I'll have to be the first to give in. Pathetic, huh?"

"Not at all. The rest of us don't have main care of a two-year-old with the energy of her father."

"Except her father."

"He was overdosed with energy at birth. Don't try to keep up with that."

"As if I could. Are you ready for the chaos tomorrow?"

"Won't bother me, but I think Duncan will be glad when it's over."

"Oh, he hates these things. Only respect for his parents keeps him from refusing."

"Wouldn't they understand if he did?"

"Sure, but ... I think he's not comfortable refusing anything in his father's house yet. He respects him. I can see he does. But he keeps a distance. I hope that will change. Gene adores him so."

"It'll take time, Suse. He hasn't known him long and doesn't see him often."

She nodded and turned quiet. Evan wondered if she was looking for more from him, better advice or ... or something he didn't catch that she needed. Duncan hadn't said anything about his father, who he'd just learned was his father two and a half years earlier, since then. At least nothing of much importance. Evan could see the respect, as well. It was apparent. Still, he was wary. Given his relationship with Tom who had pretended to be his father all those years, Evan couldn't blame him. He was close to John, though. He'd dropped all defenses with Susie's dad. In time, he and Gene could very well become close. They needed to see each other more often.

Susie stretched her back and shoulders, and Duncan looked over. With a word to his sister, he did a quick front crawl over to his wife and raised a dripping hand to her face. "Y' are getting too tired." At her nod, he pulled out of the water, stood, and offered his hand to help her up. With a look to where Stu was teasing Laura, he hesitated.

"I'll stay until they give in." Evan watched his expression. "But you know he wouldn't actually try anything."

"No' in general, bu' he is not quite himself tonight. Danny isnae, either."

"I had a feeling. And Mike and Collin are about the same. Go ahead. I'll stay."

"Are y' sure? I can find Caleb if y' would rather."

"It's fine. Doug and I will kick them out if it gets much later."

Duncan wrapped a towel over his wife and rubbed himself mostly dry and they threw good nights as they left. So perfect together. The understanding between them was completely natural, totally ingrained. They were both more relaxed while with the other than they ever were on their own. He was enamored of that kind of relationship. He wanted that. He supposed everyone did, if they let themselves believe in it.

Evan didn't quite believe it was anything but rare. Although Duncan's parents appeared to have the same thing from what he could see. Susie's parents had, also, until John lost his wife. Much too early. Gene and Linda had given each other up in order to keep their son, for so many years. If that was the kind of price to pay for that kind of relationship, Evan figured he'd do just as well with something more normal. There was only one person in the world worth that much risk. And she was Duncan's wife.

Pulling his head out of where he didn't want it, he went over to the hot tub. He wouldn't be able to stay in long as tired as he was, but he could watch the activity from there until he could make himself kick them out.

Within a few minutes, Laura got out and told her tormentors she wanted soothing company for a while. She came over and joined him. "Do y' mind?" Her eyes were playful, not tired.

"Of course not."

She made her way down into the steaming frothy water and lowered to an opposite seat. "I 'ave been wanting to apologize abou' Aunt Loretta."

"For what?"

"I know she is tryin' t' push you at me. I told her I am no' old enough and tha' y' are like a brother t' me, bu' she worries and thinks I need someone calm and stable."

Evan grinned. "Calm and stable would bore the heck out of you."

"Tha' is wha' I told her. I mean, y' donae bore me. I mean I..."

"I'm honored you think of me as a brother."

"DJ feels like y' are, so y' are to me, as well."

He looked over to where Doug and Mike were now sitting at the edge of the pool. "About ready to call it a night? I'll walk up with you."

She smiled. "Always such a gentleman. Y' are so sweet."

"Nah, getting tired and looking for an excuse."

"Well, come on then, bu' we cannae leave the happy boys alone. I will 'ave t' kick them ou' so they donae drown themselves."

16 February

Evan kept track of his friend through the current of people revolving through the McGuire residence. Although being in the midst of a crowd of screaming girls grabbing at him while he signed his name and gave them hugs and had his picture taken with any who could get close enough after their last Edinburgh concert date the day before didn't bother Duncan in the slightest, this crowd was different. He was torn between his role as the son of the highly respected ambassador hosting the party and just one of the band, also their biggest sex appeal draw. Duncan would argue if Evan called him that out loud, but it was true. Mike was, also, particularly since the lead singer most often got the most attention, but otherwise it was Duncan girls screamed for in the fanatic way that said he could play one string at a time off tune and still have their attention. His incredible skill with his guitar only added to the mystique.

Here, it was being the one member of Raucous actually from Edinburgh. Not only that, but the newly-found son of Gene McGuire. According to Danny, there had been a lot of talk about his mother's recent marriage to Duncan's father after she divorced Danny and Laura's father. Gene now claimed them as his own. At least he claimed Laura since she was willing enough to change her name from O'Neil to McGuire. Danny was still O'Neil. He said it was who he was and he saw no reason to pretend otherwise. Duncan said Gene claimed him anyway, enough to name him as part heir along with Duncan and Laura. Evan could see a fair amount of distance between Danny and Gene, but it appeared better during this visit. He figured it was partly out of high esteem for Linda. But more so, he thought, because Gene was Duncan's father, and regardless of how Laura was teased for adoring her eldest brother, Danny was nearly as bad.

Sipping the strong coffee, Evan noticed Danielle tug at her dad again. In the middle of conversation with three young women he obviously knew, Duncan picked her up and kept talking. It was so second nature by now, he looked as though he'd been a dad forever. Often, Nella wanted only to hold onto him for a few minutes before she got down again and looked for adventure.

Adding father and husband to his rock guitarist/ambassador's son image looked as natural as everything else he did. Even while he talked with everyone who insisted on his attention, he kept track of where Danielle and Susie were. It wasn't an easy task since Nella loved to swerve around the legs of guests and harass anyone she saw who she knew, and nearly as many guests stopped Susie to talk while she tried to keep up with her daughter. Evan often took over and told her to relax while he kept an eye on Nella. Or one of their band mates did, or Uncle Danny. There were plenty of eyes watching her, but the child acted as though she didn't know they were, or didn't care. She was very much at home in her grandparents' house.

Since Danielle was still for the time being and Susie was enveloped by a crowd of Laura's friends, Evan went to refill his coffee. One of the young maids insisted on doing it for him and he took a seat at the empty kitchen table, glad for a moment of quiet.

It didn't last long. As she set his cup before him and Evan thanked her, two female voices floated into the room, and then stopped. He recognized one of them as an old classmate of Duncan's.

She smiled, a genuine smile. "Y' are Evan, am I right? I am Marjory. We me' earlier."

He stood and gave her a nod. "I remember." How would he not remember? Her bright brown hair with tinges of red and pretty features highlighted her friendliness. Duncan had shown her respect. That meant a lot in Evan's book. He offered a chair and held it. The friend pulled out her own before he could offer.

"Are y' hidin' from the crowd?"

"I guess you could say that. Only for a minute or two."

"Are we botherin' y'?"

"Not at all." He sat back and enjoyed the conversation, though now and then he had to ask for a translation of a word he didn't recognize. They mainly talked about the band and the States until he managed to turn it around to find she was a nurse at Edinburgh Hospital, that she and Duncan had trained together for a short time at a local physician's office. She was fully impressed by his skill and the way he moved so easily from one field using catgut to another. With a laugh, she emphasized that she did know neither used actual catgut anymore, and it wasn't actually from cats, to her great relief as her two cats were her great loves so far. Evan decided not to mention that it sometimes was still used for instruments because of the higher quality sound.

"I supposed I should le' y' rejoin the party, yes?" She peered into his eyes and nudged a foot into his.

Evan decided it might be a good idea. Standing, he held her chair and then her friend's.

"Will it bother y' if we walk out together? I donae want t' give any wrong impressions if it will affect y' in any way."

"I can't see how it would."

"Och well, I have broken off two engagements in the past year. Many here know I 'ave. I amnae a huzzie, as many might think. It is only that they too often change toward y' after they think they have y' wrapped around their finger and belongin' to them. I willnae be servant to my husband. When they star' thinkin' I should be, I le' them loose. I' is nae more than that."

"And you shouldn't be servant to a spouse. I nearly got into that once myself." Evan was much more fully engrossed by her than he wanted to be.

"I cannae see y' puttin' up with that."

"Not for very long."

She stepped closer. "Y' donae treat your women tha' way?"

He breathed in her perfume. Roses. Light, not overpowering. "I was raised by a very independent woman. I wouldn't dare."

Marjory grinned. "I think I might like t' meet her. And d' y' have a girlfriend?"

"Not currently." Not since she'd broken up with him over the phone one night in the middle of tour. The rumors. Or the distance. He wasn't sure.

Marjory took his arm and set a hand on his chest. "It is a shame y' are only here for another day or so."

A bold girl to touch him so intimately, not that he minded. "It is. Although I'd have to ask..." He hesitated, afraid it would be far too pointed, too suggestive.

"I havenae dated DJ, if y' are wondering. We were friends only."

"I was wondering."

She grinned. "Because it would make a difference t' y'."

"It would. If I was staying more than another day." He felt her move in and stepped back. "I think we should rejoin the party."

Marjory stayed at his side as they returned to the crowd. He saw a couple of curious looks from people he didn't know, but he saw no reason to hide the fact he was talking to her. So what if she'd been engaged? He had been once, also; nearly twice. Marjory wasn't married. And she hadn't dated Duncan.

He scanned the room for his friend. Evan would know by Duncan's expression whether or not he should avoid her. Mike and Stu were surrounded by a group of girls. Doug sat with an older couple and a teenage boy who looked enthralled with the conversation. Adam was with Gene and a few of his coworkers. He didn't see Duncan, or Susie.

"You are DJ's friend, yes? The one who pulled him into your band?"

Evan turned to a face he somewhat recognized and gave his name.

"I am Alana Wiley, Gene's youngest sister. I stayed with our brother David often as I was younger. He is Collin's father."

"It's nice to meet you." He offered his hand.

She held onto it with both of hers. "I saw the boys together often as they were growin'and took photos as I could to share with his father, as well as tellin' him stories of DJ, to try t' help him feel a bit closer."

"Duncan's glad to be in touch with Collin again, I know."

Marjory set a hand on his back. "I am goin' t' excuse myself now, bu' I will be around. I hope we can talk la'er."

"Of course." Evan gave her a grin and watched her move away. She had an elegant walk: elegant and seductive, not openly, only suggestively.

"You know much about his past."

Evan forced his attention back to Duncan's aunt. "Yes."

"Linda cannae stop talking about how glad she is tha' the two of you ran int' each other as y' did. She says y' may have saved his life." Her eyes were searching, misty.

"No, he was doing all right. He holds his own well."

"He always did, bu' we are glad he doesnae have t' do so now. Y' have been a good friend to him. We are all grateful."

"It's very mutual. No gratitude necessary." Evan caught a glance of Danielle pushing through the crowd with Laura on her heels, but she was stopped by a woman who tried to talk to her.

"He is glad t' have you here today, and his band mates. They are lovely people and y' all get along well, it seems."

"Usually. We have our moments." He saw Danielle start a minor fit. She pushed Laura away, shook her head.

"Oh, an' of course. Even DJ and Collin had their spats and

sometimes wouldnae speak t' each other for days. Tha' is the wonderful thing abou' boys, though. They spat and ge' over it and are still best o' friends."

"If it's a good friendship, yes. Duncan and I have had our moments, also. I wasn't always sure we'd get over it." Nella got louder. Evan didn't see her parents anywhere.

"Ah but there is respect there. We can all see it, on both sides. Tha' is what matters most, as I 'ave always said, with any relationship."

"Yes, I'd agree with that." Nella pushed at Laura, hard. "Sorry, excuse me a minute." Evan made his way to the child and crouched down to get her attention. "Danielle, you're not being nice to your aunt." She wrapped little arms around his neck and he picked her up. "You're a tired little one, I think."

"No. Want my *Daddy*. Aun' Laura say *no*."

"I didnae say no, Miss Danielle." Laura threw her a look. "I said Daddy is busy. He will be back in a minute."

"*No*. My daddy *no'* busy for Dani-nella."

Evan noticed nearby heads turn and stroked her hair to help calm her. "Okay then, let's go find your daddy."

Laura told him Duncan and Susie had taken a walk around the garden to get some breathing space and fresh air. Evan expected they might be a while, so he strolled about the room. As long as he kept moving, she would stay patient. At least for the moment. As heavy as she was in his arms, he thought she might fall asleep. He could hope.

When they were stopped, he made sure to say they were going to find her daddy so she wouldn't protest, and he didn't stop for long. Marjory rejoined him and walked along beside. Nella let her head rest on his shoulder as her arms loosened their grip. It worked fine until Mike came over and her head jerked up at his voice.

"Hey, little one. Why don't you come to me a while? Give Evan's arms a break."

She shook her head hard and shoved her face into Evan's neck.

"Well, that was insulting."

Evan gave him a grin. "We're going to find her daddy."

Nella's head popped up again. "Yes. My daddy is here. Yes."

"No, he's not here. He ran away." Mike tickled her. "You get to be mine now and stay with Keith."

"*No*. My daddy is here. *Yes*. He *not* run 'way from Nella."

"Donae torment my niece." Danny shoved up against Mike. "Come, li'l Nella bird. We will find something t' entertain ourselves, yes?"

Again, she shook her head and clung to Evan.

Evan wasn't sure Danny appreciated it, but he'd promised her, so he started walking again. It was fair enough, as Duncan would say. She would be his if, God forbid, anything happened to her parents. They hadn't asked Danny or Laura or their parents. They'd asked him. He wanted to be the most important to her, after her parents, even if he wasn't family. Susie had told him, when they revealed they were expecting, that he had to be there, her daughter had to know him. The memory of her words were etched into his soul. They touched him more than he could ever tell her.

Spotting his friends as they came in the parlor door, Evan headed that direction. Susie's cheeks were pink with cold, but she was radiant and smiled to whoever it was she recognized and talked with while she grasped Duncan's back and cuddled against his side. Evan hated to interfere but figured he'd stalled as long as he dared. He made his way around behind the group and took Duncan's side. "I found something that belongs to you."

Turning with a question in his gaze, he grinned at his daughter's face tucked into Evan's neck. "She looks comfortable enough."

Nella popped her head up and lunged at him.

Evan shrugged. "She got mad at Aunt Laura for keeping her away from you. Thought I'd take over for a while but my luck was running low." He caught Susie's eyes. "Tried to give you the time I could."

"I'm sorry. We would have come in sooner if we'd known. Was she being horrible for you?" Her cheeks were even fresher pink close up.

"Not for me. Laura looked a bit exasperated."

Susie sighed. "Oh Danielle. You'll have to tell your aunt you're sorry."

Duncan chuckled. "Laurie exasperated me oft' as she pleased when she was little. Fair enough for Danielle t' return the favor."

"That doesn't make it okay." Susie brushed curls back from Nella's face. "I think you're tired. Time for a nap. And then you can apologize to your aunt."

"I nae tired." Nella shook her head and gripped Duncan's neck again. She refused to go to her mom. Evan didn't think Susie appreciated it any more than Mike or Danny had.

Susie stood beside the doorway that connected Danielle's room with theirs as her husband calmed Nella with a song: a cappella, and so gorgeous. Finally, he rose from the low, small bed Linda put in just for Danielle and came to her.

"I think she is out for a while."

"I'll have to stay. I can't leave her up here alone."

"I will stay with you." He pressed closer. "Y' are still cold. I kept y' outside too long."

"I didn't object, did I?" She teased the skin between the V of his navy shirt. He wasn't wearing a tie as many of the men were; the shirt was open two buttons, enough to be terribly sexy and still sophisticated enough. "You should go back to your company. I'll sit and read. It's fine."

He gave her a light kiss. "An' maybe I want t' find better things for y' t' do while she is asleep. Yes?" His lips moved to her neck.

"With a house full of people?" She closed her eyes, giving in to him, at least for a moment.

"The door will lock." He kissed the curve of her shoulder. Fingers slid beneath her blouse.

"I am sorry."

Susie opened her eyes to find Marta at their door, blushing deeply. She offered, at Linda's request, to stay and watch Nella. Duncan joked that she was taking their excuse to hide for a while and she blushed again, and apologized. Susie fussed at him.

Thanking Marta with a grin on the way out, Duncan stopped at the landing halfway between floors and set a hand aside Susie's face. "Y' know how often I have heard about you today? Abou' how lucky I was t' find you?"

She rested her hands on his stomach. "They don't know me well."

"They only know the tip of it." He brushed her bangs with his fingers. "I have stopped worrying abou' what they think of me, about whether I am what Gene McGuire's son should be. They are all so impressed with you, they give me more credit than they should."

She gripped his shirt at the waist, felt his warmth through the fabric. "I think you're exaggerating, but I love you for it. They are impressed by you. Part of it is the respect they have for your father, but mostly, it's just you." She shrugged gently. "I wish you could see yourself the way the rest of us see you. But then, I wouldn't want it to go too far to your head."

He caught her hand and kissed her fingers. "Stay by my side, my luv. I want t' show y' off as much as I can while we are here, and I 'ave shared y' enough for today."

"I'm always by your side. Always. And I'm proud to be." Accepting a kiss, although she heard voices down below, someone entering or leaving, Susie wrapped her arms all the way around him and half wished Marta hadn't interrupted.

"They are still together so far, as I see."

Claire's voice grated into her ears and she pulled back to look down at her and her parents. The witch's father warned her to be civil as Duncan grasped Susie's fingers again to walk the rest of the way downstairs. He said hello to Claire's parents and fully ignored Claire.

"I hear y' have a wee one about. Didnae take long, and I thought y' were going t' wait some time, DJ. I' is what y' said." She threw a look at Susie.

Susie refused to speak to her. Gene said she should be at home, do as she pleased. He would understand her unwillingness to speak to Duncan's ex who was so intolerably rude the last time they saw each other.

Duncan gave the witch the *don't screw with me* attitude Susie had seen so often. "I suppose the odds were against it takin' as long as we planned, considering. Fate can only be held off for so long when y' tempt it too often." He slid a hand up Susie's back and nudged her in closer.

He was rotten, thoroughly rotten when he tried to be. But she had to bite her tongue to keep from laughing at Claire's reaction.

"Lovely, DJ. Such a gentleman, as y' always were. I am sure your father enjoys y' talking in such a way around his company." She flicked her hair and it fell back to where it had been. As Mike often did. Somehow Mike didn't look half as pretentious when he did it.

"I havenae seen that he is concerned." As he offered to show her parents, Gene's colleague and his wife, to where Gene and Linda were, he slid his hand up to Susie's shoulder in a loosely protective stance. She knew that well, also. When they were on the road, he often came up and slid a hand over her shoulder whenever she started to feel uncomfortable with some guy who stood too close or looked at her in a way she didn't like. Duncan always noticed, but he said nothing. The hand on her shoulder and the look he gave them worked well enough.

"Hey." Stu jumped in front of them. "We were starting to think you decided to nap with your daughter." He glanced at the newcomers and at Duncan's hand on her shoulder. "Sorry, am I interrupting?"

"Nae, y'are not. Danielle didnae settle in easily." He introduced Stu to the parents, not to Claire. She introduced herself.

Talking only long enough to be polite, Stu exchanged a look with Duncan and asked if he could steal his wife. Barely waiting for the okay, he grabbed her by the hand and moved to a somewhat clear spot. "So you don't like them much, right? Or he doesn't."

"That's the ex I knocked to the floor the first time we were here."

Stu laughed. "Is it? Glad to know. I kinda hope she'll give you reason to do it again, 'cause that, I'd like to see."

"Might not take much. She's already starting. Do me a favor."

"Anything for you." He winked.

"If you see her around Laura, go interfere. It wouldn't take much for her to do it, either."

"Will do." He stepped back and gave her a slight bow.

"Stop that." As she fussed, Susie saw Claire come up to them, behind Stu. She warned him with a glance.

The witch took his arm in both hands and pressed her chest against it. "Y' are the piano player."

"Keyboards. I can do piano but it's kinda hard to carry one around on tour." He pulled back as much as he could.

"And what made y' do that instead of guitar or drums or something more ... well..."

Susie wanted to belt her again. Harder than the first time. Across the jaw.

"Manly?" Stu held his chin up, his back straight. "Hey, you're not the first to say it."

"I didnae mean any offense."

"And I'm not offended. I like my instrument and I know how to use it."

Susie saw Claire wonder how hard she could flirt with him and get away with it. She didn't want to hear it, even if Stu was baiting her. "Actually, he plays guitar well. Very well. Also the drums. Bass. Sax."

She focused on Stu. "I forget what else I've seen you play. Miss anything?"

"I can do a half decent violin and a passable tuba, though since the thing is bigger than I am, I don't care much for it."

"Yeah well, I prefer you on the keyboards. Or piano. I could sit and listen to that all day. Which reminds me; you haven't played the Grand at Adam's lately, have you?"

"Now and then. When nothing's going on."

Susie started to ask if he'd invite her to go listen next time but Gene joined them. A rescue, she figured, since he stepped between Claire and Stu. Susie used the chance to reclaim Stu's side, to claim him, as a dig at the witch. Susie would warn Mike, also. She couldn't have them.

Conversation about instruments continued and Stu reminded her he'd played both clarinet and flute for his job at the music store. She'd never heard either. Gene offered to let Stu use his violin, or their piano.

Duncan broke away from Claire's parents when Collin joined him and they both came over. He took Gene's side instead of reclaiming her from Stu. Collin stood between him and Claire. As his dad explained their conversation and admitted to being unsure how someone could learn so many instruments, Duncan said his friend juggled them as well as he juggled women, and that was far more impressive, as far as he was concerned.

"Aye and y' wouldnae know how t' do the same?" Claire eyed him. "From all I hear, y' do it well yourself."

Gene's jaw clenched. Susie couldn't imagine why the witch would infer such a thing in front of Duncan's father. She figured Claire should be glad she was female; otherwise Gene would likely have her by the collar as he'd done to Mitch for the same kind of insinuation against Susie.

"Y' never did know how t' discern fact from fiction and still donae, I see." Duncan moved around behind Susie and wrapped his arms around her stomach. "I do well to juggle my wife and my daughter. They both keep my hands qui' full enough." He kissed her neck.

"No damn kidding." Stu rolled his eyes. "At least one of them is always hanging on him, sometimes both. Can't imagine how he gets any writing done."

"Easy." Susie couldn't help it, even if Aunt Loretta joined them. "I sit behind him while he's writing so I can hang on him and he can work."

"Aye right, sometimes I can still work that way." Duncan squeezed her lightly. "And other times I figure work will wait till early morning when she is sleeping. Tha' is mainly when I write." He directed his statement at his father. Susie had to wonder if he thought Gene might actually believe the rumors. She knew he didn't. She knew he had far more faith in his son than to ever think he would.

"Or when the little terror has your wife's hands full."

Duncan grinned at Stu. "Ah and why do y' think we are always taking her down t' entertain you?"

"Yeah, yeah. Rub it in. All my girl juggling isn't shit compared to what you have and I'm already jealous as hell. I don't need to know what you're doing while I'm terror sitting."

Gene smirked and rubbed his chin. Claire walked away. Stu apologized to Loretta for his language, which she brushed off as nothing. She said between the boys she helped raise and her husband, she'd heard it all and then some.

As conversation continued and Danny came over to join them, he and Collin mentioned something about a Highlands camping trip for boys only over a long weekend. They wanted Duncan to come back for it over the summer. She agreed it would be nice if they could work it around the band's schedule, which was rather full. They agreed to work their dates around Raucous and Gene said she and Nella would be kept busy by the women of the house. She assured him she wouldn't at all mind a return trip to Scotland, without touring this time. Collin seemed surprised she didn't object to letting Duncan go off with them alone. It was only a few days and she'd be there in the same country. She couldn't object to that. It would be nice for him.

Duncan heard the conversation around him but didn't pay much attention. His attention was across the room where Susie held his cousin's newborn. He could see her longing. It was at least the second time she'd claimed the baby, maybe the third. The way she caressed the tiny arm and fingers gave him a longing, as well, one he didn't want. She was a natural mother, purely content with a baby in her arm. He saw it with Keith, with Danielle, and again with this baby of a cousin he barely knew. He couldn't help wish it was his second child in her arms instead. He wanted more children with her. More of his own. They'd talked about two or three. And they couldn't. She couldn't. Not of their own.

She smiled at the mother as they chatted and she swayed lightly. Soothing the infant who looked plenty calm and content. Babies were rarely not calm and content in her care. She was relaxed with them and they could feel it, feel the love she gave them. Susie could pick up a baby out of a stroller on the sidewalk and the child would feel comfortable.

"Better stop watching that. It's bound to lead you smack into trouble." Broden, his old buddy who'd waited till most of Gene's acquaintances had left to come by, nudged him.

"Aye it might."

"Aye?" Mike laughed. "Damn, you've been here too long. You're starting to sound more like one of them."

"Am I nae?" Duncan wished Collin wasn't close enough to hear.

"Yeah in a way, but no, not too much. You're too Americanized by now. You fit and you don't. Kinda like I feel when I go back to New Hampshire. Grew up there but I don't fit it anymore. It's different to me now."

"Right, and yet it is always a part of you, deny it as you wish." He returned the grin and looked back over at his wife as she lifted the baby over her shoulder and rubbed his back. A boy; a braw round boy with short tufts of blonde hair. He wouldn't mind having a son to carry on his name, now that he had a name worth carrying on.

"Hell mate, your wee one is old enough by now. Do your husbandly duty and give the girl another. She looks as though she wouldnae object."

Collin shoved Broden and told him to mind his own business. Never one to give up easily, Broden kept it up. With only Mike, Evan, and his two Rugby mates in the current group, his tongue was far too loose.

"Or do y' have too many girls on the road t' be able to keep up with your li'l wife these days?"

"I have no other girls and I donae want any."

"Aw come, I amnae glaikit, y' ken. I 'ave known y' too long, mate."

Duncan set his gaze on Broden, the *knock it the fuck off* gaze his old mate would well understand. "I was single when y' knew me. I amnae now. And y' know when I make a vow, I keep it."

"What did he just say?"

Mike was interfering, changing the topic. Duncan knew he was. "He said he wasn't brainless. I amnae sure that is true."

Broden laughed. "Ach, I give. Couldnae ever win wits with you. Donae know why I keep tryin'. But on the serious side, areyae gonna give the lass another bairn one o' these years? The first turned out a bonny lass despite 'er father."

"We may adopt before long. She hasnae brought it up yet."

"Adopt? Why in the hell would y' do it tha' way when y' could have a stoatin' time the regular way?"

"It nearly killed her the first time. We made sure she cannae take the chance again." Duncan heard the silence and the soft apology, the assumption she'd been fixed so she couldn't conceive. He couldn't make himself argue. It didn't matter which of them did.

She was on her feet now, swaying to calm the fussy bairn. Susie spoke beside his ear, stroked his back, in no hurry to give him back to his mom. Duncan figured the adoption conversation would come up soon. He hoped that was the only baby conversation that would.

Marjory set a hand on his back and asked if the conversation was boys only. Ev's eyes were on her. He'd been horribly distracted by her much of the day. Duncan told her absolutely she could join them, and he drew his friend in to talk more. He could see them together. She was elegant enough for Ev, still with plenty of fire, and very much hands on. Despite what Susie thought, Ev was into hands-on girls far more than he was himself.

A shame Marjory lived across the ocean. The four of them could do well with double dates and joint travel. He and Ev both had that in mind. His friend just had to find a girl who would get along with Susie and not be bothered by how close she and Ev were. He figured it should be doable.

Before long, he pulled his mates into a separate conversation and added distance from Ev and Marjory. Ev took the hint well. He asked her if she wanted to step outside for air.

Convinced her daughter was asleep, Susie ran through the shower, savoring the hot water that plummeted over her chilled skin. The house was warm enough for most. She knew Duncan was warmer than he wanted to be and the other guys changed out of their shirt sleeves in favor of T-shirts as soon as the older crowd dispersed. Her husband simply rolled his sleeves higher and undid an extra couple of buttons. Still she was chilled, except when Nella had grown tired again and snuggled against her. The girl reflected heat as much as her father did.

She enjoyed sitting around the living room with his family and her band in the relative quiet after the noise of the day. Marjory stayed also and sat with Evan. Her husband apparently didn't mind, even when she stayed after Susie headed up to bed. Danny's girlfriend came by toward the end of the night and was still there. Amy didn't talk much, but she did laugh at Stu when he flirted and Danny pushed him away. And Collin was still there. Susie figured he'd be hardest for Duncan to get away from.

Drying well, Susie wrapped into the long, thick towel. She loved having the guest suite with private bath and connecting smaller room. Actually, there were at least two, maybe more, in the house. Since she didn't have to traipse into the hallway after she showered, she didn't have to pull her pajamas and robe on in a steamy bathroom. The bedroom was cooler, though, and she shivered and hurried to the bed where she left her nightgown, the skimpy black one her husband appreciated.

Before she could unwrap the towel, the door opened. Duncan scanned her as he turned the lock. "I hoped y' were no' asleep yet."

"Hm, no. I'm waiting for you to continue where we left off earlier. If you're still interested."

He stared a moment, then closed the distance. Without touching her elsewhere, he teased her lips ... and moved back just enough to unbutton his shirt and pull it off. "I am goin' t' run through the shower. Stay like this. I will only be a minute."

Susie studied the bare skin of his back as he walked away, the taut muscles and lean waist... She lowered onto the bed when he disappeared from sight, listened to the water turn on, the changing rhythm that said he was moving underneath the flow. Heard it stop. Silence said he was drying off. And he came back. He hadn't bothered to cover himself and her eyes wandered as he drew closer. His mouth returned to hers as he unwrapped her towel and slid his hands over her bare shoulders, leaned in, and pressed her back onto the bed.

Too many girls on the road. Broden was a bit dim, despite his objection. How could he have missed how often Susie was at his side, how often she had his hands on him somewhere? How her eyes so constantly touched his: teasing, appreciating, or only connecting. She was always fully tuned into him. Duncan could feel it as well as he could see it. They were like opposite magnets. Incredibly strong magnets.

Why in the hell would he want some fling when his life partner was nearly always more than willing? Even when she wasn't, he could hold her close, stroke her soft skin, touch her concave stomach, the swell of her breast, the small jaw and neck, or rest his hand on her thigh as he did now with her naked body pressed against his. She was nearly asleep. He loved that she would sleep naked with him. Nothing between them. No clothes. No walls. A few things in their past maybe, but nothing that mattered. His too many flings. Her... It didn't matter.

Duncan kissed her shoulder. She nudged closer.

She'd even given up her own career to be wherever he was. She would move to Scotland with him if he asked, as Ev said she would. She was his world. She and Danielle. His center of the universe. It had been music before he met her. She allowed him both.

"Babe." He ran fingers alongside her face, along where her dark hair streamed from above her ear down behind it, behind her head, down her back, accenting and contrasting with her soft pale skin. Her physical aspects were a mirror of her inner being: the dark and light, the fire and gentleness, determination and wariness, strength and need. She'd joked about his Gemini sign giving him two personalities, but he saw it more in her. It kept him on his toes, intrigued him, turned him on, like a storm, like the beauty and danger and silence and noise of a thunderstorm. "Have I told y' often enough how much I love you?"

"Mm. I love you more." Her breath was a whisper, sleepy, her eyes still closed.

He rolled her onto her back, leaned in, brushed her forehead with his thumb. "Y' cannae. It isnae possible."

With a soft grin, she lifted up to meet his lips. "Why do I have the feeling you're not ready to sleep yet?"

He wasn't, but she was. "Nae, go t' sleep Babe. Y' are tired."

"Hm." She kissed him again, this time with a hand behind his head pulling him in.

Duncan felt his body tense, tried to fight it. She was tired. She ...

she stroked the hand down his shoulder, slid it under his arm and around his back, pulled him closer. Kissed him deeper.

"Suse..."

"Shh. Come here."

Evan walked Marjory to her car and tilted his head up to look at the multitude of stars peppering the dark sky.

"Magnificent." She stroked a hand down his chest.

"Yes. The first time I've seen them so clearly since I've been over here."

"It is rare, we have so many clouds. But I didnae mean the stars." She moved closer, slid her other hand around behind his neck. Her fingers were cold. Her hazel eyes, highlighted by the security lights around the mansion's parking area, blazed. "Do y' know how tempted I am t' move to the States, close t' where you are? Would y' mind?"

Move? Too far too fast. He couldn't let her do it, not for him. "You've known me for one day."

"It feels longer."

"Marjory..."

"My name is far prettier with your accent than it is normally."

It was the accent. The fact he was foreign. Or his job. He could hear Stu tease Susie about falling for Duncan because of his accent. Of course it was more than that, but there was a certain draw a foreigner had, something exotic about it.

"You're quiet all of a sudden."

He grabbed a deep breath and slid an arm around her waist beneath her wool jacket. The green and blue plaid wool jacket. Evan tried to decide whether to kiss her as he wanted. She was pushing things already, but...

She moved in, raised her face to his. "I am teasin'. Abou' the move. It is a joke. I would 'ave t' at least sleep with y' first t' see if we are all that compatible. It matters, yes? If the sex is gud enough?"

He loved how straight forward she was, how she'd had her hands on him so often. "Yes. I may have to come back again and ... maybe we could find out."

"Hm. Y' might start with a kiss and we will see from there."

Maybe he was the one pushing too fast. She loved to tease. He often wasn't sure whether or not she was serious. But she was about the kiss. She leaned in. He met her lips. They were cold. But she warmed fast, pressed in. Her hand wandered on his chest, teased.

Still, as much as he enjoyed her company, and as nice as it was, he didn't feel much emotionally. It was nice. Nothing more.

She dropped her head to his shoulder upon release, gripped him tight. It felt like she had a decent emotional response. "Maybe I amnae teasing."

Evan was just as glad now to have an excuse. He was headed home the day after next.

"Come back t' my place. DJ will figure ou' where y' are. I will have y' back here early in the morning, whenever y' want."

"Marjory. I can't."

She met his eyes. "Tell me y' havenae had one night affairs. In your travels. Y' are single and..."

"I have. Not with you. You're ... Duncan's friend. Can't do that with you." He had to wonder if he'd change his mind if he was more turned on by the kiss. Probably he wouldn't.

She accepted it, though, grudgingly, and asked if she should give him her number, if he would use it. Truthfully, he agreed he would. He did enjoy her company, her thoughts. He would call.

17 February

Susie kissed Danielle's head and thanked Linda for babysitting. Before they headed back to the States that afternoon, Duncan wanted to take his band mates up to Arthur's Seat. She argued it was too cold, but his return argument that the exertion of the climb would keep them warm swayed her to give in. She thought about letting the guys go without her, but it would also be a celebration of their highly successful first overseas tour, and even Adam was making the trek. She couldn't skip that.

Sheltered in so many clothing layers, Suse grew too warm inside the house and was glad to get out into the cold Scottish wind. She was constantly amazed at how much wind there was. It seemed to never stop. She enjoyed the brush of it against her skin, the way it made her inhale so deeply. It had been nicer, though, during their last visit, when it wasn't winter.

Duncan tilted his head up and closed his eyes as his hair blew around his face. He wasn't ready to leave. Although he would never say as much, Susie knew he wasn't. Guilt at keeping him away from his homeland crept in and made her shiver. Not that it was only her keeping him there. Raucous was extremely important to him, more than he let people know. It was a part of who he was by now and he was a part of what Raucous was.

"If it is the wind y' are enjoying, bro, y' will ge' more of it up top o' the hill."

Duncan threw Danny a grin. "I will enjoy it there, also."

"Y' are gyte, y' ken."

"Ah, I remember that one." Stu slid an arm around Susie. "He says he's crazy, right? *Y' are gyte, y' ken.*"

She laughed at his imitation. "That's a good one for you to know, I'm sure. But your accent's wrong."

"Hey, I haven't had as many years to work on it as they have. And my Scots accent is about as *gud* as your husband's American accent."

"No, it's not."

"It is since he's been here a while. Gotta think about what he's saying too often now."

"Nice, isn't it?"

Stu rolled his eyes. "So is that why he won you over me? You coulda told me. I woulda worked on it all those years before he came along."

"Yes, it's the accent, Stu. That was it." She moved in against her husband and set her hands on his chest, beneath the unzipped jacket. "It may have been a bit more than that, too." Unable to resist, she met his lips.

Evan got out of the car and looked up the hills of Holyrood Park to Arthur's Seat. He'd been to the top already, when Duncan asked him to go with on their quick trip home after his aunt had been injured. More than willing to go up again himself, he'd thought about arguing in Susie's favor that it was too cold. For her, it was. She was shivering already, even with her husband's arms around her. He couldn't contradict Duncan, though. Even if he had looked after her for so many more years than Duncan had known her, he couldn't.

"No way." Stu's mouth gaped when Laura pointed to where they were headed.

"Donae be a baby. I' is only a wee hill."

"Wee? There's nothing *wee* about that, and it's not a damn hill. It's a mountain. Hell, we have mountains in New Hampshire, too, but we don't go around climbing the damn things in twenty below zero. I don't even climb the things in livable weather."

"It's not nearly twenty below. It's not even twenty above. Closer to forty." Doug threw him a look. "And a lot of people walk the Appalachian trail in worse weather than this. At least there's no snow."

"Stop trying to sound macho. Hell, they're not serious. Where are we really going?"

Susie moved over to him and slid an arm around his back. "Up there. Serious."

"No way."

Danny tilted his head. "Y' are saying y' cannae do it?"

"I'm saying it's nuts."

"Susie 'as done it twice. Are y' goin' t' let her show y' up?"

"No she hasn't."

"I have. Both times I've been here. The second time was before sunrise and we watched the sun come up over the Forth. It was gorgeous."

"And you walked all the way?"

"Yep." She grasped his hand. "Come on. You'll be fine. I promise." With a wink at her husband, she dragged Stu along beside her until he gave in and started to get into the spirit of it, bumping against her as they walked, teasing and flirting, and telling Duncan he was claiming her for the entirety of the journey so they could keep each other warm.

Susie chuckled. "Only if you can keep up with me. Good luck." She jogged up away from him.

"They're like a couple of little kids." Mike shook his head.

"They are, pretty much. Compared to us old folks." Evan threw a grin since Mike was already touchy about being so "damned close" to thirty. Evan was closer than Mike, by two months. They would both reach it by the end of the next year. Doug would be thirty this coming September. Stu was the baby other than Susie, as he'd just turned twenty-six the month before and she was two and a half years behind him at nearly twenty-four, four years behind her husband. Evan had a hard time imagining she had grown that old already, and yet at other times, he had a hard time seeing her as young as she was. He especially had trouble with the realization she was mother to a two-year-old. It was good, though, he supposed. Since it worked out well and she came through the pregnancy fine, other than a few scary moments, she would have more alone time with Duncan as they grew older and Danielle left home. Susie wanted to travel. With the band was all well and fine, but she wanted more than that. Raucous would never keep going beyond the time Nella was grown and they would then be free to run wherever they pleased. Possibly, Evan could find a girlfriend who would get along with them well enough to do some combined travels.

Nearly halfway up, Stu plopped down on a rock alongside the path and insisted the girls needed to rest. Laura said she absolutely did not need to rest, but Susie gave in and sat next to him. Evan didn't see that she needed it, either. He knew she worked out as much as she could during the tour, but he figured it was keeping up with Danielle and Duncan that kept her in shape. Her arms had strengthened; her energy seemed fine. She hadn't gotten sick this tour as she did during most. She claimed it was the Scottish food, that it didn't bother her as much as the road food in the States. He guessed that could be true, but more likely it was because she was so much less tense this time. There were fewer issues with fans; they had plenty of crowds but they were more respectful for the most part. They had time to sight-see in between. And she'd found a balance between being management and being their guitarist's wife. Evan hoped that would continue when they went home.

When they started again, he switched his thoughts and focused on the climb. With Stu, Danny, and Laura taking much of Susie's attention, he was able to walk beside his friend and enjoy the enlarging vista of Edinburgh as they gained height. He and Duncan didn't talk much. It was unnecessary in the midst of the cold wind and the splendor of rolling hills and the chatter of their group.

"Come with me." Duncan led him off the path as he let Doug know they would catch up in a few minutes.

Evan followed carefully, watching where his feet landed, aware of the long roll down if he lost his footing. They tramped through untrampled foliage, around a clump of stark-bare bushes, next to some patches of browned thistle.

Duncan stopped. "Look in the direction of the hills." He pointed, as though it was necessary.

"The Pentlands?"

He questioned Evan with a look.

"If I remember from last time, that's what Susie called them. You know she's been studying Scotland."

"Has she?"

"Mainly when you've been working with Adam in the studio. It's amazing how much she knows already."

He nodded and returned his gaze to the distance. "Follow the left edge o' it down and forward."

"What are we looking for?"

"Y' see that patch of trees behind the cleared land? Beyond that is a small loch. Y' cannae see it, but it is there."

"Is that where you and Collin used to swim?"

Duncan turned his eyes to him. Only for a second. "It is where I grew up. Where the house still stands, as far as I know."

Evan stood quietly, trying to memorize the layout and remember the path from the trail. Where he'd had to deal with Tom. Where he received the scars. Duncan hadn't spoken of it in months, a year, maybe. Evan figured he'd let it start filtering out of his thoughts. He could have been wrong. "Why did you want me to know?"

His shoulders rose and fell. "I cannae come up here without thinkin' how I used t' climb up and look at it from a distance. T' try t' see myself away from there forever." He crouched and pulled a bit of browned grass from the heath. "Danielle may want t' know where it is sometime in the future. When he is no longer there t' bother her."

"Then you can take her."

He was silent a moment. "I amnae sure I would be able, or would want t' know she was there. Will y' remember where t' find it?"

The address Duncan gave him was etched instantly in Evan's mind. He'd find it for Nella if ever necessary. "Yes. I'll remember."

Nothing more was said as they caught up to the others at the top, even when Susie looked over, a question in her gaze. They joined her where she stood close to the edge, overlooking the Forth and Edinburgh. Duncan reclaimed her from Stu and pulled her into him.

And he took her up farther, to the narrow, highest peak.

Laura switched from taking photos of the band to aim the camera at her brother and sister-in-law, entwined, faced out and away. Evan was struck by the thought that eventually, they would be. After Raucous waned, Duncan and Susie would very well separate from the group, turn toward their own life with their daughter, and be less involved with their band mates. With Evan. Not if he could help it.

His chest filled sharply and he went over to join Mike and Doug as they wandered around the flatter areas. They had the house, though. The Victorian next to the apartment building would soon be ready for them to move in. Once she was settled there, Evan didn't figure she'd leave easily. At least she wouldn't be far away. Unless Duncan eventually talked her into moving to Scotland. As he'd told his friend, he was willing to move, also. Maybe he'd find a Scottish girl. Someone like Marjory. Except one who could fuel his passion better.

"So." Adam cleared his throat and waited for their attention. He let them filter in closer from their different observation points toward where he stood at the stone marker. "I wanted to wait and tell you at the right time and this seems as good as any, considering where we are." He looked over at Duncan. "*Darkness Falls* was released here mid-tour, as Axis promised. I'd hoped they'd do it sooner, but at least they did it. Yesterday it hit number one in the UK."

Duncan was quiet through the loud congratulations, until he touched Susie's eyes. "This was for you. Everything else now is icing."

"No." She wrapped around him. "This is only the beginning. Everything up to now has been the rehearsal."

Evan wasn't sure she should have said it in front of the rest of the band. They'd had number ones with Doug and Stu's writing and Mike's lead. Making it sound like Duncan's second number one, their first in the UK and one he sang, was the climax of the band's career wasn't a good idea. Mike seemed to be the only other one considering that thought. But he was considering it.

Gusto

20 February 1978

Susie leaned back in the metal chair, a leg propped in front with her arms wrapped around it. The basement was chilly but she put it out of her thoughts and let the music swirl around her tired brain. The new songs Duncan and Stu worked on here and there during tour were coming along well. How the band already had energy to practice for the second leg of the "Your Way" tour, this time around the States, she didn't know. And to try to throw in two new songs seemed slightly insane to her. She was wiped out, head to toe. By the time she started to normalize, they'd be on the road again.

Glad her dad had dropped in and was entertaining Danielle with her building blocks, Susie pulled her sweater more tightly around her front and closed her eyes.

Her conversation with Lisa they day before kept invading. Blue River was in a precarious spot. Their drummer's wife didn't seem to care that she was helping to push it off the edge. Susie liked Lisa. She was nice company. Her children were adorable. But no matter what she'd promised in her vows, why Lisa stayed with Tony when neither of them had any respect for their marriage, Susie couldn't understand. And now maybe she was pregnant again although she hadn't been with her husband in months. Susie couldn't even ask whose it was; she had a good idea and didn't want to know if she was right.

Maybe pregnant again, with a third child she didn't want. Susie had a fleeting thought of offering to adopt the child, but she didn't want entanglements with Tony Diaz even if it wasn't his. He and Duncan had no use for each other. It wouldn't work out well.

Susie did hope Blue River could struggle through, even if they had to replace their drummer. Greg was a big part of the problem, but as the lead singer and main songwriter, if he left, the band was done. And she liked Greg. She liked his voice. He annoyed her at times, but she found him charming in an odd way. She especially liked his music, their music. It would be a shame to lose it.

Mike's voice broke through and surrounded her senses, backed by instruments and harmonies. She could pick out each instrument, each voice, even though they were completely in tune with each other, but this time she focused on the whole, letting it all blend. Nothing relaxed her more. Nothing could sweep her away more than ... well, one thing did. She was amused by the fact that both centrally involved her husband.

"Susie."

She opened her eyes to Ali's voice and accepted a big hug. "Hey, where have you been? I haven't seen you since we got back."

"Oh, I know." Ali pulled a chair closer as she grinned at Doug. "This final semester is a killer, and the bad thing is that I won't be actually finished at the end of it."

"Why?"

"I still have my teaching internship to do. The few days I've been able to work at the school around my classes and work schedule aren't enough."

"Wouldn't your parents give you the time off?"

"Of course, but they need the help and it lets me pay off part of my school loan early. I want that as paid as possible before ... well, before I have other things going on I don't want it to interfere with."

Susie knew exactly what she meant. Ali's attention was more on her boyfriend than on the conversation. "I'm sure Doug won't care if you still have a loan to pay after you're married. I can't imagine..."

"After we're married?" Ali threw her a questioning gaze. "Do you know something I don't?"

"Oh. No, I mean ... I guess I'm assuming what I shouldn't. But I can't imagine the two of you not together."

Ali grinned with a shrug. "I'm only teasing. And I can't, either. It was so hard to have him gone for over a month and not be able to just drop by or have him call every night to talk for an hour as he usually does on tour. I often thought about forgetting everything else and going."

"I'm sure. I can't imagine doing it. But it's good that you can. I have so much respect for both of you for putting your career first."

"Well, we both know the band won't last forever. Doug doesn't want to go back to store management. One of us should at least have something more permanent, right?" Ali shifted and gazed up at him. Her face showed how much she had missed him, how much she cared about him.

Susie considered her words about Ali's career. Maybe she shouldn't have encouraged it. She'd certainly put her own career aside for her husband's job. They didn't have anything more permanent ready for when the band dissolved with time. But then, Duncan was learning production. He could always head that way. And she could go back to teaching dance as extra income. There was plenty of time for that. She didn't have to have it now.

She missed it. At times. But she had no energy for it unless she stayed home when he toured. She didn't miss it enough to be away from him so often.

Danielle saw Ali and came to talk to her about what she and her grandpa were building. She gave Ali a hug and continued with stories about Scotland, the pool in the house, the Nessie monster, and the "big, big castles" that she'd loved.

Ali brushed fingers through Nella's hair. "I missed you, little one."

"Yes." Nella nodded. "You come, too, we play all over, with your Doug."

"Maybe I will next time. Okay?"

"Yes. Next time. We go in summer. And Daddy and Uncle Danny camp outside. And Mum and Aun' Laura and Nella swim in big, big pool in Gr'pa's house."

Susie explained to Ali about the Highland camping trip and returned her dad's grin as he took her other side.

"Oh honey, I meant next time the band goes. I won't interfere with your family trip."

Nella frowned and tilted her head. "Yes, my band fam'ly go back t' Sco'land. Yes. And you come with your Doug."

Ali chuckled and hugged the girl again. "I'm glad to be part of your band family." She turned to Susie. "Is it just me, or is she picking up Duncan's accent?"

Her dad leaned in. "I'm apparently not the only one who hears it. She absorbed quite a bit of his culture while she was away, I think."

"Maybe." Susie hadn't noticed, but maybe she was too used to it. "That's good. She should feel home in both countries."

Ali eyed her as Danielle ran off again, grasping her grandpa's hand. "Doug says you loved it there and he wasn't sure you wanted to come home."

"I do love it." She saw what Ali didn't quite ask. "But this is home. He knows that. Duncan, I mean. He knows I need to be here. We'll visit his family a lot and he says that's enough." Susie had the feeling Ali wasn't convinced. Part of her wasn't, either. They weren't hounded by fans there. They walked along the sidewalks unbothered, in cities, along the beaches, everywhere. It was refreshing as opposed to the constant worry about being noticed anywhere in public.

She sighed. It didn't matter. This was home. It was even home to Duncan, so he kept saying. Susie hoped he didn't say it only for her sake. He'd been quieter since they'd returned.

A pair of little arms enveloped her, startling Susie from her thoughts. She pulled Keith onto her lap and hugged him tight. "Hey sweetie, I missed you. What have you been doing?"

"My mom had to work. We went to travel, too." He looked more like Mike all the time, including the dark blonde hair Kate kept hoping would turn brunette.

"I know, honey. What did you do on your trip?"

He shrugged. "I watch my mom and Miss Kara work."

Susie greeted her friends and hoped he did more than that on the week-long location shoot in Florida.

Kate rolled her eyes. "And you played in the sand and made sand castles."

"Yes." He smiled big when Nella ran up to him.

"Look, my mummy! Keith home now!" The girl tugged at his arm. "Come. We build castle. You put big part high. I no' reach. No."

Keith jumped down and started to follow, but Mike swept his son into his arms as Stu came over and grabbed Kara, lifting her off her feet for a second. "Kara Mia. Damn I missed you. How was your trip? We're taking a break. Come tell me about it."

"He'll never concentrate on work now." Mike frowned at their backs.

"Will you?" Kate eyed him, glancing at the way he still held his son. "He's kind of big to carry around, and he wants to play with Nella. Let him go on."

"Do you *not* realize how much I missed him? Especially since at least half the time I tried to call you didn't answer."

Keith gave him a hug. "I missed you too, Dad."

"Dad? When did we move from Daddy to Dad? Did you grow up

that much in five weeks?"

"I taught him. Figured it was time." Kate raised her chin and turned it in dismissal. Then she looked back at him. "Oh, and it's your turn for the next month. I have another job lined up."

"Kate, we're back on the road again next week."

"Yeah, so am I. And it's your turn."

Susie stood and stretched her back. "Good, we get to take him with us this time." She mussed Keith's hair. "Nella will be glad, and so will I." Trying to deter further conversation about it in front of the boy, she took her husband's side. "So Adam called before we came down. He'll be here toward the end of practice and needs all of you to stay and talk a few minutes."

"We might have t' go find Stu and bring him back."

"He'll be back. He knows how much work there is to do."

"Y' are sure? I wouldnae be if I 'ad been away from y' for over a month."

She grinned. "Well, he might not be right away. Maybe we could take a break, too, and leave Nella with Evan. You're tired. I can hear it."

"And y' think if we go up alone, tha' will change?" His eyes pierced hers.

"I think if she comes up, you won't be able to rest. You should have sent her back to bed when she got up at five."

"Damn, are we taking a long break?" Stu's voice came from behind her. "Cause if you two are heading upstairs, so are we. I was trying not to hold everyone up, but..."

"We're going back to work." Mike set Keith down and rubbed his head before the boy ran off to Nella. "Hell, it's not like he's going to rest, anyway." He threw a smirk at Duncan. "And if you two insist on doing the new songs, we better learn them."

Stu shrugged. "Duncan and I know them. The rest of you can work on them while we go..."

"Never mind." Susie went to reclaim her chair. "Go back to work. Adam will be here soon." As she settled in amid Stu's comment about their slave-driving manager, her dad set a hand on Duncan's shoulder, complimented him and Stu on the new songs, and told her he had to be going. She stood again to give him a hug. He made it a longer one than she expected and asked if they would join him for dinner out the following night. She hesitated until he assured her the path would be clear and that Chief Carr and his wife would be there, also. He had a date, set up by his friend. Susie couldn't quite refuse. Duncan readily agreed.

As he headed back to the office, or to wherever he was going, Susie realized she almost never asked anymore what he was doing. She felt a separation from him different than it used to be when he was always gone. With a twinge, she realized it didn't matter like it used to. A good thing, she supposed. But it would be nice to go out and have adult conversation with her dad and his friends and her husband. Evan already offered to keep Nella.

Resettling between Ali and Kara, Susie asked where Kate was.

"Better things to do. Quoted."

Susie nearly laughed at Ali's expression, as annoyed as it was.

"Yes, I was thinking the same, except..." Kara shrugged and kept her gaze on Stu. "The apartment's kind of empty right now and I'm too tired to unpack."

"You didn't answer Stu about the trip. How was it?"

"He didn't exactly give me time." She crossed her legs delicately. "The shoot went well and I made a few connections. My schedule's getting so loaded it's crazy."

"That's good, right?"

"Yes, although it would have better while I was still single. Balancing with Stu is getting impossible."

Susie heard warning bells. "Oh, well, after this leg of the tour, we'll be home for a while and it'll be easier. They'll go back to writing and normal practice, and Duncan and I are going to Scotland for a while to visit, so you'll be able to have him most any time you're available." She tried a grin, but Kara was still focused on the stage. "And we'll take a couple of days off before we leave next week."

Kara sighed. "Yes well, I have to go away in a few days so I won't be here when's he's off. There's a big shoot out in Arizona. A nice job with some top name models. I'm honored to have been asked. Stu's not happy, of course."

"Maybe he can visit you there on his time off?"

"No. We've stopped him visiting me. Too much commotion since his face is too well known by now."

"Yes, I know what you mean." Susie saw Ali's glance but put her own attention back on the guys. She hoped dinner with her dad wouldn't turn into a madhouse with fans. His date might not appreciate it much more than Susie did.

Kara shifted again, switching legs. "It's getting hard, though. You know how he is. So ... needy ... physically."

Susie glanced over and away again.

"Sorry. I just mean separations are hard for him, since ... I know he's being faithful. And I've been surprised, actually, that he is. Unless I'm being naïve, but I don't think I am. I generally know."

"He adores you, Kara. He wouldn't do that. I wasn't sure at first, either, since this is the first time I've ever seen him committed, but he's being good." She hoped Kara caught that she was teasing since Stu's girlfriend often called him a little boy inside.

"You would know, I guess."

"With as close as we all are during tours? It would be hard not to."

Kara nodded in thought. "Did he drive you nuts?"

She chuckled. "Now and then. He kind of hung on me at times. Just, yes, he does need a connection or something. It's sweet, though."

"Yes. It's adorable." She dropped her eyes. "I just don't know..."

The music stopped abruptly and Stu and Mike argued for a few seconds before Doug mediated and they jumped right back into the song. Kara became quiet, listening to the band, or just to Stu. Susie wasn't sure. She wasn't quite as into the music and Susie was, since she more often listened to jazz and rhythm and blues than to rock. Kara had shared some of her favorites and while Susie enjoyed it, it didn't get into her soul the way Raucous did, and those similar to Raucous. Rock: not hard, not pop, not metal or punk or acid, just rock. Like Blue River. Like Journey. Axe. Chicago. Well, she supposed Chicago might border into pop and maybe the others, also, but not the same as Leif Garrett and Andy Gibb and Donny Osmond and such. She enjoyed that, also, but Raucous was pure rock. She loved that purity of sound.

Blue River. Duncan hadn't heard from Steve, their lead guitarist, which was unusual. Susie wondered if it was due to Lisa or because they were struggling so much they wanted to be left alone through it. Maybe she'd suggest Duncan give Steve a call.

"Mind if I join you?" Adam pulled a chair up beside Ali, facing inward to see Susie, and saying hello to the other women.

"You have to ask?" She grinned at him.

"You look pretty absorbed into the music today. I didn't want to interfere with that."

"Oh, I'm tired. Probably look it. *Nella*, don't throw them." Susie raised her chin at her daughter's pout, waited to see that she set the Lincoln Logs back on the floor, and gave Adam her attention. "So this is sounding good so far."

He glanced up at the stage. "I had no doubt it would. This is one of Duncan and Stu's, right?"

"Yes, they just started on it, though."

"Think they'll be ready to start recording again next month?"

She stared. "Already? With the tour in a couple of weeks?"

"It'd be the end of next month, of course, just after we get back."

"They don't have much yet. They did some writing on the bus, but..."

"Stu and Doug have a ton we haven't used and Duncan has quite a few put back, doesn't he? Would he be bothered if Mike sang most of them? I'm thinking an equal split of McGuire, Lowe, and Lawrence songs for the next, or as equal as we can get since Stu writes with both of them. Unless Evan decides to jump in as I know he could."

"He already is. He and Duncan were... Wait." She accepted Ali's offer to trade chairs so she could hear him better. "You didn't actually get that cleared with Axis? They'll never go for it."

"Actually..." Adam tried to hide a grin. "They're allowing whatever we want with this one. Now, it does fill their contract, so if Axis doesn't like it or it doesn't do well enough, they'll drop them. But I wouldn't let that worry you. With their chart standings, they can get picked up again..."

"Anything we want? Including Duncan's songs? You are kidding?"

"Not kidding." The grin widened. "Seems the highly successful UK tour, combined with the still-high chart ratings of both *And It Comes* and *Darkness Falls* over there and *Intoxication* over here, has convinced them we might be onto something, that maybe they don't want to alienate one of their best songwriters and money producers. Especially one as popular with the fans as he is."

"Unbelievable." She shook her head. "I knew they would get there, but I expected it would take longer. Anything we want."

"Anything we want. So, about Mike singing them?"

"Oh. No, he wouldn't at all care. He'll be thrilled they're getting done. But you should ask him, of course."

"No question. This is what we've been waiting for. They can decide between them. I'll go with whatever they want, with some possible input. And I have a fantastic cover artist who will create whatever we need for what we decide to do..."

Susie threw her arms around him. "You're some kind of superhero, you know. No one else could have done this for us so fast, maybe not at all." Releasing him, she noted he was unsure what to say. "Late next month?" She got a nod. "They'll be ready. I'll have them working on the bus when they're not too tired."

"Great. But I have to let you know I won't be on this leg of the tour. I have a tour manager I think will be okay with Roy, but you'll be more on your own with this one. Ready for that?"

Susie hesitated. More on her own? With Roy.

"Sorry to do that to you, but I have obligations, something to make this whole thing easier and I have to be here."

"It's fine." She hoped she sounded convincing.

"I'm sure it will be. Don't worry. Think they're ready to take a break and talk about it?"

"I'll tell them they are at the end of this section. It's been giving them trouble and I don't want to interrupt it."

"No problem." Adam studied her. "Nice to see you coming into your own, Suse. I've been waiting for it. Knew you would."

She frowned and considered his words as he turned to face the band. Into her own? She must have sounded much more convinced than she was. Four weeks of managing alongside Roy without Adam as a buffer and with another new tour manager didn't make her feel at all confident. But the next album was all theirs. No covers. No objections from Axis. Fully Raucous.

"I guess that means long hours for him as soon as they get back?"

Susie turned to Kara. "Well, yes, but that'll give Stu something to think about while your schedule is full. And if you give me enough warning about when you have time off, I'll try to have them arrange for the same days. As much as I can. It always depends..."

"No, don't try to work around me."

Studying Stu's girlfriend who had become her friend, Susie wondered if she should suggest they drop the idea of doing the new songs on tour. If they kept it the same as it was, same set list and all, they could make their practices shorter, take more time off. It would also give her more time *with* her husband instead of only watching him or being within a group. She couldn't quite do it. They were incredible songs. It would be a bonus for the US shows, for fans having to wait so long for a tour after the album release. And it would be great promotion for the next album, the one that would be only Raucous material.

As she'd told her husband, up to now had only been the rehearsal. With all their own music and their own say as to what went on their albums, Raucous was positioned to kick into the top of the charts consistently, and dramatically.

21 February

Duncan would just as soon have stayed home to work. He agreed to dinner with John plus his date and Chief Carr and his wife, expecting it would be nice for Susie to spend the time with them, to have something outside the band, something more normal. Instead, as soon as they got home and tucked Danielle in, she went off to bed, to read. She'd hardly said a word to him.

Not that it was his fault John's nearly blind date had been so competitive. Everything said about what Susie had done was met with something more, and bigger. John bragged how Susie had become a main dance teacher so young. His date came back to say she'd published a scientific article a year earlier than that, one that was highly respected by her peers and made a big impact in her field. Duncan suspected it was an exaggeration but said nothing. The chief asked how Susie's management duties were coming along and whether she felt more comfortable with them yet, and in the middle of his wife saying only that she was getting there, with a lot of help from Adam – a huge understatement – the woman jumped in to say she'd been made supervisor of the whole team by the time she was twenty-three. John slipped it in that the "whole team" consisted of about five people and asked the purpose of the research. He didn't "get" it and the woman looked at him like he was an idiot instead of bothering to see that what he meant was that it was pointless.

Why she'd feel the need to compete with the daughter of her date, Duncan couldn't imagine. And why, when Susie tried to talk with the chief's wife about Danielle, the woman interfered with advice, he understood less. The woman didn't even have children. She had relatives with children, she said, and they would have turned out better if her relatives had listened and taken her advice.

He got Susie out of there and back home just as fast as he could manage, in all politeness to John and the chief. Still, she was distant.

Duncan figured he might as well work since Susie and Danielle were both in bed. Adam wanted them to start recording soon after tour.

Susie rubbed her burning eyes and checked the clock. He was still up working. She wanted to sleep, but she hated to try to sleep without him beside her. It never worked well.

She got up and pulled her robe over her shoulders but didn't bother with her slippers. The cold floor, once she got farther than her bedside throw rug, made her hurry out to the carpeted hall. To the carpet that needed to be replaced. She'd never liked the beige color or the rough texture. She wanted soft and ... something prettier but not terribly hard to maintain. The biggest reason she hadn't bothered yet was because she couldn't decide on the color. She didn't want overwhelming color to clash with her peach walls, but she didn't like neutral much, either. A brown, maybe, but she didn't want too dark. The place was small ... and it wouldn't matter soon. Their house was nearly ready. The carpet in the apartment could be someone else's problem. Evan's in all likelihood. It was time for him to have his own place. He and Duncan had talked of him taking over the apartment. Susie heard something about adjusting income and such since the band profits were paying for the building but if Duncan no longer lived there, he shouldn't have to help pay for it. Duncan shrugged it off. He would still use the basement for practice. Susie would still workout there. It was fair enough for him.

Evan would have to paint. Peach walls weren't something Duncan would choose but he said he didn't care one way or the other. Evan would. He'd probably turn them back into a neutral, and she'd help him do it since he helped her turn them peach when she moved in. He hated doing trim work.

Coming up behind her husband, Susie could see he wasn't working. His guitar was in his hands, somewhat, but his head was against the back of the couch, eyes closed. She walked around in front of him and grasped the neck of the guitar.

He jumped.

"Just me. Coming to bed? It's after midnight." When he released the instrument to her care, she set it in the case, sat next to him, and rubbed his back.

"Are y' still awake?"

"Yes. Waiting for you."

"Babe, I am sorry. I expected y' were asleep and I was thinkin' of ... now I forget. It was in my head."

"Remember it tomorrow. Come to bed with me."

Forcing himself up, he shoved a hand through his hair, then closed and latched the case. He cuddled in next to her and was asleep again within a few minutes, or less. She closed her eyes and rested a hand on his chest to feel him breathe.

He thought she was annoyed with him. He always stayed up late when she was, but she wasn't. It was nice that he would spend his precious free time having dinner with her dad and his friends, for her. She knew it was for her. And it was nice to have dinner unbothered. They were always left alone when out with the chief. Everyone knew him; they knew he wouldn't stand to have his personal time interrupted, or theirs either if they were with him. If her dad would find a dad she could stand, Susie would enjoy going out with the two couples.

And it wasn't even the woman's interruptions to brag on herself that got to Susie. It was ... she couldn't admit it to her husband because he would feel bad, but it was the way she'd followed her own passion, the way she exuded confidence in her work. Even if it was nonsense work, as Susie saw it, the confidence in it kind of made up for that. She didn't feel the same with her own.

She did. With her dancing. At least mostly. She didn't at all with her management duties, and trying to tell the chief, in front of her husband, that she was starting to feel comfortable made her realize she didn't. Susie had only ever been really good at one thing and she hardly did it anymore, and then only for herself. It was the contrast with the woman's self-confidence that bothered her. Susie had learned to look like she was and often to act like she was, but it was largely an act.

And Adam wouldn't be on the next leg of the tour. She had to take charge more.

22 February

"Y' know I didnae expect it to be in such bad condition to be taking so long."

Susie wrapped her arms around her husband from behind as they stood studying their house. It was still only part theirs. They had earnest money down and the contract had been accepted upon final repairs. She would soon be able to fill it with their own furniture, their own curtains and decorations and beds. She set a light kiss on his shoulder, just above the collar of his black leather jacket. "I still think you shouldn't spend so much on it." She cuddled closer and slipped her hands underneath the leather, borrowing his heat.

"Do you still like the house?"

"Oh, you know I love it, but it was already enough without the repairs boosting the price and..."

"I donae care." He turned to face her. "A family should 'ave a house, not only a tiny apartment. Danielle needs the yard t' run off energy and not wear y' out so much."

Susie chuckled. "Think she won't?"

"I will have a bench swing put out in back so y' can sit out there and keep an eye on her as she runs full speed." He traced the line of her forehead. Slowly. Holding her gaze. "I have been thinking. The yard is big enough she doesnae need it all. What if we put in a dance studio? Big enough to hold one class at a time. And then y' could go back to teaching."

"Oh. That would take a lot of space, not to mention the expense I'm not sure I'd ever make up..."

"Babe, I donae care about the expense. You do know y' donae have t' worry still about paying bills and such."

"Well, things change. I just don't want to make it hard when..."

"Suse." He rested his warm hand against the side of her head. "Unless y' plan to buy a mansion bigger than my father's and throw money away on a bunch of stuff I know y' donae even want, y' willnae have to worry about it. I have it managed well. Even if it all stops tomorrow, we will be fine with the house and the studio, even if it doesnae ever make money. And I want t' support you the way you have supported me. You have given up on your dancing all the way now and..."

"It doesn't matter." She brushed his lips. "I can work out in the basement whenever I need. I'm still dancing. And between Nella and the band and ... I've been wondering ... you know she's two already and maybe it's time to think about ... if you're sure..."

He grinned and raised her chin with his fingers. "Time for what, my luv? I willnae bite your head off, y' ken. Y' donae have t' hesitate t' ask me wha' y' want, wha'ever it is. An' y' know y' donae."

"Hm. Are you trying to come onto me with that accent, Mr. McGuire?"

He pressed closer, a hand against her back. "Woul' y' mind if I am?"

"I don't think I would mind. How long is Stu keeping Nella?"

He teased her lips. "I think he will keep her if we go up t' the apartment and donae answer the door. Or he will take her t' Ev. She will be fine either way." He made the kiss longer. "Now. Tell me wha' it is y' think it is time for."

"Oh. I think that can wait." Susie slid both hands up over his shoulders and kissed his neck, his jaw, moving slowly back to his lips. At catcalls from somewhere behind them, she backed up. The sidewalk. A quick glance revealed several girls staring. "Let's go in."

"Y' are embarrassed t' be seen hangin' all over your husband, are y' now?"

"Not at all." She pressed back against him. "But I kind of thought we were ... uh, taking this farther. Can't do that out here without getting arrested. Great headlines that would make."

"I donae know, Babe. Maybe it would be. Raucous guitarist arrested while makin' love with his own wife in his front yard. See photos of the melted snow outlines. Could be gud publicity. Wha' do y' think, my luv? Do we give i' a go? Adam woul' bail us ou' o' jail." He nuzzled in against her neck.

"Not in this lifetime, cowboy. Try me again in our next."

He laughed and grasped her hand to lead her toward the apartment's front door. Not bothered by the suggestive comments, lurid as some of them were, he threw his fans a smile, said hello, and took Susie inside.

She was eternally grateful for Chief Carr and the way he and his men made it clear around town that anyone who went into their yard would be immediately arrested. It had already happened a few times, often enough the papers had spread the truth of the warning.

Susie considered stopping at Stu's to make sure Nella wasn't in his way, but Duncan made no sign of thinking the same and she took his lead. As their door closed behind them, she locked it and pulled out of her jacket with a shiver.

He took it, hung it up along with his own, and wrapped his arms around her waist. "Come, my luv, I will warm y' up well. After y' tell me wha' it is y' think it is time for."

"Oh." She met his lips. Briefly. Snuggling close. "As I said, that'll wait." Her lips found his neck; she felt the stubble trying to grow back in and moved farther down, to the base of his shoulder, as she slid her fingers up to his chest, enjoying every hard curve along the way from his stomach.

Duncan pulled back enough to find her eyes. "Tell me, Suse. And then we will continue this." He grasped her hands, held them against his chest. His expression said he wasn't about to give in.

She dropped her gaze, bit her lip a moment. "Well. The house is plenty big enough and it'll be done soon ... and Nella's two now and..."

"Babe. Y' donae have t' convince me. Just tell me wha' it is y' want. Y' know I would give y' anything I can."

"I want another baby." She clarified at the slight fear in his eyes. "Maybe it's time to check into adoption? It'll take time, and I don't want them too far apart. I want ... I want another baby, Duncan. I wish I could have yours. You know how much I wish I could, but at least..."

"Alright, my luv." He brushed her lips. "I know. And I am more grateful t' y' than you know for wanting it so much and for agreeing no' t' try it yourself."

Agreeing? Susie wasn't sure she agreed. He hadn't given her much choice.

He kissed her. Softly. "It will be mine, Suse. When we get a baby, he will be mine. And yours. Donae think of it any other way. It is love that makes a good parent, that creates a bond, not biology."

"And yet you accepted your father and changed your name to his when you hardly knew him, because he's your father. Something in you recognized that."

"Tha' isnae why I did, Suse."

"Isn't it?"

"Y' didnae know?" He released her hands with a sigh and ran fingers back through his hair. "It was because of the way he talked t' you, the way he looked a' you. With respect. Approval. I could see how he approved of you from the start. And because y' approved of him. Y' liked him well."

"Duncan..."

"Did y' nae?"

"Yes, but ... he was so like you. His whole manner. He's so like you. That's what I saw."

"Y' are seeing something I donae, but I trust your thoughts. Y' thought I should try t' accept him. Y' said I should."

"Oh. But..."

"And I didnae want t' give y' the name of that man I detested. I nearly didnae let myself propose t' you because I did not want y' dragged into that."

Susie shook her head and set it against his shoulder. "I love you. Your name didn't matter. It still doesn't. I love *you*."

"It mattered t' me. Everyone around knew who he was, knew wha' he was. When they ask your name and look a' y' like..."

She met his face again, found traces of the old pain in his eyes. "I'm sorry. You deserved so much better."

He kissed her. A slow, deep, gentle kiss. And he held her in close. "Suse, tha' day Gene grabbed Roy by the collar and made him apologize t' you, I knew he would be a good father-in-law, would look after y' well, would care for you. I took his name so y' would have one you could be proud of, tha' my children could be proud of..."

She pulled back. "Duncan. No matter what your name is, your daughter will always be proud of it, because of you. Same goes for me. But yes, I am proud to be a McGuire with you, because of you. And because of Gene. I hope you are. I hope it wasn't only for us."

"Part of me wishes I hadnae, since Danny is still O'Neil. It feels wrong t' have it different than his."

"But Laura changed hers."

"And she will change it again when she is married. Danny willnae."

"It doesn't matter, you know. Like you said about love connecting a child with his parents, it does with siblings, too. And this baby, if we get one, will be as much Danielle's brother or sister as if we..."

"Yes. Bu' they will have the same name."

"And if they didn't, they would still be siblings. We'll teach them that doesn't matter; it doesn't matter if one is biologically related and the other isn't. We'll teach them that. I won't have one of my children feel less my child than the other. I won't. If we had taken Keith in like I thought we might for a while, it would be the same with him."

"And it nearly is. He feels like he is more yours than anyone's. I can see it. Ev has said the same."

"Not in front of Mike."

"No, my luv, we wouldnae. Mike is techy enough." He gave her a grin and grabbed her in a tight hug. "Y' are right, and I am worrying about nothing."

Worrying? About him and Danny she hoped. There was no need. Danny adored him. "So, is that a yes? About adoption. You do want another child?"

"I would love t' bring another child into our lives. I think Danielle will love it, as well. I want her to have it as you do. We will find out where to start. Tomorrow. Tonight..." He kissed her head, moved to her jaw, to above her ear. "Tonight I want y' to myself." He met her lips in a deep kiss, long, lingering, encompassing her fully. She felt her knees start to give and gripped the sides of his shirt.

"I love when y' do that, y' ken." His voice was breathless.

"When I do what?" She teased his lips.

"When y' fall in against me as though y' couldnae stand up wi'out my arms holdin' y'."

"I think I couldn't. You drive me crazy when you kiss me that way. Don't ever stop doing that."

With the lightest grin, he took possession of her mouth and lifted her into his arms. Breaking the kiss long enough to move back to their room and lay her on the bed, he lowered over top of her body. "Danielle is staying at Stu's tonight. Her things are there already. He promised her pancakes and bananas in the morning."

She pulled him in closer. "You know how much I love you?"

"Maybe. Bu' y' can show me if y' wish. T' be sure."

23 February

Duncan grabbed a deep breath. He'd asked Susie to come next door so she wouldn't be alone, but she wanted to stay in. Danielle was tired and grouchy. He argued that Keith would help entertain her; Keith was somewhere with his mom, she said. He said he would keep her from acting up too much, or Stu would break her out of the grouchy mood as he always did; they were supposed to be working, she said. He knew she was only trying to hide her own thoughts about the adoption meeting they'd just come back from, as though he didn't know. Maybe she was right, but they wouldn't give up.

He couldn't convince her to go with him, so he left her watching the People's Choice Awards which she'd taped the other night, and headed over to Ev's. They'd watch the Grammys later, likely with company.

He was late to Ev's. But then, he hadn't promised he'd be there the same time Stu was. If Danielle hadn't been so fussy, he would have left Susie to handle her, but since she was already frustrated, he couldn't do it. He'd settled the girl in her room with crayons. With any luck, she'd decide on her own to take a nap.

Guitar and bass greeted him until Ev saw him and set his Gibson to the side. "How'd it go?"

"Hard t' say." Duncan set his Mustang against the arm of the chair as he sank into it. "It is a long process. A lot of paperwork. A lot of checking us out. The lady did not seem optimistic. If we wanted an older child it would be easier, but Susie insists on a newborn, to start at the beginning."

"Of course she does. The list is long?"

"It is." He pushed fingers back through his hair. "And we are not favored candidates. Because of my job, the travel, and not being a citizen but only a legal resident. I amnae sure that will not disqualify us. And even if we make the list, and make a good match with a coming child, the parents cannot give up their rights until four days after the child is born. Many change their mind, she said. And if they cannot find the father to ask first, we could have him for several weeks and have to give him up again if the guy turns up and wants custody. I cannae imagine what that would do to Susie. Once she has that baby in her arms, in her home, it will be hers in her mind. To have it taken..." He grabbed a deep breath. He would feel the same. The thought of having their child taken away to give to some man who wasn't even around when he should have been was beyond what he wanted to deal with. "Now I am not so sure I should have agreed to this."

"How can they do that? To the new parents or the child?"

"I donae know. It seems cruel to both. Susie would never recover from that."

"She would." Ev didn't sound horribly convinced. "She could get through anything she had to, but no, I can't imagine either. What does she say about it?"

"Nothing. She will say nothing. It's why I am so late. Danielle was throwing a fit because she didn't want to leave her grandpa's house, and Susie has been too quiet since we left the meeting, so I waited until Danielle settled."

Stu dropped his ankle off his knee and leaned forward. "Should we go over there to work so she's not alone?"

"No, I asked. I think she was just as glad t' get me out for a while." He grabbed his guitar. "What are we working on?"

Susie set her book aside when Danielle stumbled out to the couch rubbing her eyes. "Come here, baby. Have a good nap?"

"No."

"No?" She lifted Nella onto her lap and brushed hair out of her face. "Why not?"

"I have no' good dream. Wan' my da'yee."

"Daddy's working. He'll be home soon. Want to tell me about your dream?"

She shook her head and cuddled down against Susie's chest.

"Okay, so how about if we turn the radio on and you come help me decide what we'll make for dinner? You want your favorite tonight?"

Her head shook again.

Susie rubbed the little hand gripping her shoulder. "Sweetie, it was just a nightmare. Don't worry. It's not real."

"No' like it. No."

"I know, baby, but it's all right. You're awake and it's over now. Sure you don't want to tell me about it?"

"No. I want my da'yee."

Susie checked the clock. Two hours. She supposed it was okay to go interrupt for a few minutes and give them a break from writing. "Okay. Let's go find daddy, then." It was a struggle to get to her feet holding the clinging child, as heavy as she was, especially since Danielle was still drowsy and let Susie support her full weight.

She knocked and walked in. They weren't playing. They were discussing something about dissonance and half tones. Duncan set the guitar down. "Make her walk, Suse. She is too big for you to carry."

Susie explained as he came over to take Danielle. Nella clung to him, her little arms wrapped snugly over his shoulders.

"What is it, my sweet?" He kissed her head. "You arenae supposed t' have bad dreams. I'll have to talk to the dream fairy and tell him no more bad dreams for my Danielle."

She nodded against his chest.

"Sorry we're interrupting." Susie looked over at Evan and Stu. "I'll take her back as soon as she settles down."

"Hey, no way. Come on in and listen to what we have. Give us an opinion." Stu jumped up and pulled a chair from the table, sitting in it himself and beckoning her to the couch.

"You don't have to move."

"No problem. You know I don't stay still for long. Want tea or something? Think Mike's got J.D. in there if you want that instead."

"No, but thanks anyway."

"Heard you had kinda a rough day. Sure you don't want it?"

"I'm sure I don't." She accepted the space on the couch next to Evan and glanced at Duncan where he stood talking to Nella. "It'll be all right. Look at them. How could anyone look at them together and say we shouldn't have another? Nella will convince them we're decent parents, right?"

"More than decent, Angel. I can't imagine they'd turn you down but if they do, it won't be because of your parenting. You need to remember that. It would be technical, not personal. Don't let yourself take it personally."

"How isn't it personal when someone says you're not good enough? It's what she was thinking. I saw it."

"If she was thinking that, all she saw was his job, the rumors, the image. Not you. You can't take it to heart. You can't think it's *you* as you are that she objects to."

"I know what you're saying, and thank you." She gave him a light grin. "I'll try hard to remember that. You might have to remind me."

"And I will." He grasped her hand and lowered his voice. "Suse, if they say yes, are you going to be okay if you get a baby and they take it away again?"

She grabbed a deep breath and dropped her eyes. "No." She raised them again, to her husband's. He was watching, in between keeping Nella at a distance enough she could talk to Evan freely. "But it's a risk I'm willing to take. And you know, I'll still have these two either way. So yes, I'll deal with that if I have to." A thought struck her and she looked at Evan. "Of course, you know that means if anything happened to us, you'd have both of them. If it works. They couldn't be split up."

"That's not going to happen. Don't bother worrying about it."

"But if it did…"

"No one in the world would be able to take them from me. I would fight to the ends of the earth to keep them if needed. Even if you end up adopting three or four."

"That might be more than I can handle." Susie looked over at Stu as he fidgeted with his bass. "I'll go take her so you can get back to work."

"Hey, don't mind me. I'm listening. Just had a thought in my head so I'm doing both. And my guess is you could handle a house full if he's willing to go that far."

"Could I? On days I'm not sure about this *one*." She got up and went to her husband. "Come on, baby. Let Daddy get back to work." With some coaxing and the promise they'd stay there and listen to her daddy play, Nella gave in. Duncan refused to hand her into Susie's arms. He carried her over to settle on the couch.

Susie leaned her head in against her daughter's and felt herself unwind. They played a bit, stopped and discussed it, then played more, and whichever they were doing, Danielle kept her attention on them. Susie wondered at her sitting quietly so long. Maybe the nightmare had really bothered her and still was. It was unfair, she thought, for such a little child to have nightmares. She wished Nella would tell her about them so she could try to figure out what worried her so. She would never say.

At a knock, Susie offered to get it so they didn't have to stop. Danielle frowned when she moved but curled up and kept watching her dad. Something had to be wrong with her.

Kara gave her a light smile as she opened the door. "Hi Suse, I'm looking for Stu. Sounds like I found him."

"They're working on one of the new songs. Come on in." She closed the door and noticed Kara's hesitation.

"I don't want to interfere. I just haven't seen him much and I'm off early today. Thought I'd see if he had time, but..."

"He can make time. Go tell him."

"Oh, no. If he's working, he won't even notice and if I pull him away, his head will still be in it. Not worth it, you know?"

"They're all like that. You just have to learn how to pull their attention away."

Kara eyed her. "Your husband isn't. He always has an eye on what you're doing if you're within even a hundred feet of him. No matter how much he's into the music. He still notices."

"When we're out he does. Not so much when we're home and he's not worried about who's around."

"Really? Because it seems like he ... well, it's not my business. It just gets frustrating. Doesn't it?"

Susie gave her a light shrug. "Sometimes. But I let him know when it does and it gets better again." She led Kara in and saw Duncan and Evan look up to acknowledge her. Stu didn't notice. The song was going well, coming along fast, and Susie knew his head was fully into it, enough a pack of wild dogs could ran past and he wouldn't know. But Kara wanted his attention. The song could wait.

She walked around behind him, leaned down, and wrapped her arms over his shoulders. "Hey, take a break."

He looked up at her curiously. "I'm fine."

"Stu, your girlfriend's here. You might want to notice she is. Girls like that, you know."

He turned his head the other direction. "Hey. You're home early."

"Got yelled at about it, too, but I was hoping you might have the night off or be able to take it off like I did."

"Um. Sure. Can you give me a few minutes? We're just getting this as it should be."

"It can wait." Duncan caught Susie's eyes as she sat next to Nella again and felt her head. "Is she warm?"

"A little. No wonder she's been so quiet. Nella, you should have told me if you don't feel good."

The girl cuddled in against her. "I listen Day'ee play more."

"Oh sweetie." Susie stroked her head. "Come on, let's go home so you can lie down. Daddy will come soon."

"No. I want my daddy."

Duncan stood, threw the guitar strap over his head, and pushed the instrument behind his back. "Come on, then." He picked Nella up and looked over at Kara. "Good timing. Stu is all yours tonight."

Kara studied Danielle's face. "I hope she feels better."

"I am sure it is nothing. Go make him think of something else. He needs the break, wha'ever he says." He glanced at his friend. "I will work on it and take notes on what we have done. Let it go for now."

24 February

Duncan held his daughter close against him with a hand covering her face. On hindsight, replacing the Pinto with a black and red Cobra hadn't been the best idea. It stuck out too much. He'd heard the Pinto had sold for a ton more than it was worth only because his name was attached as the former owner. It wasn't his. He'd never owned it. It was Susie's. That point didn't seem to matter. She didn't like to drive the Cobra, but then she always preferred him to drive instead, anyway. He'd suggested she keep her car so they'd have both, but said she was always with him or one of the other guys if she went out, or with her dad, so there wasn't much point.

A small crowd that recognized his car had formed outside Doc's office between the time they got there and the small amount of time it took to determine Danielle had another ear infection, plus tonsillitis. Some of them followed to the pharmacy where more joined in.

As much as he hated the idea, Duncan figured they'd have to start letting someone else run errands for them, or he'd do it himself, without his wife and daughter. Susie had tried to get him to take Danielle home and let her go but she was bothered nearly as much as he was, and she minded. In all honesty, she hated it. She hated being surrounded and badgered and stared at and asked questions. She wouldn't say as much, but he knew.

Even so, she went in to the pharmacy while he kept Danielle in the car. Susie insisted he'd never get out again and she wanted Danielle home in bed.

He switched the radio off when Debby Boone's voice came on. Again. Yeah, so she'd won a Grammy. Yes, the song was nice, lyric-wise. But her voice grated his nerves. And they played the thing non-stop, nearly as much or maybe more than *Hotel California*, also a big winner. It was an okay song. At least he enjoyed the sound of it. Not one of the Eagles' best, as far as he was concerned, but it was the Eagles.

More people gathered around the car. Looking in. Some with cameras. He did his best to keep Danielle's face close against his chest and covered as well as she would allow as he worried about his wife coming back out on her own. He wondered if he should go in with her. And yet he didn't want his daughter in the middle of it feeling as she did.

He checked his watch. Fourteen minutes. Those standing around outside called to others passing by and made the crowd stronger. Several went inside. Damn. He had to go in. A tap on his window made him nearly yell at whoever was that brazen. It was Beau. Duncan rolled his window down just enough.

"You all right?"

"How did you know we were here?"

"Your doctor called Evan. He called me. I'll try to clear them away."

"Susie is inside. Go in with her. We are fine." He put the window back up as their 6'4" guard pressed through the crowd. Duncan breathed easier.

"Mum come back now." Danielle raised a hand to his face and looked out at the crowd.

"She is coming, my sweet. She is getting ice cream for you, to make your throat feel better."

"Lots o' people. My mummy not like it. No."

"It's alright. Beau is with her. Rest your throat now."

She nodded and lay her head back against him.

Duncan watched them come out; their bodyguard towered over Susie, pushing people back. He considered locking Danielle in and getting out to help, but Susie would yell at him if he left her in the car alone. So he waited and leaned over to unlock the door. He stroked her cheek and her hair when she was next to him again, the door locked behind her.

"Beau said Chief Carr has officers coming to clear them out of the way so we can go. Here, baby." She pulled a red popsicle out of the bag. "This will help you feel better. Come sit with me so Daddy can drive."

Afraid moving Danielle from where she cuddled against her side would wake her, Susie leaned her head back against the couch and took a deep breath. The irritation in her own throat was nothing more than sympathy pain. Tour was starting in two days. She was *not* going to be sick now. And she sure hoped Duncan wouldn't catch it. It would be worse for him to have to fight it while on stage.

She couldn't imagine where Nella had picked it up. She hadn't been around anyone but the band. And Kate and Keith. But they seemed fine. Maybe she would allow herself a nap while Duncan was out. Her eyes closed and she concentrated on the tick of the clock to try to quiet her harried brain.

The door startled her.

"Did I wake y'?"

She tried to find her bearings and looked up at the clock. Over an hour had passed. "Oh. I guess. You're back early."

"Mike is down with it, also. We had t' send him away and took care of what we could. I think a' least one of the new songs will ge' thrown out for now. We needed today and tomorrow t' be sure it was ready."

"Mike's sick?" She sat up as much as she could and felt her daughter's head. Still warm. "Is Keith?"

"Apparently he came back with it from Florida. Kate had 'im on something to help him feel okay."

Susie rolled her eyes. "Wonderful. How are you? And the other guys?"

"Good so far." He sat next to her. "And y' were asleep. Are y' catching it, also?"

"Oh. No, I ... I hope not. But you should stay farther away..."

"If I didnae get it from Danielle, it willnae matter." He tilted his head and eyed her. "Y' arenae feeling well."

"I'm okay. Try to get her back to sleep if she wakes. I have to get up." She was half surprised he didn't question her more, not that it would matter. They couldn't reschedule.

25 February

"So where's your husband?" Kate watched her son give Susie a big hug and then make a beeline to where Nella sat at the kitchen table, coloring quietly.

"Next door. Want tea or juice or something?"

"Nah, I'll wait and grab a Pepsi when I can make myself go back to my apartment. Mike's being such a grouch I had to get out a while."

Susie turned from where she was pouring herself and the kids grape juice. "He's at your place?"

"For a couple of days. Trying not to spread germs to the other guys."

Susie hoped it wasn't too late for that. She set the small cups in front of Danielle and Keith and took hers out to the living room. She needed to sit.

Kate of course followed. "Nella looks good today."

"Yes, much better. Her ear is still bothering her but it will for a couple of days, like usual, I suppose."

"That's the one that was plugged when she was born, right? The left one? Is she gonna grow out of that?"

Susie took a swallow and tried not to grimace. "I hope so." So much for asking Kate to take the kids to her place so she could rest. Mike didn't need the commotion, either.

"Yeah, I hope she does, too. Makes me feel worse when Keith shares his colds with her." Kate brushed the thought off fast. "So Mike has a nanny hired for tour."

"I know."

Her friend snickered. "Of course you do. Anyway, I've met her. She seems good with him."

"She is. Mike wouldn't have hired her otherwise. She's the sister of one of my students. She used to entertain them during classes."

"So you approve of her. That's good."

Susie took another swallow and considered telling Kate to go back down and take care of Mike. She wanted to lie down, and not talk.

"That'll help other than tour, also, since I've decided to give myself an early birthday present. Kara got invited to go to Paris, you know, on this big deal of a photo shoot, and..."

"Wait. Paris? Stu didn't say she was going to Paris."

"Uh, no. He doesn't know yet so don't say anything. She's not sure she's going. Says it depends on him and ... well, not my business except I told her she'd be crazy to pass this up for some guy."

"Kate, Stu is not *some guy*. He's..."

"Yeah, one of the band. Whatever. But..."

"He's more than that. And they're already having problems trying to find time together."

"So maybe it's time for her to move on. Not everyone is so damned hooked to this band, you know. Just because you are."

"This isn't about the band. It's about Stu and Kara. They're good together. Why would you... What did you tell her, Kate?"

She shrugged. "What are you worried about me telling her? That he will never put her before his work? Why shouldn't she know that if she doesn't already? Which she probably does as long as they've been together. Why pretend otherwise? They're all the same. Nothing matters to any of them as much as the damned band does." She hesitated when Susie shrugged her hands. "Well okay, it's not so true with Duncan. I know you matter to him as much."

"More. Thank you. So does his daughter."

"Of course, but otherwise..."

"Don't try to break them up because you're mad that Mike cares so much about the band. Don't do that to Stu. He loves her, Kate. It would devastate him."

"Hell, he's a man. He'd get over it and move on to someone else." She looked over at the kids coming in and pointed to the back of the apartment. "Go play in Nella's room. Lead her that way, Keith. We're talking."

Susie clenched her jaw in order to stay silent. They wouldn't pay attention. There was no reason to keep them at such a distance.

"So anyway..." Kate shifted, switching legs from their crossed position. "She asked if I would go with her and be her roommate. Since I wasn't asked to go, although I don't know why I didn't get it over Jaycee, the tramp, or actually I do know why I didn't, I'd have to pay my flight and meals but the room is paid for. She's nervous about going alone since all the other models are from different agencies."

"Why doesn't she ask Stu to go?"

"Are you kidding?" Kate threw a look as though Susie was some kind of moron. "She's going to be there for two or three weeks, depending. You think he'd leave the band for that long?"

"When is it?"

"End of April. So only a month early to celebrate myself. I figure, why not?"

Why not? Other than that she'd have to leave her son, again, for three weeks.

"I'm not asking you to keep Keith, Suse. Mike and his *nanny* can handle it. She is legal age, right? I wasn't sure. I'd hate him to end up in jail though I guess Adam would just get him out of it."

Susie rubbed her head. "I didn't say anything about you asking me, and Keith is not a problem for anyone. He's wonderful. I'll keep him any time. Megan is *only* his nanny, if you actually need to know what Mike is or isn't doing. She offered to help with Nella, as well, and if you say one slightly suggestive word about Duncan's *nanny*, I swear I'll punch you in the jaw. Fair warning."

Kate laughed. "Hell Suse, I know that man is far too wrapped around your ass to bother with anyone else. Trust me, I know. But I'm not sure I shouldn't suggest it just to see if you really would."

Susie half considered just why Kate was so sure when she didn't used to be, but she let it go. She wanted to rest. "Anyway, why are you telling me all this when she hasn't even talked to Stu about it? At the end of April, he may be able to get away at least part of the time to go with her. You might want to wait before you make plans."

"Great." She stood. "And again, you're looking out for the band member over me. Thanks."

"I'm doing no such thing. I don't want you to be too excited before you know it's going to happen." Susie needed to stop talking. Her throat burned.

"Yeah well, maybe there are things I know that you don't." She shrugged. "I'm heading down to get myself together. Big date tonight. Mike's bitching about that, too, just 'cause I let him stay in the extra room."

"Have fun." Susie took a swallow of juice and forced herself up.

"Want me to take Keith or should I leave him with Nella?"

"He's fine here. I'm making pizza tonight. He loves to help."

Kate rolled her eyes. "Like he's not girly enough without encouraging him to cook."

Susie swiveled. "Girly? Damn, Kate. Don't ever say that where he can hear it. And maybe just don't say it. He's not girly. He's quiet. It's not the same." Damn, her throat burned.

Kate chuckled. "Yeah, and Evan likes to cook so it can't be girly, right?"

"Evan doesn't care what you think. Your son does. Be careful what you say to him." The kids headed their way talking about being hungry and Susie cringed when Keith stopped at a distance and waited to see if his mom would send him away again.

Luckily, she went over and kissed the top of his head and said she would see him in the morning before he left with his dad. He didn't bother to react, other than a nod that he heard her.

"Hey." Susie motioned him over while Kate closed the door. "Want to help me make pizza tonight? We can let Nella put the olives on this time, I think. What part do you want to do?"

"The sauce and the cheese and the hamburger and pep'roni and the 'matoes."

"That doesn't leave much work for me." She grinned and rubbed his head.

"You have Nella. That is lots of work."

She hugged her daughter against her leg. "Yes, but she's worth it, huh?"

He nodded and led the way to the kitchen. Susie had wanted to lie down first. She needed a few minutes. But they were hungry.

26 February

Susie pulled back the blankets from the hotel bed, kicked her shoes off, and lay down. Mike was coming out of it. His spunk started to come back on the eight hour bus ride to Pittsburgh. Stu was down hard. So was she.

Duncan told Nella to stay quiet and came to sit beside her. He ran a hand over her forehead. Again. He'd done it several times on the bus as she drifted in and out of sleep, usually leaned up against him although she kept warning him to stay away. "Not better a' all yet?"

"I'm okay. Just give me a few minutes." Her throat hurt. Her body ached.

"Y' need to stay in bed tonight. Donae come to the show, Babe. Stay and rest."

"I'll be okay by then." At least with enough pain reliever, she would be.

He kissed her head. "We will see. I have t' go to sound check. Sleep a while. Beau will be with Megan and the kids in the adjoining room.

Ge' him if y' need anything. I have the doors propped so he can check on you."

She didn't answer. She closed her eyes, horribly glad Mike had hired a nanny. Megan was good with Nella. Beau wouldn't let anyone in. Susie could sleep until show time. She hoped Stu would skip sound check, also.

Part of her wished she'd listened to her husband and stayed at the hotel. But as she told him, if Stu could go on stage and play, she could very well sit backstage and keep an eye on Roy. At least she had made herself allow the kids to stay with Megan and Beau instead of having to watch them, too. Beau promised on his life he would allow no one in the room and they'd be fine.

Fighting to keep her eyes open, Susie listened to her band from a little couch instead of from up where she could see them. She was trying to stay away from the roadies as much as possible, in hopes she wouldn't spread it. Roy paced up along where she normally sat, looking out at Raucous with a frown. Why he frowned, she couldn't imagine. They sounded incredible as always, even though Doug had the beginning effects of it and Mike had little energy. And Stu ... the poor baby looked worse than she felt. She couldn't bear to have to watch him out there, although she knew he'd do all he could to help make the show worth what their fans paid to see them.

"Ginger ale?"

She looked up at one of their guards offering her a can with light condensation around the bottom. "Lenny, right?"

He nodded. "Would you rather have something else?"

"No, this is good, thank you. But I didn't ask..."

"Adam's orders. He wants you to stay hydrated."

Susie opened the can and looked back up at the young man. "Adam's?"

"He's staying in touch with us. Anything I can get you?"

"No. Thank you." Susie watched him head back into the wings as she pondered his statement. Adam was staying in touch? With their roadies? She wondered if Roy knew.

When the stage went quiet two-thirds of the way through the show, she opened her eyes and looked in that direction. Fans yelled and applauded. Voices backstage murmured. The guys were quiet. It wasn't over. And it wasn't time for their finale. What were they doing?

Susie got up, using the couch arm as support, and headed to where Roy had his hands on his hips, nearly boiling. "What's going on?"

He barely gave her a glance.

"Roy? What's wrong?"

"Wrong? None of them can listen worth a damn. I told them not to do this."

"Do what?" She gratefully accepted a chair brought to her and had to wonder if she looked as bad as she felt.

An electric guitar chord filled the near silence. Duncan's guitar. Doug came off the stage, followed by Stu and Mike. She asked Mike what was going on.

"They planned this last minute. Giving us a break so we can try to make it to the end. Your husband's idea. Stu, for hell's sake, go sit down." He took their keyboardist's arm and pulled him over to find a chair and drinks.

The chord wavered, grew in strength, slowly. She wished she could see them. Acoustic guitar joined in. Evan. A soft, slow melody she didn't recognize. Duncan gave him only a hint of a backup. She had heard it. Sometime, at some point she couldn't remember. The lights began to brighten; two spotlights. Susie pushed herself up and edged to Roy's other side where she could see them both. They faced each other. And they shot into action, amid wild screams from the audience.

Evan took lead. Even with his acoustic, he was the main focus. She remembered where. When Duncan had just joined and was still trying to decide whether to stay. She'd walked down to the basement and found them playing together, only the two of them.

It was amazing.

"Get off the damned stage already."

She forced her eyes to Roy. "What is wrong with this? Are you kidding? You don't hear the reaction?"

"This is a band, not a duet. We don't need the spotlight on..."

"Hell Roy, you keep saying Evan needs to be highlighted for his guitar work. He is. Listen. How can you object when it seems to be what you want most?" She had to stop. Her throat burned.

"And you don't?" He glared into her eyes, towering his height and bulk over her. "Tell me Evan highlighted isn't what you want. Not that I'll believe you."

"I don't care what you believe." Susie dismissed him, turning back to focus on her husband and her best friend. They were amazing together. They read each other perfectly. They were in sync and connected and fully appreciative of each others' ability. And they were both exactly where they wanted to be. She wasn't sure she had ever in her life seen anything more incredibly sexy.

A light touch on her back pulled her away again. Doug grinned at her. "Nice, isn't it?"

"Amazing."

"Yeah, I think we should consider making this a routine thing."

"I agree. How are you doing?"

"A lot better than you are from the way it looks. Go sit down, Suse. I better get back out there. My turn to give them a rest." He headed out along the dark edges of the stage.

The guitars paused, then waned, pulling back. And the drums took over. She couldn't help but grin. Definitely, they should make this routine for shows. She didn't often get to hear Doug show off, either. It was nice. And the fans loved it.

"*You.*"

Susie sighed and wondered who Roy was irritating now. She looked over to see Stu return the stare and pull himself off the couch with Mike's help.

"At least *act* like you're singing out there."

Stu shrugged hands toward the manager. "Act like I am?" He grimaced and pushed a hand against his throat.

"Or *do* it. If you need more drugs, take them, but give these people the show they came for."

Susie moved in between, facing Stu. "Ignore that."

"*What* the hell do you mean, *ignore* that?" Roy shifted to where she could see him, his voice loud enough several roadies stopped to watch.

"I mean he should ignore it. He doesn't need to act like he's singing when he feels so bad he can hardly stand up." Their stage manager interrupted to say Stu and Mike needed to go back out. Susie gave him a nod. "Just do what you can, Stu. Back off as much as you need. It's all right."

"*Don't* tell them to disobey my orders. They can *call* you their assistant manager all they want and Adam can play like he's getting your advice to *placate* you as he wants, but you and I *both* know *I'm* running this show, so don't act like…"

"I *am* assistant manager. They chose me because they *trust* me. I *am* doing the job. So *stop* yelling at me. I am *not* up to this tonight." She shut him out and faced Stu, a hand on his arm. She wasn't sure if it was more for his support or her own. She needed to sit. "Ignore him. Listen to me. Do what you can and no more. Leave the stage if you have to. They'll manage." She caught Mike's surprised glance and met it. "I'll send someone out to pull him off if I need to."

Roy barely waited until they were out on stage before starting in. "You do *not* own this band as you think you do. I didn't put all of this time into it for *you* to try to take over like you know what you're doing. I'm telling you now to *back off.*"

Her throat stung. Her head was fuzzy. Her legs were weak, as was the rest of her. But she was not backing down from him. She met his stare. "You don't own them, either, and you're being well paid for your time. So back the hell away from me because I am not afraid of you and your threats mean nothing to me." Susie managed to hold his surprised stare until he walked away.

She accepted the chair Lenny brought her, along with the ginger ale she'd left behind to watch the guitar duet. There was a slight shake in her hand as she raised the can to take a swallow.

"Do you want me to walk with you back to the dressing room?"

"No. I'm not leaving them. If Stu can do this, so can I."

Duncan took Stu's side as they left the stage. Their keyboardist was pale, too pale. He shouldn't have pushed so hard. Mike had taken over on bass a couple of times, allowing Stu to stay at the keyboard, on a stool he usually wouldn't use, at least hitting a few notes on occasion. When they needed him to really be there, he was. But they could have worked around it if he hadn't. "How are y' doing?"

Stu rolled his eyes. "I've had better days."

"Y' should have stayed off when we gave y' the break."

"Right. With our assistant manager saying what she did? How could I? Damn I gotta sit down."

Susie met them and set a hand on Stu's forehead. Duncan wasn't sure she'd be able to tell if he was hot, as bad as she looked. Ev took over with Stu and got him to sit down and Duncan ran a hand over Susie's head. She was hot. Clammy. He put an arm around her and helped her back to the dressing room.

He wanted to ask what Stu meant about what she said, but he didn't want her to talk. She wouldn't have told Stu to keep going if he wanted to stop. Duncan couldn't imagine she would.

2 March

Five days on the road and she was still fighting the virus. Stu had his energy back, and Nella had way too much of hers. Evan and Duncan seemed to have been spared although she did notice her husband was quieter and rested more often than normal the past couple of days. Now though, as she watched sound check from a seat in the auditorium, Susie couldn't tell any difference.

He and Evan had kept the duet broken by Doug's drum solo since their first show. And they'd added Stu's keyboard solo at the end of it since he felt better. Roy complained still. She knew it was only because it had been Duncan's idea and for no other reason. It highlighted Evan well. Duncan still held back and let his friend shine. As he said, he had enough solos here and there within their songs; he didn't need more.

Checking on Danielle and Keith, two rows in front of her beside Megan, Susie allowed her eyes to close and pulled a leg in front of her to rest her head on. Luckily, her throat was mostly fine, but she couldn't shake the fatigue. Two days of sleeping on the bus didn't help. Their schedule was tight, since Adam kept the US leg of the "Your Way" tour short, and they used hotels in Lexington and Williamsburg only for short naps and quick showers before being shuttled to venues, showering again in dressing rooms, and jumping back on the bus to hit the next destination.

If she remembered, they were at Myrtle Beach at the moment and would be in Raleigh the next night. Then Chattanooga, Tallahassee, Shreveport, St. Louis and … Lincoln, Nebraska. The band would fly home from Lincoln after the show on the eleventh while their buses would go on to Pocatello, Idaho to meet them on the eighteenth. Home sounded good.

"You should be resting."

She opened her eyes to Adam's voice as he lowered beside her. "What are you doing here?"

He pressed a hand against her forehead. "Heard you were still down with this. Why aren't you in the bus resting instead?"

"Doing my job. And you didn't answer me. Thought you had obligations."

"Yes, but you need to take time off and I was told you refused. You're feverish, Suse. You should be lying down and giving yourself time to get over this."

"It's off and on. Don't mention it to Duncan. He hasn't noticed the past couple of days. Think he's fighting it, too, although he won't admit it and seems to be better now."

"I'll make you a deal. I won't mention it if you take time off."

"I can't. Roy has been ... well, I have to keep an eye on what he's doing. He tried to push Stu..."

"I know." He stopped one of the guys walking around and told him to find juice of some kind. "That's why I'm here."

"You didn't need to come. What about your project you said couldn't be left?"

"Robin's watching over it." He nodded at a greeting from one of their techs.

"Robin?"

He raised his eyebrows. "My girlfriend."

"You have a girlfriend?"

Adam chuckled. "For about two years now. You met her. At that birthday party when you were expecting Danielle."

Susie thought back. Two years? Was she so feverish she knew he did and couldn't recall? The party, when she got sick and had to leave. "Oh. Robin. Yes, I remember her. Pretty girl. Quiet but very together. I remember being jealous about how sophisticated she looked, especially since I was so sick and not graceful at the time."

He laughed. "Well, she does public appearances well. She's been trained for that all her life."

"Two years? Why didn't I know this?"

He looked over at someone behind her and thanked him, handing Susie a glass of something with a straw. She opened the lid. The voice behind her said it was grape juice and walked away as she tried to thank him.

"So? Why didn't I know?" She took a sip and enjoyed the sweet coolness.

"We're not making it public. Keeping things quiet for now."

"Why?"

"Well, between the two of us, she happens to be the daughter of a rival record company owner. My father and hers don't particularly like each other. Not that I care a great deal what my father thinks, but for now, we don't want to make waves. We're afraid it could interfere with what I have planned."

"And that's okay with her? To keep it quiet for your plans?"

"Seems to be. She's incredibly supportive. Even made me come take over for you when she heard how sick you were, and when she heard what you said to Roy, the way you backed him down. She's glad you did."

Susie frowned. She'd managed to keep her husband from finding out that she yelled at Roy. How did Adam know?

"Don't worry. I won't tell him." He continued at her silence. "Duncan, I mean."

"Oh. Well, I just don't want to cause trouble between them. More than there has been. And it doesn't matter. Roy's just blowing off steam..."

"Um. Actually, he's doing more than that, but I can't prove it was him." Adam reached down into his briefcase and pulled out a paper.

Susie scanned the headline: *Raucous Assistant Favoring Her First On List?* A picture of her checking Stu's head accompanied the following article. "First on list? What is this? I'm too tired to read it; just tell me."

"It mentions the way Stu says he's next on your *list* and how you were, quote, babying him, unquote, before and after the first show. It also guesses what that list might be, with some rather ... vulgar interpretations."

She grabbed a deep breath. "Roy."

"My first guess."

Susie gave it back to him. "Hide it. They don't need to see it. It doesn't matter."

"That was my thought, but I will address it with Roy..."

"No. Leave it alone."

"Suse..."

"It won't hurt them, and I don't care what people think of me."

Adam was quiet a while. "Maybe you don't now, but what about when you go back to teaching? You think it won't affect that? Or your daughter?"

Susie didn't answer. By the time it came to the point she could teach again, she couldn't imagine anyone would bother to remember. It would go away like all news. People would forget. They forgot much more important things. And Danielle would know better. "Ignore it."

11 March

Duncan saw her set her plate aside. She hadn't eaten much. Not nearly enough. Susie had recovered from the virus by now but she was still fighting fatigue. The buffet offered at their Lincoln Nebraska show was one of the nicer ones so far. He'd eaten too much. Danielle had dug in well. Keith returned for more vegetables; Mike had to push him to eat some kind of meat along with the vegetables he loved. Susie only picked at it, although it wasn't overly greasy.

He went over to where she was talking to their publicist and slid his arms around her from behind. "Are you feeling alright?"

She raised a hand behind his head and gave him a quick kiss. "I feel fine. Paula was just saying she has a radio station interested in an early morning interview if you guys want to do it. You were supposed to be able to sleep in tomorrow, though, since our flight out isn't until one."

"Ask them." He was talking to Paula but she deferred to Susie. For some reason, the woman never asked the band anything directly. After her rough start in getting to know Susie, she now insisted on going only to her.

His wife turned in his arms. "How about I ask you first? Are you too tired? Or will you be at seven o'clock tomorrow?"

"I will be up anyway. Does not matter to me." He stroked her hair. "Will you keep Danielle and Keith at the hotel and sleep?"

"Oh. No, if you do it, I'll be there."

"You do not need to be."

"Why? Hoping there'll be a cute blonde you can flirt with?" She teased with a grin. "You can, you know. I'll look the other way."

"I prefer brunettes. If there is a cute blonde, Ev can have her."

"He prefers brunettes, too."

"Nae he doesnae. He might say he does but I know better."

"Really?" She slid a hand down his chest. "You do know I'm going to use that information against him."

"Good, Babe. And he will stop talking to me." He let himself caress her, from her waist down to her thigh. Her back faced the wall. It was safe enough, not that they guys hadn't seen him do it often enough.

"I don't see that happening, but I won't tell him you told me."

Paula started away. Duncan stopped her, apologized for interfering. She said she was done until she knew whether or not the interview was a go, so he turned and called over to his band mates to ask. They all readily agreed. Mostly. Stu agreed, but after a groan about the early hour. Roy jumped in, said it was his call. Ev backed him off. Nearly every day by now, Duncan wanted to be able to just knock the asshole out. He supposed he wouldn't. At least Roy knew to stay out of his face and be careful what he said to Susie.

His wife didn't object to his caresses. She did call over to Danielle to stay out of the cookies. Doug grabbed the girl and took her away from them.

"You might want to stop that now." Susie pressed in close.

"Nae I think I donae want to stop." He slipped his hand underneath her shirt. "We have nearly two hours."

"Hm, an hour and forty minutes."

"Gud enough. Want to take a walk with me?"

"Yes."

He grinned when her blue eyes peered into his. Duncan expected her to fuss at him, to tell him to wait until after the show. Her yes was an answer to more than a walk. Taking her hand, he asked Ev to keep an eye on Danielle.

The last thing Susie expected when they returned was Lisa and her kids. And Greg. Not Tony. Lisa came over and hugged her, told her Greg was from Nebraska, not far away, so they combined a trip to visit his family and to stop by to see Raucous.

Susie picked Joshua up from where he clung to his mom. He wasn't very big for a one-and-a-half year old, not as heavy as Nella had been or close to as heavy as she was now. The boy was frail as compared with Nella and Keith, but then Tony wasn't big, either, not that Duncan was all that big and Lisa was bigger than Susie. Barely taller, but sturdier. She had to wonder if Joshua had a health issue, if Lisa had checked. He was too frail, along with being so timid. Keith was shy, but Joshua was timid. She wished she could keep him for a while. She could imagine what Duncan would say to that.

Susie asked where Lisa's husband was.

"Off with his girlfriend somewhere, as far as I know."

Duncan heard her and looked over but kept his distance. Susie wasn't sure how to answer. And she didn't have to. Lisa jabbered about Blue River and Greg's newest songs and how great his family was to her and her kids, how much he helped her with them. Greg came over for a hug. Susie didn't much want one but she was polite. Joshua reached for Greg and he took Susie's hint, and took the boy over to talk to Stu.

Susie watched her daughter treat Tonia and Joshua as though she was the hostess of the event. She yammered at Joshua until he agreed to go play.

"She's doing well with this." Lisa's eyes were also on her.

"Yes. It doesn't bother her in the slightest. Keith doesn't always like it, but he does fine most of the time."

"You and Mike are lucky. Neither of mine like it. It's getting too hard to be on the road with them. I'll probably stay home for this next tour. Most of the time, I stay home now."

"You're touring again?"

"They are." The way Lisa said *they* meaning her husband's band put Susie's teeth on edge. "I don't think I am. Joshua really hates it. He likes his own bed and his own schedule and heaven forbid you throw him from it. He's a sweetie, he is, but he's so particular."

"That would make it tough." Susie wondered if the baby she and Duncan adopted would be the same, if it would make touring hard.

"So." Lisa glanced around and leaned in, her voice low. "What's up with you and Stuart? Are the rumors true?"

"Of course they aren't."

"No? Because I've always wondered. You two are..."

"Friends."

"Only? You can tell me, you know. I wouldn't repeat it, not that people don't believe it anyway."

People believed it? Susie had let herself think they didn't, really, just because of the press coverage. She figured most would know better. At least her friend should know better. "Only friends, Lisa. I would never cheat on my husband and I have absolutely no interest in doing so."

Lisa's shoulders straightened. "Well, you never know. Things happen. You think he's being that faithful? No one believes he is."

"*I* know he is. So am I. And you can look at me that way all you want, but it's true. Why in the world would I want anyone else, ever? He's..." Susie looked over at him as he grabbed Danielle away from the cookies again and tickled her. "He's my other half. I adore him. And I love him to the ends of the earth. I also trust him because I know I can."

Lisa still looked doubtful but it didn't matter. Susie half thought about telling her friend just where she and Duncan had been a few minutes before, that they'd made love in a little vacant room and sat close enjoying each other's company as long as they dared.

Megan and Beau kept all of the kids in the dressing room while Lisa and Greg went with the band and stayed in the wings with Susie. Before he went on stage, Duncan grabbed Susie around the waist, ran a hand through her hair, and kissed her.

Catching Lisa's eyes as her husband went on out with his band mates, Susie felt incredibly sorry for her. Greg tried to comfort her. He joked with them both. But he could see it, also. Lisa wasn't close to happy. When she assured Susie she wasn't pregnant as she expected, it was hard to tell whether or not she was glad she wasn't. Greg didn't seem glad she wasn't. Susie found it hard to make herself talk to him.

21 March

Ali settled beside Susie on the sidelines of the hotel's meeting room and pulled Nella onto her lap while Keith cuddled against Susie's legs. Glad Easter break afforded her the time off from her school internship to spend the week on tour with them, Ali tried to take in every nuance of Doug's job. This was a little interview, by a paper out of Lakewood, Washington. The reporter said he was only a "hop, skip, and jump" away from Takoma where they would be playing later that night and he couldn't resist the opportunity to interview the band from Lakewood, Massachusetts. So far, he'd asked about the comparisons between their areas. It was hard for the band to answer since much of what they saw of the Takoma area was from the highway and inside the arena. They did give a nice shout-out to their adopted hometown. Doug, Stu, and Mike were asked about their homes in New Hampshire, Evan's about his in Pennsylvania, and Duncan about Scotland. The guy had a penchant for places, Ali guessed.

From what she knew, Raucous never saw much of most of the areas they played. Ali was glad they had extra time in Eureka, California, though, with a day off in between after the Elko show. They'd wandered down to the beach, at Susie's request, and Nella and Keith grabbed handfuls of agates to take home. She and Doug, Susie and Duncan, and Evan and the two kids rented a van to drive up through part of Redwood National Forest afterward while Mike and Stu chose to sleep instead. Ali could never have imagined trees so tall. She'd only been half interested in going, but since Doug wanted to go, she agreed. And she was glad she did.

Now it was all business again and she turned her thoughts back to the interview, watching the guys, studying their different reactions. And the way they had lined up for it: Mike in the middle with Stu to one side and Doug beside him on one end, while Duncan took Mike's other side with Evan next to him anchoring the other end. It was too appropriate, really. The most outgoing were in the middle with the more silent support team at the ends.

Ali had been watching their interactions for the past five days. It was different on the road than it was at home, especially between Evan and Duncan. At home, Evan appeared to take the lead as though they were on his territory and gave Duncan a strong anchor. On the road, it looked reverse. Of course, she knew Evan had a problem with stage fright, although it didn't show once he was out there, but it was more. Duncan purely belonged on the road, on stage, behind the camera and answering questions. It fit him as well as Susie fit him. Ali wasn't sure Evan felt the same. He wanted it; she could see he did, and his duet with Duncan where he was fully highlighted was incredible. But it wasn't natural. That's what Susie had meant. She mentioned to Ali once that they wouldn't be out there if Duncan hadn't joined. It was because of Evan. He needed his friend's push, the anchor he provided.

Doug, Mike, and Stu would be fine either way. She had no doubt they would be. If Raucous ever disbanded, Ali could easily see them bringing in another musician or two and continuing. And Duncan could move along, as well, jump into one of the many other bands that had offered him lead guitar. Evan needed Raucous. As it was.

"So from what I hear, the spotlight solos thing is new this tour." The reporter leaned forward slightly and moved his gaze from one member to the other. "Was it, as I heard, quick thinking on the part of

                    LK Hunsaker

your manager to cover for someone who was sick, or is that only rumor?"

Ali saw Evan glance at Roy. Mike started to answer but Duncan cut him off. "It was last minute. Ev and I have been playing that piece together for years. Abou' time it was used. We hadnae thought to keep doing it through every show, bu' the audience seems t' enjoy it." He looked over at Doug. "Gud thing it worked all right. We threw Doug on the spot withou' giving him more than a couple hours' notice."

It was the second time Duncan had yanked Doug into the conversation. Ali appreciated it, since the guy mainly ignored Doug and Stu. He'd pulled Stu in once, also, as did Mike. Duncan did it much smoother, though, and he easily managed to answer about the duet without contradicting Roy but without affirming it. Doug teased her now and then about having a crush on Duncan, since she blushed so easily around him. It wasn't that, really. Maybe to some extent, and she had been pulled by his looks that day he walked into her parents' cafe, but she'd also been a bit frightened of him. She wasn't frightened at all anymore, but then he'd changed a lot. She appreciated the change Susie had pulled from Duncan. She also appreciated the change he pulled from Susie. Ali had always felt a little edgy around Susie before, just because Susie was so edgy and a little too uptight. Ali especially liked how close she now felt to Susie, and that she could tease her without worry.

When Duncan grinned at her, Ali realized she'd been staring at him during her thoughts. She felt her face warm but managed to grin back. Doug noticed. Darn it. One more chance for him to tease. She hated blushing so easily, especially since her thoughts weren't as they must have appeared.

Doug took over the answers about his solos and how they were bits and pieces of songs by other bands, with added embellishment to make them work as solos. He refused to say which songs were from other bands. "Tonight's will be part of a new Raucous song. Hopefully, you will recognize which one it was when you hear the album." He looked over at Evan.

Ali moved her gaze between Doug, Evan, and Susie. Evan kept his expression even, giving nothing away. Susie grinned. It had been planned. How exactly, Ali didn't know. She did know that every song Doug did for a solo was one of her favorites.

When the reporter turned to his next question, Ali leaned in toward Susie. "Was that your idea or Evan's?"

"It was a joint effort." Susie put her attention on the interview for a second before finishing her answer. "Evan told me Doug was changing songs and that he should do one of theirs from the coming album. I suggested Doug should use the new one he and Stu wrote because it already has a great solo in the middle." She shrugged. "Sorry it kicked out one of your favorites, but between the article and what Mike will say about it on stage, it should lead people to be sure to pick up the album to see if they can identify it. It won't be a single so they can only get it on the album."

Ali's jaw nearly dropped. "How do you know he's doing my favorites? He said he wasn't saying."

Susie rubbed Keith's head as he lowered from standing next to her to sitting on the floor. "I asked."

"So did Stu. Doug didn't tell him."

With a grin, Susie returned attention to the interview and a quiet conversation with Adam.

The guy also had a penchant for sports, as he asked about their favorite teams. Mike said he followed the Bears. Doug the Bruins. Evan the Red Sox and the Patriots. Duncan hesitated but said the Red Sox, to which Evan looked over with a grin. He shrugged. "So y' have convinced me to switch."

Asked what he switched from, Duncan said he'd been a White Sox fan since he'd lived in Chicago for some time but he'd rather go along with his friend's team now than against it. And it was now the home team for him, as well.

Stu shrugged, also, at the sports question. "I'm not too much into sports, but damn, I saw Eric Heiden just break the record. Gotta give that guy credit. He's damn fast on those skates. Like Apollo with those winged shoes."

Mike cleared his throat and leaned in to say something to Stu behind his hand.

"What?"

"Hermes. Apollo is the sun god. Hermes is the fast messenger the winged shoes."

"Yeah okay, whatever, Mr. English professor. Anyway, that was impressive."

Ali ducked her face into her hand and peeked out from between her fingers.

Mike shook his head. "You'll have to forgive him. While the rest of us were listening in class, he was writing music in his head. And in his textbooks. The paper he was supposed to use for taking notes. Anything he could write on."

Stu shrugged again. "Hey, I stopped writing it on my shirt sleeves when I got busted for cheating, which I was not doing. Had to get the melody down and that's what I had."

Ali just wanted to hug him. He was so cute. And she'd heard the stories from Stu's mom about how many shirts he'd destroyed with ink, until he was unfairly busted, and how she ranted up and down about it. She let him keep wearing the shirts, to make a point. Stu was lucky to have understanding parents. She could just imagine the fallout if she'd done the same. She wouldn't have dared.

Duncan had to give Ali a hard time. He'd embarrassed her by letting her know he saw her stare. She embarrassed far too easily, although not as much as at first, and he was glad of it. Among all of the girls who were around on a regular basis, she was the best friend of Susie's, a real friend, trustworthy, unconditionally loyal. And Duncan liked her better than he did Kate, Kara, or whichever girl Ev was hanging with on whatever week. He was just as glad this newest one was out of the picture already and he'd told Ev he was.

With the reporter leaving the room, Duncan went over and slid an arm around Alison as she stood next to Doug. "Y' like this color, do y'?" He pulled at his shirt, just above where he had it buttoned low, and tugged it away from his skin. Light blue. Too light for his own taste but Susie convinced him it looked nice with his coloring.

Ali's eyes flickered to his chest and she blushed again. "Yes. I do like it. But don't use that accent on me or I'll have to tell you again you're absolutely not cute."

"Nae?" He smiled, a teasing smile.

"No."

"Ah, I am hurt."

"No, you're not."

Doug scratched his head. "You're playing with fire, but go ahead. I'll be over there if you need rescued."

"He just gave me permission t' flirt with y', y' ken."

"Yeah, but I didn't. And you know, I was ... when you looked over earlier, I was only thinking about how nice it was that you pulled Doug in, and Stu..."

"I know." Duncan moved his hand from her back to grip her fingers and kissed them. "Donae worry. I know you are fully devoted to Doug and I know he never has to be concerned. I respect the hell out of you for that. It is why I can flirt with you when I will not with others. I am less sure of them."

"You flirt with girls in the audience well enough."

"Ah, I have my wife's permission for that."

"Permission. Right. More like encouragement."

Duncan couldn't help but laugh.

"But thank you. I'm flattered." Ali gave him a hug.

"I hope you will always stay close to Susie. Whatever happens with the band and such. She adores your company, and there is also no one I trust more not to hurt her."

"No one?" She pulled back with a curious look.

"Ah well, Stu and Doug as much so."

"And Evan."

Duncan felt a touch of hesitation. She saw it. He had to cover. "Other than their bickering, y' mean?" With a grin, he added distance. Good enough answer. Their bickering did hurt her. He knew it did. He wasn't sure it wouldn't be more than that, though. The thought nagged him now and then. There was still something between the two of them that would have to come out in time, and he knew she would end up hurt. He only hoped he would be able to help fix it again.

25 March

Susie stood on the banks of Wounded Knee Creek and let the history of the place engulf her. She told Duncan that Beau could go with her instead so he could rest before the night's show in Rapid City. Knowing where she was headed, though, he refused. He wanted to be at her side.

She was glad he was. Over 350 Lakota Indians had been massacred right there on the banks where she stood. In 1890. Nearly a hundred years before. Still, it felt closer, at least to her.

Feeling the heaviness of the place, the events, she lowered to the ground and crossed her legs in front of her. When one of the Lakota women had asked her heritage, after a minute of studying her face, Susie said her father was Shoshone and Cherokee, full blended Indian with nothing else as far as he knew. The woman slipped a beaded necklace over her head. And she left her alone to wander.

Susie fingered the necklace and considered why people were so widely afraid of those who were different. She'd fought it through her childhood. Not to the extent her ancestors had, and she was grateful for that. She was also grateful things were turning around for the Native tribes, that they were finally protected, educated, left alone on their land. Still, there was a long way to go. It had even split her family apart, her parents from their families, on both sides. It was never one sided. She'd seen it too often. Her dad had a huge struggle trying to fit in with the business world, never mind how suited he was for it. But he looked every bit full blooded Indian other than his very short hair. It often scared people. She didn't understand why the differences couldn't look fascinating as they did to her instead of causing such fear. Her dad could be hard, yes. She knew he could. But there was such incredible honor in his strength, an innate feel for justice. Like there was in Duncan. He was so much the same.

Danielle held onto her dad's hand as they walked around close by to give Susie space for her thoughts. Keith had wanted to go. Mike refused. He said they needed family time alone. She wasn't sure Mike wasn't afraid he'd learn too much, be too disturbed by it.

They didn't tell Nella more than that it was the home of the Lakota people. At two years old, that was enough. She'd learn as she grew. Susie had to wonder if it would mean much to her, if Nella would turn away from it as her grandpa did. Or if she'd embrace it as Susie had, at least to an extent. She wanted to be what her dad had worked so hard to give her. She just wanted to *be*, not to be holed into a little group, any little group. She wanted wider horizons.

With a sigh, she picked up a handful of sand and let it sift from her fingers.

Duncan walked over and crouched at her side as Nella searched for shells. "Are y' alright?" He ran a hand down her hair. She'd left it loose and flowing down her back.

"Yes, but I'm glad you came with me."

"Babe, y' know there is nowhere else I would be right now bu' at your side."

"Some day..." She bit her lip and waited through Nella interrupting to show him what she found. And until he sent her to find more.

"Some day what?"

"I want to see where Dad grew up. I want to ... maybe visit my grandparents, or at least see if they're still alive. Maybe they're not. Maybe they won't want to see me, but I want to try."

"And what will your dad think of that?"

"He'll understand. If I tell him. I might not."

Duncan frowned but didn't argue. He stood and extended a hand to help her to her feet. It was time to go. He had to get back and ready to work.

She supposed she'd have to tell her dad when she finally got the nerve to go. Maybe he'd even go with her, although she doubted he would. He hadn't seen his parents since he told them he was marrying Susie's mom, an Irish girl, daughter of a wealthy and locally powerful couple. Not since they made him choose their way of life or hers. Susie wanted them to know, if still possible, that they chose neither, but something their own. She had to think they would respect that.

Danielle bee-lined to a little stand with jewelry and by the time they caught up, she had a jade necklace between her fingers. The old woman behind the stand smiled and said the child had good taste already.

"Funny. I've never seen her interested in jewelry before."

The woman glanced at the necklace hanging down Susie's blouse. "You were greeted already, I see, as one of our own."

"Well, kind of. I'm not Lakota."

"No, I can see that you are not. Cherokee? And something else."

"Shoshone."

"Ah, of course. It's in your eyes. The shape, not the color."

"Mom was Irish. The color is hers."

"Irish? Anglo-Irish, then, with blue eyes, not Gaelic Irish."

"I think. She didn't say much about it."

"You are, then, from both an invader's heritage and an invaded heritage."

Susie couldn't answer. She'd never thought about it. Even with the history she'd read of Ireland and the knowledge of the way the Normans and British invaded and took over the Irish natives, she hadn't made the personal connection so closely. But she knew the English colonists weren't the only ones who invaded Cherokee and Shoshone tribes. So had other tribes, more war-oriented tribes. She couldn't fault the colonists when tribes had been doing it to each other maybe from the beginning. They stole women and children from other tribes to build their own and make them stronger. It had always happened to someone, somewhere. Everywhere. Was anyone on earth not both from an invader's and an invaded heritage? She had her doubts.

The woman studied her closely. "Too much sadness in your eyes. And this is your husband and child. Such a beautiful gift you have been blessed with. No reason for so much sadness."

"Oh." Susie stepped farther from her daughter, closer to the woman. "No, it's just ... this place ... I can feel it, like I can in parts of Pennsylvania where I'm from. The battle regions. It's..."

The woman grasped her hand. "You are open to the other world, more than most."

"What?"

"You feel it deeply within, as though you were part of it. More than most can feel."

She couldn't answer. She didn't begin to know how.

"You would be a valued soul in the old ways, in the old world, when we still knew what to value. Honor the gift, but do not let it consume you." She cast her eyes around the area. "This place was full of sadness. At times, it still is. Yet there is a power and strength that comes of it. All loss leads to life again. We must dwell on the life to come, not the life that is no more. Always move forward even while remembering backward. It is something you need to remember." At that, she moved over to Duncan and Danielle.

He bought his daughter the necklace she'd grabbed and a bracelet to match, plus a rubber tomahawk Nella insisted Keith needed. As they were leaving, the old woman stopped Duncan and slid something over his head, tucking the charm down into his shirt and patting it.

"You are a good, strong man. You would have made a fine warrior. Wear this. And return to visit. Remember the pure soul can do as it wills."

"I am honored. Thank you." With a light nod, he escorted his family out, back to their own world.

Ostinato

5 April 1978

"Baby, you should be in bed." Susie ran fingers through Nella's bangs as her daughter leaned against her side.

"No, my da'yee nae home now."

"Danielle, I told you he would be late. He's working. He'll come tuck you in when he's home." She forced herself up and reached a hand to Nella. "Come on, sweetie."

"Nae, I nae tired, my mummy. My da'yee nae home."

"You are tired. You sound just like your dad when he's tired. Come on. Time for bed."

"Nae, I see dance too. Yes." Danielle patted the space beside her as Susie always did when she wanted her daughter's company.

She couldn't resist. In the couple of days since they'd been home from tour, Danielle had stuck to her. It was odd. But then, Duncan had been working nearly non-stop, learning more of the production part of the album and helping Adam with ... she wasn't quite sure all he was doing. But he loved it. He loved the technical part of the music nearly as much as the artistic part of it.

Settling again, she wrapped Danielle in against her and waited for the commercial to end so they could go back to the feature on Baryshnikov. An exquisite dancer. Susie was more interested in watching him, studying his technique, than in the interview stuff. That was interesting, too, though. She'd had no idea Russian dancers were so restricted as to what they could dance and where and what music they could or couldn't use. She couldn't imagine. It frustrated her that Axis held so many strings over Raucous. As Evan told her time and again, Axis was paying the expenses and that made it their right. But Raucous was making the money for them. So were their other artists. Still, they did have some say, some control. More now than before, now that they were bringing in a lot of money for Axis. Having no control at all, she couldn't begin to imagine. Stifling art was ... well, it was wrong. Maybe they could break away from that soon, start paying their own expenses so they could make all of their own decisions.

Of course, she didn't know exactly what that would entail. She did have a basic knowledge of how expensive it was to put an album together, and a tour, and the publicity. And then who did you trust to do all of that for you?

Maybe she didn't quite want that. But Evan could handle it. If he would.

She found herself drifting off and had to force her eyes open after each commercial break. When he came home, Susie looked up at the clock. Nearly eleven. She was ready for bed. But she had to tell him about the rejection from the adoption agency that came while he was out.

Duncan picked up his daughter and asked why she wasn't in bed.

"Waiting for you." Susie stayed where she was. Baryshnikov was performing a bit of his newest ballet, Don Quixote.

He sat next to her. "I am going to get jealous if you ignore me for that dancer when I have been away all day."

"You're later than I expected."

"Yeah, I am sorry. I will go in later tomorrow than I had planned."

She looked over. "Tomorrow's Sunday. You should be off."

"Ah well..." He stopped at her look. "Let me get her in bed while you finish watching this. It is almost over?"

"Yes." She gave Danielle a hug and told her good night, then leaned back against the couch. He was supposed to be off on Sundays whenever they weren't on tour. She wanted him home.

He was back within a couple of minutes and waited the five more until the show ended. "What is wrong, Babe? Are you upset with me for being late?"

She told him. Straight out. About the rejection. And she managed to hide how she felt. Mostly. Or she was just too tired or too frustrated to bother to let it show.

"Donae worry, my luv. We will try again." He kissed her head and helped pull her to her feet. "Come to bed now. We will find another one to try tomorrow."

"You're working tomorrow."

He caught her eyes. "Nae, I think I amnae. I will call Adam in the morning. He can manage withou' me for a day."

7 April

Susie shoved a hand through her hair and dropped her chin on her fist, staring at the stack of paperwork needed for the new application: birth certificates, proof of education and work history, a description of their apartment, the statements from Doc that they were both physically able to care for a child, as though Nella wasn't proof enough, and beginnings of a scrapbook of their lives that showed who they were. Why was she bothering? They'd already been turned down by the first agency. Why did she think a different one would accept them? They'd have to wait until he changed careers, if he ever did. Or they'd have to take an older child. Maybe both. Maybe they'd have to wait a few years until Danielle was older and then adopt an older child to be closer to her age.

But she didn't want that. She wanted a baby, a newborn.

She wanted her own.

Pushing away from the table, she tried to push the thought from her mind. Even if it could be reversed, he wouldn't try. She'd never convince him it was safe. Maybe she could go in and find a sperm donor and prove it. Except she couldn't do that, either, and she would never hurt him that way. Even if it did hurt her that he was unwilling to trust her enough to try again. She wanted her own. She knew she could.

She paced around the living room and stopped when the door opened.

Duncan gave her a curious look as he let Adam in. "What's wrong, Babe?"

"Nothing. Did you need me? I was going to be down soon." She asked Adam.

He glanced at Duncan before answering her. "Actually, we're all going out to the house. Is this a good time for you?"

She ran a hand through her hair, wondering if she'd bothered to brush it. "Why?"

"Come on, and I'll show you."

"Nella's in her pajamas still and Keith's here..."

"I will get her ready and he can come with." Duncan told Adam to go on down to Doug's and they'd be there in a few minutes. He asked again what was wrong. She said it was nothing.

Susie took her time to change into something more decent and brush her hair, pulling it back into a quick half braid. She had to pull her thoughts away from where they'd been. He could see she was annoyed.

Why shouldn't he? She was annoyed. They were never going to get a newborn with his job and all the talk about her. No matter how false it was. Maybe she should have listened to Adam when he said she would care. But why should they be denied a baby who needed a loving home when she could have just had her own without anyone's permission? She was a good mom. Not great, but good. And he was a wonderful dad.

Her eyes began to mist and she grabbed a quick, deep breath and shook her head. No. She couldn't do that. She had to go out to Adam's.

Her daughter was ready to go by the time she went back out to face him. She ran up to Susie and showed her something made from several colors of Play-doh all squooshed together. "*Look*. I make it, yes. All myself." Nella held it in the palm of her little hand.

"Very pretty. What is it?"

The girl frowned. "Not pretty, no. It's *biii*g and strong and not dang'rous. I put one *biii*ger in backyard. I paint all colors on. Daddy say no." She frowned again.

Susie tried not to grin at her pout. "Hm. It's ... a seesaw."

"No, silly. No sitting place. See." Nella shoved it closer to Susie's face.

"Okay. It's ... an abominable snowman with a rainbow coat."

Danielle laughed. "No, my mummy. A rock. A *biii*g rock. Like I'land with water and birdies and I climb high, high, *high*."

"Is it? Well, sorry baby, but Daddy's right. No big, big rocks in the backyard. It's not safe."

She frowned again. "I do have rocks. And sand and water and birdies..."

Susie grabbed her in a hug. "How about we say yes to the sand and water? And we can put out bird feeders for your birdies. Okay?" The girl looked only part placated. "And maybe something to climb on, too. We'll see."

"*Yes*." Nella pulled back and nodded at Keith. "I climb, too. My mummy say yes."

Duncan swooped her up into his arms. "Okay, my sweet. We will talk abou' climbing later. Ready t' go?" She nodded and hugged his neck.

Susie brushed a hand through Keith's hair and appreciated his grin
in return. She was a good mom, even to her friend's son. She deserved
to have another of her own.

Getting out of the car, she wandered toward the new building next
to Adam's house, with an enclosed walkway connecting them. Susie
didn't have to ask, although the guys were chattering about just how
much space he needed to live in.

When he took her side, she looked over at him. "You built a
studio."

A grin pulled at his mouth. "I built a studio. This should make
recording a whole lot easier without having to travel two hours each
way."

"This..." She returned her gaze to the rectangular building covered
in a soft gray vinyl siding to match his house and surrounded by freshly
turned dirt covered in straw. Over grass seed, she supposed. "This had
to cost a fortune."

"Wait'll you see inside. Come on."

Susie wasn't sure if that was avoidance about the cost or that she
had no idea yet about just what it cost. Either way, she hoped Raucous
would keep producing long enough and well enough to be worth his
time to build it. And what about when they stopped, as they eventually
would? Adam would move on to another band, she supposed. The
thought made her heart heavy.

He talked to the guys about details as they headed to the entrance.
Sound proofing. State of the art. Acoustics. He even had a duplicate of
Doug's set so he wouldn't have to move the thing. "I'm doing all I can
to keep things as easy as possible, the least stressful as possible. You
can produce better if you're not hauling stuff and running back and
forth and..." He glanced at Susie. "And worrying about being separated
over two hour drives."

"Adam." She was flattered, but felt guilty. "You didn't ... I mean..."

"This is something I've wanted for a lot of years. I finally had the
excuse to do it."

She held Keith's hand as they were given the grand tour and while
Nella stuck to her dad. Not only new drums sparkled in the recording
room, but new amps in the same brands as they guys already had, new

microphones, including the filter for the lead singer, headphones, and a gorgeous piano. A grand. Even though she didn't play, she couldn't help going over to touch the shining white and black keys.

"Go ahead. It sounds incredible."

She looked at Adam. "No, I don't know how."

He shrugged. "With this thing, just touch the keys and the sound is rockin'."

Susie chuckled at his excitement. "Then it should be played by someone who knows what he's doing." She met Stu's gaze as he took her other side. "So play something. I have to hear this."

She stood beside him and listened a while as he played a bit of Mozart for her before moving to one of theirs, then wandered more, her ears still on Stu, her thoughts swimming. Adam had gone all out for them. Maybe not only for them. He said he'd wanted it. Maybe he already planned to do more than work only with Raucous. After as much as he had to have put into this thing, she figured he should.

It felt ... amazing. And suddenly just a little too overwhelming. A reminder of how serious this was, how far up they actually were, how they would always be a well-known part of music history. Her guys. Her band.

Her husband.

Maybe she shouldn't push him about having another child. He had enough on his hands. Practice, recording, touring, writing, and some producing. She couldn't even manage Nella well without his help since she was such a handful. Maybe they should leave well enough alone. Except she'd already given up her career for his; did she have to give up her dreams of a big family, also, or at least bigger? When she'd looked at the Victorian so often, she saw it with a big family, several kids, three or four. She'd settle for two, but she wanted at least that.

Her chest raised suddenly and she walked out of the recording room and into the producer's room. There was a window at each side. The shutters on the one they saw as they entered were open, closed on the other side. Susie wandered over and peeked through the wooden slats. Then she pulled the blinds up all the way.

"You can come use it as you wish."

She startled at Adam's voice behind her. And turned back toward the large in-ground pool. Right outside the studio. And covered by a glass dome.

"The doors around it open for summer use. For winter, it's heated."

Susie turned back to him. But she had no idea what to say.

"Really. Come over anytime, or bring your suit when they're here working and..." He nodded for Duncan to come see what they were talking about when he joined them.

Her husband again gave her that curious look as he took her side.

"Thought it would be good to help you all relax your nerves when things get tense." Adam shrugged. "And I earned huge points from Robin. She used to be a competition swimmer."

"Is she here?" Susie looked through the producer's window at Doug trying out the drum set.

"She's at work, but you're all invited to stay. She won't be long. We can order in, have a last-minute grand opening party and get back to work tomorrow."

Susie thought about the paperwork sitting on her table. She'd wanted to finish it before bed. But she supposed that would wait, also. Maybe it would wait a few years. The studio had to be paid for. They had to keep going strong enough to be worth Adam's time. And his money. There was no way all of this came from Raucous. He didn't take a big enough cut for that.

9 April

Her disguise worked well enough. And she loved being out with Alison, just them and Nella and a couple of Ali's cousins. One of them had a seven year old who was great at entertaining Nella. The other had a two year old, well behaved, and a new baby. Four months. A sweet little boy who smiled a lot. They both teased Ali about catching up, pushing Doug for a ring and having a couple of kids. Ali said she would never push Doug to do anything, that she was content at the moment.

Susie wasn't quite sure she was as much as she said she was. But the baby didn't seem to pull at her like he pulled at Susie. Ali wanted to finish school before anything else. That was more important to her than hurrying to be a wife, or a mother. Maybe Ali wasn't entirely interested in being a mother. Susie grabbed the baby more often and hated to give him back when he wanted his mom. Ali, at the first sign of a cry, gladly returned the boy. She spent more time talking with Danielle than with her cousin's children.

As nice as the day was, Susie was glad to get home. It was nearly dinner time, so she gave Ali a hug and hustled Danielle up the stairs with the request of helping her get dinner for daddy. He'd said he'd be early, closer to six than to eight as he had been doing, since production had moved to Adam's.

She was worn out by the time the meatloaf was ready and Nella had bathed and was fidgeting in everything under the sun that she wasn't supposed to mess with. Nearly seven. Susie figured the child was hungry and so went ahead and got her dinner. She was hungry, also, but she wanted to eat with Duncan. Nella was happy enough to have Susie sit at the table and keep her company as she nursed a glass of tea. She chattered about shopping and the other kids and her new shoes and the baby and Ali until Susie wanted quiet. And to eat.

As her daughter finished, she set the plate in the sink and took Nella's hand. "Come on, baby. Let's go see if Daddy is next door and forgot what time it is. Okay?"

With a bound, Nella half pulled her, but stopped. "I no' dressed. No."

"You're dressed enough to go next door."

"No. I not go ou' no' dressed."

"Oh Danielle. You do it all the time."

"No. I big now. No' baby like Ali's baby. No."

"It's not Ali's baby. It's her cousin's baby. And they won't care if you're in your pajamas."

"No. I not." The girl planted her feet and frowned.

"Fine. Put your jacket on, then, so your pajamas don't show if you want to be shy all of a sudden." Susie grabbed it from the rack.

Nella tilted her head. "Jacket no' for 'jamas, silly. No."

"Oh Danielle, I'm tired. Can we just go for a minute, please? You don't have to go in. Just come."

"No." She pulled back.

Susie considered picking the kid up and carrying her over, but she was so heavy and liable to fight against her. "Fine. Go play in your room."

"No. I ge' dressed and we ge' daddy."

"No, you're not getting dressed again. Just go play." Susie picked up the phone. Mike answered after the first ring. "Hey, is Duncan over there?"

"Nope. Not home yet? And you really couldn't just walk over here?"

"Apparently it's not okay anymore for a two-year-old to wear pajamas across the hall and it's not okay to wear a jacket over pajamas to walk the three steps across the hall."

Mike chuckled. "Yeah, I remember hitting that point. Fun, isn't it?"

"Not so much tonight. Is Evan there or did he go with?"

"He's on a date. Need something?"

"No. Thanks. I have to go see what that noise is about." Susie hung up and hurried to the hallway. "*Danielle*." She grimaced at the dent in the wall, and the shoe in Nella's hand. "What are you doing?"

"I make tunnel. See?" She pointed at the dent. "I get little, little baby from tunnel. New sister for Nella. Yes."

"You what? *Stop* that." Susie grabbed the shoe from her hand after another bang against the wall. "Babies don't come from tunnels in the wall. And *don't* put holes in my walls."

"Yes. Ali cous'n say baby have too li'l tunnel. I make big, big tunnel. No' hard. No."

"Oh Danielle." How on earth did she pick up on that conversation? The girl had used the word tunnel in front of the kids to hide what she meant. Not well enough. "Daddy is not going to be happy about this dent in the wall. Go on in your room."

"No, my mummy. Daddy too happy. He tell my Evan Lee. I have baby brother. Yes. I hear. Yes."

Susie had to hold her breath a moment. She heard Duncan talking about a baby? Too happy. She meant he *was* happy, too: an argument. But what if they didn't? What if they were rejected again? And again?

She had to change the subject. "Okay baby, how about you bring a book for me to read to you? We'll tell daddy about the tunnel when he gets home, but Danielle, don't bang on my walls. No tunnels in the house. It doesn't work that way; it only makes mommy sad."

Nella frowned and hugged her.

After three books, Susie turned on the radio and went to put the food away and clean the dishes. She'd pull it back out when he got home if he still wanted it. Billy Joel sang *She's Always A Woman* to keep her company, which was her favorite song on the LP and she sang along with it. It faded too soon into Staying Alive, which made Nella dance. Susie watched the girl between putting dishes away; she had incredible rhythm already. She didn't like *Two Tickets to Paradise* as well, but Fleetwood Mac brought her back to her feet. Nella was right. It made good dance music. Maybe Susie would use it next time she worked out.

The newest Wings hit came on. *With A Little Luck*. Susie liked Wings. She'd have to pick up the album. And it would make a good theme song. She could use a little luck with the adoption, if she bothered to finish the paperwork. Maybe she wouldn't.

Duncan got home just after nine. He ate with Adam earlier. Susie told herself she should go ahead and eat but she didn't want it anymore.

10 April

She sighed and returned the receiver to the cradle. Another delay on the house. Just how long did it take to repair a house? It wasn't a castle or anything. Something with the wiring, but they could go ahead and move in and let the workers work around them. She didn't think so. Not only did she not want strangers in her house with her and Danielle there, but bad wiring sounded scary. They said it wasn't, not as long as ... something that didn't quite register. Still, she'd rather wait until the workers were done and out.

"Nella, are you ready?" Susie started toward the girl's room. At a knock on the door, she decided to check on her daughter first. She wasn't there. Following the noise, she found her in the music room pulling at the Mustang's guitar strings as it stood propped on its stand. "*Nella.*"

The child jumped; a guilty look crossed her face.

"You know better than to mess with daddy's guitar. Come on out of here." She heard the knock again while waiting for the girl to shuffle back to her room. "Get dressed so we can go." Maybe they'd have to find a child sized guitar for her. Something inexpensive and not valuable or sentimental. Duncan's Mustang was off limits. Susie would be bothered less if anything happened to the Telecaster she got him for his birthday a few years ago, or the new Strat he'd picked up a few months ago. The Mustang he'd carried with him since he first started playing, that was off limits.

"Okay, I'm coming." She called to the other side of the door although she doubted they'd hear her. Opening it to Ali, she started to apologize for taking so long, until Susie noticed Janet beside her.

Ali gave her a hesitant look. "Hey Suse. Are we interrupting?"

"No." She returned her attention to Janet, a very round Janet with a hand underneath her stomach in support.

"She was downstairs when I came in. Kate blocked her entrance, but I thought..." Ali still studied her as though expecting Susie to be angry. "She said she needed to talk to you. I hope it's okay. If not, I'll escort her back down."

"It's fine. Doug's next door."

Ali gave her a light grin. "I know. I'm going to go bother him. Are you coming over?"

She glanced at Janet. No way would Susie take her in where Evan was working. "I'll be over in a few minutes. Would you mind taking Nella with you?" In case she needed to kick her ex-manager out.

With Ali's agreement and a call to Danielle that Ali was there, Susie let Janet in and asked her to sit. She looked like she needed to sit. Closing the door behind them, Susie made herself sit opposite Evan's ex. "I didn't know you were expecting. Congratulations."

"Thank you. One more month to go. And thanks for letting me in. I wasn't sure you would."

"Want tea or water?"

"No. Thank you. I'm not staying. I know you don't want me here." She fidgeted. "I'll make it quick. I have a favor to ask."

Susie nearly laughed.

"I know. I don't deserve to ask. And I know I was horrible to you. I am sorry."

"It doesn't matter anymore. How's Jared?"

"As rambunctious as ever. Luckily, he gets along with my husband. I have trouble with him. Hard to believe he's eight already." She continued at Susie's silence. "And Danielle? From the glimpse I got as she ran past, she still seems to look like her dad. Especially that hair. It's gorgeous."

"Thank you, and yes, she looks more like him all the time."

Janet nodded. "Well, guess I better get to it. I'd like you to come teach for us again."

"You have to be kidding."

"I understand, but it's a special situation. And I wouldn't ask, but it's not for me, or for the studio. It's for one of our students. She's fifteen. A beautiful dancer, but her teachers are having a hard time."

"Janet, the last thing I need right now is a troubled teen who causes problems..."

"No, she's not troubled. I wouldn't ask that of you. I have teachers who are good with that sort of thing, stronger natured. This girl, she's very sweet, well-mannered, but she's mute, and partially deaf. She somewhat hears music but words are muffled so sometimes she can catch them, mostly not. She knows sign language and I offered to send a couple of my teachers to learn it, at the studio's expense, so they can communicate with her. One tried, said it was too hard to learn and not worth it for one student. But Susie, this girl ... she's good and she loves it so. It's in her soul like it's in yours. She's ready to go onto Pointe but they won't do it. They're afraid she won't understand what they're saying well enough and she'll injure herself."

"How long has she been there?"

"Just over a year. They moved to town recently from a bigger city where they had facilities to help her. She does well just following what the others do, but it's not enough." Janet dropped her eyes and took a breath before returning her gaze. "I thought ... I kept thinking it would be nice if you were there. If you remember sign language well enough. I know you and Evan still use it at times, so I thought you might. She deserves better than we can give her. I know you're busy and the band's doing great, but maybe just now and then as you can work it in? Something to help her get started en Pointe or ... whatever you're willing to do. If you are. And of course I have no right to ask."

Susie stood and paced over to the window. A young dancer. Nearly deaf and mute. She had to be a fairly strong girl to have survived the studio that way for so long. But Janet's comment rankled her. *Stronger natured.* Only Janet would be insulting, again, while asking for a favor.

"Are you still dancing at all?"

She turned at Janet's voice. "Some. Enough to stay in shape."

"I was afraid of that, that you'd quit. It's a shame, Suse, as good as you are."

"I'm happy with things as they are."

"Of course. You and Duncan seem to still be doing well. I know not to believe the papers..."

"More than well. He and Danielle are everything to me."

She nodded. "And how is Evan? Other than what I read in the papers. Is he okay?"

Susie considered not answering. Evan was not Janet's business. But she couldn't be quite that rude. "He's fine. He's writing now, with Duncan and Stu. They pulled him in to do more of it. It's nice."

Janet's response was interrupted by the door. Duncan. And Evan. Her husband came to her. "Ali said y' had company."

She kept an eye on where Janet stood to face Evan and repeated the request for Susie to come back to the studio.

"No way in hell." Duncan stiffened and threw a look at Janet. "How dare y' ask her after what y' did to her? She is not going back there."

Susie wrapped a hand around his arm. "It's a special situation."

"I donae care if the whole thing will go under without y'. Y' arenae going back. I will build y' one of your own..."

"No." She caught his eyes. "I mean, I don't want that right now. But..." She looked back at Janet. "Let me think about it and talk to him. We'll see what we can work out." Susie watched Janet rub her swollen abdomen and had to grit her teeth. Janet was not a good mom, but no one kept her from doing it again.

Duncan slid an arm around her and kissed her head. She met his eyes. "It's okay." She wanted Janet out of her apartment. She wanted that more the more often Janet looked over at Evan. "I'll get back to you. Is your number the same?"

"Yes. And I would truly appreciate it. For her sake." Janet headed toward the door and paused beside Evan. "It was nice to see you again. I'm glad you're doing well."

"Thank you. And congratulations." His eyes cast toward where she still rubbed her stomach.

"I'd rather it had been yours." With a sad half-smile, she left.

Susie watched her friend hide whatever floated around his brain. No matter what he said, Evan wanted a family. She knew he did. As the door closed, she went to him. "I'm sorry. I should have asked Ali not to say anything."

"You have no reason to be. I wouldn't have had to come over. I just wanted to be sure she wasn't bothering you because of me again."

"Why would she now?"

"She's called a couple of times recently."

"What? Why?"

"Just to talk. Funny she didn't mention she was expecting."

"Hang up on her."

He touched her arm. "Don't worry, Angel. She's married. There's no danger."

"There could be if the press finds out she's calling you, since she's married *and* expecting."

"Worried about my reputation?"

"No. But ... well, I don't want to have to worry about your reputation. Your mom would blame me as a bad influence." She shouldn't have said it. It just came out.

Luckily, before he could figure out how to counter, Duncan wrapped arms around her from behind. "Men like women who are a bad influence. As he said, donae worry. His reputation was ruined long before y' ever knew." His teasing tone brought a snicker from his friend. "Why does Janet want y' back, Babe?"

Explaining the request, Susie could see he at least understood why she didn't tell her no immediately. Still, his whole expression said he did not want her at the studio. She had to change the subject, and she couldn't help being nosy about Evan's date the night before. A nothing date, he said. He wouldn't ask her out again.

12 April

Duncan let himself into Ev's apartment. After eight at night, if Susie and Danielle were not home, they would be at Ev's. Or Stu's, but he'd just come from there. Their new songs were coming along well. During production, he'd noted a couple of things he wanted to run past his friend. Stu so easily thought in several musical parts all at once, better than the rest of them. If he could get him away from Kara more often, Duncan would have him in the studio where he belonged.

Susie was there, sitting next to Ev. Maybe Duncan should pull him into the studio more often since he had available time.

"Hey." She met his gaze. "How'd it go today?"

"Decent enough. Stu and I have a few changes we want to work out tomorrow. Have plans?" He asked Ev.

"I do now. What time are we starting?"

"Early as we can get everyone there."

"Six a.m.?"

Duncan gave him a nod. "Right, and if you can get Stu there by then, I'll owe you a Red Sox game, front row dugout."

Ev chuckled. "Might be worth trying. It's been a while."

A "while" was an understatement. They hadn't been to a game together since ... the one where Duncan stepped in with Susie and asked her to dinner. She agreed they should find time for another.

Danielle reached up with little arms and a pleading expression, so he picked her up and gave her a hug. "Ready to go home, my sweet?" Getting a nod and a nose nuzzled into his neck, he asked Susie the same. She started to get up and accepted his free hand to help.

As he discussed actual practice times with Ev, he was distracted by his wife cuddling in nearly as much as Danielle. She slid a hand up his back and ran fingers through the ends of his hair. A good sign. She'd been distant lately. Of course he'd been working a lot and he knew she usually had both Keith and Nella all day long, plus Kate fairly often. He wasn't sure why Kate wasn't modeling more, but she appeared to have at least as much free time as Ev. Or more. Still, the kids were always with Susie, and Susie was still working with Adam and with their publicist on upcoming album promotion and tour plans and he thought a few other things he didn't even know about.

She hadn't mentioned the adoption paperwork in a couple of days. Maybe he'd ask once Danielle was in bed.

Susie stroked Duncan's hair behind his ear and smoothed it down as he read Danielle a book to help her settle for bed. He was tired. She considered asking him to take the next day off, but he'd already arranged with Evan to work. They would be in the basement, though, so she and the kids could hang out down there and be almost with him.

Reaching the end of the book, he told Nella it was time for bed. She argued. He hushed her easily and carried her back to her room. Susie took the empty popcorn bowls to the kitchen, dumped the unpopped kernels and extra salt, and washed them out. He wasn't back yet, so she went to see if Nella was causing trouble. She had to grin at her daughter's little arm wrapped around Duncan as well as she could reach as he lay beside her, eyes closed. Acting asleep so Nella would, Susie guessed.

Then she wasn't sure he was acting. Nella was asleep. Her sweet face was so peaceful, angelic. Susie went to Duncan and touched his shoulder. He didn't move. She leaned closer and rubbed her hand down his arm. "Are you awake?" He shifted, inhaled deeply. "Duncan?" At his stir, she stroked his hair. "Come to bed. It's your turn to be tucked in."

He got up and stretched his shoulders, checked Nella, and slid an arm around Susie to go with her.

"Go on to bed. I'll get the lights." She was a little surprised he didn't argue, and she didn't take her time. Still, he was in bed by the time she got to their room. He hadn't showered. Unusual. With a sigh, she got ready quickly and slid in next to him. He stirred enough to pull her in. An offer. She knew it for what it was. But he was too tired.

"Good night." Susie kissed him with his mumbled reply, stroked his face over the whiskers that were longer than he usually allowed and that Nella fussed about, and settled against his side.

13 April

Again, she had barely slept. Janet's request to work with the girl at the studio kept nagging. Duncan didn't want her to do it unless it was in their building; he said they could work in the basement. But the guys were using it so often now with the album push and the changes they were working on, and she was afraid of who might come with the girl, that it might be a set up. Paranoid. She was getting too entirely paranoid. She didn't want to go to the dance studio. She kept waking up with old memories of the place, of the way they'd treated her. So she would decide to refuse. Then she'd have dreams of Jeremy and what a struggle it was for him to fit in when no one would bother to learn how to talk to him. She partly felt like this girl had been sent to her for a reason.

But the studio?

And she was tired. And Duncan was tired. Danielle was unfatigable. Tired wasn't in her vocabulary. She ran all day until she dropped. There were the constant band meetings with the publicist and cover photographer who wanted to get them scheduled for a photo shoot and Stu working around Kara's schedule as well as he could while trying to give in to Duncan to work at production. Not to mention how clingy Evan was recently. She had no idea why. It was partly helpful because he was great with Nella, but she felt ... overwhelmed.

And yet she couldn't say no.

Her paperwork wasn't done. For the adoption. And she didn't have the energy to think about it. Still, when Janet called again, Susie gave in. She would go meet the girl on Friday.

Kate kept telling her she should, that Susie should go back to work, her own work, and stop letting her whole life revolve around the band. She was a dancer and she should dance. She'd also told her, when she'd picked Keith up from staying overnight, again, to stop giving her advice about Keith, that she had no room to give parenting advice when she had such a hard time controlling her own child. *At least Keith behaves, and he stops when I tell him to stop.* The words echoed through Susie's mind. *Maybe you aren't the perfect parent you think you are.*

She sank into a chair. Maybe Kate was right. Except Keith listened to Susie just fine. He was easier. Kate was lucky. Or maybe she was right. Not that Susie ever thought she was perfect at anything. Kate knew better. She had to know better. But how right was she? Nella was a little terror, as Stu called her. Sweet. Charming. Beautiful. Loving. But a little terror. Maybe she didn't know what she was doing. If she did, Duncan wouldn't have to come home after a long day of work and put the girl in bed because Susie couldn't get her to stay in bed.

She did miss dancing. Going back to the studio would only fuel that, remind her of the one thing she always felt she did well. Did she dare ignite that passion she'd let fizzle out to no more than a lightly glowing ember? But how could she refuse?

Duncan studied her as she pushed her shoes off and removed her jacket to hang on the rack. She'd been too quiet all night. When he asked earlier, she said she didn't want to go out, she had things to do, but he and Stu wanted a break from work. They wanted to take their girls out and have some fun, partly as a thank you for how patient they'd been the past week. Susie talked with Kara during the night, but not much with him or Stu. She did give in once when Stu pushed at her to dance with him. They were cute together on the dance floor. Duncan loved to watch them. But after someone commented about her and Stu where she could hear it, Susie wouldn't do it again. She did dance with him, but she didn't seem very interested in that, either.

He told Danielle to go get ready for bed and stopped her when she started to complain. Susie headed into the kitchen. He followed to find her gathering up paperwork she'd set aside when he begged her to go out with him. "Babe, what has been bothering you all night?"

She shook her head and turned the burner on under the tea kettle.

He wandered up behind her. "Talk to me."

"I'm fine." She turned when Danielle came in and went to take her back to her room.

With a sigh, he leaned back against the counter. Then he glanced at the folder and walked over to open it. Adoption paperwork. Was that it? If she was going to get this upset every time she worked on it ... and she would. He knew she would. Especially if they were turned down again. They had Danielle, and she was an incredible child. He felt lucky to have what they had already. How could she not see it the same?

Taking over with Danielle and singing to her for a few minutes until she was sleepy enough to stay in bed, he went back out to find his wife. The folder was off the table. The stove was turned off. He didn't see her. Switching off the kitchen light, he went back to their room. She was in bed reading. It must have taken him longer than he thought to get Danielle down. "Tired?"

She looked up at where he stood in the doorway. "I guess."

"You didnae get your tea."

"I changed my mind." She went back to her book.

Duncan sauntered over and sat at her side. "Do you need help filling out the paperwork?" At a question in her eyes, he continued, although she knew darn well what he meant. "For the application. It is a lot of work. If you want me to help you..."

"No."

"Suse." He took the book from her hands, set the bookmark inside, and laid it on the bed stand. "Donae worry. If we are turned down again, we will try again. One of them will be smart enough to see you are a wonderful mum and I will do well enough..."

"I'm thinking ... maybe...."

"Maybe what?" He touched the side of her head, let his fingers slide down her hair, onto her shoulder.

"Maybe we should wait."

His movement stopped; his eyes met hers. "Why?"

"This is a waste of time. They'll tell us the same thing: your job is too hard on a child, unless I stay home for stability, and I don't want to stay home. I don't want to be a single parent. I want us to do it together, and they're never going to..."

"One refusal doesnae mean never."

"I can't..."

"You knew it would be a hard, long process. You said you could handle it."

"I *can* handle it. I *am* handling it. I'm being sensible here, so don't act like I'm a weak little girl you have to..."

"Suse, I donae think you are weak. I have never thought that." She knew he didn't. If she mentioned it, it had to be only because she thought she was, but why she'd think she was weak was beyond his comprehension. "Babe, what is going on in your head that y' arenae telling me? There is something. I have seen it." It was in the way she'd stopped looking directly at him, her body language, stiffer than normal, with less contact than normal. She had plenty of contact with Ev. He was always around when Duncan got home at night, or she was over there. She was friendly with the kids, hugged them often. But even now, she was pulled back from him, her shoulders tensed, her eyes anywhere but on him. It had been that way for over a week, since they'd been home from tour. Or since they'd received the rejection. He tried to pull her eyes to his. "Suse?"

"I just think maybe it's not the right time. Maybe that refusal was a sign." She still refused her eyes.

"Babe, what is this about? I know you can handle it. So what is this about? Have you changed your mind about wanting another?"

"No, but..." She fidgeted with the sheet, straightened it.

"Then let me help you fill it out this time, or I will do it since you did the last one."

"You have too much going on already." Her voice was sharp.

Maybe that was it. A lack of attention. He touched her face. "I have been busy. I am sorry, bu' if you want my attention, y' know how t' ge' it. Tha' hasnae changed." He gave her a teasing grin and lowered his hand to the edge of her nightgown along the top of her breasts. "I donae mind anymore than I ever have."

"It's not that."

"Nae?"

"No."

He stopped teasing. She wasn't in the mood. "Then tell me why."

"Forget it. It doesn't matter. I just ... maybe I just need a couple of days before I go back to it. I'm still tired from tour and..."

"It does matter. You are upset and you refuse to tell me why you are."

"Let it go, Duncan. I just want to read a bit and go to bed. Work on something if you need to. It won't bother me." She picked up her book again. A hardcover, which she usually didn't get. She preferred paperbacks.

He lifted it enough to see the front. *The World According to Garp*.

"It's Adam's. Just out. He started it and changed his mind, so asked if I wanted it."

When had she seen Adam when he wasn't there? Not long ago, he suspected, since she was only a few pages into it. He took it from her hands. Whether or not she wanted attention, he did. "Tell me. If you donae want to do this now, say you do not. It is alright."

The blue eyes pierced his, an accusation. "You mean you don't want this? If you're just going along with me..."

"No. Suse, I do want this, but only if you are ready. If you arenae, we will wait, but I want to know what changed your mind about having a child when you were so set on it."

"I didn't."

"Then what is this about?"

"Nothing."

"Donae tell me nothing. What is it?"

"Duncan..."

"I willnae let it go. You will have to tell me."

"Just stop; it doesn't matter."

"It does matter. Tell me."

"Does it? Or did you make sure it wouldn't happen because you don't really want another one? Did you know they'd turn us down? If you're only going along with me because you know it won't work..."

He stood and walked away, to the door. Didn't want another one? He damn sure wanted another. He wanted hers. Theirs. He'd been sick to his stomach for a full week before the vasectomy and plenty long after because he wanted it. But not at the risk of her life. His jaw was clenched. His stomach began to hurt. How could she even think it?

Forcing back his emotions, he felt his head shake. "I would never do that to you. I would never lie to you. You know I would not."

Silence echoed through the dim light of the room. She knew better. She was too upset. She had to know better.

"I know." Her voice filtered through. Barely. "I'm sorry. I know. I just... I told you I could. I want *your* baby. I want *our* baby. I don't want... I don't want some stranger telling me I shouldn't have a child, that I'm not fit. I want ... I want my own. And I told you I could."

Her own. She wanted her own. And she was still mad at him that he refused to risk it.

He went out to the living room and dropped onto the couch. Then he got up again and grabbed a beer from the fridge and stood in the dark kitchen against the counter. Her own. That's what the silence was about, the recent avoidance. She was still mad at him for the vasectomy and working on the adoption only rubbed it in.

And he could do nothing about it.

Except maybe try a reversal. But he couldn't do that, either. It wasn't worth losing her.

He sipped his beer in silence. What more could he do? How did he convince her it wasn't worth risking her life, that he couldn't imagine ever living without her? That Danielle needed her as much as he did. They had a beautiful daughter. He was happy with that. He would be happy with more, as well, but she was such a gift, a Godsend, as her mother was, how could he not be happy enough with that? How did he make Susie understand he'd wanted for so long to have everything he now had that he couldn't imagine losing either of them. Not even for the chance to have another precious child he would adore. He'd had nothing for far too long. What he had now was more beautiful than he could have imagined. He couldn't risk it.

She appeared at the kitchen doorway. Stood. Silently. In only her thin nightgown with the bare glow of the living room nightlight accenting her from behind. He loved her with a passion he also could never have imagined. She was everything. His whole center.

As though it would do any good, he tried again to make her understand. "I am sorry, Suse. I am sorry it is so risky for you. I wish I could give you as many of your own as you would like, and I would. But I amnae sorry that I love you too much to risk losing you. I cannae. I didnae do it behind your back. You were there, and I know you didnae approve, but I cannae risk it." He swallowed hard and set the bottle on the counter. He wanted to grab her and take her to bed and show her just how much he needed her. "Tell me I willnae lose you because of it."

"Lose me?" Her voice was a near whisper in the dark.

"You still could. Conceive. If you found someone who could still give you that, who was willing t' take the chance."

Her head shook. She began toward him, slowly. "Never." Still, a whisper. And she was there, in front of him. "I'm sorry. I was frustrated. I was having doubts, about myself, my own ability to be a parent and maybe it was a sign that I shouldn't be, but I want it so much, and ... I love you so much I just wanted ... more of you, more...." She moved in closer. "I never want anyone but you. You know I don't. I would never let you go, for anything. Never. And it's okay. I just ... I..." She bit her lip and slid her hands onto each side of his head.

Duncan felt himself melt into her. Never anyone but him. Never. The kiss was deep, and long, and needy. He partly released her and bit her lip as she had. Every time he saw her do it, he wanted his teeth to take the place of hers, to nibble her lips, her ears, her...

"I'm sorry." She caressed his nape. "I love you. And if we have just the three of us, that's okay, too. It is. I ... I just got too obsessed. Too... It doesn't matter. I'm sorry. I just can't think about it anymore." She moved her mouth to his neck and planted kisses in a line back to his lips.

His body tightened as the kiss deepened, as he traced her contour with his palms, as low on her thighs as he could reach.

"Come to bed, my love." She whispered in his ear and nipped at his earlobe. "I want you. I need you. Only. Always. You know I do. You know how much I love you, how much I adore you."

"Show me." He reached under her thighs and brought her body up to his. Her arms wrapped over his shoulders, her legs around his waist. He carried her back to their bed. In the morning, he would finish filling out the application and send it off.

14 April

He woke her with a kiss and she pulled him in. "Go back to sleep, Babe. I only wanted to let you know I am taking Danielle with me. We will be back soon."

"Taking her where?"

"Out for breakfast. It has been a long time."

"The two of you? With Beau?"

"Yes, he will be there. Donae worry, my luv. She will be fine. Go back to sleep."

"Have fun. Be careful." Susie ran fingers through his hair. "I couldn't make it without you, either. I love you."

He grinned at her reference to the conversation the night before. He'd told her not to listen to Kate. Susie actually thought Kate was right about being a better mother because Keith listened better, behaved better? She wasn't, and he didn't. He did with Kate, but as he told Susie, it was intimidation. He listened well to Susie, but it was largely respect and his appreciation of how nice she was to him as opposed to Kate. He didn't listen all that well to Mike. Duncan had seen it plenty. The boy pushed him often. Mike wasn't volatile, even if he was snippy. Keith knew he could, and it was healthy for him to know he could to an extent. Susie had cringed when he mentioned Kate's intimidation. Duncan assured her the boy would be just fine with Mike's guidance, and Susie's. He was smart. He knew where the true respect came from.

Danielle behaved well for everyone but Susie. She took it as failing. Duncan never would have guessed she could think so, and told her as much. It wasn't. Danielle felt most comfortable with her mom, so she tested herself most with her mom. Susie tried to argue with him, said Danielle was more his than hers. In some ways, she was right, but the girl was always trying to prove herself to Duncan. He could see it. He had done the same as a child. With Susie, though, Danielle was fully herself and fully knew she could be. He had been that way with Loretta and Terry, although he hadn't known at the time they were his aunt and uncle. They were comfortable. Strong. Steady. He could be himself there. With his mum, he was always protective.

Regardless of how most people saw Susie, Danielle knew better. She knew her mom could handle her full stubbornness and she knew she was free to test her ground and her limits both.

After breakfast, Duncan would take his daughter to the adoption agency and drop off the paperwork himself that he'd finished earlier. He'd chat with the receptionist and anyone else he saw who might have any influence. And warn Danielle to be on her best behavior. He'd have to watch for comments that would tell his daughter what they were trying to do and fend them off, but he wanted them to see the girl and how well she was doing before they saw the paperwork and made judgments about his job or the rumors.

The rumors about Susie would have to be stopped. Maybe he would find time to talk with Roy, as well. Alone.

15 April

"We are going out tonight."

Evan looked up at his friend as he pulled the guitar from his hands. "Going where?"

"Out." Duncan pushed the foot Evan had propped over his other leg. "Let's go."

"Okay. Mind telling me where?"

"There is a place about twenty miles from here. Private, invite only. Adam says it should be safe to go hang out, with the right kind o' girls, not a mob of fans."

Evan studied his friend. Girls? "This is your wife's idea. The two of you are taking me girl hunting? I don't think so." He tried to reclaim his guitar.

"Nae, she isnae going. You, me, Mike. Maybe Doug if he can convince Alison to go. Stu wanted t' go but Kara had other plans in mind. Robin and Adam are hanging out with Susie tonight, talking business. We're going t' go out and have fun before full-out recording begins. Get up. Let's go."

"This isn't necessary."

"The hell it isnae. We have barely been out together other than work in the last year or more, Ev. Donae let me down while I have permission to go. I am allowed t' flirt if you are there with me."

He couldn't help but laugh. Permission to flirt. Only Susie would send her husband off to a club to meet women and flirt. Even if it was for Evan's sake. And he knew it was. He'd pushed for her attention too much recently. Still, he missed hanging out with Duncan just hanging out. Watching girls. Listening to someone else's music. Flirting. As they used to.

Susie felt Duncan sit next to her and opened her eyes. She was still on the couch, despite knowing she'd told herself to get up and go to bed. "Hey. Have fun?" She leaned up to touch his lips.

"Yeah, it was nice. Doug and Ali came part of the time and left again. I think he wanted her alone." He stroked hair back behind her ear, off her face. "Mike was the life of the party. Had girls all over him and loved every minute. Classy girls, not clingin' screechers like he always bitches about."

"And Evan? Did he seem to have fun?"

"Oh I think he 'ad fun, alright. Spent a good amount o' time talkin' with a drop-dead gorgeous girl with bright green eyes. Smart. Sophisticated. Damn nice build and a hell of a wicked smile. He 'as her number. I am sure he will use it." Duncan traced a finger from the shoulder hem of her tank top down over the curve of her breast, nudging her robe out of his way.

"And just how closely were you looking at her?"

He snuggled in. "Close enough, y' ken. She 'as a li'l birthmark righ' abou'..." He moved the robe off her shoulder and kissed the indentation where her bra strap usually sat. "Here."

"Does she?" Susie tried not to laugh.

"Shaped like Ireland a bi' and she 'as a touch o' Irish in her. Was impressed tha' he 'ad been there. Think she woul' like 'im t' offer t' take her." He kissed her neck and let his hand wander down to her stomach, around her waist, finding her skin.

"I just bet she would. You didn't drive home, right?"

"Nae, Beau drove. Tha' is wha' he was there for."

"Oh. I didn't know he went."

"Adam insisted we 'ave a driver who could also be securi'y if needed. Beau 'ad planned t' wait in the car. We made 'im come on in with us. Had a lo' of fun when he loosened up, even with drinkin' only cola all night. And it 'as been some time since I 'ave seen Ev feelin' as good as he was. Since he was in college, if I remember." He nuzzled into her hair.

"You need to do it more often. Don't make me push you. Just go. You know I won't mind." She leaned back to find his eyes and brushed fingers through his hair. "As long as you don't do more than flirt and you come home to me when you get this, uh, revved up."

He moved his hand back around her front, slid it up to below her breast. But he held her gaze. "I will never do more than flirt with anyone else. Y' know I willnae. And I was achin' t' come t' you. The drive back was long and I was thinkin' all the way home o' how beau'iful y'are an' how much I wan'ed t' touch your skin..." His fingers crept up farther. He leaned closer.

"Go shower. You smell like smoke and alcohol. Not a turn on."

He laughed. "Yeah, and then?"

She ran a finger down his chest. "Then you can try again."

"Fair enough, my luv." With a grin, he began to slide away from her. She grabbed his shirt and pulled him closer for a deep kiss. She could taste the alcohol on his tongue and smell the stale nicotine on his clothes, but she had to hold him in for a moment before releasing him to the shower. And following him.

21 April

Susie was wiped out by the end of the first full week of recording. It was more from keeping Danielle out of the way and entertained than from sitting and discussing it with Adam. Of course, it was also from sitting so much. And maybe from the irritation of having accepted Janet's request.

Checking her watch as she raised her restless daughter to her lap, she was surprised to find it was nearly eight. "Are they about done for tonight?"

Adam tilted his head at Nella as she pushed to get back down again. "She's had enough for today, I guess." He glanced into the studio. "Yes, I think they've had enough, too. I'll let them know in just a minute."

"Thank you. Okay, baby. Daddy's almost done. Just sit with me a few more minutes." She felt the expanding and contracting of the little body against her chest, the stubborn little head drop back against her shoulder. And as soon as Duncan came out, Nella jumped down and ran to him.

Adam stood and stretched his shoulders. "I know it's been a long week, but what do you think about putting in some time tomorrow?"

Mike shrugged with his hands. "What's the big rush on this?"

"Summer fairs. If we have it out, or very nearly out, by August, we can hit a bunch of them on a low budget, whirlwind state fair tour and grab people who aren't as likely to go to a concert at an auditorium. If they're out at the fairs, anyway, it costs them nothing more to have a seat and listen a while. Different audience to some extent."

Whirlwind tour. One of the reasons she thought it best to push off the adoption paperwork she hadn't bothered to touch again yet.

They all hesitated about returning on Saturday after such a long week, but they agreed. Except Stu. She wasn't sure anyone noticed he didn't. "How about not too long tomorrow? Is that okay?"

Adam gave her a light frown. "You have plans for your husband?"

"Well, maybe. At least I have plans for me. And I know I don't have to be here..."

Duncan shifted Nella to his other arm. "Are you going t' let me go to the studio with you to talk?"

"I hoped you would. But you don't have to, if you need to be here..."

"We will make it no' too long tomorrow." She could see the matter was settled and at the same time realized how she'd missed him during the week while he'd been stuck behind the glass so much. Even if she was there most of the time. As soon as he came out, every time, his daughter clung to him. Now and then Evan pulled the girl away, or tried. Sometimes it worked. Mostly it didn't.

As they headed toward their cars, Susie made her way to Evan's side. "Hey, would you mind babysitting for a while tomorrow night?"

He touched her eyes and paused.

"You can say no if you're too tired and need the break."

He glanced over to where Duncan talked with Stu as he put his daughter in the Cobra. "I would, but I have plans."

"Okay."

Mike threw a glance between them. "You're not even gonna ask what his plans are?"

She shrugged. "Should I?"

"Always used to."

Trying to figure out how to answer that, Susie noticed Evan throw Mike a warning glare. And he returned attention to her. "How about Sunday? Trying to get time alone or you have something up tomorrow?"

"Don't worry about it."

"Sorry..."

"Don't be. I was teasing. Have fun on your date in case I don't see you tomorrow." She took his arm and leaned in. "I hear she's classy but fiery and has an incredible body: a nice combination. My husband was plenty impressed." With a wink, she went to catch up with Duncan.

22 April

Susie was glad she left Danielle with Mike and Keith. Evan asked to go with them to the dance studio and she didn't know quite why, but it made her less nervous. She'd barely used her sign language since they lost Jeremy. He would likely remember better.

Janet greeted them and gave Evan a long gaze until Susie asked if the girl and her mom were there yet.

"Yes, in room three. Let me call Mr. Gibbons down. He wants to be there to discuss it."

Susie cringed. "I thought he left."

"He did, but he came back recently. Sorry. I should have mentioned that but I was afraid you wouldn't come."

Duncan ran a hand along her back. "Anything else she should have known already?"

"No. I don't think so. Excuse me a second." Janet pulled her eyes from Duncan, glanced at Evan, and went into her office.

"Hey." Susie grabbed her husband's attention from where he watched Janet. Everything in his stance said he did not want to be there, or at least didn't want her there. "It's fine."

He started to answer but a couple of girls moved in and pressed paper and pens at them. They were soon joined by a few more, which drew attention...

Susie felt a bit surreal standing in her old studio largely ignored while her guys did their best to keep up with autograph requests from dance students and young teachers she didn't recognize, as well as a couple she did. They all chattered at once, trying to get individual attention from the Raucous members they seemed stunned to actually see in real life, never mind they were always about town. They searched fanatically for anything they could get signed and called out for a pen to share and pushed against each other trying to be the closest. Funny. She hadn't thought about them getting mobbed in a place they'd been so often only a few years ago. She had nearly dropped right back to the days they could all walk around unbothered.

Moving away from the crowd, Susie glanced over at the reception counter. Two of the teachers returned her gaze then turned their heads. The two who had been most instrumental in trying to push her out. And yet they stared at her husband and best friend, inched a bit closer, stopped, spoke to each other as though trying to decide whether to show how much they wanted to talk to them, whether it was worth Susie seeing how much they did. It was nearly impossible not to laugh. Another joined them, one who had never even deemed to speak to Susie, and turned a haughty stare toward her.

Duncan edged out of the crowd and took her side. Even with the girls still nearly on top of him, he leaned into her ear and pulled her close. "Ignore them. They donae matter."

"I know." She touched his eyes. "I'm just wondering if they'll find the nerve to come talk to you as I know they want to. And it's horribly petty, but I'm glad they don't seem to have quite that much nerve. They don't need to be close to you. They can be jealous from over there."

He grinned. "Want to make them more jealous yet?" Before she had time to answer, and paying no attention to the clamor for his signature and a photo and whatever else, he pulled her in tighter and gave her a light kiss.

"Mm. I bet they wish they were in my shoes about now."

"Y' think they do?"

"I'm sure of it. And I'm horrible to be glad they can only wish they were."

He brushed her lips again. "Yes, y' are horrible." He slid his hands down to her hips. "Rotten." His voice was a breath in her ear. "And I am so in love with y' I donae care."

"No? Even if it looks like I'm using you to get back at them?" She raised a hand to brush through his hair, the other on his chest.

"G' ahead, Babe. Use me as y' wish." His eyes peered into hers, a touch of amusement mixing with that look. The one that always made her want to take him somewhere private. "I am all yours t' do with as y' please."

Her stomach twinged. Nearly four years of marriage and the man still made her feel like a teenager with a horrid crush. A couple of girls nearby giggled and whispered. Another's jaw dropped.

He glanced over. "I think I said tha' a bit too loud."

Susie felt her cheeks get warm. Duncan kissed the side of her head and shrugged at the girls. "We are married. It is allowed."

They giggled again and he went back to signing his name and talking with them. Her hand on his back, fingers entwined in his shirt hem, Susie looked over at Evan. Janet returned, again checking him out through the crowd.

Gibbon's voice overcame the chatter. He protested Duncan and Evan's presence and disruption but Janet interceded and led them to where Reanna, the fifteen-year-old, was warming up. She was delightful. A cross of animation and control, dignity and a beaming smile, she would be a wonderful student. If Susie could stand to be there. They talked about Susie's odd schedule and how there would be weeks she wouldn't be able to make it and that she might have to bring her daughter in at times. Susie noted Janet's look, but nothing was said.

Reanna readily agreed to show Susie where she was in her training. Janet was right. She was a beautiful dancer: graceful, elegant, with sharp technique and strong ankles. And she had the soul for it. The music was loud. Her mom said it had to be in order for Reanna to barely hear it, and still, she heard it muffled, as far as the doctors could tell. Susie said she was plenty used to loud music and it was fine. Surprisingly, she remembered her sign language better than she expected.

With plenty of reservations still, Susie went back to the office with Janet to sign paperwork. Her guys valiantly agreed to wait in the lobby and sign more autographs. She figured it was okay. There were only dancers and their parents around. It wasn't too public.

The pay offer was better than she expected. Janet balked when Susie insisted her pay check go not to her but into a special fund for students who needed temporary financial help. Susie wouldn't back down. Either that or she would offer to let Reanna come to her building to teach her. Free. With Janet still arguing, she broke down and offered to let a few others join the class, those who could only do occasional classes or who couldn't join a regular class for some other reason. She figured the offer to bring more money to the studio would work. And she was right. Janet gave in.

"Don't you want to have your own money again, though?" Janet leaned back in her chair, a too-smug look on her face. "Even if he is doing okay by now, wouldn't you rather know you were helping to support your family?"

Helping to support her family? Did Janet seriously think she wasn't? "Do you have any idea what the assistant manager of a successful rock band makes? Do you think I don't get paid for it? Not that I would need to be since supporting Duncan is supporting my family and taking care of Nella is supporting my family, but Adam insisted." She paused to let that sink in, and nearly told Janet just how much of *her own* money she made. "I don't need this job or the studio's money. I'm doing this for Reanna. And to teach again."

Janet's expression changed. The haughtiness she always lorded over Susie because of her wealthy family and status as studio manager was gone. She and Duncan were doing more than okay between his album percentage, songwriting royalties, and producing fees, plus her managing income. They could buy her parents' overdone house and everything in it and hardly notice.

"So." Janet recovered enough to assume an authoritarian air. "If he agrees, are you going to insist on watching over the account? Want me to send statements and such?"

"No, but you watch over it. Not him. I don't trust him."

"And you trust me?"

Susie gave her a minute to wonder, and then shrugged. "I always trusted you. You know I did. Maybe it'll work better this time."

A shamed look brushed across her face. "Except with Evan. You never trusted me with him."

"No. Except with Evan. But this studio is much more a part of you than he ever was. I always knew that."

Janet cringed only for a second. "I guess you're glad I have this ring on my finger and this child on the way as a deterrent?"

"Doesn't matter."

"No?"

Susie tried to look as confident about that as she wished she was.

Janet gave her a sly grin. "Still chasing girls away from him?"

"I haven't had to. No one else has worried me. But if I need to, I will, until he finds someone good enough for him. Because he will, and he deserves that." She stood to go. Susie didn't care at all what Janet thought about her possessiveness. She would fight any woman tooth and nail if she expected Evan to get hurt. And she would never apologize for it.

"We haven't signed paperwork yet."

Susie set her hand on the doorknob and turned. "It needs to be redone to figure the fund in, and make sure it doesn't put me on some kind of binding term. I won't sign it if it does. Send it to me and I'll bring it back in."

Janet stood, a hand supporting her stomach. "You've changed. I don't even know you anymore."

Had she? Susie supposed she had. "You never really wanted to know me. I was only a tool to get to Evan. So don't expect this to change things between us. I won't forget that. At least when fans do it to me, I see it coming." She walked out, closed the door, and made her way through the crowd of girls to her husband. She needed him more than they did.

"Well?" He ran a hand down her head.

"She's mad at me again, but this time, I get my way." Susie wrapped around him and waited for the guys to thank their fans and head away from them.

25 April

Susie greeted Kara when Stu's girlfriend joined her in the basement, surprised to see her. She had an unexpected half day off, she said, and figured she'd see how busy Stu was. Susie offered to get them to either make it a short day or take a long break in between.

"Don't do that on my account."

"I'm not. I'm doing it for Stu." She grinned to show she was teasing. "Actually, it's coming along and they can use the break." There were still songs that weren't ready, but with recording what they did have ready and letting the producers work on mixing as they went back to the basement to work on what still needed it, they were moving along well.

"I hear you're back at the dance studio. Won't that be hard with Danielle, with as many hours as they're doing here and his production work added? I can't imagine why Stu thought he had to do it, also, although he says he's just hanging around and deciding whether he wants to."

"Duncan asked if he would. He has such incredible..." Susie stopped and studied Kara's face. "He said he only would while you're at work, not if you aren't. Have we mixed up the schedule so it's interfering?"

Kara snickered. "No, you know, it doesn't matter at this point. But thanks for worrying about it. I'm glad you at least do."

"Kara, you have to let him know. If he's not..."

"Forget it, Suse." She gave her a hug. "I really appreciate everything you've tried to do. I don't know how you handle it all so well, but you're rare, and they better know how lucky they are to have you." Kara shifted, uncrossing her leg to cross the other. "Are they going to take a break soon or should I come back? There's something we have to talk about and he wasn't in the mood to talk last night."

Although Susie was wary of Kara's intentions, she went up close to Duncan and waited for him to meet her. As soon as she explained, he told them they were taking a break.

"*Nella.* At least give daddy a few minutes to rest." She shook her head when the girl pulled him over to show off whatever she and Keith had created with a mixture of blocks and assorted things that had to have come from Kate's.

"Kara Mia, did you call in sick today like I asked? You missed me already, right?" Stu grabbed her and gave her a light kiss.

"I'm sorry to interrupt." Kara threw an apologetic glance to the other guys. "I didn't mean to..."

"It's fine." Doug stretched his arms. "Honestly."

Stu tilted his head toward his friend. "The old man, here, is getting sore arms. I'm sure he's thankful."

"The three years I have on you isn't the problem."

"Three and a half."

"Either way, sit behind the drum set for a week straight all day long and then spend your evenings helping to restore the diner. If you're not sore, talk to me then."

"Hell, hire someone to do that. Not like you can't."

"They won't let me. It's not my place."

"Well then, just say you're too tired..."

"They're not asking for the help. In fact, they've objected at least a hundred times so far, worried it's too much."

"Well then?"

Kara took Stu's hand. "We need to talk a minute. Can you badger him later?"

"Just talk?" He wrapped an arm around her waist. "I hoped you wanted a longer break than that."

"Stu." She pulled back. "I have a job offer and I need to talk to you..."

"Yeah? Cool. What are you doing this time? No nude poses, right? Still saving those for me?" He pressed against her again but turned to where Mike and Evan were talking to Doug about the diner. "Hey, I'm serious. Pay someone to do it. Save your arms for the drums."

Mike shrugged his hands. "Her parents said no. Do you listen?"

"I can't imagine why. Hell, he's nearly family and half of what he eats comes from there. Starting to show, too, by the way."

"Stu." Kara set a hand on his stomach.

"Sorry. So where's the job this time? Gonna let me sneak in to meet you somewhere? Or is it around here?"

"No. It's..."

Susie thought about bopping him upside the head when he again turned to the other conversation.

Kara sighed and pulled away from him. "I'm going to Paris. For three weeks, nearly four."

"Just a sec." He partially turned to her then continued the discussion.

When Kara walked away, Susie went up to him and put her hands on both sides of his face. "Hey, your girlfriend is leaving. Wanna pay attention to her for more than two seconds?"

Stu turned to find her and started to follow. "Wait, I thought ... what about the job? Where are you going?"

Kara only half-turned back as she paused. "To Paris."

"Paris? To model?"

"That is what I do." Her voice held a controlled edge.

"Yeah, so when? Not soon, right? Because we're in the middle of this thing and it needs a ton of work."

"Next month. And don't worry about it; I'm taking Kate. She'll love the experience since she understands it, and..."

"Next month. Wow, that's bad timing. They can't move it?" He moved closer to her.

"Yes Stu, they're going to move the whole photo shoot with models from around the world that has been in the works for months just because you're busy."

"I didn't mean that. I just meant I can try to..."

"Forget it. We'll talk later."

"Hell, I'm on break. Tell me about it now and we can save tonight for better things."

She stared for several seconds, and shook her head. "I won't be there."

"You're working late tonight?"

"No. I mean I won't be there. I'm going to go grab a few of my things and I'll come back for the rest. I'm sorry. I can't do this anymore. I've tried. I've been supportive. But I'm not getting that back from you. I can't talk to you anymore because it's nothing but this."

He crept up closer to her. "No, Kara, it's the recording. I'm always like this when we're recording. You know..."

"It used to be only during recording, Stu. Now it's always. And I could deal with it. I could deal with the time you spend if you would just still see me. But you don't. It's like I'm a stranger to you all of a sudden."

"No." He caressed her face. "No, you're ... you're my heart. I'm sorry. I've been distracted. I'll cut it short tonight. Wait. Wait and we'll talk. We'll go to dinner..."

"Where your fans will recognize you and you'll spend more time with them than with me. No." She shrugged out of his grasp. "This has been coming a long time and you didn't even bother to see it. I can't keep pretending it'll work. I'm sorry. You used to be the best thing that ever happened to me. And I'm sorry you're not anymore." She ran fingers down his hair. "Don't argue. I've gone too far with these thoughts to turn back. It's over." With a quick kiss, she turned and left.

Silence flooded the room as he stared behind her.

With a deep breath, Susie went to him. He touched her eyes. "This ... this isn't real. She didn't just... Hell, she didn't say anything. Nothing. She could've told me."

"She did." Susie watched his disbelief. "I tried to warn you."

He covered his face with his hands and talked through them. "It felt so damned secure. The ... what you said, what she said, it didn't ... it didn't sink in. It was too secure, too right. Damn."

In the silence, Evan suggested they pick up again the next day.

"I have to go stop her."

"No." Susie grasped his arm. "She told you not to."

"Damn, I don't care. She can't just say that's it and ... and that's it."

"Yeah, she can." Susie argued with herself. Maybe she should encourage him instead to try. But it wouldn't work. Kara was a determined soul. She'd made up her mind. It was too obvious. And she didn't want to see him grovel, to Kara or to anyone. "If it was really that secure, that right, she wouldn't have walked away. She would have fought harder. She would have made you listen. I know. Because that's what I would do if I had to. I'm sorry. I know... I'm really sorry. But you can't follow someone who doesn't want to be followed."

At his expression, she held him in. When he pulled away and started toward the back of the room, she followed, to the stairs, where he plopped down, head in hands. Susie sat beside him, quietly, just to be there.

After several minutes, Nella found them, her eyes on Stu, her dad right behind her. She knocked on Stu's head until he raised it and then grabbed him in a hug. "Come, my Stuey. You come an' eat with me and mummy and my daddy. Yes. Daddy say you hungry and you need t' eat. I make jelly and butter san'ches and big, big cookies with chips. No veg'tbles. No."

Stu looked up at Duncan. "Not fair buttering me up with the little one when I wanna just feel like hell."

Duncan gave him a light grin. "Y' can do that later. Come on up with us." He offered Susie a hand. "Danielle and I are makin' lunch. Y' get to sit and relax, as well. It is time y' did."

She had to wonder if her husband was trying to make a point, to show Stu how you had to put a woman's needs first now and then if you wanted to keep her. No, he wouldn't. He was only allowing his friend time with her. When Nella pulled Stu to the lead on their way upstairs, she paused to give Duncan a quick kiss.

He caught her eyes and spoke beside her ear. "I hope one day he will find wha' I have found. I' will do 'im as much gud as i' has done for me."

"I think you need the rest more than I do. You're tired."

"An' maybe I am only tryin' t' turn y' on."

"Not when you've just invited Stu up, you're not."

He chuckled. "I think we all need the day off. Yes?"

Stu didn't stay long. He allowed Susie to give him another hug and said he was going to go sleep it off, alone. She didn't figure Doug would let him be too alone.

Evan came to the door as she walked Stu out. He set a hand on their keyboardist's shoulder and told him something better would be ahead. Susie didn't figure Stu believed it, but he gave him a nod and shuffled down the stairs.

"Looking for me or for my husband?" She gave him a grin.

"Both. Am I interrupting?"

"Are you kidding?" She led him in and let him close the door. "Nella, how about picking up what you're not still using? I can hardly walk in here."

"My *Heavenly* Scott." The girl jumped over a stack of books from where she'd been telling her dad a story about what her Fisher Price people were doing and grabbed Evan's hand.

Susie shook her head at the nickname Nella wouldn't stop calling him since she'd learned his middle name. Sometimes she actually said it *Evan Lee* instead. "Nella, your Lincoln Logs, please, and maybe the crayons, too, if you're done with them? And put your books back on the shelf."

"No, I not done. Look." She pulled on Evan.

Duncan grabbed the chance to escape and suggested she tell Ev what her *peoples* were doing. He shrugged at his friend with a smile by way of apology and grabbed the crayons scattered on the table.

"Don't do that for her. She needs to learn to do it."

"There is plenty for her t' do still." He tossed them in the little container Susie got to keep them in since her thin cardboard boxes didn't hold up well enough.

"But she won't if she knows you will."

He closed the container and slid a hand down her arm. "I donae always." He stopped further protest with a quick kiss. "Relax, Suse. She is only two. There is time t' teach her t' take care of herself."

She supposed he was right, but still, when he wasn't around, it made it harder for her to get Nella to listen. Susie didn't want to keep picking everything up herself. Or fighting with her daughter to do it. She'd have to talk to him more about it when they were alone. She wouldn't argue with him in front of his friend. Their friend.

By some miracle, Evan got the girl to pick up her Lincoln Logs, then left her to it and came to join them. "What would you think about going out tonight?"

"Where?" She glanced over at a loud thunk. "*Danielle.* Don't throw them."

"I picking up, my mummy. See?" She threw another toward the can and it bounced off the edge.

"Carry them over and put them in. Don't throw them. You know better." With a sigh, she tried to ignore Duncan's amusement.

"I have a sitter for you. Mike said she's welcome to come entertain Keith. Looks like you could use one about now."

"Now?"

"Tonight. If you're interested. Just called Stephanie to see how soon she'd be free since we have the rest of the day off. She said she'd take off early and could be ready by five. I was thinking dinner and maybe going back to that club."

A double date? Susie couldn't remember the last time Evan had offered to go on a double date.

"Sounds good t' me, Ev." Her husband ran a hand down her back. "What d' y' think? Would y' mind a night alone with two o' your favorite men?"

She pressed closer to him. "A real date night? I'm not sure I remember what that is."

Evan raised his eyebrows. "Then I think it's way past time. And I think you'll get along with Stephanie. Anyway, I hope you will. She looks forward to meeting you."

"Wow, you're moving fast with this one. Must like her a lot."

"Or maybe I want to know if you approve before I move too fast."

Susie gave him a smile. "There's no way I can turn that down."

Evan slipped his arm around the back of Stephanie's chair, his hand on her shoulder. She was talking with Susie about children, comparing Danielle's two-year-old behavior with her niece and nephew she helped care for. They'd gotten along well at dinner and chatted with each other more than with their dates. He was glad to see it. Susie had moved up beside him as soon as she had the chance to let him know she approved and was happy to see him so content. He kissed the side of her head in thanks.

She looked radiant tonight; they both did. Stephanie was about three inches taller than Susie and her auburn hair was shoulder length and wavy. She wore dressy flowing pants and a shiny fitted blouse that showed only a touch of cleavage. Susie had pulled her straight black hair back along the sides, letting the rest of it flow down to her waist, the way Duncan most liked it. She was in a skirt that nearly hit her ankles and a loose gauzy blouse showing nothing but the necklace and earring set Duncan gave her recently, just because. They looked so different, but as they talked, it became apparent they had a lot of commonalities. Evan wasn't sure if that was comforting or disturbing.

"Can I steal her from y' a minute or so?" Duncan leaned in to interrupt their conversation.

Stephanie smiled at him. "Of course. I'm sorry, I didn't mean to monopolize her time."

"No, it is fine. Bu' this is our song and I would like t' dance with my beautiful wife."

"Your song?"

Susie nodded. She'd glanced over at Duncan when *Just You 'n Me* started. "From our first date. When we didn't separate after another song ended, the band made a comment. Duncan asked for something from Chicago and this is what they played." She let him pull out her chair and took his arm to walk to the dance floor.

Evan watched as he had the first time they'd danced together, at the first show Duncan played with Raucous, to Paul McCartney's *My Love*. The night Evan realized he might actually lose her to his friend. They stood as close as they could get and still be able to move somewhat individually. But they moved as one. Always. She spoke into his ear and he nodded, kissing her beside her ear and then on the lips, and sang part of the song to her: *promise you'll never leave me*. She held his eyes and looked at him as though he was the only person in the world she could ever love. Evan supposed that might be true.

"They look nice together."

Stephanie's voice pulled him back. "You should see them when they're actually dancing. It's amazing how well they read each other. Haven't seen it recently. I hope they still do."

She watched them a while longer and leaned in. "I've heard the rumors. Of course, I know some of what I've heard about you isn't true, and I suspect they aren't, either..."

"Which rumors?"

She brushed hair behind her ear. "About him not being faithful. Everyone says he isn't, and I overheard someone mention it tonight as I walked past, but..."

"Not true." Evan straightened in his chair. "He is absolutely faithful to her."

"Yes? You're sure he is? Because she's so sweet. I can't imagine how it would hurt her..."

"He would never cheat on her. It wouldn't happen. Yes, I do know that for sure. The rumors are only wishful thinking on the part of jealous women hoping for a chance. They try often enough. She knows they do. And she gets her share of offers. But no, neither of them ever would. Not everyone in the business does."

"Good. I'm glad to know." She stared into his eyes. "So if I hear the same about you?"

"I don't, either." He checked to be sure no one was close enough to hear. "I did once. It was because I was with the wrong woman, but it's not an excuse and I'm sorry I did."

Stephanie pressed in, squeezed his arm. "So if we take things farther, I could know you wouldn't?"

"I wouldn't to you. And I haven't. Not since we met."

She kissed him lightly and stroked the hair behind his ear. "I never move this fast, Evan. Never. But I was so glad you called today. I think about you every day. I wonder what you're doing, how your album is coming along, what it would be like to watch you play. I listen to your albums every night and wish I could watch your fingers stroke the strings and ... and I have never been so turned on by a man I haven't even slept with. Not that there have been many. There haven't. I'm..."

Evan interrupted to invite her to the studio on Saturday. It would be a short day, or so Duncan said. Perfect time for Stephanie to watch him play. Susie would be there at least part of the time, before she had to go in for Reanna's dance lesson. That meant Danielle would be there. Perfect opportunity for him to let Stephanie know he would become Nella's guardian if ever necessary. Her reaction to that would matter. There was no point in taking it farther if she didn't get along with both Susie and Nella. She seemed a bit stand-offish with Duncan, but that could be worked around and his friend wouldn't bother to let it worry him, and she might be friendlier with him now that Evan clarifed the rumors.

Stephanie agreed to practice and to dinner afterward, and she hinted about after dinner. Her fingers roaming his skin added to the hint.

He had to get up. "Would you like to dance?"

29 April

It was coming along. Too slowly, given Stu's disinterest in being at practice. They were due to record again the next two days. Duncan wasn't sure it would be ready. Of course, with the studio belonging to Adam, they could change the schedule, but that would put them farther behind and would mean pushing harder to fit in whatever time he could manage to help produce. Especially since they were all taking the second and third off. Susie didn't know yet. He figured it was time to tell her, as soon as she returned from the dance studio.

He was distracted, as well, with her being at that place. Beau went with her. She'd balked at the idea but he insisted. Either that, or he'd go and miss practice. She gave in with a sigh. Their guard didn't mind. He worked other odd jobs around when the band needed him, but Duncan had the idea he would work for them every day if they asked.

At least Ev was fully together, showing off his best for his girl, Duncan figured. Fair enough. He used to do the same when Susie was at practice, back just after they met. Stu was fully off. Even Duncan couldn't help but cringe at the bad phrasing.

"That sounds like hell." Mike pushed a hand through his hair and looked at Stu. "C'mon, man, get it together."

"Yeah, 'cause you never screw up, right? Give me a break."

"Not for four days in a row. You're better than that. Start acting like it again."

Stu propped himself on Doug's riser, in front of the bass drum, and dropped his head into his hands.

Mike moved closer. "Damn, are you still in there somewhere? Try sleeping for a change."

"Fuck off."

"Yeah great. That's going to help." Mike raised his hands at Doug. "Can you *do* something with him?"

Stu jumped up again. "Get *off* my ass. Think we didn't have to deal with your shitty moods often enough when Kate was screwing you around? You got no room to talk."

"I still did my job."

"Yeah, whatever. You're Mr. Perfect. Got it. I'm not, and I'm taking a break." He started off the platform.

"Sounds like a good idea." Susie's voice stopped Mike's next comment. Kate was with her. And both kids.

Stu shoved a hand through his hair. "Sorry. Didn't realize you were there."

"Don't worry about it." She sent the kids to go play and waited while Danielle detoured to give him a hug first. Susie said hello to Stephanie, introduced her to Kate, and came to the front of the riser. "What's going on?"

"Think you can get him to pull his head back into this?"

She gave Mike a light grin and went up to Stu.

"Go ahead and lecture. I've already heard it."

"I'm not going to lecture you. I do wish you would sleep, though. You look exhausted." Susie set a hand on his face. "No wonder you can't concentrate on work. Are you at least eating?"

Duncan wasn't sure Stu wouldn't collapse into her arms as his shoulders slumped.

"Answer me."

"You said you weren't going to lecture."

"Fine. Come up and eat with us tonight, then, so I know you are."

"I don't need to intrude..."

"You're not. And I'm not letting you refuse. Take it as an order from one of your managers if you want."

"Yes, ma'am." He glanced out at Kate. "Damn, she's gonna be pissed at me."

"No reason to be. Truth is truth. Are you up to working a while longer? I'll get dinner started in a bit but I thought I'd unwind with my favorite music first."

Duncan moved closer now that the subject changed enough. "How did the lesson go?"

Susie rolled her eyes. "The lesson itself was fine. She's wonderful to work with. They're taking full advantage, of course, and had eight other women in there, at all different stages of progress. That made it hard, but I pulled her aside as much as I could to really focus on helping her. It was the rest of it that ... well, it'll wait." She held him. Tight. She needed to talk. But she backed away to let them return to work.

Stu settled down and got some decent work done, but he was tired. Exhausted, as Susie said. And Duncan wanted to know what happened at the dance studio. Susie talked with Stephanie and Kate but barely, and the annoyance still covered her face. He called for a break sooner than they should have and pulled a chair up next to his wife. "What happened?"

"I'm not sure I should go into it here. It'll wait."

"Oh no, you gotta tell him." Kate nearly giggled. "This is too good not to share. It's the only reason I came down with you."

Susie gave her a 'not-amused' glance. "It'll wait."

"Babe, you should not be there. Tell Janet you can work with her here."

"No, it's not that major, just frustrating. Embarrassing, really."

"Embarrassing?"

"It's wickedly funny." Kate pushed at her arm. "And you had to have expected it."

"No, it's not funny, and I didn't. They're supposed to be professionals setting a good example for the students, not a bunch of immature silly teenagers, especially when they're mostly older than I am. I wouldn't even have acted like that when I was thirteen, much less..."

"They're making comments about us." Doug lowered next to where Stu had plopped on the floor, leaned back against the riser. "I did expect that, since they were doing it to you before."

"Well." Susie glanced at Duncan and returned to answer Doug. "Yes. Mainly just asking regular questions about you, and I did expect that. It's not like I'm not used to it, so I gave them the regular answers and figured that would be the end of it."

Kate giggled again. "Yeah, but you had to know they'd ask about him, right? Hell, I would if I wasn't your friend, and I'm older than you are, too. *Look* at him. Of course they ask."

"Honestly?" Susie rolled her eyes at her friend.

"Of course. And hell, I wish you would've answered and then told me what you answered. Curious minds, and all. You had to be tempted."

Susie brushed a hand through her hair and took a deep breath. "It's not their business, and I can just see that getting into the papers."

Stu looked up as though he'd just heard the conversation. "Okay, so now you gotta spill. About your husband, right? What in the hell else would have you so flustered?"

Evan tried to hush Stu. It was a hint to Kate to hush, also.

Duncan rubbed a hand over his wife's back. "Doesnae matter, Babe. Do not let them get to you. I donae care what they ask."

She found his eyes. "I care. It's not their business."

"Since when does that matter?" Kate leaned forward and whispered in Mike's ear.

He shrugged. "Wish I could say I was surprised. Not a big deal, Suse, and we've all been asked. I bet Ali has been, also. I know Kate has and I'm quite sure she's answered. Like he said, ignore them."

"Hey." Stu shrugged with his hands. "Damn, asked what?"

"Nothing. Okay, it's nothing." She pulled a leg up in front of her. "Enough break time yet?"

Kate tilted her head at Stu. "Wow, you're slow tonight. And I shouldn't even talk to you. Nice comment earlier. Thanks for that."

"I said I was sorry. Just being bitchy in general. Have you heard from her?"

"Every day. And she's not coming back, so you might as well get over it."

"Kate." Susie pivoted toward her. "Could you be a little more understanding?"

"Yeah, right. It's his own fault..."

"Okay." Susie stood. "I'm going up to make dinner." She went to Stu and crouched beside him. "Come up with Duncan. Don't make me tell him to drag you up."

"He will come with me." Duncan waited until she stood again and brushed a hand along the side of her face. "Leave Danielle here and we will bring her. Go shower and rest as y' need."

Duncan called Susie's name as he walked in with Stu. The music was too loud.

"Shh." Stu held up a hand and crept toward the kitchen.

Following, Duncan realized why: she was singing *If You Leave Me Now* with the album and doing a damn nice job with it. He gave in to his friend and enjoyed her voice through nearly the end of the song.

She jumped as she saw them.

"Hey, don't stop." Stu pressed around him. "Keep going."

She gave him a frown and went past them to turn the music lower. "Where's Nella?"

Stu interrupted. "You gotta start singing with us again. You know your voice is a huge turn-on to me, right?"

"Is it? Good reason not to, then." She paused beside Duncan and set a hand on his stomach. "I'm making spaghetti since it's fast and easy. Hope that sounds good. Where's your daughter?"

"I left her with Keith to finish her building. Mike is keeping her long enough to have hot dogs and tater tots, and to give you time to rest. It is nice to hear you sing again."

"Yeah it is." Stu rubbed up against her arm. "So while Nella isn't here, what in the hell were they asking you that had you so flustered?"

"Never mind."

"No, come on. Maybe I am slow today, but I'm tired and I'm bitchy and it's gonna bug the hell out of me, and having anything else to think about other than how I screwed up with Kara might be good, you know? So spill. It's just me, and I've told you all kinds of embarrassing stuff. We're buds, right? And I know you're gonna tell him."

"They wanted to know how he is in bed, with detail." Susie shrugged her hands. "Happy now? Did ya want to know that?"

Stu laughed. "Yeah, and what'd you tell them? Damn, wish I'd been there to hear you answer."

"I didn't. Why would I answer that? What makes them think they can ask me something like that about my husband?"

"Why? He's a damn big name, Suse. Of course they want to know. I mean, on top of the name, his looks are kinda hard for them not to notice..."

"Yeah, maybe so. I mean..." She turned her attention to Duncan. "I know you are, but still, it's so horribly rude and they couldn't think I'd actually answer that. But I can't tell you how often I was asked, that, among other things, like the stupid rumors and of course I said they weren't true but what else would they think I'd say?" She broke up a handful of spaghetti and dropped it into the pan of steaming water, then stirred the sauce. "I was prepared for the snubbing and such, but I ... I guess I just thought I could be a teacher since that's what I was there for."

"You're too much more than that." Stu lowered onto a chair. "You can't expect to be able to go back to being an everyday person no one pays attention to. It won't happen."

"It will. Eventually..."

"Nah, I doubt it. That's why Adam keeps pushing to counter the rumors as much as possible. And why Ev does it so much. He knows. And he does. Not sure you know how much he does, but he's on Roy's ass a lot to get him to shut the hell up about you."

At her frown, Duncan took the spoon from her hand. "Do you want to keep teaching there?"

"Yes. For Reanna. But I don't... You know how awkward it is to be asked something like that? Not to mention how the girls who heard you tell me I could use you anyway I please had spread that around."

Stu choked on the tea he'd poured himself. "Damn, he said what? In front of others?"

"I didnae expect them to hear me."

"Anyway, maybe it doesn't bother Kate, but it bothers me and ... what do I do to stop it other than not answering, which didn't seem to work?"

He shrugged. "Then answer them, and maybe tha' will work."

"Right."

"I am serious, Babe." He slid his hand down to the small of her back and brought her body in next to his. "Tell them I am incredible in bed and everything y' could ever want and y' are always more than satisfied. I bet they donae ask y' again." He teased with a grin.

"Uh huh. And you think I'm going to say that?"

"It doesnae have to be true."

"Oh, well, true isn't the problem. It is true." She ran a hand along his face. "But I'm not saying that."

"Damn." Stu half-choked again. "That's more than I needed to know."

She tilted her head toward him. "You asked."

"Uh, well, yeah but ... hell, Suse, tell 'em that. He's right. I bet they don't ask again, either."

"I'm not talking about my husband that way. I'm not some groupie who's only with him so I can brag about it."

"Groupie or wife, any man in the world would love to have a girl say that about him." Stu shrugged. "Hell, I'd love to have a wife say that about me, especially if it was true, and even if it wasn't."

"Because you're a huge pervert." Susie studied him as he laughed. "And I thought you said you'd never get married."

He shrugged. "You say I will, and I tend to think you generally know what you're talking about."

To change the subject, Duncan told her she should forget about it for now and think about packing. They were heading to New York City on Tuesday. He and Adam arranged tickets for the American Ballet Theater's production of Don Quixote at the Met. It featured the Russian dancer Susie had been keeping up with since he defected, Mikhail Baryshnikov. She literally jumped on top of him when he told her, enough he had to take a step back to steady himself.

From her reaction, he figured it topped his father taking her to the Scottish ballet the first time she was in Edinburgh.

"It is absolutely true."

Duncan stroked hair from her face as he held her in close, her skin against his, her heartbeat starting to calm. "What is true, my luv?"

She raised her head from his shoulder. "You *are* incredible in bed and everything I could ever want. I love you more than I could ever tell you."

A deep breath filled his body and he kissed her. "I love you more."

"Oh Duncan, that's not possible. It's not at all possible."

"Will you still say that after I tell you I went behind your back to do something you said you were not sure anymore you wanted to do?"

"Mm, probably." She kissed his neck and trailed her lips down to his shoulder.

"We have a meeting with an adoption agent just after we get back from New York." He felt her pause. "I sent in the paperwork and gave you more credit for being a wonderful mum than you had given yourself. They want to meet with us. Here. To visit with Danielle in her home. I have spoken to the woman on the phone. She sounds as she might be interested in us."

He couldn't quite tell what she was thinking, until she leaned in and claimed him again. "Y' do still want it?"

"Yes." Her eyes were moist as she raised her hands to the sides of his face. "Thank you. I couldn't... Thank you."

6 May

Evan stared at the advance copy of Vestor Presley's biography about his nephew but couldn't put his mind on reading it. He wouldn't tell Adam that, after he'd gone to so much trouble to get it for him a month before it would be in stores. And he looked forward to diving in and getting deeper into Elvis's world. But his mind was on the meeting next door. The adoption agent was there, posed as a business acquaintance so Danielle wouldn't know. Susie insisted they didn't tell her until it was an actual possibility.

"You gonna read that or just stare at it?" Mike plopped down beside him.

His friend didn't look ready to go out, covered in baggy sweats and an old T-shirt. "Aren't you heading to New Hampshire with Stu and Doug?"

"After the way my family ignored my son at Easter? Not a chance in hell. I don't care if I never see those people again."

"Not even your youngest sister?"

Mike shrugged. "I told her she could visit any time. Of course, it would be more for Stu than for me if she does. Probably the only reason she talks to me, to try to get to him. Maybe I should call and let her know he just broke up with Kara and could use some company while he's up there."

"Thought he wasn't interested."

"Hell, only because she's my sister and he says that's out of bounds. Same reason he flirts with Laura and with Doug's sister, but would never actually hit on them. But it's not hardly the same. I don't give a shit. He'd be better for her than most of the jerks she's dated. And my parents would be livid, which I wouldn't mind."

"I doubt he's in the dating mood yet. Kara was good for him. A shame it didn't work." Evan set the book on the coffee table. "Should I ask if Stephanie has a friend who can join us tonight since you're home? I'm sure Susie would take Keith."

"He's staying with Kate for a couple of days before she leaves for Paris." Mike scratched his head. "Exactly what I need: a girl desperate enough to not only accept a blind date, but a last-minute blind date."

Evan grinned. "Okay. Thought I'd offer."

"Hey, I'm serious. Sure. If you don't mind the barge-in. Desperate might be good. Just make sure she doesn't mention who I am so her friend only accepts because of the band."

With a nod, Evan went to his room and grabbed the phone. He couldn't promise it wouldn't be a Raucous fan since Stephanie was, and it was getting hard to find dates who weren't.

Mike's date for Don Quixote was not only a new Axis artist, but an overzealous Raucous fan who kept talking about the band all night, even through Mike hushing her. Stu's date was a friend of hers, very quiet, enough Evan had no idea if she was a fan or if she even wanted to be there. Both were arranged through their publicist who used the event as a "Raucous supports other artists" campaign, and to try to show them in a "classier" light. Evan supposed the fact that Duncan commandeered tickets for John and his date and that their own "manager" refused to go was overlooked well enough.

Susie had been awestruck the whole time. Her eyes remained affixed to Baryshnikov every second he was on stage. Evan had to wonder if it made her wish she'd followed that path as she could have. If so, she didn't say. She'd clung to Duncan's arm both while sitting and while wandering before and after the ballet and at intermission. Thrilled to her core. Evan wasn't always sure if it was the ballet or her husband in his tuxedo that had her more elevated and more social than normal. They were beautiful together, with their dark hair and blue eyes, their nice builds, their difference in height lessened with her heels. Her long black shimmering dress that curved in with her waist, out around her hips, and back in above her ankles, with a touch of flair at the bottom. As modest as her neckline was, with extra material draped across the breast, it was still a knockout. He had to admit it: they made a stunning couple, perfectly matched.

And Stephanie had been the perfect date. Elegant. Friendly to his friends. Glad to accept his arm when he offered, but not clingy. She'd loved the ballet. Evan had doubts about asking her to go since they were staying overnight, afraid she'd take it wrong, think he was pushing too fast. She didn't. She offered to pay her own room, which he refused, asked him in long enough for a nice good night kiss, and let her fingers slide from his as he left. Much of him wanted to stay, or at least ask to stay. But it would come in time. If it worked well enough. He had every thought that it might.

Pulling away from that particular thought enough to dial her number, he couldn't help but grin at the way she sounded so happy to hear his voice. And she readily agreed to find Mike a date.

"Ev."

He looked up at his friend at his door. "Steph, hold on a second."

Evan covered the receiver with his palm.

"Sorry t' interrupt. Can y' come over for a few minutes?"

"Sure. What's going on?"

"Since we chose you as Danielle's guardian, if y' ever needed t' be, and y' would be for the baby, the agent wants t' meet you. Finish your call first. Take your time. The door is open, come on in." Duncan walked away again.

Evan frowned at the stress on his face, and in his voice. He uncovered the phone. "Sorry, I have to go, but I'll see you later."

"Everything okay?"

"Hope so. I'll talk to you tonight. Have a good rest of the day."

"You too, Evan. I look forward to seeing you."

With a quick explanation to Mike, he headed next door, then paused, gathering himself, and sent a quick prayer that he wouldn't screw this up for the people he loved most in the world. He knocked as he went in and Duncan stood to introduce him to the woman, a stern looking middle aged woman who looked him over as she took his hand.

"Have a seat, Mr. Scott."

Evan did his best not to react to the woman giving him orders in his friends' house.

"My *Heavenly Scott*." Danielle ran over and jumped in his lap, nearly hitting him in the face with a piece of paper. "*Look*. I d'awing you at pac'tice play 'tar. *See*." She pointed at the scribbles that almost looked like it could be a person. "And my daddy and my Stuey and my Doug. On stage. All 'gether."

"I think your daddy is bigger than the rest of us here. He's not, though."

She frowned. "Yes. My daddy is biggest. Yes."

Evan chuckled with a glance at his friend and gave her a hug. "Okay, little one. You may be right. Do I get to keep this?"

"Yes. You keep safe in your house and have ever and ever."

He kissed her head. "Thank you. I will."

"Danielle, can I see it?"

She turned her head toward the woman. "It for my Evan Lee."

"I'll give it back. I just want to look."

With a sigh, Nella got down and took it over to her.

"You listen to your daddy's band a lot?"

"Yes. And Keith, too. Building blocks and play jacks and dance like mummy, and … and … I play 'tar and p'ano and … and 'boards with Stuey."

"You want to learn all of them?"

She nodded, bouncing her curls. "Yes. All. Not drums. No. Drums too big. I too small for drums."

"What else do you like to do?"

Nella frowned.

"Other than music and coloring, what do you like to do?"

"I build big, big castles like in Sco'land. And my daddy build a jumpin' gym for me in my yard, my big, big yard in back. We live in next house. Yes. I have big, big yard and … and sand and birdies and rocks and…"

"No rocks, Nella." Susie interrupted. "And you mean a jungle gym to climb on."

"Yes. C'imbing gym. My mum say no big rocks. No." She pouted.

The woman's stern expression chipped into a grin. "You stay next door with Evan sometimes?"

"Yes." She nodded again and looked over at him. "Evan Lee my mum's friend and my daddy's friend and my friend. He be here ever and ever. Yes."

The woman glanced over at him. "Is that so? What if he gets married and moves away and has his own kids?"

Nella tilted her head at him. "You not move. No. You stay ever and ever. Yes."

"I'm not moving away, little one. And if I ever have kids, you'll have more friends to play with."

"Yes. You have li'l one, too, like me and like Keith, and we play 'gether at you house and my big, big yard. He play in my yard with me. Yes. No big rocks. He not get hurt."

He did his best not to laugh about the rocks. "You'll help look after him?"

"Yes. 'Cause I big now. No' like Keith. No."

"He's older than you."

"Yes. And Keith is boy, no' a girl. I no' get big like Keith. My mum no' big like my daddy. No."

"Sounds like you need a nap, baby."

Nella swiveled toward Susie. "I no' s'eepy."

"How about a couple more questions?" The agent pulled Nella's attention back. "What do you do when you're at Evan's house?"

She tilted her head again, confused by the question.

"You stay there sometimes without your mom and dad, right?"

"I play with my Evan Lee and play 'tar. My hands li'l too much. My Evan Lee read books and I read too. I not read words. No."

"But you can write your name." Evan couldn't help but brag.

The woman raised her eyebrows. "Already?"

Susie cut in. "Somewhat. She gets some of the letters in there and sometimes in the right order."

"You're teaching her already?"

"Well, I help when she asks. Mostly Evan is teaching her. Keeping her busy and out of trouble, I'm guessing." She gave him a grin.

"I no' trouble for my Evan Lee. No." Nella frowned at her mom.

"I know, baby. I'm being funny. How about lying down a while? I can hear you're tired."

"No, I no' tired."

"Danielle." The agent interrupted. "How about you go draw me a picture of your new backyard? Here, you can give this back to Evan."

She not only gave it back to him, but jumped on his lap again, gave him a hug, and asked if he would take her outside.

"I'll take you outside after you obey your mom."

With an exaggerated sigh, she went back to the kitchen.

"She talks well for a two and a half year old."

Duncan nodded. "She has her mum's brains."

Susie threw him a look. "We talk to her a lot. Not baby talk, but real talk. Keith is advanced, also, but he's quiet so it's harder to tell."

The agent wrote a few notes and looked at Evan. "Do you have plans for marriage and children in your future?"

"Possibly."

"You're not sure?"

"I'd have to find the right woman first. But yes, I hope to."

"And at that point, you'll still be willing to take in Danielle and the new baby if the adoption works out?"

"Of course."

"And if your future wife doesn't agree?"

"I wouldn't marry anyone who would object."

"So, let's say you fall in love with this incredible dream woman and she's everything you want, except she doesn't want kids. You'd give her up for the slight possibility you may have to take over for your friends?"

"Honestly? I wouldn't consider marrying a woman who doesn't want children, and who wouldn't be good with them. That's very high on my must-have list."

"Children?"

He dropped his eyes a moment. It went against everything he'd been saying. Almost. "Yes. A family. At least a couple of children. More would be okay, also. Although I'm in no hurry."

Susie gave him a quick grin. She knew. She'd told him more than once she knew he did. Evan supposed he'd never be able to deny it now. And Duncan's expression said Evan would hear about it later, when they were alone.

"Well, then." The woman scribbled more notes. "I've already asked them, but I need to ask you, as well: if and when the music career ends, as I know it often can with little warning, what would you do next?"

"I have a degree and experience in business management. I'd head that direction."

"Would you move away for a job?"

"No. I've promised Danielle I wouldn't. I'd find something around here."

"But if you, God forbid, had to take custody of her, and the music ends, then what? You'd stay here?"

"I can't say I've considered it, since I don't expect that to happen."

"If you had to consider it?"

He frowned, refused to look at his friends. It wouldn't. But he played along. "Well, I guess I'd have to figure it out from there. The children's needs would be at the top of the consideration."

"And if I weren't an adoption agent trying to assess your worthiness as a guardian, would you still say that?"

Evan was stunned into silence. She thought he was lying?

"Of course he would." Susie answered for him. "He is one of the most honest people you'll ever meet. And he's always put others in front of himself. Too much, really. He did it for me, for his brother. For so many. It's who he is. I would never trust my children to anyone I didn't know would put their needs first. I wouldn't."

Duncan glanced into the kitchen and jumped up, hurrying toward the door. Evan followed and saw him grab Nella off from where she'd pushed a chair up to the counter.

"Wha' do y' think y' are doing up there?"

"I want cookie, my daddy. I get it. I a big girl."

"Danielle. You *donae* climb on the counter. Y' have been told."

"I big. I can do it. Yes."

"Nae, y' cannae since we have told y' you cannae. You ask if y' want a cookie."

With an exaggerated sigh, her shoulders rose and fell. "I have a cookie, p'ease, my daddy?"

"No' now, y' willnae."

"Bu' I ask nicely."

"After y' broke the rules. Come on, time for your nap."

"I no' tired. No."

"Donae conter me." Duncan gave Evan a look of frustration as he took his daughter back to the living room and excused himself to put her in bed.

The agent watched the scene then asked Susie about Nella's grandparents and if they were part of her life. She admitted the the three of them, and her aunt and uncle, were all very close to Nella, that Duncan's parents talked to her on the phone a lot to stay connected.

"Can I ask, then, if they are so important to you both, why you didn't choose family as your children's guardian if needed instead of a friend?"

Evan tensed. His first thought was, *Don't call me your family*. And then, in less selfish mode, he hoped she could explain to the agent's liking and he'd stand by whatever she said.

"Easy." Susie glanced at him. "Evan's here every day, and I don't mean here in the apartment, but around, and she sees him most every day. She knows him best after us. She loves her aunt and uncle, but Evan's already like a second father to her. She would be most comfortable with that, and she'd stay here, in the US, instead of moving overseas."

"And did your husband argue with you?"

"Not at all. He trusts Evan with his life. He has since they met. And he knows Evan would take her over to visit his family."

"They would be all right with him doing so?"

"Yes. They'd be glad to have him, even without us, just to visit and travel. They'd be glad if he did and they've told him that."

"So he's more family than you've said."

"Oh." Susie glanced at him again. "Well, he is to Danielle. And he will be to any other children we would have. He's our best friend. We both have tremendous respect for him. There's no one in the world I would be more comfortable leaving my babies with."

The agent nodded and looked at Evan. "Would you object to my stopping in your place and having a quick look around?"

"Not at all." He stood. "You can come over now if you'd like."

"You're sure?"

"Of course. It'll give Susie time to go check on Nella, as I know she wants to do." He gave her a grin and waited for the woman to follow him. He announced as they were walking in to let Mike know, introduced him as Keith's father, and told her to check what she liked.

She skimmed the place, including the kitchen, and suggested it didn't look much like a bachelor pad. Mike said it was far more a nursery since his son lived there much of the time and Nella was there often. That brought up a conversation about Keith, and Mike didn't hesitate to give Susie credit for half raising him and said he'd willingly stay with Susie full time if Mike allowed it.

Back in the hall, she stopped Evan. "Now that we're alone, tell me your honest opinion about Duncan and Susie adopting another child so soon. She's young, don't you think? And her hands seem full already, particularly with his career being what it is."

"She is young, but she's always been mature for her age. And I think Nella would be less a handful if she had a brother or sister. She likes attention. She's very social. They could entertain each other."

"You're saying they want another child to help entertain Danielle?"

"No. Not at all."

"Then why do they? Already?"

"They expect it to take some time. They know the process, the waiting list. They want them close in age..."

"They could adopt an older child."

"Yes, but she wants a baby. Susie is a natural mother, a nurturer. She always has been. That's part of why she teaches, because she loves helping children along, being part of their lives. She needs to nurture the way Danielle needs attention."

"She could do that with an older child."

"And she would. Gladly. But there's a bond a baby forms with its main caregiver and she wants that. You know she plans to try to nurse. She's heard it can be done."

"It's rare."

"I think it's rare for anyone to try."

"She nursed Danielle?"

"Until she was nine or ten months old. Even with the touring. She wanted to go for a whole year, but she lost weight and her doctor told her to stop. Even then, she pushed it a while after he told her to stop because she insisted it was better for her baby. She is a wonderful mother."

"And Duncan? I've heard the stories about him. I have to say I'm concerned about that. It wouldn't be good for a child to have to hear about ... infidelities, especially if it causes a divorce."

"They aren't true. He doesn't cheat on her. Never has and won't. And divorce is not even close to a possibility."

"You can't be sure about these things."

"Yes. You can be with them. It won't happen." Avoiding further private conversation, Evan knocked as he opened the door. Susie had her arms around Duncan's shoulders, her face buried in his neck. His hands were under the back of her shirt. "Sorry. Should have waited for you to answer."

"'I' is fine. Come in."

The woman didn't stay much longer. She finished writing notes and thanked them all for their time, with a quick "I'll be in touch."

As the door closed behind her, Susie wrapped back into her husband and held him.

"Maybe I should offer to babysit tonight instead of going out?"

"No." Susie met his gaze. "Go ahead, and you should go get ready. Thank you. I didn't expect she'd bother you for so long."

"It's fine, Angel. Anything I can do. And I think it went well."

"She's going to turn us down. Did you see her face, all the disapproving looks? She'd made up her mind before she ever came."

"Donae be so sure, my luv." Duncan kissed her head. "I think there is a gud chance."

"Do you?"

He set his hands alongside her head and gave her a soft kiss. "Yes. An' if she turns us down, we will try again. I' will be alright. Donae le' it get you down."

She inhaled sharply, let it out slowly. "And if it doesn't work at all, I still have you, so it's still okay." She clung to him again.

Duncan took her hand and led her to the kitchen, found the chilled wine, and poured two glasses. She was quiet, bothered. She didn't at all believe they would say yes. And he didn't want her to go back to thinking how much she wanted to have her own.

He moved in and kissed her neck. "Donae think of it anymore today, Babe. It has been a long day already." He moved his lips to her shoulder, pressing in until he felt her chest against his. She needed to unwind. He hoped some mild, or a touch more than mild, flirting and the glass of wine would do it.

"Why did she stay so long if she was already set on turning us down?"

"She wouldnae 'ave stayed so long if she was. Waste o' her time. Tha' means she isnae se' on turnin' us down. We will know when we know. Donae dwell on it until then." He returned his lips to her neck. Traced a finger around her shoulder, up her nape, down the center of her back. He brushed her lips. Softly. Tasted the wine on them.

She took another sip, set it down, and pressed her mouth hard against his. Her tongue reached in. Her fingers pulled him closer and slid down his back, to the top of his jeans, under his shirt, pushing it up...

He pulled back to see her face.

"Nella should sleep for an hour or so." She tugged at his shirt until he took over and pulled it off. Her hands slid up his bare chest; her mouth returned to his. And she grasped his hand to lead him to the bedroom.

12 May

Grabbing the phone, annoyed by the interruption, Susie was surprised to hear Kara's voice. She returned the greeting carefully.

"I'm sorry." Kara hesitated. "I know I'm probably the last person you want to talk to now, and if you want me not to call you, say so. I'll understand. I know how close you are to Stu..."

"It's okay, but I thought you were in Paris." She pulled the phone cord into the kitchen and returned to her chair, and the paperwork.

"I am. But I called him this morning, or I tried to, and he wouldn't take the phone. Doug says he's fine, not to worry. He's okay, then? It didn't matter that much, right?"

He wouldn't take the phone. Susie bit her lip and wondered how much she should say.

"Suse, I just … I can't talk long but I want to know he's all right. He does matter to me, and I was so abrupt, and … maybe I'm worrying about it more than I should. I heard he was dating already."

"It was a business event, with a date set up for him. He barely spoke to her." Maybe she shouldn't have, but Susie couldn't let Kara think it didn't matter.

"Oh. Well…"

"Why did you call him, Kara?"

"Like I said, just checking. He could have taken the phone for one minute."

"No he couldn't." Susie got up again and paced. "Don't think it doesn't matter. He's finally starting to work again. He has to be pushed into going, but he's…"

"He has to be pushed to go to work? That's a first."

The humor in her voice grated Susie. "He's not okay. He's devastated. But he will be okay."

"Suse, you know I tried. You know I've been trying."

"Yes, I know you did, and I understand. But you can't think this isn't going to bother him like it isn't a big deal, like he didn't care enough. You can't think that. Even if he was distracted. It's not because he didn't care. It's just … that's who he is. You're the first one to put up with it so long."

"I love him, Suse. You know I do. But…"

Susie brushed fingers through Danielle's bangs when she came up to find out who was on the phone. "It's not always enough. I know. And we won't let him wallow in it too long. We're here for him."

"Yes." Her voice shook. "I'm glad you are. You, especially. I'm glad you're there. He adores you so."

Susie couldn't answer. He'd been at their place every night except when he was home for his parents' anniversary party or when Doug and Ali pulled him away. He wasn't all right. At least he was working.

"I am sorry. Truly. More than you know."

Susie nodded, trying to regain her voice enough to answer. "I know."

"Mummy, we go now listen to music. Yes. No papers more." Nella tugged at her hand.

"Okay, sweetie. Just a second. Go get your shoes on." She made herself return to the conversation. "I have to run. Nella's been patient but she won't be much longer. I do hope you have a wonderful time."

"Thank you. Can I call you now and then? Just to check in?"

"Sure." Susie had doubts she would get more than one or two calls. Maybe she shouldn't have agreed, though. Hanging up, she grabbed a deep breath. A very long day. She was ready to step away from the scrapbooks the adoption agent wanted, not only recent but from their childhoods. That part was tricky, even with photos Laura had sent her and information Susie gathered from Duncan's parents about his relatives. Also on the table was some band business and the citizenship study book. She couldn't believe all the stuff he had to know in order to try to get dual citizenship. She was a born citizen and she didn't know half of it. They'd been studying at night before bed, since they would have a better chance at adoption if he was a citizen. He'd hesitated, not willing to give up his Scottish citizenship. So they were going for duel, which they were told was harder to get than full. Susie thought it might not be so hard with his father's help, if Duncan would accept it.

She sighed. Even with accepted help, it would take them one to three years, if they were approved, to have a baby. One year was fine. Three ... three was too long. Nella would be nearly six by then. She didn't want them that far apart. They should have started sooner.

Or he should have listened to her and let her have her own, as she knew she could.

"Come. We find Daddy and listen to music. My shoes on. Yes." Nella held up one foot to show her.

"Yes, let's go find Daddy." Susie tickled the child as she caught up, slipped into her own shoes, and grabbed her keys. By the time she got down the three flights to the basement, Susie wanted to take him away from the guys and hold onto him. She hated the occasional flare of anger that welled and kept growing throughout the tedious process.

He should have let her have another of her own.

Trying to brush the thought aside, again, she sat next to Ali and watched Nella run over to irritate Keith. The boy had been building something tall and precise. He frowned when she knocked it down.

"Danielle! Don't do that to him."

Keith shrugged. Then he handed Nella some pieces and started something new.

Susie caught Evan's smile and shake of the head. They were between songs and he signed to her: *so much like her mom*. She decided not to answer. If she'd treated him that way when they were young, it was truly a wonder he was still as nice to her as he was.

"Is everything all right?" Ali studied her face.

"Oh, just a very long, frustrating day. More problems with the house. Another week or two or three before we can have it inspected again. And to top it off, Kara just called me."

Ali turned to face her more directly. "Why? Is she changing her mind?"

"No. She was checking on him, and wondering if we're all mad at her, I guess."

"Of course we are. Did you tell her that? He's crushed, the poor baby. It breaks my heart."

Susie wondered if she wasn't being quite loyal enough to Stu by refusing to be mad at Kara. "Well. It's not like she didn't try to warn him. So did I. He chose not to see it, which means there's someone better, someone who can put up with him without it being a big issue."

"She could have if she'd wanted to. He wasn't the only one unavailable, you know. Maybe you didn't see as much as I did since I was at their place so often. There were plenty of times she was too tired to bother with him when he tried to get her attention, and yet if a friend called, she'd be on the phone for an hour." Ali sighed. "Yes, he deserves better, but still, I hate to see him so crushed."

"I didn't realize."

"She kept trying to make it all his fault, but it wasn't, Suse. He did try, more than he'll admit. She ran over top of him and he just looked the other way. He's really better without her, once he gets over it. I was worried about how far he'd let her go and how much she'd take over."

Susie looked up at Stu. He was talking with Mike, calm. Too calm. Too disinterested. It broke her heart to see it, also. He'd never said anything. All those times Susie was warning him, he'd never mentioned the other side of it, had never said one negative word about Kara. Ever. She was crazy, then. It was her loss far more than his.

"So what about the rest of your day? Didn't you teach?"

"Yes." Susie rolled her eyes. "That was probably a mistake." Susie explained about management hardly speaking to her and other teachers and students asking for stuff from the band and she refused so they wouldn't overwhelm her with it so they were all mad and she'd quit but it would be unfair to Reanna, who was so wonderful. How she hated that it was so much about the money and not about the students, the dance.

"Maybe you should take Duncan's offer and build a small studio behind the house."

"Maybe. After a while. I can't now. It's too much on top of everything."

Ali didn't push, and Susie melted into the music, even with the starts and stops, the changes and light arguments. Kate didn't understand. The band didn't wear her out. Everything else did. She needed them.

Mike called a break. As the others pulled away from their instruments, Stu remained where he was, behind the keyboard, and messed with a section they'd just been working on. Doug stopped and told him to sit a while. He shook his head and kept working.

Susie went to him. "Hey. You know what a break means?"

"Don't need one." He continued, repeating and changing a couple of measures.

She pushed between him and the instrument and gave him a hug.

"She tried to call me last night." He pulled back. "I wouldn't take the phone. Should I have? Think she might want to work things out?"

"No. I think you were right not to."

"Was I? Then why do I feel like total crap today?"

Susie stroked a hand down the side of his head, as she did to Danielle when the girl was upset. "There's someone better, Stu. I know you don't believe it now, but there is. And then this won't matter anymore. And you'll kick yourself for wasting the time feeling like this. You were right not to answer. Move on. She let you go. You have to let her go. There will be someone who suits you better, who would never dream of walking away from you. I know there is." She hugged him again. "Besides, some day I'll owe you a lot of babysitting favors and I want to return them, so you'll have to find someone willing to put up with your ass long term."

He chuckled. "You know, the more time you spend with the street rat, the more you talk like him. Kinda funny. And horribly cute."

"Is it?"

"And I didn't even get punched for calling him that."

"Hm, I'm being nice today. Don't count on that again."

Duncan watched her walk past him without even a glance and go to Stu. Had he done something wrong? She had hardly even looked at him when she came down. She'd watched Mike as normal, and the others, talked with Ali. And she was avoiding him. He went over to his daughter.

"Daddy! Look! I build *big*."

"What is it that you built?" The cardboard blocks didn't look like much of anything except a big stack. They were in order, though, by color.

"Nella's house. Yes. You live here, too. My mummy, too."

He tilted his head around the side of it. "'Y' might need to add a door so we can get in."

"No. We jump higher and higher. No one comes in. No 'porters. No cam'as. Only Nella and Daddy and Mum and ... and Keith and Evan Lee, and Stuey, and Mike and Doug and Ali and..."

"Danielle." Duncan crouched and pulled her into one arm. "Do you worry about reporters getting in the house?"

"No." She shook her head hard. "They not get in my house. My daddy not let 'porters in my house. No."

He pulled her eyes to his. "'Y' are right. I will not let them in our house. I promise. You do not have to worry. You know I'll always take care of you."

She nodded. "My mummy, too. Mummy not like 'porters."

Maybe that was it. Maybe something had happened at the studio, or on the way home. "Yes, my sweet. I will take care of your mum, too. Do not worry. I will not let anyone bother you or your mum. Okay?"

She wrapped her arms tightly around his neck.

Maybe it wasn't worth it. Maybe it was time to back out, to go find somewhere normal to live, something to do out of the limelight. Then Susie could teach and Danielle wouldn't have to worry about reporters, or about her mom's reaction to them. And maybe they'd have an easier time adopting.

Duncan balked at the idea of leaving her home alone with Nella while he and Ev and Stu went out again. She had things to do, she said. And she didn't want to be out. But she wanted him to take Stu and hang out with Ev.

"Maybe next time." She ran fingers down his face. "I want to get this scrapbook together and it's been a long day and I just..." With a shrug, she pulled back.

He would have refused if Stu hadn't heard the suggestion and pushed him to go. Said he needed to girl hunt, was tired of being bitchy. Duncan supposed if it would help pull him back to normal, it would be worth it. But he wanted Susie to go. "Come with us, Babe. Stephanie is meeting Ev. It would be nice for you to sit and talk with her. You enjoy her company."

"Yes, but I'm too tired tonight. Go ahead. Have fun. You deserve it as much as you guys got done this week."

Knowing she wasn't going to change her mind, he gave in and promised he wouldn't be late.

Susie was asleep when he got home, with Danielle curled up in the bed beside her. The girl popped her head up. "Sh." She put her finger to her lips. "Mum sleeping. I sing her to sleep. Yes."

Duncan sat next to her and stroked her dark hair. "Were you good for your mum?"

"Yes, my daddy. A good girl. My mum not happy, no. I sing to her and make her sleep."

Not happy? He studied his wife's face. She looked peaceful enough. "Come, my sweet. Time for you to sleep, as well." He offered his arms and carried her to her room, pulled back her blankets and tucked her in. She let him bypass a good night song, so he kissed her forehead, told her to have sweet dreams, and returned to his wife. He showered just long enough to get the smoke off and lay beside her.

Wanting to wake her and ask what she was not happy about, Duncan decided to let her sleep instead. He lay awake and stared at the ceiling for some time. Maybe he should have let her try again. His head shook automatically. No. The adoption would work. She'd have another baby to hold, to love, and then she'd be fine. He prayed it wouldn't take three years, and that she wouldn't again decide to want more. Not that he'd mind. He would love to have a house full, once they got into the house. But this was too hard; watching her struggle with it was too hard.

Turning toward her again, he couldn't help moving closer and running a hand over her head, down her shoulder.

She started, opened her eyes, and moved in against him. "I'm glad you're home. I missed you."

His eyes clenched. Missed him. She'd missed him, even as much as they were together.

13 May

Evan tried not to yawn as he stretched back onto the metal chair, trying to get as comfortable as possible. Maybe it was time to replace them with something nicer, or go further and set up an actual meeting area in the basement with easy chairs and couch and such. Susie wasn't using the space to teach, anyway. If she ever did again, they could move the furniture. As often as they sat in the basement and talked, that expense to be more comfortable wouldn't be unreasonable. They could even put an imitation fireplace down there, for heat during the winter. For their audience: Ali, Kate, the kids ... for Susie, so she wouldn't always have to be so wrapped up during the cold months.

They could also add a large throw rug under the main seating area. Susie had already put one in the area beside the wall where the kids played, along with a small table and chairs set and a little shelf with books and games and coloring supplies. Evan figured it wouldn't be much more of a stretch to make the adult area just as accommodating.

Of course, what Susie most wanted, as far as accommodating, Evan couldn't do. Not yet. Roy paced around behind Adam and Doug and Mike, where Evan could see him. He never paced behind Evan.

"Is Stu coming?" Adam tapped a rolled-up paper against his leg.

"On his way. Had to pull him out of bed and shove him in the shower." Doug looked over at where Duncan plucked at his Mustang. "Did you have to introduce him to those girls?"

"Nae, I didnae introduce them. They introduced themselves quite alright."

Adam stiffened. "Please tell me they aren't still in the apartment."

"How did you know they were?" Doug accepted the sheet of paper and unrolled it.

Roy stopped pacing. "Everyone's going to know soon. That's a press release. Just came in early this morning."

Evan eyed him. "How? With your help?"

"My help? Why would I bother with such a nothing story? So a couple of girls came back with him? So what? Makes him look available again."

"He is available again." Mike cast a glance at Evan. "I actually agree this time. What does it matter?"

"Um." Doug turned his gaze to Duncan. "That's not the problem." He handed the paper over.

Evan moved closer to his friend and read it at the same time. He cringed.

Duncan shrugged. "Yeah, so wha' is new? There have been stories as this before."

"Not with photos, only rumors."

"Sorry I'm late, but look what I found at my door." Stu's arm was around Susie and he had Nella's hand on the other side.

"We weren't at his door." Susie pulled away and claimed the chair Duncan had left for her. "Nella heard his door close and yelled at him as we were heading down."

"Yes, I found my Stuey. Early morning." Nella climbed up on her dad's lap as he set the guitar out of her way. "We have pancakes, my Daddy. You go early too much. You come eat now."

Duncan rubbed her head. "I will come in a bit. How about you go and build a big house, my sweet?"

"No. I sit with you and talk music. Yes."

"No' today. Go on over with Keith. He has been waiting for you." He set her down and gave her a light push.

"Yeah, this isn't good." Mike scanned the paper he'd grabbed from Duncan. "Stu, damn, wake up."

Their keyboardist opened his eyes. "What? I can hear with my eyes closed. What isn't good? Can we make it quick? I gotta get some sleep."

"Should've sent them home sooner last night."

Stu shrugged at him. "This morning, and you're just jealous. Twins. Damn."

"They werenae twins."

"Yeah, I know, but they said they were and that was good enough."

"Anyway." Adam cleared his throat with a glance at Susie. "I don't care what you're doing in your free time, but you might consider being more cautious about where you do it. As in, bringing them back here might not be a good idea."

"Why?" Stu yawned through the question and slid down farther in the chair. "I live here."

"Yes, but so do your band mates."

"Yeah, and?"

"Including your married band mate who was there without his wife."

"Okay." Stu shrugged. "And?"

Mike gave him the paper. Susie looked at Adam waiting for explanation. When it didn't come, she got up and stood beside Stu to read over his shoulder.

Evan watched her face. She didn't look at all surprised.

"*Hell.* What in the hell is this bullshit?" Stu straightened up and looked at her. "Hey, they were both with me. Not that I'm bragging at this point, but this is all lies. He didn't ... hell, he wouldn't..."

Susie moved back to her chair. "I know he wouldn't. It's not your fault. I'm the one who refused to go."

Adam studied her. "You're awfully calm about this."

"Not the first time. I'm sure it won't be the last."

Roy pivoted and stared at her. "Why should she care? She had company of her own. Had a reason to send him off alone, right?"

Evan saw Duncan stiffen and Susie set a hand on his arm. "Company of my own?"

"Roy. Let me, as I asked." Adam leaned forward, toward her. "Someone call you last night?"

She met his gaze. "Yes. Why?"

"A different reporter says he called and got a man's voice, while they were out last night."

"So?"

Roy chuckled. "She even admits it. I've been telling you forever..."

"*Stop* there." Duncan gave him a glare and turned to his wife. "Did John come over? He said he might."

"Yes. He answered. Nearly wouldn't give it to me, told the guy not to call again. But he did and I picked it up and he asked if I knew that you were out with another woman."

"He what?"

"I told him I knew you were out with your friends, as I suggested you should, and not to call me again. When he kept talking, I hung up and left the phone off the hook." She looked back at Adam. "Why?"

"You told him it was your idea for Duncan to go out?"

She shrugged. "Just that yes, I knew, and I didn't care, or something of that nature. I don't know exactly. I was tired and Nella was being horrendous and it pissed me off that he'd call my house and accuse my husband of cheating. So I can't tell you exactly what I said."

Adam nodded. "Well. We're going to have to do some damage control on this one, since they're going to make it sound like you sent him out on purpose to have time... Well, we can't ignore this one."

Susie shoved a hand through her hair. "Don't they have anything better to think about? No cats up a tree getting rescued or something?" She found her husband's eyes. "You know if they accuse me and make it sound convincing, it'll completely blow any chance we have of adopting."

"We'll counter it."

She turned back to Adam. "We can counter it all we want. I can say it was Dad and he can say it was him, and they'll never believe it."

"We say it anyway, Babe."

"Why? You don't. When they do it to you, you say nothing."

"It is different."

"Why is it?"

"I am out there on the stage. It is expected; at least people expect the rumors of me."

"And there haven't been photos." Adam grabbed a deep breath and focused on Susie. "There's more. Someone faxed me a photo of you and some guy where you're handing him a piece of paper. They're saying it's your phone number or a meeting place."

"What?" Susie took it from him and frowned. "This is ... at the studio. Yesterday morning. He's Reanna's father. I was giving him dates I was available to teach. How did they get this? I didn't see any photographers."

"Could have been some student who took it, or a parent, a teacher..."

Susie got up, dropped it on her chair, and started away. Duncan caught up with her.

Evan couldn't hear what they were saying, but they were both frustrated, upset. "Adam." He kept his voice low enough they wouldn't hear. "Counter it. Tell the truth, all of it, to someone you think will listen. If you need her dad to back it up, let me know. And I'll contact Reanna's father to ask him to do the same."

"Hey." Stu raised his head. "Yeah, so will I. And I have the twins' numbers, at least one of them, if you need."

Adam glanced over at the couple arguing, or at least debating. "We should ask them..."

"No. Just do it." Evan felt the band's stares, but he wasn't backing down on this. "She's right. If we don't convince someone there's at least a good chance it's true, they have no chance in hell of adopting."

"Think they will anyway?"

Evan glanced back over with a sigh. "I hope so."

19 May

Evan was unsure why he needed to be present again for the continued home study, but he did his best to stay out of the way. John was at least relaxed, and that helped Susie stay relaxed. Nella was at the top of her stubborn form and annoyed by the stranger in the house she didn't seem to like.

He hoped they would be accepted this time. He wasn't at all sure she would try again. He was afraid she would let it go and live with the fact that since she couldn't conceive again, they would have to stop at one. Evan wasn't sure she shouldn't. If they ended up with another as fiery and headstrong as Nella, she would have her hands far too full. Or she'd have to quit as Raucous's manager. Or Duncan would have to quit producing in order to be more help with the kids.

Evan didn't want either option.

Maybe Susie was right, though. Maybe Nella having a sibling would calm her down. He hoped.

He checked the clock. Stu and Doug were scheduled to "stop by" in a few minutes, so the agent could meet them, watch the interaction. And she said she would do surprise visits, as well. If they were at practice, since Susie was part manager, she might drop by then. No warning.

It made Susie nervous every day, all day. She'd lost too much of her spontaneity Duncan had helped her gain, became too closed again.

Evan would be damned glad when this was over. Preferably with a new family member. An easy-going family member.

Of course part of it was the newest rumors about her and Reanna's father. He'd been identified. He was also hounded and criticized although he'd said the same; it was her teaching dates and nothing more. Too many didn't buy it. They figured a dance schedule would go through the center itself, not personally through a teacher. In general, they would be right. It was hard to counter. Evan had spent much of his time working with Adam and their publicist trying to counter it.

At the knock, he offered to get it and Duncan gave him a thankful nod.

"How's it going?" Doug paused by his side.

"From the questions and look on her face, not well. They heard about the recent photos, of course. I'm not sure she believed the explanation."

"Well, not to be the bearer of bad news, but word is out they're trying to adopt, also. It was in a little local paper, which means it'll spread soon."

Evan grabbed a deep breath and glanced at Stu. "Don't say anything about it while the agent's still here."

"Maybe she's the one who spread it." Stu glanced across into the room.

"Shouldn't have."

"Doesn't mean she didn't."

" Just don't mention it in front of her." Evan hoped Stu would pull himself together at least while he was supposed to be his normal charming self and lock his current attitude away. Nella came over and jumped at him. Stu picked her up and gave her a hug. Maybe she would keep him in a decent mood.

"My Stuey, I not see you in long, long time. No."

"Three days, little monkey. That's not a long time."

"Yes. You take me and play 'boards now? I not be here now. We go play downstairs." She jerked her body toward the door.

Duncan came over to introduce Stu and Doug as the agent stood. Nella at least stayed quiet through it, but she wouldn't answer when the agent asked why she didn't want to be there.

"She is in a mood today." Duncan addressed Stu.

"Is she?" He tickled her side. "Gotta change that now, don't we?

Tell you what. You be nice to your dad's guest and we'll go play the boards later."

"No. I not be nice. I not want her in Nella's house. No 'porters. Daddy say no."

"Danielle." Duncan took his daughter from Stu. "Mrs. Hile is not a reporter. Is tha' why y' are being this way?"

"My daddy, she is 'porter too. Yes. See. Writes down on paper. Yes."

He gave her a hug and addressed the agent. "I am sorry. We didnae know why she was bothered by you."

"She's bothered by reporters?"

"Nae, she is rarely bothered by anything, bu' her mum is. She knows her mum doesnae want reporters in the house and I promised her there would not be, that I wouldnae allow it."

Nella locked eyes with him. "Yes. No 'porters in mum's house. Not in Nella's house."

"And tha' is why y' are mad at me today?" He shook his head. "Danielle, Mrs. Hile is not a reporter. She isnae."

"Maybe it's time to tell her who I am?"

Duncan looked at the agent and then over at Susie, who came to join them. "Only if there is a good chance it will work. No' otherwise."

"There is a chance. I'm trying hard to lean that direction, although my superiors are against it. But from what I see ... so far, there is a chance. I would like to know what she would think of it."

Evan saw him hesitate, look at Susie, asking her silently. She rubbed a hand over his back – an agreement with whatever he decided, without having to say so.

Duncan stroked his daughter's hair. "Danielle, you have been talkin' about wanting a brother or sister, yes?"

"I get a brother or sister?" The child nearly bounced as she looked between her parents.

Susie took her hand. "Mrs. Hile is here to see if a baby might want to come live with us. If he does, you would be his sister. Would that be okay?"

"And he would stay ever and ever here with me and my daddy and mummy and..."

"I hope so, baby. We're trying. We don't know yet."

"*Yes.* I want a baby. *Yes.* My brother or sister. And I a big girl and I help and I hold bottle like my baby doll and we play 'gether with Keith. Yes." She nodded until Evan was afraid she'd hurt her neck.

Duncan eyed his daughter, silent. Evan could see what he was thinking. The child would be horribly disappointed now if it didn't happen, and he'd have both of his girls upset.

Stu took her again to help her settle in while and Doug talked with Mrs. Hile. Duncan and Susie took the chance to disappear into the kitchen. Evan wanted to follow, to assure them it would be fine, that Danielle's reaction would help. But he wouldn't intrude.

He listened to the talk, joined in when he had to, and made a note to remember anything she said his friend would want to know.

Finally, the agent stood to leave and asked if they were coming back. Evan went to get them. The woman followed on his heels, seeing as soon as he did that they were wrapped together, Susie's arms around Duncan's shoulders, accepting a kiss. Luckily not one of their more passionate kisses, but loving, comforting. Evan announced their presence.

Susie moved back. Slightly. Still hung on to her husband.

Duncan threw his friend a look. Ev could have announced the woman was barging in. He wanted her to leave. He wanted them all to leave and let Susie have time to unwind, to let him have time to unwind. The last thing they'd wanted was to tell Danielle until they were accepted and up high on the list. He couldn't, though, let Danielle think he'd broken his promise. And it worked. She was much friendlier to the woman after finding she might bring a baby.

Susie told him, after they escaped to the kitchen, that Danielle would have the wrong idea now about how babies joined families. He figured that was fine for the moment, until she was old enough to need to know better. The thought of her knowing quite that much, and more as she got older, was not something he was ready to consider. The boyfriend stage was going to be hard as hell on his nerves. He hoped they'd get a boy through adoption. One girl in the boyfriend stage would be bad enough. He was often amazed John liked him as well as he did, considering. Susie could have had so much better, and she was still so young to be mother of a two year old trying to have a second child, on top of her work duties and the extra stress that came with his job. Duncan often worried about her dealing with so much so soon.

Her dad had to worry, as well. He had to know she could have had an easier path than the one Duncan gave her.

She looked up at him. "Is that not okay?"

He'd missed something. "Sorry. I was lost in thought. Is what okay?"

She grinned and leaned closer. "If Mrs. Hile comes to practice tomorrow."

He turned his attention to the agent. "I thought it was agreed already you would stop in as you wished."

"Yes. For the first time, though, I thought I'd give you some warning."

"Not necessary. You will have to page Adam to let him know. The door is locked. He will come and open it for you. I think he will be here most of the week. Next week we are in the studio. You can arrange that with him, as well. He will not warn us if y' ask him not to."

The woman eyed him. "Are you as open as you're acting? Or are you acting like you are for my benefit?"

He felt himself stiffen at the suggestion but forced it not to show. "We 'ave nothin' t' hide." Damn, he'd let his accent slip too far. Susie rubbed his back.

"And yet you're tense all of a sudden."

He nodded with a deep breath. "T' be honest, I find this all a li'l insulting. No one checked us ou' when she was expectin' Danielle t' be sure it was okay. Y' can see Danielle is healthy an' happy. If we 'ad another on our own, we wouldnae be goin' through this. It feels as though our child's welfare didnae matter the same as someone else's child does, and I donae understand the idea of it. We could have five of our own and no' be checked if there is not a problem."

"So why didn't you?" The woman flipped through her paperwork. "It seems pretty evasive, no more than that you can't. I often find 'can't' to be rather overused, often as a convenience. Why can't you, since, as you said, Danielle is healthy?"

Susie glanced up at him and over to the woman. "I can't. I had a hard time carrying Nella long enough. It nearly wasn't long enough. I would, if it was possible. I'd love to. I might even give him the five kids he mentioned if I could carry them. But I can't. We don't have that option. You can verify that with my doctor if you need."

Duncan's annoyance dropped, faded as he wrapped his wife in his arms. "Her mother died in childbirth with her second attempt. They lost both her and the baby. We came too close to losing Susie the first time and so we made sure history wouldnae be repeated." He kissed her head. "She was willing t' risk it. I amnae. And she will be less angry with me for agreein' with Doc that she cannae if y' will say yes to us."

Susie touched his face. "I'm not angry with you."

He wasn't about to argue in front of the woman, but she was.

"You're agreeing to the adoption only so she won't be angry?"

Duncan stared. That wasn't close to what he said.

"That couldn't be further from the truth." Ev shifted from where he'd been standing at the doorway, switching his gaze between the kitchen conversation and the other room. He moved closer. "He wants it as much as she does. He won't say so, in case it doesn't work, because he doesn't want to add to the fact that Susie already hurts enough knowing she can't..."

"Ev..."

"You won't say it, so I will." He looked the agent in the eye. "As he said, they have nothing to hide, other than protecting each other and Danielle. He won't say anything that might hurt either of them. But I know how much he wants this."

Duncan wasn't sure whether to deck him or thank him.

"Besides, he can say or think she's angry all he wants, but she knows it's because he can't stand the idea of losing her. She's angry about the situation, not at him. Does she look like she is?"

"Yes." Susie's voice was nearly a whisper. "It's the situation that makes me angry. I'm a good mom. Ask anyone who knows me. Ask Danielle. Ask Keith. He's more mine than his own mom's and I'd take him in with no hesitation. I'm a good mom. My children come first. I don't want Danielle to be an only child just because I can't do it again, physically. Otherwise, I'm much better able to be a mom than a lot of those women who have them on accident and don't really want them. I am angry that I'm unable when they can have six or seven and hardly pay attention to them. It's not fair. I am angry." She looked up at Duncan, her eyes moist. "Not at you. I love you, and I adore you, and you know I do. Even if you are too overprotective at times."

He pulled her back in and kissed her head. He wanted to do better than that, but they had to get the woman out of the apartment.

"Well." Mrs. Hile made notes again and returned her gaze. "At least now it all makes sense: what I've seen, compared with what my superiors expected as the reason. And I agree with you. My job is try to balance that unfairness as much as I can, to be sure children will be well-cared-for and truly loved." She closed her notebook. "I'm going to get out of your way now and I'll be in touch."

He and Susie walked her out and wished her a nice evening. What her superiors thought was the reason? He should have asked, but he could imagine because of his job they figured Susie was some pampered type who didn't want to be pregnant in the public eye or to be bothered with nearly a year of the inconvenience. The shakiness of Susie's voice while explaining sounded nothing like an act. The agent had to know it wasn't.

26 May

Duncan was right. She was upset.

Evan stood in the basement and watched her dance. To Aerosmith, *Draw The Line*. Their newest LP. Mike had listened to it a lot when it came out a few months before. While Evan liked the guitar work on it, he wasn't crazy about Tyler's voice, and especially the scream thing. He'd often left the apartment rather than have to hear it repeatedly.

But this ... the way Susie combined her ballet movements with the metal sound and club moves ... this made Aerosmith sound sexier than he'd ever found them to be. Susie must have found them to be with the way she blended into it.

He wandered closer as she moved into *Get It Up*, and although he knew she only danced the way she was when she was upset, Evan couldn't help but enjoy watching her fire, her passion, her inner... He couldn't quite think of the word for it. Sensuality. But more. Her appreciation of the humor of the song, of the double meaning and innuendo.

She looked over at him and paused. He told her to keep going. She checked to see that he was alone, and kept going. Damn, she was beautiful. She was fire, inside and out.

At the end of the song, breathing hard, she wiped sweat from her forehead with her shirt sleeve and reached out a hand. "Come on."

"No. I'll watch from here. Or I'll leave if I'm interrupting."

"Come on, Lee. It's been forever. You remember how." Her blue eyes dared him.

Did he? She was right; it had been forever since they'd danced together, more than a simple slow dance. "I'm not sure I do."

"Oh.. then it's time to remember. Come on." She pulled at him, gave him no choice.

He tried to tell himself he couldn't, or shouldn't. She was Duncan's wife. But she was still his friend. The phrase *Duncan's wife* swam in his head as he followed her lead into the way they used to dance, when she wanted to practice with a partner and insisted he learn. He'd kept up well enough at the time. And it came back easier than he expected.

She smiled as they stopped at the end of side one. "Told you you remembered, and you're just as smooth as you always were."

"I think you're being too nice, as you always were."

"And you're still telling me I don't know a good dancer when I see one?"

He studied her face. Through her teasing, he could see her concern, her struggle. "I wouldn't dare. Is this Mike's album?"

"No, it's mine. I picked it up after I heard Mike's. Anyway, I had it picked up. Dad gave me the same look you are."

Evan doubted it highly. At least he doubted it was for the same reason. "I like it worlds better right now than I did."

She laughed. "Thank you. I'm flattered." Susie wiped her brow again. "Try another?" She went to her stereo and flipped it to the other side.

"Want to talk first?" He waited to catch her eyes. "What's bothering you? Or do I have to ask?"

"Probably not. But there's nothing to say about it. It's not going to happen. I know it's not. But you know, it's okay. I have Danielle and she's incredible and it's more than a lot of people have and I'm lucky to have her. I'm lucky to have Duncan. I have no reason to let it bother me. So I guess I won't. Right?" She shrugged and placed the needle on the album.

He stood back and watched again as she danced. The mood of *Kings and Queens* fit her mood. And the theme fit well enough. Holy wars. Some deciding who should be allowed to do what. She could say she wouldn't let it bother her. She could tell herself she was lucky and fine with how it was. That didn't mean she could convince herself.

She was breathing harder again at the end of the song, with as much power as she'd put into it. He went to her, took her hand, met her eyes. "Talk to me, Suse. You don't have to hide it from me. I know better."

Her shoulders rose and fell. And she went back to the stereo to turn it down. "The thing is ... that it's not just for me. Duncan wanted three or four kids. I know he did. He loves being a dad. And it's my fault he can't. I'm keeping him from it..."

"No, you're not." Evan stepped in front of her, close, and raised her chin. "Suse, it's his job making it difficult. You know that."

"That's not what I mean. The adoption, yes. But we shouldn't have to adopt. I... He wanted his own. I should be able... With all he's been through and then to find that he's a wonderful father as I told him he would be... I feel like I'm letting him down because I can't. And I can't help thinking maybe Kate's right. Maybe the agent sees what she does, that I can't control the one I have well enough and I don't deserve to have another and now I'm stopping him from having more not only because of my physical weakness, which infuriates me because I try so hard to take care of myself, but also my ... my lack of ability to..."

"Angel." He slid his hand to the side of her head. "I can't imagine why on earth you would listen to Kate."

"Because she's straight with me. She doesn't hold back like others do, like you do, in fear of hurting my feelings. Nothing against you. I love that it matters to you that you don't, but..."

"You think I'm not honest with you?" As he asked, he felt a twinge of guilt. He wasn't, quite. He couldn't tell her how he had to keep reminding himself she was Duncan's wife.

"I think you tend to be too careful about not hurting me. I'm stronger than that, Lee. You can just say so if Kate's right. So tell me. Honestly. Are they right not to think I can handle another child?"

He wanted to wrap her in his arms and hide her away from it all. Maybe she was right. Maybe he was too protective.

"Lee?"

"No." He let his hand slide down to the back of her neck, felt the moisture and heat on his fingers and palm. "Suse, no, they aren't, and I'm not convinced they won't. I know Duncan feels without doubt you can, or he wouldn't be trying so hard."

"Because he wants it that much, like you said."

"Oh Suse. You know I only said that because the woman needed to know. Don't let it make you feel bad. You shouldn't. None of it's your fault. Your condition isn't your fault; you didn't choose it and you didn't do it to yourself. Like you said, you try. Give yourself credit for that and don't dwell on what you can't do."

"Right. Easy for you to say, but what if it was your wife who couldn't? Because I know you want children, also."

A sharp sting pulsed through his system. Yes, he did. With her. And he couldn't have that, either. He couldn't even have half of it. "I think ... that Duncan is incredibly fortunate to have what he has, and he knows he is. And I think he'd rather know you're happy with what you have, that having him and Danielle are enough for you, than to think you'll be unhappy forever if you don't have more."

She shook her head. "I'm not..." Her eyes watered.

"That's how I would feel. If it was me." He was pushing too far. He knew he was. And he held her gaze. It was as far as he could go.

Susie bit her lip and breathed in deep. Her eyes rolled toward the ceiling. "I've been such an idiot."

Had he gone too far? An idiot how? Did she see it? Finally?

"I'm ... going to go up and shower and... He should be home soon." She walked away to stop the record and turn off the stereo. "Thank you." She came back, gave him a hug. "You're right. I've been an idiot. And they are enough, more than enough. I can't let him think otherwise." She grinned as she pulled back. "I've always said you were one of the smartest people I've ever known. Walking up with me?"

He shook his head. "No, think I'll work out a while."

"Be careful. Don't overdo it since no one's here as backup."

"Suse." He grasped her hand as she started away. "Kate's wrong. You absolutely deserve to have another. And you would handle it well. Nella is a wonderful child. Much of that is because of you."

With another grin, she wrapped an arm around him and kissed the side of his face. "Thank you." It was breathy. Quiet. And she slipped away. Upstairs to shower and wait for her husband.

Evan forced a deep breath, deep enough it pulled at his lungs, and went to the weight bench.

Susie propped herself over her husband and stroked hair from his damp forehead. He needed a shower again. So did she. It would wait. She wanted to lie there and hold onto him, enjoy his skin against hers.

"Wha' has y' in such a mood tonight?" His eyes sparkled as his fingertips teased her waist.

"You." She kissed his chest.

"Mm, and I 'ave been here every night."

"Yes. And I'm glad you are. I just want to be sure you know I am." She saw his confusion and kissed him again, on the lips. "I love you, Duncan. You are the most incredible man I've ever known and I'm so terribly lucky to have you. I don't think I've seemed recently like I know I am, but I do know I am."

He turned her onto her back, leaned in, and ran a thumb over her cheek. "Donae give up, Suse. I havenae."

"It doesn't matter. It does, but it doesn't. It's fine either way. Knowing how hard you tried, how wonderful you've been, how wonderful you are ... that's what matters. And I love you for it. I already have more than I deserved to have. You ... you are everything to me."

He studied her a minute then wrapped her in his arms, cuddled her close, kissed her head. "I love you more, Babe. And I am still working on giving y' all y' deserve. I need a hell of a lo' more years t' do so, bu' I will keep trying."

1 June

Evan pulled Nella onto his lap when she came over to talk to her dad. "Sit with me, little one. Your dad's trying to get his phrasing right." He threw his friend a grin.

"Look. See." She shoved a piece of paper in his face.

He lowered it to where he could focus on what she'd drawn. "And who is it this time?"

She frowned and pointed at each stick-like figure with looped lines he guessed must be clothing since each was a different color. "My daddy and 'tar. Mummy. Dani-nella. And new baby. See. I hold my baby like big girl."

Evan saw Duncan's eyes raise. Hardly a day had passed the girl didn't talk about the new baby. They'd told her time and again it could be a long wait, but she wasn't listening. They hadn't heard anything in the past week, although it had spread fast that they were trying. The more often Duncan saw the mention of it anywhere, the more sullen he became. And worse when Nella brought it up.

"Sorry I'm late, but you will never guess who I just got off the phone with." Adam plopped on a chair next to where Susie was juggling the schedule book and directed the question at her. "You're not going to ask?"

She grinned. "I don't know. I enjoy seeing you so hyped up you can barely keep from jumping up and down. It's cute."

"Cute. Thank you." He cleared his throat. "Anyway." He glanced around the basement. "Where's Stu?"

Doug answered. "He's on his way. Had to nearly pull him out of bed."

"He is going to come out of this soon, I hope. I don't mean to sound like I'm thoughtless or anything, but…"

"We know you're not." Susie sighed. "I hope your news is something that will help pull him back in. Once he gets absorbed in the music again, he'll feel better."

Evan hoped she was right. Their keyboardist had barely been with them since the break up, working fine, technically as good as always, but without the usual spirit that made him stand out. Evan started to miss his energy, although he never would have believed he could.

"There he is." Mike looked over to where Stu was dragging himself in, yawning.

"Sorry. Waiting on me?"

Susie raised her eyes from the paperwork. "Sleep at all last night? You don't look like you did."

"Nah. Not really. Can we make this quick? I gotta try to crash a while." He sat on the floor, against the stage, knees pulled up, arms slumped over them. A closed mug of what Evan hoped was coffee at his side.

Adam studied him. "We have a long day ahead. Are you going to be able to stay awake through it?"

Shrugging, Stu scratched his head. "Guess I will."

Susie moved over beside him and rubbed a hand over his back. "You'll feel better after a shower."

"Yeah, you better stop that. You'll turn me on since I haven't had any in, well, since that article that got your husband in trouble."

She smacked his arm. "Behave. And we only asked you not to bring them here. Take them elsewhere. We didn't say you couldn't."

"Damn. Nothing like my manager telling me to go out and screw someone. Especially a hot chick manager." He chuckled when she hit him again, harder. "Sorry."

"I think y' have been spendin' too much time with him." Duncan went to her, reached for her hand, and helped her to her feet. "He is startin' t' think again he migh' be able to steal you away."

She leaned closer. "Well, you know, if I wasn't already so hooked to you, maybe he could."

"Great." Stu scratched his head again. "Tease a man when he's down."

Adam glanced at Evan. At the nod, he grabbed paperwork from his leather binder and explained briefly of how Axis and Roy bumbled getting word of a big offer, but it finally got to him. "So, if you accept, we have to be in Utah early next week." When no one interrupted, he continued. "To perform two songs on the *Donny and Marie* show."

Susie found her voice first. "Are you kidding?"

Adam grinned. "I wouldn't kid about that. National television. Not only national television, but their end of season two-hour special. Star packed. And they want you. They want you enough to keep trying through blundering idiots not getting us the word. I called as soon as I got it this morning and promised an answer before noon, although I made it sound pretty clear we'd accept. It would be foolish not to."

Mike stood. "Hell, of course we're accepting. Damn. National television?"

"That is the consensus, I would guess?" Adam waited while they all chimed in, as though he had to ask.

"Get yourselves together and let's get to the studio. There's something we need to do first thing." He looked at Susie. "And we need your help."

"Okay."

"I'm holding you to that okay even though I have a feeling you'll change your mind."

"Adam, you know I'm willing to do what I can to help."

"Does that include singing with your husband?"

Evan watched her hesitate.

"It would only be for the recording. They want us to do *Intoxication* just as we do it on the road. But they also want *And It Comes*. Except they want it to be a duet, with Marie singing harmony." He checked Duncan's reaction. "If you're willing. They were pretty persuasive about it, so if we refuse..."

"No, it is fine. An' they want a track of it arranged as a duet?"

"Exactly. So if Susie does the harmony for Marie's part and we send it, it will make things easier at show rehearsal. I'd like to have it done today so I can overnight it and give them plenty of time. Still willing?"

"Yes, but..." She looked at her husband. "I'm not used to doing harmony. Not to mention he'd have to write the part and I'd have to learn it by tonight."

"By about four o'clock, actually." Adam checked his watch. "I need to get it mailed out."

"I'm not sure I can."

"Of course y' can. Come." Duncan started away, grasping her hand. "We will go and start working on it." When Nella ran over to him, he picked her up and took her to Evan. "Mind keepin' her here for a bit?"

He reached out and claimed her from her dad. Luckily, she didn't complain with more than a pout, which stopped when Evan said they could work on guitar together while her mom and dad did.

Before she left, Susie verified that Nella and Keith would be going, also, and told Doug Ali had to go, since she was such an Osmond fan. Adam agreed and said he'd arrange it.

"Stu." He waited for his eyes. "I'm sorry this is so soon after..."

"Hey, no problem. I'm sure there are tons of girls out that way willing to entertain a single guy going on national television. Since I'm allowed and all, and my manager says I should."

"How about you don't say that where anyone will hear you? Go get a shower. I'll see you all at the studio in, say, two hours? Less if you can make it less."

Evan couldn't keep from showing his appreciation of the duet. Even if it was only a proof recording, it was nice to hear her sing again. And she hit the harmony dead on. Duncan, of course, arranged it to fit her voice, although Adam gave him instruction for what key Marie sang in so he figured they must be fairly similar. And he made it highlight her over him. How he did it so fast and so well, Evan didn't know. But he told Adam he wanted a copy of it. This had to be saved.

Susie enjoyed singing with her husband, also. It was so obvious the rest of the band threw each other looks. Maybe they could get her out there again. Now that Nella was two, they could hire someone to do tours, someone Susie could trust to care for her backstage. She needed to be out there with them, as one of them, not only as management. Or instead of management. They could hire someone for that, also. It wore her down.

When the mail came earlier with a bunch of returned envelopes due to insufficient postage, Adam told her it had gone up to fifteen cents. They had to mail all of the replies to fans again, in new envelopes, with new postage. She apologized far too much for such a small thing, said she hadn't heard it changed. Evan suggested they get someone else to do those things; there was no reason she should. She took it as an insult, as though she couldn't handle it. He didn't mean anything of the kind and Duncan jumped in to say he didn't, that she was distracted lately and had enough to do and that should by all rights be someone else's job, not hers. They weren't still a struggling bar band. They could afford office help.

Singing, although it made her nervous, would fit her better than juggling those details; she was an artist, not a business woman. She could do both fine, but Evan didn't figure she should have to anymore. She'd done it enough through the years of helping the band when they couldn't afford the help. She'd paid dues that weren't even hers to pay. It was time for that to stop.

"So?" When the music ended, she looked at him, asked his opinion first.

"Incredible. Maybe too incredible. Marie may not want to even try to measure up to that."

She laughed. "Yeah, I'm sure. But thank you."

"Time to record it." Adam broke in from the control booth. "Perfect, Suse. Let's do this so we can get to other things."

With Danielle finally asleep, Duncan pulled the blanket higher around her shoulders, kissed her forehead, and went out to find his wife. She was in the kitchen, cleaning a sink that he couldn't see needed to be cleaned. With a grin at her habit of doing so, he moved up behind her and wrapped his arms around her stomach. "I think it is good enough, Babe. Come an' sit with me." She smelled of sunflower lotion, a scent he had come to love. When they finally had their house – if the contractors ever decided to finish it – he would plant her a field of sunflowers around the edge of the back yard. Most of the planting, she would do, since she loved to play in the dirt and help things grow, but the sunflowers, he wanted to do for her.

She dried her hands and turned to run her fingers up from his stomach to his chest. "Just keeping my hands busy while you were." She reached up to kiss him. "She'll never be able to go to sleep on her own, you know, if you keep spoiling her that way."

"I am sure she will, as she gets older and doesnae need me as much."

"Oh, I can't see her ever not needing you as much. Differently, maybe, but still as much." She brushed fingers through his hair.

"Suse." He moved his lips close to her ear. "Would y' consider singing with me? For the album. I will not ask y' to sing on stage since I know you donae want that, but today was amazing. I have never enjoyed myself as much while singing as when y' join me."

"Maybe. I had fun today, too. Of course, we could do that and not record it. Just to do it."

With a light grin, he let it go for the moment. They had time. As she got more comfortable, she might change her mind.

Tired of conversation and overwhelmed with the day's last minute song change and studio work, he pushed thoughts of everything else aside and focused on her scent, on her skin against his, her closeness. He kissed her, glad she allowed him to make it deep, long. She would know what he was asking. She always knew. Rarely did she ever turn him down.

She broke the kiss and ran her hands back down his chest to his stomach. "Come to bed."

4 June

They should have gone to the studio. Ev insisted it was Sunday; they needed a break, a day off. He didn't mention Duncan's birthday, number twenty-eight, but as they rarely took a whole Sunday off anymore, Duncan had the feeling that was partial motivation. They should have gone to the studio.

On the other hand, it was nice to have his wife at his side all day instead of at a distance as he worked and she talked with Adam. Or with Roy. Whatever had gone on during their last tour between Susie and Roy had calmed things between them. She'd only said she refused to back down when he told her to and nothing more. He supposed that could have been enough. With blustery hotheads, often it only took standing up to them to make them give up. Rarely was there much behind the bluster.

"Hey, got a surprise for you."

Duncan looked over at Stu and took a swallow of his beer. "I donae like surprises."

"Yeah, you're gonna like this one. Trust me." He nodded at Susie in a suggestion she should come closer. "While you've been busy producing and all, I've been stealing your wife."

"And I am supposed t' like that?"

"Hey, once she gets over you, she'll choose me and you know it."

Susie chuckled. "Yeah, well. You better have a lot of patience if you're waiting for that."

"Not like I'm holding my breath, or anything else, while I'm waiting." Stu shrugged and pulled his guitar from its case. Danielle made a beeline for him and asked if she could play. "In a while, little monkey. Right now it's your mom's turn."

"No, my mum no' play 'tar."

Duncan moved closer as Stu explained she didn't play guitar but she did sing, and that he and Doug talked her into trying a couple of their songs that Mike only "screwed up." Mike gave him a look but didn't look surprised that Susie was singing with Stu. Neither did Ev. Was he the only one who didn't know?

She studied his face as she sat close to where Stu tuned his instrument, using the tuner only for low E and his ear otherwise. He'd been working on doing it by ear only and nearly could. Duncan had no doubt he'd get there.

"That one is off." He took another swallow.

"D?"

"G. It is flat."

With a frown, Stu grabbed the tuner again and put it on G, then sighed at the difference and tightened the string. "Show off."

Duncan didn't bother to answer. He settled onto a chair, accepted Danielle's plea to sit on his lap, and put his bottle on the floor beside him.

The song was unbelievably beautiful. She had just the right tremor, the right crescendo and decrescendo, perfect pitch, and a newly developed style, more professional. Stu had taught her that, as well? And it was a love song. She focused on him as she sang.

As it ended, he lifted Danielle off his lap and went to her, squatted in front of where she sat, one leg underneath her on the couch, and raised a hand to her face. "Beautiful. It was absolutely beautiful, Babe, as though it had been written for you."

Stu grinned. "We kind of readjusted it for her range."

He nodded but kept his eyes on his wife. "You should do it on stage."

"Oh. No. It's for you."

"And she has a couple of others ready if you want to hear them."

Duncan glanced at Stu. "Y' know I want to hear them." He backed away again, only far enough he wouldn't be in her face. The other two were just as nice. Stunning.

He was nearly unable to speak when she said that was all she had time to get ready. And she handed him a cassette. "Happy Birthday. Adam helped us slip into the studio one day while you were working with Evan here. It's a combined effort. Not to mention Mike's help with voice instruction."

"I thought I heard professional coaching." He looked over at their lead singer. "Y' could do that as a living."

Mike shrugged. "Maybe some day. Of course, she's easy to work with. Learned fast. Nice, isn't it?"

"Stunning." He pulled her up from the couch and gave her a light kiss. "Thank you. This is worth havin' a birthday. And when we are less busy, I want you to sing with me more. At least to record it like this, if not for more than that. Yes?"

She nodded and stroked his hair. "When I talked to your mom today, I thanked her."

"For what, my luv?"

"For you. I think I made her cry. I didn't mean to do that. I just wanted her to know ... how much her sacrifice, what she did to keep you safe, means to me. How much you've changed my life, how much better you've made it. I wanted her to know."

He couldn't find a way to respond. He imagined his mum very well did cry, with as much as she'd gone through, had worried, had given up. "Suse." He caressed her face, along the edge of her hairline, back to her nape beneath her unbound long shiny gorgeous hair. "I imagine you made her day, her decade even. You are the most beautiful soul I have ever known, to think to tell her such. You may have repaid everything to her I will never be able to do."

"Oh that's not true. She is so proud of you. What more could a mom want than to be able to be so proud of their children? To see they turned out so well? She couldn't want more than that."

"You're still damn sexy for an old man." Kate pressed against his arm as Duncan watched his wife laugh with Ev and Adam across the room. "And you know, since you've been married a while now, you can start flirting with me again. It's not like she's going to worry about it like she did before you were married."

Duncan eyed her. He was infinitely glad Susie hadn't let her old roommate 'update' her clothing style as Kate was trying to do when he met them. Kate's cleavage was hard to avoid, with the way she had it pushed up as far as possible. "She was not worried about it."

"Uh huh, which is why she kept dragging you away from me."

"It was an excuse to be able to drag me. It turns her on to be forceful." He glanced over at his wife again.

Kate laughed. "Yeah, I'm sure it does. Susie? Forceful? That's gotta be the funniest thing I've ever heard."

"Y' donae think she can be?"

"No. But I appreciate the wishful thinking and I wish she could be. I imagine you'd love it." She pressed harder against his arm. "I can try to teach her. I know how to be forceful."

"Yea' I am sure y' are right."

"Wait. Right about which?"

With a grin, he walked away, leaving her to think what she wanted. It wasn't getting married that stopped him from flirting with Kate as he used to enjoy, but what she had put Susie and Mike through afterward. What she was still doing to her son. Duncan didn't mind having Keith around so often, even overnight. If it ever came to it, he would take the boy in full time without argument. Still, his mother should be a mother, full time, not only when it was convenient for her. He would get along with Kate. He would still enjoy her spunk. But he'd lost too much respect for her.

Little hands pulled at him when he stopped to talk with Doug and

Ali. "Yes, my sweet?"

"Pick me up."

"I donae think so. You are getting too big for me."

"Daddyyyy. *Up*. Pleeeease."

Setting his glass on the table behind him, he lifted her high in the air to make her laugh and settled her in his arm. Her legs wrapped around his waist and she set a kiss on his chin.

"Nella, you're going to make Daddy tired." Ali pulled at her fingers.

"No. My daddy not get tired. My daddy never tired."

Mike pressed in from behind. "I don't know, little one. He's an old man today. You know he's twenty-nine, right? Thirty is creeping up fast."

"My daddy *not* old." She frowned at Mike and shook her head. "No."

Doug laughed. "She'll be saying that when she's forty and you're sixty-six, I would guess."

"And she will be right. How can you get old when y' have such a cheerleader in your corner saying you are not?"

Danielle ducked her head into him and he gave her a squeeze. Regardless of how often Susie chastised him for giving in to the child too often, Duncan couldn't find it in himself to turn down any affection she offered. He made her listen when she was told to do something. She was learning manners well. She had a beautiful loving, giving nature, despite her stubborn independent streak. She would be fine. He knew his daughter would become a wonderful adult with her courage and social abilities and her intelligence. He had no concerns, other than how attention-needy she was. He only hoped she would still listen to him when she became dating age, and allow him to warn her off those he knew were after the wrong things. Nothing frightened him more than his daughter being subjected to the kind of men he'd seen far too many of. He knew Susie would be just as frightened of the idea when it came that time. Trying to calm her about it would be difficult since he doubted he'd be too calm about it himself.

Susie caught his eyes and grinned at him, set a hand on Ev's arm, and came over. "Nella, why are you making Daddy hold you again?"

His daughter hugged his neck.

"Wow, you're going to have trouble on your hands when ... that other thing comes through."

He looked at Mike. "No, I do no' think we will."

"No?"

Ali cut in. "Any more word on it?"

When Susie shook her head and rubbed her daughter's back, hiding her thoughts as well as possible, Duncan set Danielle down, squelched her protest by asking if it was time for ice cream, and wrapped his arms around his wife.

Diane's call for cake and ice cream pulled attention away from where Susie held him and gave the others an excuse to back away. Ev was right; Danielle was much like her mum. Duncan couldn't deny whatever affection his wife wanted, either. When she was ready to release him and join the group in the kitchen, they would. He wouldn't push. And he didn't want to push. He wanted to hold her.

"So you should've brought your girlfriend." Stu pushed into the conversation, in between Ev and Diane.

"Girlfriend?" Diane threw a look at her son. "I haven't heard of this."

"Just someone I've gone out with a few times." Ev swallowed a sip of Coke. From his expression, Duncan had a feeling he wished he'd accepted the offer of Whisky to go with it.

"Still, it would have been nice to ask her. It's been some time since I met anyone you were dating. I'm glad to hear you are."

"Duncan doesn't like crowds for his birthday. I imagine he's barely tolerating all of us being here."

He tipped his bottle toward his friend. "Barely tolerating all of you is habit by now."

"Tolerate." Stu laughed. "You are so full of shit. You know you love us being here. And besides, his girl is really hot. Even if you are stuck, you can't say you don't enjoy looking. I know better." He pushed on Ev. "Or are you dating someone different now? Is she a dog? Is that why you didn't bring her?"

"Stuart." Diane scolded him. "It doesn't matter how she looks. It only matters that she's a nice person and they get along well."

"Like hell it doesn't matter. Any man who says different is a liar. And why would he date a dog when he could have any girl he wants?"

Ev rolled his eyes. "All right, you can stop."

"Hey, it's true and you know it is. He tries to play it off but damn.

The way they follow him around, he probably has seven or eight girls he's seeing and couldn't decide which to bring."

Duncan couldn't help but laugh. Ev's seeming unavailability although he was technically available worked opposite of what he was trying to do: it attracted them by the droves. He already had a reputation for being particular, stand-offish, and according to some reporters, a snob. He wasn't a snob. Not exactly. He was particular, and it showed.

"I did not raise my son to treat women that way." Diane moved her focus to Ev. "And I'm still waiting on a daughter-in-law and grandchildren."

"Ignore Stu." Susie slipped a hand around Ev's arm. "Of course he knows how to treat women. It's why they're so interested. They can tell he does. And he should darn well wait for the right one, one he's attracted to and not only nice. He deserves that." She looked up at him. "Of course, I like Stephanie so far. You can bring her over whenever you like. He'll tolerate it just fine, and I'll do my best to keep him from appreciating her looks entirely too much, since I know he does." She looked back at him, a teasing scold.

"Hey he can't help it. She's really, uh..."

Ev threw Stu a warning look and Duncan nudged his arm. "Better change the subject before we are both in trouble."

"Hey I don't know. Getting in trouble with you could mean a whole hell of a lot of fun. Think we should try it."

Susie rolled her eyes. "I think you already have. How about waiting a while before you try it again?" She moved back to Duncan and ran a hand up his waist to the back of his shoulder. "It's probably a good thing Danny's pulling you away from him for a while. With the mood he's in, it could be trouble."

"Aye an' y' may be right." He teased with a grin. "Nae even a fiery Scotsman wants t' make an Irish Injun lass too upset with 'im. We may be braw bu' we arenae gyte."

She chuckled. "Practicing so you'll fit in with them again?"

"Nae my luv. Tryin' t' get myself ou' of the trouble he 'as already pulled me into. Is it workin'?"

She slid both arms up around his shoulders. "We'll see." Her eyes sparkled mischief.

He heard Diane question what he'd said and Stu translate some of it with Ev's help and conversation turned to their coming trip to Scotland for Duncan's 'boys weekend' with his brother. He'd invited Ev but his friend declined in deference to allowing the time away from the band with his brother and cousin and a couple of old friends. Laura already had plans made with Susie and Danielle: shopping, more sight-seeing, swim parties with her friends. He wasn't sure what else, but Susie would stay busy. Maybe more than she wanted.

He knew she wasn't happy about him being away for five nights without her, but he couldn't refuse Danny. It had been close to ten years since they'd done it, and he wanted the time with his brother and friends up in the hills under the Scottish sky. He looked forward to it more than he had when he was younger and used it as an escape. This time it was only for pleasure. He needed no escape.

Duncan tucked Danielle in and kissed her forehead. She was wound up after cake and ice cream and so many people stopping by the apartment, so he sang to her for a few minutes to settle her in.

He and Susie had stolen time during the day to go check on the progress of their house. Susie preferred to go when the workers weren't there so she could wander freely. A couple more weeks, they said, and it would be ready. He couldn't wait to move his family next door, to have more space, more privacy. By this time, he figured it would have been faster to tear the thing down and start fresh. But she loved it. As it was. She loved the historical feel, knowing how long it had been there. It would be worth the wait. Although with as much as they had to fix: flooring, walls, electric, water pump, shingles, updated HVAC, plus new kitchen appliances, not to mention foundation work ... it wasn't going to be too original. Still, it was what she wanted.

With a caress of his daughter's head, Duncan went out to find Susie. He didn't actually resent his birthdays any longer. He wanted many more years of them just to be able to spend them with his family, to watch his daughter grow into a beautiful young lady, and to joke about his wife's hair as it turned from nearly jet black to silver. She would still be as exquisite to him as they day they met.

18 June

Ali had readily agreed to go to Utah. She more than agreed. She had jumped on Doug, congratulating him and the band all together. Susie was glad to have her there. Even with as many other singers as they had already met, Donny and Marie were icons. Their brothers were there, also, for the extravaganza show. It was a bit nerve-wracking, but so much fun. And the long hug she got from Donny as they were leaving was something she wouldn't forget. Even if he was a kid. Not a kid, really, but a few years younger than she was although he was a fair bit taller.

Ali talked about it all the way back to Massachusetts. Susie imagined she'd be talking about it for months. She grinned as she changed into her dance clothes. The grin slipped away again. She didn't want to go teach. She did want to teach; she didn't want to deal with those people.

They'd been home for two days. The first thing she'd done was go through the mail, but there was still no word from Mrs. Hile.

Nella nearly jumped on her when she went back to the living room. "Mummy, I hu'gry for fries and burger. Yes. We make fries and burgers? I pat them and pat them." She imitated the way she liked to shape the hamburger into patties.

"Honey, I have to go to the dance studio a little while. Daddy will make you a sandwich to hold you until I get home, okay?"

"No, my daddy no' here. He downstairs with Stuey. You not leave Nella all 'lone. No."

"Downstairs?" Why was he... The rest of what she said sank in. "Leave you alone? Have I ever left you alone, silly girl?" She squatted to catch her daughter in a hug. "Come on, let's go down and see if you can stay with daddy."

"I hungry, my mummy. My hummy no' tappy. No."

Susie chuckled. "You mean your tummy is not happy."

"Yes. I say that. Not 'appy, no."

She checked the time. She was already going to be a minute or two late, and she now wished she'd kept her own car. She'd have to drive the Cobra and she always drove it slower since it was his and he loved it so and doing anything to it would be a hundred times worse than doing anything to her own car. He said it wouldn't be; it was only a car, but she knew better. She should have kept her Pinto.

With a sigh, she went to throw a peanut butter and jelly sandwich together and set it on a napkin. "Here, baby. We'll take this downstairs.”

“No, I not want butter jelly. I want fries and burger.”

“We’ll do that later. This is just a snack. Come on, Nella, I’m going to be late.” Susie managed to draw the pouting child out the door and down to Stu’s. No answer. But she heard music and knocked again as she opened it. They were heavily engrossed in the song, with Doug listening in, plus Ali and two girls she didn’t recognize. Susie wondered if they were Stu’s “twins,” except they weren’t supposed to be at the building.

Doug spotted her and came over. “Sounding good, isn’t it?”

“Yes. But he’s supposed to be watching Nella.”

“Stu had a thought and yanked him down here. He probably didn’t plan to stay this long.”

“Who are the girls? Stu’s?”

“Ali’s cousins, in town visiting. He doesn’t bring girls here anymore. Says he wouldn’t forgive himself if he hurt your adoption chances even worse.”

Susie saw one of them lean in closer to Duncan, admiring him. “He probably shouldn’t worry about it at this point. Would it be okay if I leave Nella here?”

He stroked a hand down the girl’s head. “Of course. Do you want to take that to the table? I’ll get you some juice.”

Nella shook her head. “No. I want fries and burger. I not want peanut jelly and juice.”

“Oh, Danielle, please just be good. I have to go.”

“I go too, and get fries and burger.”

“I don’t have time...”

“Yes. You do have time for Dani-nella. Yes.” She scrunched her eyebrows in a scold.

Susie grabbed a deep breath. “Fine. Come on.” Her husband still didn’t notice she was there, and Nella didn’t need to see that girl flirting with him, so Susie asked Doug to let him know where they were.

If Reanna wasn’t such a wonderful student, Susie would have walked out. Too many students in the one class. Too many ages and ability levels. That wasn’t what she meant when she offered to teach more than only Reanna. Then the girl hadn’t even shown up for class, with no warning. Susie wouldn’t have bothered if she’d known. And

Danielle was unbelievable: interrupting, wandering too close to where they worked, calling to her every few minutes. Susie was exhausted.

She stopped by the studio's office to ask where Reanna was and why she hadn't been told she wouldn't be there.

Janet asked her to sit, and asked if Danielle could stay outside with one of the girls for a few minutes. Susie absolutely refused. She didn't know any of them well enough and the photo incident was still heavily on her mind. At least one of them wasn't to be trusted, probably more than one.

"Okay, well." Janet glanced at Nella when she wandered over to look at the Newton's Cradle sitting on a low filing cabinet. Susie showed her how it worked and sat again. Janet looked uncomfortable with having Nella play with it but Susie couldn't care less. She repeated her question.

"Reanna's been pulled out of the studio. She won't be back."

"What? Why? She was doing so well."

"She was, but her father ... the harassment got to him. Because of that photo. With you..."

"Janet, you know I was giving him my schedule..."

"Of course I know that but it hardly matters. The fact is it was an embarrassment to the whole family and ... well, they're moving back to the city. They came here for the quieter atmosphere, for the friendliness of the place, and ... well, that didn't work for them. Because of ... events."

Events. It was an accusation.

"But we'd still like to have you come. Your students are enjoying the class and it's nice to have the flexibility..."

"No." Susie got up.

"Suse, you enjoy teaching..."

"Yes, but not like this. You took advantage. You knew she wouldn't be here today and you didn't let me know..."

"Everyone else was still here. You still got to teach."

"Janet, you don't get it." Susie considered trying to explain, but it was pointless. "Nella, come on. Let's go find daddy." She was glad her daughter at least listened this time. She gripped Susie's hand with a beautiful trusting look on her face.

She made her way out through the lobby, pretending she didn't hear someone asking her for some favor or other, about the band. Why should she? It would likely backfire, also. All she'd tried to do was to help Reanna, to be the teacher she needed, and it was working despite Janet pushing everyone else on her. The girl was a natural en Pointe. Duncan had been right. Susie shouldn't have agreed. She should have pulled the girl to the apartment to work, out of the studio, away from whatever spy was there.

Personally, Susie was relieved not to have to go back. But that girl, the beautiful fifteen-year-old dancer ... she'd loved the smaller town; she'd said as much. Stupid rumors. Lies. Pettiness. And for what purpose?

By the time she got back home, all Susie wanted was to get inside and crash on the couch and watch brainless television.

Danielle tried to knock on Stu's door. "No, we aren't going to Stu's. Let's go." She pulled Nella away from his door and nudged her toward the stairs.

"My daddy with Stuey. Yes."

"He might be home by now. Let's go find out."

"No. He not home. He with my Stuey. I play too."

"Danielle Lynne, I'm too tired for this. Upstairs. Now."

"No."

Susie swept the girl into her arms. "Yes. Are you going to walk or do I take you up?"

"No. I not walk the stairs. I see my Stuey."

"Not tonight, you're not. You're going to bed early." Susie kept one arm tightly around the child and held the railing with the other. Danielle fidgeted, made it even harder to hold her. Susie was tempted to let her go to Stu's and if Duncan was still there, he could deal with her. But she wasn't giving in.

At the top, she had to hold onto the girl's hand to keep her from running back downstairs while she found her key, and she pulled Nella inside as she threw a fit. "Danielle, *stop*. Go on to your room and settle down *now*."

"No, I *not* go my room. I go see Stuey and my daddy play 'tar. *Yes*." She tried to shove past.

Susie closed the door and stood in front of it. "Go to your room."

"*No*, I go *down* the stairs."

"You're not. Go, like I told you."

"*No*." Danielle tried to push Susie out of her way.

As she again hoisted the struggling child into her arms, Duncan came over, took Nella, and told her to stop. The girl calmed immediately. Susie felt a huge sigh of relief coming on, until she noticed Mrs. Hile, on the couch, with some man Susie didn't recognize.

Duncan met her gaze for a second and put Danielle down again. "Go on to your room. I will come in a minute." He waited until she huffed away. "Wha' is she in a fuss about?"

"I don't know. She's been like this since we left for the studio." Susie slipped her shoes off and apologized to her guests.

Mrs. Hile shrugged it off and said they dropped in on part of Duncan's writing session with his friend. She didn't say which friend. She introduced her supervisor, Mr. Garland. "Since I was having two different thoughts about this case, he thought he'd come by for another opinion."

"And I chose the right time, it seems."

Her stomach tightened at the man's expression.

Duncan rubbed her back. "He is a fan of acoustic guitar. Stu and I were working on *Crossed My Mind* today." The one Stu was playing acoustic for. "How did your class go?"

"I'll tell you later."

"I am sorry. I forgot I needed t' keep Danielle. You could have left her with me."

"No, it's fine." She turned her attention back to where it needed to be. "Can I get you anything? Have you been waiting long?"

"We have just come up. I put coffee on. Sit and relax, Babe."

"I need to check on her. I'll be right back." Before she could get an argument, Susie headed to the hall. A whiff of brewing coffee made her breathe more deeply as she passed the kitchen. With a peek in to Nella's room to see that the girl was lying on her bed at least nearly asleep, Susie took another breath and went to her room. She needed only a few seconds to gather herself. He could deal with the intruders that much longer.

She pulled out of her dance clothes covered by jeans, went in to wash her face and brush her hair, and redressed in the same jeans and different shirt. Duncan's shirt. She supposed she should put something nicer on, but she didn't care. Susie had every thought this was going to be a waste of time and nerves anyway. She wanted to be as comfortable as possible.

By the time she returned, they were all seated in the living room with their coffee. Duncan let her know he had hers and she took his side. She wanted to wrap into him, but she managed to control herself and simply thank him.

"Danielle must be sitting quietly."

Susie turned to Mrs. Hile. "She's asleep. I'm guessing she didn't sleep well last night."

"Oh? Is that a normal problem?"

"No. Just now and then."

"Have you talked with her pediatrician? There could be a physical reason."

"Doc has checked her well. She's fine. She just doesn't like to sleep and she fights it."

Duncan rubbed her shoulder. "Too many other things she wants t' do. I was the same, mum says. She will grow out of it."

He hadn't exactly grown out of it. He still tended to get up early to work on a song because it wouldn't let him sleep. But she didn't counter him. She answered about her work at the studio. They'd found out, somehow, that she was working for free and asked why. She explained as well as she could without making it a big deal.

When they shifted back to his job, the rumors, Susie stopped bothering. She let him answer the last few questions and just wished for them to leave. She hated the invasion. She hated the scrutiny. It was bad enough they got it from the press; they didn't need it inside their own home, as well. How many parents would pass their test who already had several kids?

She had to stop focusing on it. She had to try to get Duncan to stop focusing on it. They had work to do. An album to finish. A tour to get set up. New promo photos. Radio interviews. Fan letters to answer. A house to move into and then furnish. A play set to put up for Danielle and Keith. A trip to Scotland. Their hands were full enough. In a couple of years, they could adopt an older child who needed a home, a child no one else wanted. That would be better. All the way around. She could be happy with that, and she figured Doug and Evan would both have kids before too much longer. Stu would eventually. There would be plenty around.

When the band waned, Susie would go back to teaching. Little ones. Like she preferred.

Rubato

1 July 1978

"Why your *other* manager decided to say yes to a little town show in between trying to get this album done, I'll never understand."

Duncan sat through Roy's bluster and made production notes while Ev jumped in and told the idiot they'd all agreed to it, that Lakewood expected them by now and it showed loyalty to their home town. The "nothing show" as Roy insisted on calling it, for the Fourth of July celebration, didn't ever pay much, and this year the band didn't let the town pay them anything. Maybe Roy didn't understand the point of loyalty, but the rest of them did.

And it wasn't like they were going to much extra effort for it. They would do part of the set list from their last tour plus a few new songs from the coming album. It was promotion.

He was trying to talk Susie into doing at least one of those she'd recorded for him, also. So far, she was hesitating, although she'd stopped saying no outright. She did agree to the duet they'd prepared for *Donny and Marie*. She needed to sing more. With him. As much as he could get her to do it.

"*Duncan.*"

Her urgent call as she hurried toward him jolted him away from his notes and he went to meet her. "What is it, Suse? What is wrong?" Her eyes were moist and she held a letter in her hand. Another rejection? Hell. Why this time? She would never agree to try again. "It is alright, my luv." He held her close. He would try to convince her...

"No." She pulled back. "It's not bad news this time. They said yes. Look." She held the paper up with a shaky hand. "They said *yes*. We're on the list. They said yes." Her tears fell, but Duncan had to take the paper to read it himself. Neither of them had a good feeling about it when the agent and her supervisor left. The letter, though, said Mrs. Hile enjoyed the relationship Danielle had with him and Susie. She said the living environment was calm and soothing, more than adequate for a child's well-being. And the interaction between Susie and Duncan was refreshing and stable; their eye contact was honest and respectful. All good conditions in which to raise a child. There was a comment about his job, their travel, but they had both said they would be willing to quit and change their lines of work if it became harmful to the children. And so, with a very slight hesitation and a note that there would be follow-up checks, before and after receiving a child for placement, they were officially on the list. Which could take anywhere from two weeks to two years or more.

He found her eyes. "We are going t' be parents again."

She nodded, wiping tears.

He held her through the guys throwing them congratulations and patting him on the back.

Ev offered to keep Danielle so they could go celebrate. She didn't want it to be alone, though. They invited the band, somewhere family-friendly so they could take Danielle and Keith. They would all be involved in it, she said, so they might as well be part of the celebration.

7 July

"So it looks like we should be able to get this out by August fourth, which will be good timing..." Adam stopped when Stu came in and threw a newspaper down on the mixing board.

"*Look* at this." He paced while Duncan picked it up and scanned the headline on the entertainment page. A photo of Kara with some guy holding a camera. An engagement photo.

"Married. She's getting *married*. To some guy she met in Paris. She's known him for like two days ... okay, three weeks. And she's *marrying* the jerk." Stu paced again. "How do you agree to marry someone you've known for three weeks?"

Mike took the paper. "How do you know she didn't know him before?"

"It says they met in Paris. She hasn't been there before..."

"Could be a lie. A cover. She has to know you'll see it."

"Mike." Susie threw him a look. "She's not like that. And I would have accepted if Duncan had asked after three weeks. Sometimes you just know."

"It took y' three weeks or more just t' agree to go out with me."

"Well, I meant three weeks after we started dating. Not everyone is so touchy about accepting a date." She grinned at him.

"Yeah." Stu grabbed a deep breath. "Whatever. Move along, huh? So what did I miss?"

"Someday you'll find that. And Stu, it's much more her loss than yours. It is." Susie grasped his hand to bring him over to sit with the others.

Duncan kept track of the time as they went back to dates and shows. He'd have to call Danny soon, after his brother was off work. He'd missed the call the day before when he was at the studio. Plans to finalize. What still needed to be finalized, he didn't know. They had their tickets. Danny and Collin had the site and arrangements made to get there, which would include some hiking at Collin's request but not as much as Duncan would have preferred at Danny's refusal. He looked forward to getting home, and then up into the Highlands.

"Damn, Stu, just go back and play *Space Invaders* if you're not going to do this."

Doug nudged Mike to get him to stop.

"Fine." Stu bolted out of his chair and headed to the door.

Duncan went after him. They needed him there. They needed his head in it. Bitching at him wasn't going to do it. "Hey, hold on." He caught his friend's arm. "Interested in goin' out tonight?"

"Why?"

"Because you need to put your mind on something else. A set of twins maybe, if they are twins or not." He grinned.

"Right. Then I get bitched at for ... you mean with your wife this time so you don't get in trouble?"

"Nae, I mean with you and Ev. No girls, only someone else's music for a change. Hangin' out."

"Yeah? Where are we going to do that where we won't get mobbed?"

Duncan shrugged. "So maybe we ge' mobbed a bit. Without the girls there, it willnae matter."

A smile formed at the edges of Stu's mouth. "Promotion, right? Looking available?"

"If y' like. But I only meant for the fun of it."

"Hell, yes. I'm in. If you can convince your wife it's okay."

"We willnae say all that t' her. She can get over bein' mad at me tomorrow. Yes?"

He laughed. "Now you're starting to act married. Kept waiting for it. Damn right, I'm in. I've been waiting for you to get back to flirting like one of us single guys again. This should be a hell of a lot of fun."

"Ah well, I only mean t' a point, not enough to screw up the adoption."

"Or make your wife never talk to you again."

"Or that."

"I know, and I'd lose all respect for you if you ever did that to her. But it doesn't mean you can't act like you might every now and then." Stu gave him a playful shove. "You win. I'll put my head into work. But don't back out on me. I am looking forward to this like you can't believe."

They asked Mike, but he said he had no interest in being shoved and pulled and yanked when it wasn't for work. Just as well. He and Stu had been on each others' nerves too much. Doug said he'd rather enjoy the night off quietly.

They went to Gerry's. The first hour or so was filled with autograph requests and questions about the next album and the next shows and such. He was asked about the adoption and said it was going well and nothing more. There were questions about their TV appearance and about the Osmonds and what they were really like ... and then the owner and one of his bouncers stepped in and told everyone to back off and let the boys relax as they came in to do. It helped but didn't quite stop it, since more came in the later it got.

But at least Stu was distracted with all the girls hitting on him. Duncan was hit on, also, including by those in town he recognized. Did they think he would cheat on his wife in their own town? Not that he would anywhere else, either, but he couldn't imagine they thought he would be so stupid. Not that it didn't happen. He knew it did. That was part of the issue between Tony, Blue River's drummer, and Lisa. He had. And of course she found out. Why she stayed with him, Duncan couldn't fathom. She was a lovely woman, kind and gentle and pretty. Tony was lucky to have her and damn sure didn't deserve her. Duncan had told Susie as much. He couldn't even blame Lisa for being with Greg, as he knew she was, with as many affairs as Tony had on a regular basis. Why shouldn't she?

Ev was playing the single role well, although Duncan knew he was hooked to Stephanie enough it was only an act. He agreed to several slow dances, talked with one girl after another, and in between, he sat with Duncan at the bar and tried to act like he didn't mind the constant photos. Ev wasn't any more fond of photos than he was of having too much focus on stage. A shame he was so reserved about it. He'd make a hell of a lead guitarist if he'd relax and allow himself to do it. But it did work better for Raucous that he was content playing bass and occasional acoustic.

"Hey." Stu pushed against his arm. "I'm catching another ride. Do you mind if I ditch you? It's late anyway and my guess is you're ready to be home with your wife."

Duncan looked at the girl nearby waiting. Cute girl. He spoke in his friend's ear. "Is she old enough for you?"

He shrugged. "Twenty. Plenty legal."

"No' what I asked, and I did not mean only age."

"Hey, I never go for the inexperienced." He winked.

Duncan motioned for him to go on and turned to see if Ev he was ready to go. A flash hit his eyes just as a girl pressed in against him.

"Thank you." The girl smiled big and walked away.

"Could 'ave asked." He spoke to no one, since she was already too far away to hear. He would be glad to be home.

And Susie was glad to have him home. Danielle was asleep and he went in to kiss her head and then to shower to wash the smoke off, as his wife ordered.

13 July

"Danielle, you can't be sick again. We leave in two days." Susie leaned her daughter into her arm and felt her forehead. Another fever. "Oh, honey." She moved her to the couch, told her she would be right back, and pulled a blanket over top. Two days would give her recovery time, Susie expected. At least she hoped. Usually, Nella bounced right back. Of course there was always the chance Nella would feel better in two days and pass it along to Susie about then.

It was nearly lunch time, so she put water on to boil and poured a small cup of grape juice to take to her daughter, with a second glass for herself to try to boost her immunity. The child was mostly asleep by the time she returned and she didn't have the heart to wake her, so she returned the glass to the refrigerator and continued the soup. There was a dish of leftover chicken in the freezer, so it wouldn't involve more than cutting up carrots and potatoes to add to it. She always had noodles on hand since it was the one thing she always knew Nella would eat. That and hamburger. Susie insisted she try anything they were having for dinner but never forced her to eat it if she didn't like it. Kate fussed at her, said she was spoiling her too much, that Keith learned to eat anything on the table, like it or not, and it would make him less particular. Whether or not her friend was right, she couldn't do it. Trying it was good enough.

Duncan was out at a promo event for the coming album and the newly released single that had sold out in their area within the first two or three days. Adam had them restocked the day before and was hoping their promo at a few stores to sign the 45 would push it right back out of stock before the album release. He estimated what they might sell and asked for a supply barely under that, in hopes of being able to report a second sell-out. The B side was her duet with her husband, which she tried to argue but he and Adam insisted. Or at least they pushed her about it until she gave in. It was a bonus: something to make fans want the single as well as the album since the duet wasn't there. She hadn't given in to do more than the duet. Duncan was disappointed she wouldn't, but she wasn't part of the band. She was management. And she was his wife. Something inside wouldn't allow her to interfere quite that far.

The guys were unsure about the tactic of minimal stocking but Adam assured them it wasn't unusual and it would only be unfair if his stock number was ridiculously low. It wasn't. With the announcement that they would all be there the day the stores were restocked, numbers were wonderful. Susie was anxious to see how it went. If not for Nella, she would have been there with them. Ali offered to babysit so she could go, but Susie knew how much Doug's girlfriend wanted to attend, since she actually had the day off and had been able to do very little of their touring and promoting with him. Her dad was away again. Kate ... well, she didn't know where Kate was but Susie had Keith, also.

Other stores around the area and across the country were set up with signings, as well. With Duncan scheduled to be away for the next two weeks, Adam had them split up, sending a couple of them to different places at different times. He didn't want all but one member to attend any one signing. When Duncan returned, he would jump in and do the same, with a few dates already set. Susie and Nella would go to the different cities with him but stay away from the signings. She didn't want her daughter photographed. The press would know they were travelling with him, and they would possibly be allowed some photos together with Nella's face concealed, but that was as far as Susie would compromise. Her daughter had a right to privacy.

"Can I help?"

She looked down and gave Keith a grin. "Sure honey, I would love help. Do you want to scrub carrots?" Susie moved a chair in front of the sink and gave him the amount of carrots she wanted. Keeping an eye on him while she peeled potatoes, she was glad for the distraction. Danielle's illness worried her. Why did it have to be two days before their flight? Duncan couldn't cancel on his brother. It meant too much to him, to both of them.

14 July

Susie stroked her daughter's head as she settled in on the couch. At Duncan's voice asking someone on the other end of the phone for his brother, Danielle turned her head toward him, found his face, and settled back in.

"Yeah, I know it is late there and I am sorry." Duncan paced the short reach of the phone cord. "I am going t' have to cancel the trip."

Susie could imagine what was being said on the other end of the line as she watched her husband's face.

"It isnae work. Danielle has an infection in both ears. She cannae fly for several days and by then there wouldnae be point in going... She may feel better in a day or two bu' she cannae fly until it is clear. It would be torture for her and could burst her ear drum... And so have I, bu' y' will have to tell them all I am sorry... Nae, we are booked too solid the rest o' the summer... Donae cancel the thing. Go on with the rest. I can try t' get there with you next summer if y' plan it well enough in advance." Duncan rubbed a hand through his hair. "I know, Danny, and I am sorry..."

Pushing herself up from the couch, Susie took his side. "Let me talk to him." Despite the warning look from her husband, she reached for the phone.

"Suse wants t' say hello. Stay polite since it isnae her fault. Y' can curse at me more when she is done." He set his palm over the receiver. "He isnae happy. Give it back if he is rude."

She leaned in to give him a quick kiss. "You know how much I love you, right?" With a light grin at his confusion, she greeted her brother-in-law.

"Hey sis. Tell my brother he doesnae have t' keep worryin' abou' what I say to you."

"I know he doesn't."

"Yeah? So you finally got your wish, did y' nae? Y' are keeping him over there away from us."

She chuckled at the teasing tone in his voice. "Not me. I'm not sick. So far, anyway."

"Hey, donae catch it from her. Leave 'im to deal with the girl and stay away."

Susie looked over at Duncan as he rubbed Danielle's head. "Well, that's going to be difficult since he won't be here." She paused at his silence and Duncan's raised eyebrow. "I'm sending him to you. There's no reason he shouldn't go just because we can't."

"Suse." Duncan tried to take the phone.

"You should go." She kept it from him and returned it to her ear. "He'll be there. But Danny..." She tried not to let her emotions take over as her husband continued to argue. "You better take care of him for me. And you better send him back to me, 'cause you know I enjoy getting along with you and I'd like to keep doing that."

"Like I would 'ave any say in the matter." Danny sounded wary. "But it doesnae sound like he is going t' agree."

"He will. I'll convince him." She reached up to place her fingers over her husband's lips as he tried again to argue. "Not that I don't want him here, you know. And I'll want as many phone calls as I can get because I hate being away from him, but ... just take care of him for me." She moved her fingers to his hair, through the silky locks, and rested her palm on his cheek.

"Sis, we can wait till next summer if y' need."

"No, you've both looked forward to this too much. There's no reason he can't. Tell Laura I'm sorry, though. I know she had plans."

"Yea', she did, and y' are saving yourself, y' ken. I donae know how y' would 'ave stood all those chattering girls for so long by yourself."

Susie grinned. "They're not so bad. Tell her she can call and help keep me company as much as she wants."

"I will tell her."

"Here. I'll give you back to your brother."

"Suse?" Danny waited to know she was still there. "Thank you. I 'ave been lookin' forward t' it. And so 'ave Collin and the others."

"Well, I have him every day. Guess I don't need to be too selfish." She grinned at her husband despite the emotion trying to seep through. "Have fun, Danny. And take care of him." Susie handed the phone back to Duncan and half listened to the conversation as she returned to Danielle and grabbed a deep breath. She couldn't let him know just how much it bothered her to let him go alone. He would refuse to go if she did.

He came to her when he hung up. "Suse, you shouldnae have told him that. I should stay here with you."

"Why? There's no reason you should."

"Danielle is sick."

"She's always sick and it's just a virus. She'll be fine. Doc's a phone call away, and ... and Danny needs you there. He misses you. You have to go." She ran fingers back through his hair. "It's only a couple of weeks."

"Or less." He studied her face. "I can come back as soon as the trip is done instead of stayin' as we planned."

"Or we can go meet you there in about a week. She'll be okay to fly by then."

"Will you? By yourself?"

"Adam can take us to the airport..."

"Or Ev can."

"He'd attract attention."

Duncan caressed her cheek. "Bu' I would feel better knowing he was there until y' got on the plane. Or bring him to Scotland with y', so you donae have to go alone."

"Yeah?"

"If he can, around promotion."

"I'll ask." She cuddled in against him. "So only a week. I can manage a week."

With Danielle feeling so bad, it was easy to get her in bed early. Duncan took over her care. He said he didn't want Susie to risk catching it more than she had to and she should let Ev help her, and rest well. It was only part of the reason. He would miss her. Susie could see in the way Duncan held the child against him and kissed her face that he'd have a hard time being away for a week. Still, he needed to go. Danny needed to see him. His family needed to see him. It was her fault he was always away from them. She couldn't get in the way this time.

Once Nella was asleep, Susie put Journey's *Infinity* on the record player and turned it on quietly. She turned the lights down and led her husband into a slow dance. He made the movements stronger, deeper, his hips caressing hers, his hands holding her in close. She didn't pay much attention to the music. Her senses were fully infused with him, his skin, his gracefulness, his magnetic blue eyes, his long dark lightly wavy hair, his chiseled beautiful features, his scent – she loved his scent, he always smelled so wonderful, so sensual. And he still emitted pure sensuality, as she'd noticed the first time she saw him.

Raising her face to find his mouth, she moved in against him, pressed a hand against his chest, ran it down to his stomach, underneath his shirt. His skin was warm and soft where it wasn't often exposed to the elements. She lowered her lips to his neck, his shoulder.

He pulled back and went to move the needle. Taking her in his arms again, he sang *Anytime* along with the band and made his movements more passionate during the guitar solo she knew he loved. As the song ended, he set his hands on each side of her face. "I love you for letting me go. And for no' letting me go. Y' are my world, Suse. Always remember y' are."

"You think I'll forget that in a week?"

He grinned and leaned even closer. "I want y' t' never forget. Even when I amnae here where y' can see me, I am here. Always." Duncan met her lips, softly, lingering, then with more urgency, more passion.

"Duncan." She spoke against his mouth, a whisper, afraid to break it too far. "Let's go to bed. I want you closer."

15 July

In the pale dark of early morning, Susie turned off the alarm and rolled back over against her husband. "Time to get up."

"Mm. Come here."

She grinned as she raised to see his face, propping a hand on his bare chest. "You should eat before you go. I can do scrambled eggs real quick."

"It is too early." He slid his hand down her shoulder, along her back, to her hip. "I donae have t' go. I can wait until it is safe for Danielle."

"We told Danny..."

"I will call 'im back."

Susie dropped her head and nuzzled her face into his neck, caressed his bare skin, and considered agreeing with him. She couldn't do it to Danny. "You have to go. It wouldn't be fair to him. Just ... be careful and call me as much as you can."

He kissed her; a hand slid into her hair and held her in. "Are y' sure? There is always next summer."

"Yes." She felt his body moving against hers with his breath. "No."

He rolled her over and leaned in against her, teasing her lips. "No?"

"No. Yes." She grabbed a deep breath. His body tensed. Fully tuned in to hers. "You're making it harder."

A light grin skirted his mouth. "I think y' are."

"Oh. Duncan..."

"Tell me t' stay." He kissed her shoulder.

"That's not fair." She felt him press in, teasing, torturing. "You have to go."

"I donae."

She clenched her eyes at his wandering fingers. "Be with me before you leave."

"Babe..."

"You have to go. I want you to go. I don't want to be without you, but I want you to go." She kissed the spot under his jaw where hair didn't grow. "But I want you to be with me first."

Danielle clung to him and shook her head.

"I will see you soon, my sweet. You be good for your mum and be a good helper."

"I go a Sco'land too, my daddy."

"Next week y' will come, when you feel better." He hugged her with a kiss to the head.

"I nae feel bad. No." She shook her head hard and cringed, pressed a hand to her left ear, then wrapped into him, clinging.

"Come on, little one." Ev nearly had to pull her out of his arms. "We'll see your dad in a few days. I'll take you there. Okay?"

Duncan gave him a half grin and Danielle another kiss. "Be good and listen to your mum." He brushed fingers through her long wavy hair and looked at Ev. "Take care of them for me. You will be around?"

"Most of the time. My schedule is light and either Stu or Doug will be here when I'm not."

He nodded and grasped his daughter's fingers. "I will see you soon. I love you, my Danielle."

"My daddy, love you." She bolted forward and gave him a kiss on the chin.

Ev kept her inside while he and Susie moved out to the hall. Beau was waiting at the car: a rented car so it wouldn't attract attention. His wife wrapped around him and he considered changing his mind. "I will stay if y' say so." She didn't answer and he pulled back to find her eyes.

"I love you." She touched his hair, ran her fingers down and around behind his head. "And I want you to have a lot of fun. But call me. I know for a few days you'll be away from a phone, but otherwise, call me. When you get there. And before you go to bed and..."

He met her lips. Deeply. Passionately. Pulling her in. And then he stood and held her silently for a long while. "I love you with everything I am, Suse. I always will."

She nodded against his shoulder. "I love you more."

"Not possible." He gave her another kiss, softer. "Call the house if Danielle doesnae keep getting better. I will come right back."

"She'll be fine. Don't spend your trip worrying, about either of us. I'll be fine, too, even though I..." She caught her breath. "I'll miss you."

"I will miss y' too, my luv. An' we will have t' make up time when you come. Yes?"

"Count on it." She ran a hand down to his stomach. "You better get going. Tell Danny he owes me."

Duncan gave her a grin, ran fingers down the side of her face, and forced himself to head downstairs.

She couldn't sleep. He'd called from New York where he had to connect from Boston. His flight was delayed. He joked about how hard it would have been to keep Danielle cooped up in the airport for an undetermined amount of time. He would call when he finally had another flight time. So far, no one in New York paid any attention to him. He wore a baseball cap low over his face, and he'd decided to leave his guitar home, which surprised her. He said it would be easier to just go along with things instead of being asked to play if he didn't have it.

A book in her hands, her back propped against the headboard and knees pulled in front of her, Susie checked the time again. Nearly three hours since he should have flown out of New York. She wished he would call and at least update her. Trying to read was pointless; she couldn't concentrate on the story. Replacing the bookmark, one he'd given her – black leather with a bright red heart carved into it – she returned it to the night stand and dropped her head back. She wanted to cuddle in against him, feel his warmth, hear his strong and steady heart beat, kiss his bare skin. The only time they'd been separated at night since they were married was the once on tour when she was expecting and couldn't travel, and when she was in the hospital having Danielle. Although he'd stayed right there with her until she went home, so they weren't really separated then, either. She didn't like it. Her bed was too empty. It felt wrong.

At the phone's ring, she banged her head on the headboard and reached to grab it. "Hello?"

"Ah, it is nice t' hear your voice."

"What's wrong?"

"One delay after another. We go' almost on a plane and it was delayed again. Then they moved us down to another terminal and back up t' this one. I am glad you and Danielle are no' having t' deal with all of this."

"And I wish we were there with you, to keep you company. Has anyone bothered you?"

"Nae, I am keepin' my head down and everyone is too irritated to worry abou' anyone else."

"Good. I mean that you're not being swamped."

"I donae know. I' might be a good distraction about now."

"Duncan, no. You don't have security there."

He chuckled. "I amnae serious, my luv. I am quite happy being left alone. Hold on..." A voice blared in the background, some kind of announcement. "They say we will board in ten minutes. Let's hope they are right this time."

"Yes. Or they need to send you back home and try again when they have their act together."

"You want me t' cancel?"

"Yes. No. Duncan, that's not fair. Just talk to me for a few minutes."

"I am here until they call for boarding if y' wish."

"Yes."

"Suse? Are y' okay? How is Danielle?"

"Oh, she's fine. Fussed for some time before going to sleep, wanting daddy to sing to her, of course, but she settled in finally."

"And you? Y' are not going t' be mad a' me for going?"

"No. I told you to go. I'm just... You know I hate to be away from you overnight. It's crazy. I know it is, but I'm kind of used to you."

A short silence followed. "If they cancel this one, I will tell them t' send me back t' Boston and I'll grab a cab home. And I am no' asking you. We will leave it in someone else's hands, yes?"

She grabbed a deep breath, trying not to hope for another cancellation. "Fair enough."

Another announcement interfered. "They are boarding now."

"Oh. Okay. That's good." She twisted her sheet in her fingers.

"Babe, le' Ev babysit tomorrow and get back t' your dancing. It will help your immunity so y' donae catch it."

"Yeah. I should." Silence. She wiped at her eyes. "Duncan."

"I am here."

"Have a good time with Danny and Collin. And be careful out there in the middle of nowhere."

"Donae worry, my luv. I have plenty of experience bein' in the middle of nowhere." He paused at more noise. "I have t' go, Suse."

"I love you. With everything I am. Always."

"I love you, too, Babe. Go t' sleep now. Y' donae need t' get overtired."

"I'll try. Call me as soon as you get there."

"Y' know I will. I love you, Babe."

Hearing the phone click, Susie held onto the receiver for a minute or so, until it beeped at her. Then she slid down into her blankets and clenched her eyelids together. She wouldn't cry. It was ridiculous. Only a few days. It would only be a few days. But she wanted to hold him.

And she hated knowing there would be a whole ocean between them.

16 July

A banging from the front door made her look at the clock. Just past seven. Seven-o-nine. Why would someone bother her so early? She considered ignoring it ... but the pounding came again, followed by the doorbell. She bolted upright. They would wake Nella. How dare they... Something was wrong. Or ... maybe he came home. Maybe they delayed it and he came home. Did he take his keys? Maybe not. Wrapping in her robe, she checked to see that Danielle was still asleep and pulled her door closed to block out the noise. Then she hurried to the door and checked the peep hole. Evan. And Mike.

A bolt of pain streaked through her system as she opened it to them and saw their faces. "What's wrong? What is it?"

Evan took her hand. "You weren't up yet."

Stu and Doug came up behind them. And Kate. Kate never got up so early. "No, I didn't sleep well last night." His hand shook. Evan's hand shook in hers. "What is it?" A thought hit her. "Dad? Did something happen?" No. She needed Duncan home.

"Angel." Evan stepped closer, studying her face. "Danielle's still asleep?"

"Yes, I ... Evan, what? You're scaring the hell out of me. Why's everyone here?" And their faces were all grim, staring.

"Come sit down, Suse." His voice shook nearly as bad as his hand.

"No. What? He's okay, right?"

Evan swallowed hard, grabbed a deep breath. "Angel..."

The phone rang. As she stared at it, Mike went to grab it, then hung it up and left it off the receiver. Evan again told her to sit. He'd pulled her to the couch.

She shook her head. Her heart hurt. "Tell me. Where is he? How bad? I didn't ... I didn't even get over to see him before he left for..."

"Angel, it's not your dad. He's fine." Evan squeezed her fingers tighter. "The plane. There were mechanical problems."

She shook her head. "He's ... where? A business trip, but where? I don't remember. I stopped asking..."

"Listen to me. Your dad is fine. Still away. But I just talked to him. He's coming home."

"Then what? Danielle's asleep. You'll wake her..."

"Suse." Evan moved his hands to her arms. His fingers were cold. They were never cold. "It's Duncan. His plane..."

"No. There were ... delays ... but they fixed it..." She couldn't breathe. No. Not Duncan. No. Only a week. And she'd go meet him.

Kate wrapped an arm around her.

"No." She barely heard her own voice. "It's fine. They fixed it."

Evan swallowed hard. His eyes were moist. Pain flashed across his face. "His plane went down. In the ocean. They've already..."

"No." Her chest burned. Her stomach spasmed. "No. Evan, no. Not his. It wasn't his."

He moved in to wrap her in his arms. His breathing was rapid, heavy.

She pulled away. "No. I would've heard. It would've... It's not his."

"It's all over the TV." Mike. Staring. "Adam called."

Her head shook again. She backed away from them, headed toward the television.

"Suse, you don't want to watch it." Doug this time, intercepting.

She pulled away, turned it on. Her hands shook as she stood in front of the screen. Photos. A plane. Mostly underwater. A helicopter flying overhead. Wreckage. Something orange floating around it. Boats. Someone was behind her, supporting her. She couldn't look away. A flight number flashed on the screen amid the announcers talking about how they'd delayed the flight, thought they had it fixed, wondering who would take the blame.

"It's not his." She stared at the number. Not his. She knew his flight number.

"Suse." Evan. Beside her.

"No. It's not his. It's not. It's the wrong number. It's not his."

"They switched his flight. They've already said..."

"No." She refused to hear Evan's voice shake. Refused to acknowledge the eyes on her. She listened to the guy on television say recovery efforts were slow, inhibited by the cabin being mostly flooded with water, an explosion, metal pieces, no one found yet but they were searching. She felt for the families watching whose loved ones were on that flight, that number, not his. It wasn't his. It was the wrong number. A voice behind her said her dad was on his way. He was still out of state. It would be a while. He didn't need to... Her dad was on his way.

No. He didn't need to be...

Her husband's face flashed on the screen. The guy was talking about him, saying... No. She tried to walk away and couldn't...

"Suse, breathe. You're going to pass out. Breathe. I'm here. Hang on to me."

She shook her head, her eyes still the screen.

"No survivors found yet..." the guy said in between talking about her husband. "What a loss for music..."

"No." She gasped; her lungs ached at the held breath she didn't know she was holding. "No."

Evan wrapped her in his arms, held tight. He was shaking. Or she was. She didn't know. She hoped it was her. He wouldn't. He was strong. Nothing got to him. Pushing away, she looked back. The camera scanned the scene. Scrap pieces floating. Empty life vests spotting the water. Barely any of the plane still visible. An explosion. A delay. Technical difficulties. *Switched planes.*

Her legs collapsed. And Evan was beside her on the floor, holding her in. And Kate. She couldn't breathe. Gasping for air, she forced her eyes back to the screen. The voice. The wreckage. And her husband's photo was there again, repeating it. Why did they have to repeat it? He was fine. He was coming home. If it was delayed again, he was on his way home. But ... he was boarding. Her head shook. Her chest ached.

"Suse, you have to breathe. Someone go check on Nella. Get her out of here. She can't be here now. Turn off that damned television..."

"No." She pushed away from him. "No. Don't turn it off. They'll find him and they'll tell us. Don't turn it off."

"Just for a minute, Suse." Doug, crouching beside her. "Come with me. Danielle's awake. Stu will take her downstairs for now. But you don't want to scare her. She can't see that on television."

"No. *No.* She's *not* losing him. No. He's coming home. He promised it would only be..." Her breath caught. Dizziness set in with her too-fast breaths, her shaking. She felt herself being lifted and tried to fight him. "*No.* Evan, *no.* I have to... They'll find him."

He didn't answer but didn't let her down. He took her back to her room. Someone else was there. Closing the door. Standing over them. Kate.

"Where is Keith?" She stared at her friend. Mike was there. Kate was there.

"He's asleep. Suse, it's going to be okay. We're here for you." Her eyes watered. Her cheeks were wet. Kate never cried. Never. Almost never.

"He's coming home." She shoved Evan's hand away from her shoulder. "He's coming *home*."

"Angel." Evan sat facing her, kept her from getting up. "Look at me." He tried to set a hand along her face.

She pulled back. "Move. Let me up. Danielle. I..."

"Stu has her. She doesn't know. She's fine."

"*Let* me *up*." Pushing at him while he held her, she pushed harder. "Let me *up*. Leave me *alone*. I have to ... they'll find him and they'll tell us. They'll find him, and..."

"Shh, Angel." He pulled her in, against her will, against her fighting, her pushing at him. "Angel, stop. Stop fighting me. You're all right. You're going to be all right. Just breathe now."

"I'm fine. I have to go to him. He can't be alone. It's... I shouldn't have let him go. I shouldn't have told him to go. Now he's alone and ... and he can't be alone. I have to go..."

Evan gripped her from the side, holding tight, making sure Stu had time to get Danielle out of the house. She couldn't see the television. She especially couldn't see her mom like this. She'd be terrified. It was going to be hard enough ... hard enough. He had to fight his own emotions to try to keep her calm, to get her calm, as much as he could. He'd been up early, as usual. Mike had the television on and yelled to the kitchen for him. They watched together, and then Mike called down to Stu and Doug. Getting over the first wave of shock, with the announcer saying they didn't expect to find anyone alive based on the amount of damage, along with the cold water that would help hypothermia set in on top of the shock of any passengers who may have survived the explosion, Evan froze. As he was trying to decide who to call to double check, praying it wasn't his friend's plane, Adam called. He'd already done it. Verified it. Then John...

Susie. He'd rushed toward the door. He had no idea how Kate was there. It was good, he expected. Anything ... as though anything would matter to her.

"Breathe, Angel. You have to breathe." He felt her holding her breath and forced her face up to his. "Come on, Suse." He stroked her face. "Your daughter's going to need you. You have to breathe. If you pass out, you'll only have a headache and..."

"Let *go* of me." She tried to push away.

"Kate, check on Nella."

"She's downstairs." It was Mike's voice. Evan didn't dare look. She was struggling against him.

"Look at me, Suse." He tried again to find her face. She kept pulling away. "*Look* at me." Releasing her arms, he pressed his hands against the sides of her head, forcing her attention, refusing to let go when she shoved at his arms. "We'll watch for any news. You can't watch that. You can't keep..."

"He's *my* husband. He's *mine*. You can't keep me away. *Let me go.*"

"I'm not keeping you away. I'm trying to help."

"Then let me *go*." Her eyes pierced his, not seeing him, likely still seeing the news, the flashes of wreckage, the coverage of Raucous's lead guitarist. "Let me go."

He moved his hands, not sure what else to do. And she bolted to the living room. "Kate." Exhausted to a point he hadn't felt since they lost Jeremy, Evan looked up at her. "Call your dad. Get him over here."

She wiped tears and gave him a nod.

He pushed himself up at the sound of the television. He couldn't even be surprised when Kate hugged him strongly. "Think there's still any chance?" Her voice was weak.

He swallowed hard, fighting the images of what he was afraid his friend could have had to go through: the explosion, the freezing water, how long he knew... "No." Evan could only hope it was quick and maybe he didn't see it coming.

"You'll have to stay with her. She's..."

With a nod, he pulled away and headed back to Susie while Kate slumped onto the bed to grab the phone. Mike touched his back as he went by.

Ali was there, and Doug, both next to her on the floor as she stared at the set, knees pulled up in front, hands clasped around them. Approaching slowly, he caught Ali's eyes when she looked up at him. She was crying. She got up to give him a hug. "I'm so sorry. Evan, I'm..."

"I know."

"She won't talk to us. She's..."

"In shock." He grabbed the afghan from the couch, remembering how Duncan had made a point to keep her warm after the mugging attempt, when she showed similar signs. Shock. She had to stay warm. He wrapped it over her shoulders from behind but she shoved it off, her eyes glued to the screen. With a gasped breath, he crouched half behind her and half beside her, put it back around her and held it there.

"Don't." She tried to push him away.

"Angel, you have to stay warm."

"I have to go to him." Suddenly, she swiveled to face him. "Take me there. You have to take me to him. He can't be alone. I shouldn't have let him go. He can't be alone..."

Doug shook his head, his voice barely audible. "They're saying no chance of survivors. Some ... bodies have been found. Only a few. No one still alive. They don't expect..."

"He's coming *home*. You have to take me to him. We'll go find him. We'll bring him home." Her eyes were wide, unfocused.

Elevate the feet. For shock, you elevate the feet and keep the person warm. His friend's medical training. He heard his voice saying it. Evan stood and tried to pull her up with him. "Come on, Suse. Come over to the couch."

"*No*. Evan, *take me to him*. He's your *friend*. He would do it for you. He would go find you. Take me to him. You *have* to..."

"I can't, Suse. We can't. I would. You know I would. If... Come on, stand up with me." He half pulled her to her feet, blocking out her continuing requests for him to take her to her husband. No. He would do anything in the world for her, but not that. She couldn't go there. On television was bad enough.

Leading her to the couch, he tried to get her to sit. She wouldn't. The doorbell rang and he knew someone was answering it, hoped it was Doc, or someone else who could help him. He didn't have any idea what to do.

Strange voices filtered in. Flashes of light. Reporters. He looked over to where Mike and Kate were pushing them, trying to back them out the door, and went to help. They tried to ask him a question and he shoved the nearest one as hard as he could, told them to get the hell out of their building. It was just enough for Mike to get the door shut. "Call the police."

Doug was already grabbing the phone.

Susie was staring at the television again. It showed Duncan, a promo shot, and several miscellaneous pictures from shows and times reporters caught them in public. Talking about what a loss it was for music.

He went over and turned it off.

"*No.*" She pushed at him, trying to get at it.

"Suse, you don't need to watch that. It won't help anything. Damn sensational headlines. You can't watch that." With her still struggling, he picked her up and took her to the couch. She pushed at him and told him to leave her alone. He pulled her in close and held her arms still. Her breathing was rapid, shallow. "Calm down. You have to calm down. You can't do this to yourself."

"No. Evan, *no.* I told him to go. I *told* him to go. And he was going to come back, with the delays, he was going to come back and I ... I told him he should go."

"Don't." He forced her eyes to his. "Susie, don't do that. Be glad you weren't with him. Be glad Danielle had an ear infection and couldn't go." He saw Mike check the door and open it ... to Adam. Beau was behind him.

Susie gripped his shirt. "I should have been there. I should be with him now. He can't be alone. I told him he wouldn't be. He's been alone so much. I should have been there with him."

"So we would have lost you, too? And Danielle? You can't think that." Evan couldn't keep his eyes from watering. They would have been. If not for the ear infection, he would have lost all three of them.

She shook her head, sniffing, rubbing at her eyes. "He's ... he's not... He's coming home. Evan, I know he's coming home."

Adam set a hand on Doug's shoulder, and on Mike's arm, then came over and sat on Susie's other side. "What can I do?"

She at least came to her senses enough to acknowledge him. "Take me to him. Help me find him."

Adam glanced at Evan but maintained composure and took her hands in his. "They won't let anyone get close to there. The best you could do is to get to one of the rooms they have set up for families, one in New York, one in London."

"Take me."

"Suse, it would be a mad house. Reporters would be all over you."

"I don't care."

"And you wouldn't know any more than you do now. I have them keeping me informed. I've talked with the officials. The best thing to do is stay right here."

She shook her head. Sniffed. Wiped at her eyes. Adam held her in.

Evan was relieved to have help. Their producer, their friend, was calmer than he was himself. He'd thought to call whoever needed to be called already. Or at least he said he had. Maybe it was a cover to calm her down, but Evan figured it was true.

He heard the phone continue to ring. Someone had been answering. Or not. He wasn't sure. Damned reporters. They were still outside the building, he was sure, although he hadn't seen them when Adam came in. Maybe Beau held them back. Or the police cleared them out. They could keep them off the property but not off the sidewalk or the street.

Mike called his name, holding the receiver in one hand and muffling it with the other. "It's Gene. Asking to talk to Susie."

Gene. Duncan's father. His whole being cringed. Evan forced himself up. She wouldn't talk now. She couldn't. He wasn't sure if he could. Not to anyone but Duncan's family. Anyone else could leave them the hell alone. Accepting the receiver, he looked back at where Susie still appeared somewhat calm in Adam's protective hold, and moved around into the kitchen. "Mr. McGuire, it's Evan."

"Evan. How is she?"

He swallowed and grabbed a deep breath. "She's ... in shock. A few of us are here with her. Danielle is downstairs. She doesn't know yet." He paused, gathering himself. "I'm sorry." It was too lame. Sorry wasn't good enough. "Are you ... all of you..."

"We will be comin' over. As soon as we can arrange it." His voice showed his despair. "Can I speak with her a minute?"

"I ... I don't know if she will. She's... We've called Doc, for something to help calm her. He's not here yet. There are crowds outside the building. She keeps asking me to take her to him."

"Are you all right?"

Something about Duncan's father asking if he was all right was one thing too much. He couldn't answer; he pressed a hand against his eyes. And Mike took the phone with a hand on his arm. Evan slumped into a kitchen chair. He couldn't go out there. He couldn't see her like that, knowing how it was torture for her to try to accept ... not having him.

Evan couldn't imagine how she'd get over this. She'd been through a hell of a lot already, and she kept going, but this... They were soul mates. She was never quite herself when he was away, even for a day's work. This ... this would destroy her, if they didn't prevent it. And Danielle.

Danielle. So completely stuck to her dad. How would she handle this?

"Evan."

Doc's voice and hand on his shoulder raised his head. He saw him twist open a white cap on a brown bottle and hand him a little blue pill. "Take this. Mike, get him a glass of water."

"No." Evan didn't want it. He didn't need...

"I already gave one to Susie. It's just enough to help you relax a little, not enough to bother you."

With Doc's pushing, he lifted his hand to accept, not sure he would accept until he noticed his hand shake. She couldn't see that. So he took the glass from Mike and swallowed the pill. For her. He grabbed a deep breath. For her, he would act like it was all going to be fine. No matter how he didn't believe it.

Composing himself with a fake front as he did after losing Jeremy, Evan returned to the living room. She was sitting beside Ali, watching the damned news again, rocking back and forth, her eyes glossy. He wasn't about to lose her like that, let her fade into despair. It wasn't going to happen.

He strode up to the television and shoved the switch off, catching her as she flew toward him to try to turn it on again. "No." He grabbed her hands as she swung at his chest. "*No. Suse, no.* You are *not* going to sit and watch that. *Stop* it." She kept trying to get away from him. "*Stop it!*" He knew the others were staring at him like he was insane, but he wouldn't pander to her. They shouldn't be, and he wouldn't. Doc spoke to him, told him to let her be if it helped calm her.

"It's not calming her. It's eating into her. *Leave* it off." He pulled his head back when she struggled harder in order to keep hers from hitting him, and grabbed her in a tight hug that strapped her arms in against his chest. "Stop it, Suse. Stop fighting me. I'm not letting go. You know I'm not letting go."

With a gasp for breath, she stopped and sank in against him; her tears wet his shirt with large sobs, her body shook.

"I know." He swallowed to fight his own emotions. "I know, Angel. But I'm here. And I'll get you through this. I'm here." Loosening his grasp, he reached up to stroke her hair and held her while she released as much as she could release. Finally, her hands slipped around to his sides, fingers clenched his shirt. "Did you sleep at all last night?" He lowered his voice, tried to make it as soothing as possible. Her head shook. "I expected you didn't. Come lie down."

"No."

"Angel..."

"No, I can't ... be there ... without him. I can't."

"Okay. Then come next door with me. Get out of here a while. I'll get you some hot tea." Her head shook again and he caressed her back. "Or I'll just sit with you. Whatever you want. No TV. Just come over with me and rest."

"Nella..."

Evan looked over at Doug.

"She's playing with Keith. Kate and Ali are there."

"Keith's entertaining her." Evan repeated it into her ear in case she didn't hear Doug. "She loves being with him. She's fine."

"She doesn't know..."

"No."

"I don't want her to know."

"We'll wait until you're okay to talk to her."

"No." She raised her face to his. "No, she can't know. She thinks he's on a trip ... with Danny. She can't know. Until he comes home. She'll be too scared."

"Angel, he's not coming home. You heard them."

"He is. I don't care. He is, Evan. He is."

With a glance at Doc, he decided not to argue with her. She was more calm, breathing almost normally, talking to him. It was enough for the moment. "Come next door with me a while. If you want, someone here can watch the news to keep up. Just come with me." With her agreement, or at least without a fight, Evan led her across the hall. Doc went with them, and Stu. Evan didn't know when he'd come back up but he had his eyes on her, concerned, hurt. He offered to go put water on for tea as soon as they got next door. Evan wasn't sure she'd take it.

Before it was ready, she was drowsing against his shoulder, her arm wrapped in his. He had no idea what to say, so he remained silent, noticed her grip loosen, her body grow heavy. When she fell asleep against him, he shifted carefully to lay her on a pillow and pulled a warm blanket over top. Her face wasn't peaceful as it normally was when she slept. It showed pain. Grief. Defeat. Everything about her looked defeated.

Take me to him. She'd begged him, expected him to ... do what? Go fly over the scene so she could see for herself? Go to one of the information areas for families to see them all grieving, to hear it from some stranger? No. He couldn't let her do it.

"Are you all right?"

He saw Mike in a haze. It wasn't real. A nightmare. He only needed to wake up.

"Hey, come on, Evan. Sit." Mike tugged at him.

He didn't move. He had to wake up. Mike got him to a chair, nearly pushed him in it. A nightmare. Nothing more. What was it telling him? He rubbed his eyes, opened them. They were open. And they stung. He rolled his neck to loosen the muscles.

Mike crouched in front of him. "Ev, I am... Damn I know this hurts like hell. It does for me and I wasn't as close... I'm sorry, man. This is bullshit. This shouldn't have happened." He set a hand over Evan's arm. "I'll take charge for a while, all right? Just ... Doug and I can handle things. Stu ... I doubt Stu will be very useful but we'll handle things. Just get yourself through it. And Susie. Danielle." His voice caught. "Keith will help Danielle."

Evan swallowed again, took a deep breath, clenched his eyes as he raised his head toward the ceiling. It *was* bullshit. Mike was right. Not a nightmare. Mike was fucking right. It was bullshit. He felt Mike get up, move away. He forced his eyes open again, looked over at Susie. Get her through it. Right. Get her through it. That had to be his first thought; it had to consume what energy he could find. She was supposed to be on the flight. And Nella. He nearly lost all of them. He thanked God they didn't go.

"Adam's still next door. He's cancelling our appearances." Mike moved in front of him again. Appearances. There would have to be some kind of statement from the band, he supposed. Adam would handle it. If the album didn't sell, it didn't. He wasn't doing any damned appearances. Not without his friend.

Mike shoved a beer at him.

"No."

"Evan, it's going to be a long haul getting her and Nella through this when it's already so hard on you, on all of us. Use whatever you need to get through it."

"My stomach already hurts like hell."

"Right. Want a ginger ale? Something else?"

"You don't have to wait on me. I'll get something if I want it." The door opened. Doc. With his mom. How was she there so fast? He made himself stand. His legs barely held him.

"Don't drink that on top of what I gave you." Doc took the bottle from Mike and set it aside. "It's a mild tranquilizer but still a tranquilizer."

His mom interrupted with a hug. "Honey, I am so sorry." She set a hand on the back of his head. "I never wanted you to go through this like I did. I'm so sorry. He was such a good friend."

Evan politely shrugged away and checked to make sure Susie was still asleep. He put his focus on Doc. "She's already gone from shock to denial." He rubbed his neck. "She says he's coming home. There were no survivors. I told her, but... This is..." He grabbed a deep breath.

"Have you eaten yet?" His mom rubbed his arm as though trying to find life in it. "This morning. Have you had breakfast?"

"No. I'm not..." He thought of Susie's resistance to eating the food brought by well-wishers after they lost Jeremy. Funeral food. She called it funeral food and wouldn't touch it, whatever it was. He would have to make sure people didn't...

"Honey, come on in the kitchen. I'll make you something."

"No, I'm ... if she wakes up, I..."

"Mike's here. Come eat and we'll have something ready for her when she wakes up."

"No funeral food."

"What?"

He shook his head, trying to clear it. "Nothing."

Starting to argue when she told him to sit and let her take care of it, he gave in and slumped at the table. A strange half-numb feeling settled in. He shouldn't feel so ... whatever Doc gave him. He wouldn't take it again. He didn't want to feel numb. He wanted... He wanted to go outside and scream as loud and as long as he could. To yell how unfair it was. How she didn't deserve to lose her husband, too. Her mom, her sister, her dad who was almost always at work, Jeremy... She didn't deserve this, too.

"Evan." Adam sat next to him. Mike was at the kitchen entrance, arms crossed, lost in his own apartment. "If there's anything I can do..."

"I'm not doing any damned appearances."

"No. They're already being cancelled. Don't worry about business details. I'll take care of it. And anything else you need that I can do, tell me. I am so sorry. I know how close you were."

"The McGuires will be coming in soon. They're making arrangements. I don't want them hassled by... I'm guessing they're still outside the building. Reporters."

"Yes, but mostly they're fans. Grieving. Trying to show their support. I know it's not what any of you want right now, but they are trying to show their support. It's hurt them, also, and I'm sure there will be more in the days to come."

Fans. Grieving. He hadn't thought of it yet. Pushing himself up from the table, he went back to the living room, to the window that overlooked the street. He didn't get close since he didn't want to be seen. Tons of them. In black. Some crying, hugging each other, holding signs with Duncan's name. And they saw him, or at least they saw the curtain move. Their eyes shifted to the window. Saying something he couldn't hear. He walked away from it to go sit in the chair closest to Susie, to watch her sleep.

The drug was apparently making her numb enough to sleep, also. It was good. Exhaustion would make it worse. If there was a worse. Leaning back, he let his head drop against the chair and closed his eyes.

"Honey, come eat." His mom's voice pulled him from a haze. "Then you should lie down a while. The next few days will be hard. Rest when you can."

Few days. Only the next few days? He knew better. But he followed her and forced the eggs and pancakes he didn't want. They would help counteract the drug, though, help him be sharper, less foggy.

Evan woke with a start. With some convincing, he'd gone in to lie down after he ate, more to get away from everyone's good intentions than to sleep. But he had. He hoped she still was.

Bolting up, he went to the living room and heard someone ask how he felt, if he wanted coffee. The questions barely registered as he moved to the couch. She was stirring, breathing hard, her eyes squeezed together as though she was in pain.

Mike took his side. "The McGuires called in. They're on a plane now."

"Where's Danielle?" He kept his eyes on Susie. She turned, and turned back.

"With Ali. She said she'd be here all day, not to worry about Nella."

Susie stirred again. Pain covered her face. Evan went to her and set a hand aside her head, stroked her hair. She calmed, her breath slowed. He shoved moisture from his eyes and went to get coffee.

"Would have done that for you." Doug followed. Evan couldn't answer. He wanted to ... run. To change into his sweats and running shoes and ... go out and run, with Duncan. He grabbed a deep, shaky breath.

"Don't hold it all in." Doug moved close, watching him. "It's going to be hard enough. She's going to have a hell of a time with this. That's going to make it harder on you, too. Don't try to act like you're fine when you're only around us. We know you aren't."

He set the cup on the counter and rubbed at his eyes. Felt his shoulders shake. Doug hugged him. At first Evan thought to back off. He didn't... A hard time. She would have a hard time? That was an understatement if he ever heard one. He had no choice but to act fine. For her. To try to make her think it would be all right when they both knew it wouldn't be.

He yanked control of himself and backed away, wiped his face. "Heard from her dad?"

"Yes. He's in Nevada. Trying to get a flight out."

Hell of a time for him to be so far away. Evan retrieved his cup and took a large swallow. Not strong enough. But hot. It nearly burned his throat. "How'd Mom get here so fast?"

"I think she was already in town. She came with Doc."

He hadn't noticed. With a smaller sip of his coffee, he heard her voice. Susie's. He grabbed another breath and went to her. She jerked to sitting.

"Hey." Evan set his coffee on the table and touched her head.

"A nightmare. I..." Breathing hard, she scanned the room. Along with Mike and Doug, Kate was there, and Robin, Adam's girlfriend, but not Adam.

"Suse." He watched her realization that it wasn't a nightmare.

"No." She shook her head. "No. Evan..."

He held her in, tight, cradling her head against his shoulder. Her body shook. At least he thought it was hers. And at least she wasn't fighting him anymore. Part of him wished she would. It was easier to take than her acceptance. Her grief.

"Here, Suse."

Doug offered coffee. She looked up at him, but only stared.

"Want eggs? I'm warming pancakes for you."

She shook her head.

"I know you don't want to eat, but you need to. So eggs with them or not?"

She pressed her face back into Evan's shoulder.

"Yes." He answered for her. "She'll need the protein." He accepted her coffee and convinced her to take a couple of sips. He knew what Doug was doing, trying to normalize her. Evan doubted it would work. He took her cup when it shook too much and set it aside. "The McGuires are on their way."

Her eyes widened, her head shook. "No."

"Angel..."

"No, they should stay there. He ... he's closer to there and he'll need them..."

"Suse, stop. Look at me." He gripped both sides of her head. "There were no survivors."

"No, Evan. They're wrong. I know they're wrong. He's coming home."

A deep breath overtook his body. Denial. One of the stages of grief. He remembered it well, both when his dad left them and when they lost Jeremy. She needed time. It was less a shock to the system to work into acceptance. "Here." He gave her the cup again, hoped the warmth would soothe her, kept hold of it since her hands shook.

"Nella..." She looked around the room again.

Kate came over and sat next to her. "She's at my place with Ali and Keith and Stu. They're making cookies. We told her you don't feel good so she's making you cookies." Kate rubbed her back. "It's going to be okay, Suse. We're all here. I'm so sorry..."

"He's coming home."

Kate grimaced and looked at Evan.

He got up. "Come on."

"No, I..."

He pulled her from the couch and into the kitchen. Held a chair for her. Kate brought their coffee in and Doug set a plate in front of Susie. She only stared at it.

"Don't make me force feed you. You know I will. He told me to take care of you, so whatever it takes..."

She moved her eyes to him. Then threw her arms around his shoulders. "Help me find him, Lee."

He didn't want to argue with her now. He wanted to help her get on her feet. "I'd do anything I can for you, for both of you. You know that. Right now, you need to get something in your system to help counter-act the nerve pill Doc gave you."

"The what?"

She didn't remember taking it. He wasn't horribly surprised. "It helped you sleep. But eat now."

Susie managed to force herself to eat about half of what Doug gave her, which wasn't enough, but he wouldn't push yet. He would push if he had to, but not yet. They went back to the couch and she cuddled into the corner of it, pulling the blanket over her legs. They talked around her, tried to pull her in. Adam came back and gave her a long hug. Kate went down to relieve Ali with the kids and send cookies up.

Susie didn't want them. She gave her head a light shake and continued to stare at nothing.

"Nella is asking about you." Alison set the plate on the coffee table. "We told her you weren't feeling well and were resting. She thinks she gave you her cold."

"At least it wasn't a lie." She took a swallow of coffee.

Evan studied her. "You don't feel well?"

"Good. I don't feel good. As often as you corrected me about that and you got it wrong?"

"A test." He gave her a forced grin and set a hand against her forehead. "You don't feel hot."

"I usually don't. Forget that, too?" Another swallow. "My muscles ache. Started late last night. I hope I didn't give it to Duncan. He'll..." She grabbed a deep breath and clenched her eyes.

Evan set an arm around her. "You should lie down and try to get over it before his family comes. If you'd rather stay here, you can use my room."

"I want to go home."

"Okay."

"Come with me."

"Of course." He stood and started to take their cups to the kitchen.

"We'll get it." Doug took them. "And Stu is doing fine with Nella. They're keeping each other entertained."

Stu. Evan knew he was going to have major issues with this, also. They'd become very close and Stu was ... not good with loss. Or anything close to it. He wasn't recovered yet from losing Kara. It would have been helpful if she was still here with him. He supposed Doug and Ali would keep an eye on him, though.

"Where's Dad? I thought he was..."

Evan opened the door for her and set a hand on her back. "On his way."

She nodded and let him lead her to her room and pull the blanket over. "Evan."

He sat beside her and stroked her head.

"Wake me up. If you hear anything. Wake me up." A tear ran down her face.

"I will." He wiped it away and kissed her head and continued to stroke her hair until she fell asleep. Maybe her illness was a blessing, as Danielle's had been. It would force sleep.

Stu had to walk away.

Nella kept talking about her daddy, how she would go to *Sco'land* to meet him and see her uncle Danny and... And he'd kept changing the subject, but it got to him. He had to walk away. Kate was with her. Stu couldn't be. Not until he pulled himself together.

He slammed the front door of his apartment behind him then the door to his room and flopped onto his bed. "*Damn* it, this is fucking *wrong*." He spoke to the ceiling. Not the ceiling. He knew who he was talking to. And then he cringed at cursing. He knew better. His dad would yell.

With a big shaky inhalation that hurt his lungs, he dropped his arms over his face. Heard the phone ring. Refused to get up to answer. He didn't care who it was. He didn't want to talk to anyone. When it wouldn't stop, he went out and yanked the cord from the wall. Anything he needed to hear, he'd get from Adam. Everyone else could leave him the fuck alone.

He grabbed another breath as he fell back on his bed. The anger wouldn't help. His dad had told him over and over the anger wouldn't help. It didn't change anything. But it was the best he could do. He *was* angry. It was *wrong*. Duncan. Not Duncan. Damn. Why him?

"It's *fucking* wrong. Yes, I'm angry. I have a *right* to be." Stu clenched his teeth, breathed hard and heavy, to regain control. He hadn't been so angry since ... since then. Since he'd lost the one person who made the most sense to him. Slowly. Withering away far too young in that damned hospital. He should have survived it. No matter what anyone said, no matter how young Stu had been at the time, he knew. They made it worse, not better. He hated those places with a passion. Even if hate was wrong, as his dad told him. Still. He hated those places.

And he hated injustice. This ... losing Duncan. It was injustice. Yes, he was angry. Furious. Duncan's death made just as much sense as... Actually, he was much like him. Why Duncan, too? Why?

And there was, again, nothing he could do about it.

He heard the knock. Ignored it. Anyone he wanted to see or could stand to see right now had a key. Anyone else could go the fuck away. Another knock. Soft. He didn't care. Susie had a key. But she wouldn't be there. She... He pushed moisture from his eyes. He could do something. He could help her, however possible. He would help her deal with it, go on, try to be happy again at some point. Whatever happened with the band now, Stu would hang with Susie until he was sure she was okay.

"Stu?"

He looked over at the soft voice. Kara stepped just inside his room. Hell. He forgot she had a key. "Not now. Go home. Back to your fiancé." He turned away from her.

She came over and sat on his bed, touched his arm. "Stu, I just ... I wanted to be sure you're all right. You were so close to him. You loved him so. I know you did."

"Go away. You can't be here."

She ran her hand up to his shoulder, leaned in, cuddled next to him.

"I'm sorry. For everything. And I have to know you're all right."

He turned to face her. His Kara. The woman he thought he'd have forever. She'd left him. Walked out. But she was back. And so beautiful. So concerned. It was all over her face. He moved in and kissed her. Hard. Pulled her against him. It was wrong. He knew it was. But he didn't care. Wrong didn't seem to matter. It didn't keep anything from happening.

"Stu." She moved back a touch. "No, we can't. I just..."

Doug kissed Ali and said he'd be back. He wanted to check on his friend.

The door was unlocked. The door to his room was open. Doug went over to check ... and stopped. Backed out again. Kara. Just outside the door, he debated. She couldn't be there. In bed with him. Still engaged. He couldn't make himself interrupt, though. It was too late to matter. This time.

Doug went to the kitchen and paced. Why in the hell was she there? He could call Mike down. Mike wouldn't hesitate to interrupt and kick her out. But it was best left between the two of them. Maybe he could keep anyone else from finding out.

He grabbed a beer and went to the couch to wait. She wouldn't stay long. Unless she was actually staying, which he doubted. He got up again to lock the front door. No one else needed to find out. He'd take care of it, as he'd told Evan he would.

Not sure to be glad whether or not he was right, he held Kara's eyes when she came out, alone, and startled at seeing him. "Why are you here?" He didn't bother to get up.

"I came to check on him."

"That's what you were doing?"

She at least had the sense to look ashamed.

"Are you staying with him? Coming back?"

"No." She shifted her bag on her shoulder and moved closer, her voice quiet. "I'm engaged. I can't."

"Then why are you here?"

"I knew he'd be devastated, and..."

"Did you tell him you weren't staying? You weren't coming back?"

"I ... didn't have the chance. I'm sorry. I never meant for that to happen. I tried to back him away but he... I didn't mean for it to happen."

"You didn't mean too hard for it not to, either." Doug stood.

"I love him, Doug. You know I do."

"Then come back to him."

"I can't. I'm engaged. My fiancé is a well known fashion photographer, and well liked. It would destroy my career. Even if Stu would leave the band or if it stops now, I can't. It would ruin me."

As he figured. Doug didn't even want her to come back. She was too self-focused for Stu. His welfare never mattered to her like her own did. "Stay away from him. And don't tell anyone you saw him. Tell them, since they saw you come in, that he wouldn't see you. If you say anything other than that, I will counter it."

"It's a lie."

"You want your fiancé to know what really happened? Tell them Stu wouldn't see you. I'll make sure he stays quiet. Leave him alone and don't come back. By the way, I want the key." He held his hand out and waited until she placed it in his palm.

She apologized again and said she was sorry about Duncan and wished them all well. He didn't answer. As the door closed, he checked on Stu. Asleep. Doug figured it was a good thing. He turned the key over in his fingers, then set it on Stu's dresser and closed his door.

Groaning at her aching muscles and encompassing fatigue, Susie turned to her husband's side of the bed and ran her hand over his pillow. She moved enough to smell his scent on it and gripped it against her chest. He wasn't gone. He couldn't be. They'd had only four years. Four years of being together. Nearly four years of marriage. September. Their anniversary was in two months. She'd planned to take him away. Back to Maine, the two of them. She'd arranged the schedule with Adam already, swore him to secrecy. They would start at the cabin as they did on their wedding night and drive up to Maine to walk on the beach and eat lobster and... Her body convulsed in sobs. He would be back by then. They would still go. He'd be fine. He had to be.

With that thought in her head, she forced herself out of bed, grabbed fresh clothes, and headed to the shower. She needed a long, hot shower to steam out the virus and ... and try to calm her nerves. He would be home. She knew he would be home. But it hurt like hell to know what he might be going through to hang on, to return to her, to his daughter.

She held her head under the water and let the tears fall with it.

And then she backed up, took a deep breath and refused further tears. Danielle needed her. She had to let her know everything would be okay. Scrubbing her hands over her face, she realized she was cold and too exhausted to stand up, so she pushed the shower faucet all the way to the hottest position and plugged the tub. She was cold. It was mid July. She shouldn't be so cold. She watched the water gather at her feet, remembering how he had treated her high fever while they were dating by filling the tub with cool water and setting her in it, pajamas and all. She'd been surprised not to be embarrassed that he saw her with wet pajamas clinging to her skin, although they hadn't been that close yet, he'd never seen quite that much of her. She hadn't cared. It could have been the fever, she supposed. It was high enough to make her fuzzy and somewhat numb. Kind of like she felt before the nap, the dullness of the ache in her brain instead of the sharp torture of ... no, not grief, worry. She didn't need grief. He was coming home.

Pulling from her reverie, she realized the water was too hot for her feet and ankles and turned it cooler until she could stand to lower her body into it. She turned it off when it was three quarters full and leaned her head back against the hard porcelain.

A pounding on the door opened her eyes.

"Suse? Hey. *Answer* me."

Evan. The water was cooler, nearly too cool.

"*Susie.*" Fear reflected in his voice as he cracked the door open.

"I'm okay."

A pause. "Are you awake?"

"Yeah. I'm getting out." She'd scared him. She'd fallen asleep. She never did that. With a shiver, she pushed out of the water, pulled the drain, and dried quickly, trying to warm the skin that had been nearly too warm a minute ago, or what felt like a minute ago.

He was standing beside the door when she opened it. "You fell asleep." He wasn't asking. He knew.

"I ... I was cold. Just trying to warm up."

He touched her arm. "And you're cold again. Nella's been nearly throwing a fit wanting to see you. Come sit with her a while and then we'll distract her again so you can rest."

"She doesn't know?"

"No. Suse, we won't tell her. We know that has to be from you."

She decided to let it go. Her daughter thought he was on a trip. She would keep it that way, at least for the time being.

She was too calm.

Evan picked at his own meal — hamburgers and fried potatoes his mom had made at Nella's request — and tried not to study his friend too hard. But she was calm, much calmer than he felt. Maybe it was body aches from the virus. Maybe Doc had left her more pills for her nerves as he'd tried to do for Evan. But it wouldn't last. People came and went. The phone continued to ring incessantly until Evan unplugged it. Roy came in while Adam was there to protest that they'd stopped all album promo. Adam and Mike shoved him back out before Evan could get to him. Janet came, with her new baby, to give Susie her condolences. Susie wouldn't go near either of them. Doug told Janet she was sick and keeping germs to herself. Flowers were delivered from acquaintances and strangers, fans, with their sympathies, and were rerouted across the hall to keep Danielle from asking questions. The girl asked to call her dad several times. Still, Susie was calm.

Too calm. It worried him. She still said he was coming home. Throughout the day, it was apparent no one from the plane would go home alive. She wouldn't listen.

Danielle stared at her often, and often with a frown. She gave her hugs and told her to feel better and she was sorry she made her sick. Susie held her in, closed her eyes, and said that was a mom's job, not to worry. Much of the day Stu kept Nella downstairs. He couldn't be around Susie. Every time Stu looked at her, his eyes watered and he turned away. Evan couldn't think about his own pain at the moment. He had to think of her. Of her daughter. Of Duncan making him promise to take care of them. Of the McGuires who would be there late the next morning.

He had to brace himself for that. For Duncan's mom. For Laura.

The thought of it nearly made him lose his own control and he focused on the potatoes. Not fries as Nella wanted, but close enough, his mom said. Evan was grateful for her presence, his mom's. She kept conversation neutral, chatting with Danielle mainly, checking Susie's forehead to be sure a fever didn't develop, setting a hand occasionally on Evan's arm, only enough to say she understood.

After dinner, they put *Superman* in the Betamax. Trying to normalize. Susie curled up on one side of him and leaned against his shoulder while Nella took his other side. They were his now, his to look after. He'd promised Duncan.

Lying in Susie's guest room, Evan stared at the ceiling. He would get up early so Danielle wouldn't know he stayed all night. She was worried enough, reading into her mom's emotions to know it was more than a cold. Susie would have to tell her. She would be too confused otherwise, which he figured would be more scary than facing the truth.

She would have to tell her before the McGuires came, since Danny would be there when her daddy wasn't, and they were supposed to be on a trip together. Maybe it would be easier for her to say it after the McGuires were there for extra support.

Mike had warned them about the fans on the sidewalks. They were still there holding candles and small flashlights. It was nice, he supposed. Susie had wandered over to look out at them now and then, standing back far enough they wouldn't see her while it was still light out. As dusk fell, she avoided any chance of them seeing even her shadow through the curtains. It worried Evan how carefully she avoided it, as though afraid of what they would do. They were showing support. And grief. Nothing more. He thought about stepping outside to thank them, to return the support, but he couldn't quite do it. Adam did, he knew; he'd talked to them. It was enough for now.

The McGuires said they wouldn't speak to anyone since it would be hard to know which might be reporters and the band had yet to make any public statement.

Greg and Steve called during one of the times the phone was plugged in for John to get through. And Lisa. Evan told the Blue River gang to hang on until they knew what was happening and when. He couldn't imagine Susie trying to get through funeral arrangements, although it wouldn't actually be a funeral since there was no ... since they hadn't found him. Adam mentioned a memorial service and offered his assistance setting it up. Susie wouldn't listen.

A disturbance in the hallway night light drew his attention. His imagination? Possibly. He was exhausted. Still, he decided to check.

Her door was open more than it had been, so he nudged quietly toward the living room. When he spoke her name, her head turned from where she sat on the window seat he'd built for her under the bow window that overlooked the street. She had the curtain pulled open just enough to look out.

Joining her, he sat on the other side. With the house lights off, if they were seen, it would be only shadows. "Beautiful, isn't it?"

She flashed her gaze at him. The dark bags under her eyes dispelled the anger she tried to show.

He refused to let it get to him. "The candles in the dark, all of the well-wishing that shows how he mattered to them. It's..."

"They didn't know him." Her voice was flat, and she looked out again. "They don't know him. They're ... they shouldn't be here. Tell Adam to make them go away."

"Angel." He adjusted closer to grasp her hand. "They're his fans. They respect what he does, what he did, what they saw of who he was. They mean well."

"But he's coming home. This ... they don't need to do this. It looks like ... like they've given up. I don't want to see them giving up on him. He's coming home."

Evan wasn't sure how to answer. She couldn't honestly think that was true. Out in the cold waters of the Atlantic too far from the coast of Ireland to ever be able to swim that far even if he was a strong swimmer ... the image of competing with Duncan out at the beach a couple of years back grabbed at him. Not a couple of years. Nearly five. Before he married Susie, when he was still showing off for her. Despite what he said, Duncan had been showing off for her. And it worked. Her eyes hardly left him as he teased Evan and dried off. Evan could still clearly see the way she looked at Duncan. Always. She'd been fully wrapped up in him since they day they met. Like a moth to a flame. A beautiful fragile butterfly to a full-burning flame. It had always worried him, although he expected ... a different result.

Grabbing a deep breath, he stood. "Come on, Suse, you need to sleep."

"I can't."

"Doc left you more nerve pills. Maybe you should..."

"No. Evan, no, he's out there, cold, alone, and they aren't looking hard enough. They should have found him by now. He's..."

"Suse." He touched her chin to raise her eyes to his. "You know he's not coming back. If they haven't already..."

"No, Evan. He is. I know he is." Her eyes were calm, unwavering.

Denial. It was normal. Tomorrow the McGuires would be there, and her dad. She'd start dealing with the truth then. "Come to bed. Exhausting yourself won't help anything."

"No. I want to wait. I'm not giving up. I won't."

"He told me to take care of you. Remember? When he left..." Evan had to swallow his emotions back. "He told me to take care of you and Danielle while he was away. Let me do that. I wish I could do more. But at least let me do that."

She stared out the window again. "I can't be in there alone. I can't."

A beautiful fragile butterfly. Her wings drooped. But her courage was intact. For how long? "I'll stay with you."

She didn't answer. Didn't move.

Evan lifted her into his arms, with barely any protest. She let her head fall to his shoulder. Her breathing was hard, slow. Exhausted to her core. He couldn't quite take her to her bed, Duncan's bed, so he returned to the guest room and helped her slip under the covers. He lay beside her, over top of the covers, and cuddled her in.

17 July

"My *Evan Lee*. You here 'ready."

Evan turned from the kitchen counter where he was stirring pancake mix and grinned at the girl. She was in her favorite pajamas, a purple tank and shorts set that left her adorable little girl legs sticking out, and curls jutted from the rest of her hair. "Hey little one. How are you feeling this morning?"

"My ear all better now. Yes. We go Sco'land 'day, find Daddy and Uncle Danny?"

He crouched as she came over and swept her into a hug. "No, we can't go to Scotland today. I'll take you another time." Duncan had made him promise that, too.

"I feel all better. Yes." She stuck fingers in her ears. "No' hurt."

"Good. I'm glad you do."

"My mummy still sleepy. I look at her. Quiet, yes. I not wake her. I give mummy my ear cold." Nella frowned.

"It's okay, baby, she'll be fine." Relatively. He stood. "How about chocolate chip pancakes?"

"Yes!"

"Shh, Nella, don't wake your mom." He rubbed a hand through her hair. "How about you go get dressed. Then bring me a hairbrush and we'll try to tame this bird's nest."

"I not have nest of birdies in my hair." She pushed both hands through it. "No."

"You will have if you don't get it brushed. Run on, now. Pancakes will be ready soon."

With another frown and more playing in her hair, she jumped at a knock at the door and headed that direction. Evan followed. The chain was locked, but he didn't want any chance of a reporter getting a photo of her in her pajamas. Or at all. Susie would throw a fit. Especially now.

Glad it was only his mom and Doc, Evan waited through Nella explaining about chocolate pancakes and no birdies in her hair and then sent her off to get dressed. Doc asked if Susie slept well. He had to admit she didn't, but he didn't say he slept beside her.

"I hate to give her anything stronger."

"She won't take it. She's still convinced he's coming back and ... at least she was last night. Maybe today when his family comes..." He left the sentence unfinished and turned the stove on to heat the pan. "Have you heard from John? She asked again last night where he was."

"He called." His mom rubbed his back. "Apparently someone remembered who he was from some photo of him with Susie and he was hounded at the airport trying to get to his connecting flight. He missed it and the next was delayed for fog. He's still trying to get here. I'm sure he will be soon. Let me do that for you."

Evan refused to relinquish the cooking duties. It gave him something to do with his hands, something else to think about. John was hassled at the airport. She couldn't know. He asked them not to tell her. And he told them Danielle didn't know yet.

He stopped when the little brunette bounced back into the kitchen in a purple and pink tie-dyed shirt and blue pants with orange polka dots. "That doesn't match, little one. What happened to the sets your mom has put together for you?"

She looked down at herself. "No. I like this."

Evan imagined she'd stirred them up again, made her drawer look like a tornado hit it, which always exasperated Susie. "I bet you'll have to try again."

"No. I dress by myself. Yes."

"Nella." He crouched in front of her. "Your mom doesn't feel good. She still has the cold and she's tired. How about we just say yes to her today and not make her upset."

She frowned. His mom cut in. "Go get the hairbrush and we'll change those clothes after breakfast."

As they were finishing, in silence other than Danielle's chatter, Evan realized what she'd said. Nella had gone to check on her mom. Susie was still in the guest room when Evan got up. Did Nella find her there?

Setting his plate in the sink and leaving them to entertain her, he went to check. She was in her own room, staring at the ceiling with Duncan's pillow wrapped in her arms. Evan grabbed a deep breath and knocked lightly. When she only flicked her eyes over in response, he went in and closed the door. Danielle didn't need to see him sitting on her mom's bed.

"Feel any better today?" He brushed fingers through her bangs while checking the heat of her forehead. It felt normal. "Nella had breakfast. Mom and Doc are here. Ready to get up and eat?"

"I shouldn't have let him go. I told him to go." A single tear slid down her face.

Evan wiped it away. "Don't do that to yourself. Don't even think it."

"He asked... He wanted me to tell him to stay. I didn't. I..."

"Shh, Suse. Don't." He leaned closer and held her in. At least she was starting to accept it. He supposed it was good. "He knew you were doing it for him, for Danny. Don't do this to yourself. It won't bring him back."

Her fingers tightened against where she gripped his sides. "I want him home."

"I know. Angel, I know. So do I." He held her quietly for a while and then leaned back to brush more moisture from her face. "But I'll be here for you. For Nella. We all will be." He stroked her hair. "Lean on us as much as you need." He grabbed a deep breath, keeping as much control as he could manage. "You need to tell Nella today. Before his family comes. Or are you waiting until they're here?"

"No. I'm not telling her. He's coming home. He's only ... on a trip.

She doesn't need to know more."

Evan cringed. "Suse, don't do this." He set a hand on her bare arm, realizing she wore the same navy tank and bottoms she'd worn the day she was so sick and Duncan immersed her in the tub. He had to wonder if it was on purpose. And he would not let her get that sick again. "Come on. Get dressed and come eat..."

"No."

"Suse..."

"I don't want to see anyone."

"His family is coming today."

"No. Tell them not to come. If... He's closer to them, to Scotland. He'll go there first. Right? They have to be there."

Evan set his hands alongside her face. "Look at me." He waited for her eyes. "Suse, there were no survivors. He's not coming home. You can't do this to yourself. I know you don't feel good. Go take a hot shower to relax your muscles if you need to. Don't fall asleep again. But steam it out and get dressed and come eat."

She pushed his hands away and lay down, away from him. Where in the hell was John? She needed her dad. Evan needed his help. He was at a loss. She had to accept it. What would it take?

With no choice other than to carry her out of her room, which he didn't want to do with his mom and Nella there, Evan went back to the kitchen. Doc asked if he needed to check her out. He didn't see any need. Neither the virus nor her emotional condition could be cured without time. They could both be numbed, he supposed, but she was touchy about drugs, about anything that threw off her system. More unbalance was the last thing she needed.

He did his best to play host through the morning and early afternoon as people filtered in. Everyone but Stu. Doug said he couldn't yet. Nella went down to harass him a while, with Kate and Keith. Evan couldn't worry about Stu. Doug would have to do that. He tried several times to get Susie to come out, telling her who was there and that she needed to eat. Her stomach was upset, she said. He took her broth, ice water, tea. She refused it all. Kate tried. His mom tried. She wouldn't budge.

Adam tried to talk to him about a memorial service. "And we're going to have to make some kind of statement about the band. I know you don't want to think about it, but we'll have to soon. Whenever you know what you want to say, tell me. I'll take care of it, or I'll set up a press conference…"

Evan walked away. He wasn't doing any damned press conference. The press was in their faces enough. On the phone. Around the building. They already knew everything. What more was there to say?

Mike followed into the kitchen.

"I'm not doing it." Evan shoved away from the counter again to grab the tea. He poured himself a glass and offered one to Mike.

"No, thanks. And you don't have to. Doug and Stu and I can do it in a couple of days. They can wait that long."

"Think Stu's going to be willing?" He took a swallow and focused on the chill of the bitter liquid.

Mike shrugged. "Maybe not. I will, if you want. Or we let Adam handle it. Whatever you think."

"I don't care." He lowered onto a chair, slumping back against it.

"Think she's going to come out here some time today?"

"Couldn't tell you. She won't even talk to me."

"Go take a break, Ev. Go next door, unplug the phone, and lie down."

"I can't." He focused on the cold of the tea, of the glass in his fingers. Trying to stay awake. He'd barely slept, either. She stirred all night. Even when he did start to drowse in between images of what his friend must have gone through, her stirring woke him again. He expected she saw the same images. From the damned television.

"Sure you can. We're here. Nella's downstairs with Keith. You need to sleep."

"I can't leave her. If she gets up, I need to be here." He swallowed more tea, wondered if the Atlantic was as cold, or worse, thought of the cold pools they'd used to push each other, how it bothered Duncan less than it did him. He was *used to it*, his friend always said, brushing it off. Still, however used to it he might have been, the body could only handle so much cold, so much strain. If he'd even had the chance to try.

"We're here for her, too. You need to let us be. Don't let her be too fully dependent on you."

If he had the chance to try. Evan couldn't help but hope he hadn't had to struggle long, that he hadn't been in pain. He shoved a hand through his hair. "You don't understand." He got up. Forced control.

He was at Susie's place. He couldn't let her see his thoughts. If she did get up.

"Yeah, I do." Mike got up beside him. "You're her best friend. I get it. And that's great. But Evan, I know you feel more deeply for her than that and I don't think it's a good idea to..."

"To what?" He jerked his head toward his friend. "Hell, you think I'm going to hit on her now? Are you crazy? He was my best friend, too. As much a brother as Jeremy was. It hurts like hell to know he's not coming back and what he had to deal with and ... I'm not..."

Mike set a hand on his arm. "Hey. That's not what I meant. And I know. What I mean is, you've got to take care of yourself through this. You won't if you're so wrapped up in always being here. We're her friends, too, Ev. She's like a sister to all of us. Don't take it all on yourself."

With a shaky breath so deep it hurt, Evan paced around the kitchen. Yes, Mike was right, but he didn't fully understand. Ever since Susie lost her mom, she'd counted on him. Always. No matter what else happened or who was there. She counted on him.

"Evan."

Laura. At the kitchen entrance. Her eyes were red and puffy and she seemed to be doing all she could just to stand in the doorway. Evan made his way over to her and she wrapped into him. He swallowed hard as he held her, told her how sorry he was. Her body shook. She gripped him hard. "I am sorry." She sniffed in between. "I said I wouldnae do this. Bu'..."

"It's all right." He slid his hand up to hold the back of her head. Duncan's baby sister. As much dependent on him through the years as Susie was on Evan. He would do what he could for Laura now, also. "I'm so sorry, Laura."

She nodded and sniffed, wiped her nose, and raised her eyes to his. She asked about Susie.

He explained that she had a virus and was still in bed but Laura knew it was an excuse. She started to cry again. Danny came to her and took over, sheltered her in his arms, gave Evan and Mike a nod in greeting. Evan was afraid to say anything to him; he looked barely in control of himself and trying hard.

They moved into the living room. Duncan's parents were there, and Aunt Loretta and Collin and Collin's parents and Amy, Danny's girlfriend. Evan made the rounds and expressed his sympathy, gave hugs to Linda and Loretta. And they asked about Susie.

"Let me go see if she's awake." He was glad for the chance to retreat, even for a minute or two. Making his way to her room, he knew he had to get her up. She couldn't hide all day. He couldn't allow it.

She was awake. He sat beside her and touched her forehead. "Still feels okay. Ready to get up? You have to be starving since it's after two."

She shook her head.

"Need pain reliever? How are your aches by now?"

She closed her eyes and turned away from him.

With a deep breath, he lay beside her, cuddling up against her back and holding her tight, cocooning her in her blanket. Evan felt her slow breaths interspersed by sniffs that jolted her body against his. He stroked her hair. "Suse, I would bring him back to you if I could. I know, Angel. I know how you hurt..."

"No, you don't."

His breath paused. She'd at least spoken to him. "Okay, not exactly, but..."

"You don't know. You didn't send him away. You don't think he's still alive. You think... You don't believe he's still out there, struggling to live, with no one willing to look for him. You don't know. You *don't* know how I feel."

"Suse, he's not. They did look. They had a lot of expert searchers..."

"He's still out there."

Where was John? Maybe he would get through to her. He'd lost a spouse. He could help more, know better what to say. Or maybe Duncan's family would. He stroked her hair again. "The McGuires are here. You need to come out and see them."

She pulled into herself, curled up more. Her breathing sped up.

"Come on, Angel."

Her head shook. She resisted him pulling at her.

"You need to eat. Mom made chicken soup, the way you like it, with plenty of ginger. It'll help..."

"No."

Still out there, with no one willing to look. Was that why she wouldn't talk to him? Maybe he could at least fix that. "Okay. Tell you what." Evan half picked her up, enough to make her face him. "I'll hire another crew of rescue searchers. I'll make them look again."

She stopped trying to pull away. "Don't lie to me. You don't believe me. Don't lie to me."

He touched her face. "I would never lie to you. I'll call and find out how to get started, but only if you get up and come talk to his family and eat. You have to do that first."

"You don't believe me."

"I believe you want to believe that. No, I don't think they'll find him, but I'll have them look. And if you're right and they do, I will take you to him, the second they do." He leaned closer. "You know I want that, also, Suse. I want him home. I love him, too."

She bit her lip and tears escaped. Then she fell in against him and held tight.

Susie ached from head to toe. She'd pulled into sweat pants and a big T-shirt, one of Duncan's. By the time she was dressed, she had to sit again. Her body hurt. Her heart hurt more, so much more. Evan would make them look again. They'd find him. She had to get herself well so she had the energy to take care of him. She knew he was hurt. She knew he was. He needed to get home so she could take care of him.

Forcing herself out of her room, she rubbed her eyes dry, took a deep breath, and braced for the impact. She warned them she was sick. It made no difference. They all hugged and hovered until she wanted to explode, to tell everyone to leave her alone. Evan rescued her and took her to the kitchen, helped her sit. Asked again about pain reliever. She didn't want it. The body aches were a distraction.

Duncan's family joined her there. They said Collin and his parents had gone on to the hotel and would be back later. To help make arrangements. She didn't answer.

And she couldn't look at Laura. Her sister's eyes were red. Swollen. Susie couldn't look at it. Danny took the chair beside her, pushed her to eat. She had a hard enough time sitting up. Eating took too much energy. She asked about Nella. Downstairs. Doing fine with Kate and Keith. And Stu. Susie wondered how he was. He'd gotten so close to Duncan.

Her hand shook and she set the spoon down.

Evan set his palm against her forehead. "You're getting warm. You have to eat something. Or at least drink the broth. I'll put it in a cup if that's easier."

She shook her head and gripped his shirt, let her head fall against his stomach as he stood next to her. Evan would hire a new team. They'd find him. She just had to hang on until then. He would be hurt. She'd told him she didn't want to see him that way again, like he was after ... after the mugging when he nearly gave his life for her. But she did. She wanted him home where she could take care of him.

She heard them talk about her cold, about how heavy she was breathing, how hard her body was struggling just to function. But she was used to it. She almost always felt that bad with a cold. They hadn't seen it. And it was just a cold. Duncan. He needed her. And she didn't have the strength to even make it down the stairs by herself, not to mention through the crowd she figured was still there and to ... wherever she needed to go.

"I know you hurt." Evan's voice was as soft as his hand soothing over her head. "But try again, Angel. Just eat a bit and you can try more later."

He would call after she ate. He said he would. She pulled herself using the table and Evan's help, refused to look at anyone, and tried again. He was right. She had to regain strength. To take care of him.

After a few bites, while they talked around her trying not to act like they were staring although she knew they were, Susie was gripped by nausea. She started to get up. Evan argued. She put a hand over her stomach. And he helped her, walked her back to the bathroom. She closed him out, gripped the sink to assist her shaky legs, like the nightmare, the one ... before she was married, when she thought Duncan was leaving her. The white sink. The sweating. The shaking legs. No one there.

She moved to the toilet, bent over just in time. Felt tears run down her cheeks. Forced herself back to the sink as she flushed it down. Ran water over her face. In her mouth. Like in the nightmare. When he wasn't there. When no one was there and she couldn't stand up on her own.

And when she woke in his arms, he promised he would be, that he would be there.

Laura called to her through the door. Susie splashed more water on her face. The door opened as Laura called her name again. Her sister put an arm around her back and turned the water off, grabbed a hand towel to help her dry her face. She tried to guide her out to the couch. Her legs were too weak. Evan picked her up and took her to the couch, set her down gently, wrapped an afghan around her. "I'm calling Doc."

"Danielle had the flu?" Linda. At her side. "We though' it was only a cold bug. No more."

"It was only a cold. This is mainly nerves." Evan touched her forehead again. "And you're even hotter now. If you don't make yourself calm down enough you can eat, I'll have him take you in and put you on an IV. This can't continue. I won't allow it."

She shut him out and closed her eyes. Heard voices around her, but refused to listen. He said he'd be there. He said he would. Always.

Vaguely aware of Doc's voice and his threat to take her to the hospital, Susie gave in and took whatever he handed her. She closed her eyes again. She had to wake up. She had to tell Evan to call. He needed to call. She said his name.

"I'm right here, Angel."

"Call them."

"You haven't eaten."

"I will. Call them."

He leaned in and kissed her head. "I already did. I have someone checking into it. I told them I don't want any delays. Now, can I bring you more soup?"

She didn't want it. But he'd called. Without making her eat first. She nodded.

Evan waited for Nella to ask. The girl ran to Danny and gave him a big hug, then asked where her daddy was. They'd been warned she didn't know, and Susie didn't want her to know yet. Danny managed to say that Duncan had been "pulled away" and couldn't go camping, so they all came there instead.

When she pushed more, Evan interrupted and asked what she'd been doing all day. He quieted her once with a reminder her mom was asleep. Nella tilted her head to look over at Susie then finished talking about the 'boards and Jacks and cartoons and the fire truck show that Evan explained was *Emergency* reruns that Stu taped.

"Where is Stu?" Danny asked Kate.

"Staying out of the way, he said. We tried to get him to come up."

"My Stuey no' get sick like my mummy. No. I give mummy my ear cold." Nella frowned. "I no' give it to Stuey."

"He is stayin' away, now, because he is afraid of germs?"

Evan sent Danielle to get her crayons to bring out and share with Laura. With her out of the room, he explained it wasn't the germs Stu was afraid of.

"Wha' a fuckin' baby." Danny started away. "If I can be here doin' this, so can he."

Evan tried to stop him but Laura jumped up to go with. Maybe it was better. Stu couldn't avoid Susie forever. Linda sat with Nella and colored, holding her close as often as Nella would allow, and at times gazing at her as though looking for Duncan. He was definitely there, in Danielle's face. And in her attitude.

Evan sat and talked with Gene. Quietly. Out of Nella's range. Susie's father-in-law wanted to know everything, how she heard, what she said. While talking, he kept an eye on Danielle. Her coloring got harder, more scribbles than controlled, and she finally slammed her crayon down and came to him, climbed up on his lap. "My daddy nae working. No. My mum nae there too and Nella nae there and Evan Lee and Stuey. No. Nae working. We go an' get my daddy."

The girl was too smart to hold her off. She had to know. He considered telling her, to save Susie from having to do it, but he couldn't go behind her back. "No, he's not working, little one. Your mom will talk to you later, when she feels better." He hugged her. "I'm here for you, Danielle. Always remember that."

She heard voices. Scottish voices. Her family. Duncan's family.

Her body didn't ache quite as much. And she was starving. She started to get up. Nella nearly jumped on top of her.

Stu grabbed the girl. "Give your mom a minute to wake up before you pounce on her, little terror."

Stu was there. Susie ran hands over her face and looked at him. Before she could ask how he was, Danny interrupted, fussed at him for talking to his niece that way. Too many people were there. The room was full. While she was asleep. She should have gone back to her room. Laura sat next to her, felt her head, pronounced it normal as far as she could tell.

Collin. Aunt Loretta. A lot of his family. She closed her eyes again. Tried to find some balance somewhere in her befuddled brain and body. Laura said something. And Gene. But Nella fussed. She wanted her mum.

Susie reached for her and took her on her lap. "What's wrong, sweetie? I'm sorry I slept so much today."

"My daddy nae here. No. Uncle Danny and ... and Stuey and ... and *all* here and my daddy *nae* here. We go an' find my daddy now you 'wake 'gain."

Find her daddy. Yes. Susie nodded. "Yes baby. Soon."

Danielle hugged her tight. It hurt. Her body was still more sore than she'd realized yet.

"Susie." Laura. Still at her side. Her eyes moist. "Y' cannae tell her that."

Of course she could. Danielle was her daughter. Danny interrupted again, convinced Nella to go to him for a few minutes.

Nella stuck to her side through the afternoon, no matter how often someone tried to pull her away so Susie could rest. She didn't need to rest more than she was with her daughter cuddled against her. She was numb. Other than being asleep, she couldn't be more at rest. She listened, more or less. Sometimes she answered someone. Mostly, she was numb. Evan was worried. She could tell he was in the way he watched her. But it was okay. Temporary. They'd go find him, go to him and bring him home as soon as the rescue party found him.

"We go now, my mummy. I' is soon now. Yes."

Soon now? Go. Find Duncan. Nella had been so quiet, Susie forgot she was waiting to go.

Evan told Danielle her mom didn't feel good. She needed to stay home. Nella countered, said he could take her, she'd go with him.

"Nella." Susie squeezed her to rescue Evan. "I know, baby. We should be with daddy. I know."

"Of course y' *shouldnae* be." Laura's eyes widened. "Thank the Lord y' *didnae* go with 'im. I 'ave never in my life been thankful a child was sick, bu' I am now."

Susie felt her head shake. She didn't mean that. She would never put her child at risk knowingly. Evan said as much, that it wasn't what she meant. Linda wrapped her arms around her daughter to calm her and suggested they might make dinner. Susie tried to make herself object. It was her house. She should... but she had no energy. She felt like ... like nothing. Inside or out. She felt nothing. Except protective of her daughter. Her first responsibility was to protect Nella.

Adam came back, with Robin. He asked if he could do anything and she referred him to Evan. Susie managed to talk with Robin enough to be polite. She also talked with her in-laws but avoided looking at them too directly. She didn't want to see their thoughts, didn't want to see the pain of the loss reflected in their eyes. She colored with Danielle for a while. She acknowledged Doug and Ali when they came in and brought dinner. Funeral food.

Her stomach twisted as she stared at the dish.

"No, it's not." Evan lowered to her side and set a hand on her face to pull it away. "I know what you're thinking, and it's not. You're sick. Ali's trying to keep you from having to cook until you feel better."

"How do you know...?"

"I know. And you do need to eat it."

Yes. Ali brought it. Because she was sick. It was hardly the first time. He did know. He knew better than anyone. He was there. She slid her arms up around his shoulders and buried her face in against his chest. Until she calmed enough to release him. And a plate was handed to her. Chicken Tetrazzini. Her favorite thing Ali's mom made. She saw her hands shake as she took it. Saw Evan notice. He kissed her head and rubbed her shoulder.

It would be okay. Evan would help her find him and bring him home. He wanted him home, too. His best friend. He would find him.

Susie congratulated herself on putting her own thoughts behind her as she focused on his family and tried to comfort them. She managed to eat decently. She knew they were all watching her, Evan more than anyone, but she was okay. At least as okay as possible, and that was good enough.

Stu was avoiding her. Ali had to force him to stay and eat. She'd brought plenty. He wasn't okay. He'd hardly said a word. When he sat on the floor against a wall away from everyone, she went over and sat next to him. If Nella hadn't given him the cold, Susie figured she wouldn't. "Hey."

"Feeling better?" He barely glanced at her. "I mean the cold."

"No."

That got his attention. "Not at all?"

"Um, I don't know. I think the pain pill is pretty strong. For me, anyway. I feel kind of ... out of it."

"Yeah, that's probably the nerve pill." He looked away again.

"What?" She hadn't taken anything...

"You know Doc has you on a tranquilizer."

Was that what he gave her? She shook her head. It was the cold making her groggy. Stu looked worried that she didn't know. But Evan would know.

"Suse, you're gonna be okay, right?"

"Yeah."

"Yeah?"

"Just a cold. I have them all the time. You know I do..."

"Not what I meant. And wow you're out of it. He might want to give you something less intense. Or nothing."

He meant Duncan. "Oh. Yes. No, I'm okay. He's coming home, Stu. Hold onto that, okay?"

He started to speak and changed his mind. Instead, he looked over at Danny coming to join them.

"You shouldnae be down here, Sis. We can make space for 'im beside y' on the couch if y' want t' talk."

"No, I'm..." Stu glanced at her again, got up, and left the apartment.

"I didnae mean t' interfere."

"No, it wasn't you. I need coffee. Want some?"

"I will ge' it."

"No. I have to..." She let it go unfinished. She had to move around. She had to do something, other than wait. Evan had called. He'd been on the phone off and on. They'd find him. And Evan would take her to meet him. Even if Stu didn't believe her, or anyone else.

As soon as she had her coffee and took some to Gene, the only one to accept although he followed her to the kitchen and half did it himself, she settled back on the love seat. Where her husband should have been beside her. Susie allowed herself a quick clench of the eyes and jaw before forcing herself to look okay.

Evan moved up beside her and set a hand against her forehead.

"I'm fine. Stop that." She got up again and went to the kitchen. For what, she didn't know. Just to move.

He followed her. "Fine? You're fine?"

"Okay, I'm not fine, but you know what I mean. Don't act like you don't. It's just a cold. I'm not ... I'm not..." Her hands shook while adding water to the tea kettle. He told her there was tea made already and she checked for herself.

"What can I get for you?"

She looked at him but didn't answer.

He took her hands. "Should we go and give you space to be with his family?"

"No." She drew back, her eyes wide. "Don't go. I can't do this alone."

"You're not alone. His family..."

"Is his family. You're mine. I need you here."

Calming her with his agreement, he persuaded her to go back to sit down. The pain reliever seemed to be helping, but she was tired, weak. And too fragile, too close to the edge she was trying to avoid. She leaned her head back against the couch and closed her eyes. Her heavy breaths indicated she was congested, and too tired.

"We will go if y' want to get t' bed early." Linda studied her as she raised her head again, enough to shake it. "Tomorrow will be a long day. We 'ave t' make arrangements. Your producer has brought information t' help out. Will y' be up t' it tomorrow?"

Susie shook her head again.

Laura's eyes watered.

Gene came over to the nearby couch section where Evan usually sat and took her hand. "We will do it all together, luv. We will ge' through it together."

Susie stared at him. Not arguing. Not agreeing. In a daze. The nerve pills, Evan figured. Or she was holding herself in too well, depending too much on the hope the team he'd hired would actually find him, alive. Evan knew very well that even if they did find him, it would only be as proof for her. The chance of him being alive was next to nil, or worse. Still, there was a part of him that tried hard to believe her, that wanted to believe her. He wished he could. He understood why she had to believe it. He also knew why he couldn't let himself. When the full truth hit her, the numbness he saw would be gone.

As the evening passed, she seemed more aware, more herself, except too calm. Doc came back to check in. Her temperature was still higher than normal but much better. He urged her to have more juice and Kate went to get it. Doug and Ali were taking their turn with the kids downstairs. Distracting Nella. Evan didn't want her to keep asking Susie to take her to her dad.

He went across the hall to check messages now and then since Susie's phone was unplugged. Sometimes Mike went instead, but he came back. He hovered around Evan.

At a knock, Mike went to check.

John. Finally. He gave the McGuires his sympathy and touched a hand to Gene's shoulder, then took Susie's side and set a hand on her face. "Sweetheart."

"Where have you been?" A tear escaped.

"Oh sweetie, trying to get here. I'm sorry it took so long. I'm so sorry..."

She fell into his arms. The tear turned into sobs; her body shook.

She'd been waiting for her dad, as she always had. She'd always been stoic while he was away, as though she had to hold down everything herself until her dad was there to relieve her. Sometimes Evan would substitute, not always. John more often through the years saw the side of her that let go, let her emotions take over, as they did more when he was around. He was safe ground. Of course, he didn't see as much of her stoic, stronger side that way.

At least she was letting it out, giving in.

It made Laura and her mom cry again. Danny held his sister, spoke into her ear, and took her out of the apartment. Evan supposed they would go down to see Stu.

It struck Evan that Susie had been right about Kate; her friend was there for her now that she needed her. She'd been wonderful with Nella, more patient, distracting her whenever necessary. When someone else took over with the kids, Kate would come up and check on Susie, ask if she could do anything, and give her a hug.

Mike handed Susie tissue as she began to calm enough to gasp for breath, still buried in her dad's arms. Evan stood back and let her family take over. Maybe he was her family, to an extent, but not the same. Maybe he could take over with Nella a while since John was there. He wanted to make sure she was okay, too. Even if she hadn't been told, the girl could sense something was very wrong. Her occasional looks and frowns told him she did. Maybe John could convince Susie to tell her.

He rubbed a hand over her back. "I'm going to go see Danielle."

She didn't acknowledge him, other than to start crying harder again. John gave him a nod.

Evan stopped in the hallway and leaned against the wall. Closing his eyes, he forced deep breaths. Maybe she was right. Maybe he'd be back. He prayed she was, that the team would find his friend.

18 July

John looked in on his daughter and then his granddaughter. Both were still asleep. Both had been awake far too late. Danielle was both energized by the McGuires' visit and wary about what was going on. He hoped he could talk Susie into telling her this morning.

Her liveliness was exhilarating, though. Through the somber mist of despair, she was a little beacon of light. That would change when she knew. For how long, John couldn't tell. Susie never quite came back to herself after losing her mom. At times, he did still see that spark, the mischievous trait he'd admired that at times drove them both crazy, the curious adventurer. Not often enough. And Duncan brought it out. It was what finally made John settle down about the long-haired, leather-jacketed foreigner she fell for against John's wishes. He drew out the spark in her and often lit it to a fire.

He hoped that wouldn't be gone again.

With a sigh, he started coffee. The McGuires would be over before much longer. He wouldn't wake her, though. She needed to sleep as much as she would. He could entertain.

A tap on the door made him wonder if they were there already. Not likely. It wasn't seven yet. As he went to answer, he figured he knew who it was, and he opened it to Evan.

"Thought you'd be awake."

John closed the door behind him. "Barely. We were up late."

"Expected that, too."

He led Evan into the kitchen and turned the water on to fill the pot. "How are you today?"

"Still stunned. And wishing I could believe Susie when she says he's coming back. I know it's near impossible. I'm not kidding myself. I just can't put my head on the idea that this is it. This shouldn't have happened to her. She's been through so much; she's lost so much already…"

"As have you." John turned to see him slumped in a chair. "I know what you're doing. You're trying to dispose of your own pain by focusing on hers. I did it, too. But I can tell you it doesn't work. It only eats at you. Slowly. Through the years. It's not worth it, son. Keep focus on yourself, as well as on her. Acknowledge how hard this is on you."

Evan swallowed hard and rubbed the back of his neck. "I shouldn't have lost him, either. And it does hurt like hell. I'm not hiding it. Only when I'm here, when she could walk in any time. It's the best I can do."

"Understood." John added the grounds, turned the machine on, and sat next to him. "After the memorial service and his family leaves, you might consider heading to your mom's for a while, all three of you, to get away from things. Fans. Reporters."

"If she will."

"I don't mean for a long time. She'll have to adjust to being here without him and she can't run from that, but a couple of weeks to regroup without people in her face…"

"Agreed. But I doubt she will. I'll try." He got up and pulled two mugs from the cabinet, then leaned back against the counter. "I know she won't until we can convince her he's not coming back. She'll stay here to wait for the call, for some news."

"She doesn't believe he is. My guess is she's trying to ease into it."

"No. She thinks he is. I have no doubt she does. I even… I hired a rescue team to go back and search. They said it was pointless since the area was already searched thoroughly, but it was the only way I could get her out of bed yesterday."

"Evan." John bit his tongue, tried to tread lightly. "Are you sure that was a good idea? It's only feeding that thought, when she needs to accept it."

"I know. But I don't think she'll consider accepting it without at least trying first." He shrugged. "I can't tell her I'm willing to do anything I can to help and then not do it when she asks."

He supposed that was true. If nothing else, maybe it would give her more finality. Few bodies had been found. The explosion… John couldn't think about it. If there was any way to help her have finality, he supposed Evan was right. Even if it took longer. "Must cost a fair amount for that. Can I help with the expense?"

"No."

"Evan..."

"No. John, it doesn't matter. The band is doing well. What else do I have to spend it on?"

"A family some day. A house. Retirement?"

At the rumbling of the coffee maker, he grabbed the pot. "This won't affect that. And it doesn't matter right now. I have other priorities."

"Yes well, like I said, keep focus on yourself, too." John got up to accept his mug. "So how are things with Stephanie? Are you still seeing her?"

"If she hasn't changed her mind since I wouldn't take her calls yesterday."

"Why didn't you?"

"Couldn't."

John sat again. "Susie likes her."

"Yes. They get along well."

"Give her a call today."

He nodded but didn't answer. John wanted to keep him talking, keep him from dwelling too heavily on the grief. "Mike said all band appearances are cancelled." He didn't get an answer. "You are going to keep going? All of you. I hope you are."

"You know, I just can't give a flying fuck about the band right now. And Roy ... I would have knocked that asshole out yesterday if they hadn't pushed him out the door too fast." He grabbed a quick breath. "Sorry. I shouldn't have..."

"No, you're fine. Your mom might be touchy about language but you know I'm not. Not out of the presence of my daughter. I suppose that's hypocritical."

"No. It's respectful." He shifted, glanced toward the opening that led to the living room. "I figured Mom would be here by now."

"She and Ben are coming later." At Evan's raised eyebrow, he asked Diane's son if he know of her relationship with Ben. He did, to a point. He didn't seem to care.

John defended her decision to stay in Glenn Heights and only visit Ben occasionally. It worked for her. She had her clients there. Her independence, after the years of dealing with Jake Scott's tight control, mattered too much to lose. Of course, Evan was helping her take care of the old house, paying maintenance expenses and working on it himself when he visited. It would take a load off him if she'd give in and move in with Ben, as Ben wanted.

"He's offered to help with her expenses so you wouldn't have to."

Evan raised his eyebrows. "I'd rather she get it from me."

"She'd rather stop draining you. She feels bad enough to have done it while you were still living at home, going to school…"

"It's hardly draining me. It's fine. You can tell her that. And she could talk to me about it if it bothers her."

"Am I interrupting?" Susie paused at the entrance. She looked frail, wary.

Evan assured her she wasn't and asked how she felt. She only shrugged, a sign her cold wasn't leaving easily and she didn't want to say so. As Evan offered coffee, she pulled her chair close to John and gripped his arm. Her head dropped to his shoulder.

He stroked her hair as he had when she was a child and not feeling well. "How about omelets this morning?" She shook her head. "Bacon and eggs?" Her grip on his arm tightened. He leaned to try to see her face and raised it to his. "How are your body aches by today?"

Tears formed in her red eyes. As he cuddled her in, her body convulsed with shaky breaths and moisture seeped through his shirt to his shoulder. Evan left the kitchen.

"Oh, sweetheart. I wish I could fix this for you. I'm so sorry." He kissed her head. There was no point in saying anything else. It wouldn't help, wouldn't ease her pain. Danielle would get her through it, as Susie had done for him. In time, he would tell her not to wait as long as he did to start moving on, to reclaim her life, to date again. It wasn't good for her that he did and he hoped she wouldn't do the same to Danielle. Maybe his experience could at least prevent that.

Evan stepped in again and put a tissue box on the table. "Nella's awake and getting dressed. I'm taking her next door to get breakfast. Come over when you can." He rubbed Susie's shoulder. And he went to meet the little voice in the living room calling to "My heavenly Scott."

It made John grin despite his daughter gripping him as though she'd fall if she let go. Danielle would be okay, too. Evan would become a father to her. Like Diane was for Susie, except more. They were closer. It would be easier. With a sigh, he kissed Susie's head again. He'd done so many things wrong with her. He never should have been away so often. He should have seen she wasn't comfortable enough with Diane. But she was with Evan. And with Jeremy. To be honest with himself, John wasn't entirely sure Diane didn't hold a grudge against Susie for not telling someone the boy was on his bike at night in a storm. John never should have left her there so often.

And he wouldn't leave town for any job that came up, even if he had to leave the company, until he knew she was on her feet again.

By mid-afternoon, she still refused to talk about arrangements. His team had checked in. They found nothing, said there wasn't much point in looking further. The Atlantic was too cold to survive in the water more than an hour or so, at best. Nearby islands with inhabitants had been searched. Helicopters had checked uninhabited coastlines. Nothing. Anything not already found by the first search team was not to be found. Evan told them to continue until dark and then call back. It was nearing dark in the UK. He took the calls at his own place, at designated times. She didn't need to overhear his part of it. And he wanted time to compose himself before she saw him.

Nella hovered around her. Now and then she let Danny distract her, and Stu took her down to play music once. Mainly, she stuck to her mom. Gene offered to tell Danielle since Susie couldn't make herself. She wouldn't allow it. Even John couldn't get her to change her mind.

Ali tried to change the subject, asked about the house and if she wanted help decorating.

"Not until he's home. He wants to do it together."

Laura started to answer, but instead looked over at Evan, pleaded with her eyes. But what was he supposed to do? John tried again, told her she had to face reality. She got up and walked away from him.

Adam suggested they all go to his place for dinner. He had room for them all. It was a warm day; Nella could swim along with anyone else who was interested. A change of scenery. He figured it might help.

Susie refused to go. She looked out the window at the flood of people on the sidewalk. Adam took her side. "There will be no crowds there. You can sit outside, let Danielle run around in the yard or swim. It's a beautiful day."

"Is it?" She looked over at where Nella was climbing all over Danny pretending to defeat the giant and claim victory.

"I have room for the whole clan, and caterers already busy. You'll have more breathing room."

Danny turned to toss Nella onto the floor and tickled her until she cried *uncle*. Laura fussed at him. Nella looked at her aunt as though she couldn't imagine why Laura was fussing. She was having fun. She adored her uncle. He was so like her dad.

Susie headed into the kitchen to find something to drink. What did she want? Tea. No. And she couldn't deal with soda. Her stomach was already touchy.

"Are we heading to Adam's?"

Evan joined her, with her dad and Gene. "Angel, it would be good to get fresh air. Nella hasn't been out of the house in about a week."

She nodded, went to the refrigerator, looked in, found nothing she wanted.

"Hungry?" Her dad asked. She shook her head. "What do you want, sweetheart? What can I find for you?"

My husband. Just find my husband. She didn't let herself say it. She heard water running. Looked at the coffee pot still on and warm. She didn't want that, either.

"Here." Evan handed her a glass. Ice water. She took a long swallow, set it on the counter, and wrapped around him. He held her in, rubbed her back. "Do you want to change before we go? You don't need to, it's only us..."

"I don't want to go out. I have to be here if..."

"Adam is in touch with anyone we need to hear from. His answering service knows where he is at all times and they have his mobile number. You won't miss any important calls."

"Including your team?"

He hesitated, rubbed her back. "Including the search team. Don't worry, Angel. We have everything covered."

To throw fans off from harassing Susie and Danielle, or at least with the hope of that, it was decided the band would go on ahead with Adam, leaving the McGuire clan to follow at two different times. Evan wasn't sure it would work. They wanted to talk to Susie. Wanted to see her.

And he didn't want to leave without her and Nella. But Beau was there, and Danny and Collin promised to stay on their sides. Laura said she would play guard, also, and could darn well do so. Susie told him it was fine, to go ahead.

They ignored the questions and the yelling, sympathy messages and such, and a couple of members of their security team pushed them into the cars and headed toward Adam's.

Evan paced within the house as he kept watch outside the tinted front windows that showed the long drive from the small side street. He should have insisted on waiting for her. He was right; their fans stayed at the apartment building. It was Susie they wanted to see, and maybe Nella.

Finally, two more cars pulled in through the gate. Evan went out to meet them. Nella flew out at him talking about swimming and that she "couldnae swim" without her Evan Lee to be with her.

"Where's your mom?"

"She come soon, yes. Lots and lots of people ou'side our house. She no' like it. No."

"I know, little one. But she's coming?"

Laura caught his eyes. "Yea, she says she is in a bit. She wouldnae le' me stay an' wait. Bu' Danny is with her, and Collin, and her dad. She made everyone else go on ahead or she wouldnae come."

Evan's stomach tightened. But he didn't see Beau, either. He had to be with her. And he would be. From the first day Duncan told him Susie was his main job as their security, their young, large guard had shadowed her almost mercilessly. At least twice her size and a fair bit larger than Evan was himself, Beau would never let anyone get to her without going through him first, and that would be some feat. He was also very well trained in defense tactics. Duncan had said once he wouldn't want to have to go up against the kid.

"Come, my Evan Lee. We swim. Yes." She held up a bag to show him.

"And how do you have my swim trunks?"

"My mum go to your house and find them. Yes. She say you not care."

"All right, little one, you win. Go on inside and change. And wait for me. Don't get near the water until I'm there."

Laura followed her. Evan stood and watched the road.

"She is going t' wait a while." Gene took his side. "She hoped they would give up and move away if they though' she was no' coming out."

"I doubt they will. They've been there since..." He couldn't say it. "Come on in. I'll give her a call and see how long she plans to be."

"Can we talk first? The two o' us."

Something in Gene's expression made him wary, but he agreed. Linda rubbed Gene's arm, gave Evan a light grin, and she and Loretta went on inside. Evan lowered onto one of the patio chairs. Gene moved another one closer.

Duncan's father looked out at the blue sky, the slight clouds drifting here and there, the birds streaming through. All was still and calm. A beautiful day. Warm, but not overwhelming. A touch of a breeze now and then. The kind of day she loved.

"Susie used to grab a book and sit on the porch during days like these, back in Pennsylvania." Evan wasn't sure where the conversation would head, but he figured it could at least get started. "That, or help Mom put flowers in or weed the garden. I wish she could still do that without worrying that someone will see her and interfere. I guess she'll be able to once they get a fence ... once she gets a fence around her house. When she can make herself move in."

"It has been hard on her. His job." Gene kept his gaze in the distance.

"At times. But she does well with it."

"A' times she does, and sometimes she doesnae. From wha' I have heard."

Evan didn't answer. He didn't need to answer.

"Do y' plan to keep going? The band as a whole, and you in particular?"

Evan thought about repeating what he'd said to John, that he couldn't give a flying fuck about the band right now, but he couldn't be that rude to Duncan's father. "Honestly, I'm not sure what'll happen. We wouldn't have gotten that far without him and I don't know ... and even if we would be able..." He shook his head. Shifted. Swallowed hard. "I don't know that I want to. Without him. From the beginning, from the time we met, it was about the two of us doing it together. Now ... I just don't know."

Gene turned to study him. "Yet y' are close to the others, as well. I can see it. They are dependin' on you."

"They'd be all right. They'd easily enough find a couple of other guitarists and keep going." With a different manager. They'd have to find a manager.

Gene turned back to the sky, the distance. "Danielle will need a father. One who will love her the same, who will be good t' her and be there for her. I didnae give that to my son until it was too late and it was the biggest mistake I 'ave ever made. I though' I was doing wha' was best. I was wrong. I should have fought for my right t' see him. And I missed too many years. I had hoped ... that I would have time t' make it up, to get closer t' him." He grabbed a deep breath and dropped his head. "It is a regret I will ne'er be able to fix."

"I'm not sure about that." Evan also wasn't sure he should say it, to speak for his friend, but he figure it wouldn't matter now. "He has ... had a lot of respect for you. Changing his name wasn't a small thing to him. And I know he cared about making you proud."

Gene cast his eyes over. "Makin' me proud?"

"Yes. He respected you enough that it mattered if you were. And for him, that's about the highest compliment you could have. He didn't care what people thought. He didn't even care what I thought, and he told me that often enough. I could accept his actions or not. He cared about Susie and Danielle being proud of him. And you. Otherwise, people could or not. It didn't matter."

Gene raised his gaze back to the sky. "A child should ne'er go before the parent. If I could only take his place, I would do it wi'out hesitation."

"So would I." Evan again thought of Duncan's offer to go with him. If he had, maybe he could have ... helped, or protected him somehow. A foolish notion. No one on the plane survived. Still...

"Y' are his age. There would be no sense in't."

"Sure there would. Susie and Nella would still have him. She shouldn't have to be a widow at twenty-four. Nella ... she's so young still..."

"Y' would do tha' for her?"

"Yes."

Gene stared for several seconds. "I plan t' ask her to come stay a while, t' get away from all o' this, so she can again walk outside or sit and read on the porch wi'out harassment. So we can help her as she needs, give her time t' get on her feet."

Evan felt himself cringe. Take her away. Gene wanted to take them away, to Scotland. For a while, which he figured meant a long while.

"Will y' encourage her t' come? I think she willnae unless y' help me convince her it would be good."

Could he? Maybe it would be good for her, for Danielle. No press. No fans hovering. A large yard and garden. The swimming pool they both loved right there in the house. And she loved Scotland. Maybe she could feel closer to Duncan there with his family in his homeland. But could he do it?

"Y' donae want her to go."

"Well." Evan shifted in his chair and looked out toward the street. He wanted to call and ask when she was coming, to know when to expect her. But he had to answer Gene. "The thing is, he asked me to look after them."

"And I am sure he meant while he was camping since they couldnae go."

"Yes, but not only that." Evan bounced his heel, reminding him of Stu. Did he do that because he was nervous? He didn't seem constantly nervous. "Danielle is mine now." At Gene's raised eyebrow, only one like his son, Evan tried to regroup. "He asked me, if ever needed, to step in and be her father. They legally made me the guardian if ever needed. I will be a father to her, as he'd want. As he asked. And I'll take her to Scotland now and then, as he asked..."

"And if Susie marries again a' some point?"

Marries again. His heart nearly stopped at the thought. Of course it was possible. He hoped she would. He wouldn't want her alone forever. On the other hand, he couldn't imagine standing by again and letting it happen. With anyone else. He couldn't imagine caring enough about any other man to step back as he had for Duncan. He hadn't only stepped back for Susie; he'd done it for his friend.

"Y' are in love with her."

His gaze flashed over to Gene, to Duncan's father.

"I can see it, Evan. I always have seen it."

"She's my best friend's wife."

"She was. Now she is widowed."

Evan stood, paced closer to the driveway. And turned. "I'm her friend. First and foremost. I most want what's best for her and Danielle and that's what I plan to do, whatever I think is best for them. Maybe it would be good for her to get away, to spend time in Scotland, but I'd ask to go with her. Just ... because he would want me to go with her. To help with Nella. She is my daughter now, as he would want, whatever else happens. Nothing will change that."

Quiet intervened. Gene meant to take over as head of Susie's family. To be her main support since his son couldn't be. Evan wasn't sure he wouldn't try to talk her into moving to Scotland. He also wasn't sure she wouldn't consider doing so.

"Everything alrigh' ou' here?" Laura's voice came from the doorway and she closed it behind her.

"I' is fine, Laura." Gene moved closer and touched her arm. "I was suggestin' Susie come and stay with us a while. Do y' think it would be good for her?"

Laura started to answer and then turned to Evan. Her eyes watered. And she came over to him. Shook her head. Turned back to her father. "I think it will be nice t' 'ave Evan bring them t' visit as he can, as I know he will."

"Tha' is no' what I meant."

"I understand wha' y' meant, and y' know I would luv t' 'ave them. Y' know I would. Bu' y' cannae ask it of her. This is her home. DJ stayed here for her because i' was wha' she wanted. Y' cannae ask her t' leave it now." Laura turned again and found Evan's eyes. "She is going t' have such a hard time, she loved 'im so. Y' will keep her together, yes? Y' will take care o' her weel?"

He nodded.

She gave him a hug and spoke quietly in his ear. "She will be alrigh' as long as she 'as you. I know she will be. Donae le' anyone tell y' different. Keep standin' your ground as y' need. I will stand with you, y' ken. I' is wha' he would want. Y' are my brither, as weel, as I 'ave said, because y' were t' him, because he loved y' so."

Evan felt himself nod. Laura adored her father, but Duncan was always first to her, above anyone. "Thank you. And yes, I'll be sure she's okay." He rubbed her back and looked over at Gene. "I will take her to Scotland as often as she wants to go, whatever the band decides to do and whatever I decide to do. I'll work around it. He wanted Danielle to feel at home there, too. I'll make that happen, or at least give her the chance." He told Laura he needed to go call Susie, to check on when she planned to come, and headed away.

"Evan, one more thing." Gene came to him. "Thank you. For

everything y' have done for my son. Y' are always welcome, as part of the family, whatever Susie decides to do in the future." Gene stepped forward and extended a hand.

As he took it, a car pulled up and waited for the gate. John's car. With Beau in the front beside him. He moved toward it as it pulled in and parked. Danny got out of the back and held the door. She got out beside him. Her eyes went straight to Evan's. They were moist. He went to her. Slowly. Not pushing. She came to him and wrapped her arms around his waist. Her head rested against his chest and shoulder.

Yes, he loved her. He would never say he didn't. But she was Duncan's wife, and she hurt worse than ever before. His job, as her best friend, as Duncan's best friend, was to help her heal as well as possible.

Susie sat along the edge of the pool, her legs crossed, and dipped a hand into the cool clear water. Nella had finally given up. Evan was doing a few laps by himself as Nella waited for him at one end, wrapped in a towel, sitting with her grandma. Others floated around her, in and outside Adam's house. It was nicer than keeping everyone at hers where they were cramped, where she couldn't be outside without hearing the fans, and questions, and having cameras flashed at her. Ali suggested they use the Victorian since it was ready and plenty big. She couldn't make herself do it. Not without him.

The waves Evan made brushed against her wrist. Soft serene waves from his smooth movements. She wasn't watching him, but she knew his movements were smooth. They always were. Not quite as graceful as her husband's. Duncan was always so graceful, so... She clenched her jaw and watched the water move against her skin. Was he in the water, fighting to hang on? Not this long. It was too cold. He couldn't have stayed in it very long. He would have had to find a way to get up out of it. And he would. He had incredible survival instincts, incredible skills, including his medical training. He could use it for himself. He would. To come back to her, to his daughter who was the absolute light of his world. He would come back to them. Whatever it took. She knew him that well, better than anyone.

And she could feel him.

Even if no one else could. She felt him holding on.

Tears gathered in her eyes at the thought of the pain he was fighting, at how hard he was trying. She knew he was. She felt it. It hurt her physically as well as mentally. The water slapped against her wrist. How long had he fought it? Was he warm now? Was he still wet and cold? Were the waves still flinging themselves at him?

"Are y' thinking how he loved the wa'er?"

She started at Collin's voice. He knelt beside her, stared a moment, and wiped tears from her cheek. She looked away, back at her wrist, the waves.

"If y' ever feel the need, I will take y' t' some o' his favorite spots along the wa'er. He meant t' do so himself, bu' ... weel, I woul' be glad t' do it for 'im. Or anythin' else I can do for y'."

"Thank you." She swished her fingers as far as she could reach and back again, in a rowing motion.

"I wasnae sure o' y' at first, if y' didnae know. Y' seemed migh'y uppi'y for 'im. I am glad I was wrong. I am glad t' know how y' made him happy, how y' were gud fur him."

Her tears strengthened. She let them drop into the water.

"Collin, donae annoy her." Laura took her other side. "Go on now. Le' her be." She lowered her voice. "Nella is lookin' this way."

The tears got worse. Nella. She had to tell her daughter something. Laura hugged her. Susie felt her body shake. She had to stop. Her daughter...

"I am sorry." Collin rubbed her shoulder. "I didnae mean t' upset y', y' ken. I only wanted y' to know I wud still be around. When y' feel y' are munro baggin', call me up and le' me know wha' I can do."

She rubbed her eyes, tried to make herself stop, glanced over toward Nella. Evan had her. Distracting her. Munro? What? Collin's phrase distracted her, also. She focused on that. "When I'm what?"

He questioned her with raised eyebrows.

"Munro bagging." Danny moved in beside Collin but stayed on his feet. "Climbin' a mountain tha' is very high, no' only a hill. An' if she needs anythin', she will call me first." He offered his hand. "Come, Sis. Walk with me."

Susie welcomed the escape and accepted. He led her out to the back of Adam's tree-lined property, away from everyone. They ambled, silent. She felt better just moving, being so close to the fresh greenness, as some of the longer grass reached up to tickle the edge of her feet over her thin sandals.

"Gene is goin' t' ask y' to come and stay for some time."

Susie stopped when his words sank in. "For some time?"

"He is concerned abou' your mental state. He wants y' watched. Although he says i' is t' offer help."

"My mental state? I just lost my husband. How am I supposed to act?"

He tilted his head. "And y' believe now he isnae comin' back?"

Susie pulled away, starting moving again.

"An' tha' is why. We are all concerned."

"I'm not crazy."

"Nae, I didnae think y' were. Well, there 'ave been times I though' y' might be, as when y' named your firstborn after me when I 'ad pu' y' through so much. I wasnae sure then."

She heard the humor in his voice. "Nothing crazy about that. Duncan admires you, most of the time, and you're so like him. So is she. It fits."

"Admires me? I donae ken, sis. I think he pu' up with me only because I am kin an' he 'ad no choice."

"That's not true." She stopped again. "He absolutely does. I see it every time he looks at you, most every time, never mind how much he talks about how smart you are, how much talent you have, how you could so easily excel at anything you decided to do. Why wouldn't I want my child named after someone he loves so much and has so much faith in? There's nothing crazy about that."

Danny dropped his eyes, clenched them for a moment. Then he shook it off. "Can I ask y' a straight question?"

"Of course."

"When the team Evan 'as hired comes back with their report, if they donae find any trace an' say there isnae a chance, willyae hold the service and le' go?"

Susie clenched her jaw and started walking again.

He caught up and grasped her fingers. "Look a' me, Suse." He positioned himself in front of her and forced her attention. "Answer me."

"No."

A question flashed through his intense stare. "No, y' willnae answer?"

"No, I won't let go. I won't give up. No."

"Suse..."

"Danny, don't fight me on this. It won't work. And I don't want to fight with you anymore. I need you on my side. I need you to trust that I'm not crazy. I know what everyone thinks. I need you on my side. He would want you to be. You know he would."

Pain crawled across his face.

"I trusted you. Back when we met and you wanted me away from him. I trusted you to come around, to be his family, and mine. I didn't give up on that. And I was right. You are my brother, just as you're his brother, and I love you as my brother. I need you to trust me now, to stand with me even if you don't agree with me. I need you to stand in for him until he comes back. He wouldn't let them walk over me and go against what I want."

"Nae, he wouldnae. He would stand with y' against anyone." Danny looked back toward the house. His chest rose and fell hard. "And so will I." His voice was soft, unconvinced, but his gaze was steady. "Alrigh', Sis. Wha'ever y' decide, I will back y' on it."

She hugged him, felt his strength. His cologne was an odd scent. Spicy but not like Duncan's. More ... untamed. Like Danny. Like she imagined Duncan would have been when he was younger. "Can you stay a while?"

"As long as y' need. I 'ave already le' them know I might."

She backed up. "Don't lose your job."

"I donae think I will. I am a gud name by now, 'ave proved myself. They will be lenient wi' this."

Susie hugged him again. She needed Danny there. Maybe more than anyone else, she needed Duncan's brother to stay.

Evan wished she would have given in and gone for a swim with him and Nella and Mike. The movement would be good for her, but he expected it might be some time before she could make herself do anything that was so specifically related to her husband.

Dried and dressed after leaving Nella with her grandma to do the same, he stepped back outside and scanned the area.

"Out there." Doug nodded toward the back edge of the yard.

With Danny. Holding him. It was good. Danny's presence would help retain that connection. Evan was horribly grateful they now got along so well. It would help Nella as much. Maybe more. Uncle Danny was special to the girl, also. He would help hold memories of her dad together. She was so young. It would be hard as she got older.

"Are you going to try to convince her to have a service?" Ali held Doug's arm, but continually glanced out at Susie.

"That's not for me to say. If anyone has a say in that besides her, it's his family."

"You don't think she'll change her mind." Doug rubbed his girlfriend's fingers and looked over at Adam's hesitant approach.

"No." Evan invited him over. "Hear anything?"

Adam nodded. "They called while you were in the pool. They found nothing, and no reason to keep searching. They will, as long as you're willing to pay, but he said it was a waste of your money."

Evan sighed. Some little part of something inside him hoped for a different reply. Actually, a large part of him did. Even if he knew better.

Doug set a hand on his shoulder. "Call them off, Evan. He wouldn't want you to lead her on and make her think you believe she's right when all signs say different. I wish she was, too. We're all going to miss him. But you can't let that thought linger in her mind; you can't encourage that."

"No. But how do I tell her to stop hoping? How do I tell her I have?" His stomach hurt. He clenched his teeth together, his jaw, as he'd seen his friend do so often.

"Want me to relay the message?"

Evan nearly said yes to Adam. He wasn't as close to her. It wouldn't be as hard. But he couldn't. "No. I'll do it. After we eat. I want her to eat first."

John kept an eye on his daughter as Evan walked with her out into the yard. In the meantime, he gathered everyone else into Adam's living room to discuss memorial service arrangements as soon as they were done talking. Robin and Stu had Danielle entertained with modeling clay on the cement patio. Stu wanted no part of the planning. John hadn't seen him even talk to Susie all day.

"Danielle." He stroked his granddaughter's curly dark hair, still damp from the pool. "I want to tell you something, and I need you to listen well." He saw her nod and crouched beside her. "You know your mom isn't happy right now. But she is most of the time, right? She has a lot of fun with you and with her friends."

Nella nodded again. "Yes, and my Stuey make her laugh and make me laugh."

"Yes, and sometimes you can't laugh. You get sad and think you won't want to laugh again."

"No, I like to laugh. Stuey make me laugh a lot and a lot. He my friend, too, and my mummy's and my daddy's."

John noticed Stu grit his teeth and Robin set a hand on his arm. "Sweetie, it's okay to be sad sometimes. Your mom was really sad when she was a little girl. She lost someone who mattered to her a lot, someone she loved, and she was very sad. But it's okay now because she was happy again later, like she is most of the time. Right?"

The girl frowned and looked out at her mom hanging onto Evan. "My Evan Lee no' like mum be sad. No."

"No. He doesn't like her to be sad, and your Evan will help you and your mom not be sad for too long. Like Stu will, and the rest of your band family, right?" John cupped her head in his palm. "However sad you get sometimes, you remember that later you'll want to laugh again. I promise."

"And I'll be there to help you laugh." Stu gave her a half hug. "Now go talk to your mom. And give her a big hug because that always makes things better."

Susie grasped Evan's arm and allowed him to lead her back to the house. She was disappointed to see he didn't believe her, but then he'd never given her intuitions a lot of credence. It always bugged her, but she was used to it. No one else did, either. Except Duncan. He never scoffed. He listened.

And he would never give up on her. Susie imagined he would have been out there himself by now, looking, if the tables were turned the other direction. She would, but how would she start? And how would she get past all of those who would do their best to prevent her going? They wouldn't stop him. They wouldn't... Maybe she could sneak out without them knowing. But Danielle. Susie couldn't take her, and she couldn't leave her. Duncan wouldn't want her to do either.

She heard his voice negating the plan, telling her not to risk his daughter's safety. "Okay." She whispered in return.

"Okay, what?" Evan tilted his head toward her.

"Nothing. I'm just ... nothing."

He squeezed her hand until Nella ran up to her and Susie picked her up. "What's wrong, baby?"

"We go and ge' my daddy. Yes." She nodded hard.

Susie shot a look at her dad. "You didn't tell her."

"No, but sweetheart, it's time."

Wanting to yell that it was her business and no one else's, Susie readjusted her grip. The girl was getting too heavy. Evan offered to take her but Nella refused, said her mom would take her to her daddy. Susie cringed. She found her way to a patio chair and set her daughter on her lap.

"No, my mummy. We *go*." She jerked toward the door. "We *ge'* my daddy. Yes. Too long away now. My ear no' hurt."

"I know, sweetie." Susie kissed her head and held her close. "I need you to listen a minute, okay?"

"No. I listen minute t' Ga'pa. I not listen 'gain. I *go* ge' my daddy."

"Baby, we can't. Look at me, Danielle." Susie slid a hand to one side of her head and pulled her face gently over to find her eyes. "This is hard. I know. But we can't go get Daddy. I wish we could. You know I want your daddy here. But he ... he can't come home right now." She saw both her dad and Evan consider jumping in and flashed them a quick warning.

"Yes, my daddy do come home now. Too long now. Yes."

The pain and frustration on Danielle's face nearly did her in. The sweet innocent little face looking at Susie as though she would fix it broke her heart even more. She was trying to fix it, but how did she tell the two-year-old she was doing her best and it wasn't working? "Nella." Susie stroked her hair and kissed her forehead. "You know how much your daddy loves you. You know he wants to be here with you. Right?" She waited for a light nod. "He loves you more than anything. When he can come home to you, he will. You know that."

"Suse..."

She flashed another warning at Evan. "Don't. This is my decision."

Nella frowned and looked at Evan. Susie pulled her attention back. "Hey. It's okay. I know you miss him. I miss him, too. But it's going to be okay. You and me ... we'll be okay together, right? I'm right here, baby. I'll be right here for you."

Nella wrapped her arms around Susie's shoulders. Her little girl breath whispered against her neck. She was smart; she knew there was more going on. But Susie would make it as okay for her as she could.

She looked over at Danny when he called her, and Laura. When she started to move, Danielle clung tighter.

"Comin' in?"

"No. Nella and I are going to play with the clay. Tell them to decide what they want to do."

"You don't want in on the arrangements?" Evan knelt beside them.

"No. I told you. I don't want one. I can't stop anyone else, but I won't be there. The rest of you will have to do what you think is best. But I won't be there."

"Suse, you can't..."

"Yes, I can." She stood, with a struggle, and took Nella over to the table with the clay scattered about. "Sit down, baby. I'll be right back."

"No, you stay and play. Yes."

"Yes. I'll play with you. Just give me one minute. I'll be right back." Getting a frown and rather hesitant agreement, Susie left her with Stu and went back to Evan, her dad, and Duncan's siblings. "I'm staying with my daughter. I'd rather there not be any kind of service but I know I can't stop it. If there is, I won't attend. Anything." She focused on Danny. "Will you relay that for me?"

"Yea, and I will do my best." Danny hugged her and went over to put a hand on Stu's back. "Come. Y' are goin' t' agree with me."

Laura gave Susie a wary look and put her attention on Evan, waiting for him to argue, to intercede, Susie supposed. He didn't. He gave Susie a kiss on the side of her head, said he hoped she knew what she was doing, and escorted Laura inside.

With shaky legs, Susie made her way back to the table and grabbed a hunk of blue clay. "What are we making, Nella?"

"Do you want to stay tonight since Danielle's asleep already?" Adam crouched beside Susie as she sat in the dark and stared into the pool. "Robin's making up a couple of guest rooms."

"She doesn't need to. I should go home."

"Why should you? It's safe here. And it's late."

It was late. And she was tired. Exhausted: hair to toenail exhausted. They'd given in. She supposed she should at least be glad about that. No memorial service, although Gene proposed at least doing one in Scotland. An ambassador who didn't give his only son a funeral, or memorial service of some kind, wouldn't be seen a good light, regardless of how popular Gene was among his peers. But he gave in to Danny, for the moment. From what Laura told her, Danny fought hard for her, to respect what she wanted. And Stu agreed, even if no one else did, although he didn't seem comfortable agreeing.

They only gave in when Evan suggested a prayer service instead of a memorial. It wasn't an end that way, but a hope ... for whatever people decided to hope for. It was something. Laura said he couldn't agree to do nothing, either.

Everyone else had filtered out of the house afterward, to talk to her, to try to tell her they understood even if she knew they didn't. Except Evan. She supposed he was upset with her for not giving in after his team had found nothing. He would give them two more days. She tried to repay him for the whole expense. He refused. His choice, and he'd have to deal with it if he was mad. Her first loyalty was to her husband and daughter. Danielle wouldn't want her to give up, either, if she was old enough to understand.

"Should I tell Robin you're staying?"

"Oh." Susie splashed her fingers back through the water. "I don't know." Most everyone had left. Doug and Ali gave her hugs. Collin's parents said they were making arrangements to go home right after the prayer service and were thankful for the agreement to make it so soon. The twentieth. Two days. She tried to make herself talk with them before they left for the night. Collin was staying a few days longer with the rest of the McGuires. Susie gave Laura her extra room. Danny was crashing on Stu's couch, Collin in Mike's room since he moved down to Kate's for the time being. And Susie suggested Gene, Linda, and Aunt Loretta should use the Victorian since it was there and ready. Ali had gone over to help them settle in. They used the two guest rooms, not the master bedroom. That one would wait.

With a sigh, she looked out over the quiet yard. Nella had stuck to her side until she fell asleep in Susie's lap. She was on the couch. Robin gave her a pillow and blanket. And Susie had moved out to the darkness and cool air, to sit beside the pool.

She shivered. The water was getting cold. Still, she stirred it, watched it splash up on her arm.

"Come on, Suse. Come inside and have a cup of tea. Or coffee if it won't keep you up." Adam rubbed her shoulder.

Everyone had talked to her afterward. Except Evan. He avoided her. Stu even hugged her before trying to distract Nella. When that didn't work, he turned it toward Laura. Susie could almost see them together. But Stu would never do it. She was Duncan's sister. Duncan had warned him away. Stu would never cross that. Although it would be nice to keep Laura around. Stu wouldn't move. He would stay right there with the band. Susie knew that, also, without a doubt. Anyone he married would have to agree to that.

The band. Biting her lip, Susie swallowed tears back. How would she go to band practice and see him not up there on the left edge of the stage? They'd have to readjust, put Evan back on lead guitar ... no. He'd be back. They could wait. Or they could practice around his spot and he would catch up. It wouldn't take him long. If he was injured enough to not be able to play for a while, he could still catch up easily.

Another shiver and Adam got up and walked away. Or because she was ignoring him. Not intentionally. She didn't want to talk. She didn't want to go home. And she didn't want to stay there.

She felt something warm around her shoulders. "Come inside, Angel. You're getting too cold." At Evan's voice, she couldn't prevent the tears.

He knelt down and cuddled her in, held her head to his shoulder. "Time to go home. It's been a long day."

"You can stay if she'd rather. I have rooms ready." Robin. From a short distance. "And coffee. Adam always has a cup at night. Would you like to join him?"

Evan pulled her tighter when she grabbed a sobbing breath. "No. Thank you, but I'm taking her home."

Susie had slipped off to bed while Evan tucked Nella in and read her a quick story. She'd asked Laura to let him know. And Laura stopped him when he tried to leave. "She believes he isnae gone. I know it is why she refuses a service. Is there a chance she is right? She is smart, Susie is. If she thinks..."

"Laura, don't let her get to you. I wish she was. I wish there was a chance. But it's been too long. Two professional teams have looked. And she knows. Inside, she knows. She's just fighting it. It's the only way she can deal with it for now."

"Bu' i' isnae healthy. And Danny ... I donae ken wha' he thinks he is helpin' by givin' in t'er as he is, bu' I could clobber 'im..."

"He's doing what she needs him to do." Evan gave her a hug. "Don't worry, Laura. She'll be all right. They both will." He gave her time to unwind. Then she told him good night and headed back to bed.

Evan stood at the door a moment in the quiet of the apartment. He didn't want to leave. Laura was there and he was glad she was there, but still... With a deep breath, he moved to the window and looked out at the fans still gathered, still holding lit candles. They needed a memorial, a place to go to grieve him, honor him. Somewhere besides their building. Susie was going to have to give in. For now, the prayer service would work. But they would have to do more.

"Evan?" She was at the far end of the living room, in her pajamas, her robe untied. "Why are you still here?"

"Waiting to tell you good night."

With a light nod, she came to him, slowly, and wrapped her arms around. He could feel her damp, warm body pressed to his, smell her shampooed hair. And he felt guilty that Danny had been the one she turned to when she needed someone to take her side. It should have been him. He shouldn't have argued with her. He hoped he wouldn't have to again. "Go to bed, Suse, and try to sleep tonight. I know you haven't been."

"I can't. I keep reaching for him. I always... I can never sleep without him there."

"He's there. Even if you can't see him. I know he's still there with you." Evan kissed her head and pulled back, taking her hand. "Come on." He walked with her, waited while she discarded the robe, and averted his eyes until she was beneath the covers. "Good night, Angel. I'm only across the hall if you need me. Try to sleep. Your cold will get better faster if you rest."

He caressed her head the way he had Nella's, and turned out her light as he left.

20 July

She should have gone with them.

Adam's announcement about the short prayer service didn't go over well. Fans wanted more than that. Susie asked what difference it made when it would be no more than a plaque anyway. Evan saw her point, but he also understood the fans. Eventually, he wanted to get to Memphis and visit Elvis's final resting place. It was different, he knew, since the king was actually buried. Still, it mattered. Maybe in time she would agree.

They heard comments as they were leaving the service about why she wasn't there. The band didn't respond. How could they? The last thing they wanted was to let anyone think she'd lost her mind. Though maybe she had. At least temporarily. She barely spoke to any of them the day before, to anyone but Danny and Danielle. She'd hardly even looked at Evan, until she had to give in to exhaustion and go to bed. First, she held him for a long quiet time. Still, she said nothing.

Alison and her family were there. Duncan's family, except Danny who stayed with Susie and Nella. Adam and Robin. Some teachers from the dance studio, those who'd supported Susie and some who hadn't. John. Doc. His mom. Stephanie went to be with him. Janet was there with her baby, not with Jared or her husband. Kara took her fiancé, which Evan thought was fully unnecessary; Stu didn't even see her, with Doug's assistance. Kate took Keith; she said it was important for him to deal with both sides of life. Joe and Mel came. Several musicians he recognized made an appearance. Blue River with Tony and Lisa, but without their kids. Foresight. A couple of other bands they'd toured with. Others had sent messages that they couldn't be there last minute, but they were very sorry. The place was packed with flowers. A few Axis representatives had shown up. Even Roy did, only for looks. Afterward, in private, he railed on them to start doing appearances for the album again. Evan walked away.

Susie should have been there.

With a sigh, he undid his tie and the top two buttons of his shirt and made his way up the stairs. Mike unlocked their door. Evan hesitated. He wanted to check on her. He also wanted to change back to real clothes, to put the thing behind him.

"Coming in?" Mike stared from inside their apartment.

"In a minute."

"Evan, change first. Unwind. She's not alone. And she should have come."

Maybe he was right, but Evan wanted to check on her anyway. He knew she would be erratic for some time. He'd seen it before. And he would help her get through it again.

Danny answered the door and asked how it went. Evan told him about the huge crowd and how respectful they were. His family would be by soon; they'd stopped to pick up dinner since Laura wanted pizza and Gene was doing all he could to comfort her.

He started to ask where Nella was but then caught a glimpse of her in his peripheral vision: on the window seat looking out at the crowd, some of which had followed the band back home from the service. Evan sat next to her. She gave him a frown, then climbed on his lap. When he pushed her to talk, she fussed about the crowd, her mom didn't like it, and that her mom had been lying down "all day and all day 'gain" with mention of Susie being hot like her daddy and she wasn't supposed to be hot like her daddy.

Danny verified that Susie was running a fever again, but it didn't seem too bad. She'd eaten a bit of soup when he took it to her. Danielle was worried, not about the crowd, but about her mom. It was all over her little face. Evan hugged her close and told her the child her mom would be just fine, he promised. And Danny took over so Evan could go check for himself how "nae bad" it was. Evan suggested they go down and visit with Stu since he was home. It would be good for both of them, for all three of them.

He went back and knocked at Susie's mostly closed door. No answer. He peeked inside. She was asleep, or looked asleep. Evan went to her side and set a hand on her forehead. She opened her eyes.

"You're burning up."

Closing her eyes again, she rolled over, faced away from him.

He went to give Doc a call, and then poured a glass of juice to take to her. "Sit up. You need fluids." When she ignored him, he set it down and sat next to her. "Come on, Suse. Don't do this." He still got no response, so he pulled her covers back enough to raise her into his arms, against her light struggle, barely a struggle, and held her against him. "I won't lose you, too, Angel. I won't. So stop this now."

Her body relaxed, allowed his support.

Evan decided not to say anything about the service unless she asked. He did tell her the McGuires would be over soon with dinner and that several of their friends and acquaintances were heading to Adam's at his invitation, that he hoped she would go.

"I can't." It was nearly a whisper.

"Suse, don't shut your friends out. They're here mostly for you."

"I ... I hurt. My whole body... and I ... drinking anything makes me sick. I can't." Her fingers were wrapped into the bottom of his shirt just above where it was tucked in. There was no strength in the grip.

"You should be better by now." He kissed her head. "Doc's on his way."

"I'm not going to the hospital. No, Lee..."

"As long as it doesn't become an emergency, I'll agree with you. I'll do whatever I can."

Her grip loosened. He adjusted his arms to support her better as she slumped more.

"He needs me. I know he does. I can feel it."

Evan cringed. She had to stop. It felt like she was trying to go with him. He wouldn't allow it. "Danielle needs you more right now. She's frightened, Suse. Confused. Scared to death about you. She needs you. You're going to have to come out of this. For her, if for no other reason."

She didn't answer and didn't move. He held her, knowing he could let her lie down again, but he wanted to hold her, to let her feel he was there. He heard a knock on the door but didn't want to get up, and he'd told Doc the door was unlocked, to come in. Anyone else could wait.

John stepped into her room with Doc behind him. Evan repeated what she'd said about her stomach getting upset if she tried to drink anything. And he let Doc take over.

Heading over to change clothes, he ran into Nathan. Evan had seen him at the service but the jackass had enough sense not to talk to him there. He asked to see Susie.

"No."

"Evan, come on, I'm not going to try anything. I'm really not that much of a bad guy, whatever you think."

"I think she doesn't need your shit today."

Nathan dropped his head, then raised it. "I only want to tell her I'm sorry, to check on her. You know she matters to me. Even if you don't want to recognize that, you know she does. Give me two minutes and I'll leave."

Evan supposed he actually did. To an extent. "You'll have to wait. She's been fighting a virus and her fever is back. Go on down to Stu's and I'll let you know when she's up to it."

"Fever? She doesn't get fevers."

"Now and then she does. Her doctor's with her."

Nathan was visibly concerned, and he nodded. "Thanks. And hey, I'm sorry for you, too. For your loss."

"Yeah. Tell Stu. Maybe you can be a friend to him for a while, as you say you are. Think he could use it." He waited until Nathan went back down the stairs to return to his own apartment. He supposed he could have been friendlier, could have at least thanked him for his sympathy, but he didn't want it, not from Nathan Castillo, who Duncan wanted to punch in the face every time he saw him. For good reason. More reason than Evan knew, he expected. There were things Susie had told her husband he didn't know. Evan knew she had; he could often see it in Duncan's glance at something that was said.

She hadn't only lost her husband; she'd lost her greatest confidante, her best friend. As often as she told Evan he was her best friend, he knew it wasn't true. Duncan took that place in her life, also, as he should have, as her husband. He was everything to her.

As he pulled his shirt off, it hit him that Nella was at Stu's and he'd just sent Nathan there. Duncan didn't want that man around his daughter. But Danny was there. Danny would supervise.

Mike grimaced at a trickle of sweat that ran down his back and into his shorts. He hated to sweat. He'd always hated to sweat. It was the worst part of shows, the sweat that soaked his back and chest and dribbled into his shorts until he felt so disgusting he couldn't imagine why any girl would want to touch him, much less be so unparticular about where they touched him. He liked that Kate rarely ever sweated. Not at clubs. Not in bed. And not often out in the July sunshine, even in eighty-something degrees.

She wasn't now, either, that he could see. She was radiant as always, calm, collected, although her face as she stared over at Susie reflected concern. Susie wouldn't go inside, into the Victorian that belonged to her, where it was decided around her they would hold the gathering of those who weren't content with only the prayer service. Family, including Stu's and Doug's who had come down to show support – heaven forbid his family would – along with closer friends among the musicians they'd met on the road filled the back yard with some in the house. She was pale. At least she agreed to just sit and let the band play host. Doc got her fever down. Everyone was warned she could be contagious, but no one seemed to care. They still crowded around her until it went too far and Ev backed them off. Or Danny did. Danny had taken his brother's place as guard dog. Mike was both amused and ... annoyed, to be honest with himself. The band could do that fine; they had for a lot of years. But he supposed it helped Danny get through this to be of what help he could.

It was sure as hell getting Evan through it. Mike kept waiting, though. He knew at some point Evan's protection of Susie wouldn't keep holding off his own grief. Mike could see it. He knew his friend well enough. Everyone else, or most everyone else, continued to treat him as normal, strong, in control, not bothered by much of anything. They needed to give Ev more slack than that. Mike tried to help give it to him as he could. Often he was brushed off. A defensive measure. Ev couldn't let himself lower his defenses, even when someone was trying to help.

Kate was looking after him, which Mike found incredibly charming. She took him iced tea and stood beside him, watching him off and on. She knew as well as Mike did that he was barely holding it together. He wasn't sure whether Kate was more consumed with her own grief, with as much as she'd always liked Duncan, or with Susie and Evan's.

With another check on the kids to be sure Nella was okay after Keith let it slip that her daddy was "lost" and that's why everyone was there, Mike made his way over to Kate. He was glad he'd heard Keith so he could jump in. As much as he figured the girl should know the truth, Susie didn't want her to know. So he told Nella only that they weren't sure where he was and everyone was here to help wish him well. It was true, he supposed. They couldn't know exactly, not physically or spiritually.

Chief Carr gave him a nod as he scanned the perimeter of the yard where the chief and several of his men helped provide security along with the Raucous guards. Susie wouldn't stay inside as they hoped. She wanted to be in the sun, she said. Truthfully, she didn't want to be in the house Duncan bought for her without him. He wasn't sure she ever would. A shame, as she loved it so.

He stopped to chat with Chief Carr for a minute, to thank him again. For a police chief, he was pretty cool. Mike had known a couple who weren't, but then he'd known a lot of higher ups in many jobs who weren't, including several musicians with big names he'd just as soon not cross paths with again. Of course, John wouldn't be such a close friend to the chief if he wasn't a decent guy. Susie's father was nearly as particular as Mike was about friends. Acquaintances, sure, the more the merrier, in general, as long as they weren't assholes, and he liked meeting people from everywhere, especially other musicians he was always glad to talk to, other than the few assholes with more ego than talent. He hated too much ego. Nearly as much as he hated to sweat.

And he was right. As he ran a hand down Kate's back, he noticed the soft thin material barely covering her was dry, and her scent was all floral, no pungency mixed in. Gardenia. Kate loved the smell of gardenias.

She turned her eyes to him. They watered. So unusual for Kate. He couldn't help pulling her in for a hug and he assured her Susie would be all right. She wasn't so sure. Neither was Evan, although he kept telling others she would be. Yet he treated her as though she'd actually break. She wouldn't. She'd continue being a good mom to Nella and support for the band, and she'd pull back into herself. In time. He knew she would, even if Ev wasn't so sure. Stu and Doug weren't, either. They all thought she'd pull away from the band now. Mike didn't see any possibility of that, other than short term.

"They're trying to get her to move to Scotland."

Mike met Kate's worried gaze. "She won't."

"How do you know? She likes it there. It's more peaceful than all of this madness. She put up with it for him. Now that he's not here..."

"No." Mike stroked her shoulder, the silky black short sleeve down to her bare arm. Such a beautiful woman, even with her myriad of faults, even if she drove him crazy. Evan would accuse her of being more worried about losing Susie's help than being worried about Susie. He would be wrong. Mike knew her better.

"No, what?" Her bright brown eyes peered into hers.

"No, it wasn't for Duncan." He kept his voice low.

"Of course it was. She hates it, you know, the commotion, the public invasion of her life. She hates having given up dance, although she'll never say she does. She hates the shit that came with his job. Why wouldn't she leave, get away from it? I would. Hell, I did."

Mike felt himself stiffen. "You left me because of my job?"

Her face became strained, vulnerable. Also unusual. "No."

"You just said..."

"Maybe. Partly."

Because of his job? "Damn, Kate. Why didn't you say so?"

"I did. In a hundred different ways. It didn't matter enough to you..."

"Didn't matter enough?" He felt his head shake. "You know how hard I tried to make it work?"

"Not hard enough."

He looked away, into the crowd, the noise ... the commotion caused by his job, his friends. His life. It was part of him. "Neither did you. You don't mind commotion, not like she does. If she could do it for him, because she cared for him enough, so could you, if you'd wanted..."

"And he would have given it all up for her if she'd asked. Would you?"

So much of him wanted to say yes, he would.

"You can say no. You can tell me the truth. It's not like I don't know."

"Kate, the thing is ... it's impossible to answer since you were never willing to give me the chance."

"Maybe I didn't want to be the bad guy. Like Janet was. Everyone hates her because she wanted Evan to choose her over the band, because she tried to pull him away. Why would I want that?"

"Whole different thing."

"No, it isn't. You know, Mike." She traced a finger down the side of his face. "You know me better than that. You know I can't be the bad guy more than I already am, more than I have been already. No one else thinks it matters, but you know me. And it does. And I care too much about you to have you be the one hooked to the bad guy who ruins everything."

He pressed closer. "And that's why you're different than she is. Because she didn't care. It's why she wasn't worth it for Evan, and why you are for me. Not to mention she was just a plain bitch all the way around, including to him. Stu wanted to throttle her more than once because she was so rude."

She chuckled, only a touch. The idea of Stu throttling someone always gave Mike a chuckle, as well, even if he had seen his friend do it once. He'd had to stop laughing enough to interfere before Stu got hurt. It was a big guy. Stupid thing to do. But funny.

He loved to see her laugh. He always had. Hell, he loved her all the way around. He always had. With a deep breath, he moved his mouth beside her ear. "You know I love you, Kate. You know I'll work with you. I won't ask you to give anything up for me." He found her eyes. "Can we try this again? And it's not for Keith's sake. It's for ours. This... You know this is a good fit. Let's try to give it a real chance." And he needed her. Especially now.

"You're dating that friend of Evan's girlfriend."

"No."

"Don't lie to me."

"Didn't work. Haven't seen her in three weeks or more."

She hesitated, studying his face. "Did you sleep with her?"

"Does it matter? Should I ask you about...?"

"No." Her eyes dropped down his frame. She moved closer until her scent invaded his senses, her presence blocked out the commotion around them. "I've always detested the thought of you with anyone else. Always. Even before we got together. And I detest the thought of how many there have been out on the road."

Mike felt a heavy breath surge through his body. His eyes clenched a moment. "Same here. And probably not near as many as you think."

"Same here." She ran a finger around his ear, stroked it down his neck.

Not near as many. Mike didn't think, already, that there had been as many as she always made it sound. Maybe there were less than that, even. He stepped back and grasped her fingers. "Come with me a minute."

She eyed him, glanced over at Susie where Greg and Lisa flanked her, and gave him a soft nod.

He weaved them through the crowd, spoke to anyone who stopped him enough to be polite, including the young Foresight guitarist who used to follow Duncan around. They slipped around to the side of the house, behind large shrubs that blocked the street view.

Mike kissed her. Took her in. A sweet, desperate kiss. She returned it fully. Her hands pressed each side of his head. He loved when she kissed him that way, as though she wouldn't possibly let him escape, pull away ... leave. It was wrong to feel the way he did right now, during the non-memorial remembering honoring service or whatever it was. With Susie so devastated, Danielle so confused. Evan at his near breaking point. But damn, he wanted her. It was impossible that she didn't know he did, as close as her body was to his. He forced release from the kiss. "Kate..."

"Come on." She lowered her hands to take his.

"We shouldn't. Not now."

"Who's going to care? Or bother to notice? Mike ... now. I want you now."

He kissed her neck. "And tomorrow?"

"I don't know. Guess you'll have to decide if it's worth the chance."

He froze. His body changed its mind. Not again. How often had they played this game? For what? He backed away, let his eyes roam her body, the silky black blouse that even though it was rather conservative for her still looked entirely too sexy and just snug enough over her breasts, around her small waist. The dark green skirt, pleated just enough to show off her curves. The long legs. Shapely. The heels lifting them into a perfect model stance.

No. Not just for today. Not again. He shook his head again. "I need more than that."

"You mean you need more than me."

"No. And you know damned well what I mean."

"I know one night stands seem to work for you when you're on the road. That's good enough and this isn't?"

"I don't care about them. And vice versa."

"Yeah? So you'll do it for someone you don't care about but not for me? You think they want you more than I do? They only want your name. Your image. Why does that matter more, Mike? Because trust me, they don't want you more than I do. Trust me on that."

He tried to argue, tried to tell her if she wanted him that damned much, she could have him, and she knew she could. He wanted to tell her they damned sure did want him, those strangers on the road. They fought each other off just to have him for an hour, or less. Or the night. Whatever they could get. They would take whatever they could get. And she ... the one, the only one he was willing to give all of himself to, only wanted him when she wanted him. The hell with what he wanted. How could she say she wanted him more?

No. Not even if he needed her desperately today, when he was trying to keep himself together, watching everyone he cared the most about do the same, mourn, try to cope. Maybe he wasn't as close to their guitarist as everyone else was, but he damned sure missed him and always would. More than anyone knew. Just because he didn't show it...

And maybe Kate did want him more than she showed. Sometimes she did. At times she showed it so much he thought she'd given in, had decided to accept him fully. So often he felt she would, she had. But she always pulled away eventually. He never knew how long it would be each time. He never told her just how dammed much it hurt when she did. He didn't have the strength for that now.

"I can't do this again, Kate. Not now." Mike walked away. Evan would be proud of him. How often had his friend told him to stop letting her use him? On the other hand, Mike told him that about Susie plenty, as well. It did no good. And Ev hadn't even taken Stephanie's calls since ... since he was again so wrapped around Susie he couldn't see anything else. He'd barely spoken to her at the service, didn't invite her to the house.

Maybe Mike would play interference this time. He could call Stephanie, invite her over, give Ev something else to think about. The last thing Susie needed now was for Ev to start showing too many signs of just how much he loved her. Even if he said he wouldn't. It was already showing. Duncan's family saw it. They all saw it. Except Susie. So far. It had to stay that way.

Evan slumped onto his couch and pushed a hand through his hair. He shouldn't have let John kick him out, even it if was for "his own good" as her dad said. She was nearly asleep. It was late. At last, they'd cleared out most of the well-wishers. She'd done well, although whatever Doc gave her was part of that, he guessed. She was calm. She ate decently enough. Her fever had lowered; Evan hoped her insistence in staying outside even as night fell wouldn't change that. She talked to some of those who tried for her attention, as her energy allowed, including Nick, the Foresight guitarist who seemed afraid to approach her. She talked to him a moment, told him she looked forward to seeing one of their shows again sometime. The kid was nearly ecstatic, despite the reason he was there.

Dropping his head into his hands, elbows propped on his knees, Evan considered the way so many people looked at her that way these days: hoping to even get a glance. She didn't notice. Or she brushed it off as being Duncan McGuire's wife and no more. It was more, though. Susie McGuire was making her own name for herself. It wasn't all good, although in truth, no one's name was all good as far as he could tell. But there was a hell of a lot of respect thrown at her for what she had accomplished already. She didn't even see it. He thought it might be better that she didn't.

This would hurt her, though, if she didn't pull out of it. If she didn't publicly recognize his fans' need for a real memorial, it would come back to haunt her. He shivered at the phrase. And the thought.

"Oh Evan."

He started at the soft voice and light touch on his shoulder. Stephanie.

"Mike asked me to come. I hope it's all right. I'll leave if not. I just wanted to know you were okay. I know you're not okay, but I mean... I'm so sorry." She stroked hair from his face. "Should I go?"

He stared at her a moment, then glanced up at Mike. His friend didn't bother to explain himself and he didn't have to. Evan shook his head and pulled Stephanie into his arms, between his legs, let her warmth and softness surround him, let her pull his head against her stomach.

Mike said he was heading downstairs and silence took over with the click of the door. He was glad to have her there. Thankful for her arms, her softness, her concern. He pulled air deeply into his lungs to try to contain his emotions. It was harder with her being so warm, so gentle.

She slid her hands to the sides of his face and raised it, stroked a thumb over his cheek. "Is there anything I can do?"

He swallowed hard. "I'm sorry I didn't call. Or answer. And for brushing you off today. I just... It was all I could do..."

"I nearly didn't come tonight when Mike asked."

"I wouldn't have blamed you."

"Do you want me here?"

Thoughts of Myra crept in, the way he let her go, the way he didn't give enough of himself to her just because of Susie. He shouldn't have. And yet, there was something about Stephanie he hadn't seen in Myra. Strength. More of it. Less needy. Less demanding. Less insistent. More willing to let go, and it would take less. He knew that without a doubt. Part of him had to think he was crazy to take that as a good thing, but he did. "I want you here. And I am sorry."

"Have any wine on hand? Can I get you a glass?"

He nearly said yes, but he didn't want it. He stood, brushed a hand back through her hair, and kissed her.

She gave into him, pressed closer, slid a hand up under the back of his shirt. Whispered into his ear. "I've missed you."

"I've missed you too, Steph." He had. He'd missed her like crazy, wanted her arms, her smile, her gentle strength so often during the past few days he couldn't count. "Will you stay?"

"Absolutely."

Mike started to knock on the door, then stopped. Stood still. He could go to Stu's instead but Nathan was there. Nathan was one of those assholes he couldn't deal with on a normal basis, and he sure couldn't now. He didn't like him before he was such an ass to Susie and he didn't understand why she'd been so nice to him today, even thanked him for coming.

And he wanted to see Kate. Whether or not he should. He knocked lightly. It was late. Keith should be asleep. He hoped, anyway. Waited. Thought about changing his mind.

The door opened. She was in her nightgown, one that barely covered her thighs, with a glass of something in her hand. Her dark hair was down around her shoulders, her tanned, toned, beautiful shoulders. She looked him over a minute and took a swallow of whatever she was drinking. "Keith's asleep, if you came to see him."

"No. I hoped he was asleep." He took the glass from her hand, tasted it. Vodka and orange juice.

"A slow screw. Want one?" She held his eyes.

"If you still do."

She reclaimed it and moved inside to set it on the table. Mike followed, knowing he shouldn't, and knowing he wouldn't make himself resist. Not tonight. Tonight he would play her game of *I need you now and then we'll see,* but he would keep in mind that it was his choice whether or not to continue if she wanted to continue. She'd taught him well. He needed her tonight. Possibly tomorrow he wouldn't.

He slid his hands up her thighs, under her flimsy gown. She gripped the top of his shirt, hooked a finger over the collar, and walked backward, leading him to her room.

Stu stared out his window from behind the curtains. There were fewer out there now, but some had turned on her, held signs protesting her choice not to have some kind of memorial stone in the city for him. A place they could go to show their grief. Publicly. It made him sick. It was all show. If they truly cared about him, they would never harass his wife. His widow. Who he loved more than anything on earth. Along with his Danielle.

He hurt for the baby. He hurt more for Susie. Danielle was only two. She'd grow up not knowing much about what she lost, and she'd be fine. Susie.... He grabbed a deep breath, let it out slowly. He could hardly stand to be around her. It hurt too much to see how much she hurt, to know she would for ... forever.

They didn't understand. Those sign holders protesting her decision. They couldn't possibly understand how much she couldn't give in, couldn't give up. If they'd only found him, found some indication, it would be easier on her than the complete vanishing act. But then a lot of them vanished. Like the Titanic. Too many never found. Just gone. The story always resonated with him. He'd always hated mention of it. He never thought he'd be so closely touched by much the same thing.

"What say we go up and check on her?"

Stu turned to Nathan. "What?"

"Susie. People have cleared out now. Her bodyguard was sent home, from what I hear. Might be able to talk to her."

He stared a moment; the thought of knocking his friend's head off ran through his own. "Her bodyguard? You mean Evan?"

"Who else would I mean?"

"Stop calling him that." Echoes of Susie's voice telling him to stop calling Duncan a "street rat" flashed through his head. But she knew he did it out of affection. Nathan had no affection for Evan.

"Oh come on, I know you're not that close to him. And hell, he played interference any time I got around her all day long."

"Can you blame him?"

"Uh, yeah. Does he think I'm going to hit on her today?"

Stu moved closer. "You better not hit on her any day. And I don't mean only this week. Or this month. Or this year. Leave her alone."

"Shit, Stu, the girl is going to have to date again at some point. Or did you want to go for it yourself? Finally getting up the nerve you never had before?"

He grabbed the collar of Nathan's tee and twisted it in his hand. "She is my *friend*. Her husband was one of my *best friends*. A far better friend than you have ever been. He was always there for me. When Kara left me, he was there. He didn't make jokes over the phone like you did. He was there. He took me out. She sat with me, had me up for dinner, sent Nella to distract me. They were there for me, as always. Where were *you*?" Stu released him and shoved him away. "Those two people are closer to me than my family is. I love them both. And it hurts like hell to know he's not coming back. So *don't* screw with me. And *don't* say that again. I have never seriously hit on her and I never will. And you had better not, either, because I will be all over your ass, never mind Evan."

"If I donae ge' t' y' first." Danny stepped between, facing Nathan, nearly nose-to-nose. "I donae know why my brother didnae like y', bu' I know he didnae. An' y' will leave my sister be or y' will fuckin' wish y' 'ad."

Stu wasn't sure when Danny came out from the bathroom or how much he heard, but enough. He had only his jeans on, his hair wet. So similar to his brother's build, and voice, and stance. He'd even put on muscle since they'd first met, with age, as Stu kept hoping he would himself and hadn't yet.

Nathan backed up, threw his hands in front. "Hey, ease up, man. I was joking with him. Trying to lighten the mood, you know? I would never hit on a woman in mourning. I'm not that much of a scumbag." With a wary eye on Danny, he moved closer to Stu. "Sorry. Didn't mean to rattle your cage. It was meant to be funny."

"It's not."

"Yeah, got that. Relax, man. You know I care about her."

"I'm never real sure, if you want the truth." He felt himself unwind, saw Danny ease his stance. Slightly.

"Hey, what was between me and her is between me and her. She let it go. She forgave me. And she came up to me today, to talk. Told Evan herself to back off, not in quite so many words, but close enough. And you know he's gonna have to let her date again eventually. In a couple of years or so..." He glanced at Danny. "No disrespect to your brother, but she's too young to stay single forever. You have to know that."

Danny raised his chin, took a step closer. "And I wouldnae want her t' stay single forever. Bu' it willnae be you. I can guarantee y' that. I trust my brother's opinion. If he didnae like y' as much as I know he didnae, it willnae be you."

"Damn." Stu shoved a hand through his hair. "This is uncalled-for. This whole conversation. A couple of years? You think she's going to have any interest in dating in a couple of years? This is a bullshit conversation, because she won't. She was too hooked to him, too fully absorbed in him for that. No way in hell will she even think about dating again that soon. Can we just drop this?" He plopped into a chair. "And the biggest reason she is talking to you is because of me, because you're my friend and she trusts my judgment. Don't make me look like an ass again or it'll be the last time." Before Nathan could respond, he treaded to his room, grabbed clean clothes, and headed to the shower. He needed to wash the day off.

21 July

A band meeting.

How Adam could ask her to go to a band meeting, Susie couldn't fathom. Five days. She saw signs of life returning around her, but she couldn't feel it. And she still felt horrible. She wasn't going to a band meeting.

She did turn music on for Nella when she asked. *Dance of the Sugar Plum Fairies*: her favorite music these days. But then, the girl went in spurts. A couple of weeks before it had been Queen's *We Will Rock You,* thanks to Stu, who listened to and tried to imitate the newest album often enough Susie got tired of hearing it even without Nella's fascination. In another few days, it would likely be Supertramp or something similar. Maybe a BeeGees song that Stu would roll his eyes about. Or Blue River's newest. Duncan said their newest was far from their best and they needed to put more thought into their work again instead of coasting on their fame. Susie liked it fine, but it didn't grab her like their first album had. Of course Duncan was right. When it came to music, he always was. She would argue with a lot of musicians about music, but not her husband. Even if she had during their first conversation, the day they met.

With a gasp, she lowered onto her love seat, where he always sat beside her, and pulled her legs up to wrap an arm around. Five days. It felt like fifty.

"*Mummy! Look.* I jeté like cat jump. Yes." Nella did a decent jeté in time to the music, and then a few more, the concentration at getting the step just right all over her sweet little face. She would be a good dancer. Maybe she would do more with it than Susie did, actually make it a career since she also had the personality to go with it, the independent spirit. Or maybe she would do something more normal, away from public life. Susie could only hope.

Maybe she needed to go away for a while. Evan's team had been called off. There was no one to wait to hear from, other than Duncan, and he'd find her wherever she was. Susie knew that without a doubt. Just to get away from the crowd, the fans, the phone, the sympathy she didn't want or need. Gene asked her to go to Scotland. Maybe she would. He would find her there, too. Maybe faster.

"Again I pu' it on?" Nella headed to the record player.

"Nella, don't touch that. I'll do it."

"I a big girl. I record change. Yes."

"No." Susie grasped her around the waist before she got to the player and gave her a hug. "I know you're getting big, silly girl, but not that big yet. You'll have plenty of time later to *record change*." She kissed Nella on the cheek. "Don't try to grow up so fast, baby. You'll be out on your own soon enough. I like having you right here with me."

"Silly mummy." Nella bumped her forehead against Susie's softly. "I righ' here, too. Yes. My mummy always righ' here with her Dani-nella. Yes. Always and always."

"Yes, baby. Always. I'll always be right here for you when you need me, however old you get. You remember that, okay?" Susie squeezed her again, for too long. Nella started to fidget until Susie released her and lifted the needle to start it again on the song she wanted.

A knock made her frown. Nella ignored it, too busy dancing again to her music. She checked and opened it to Nathan.

He held out a box of chocolate covered cherries. "Still like these?"

"I suppose."

"You suppose?"

"Haven't had them in a while."

"Oh well then it's about time again, right?"

"Actually, I think I stopped eating them about the time you left, since they reminded me of you."

"Okay. You don't want me here. Got it. Want these, anyway? It'd be a shame for you not to enjoy them anymore." He held them out, asking with his eyes for a peace offering.

"Come in."

"Yeah? It worked? Should have tried it long ago."

"You know it's not the chocolate. I've already made peace with you, right?"

"Yeah. Being funny. Didn't work again. Twice in less than twenty-four hours. Must be losing my touch."

"What?"

"Nothing. Sure I can come in? Evan's not going to blow his top if he finds out?"

"It's my place. My call."

Nathan gave her the box, then pulled the hand from behind his back and added a second one to it. "Thought you could use it." He looked over at Nella still practicing her dance moves as they moved to the couch. "She's definitely your kid. She has some potential."

The girl stopped and looked over. Nathan said hello to her and she studied him a moment before showing him her steps, talking to him directly. Susie imagined her husband's reaction. But he would have to get used to Nathan. There was no longer a reason to protect her from him.

Susie opened the chocolate and popped one in her mouth. As good as she remembered. It was stupid to have given them up for so long only because Nathan used to bring them to her. For no reason. Only because he found out she loved them.

Nella noticed and came to investigate.

"Want one? Pull the stem out and be sure to chew it well."

She popped one in her mouth, pulled the stem out as Susie showed her, and scrunched her face as she bit into the cherry.

"Don't spit it on the floor." Susie caught it in her hand. "Dan*ielle*."

"No' good. No. I not like it. No." She kept making faces while rubbing her tongue with her hand.

"Go wash in the sink." Through Nathan's laughter, Susie nudged the girl toward the bathroom and went to dump the mess in the garbage.

"Guess she's not fully yours." Nathan laughed again as Susie washed her own hands.

"More Duncan's, really. He hates chocolate mixed with fruit. Any fruit. She's so much more like him than like me."

Nathan moved closer. "How is she doing? She seems okay."

"She'll be fine." Avoiding the conversation, she headed back to check on her daughter who was still slurping water in her mouth and spitting in the sink. "Okay, don't make a federal case of it. Come on, I'll get you a drink." She turned off the water, dried the girl's hands and face, and nearly dragged her to the kitchen.

Nathan handed her a cup of milk. "Want this? It's what I always used to wash away stuff Mom made me eat that I didn't like."

Nella gratefully gulped it. Susie told her to slow down and to set it in the sink when she was done. She took Nathan back out to the living room. She wanted to sit. She was still muscle-fatigued, still sleepy from not being able to sleep. Even so, she enjoyed talking with her ex. And she appreciated the way he talked with Nella, watched her show off, started her song again, twice, until Susie said that was enough. She loved Tchaikovsky as well, but enough was enough. It would be playing in her head all night as it was.

Nella finally settled for her Lincoln Logs, with Nathan's help, and Susie leaned her head back and closed her eyes. She wondered how the meeting was going, what they would decide to do next. No matter how hard Evan tried to convince her, she couldn't go, couldn't be part of the decision. They didn't believe her anyway, didn't believe he'd be back, so whatever they did now, they'd have to change again. They could do as they wished in the meantime. What did it matter?

The album did need to be promoted, though. She wondered if they'd make themselves do it. That didn't matter, either. When Duncan came back, they could do more promotion, all together, as it should be.

She sighed at another knock. Nathan offered to get it, but she decided that wasn't a smart idea, particularly if it was Evan. It wasn't. She opened the door to Greg and Steve.

"We've been sent to convince you to come downstairs."

"No. But come in if you want." She left them to do so, or leave. Their choice. She was tired. And the aches were trying to come back.

They followed, gave Nathan a brief hello, asked Nella what she was making, and sat on either side of Susie.

"I'm not feeling well, as I told you. You're going to catch it."

Greg shrugged and set an arm around her shoulders. "We don't have a show coming up and we're not recording. Doesn't matter. But come on down with us. We've barely seen you with that damned harsh schedule you guys have been on. We tried to catch up with you a couple of times during your tour. Didn't work."

"Adam said you were trying. What have you been doing recently?"

"Nothing."

"Why?"

He shrugged again. "The last album was shit. Everything else is coming out that way, too. Could be that was our last, at least with this line up."

"Are you serious?"

Nathan looked over. "Hey, need a bassist? I'm free."

They glanced at him and returned attention to her. Steve took over. "We could be losing Tony." Another glance at Nathan. "Play drums too?"

"Nah. Can't help you there."

"Why are you losing him?" Susie focused on Greg. She figured she knew why, but she wanted him to say it.

"Not sure we are. Also not sure I give a shit, for the most part, except..."

"Man, don't go there now." Steve cut in.

"Not like she doesn't know."

"Maybe, but still."

"Is that why Lisa didn't stay more than the one day?" Susie eyed him, her way of saying she absolutely knew, and didn't approve.

"Yeah. What can I say? The asshole doesn't deserve her, doesn't give her what she needs, the least of all respect, which she should at least have..."

"Messing around with a married woman isn't showing her much respect, either." Susie knew she shouldn't say it. She liked Greg. Still...

"Okay. Granted. But at least I'm nice to her."

"She's married. It's not okay and I'm never going to tell you it is."

He conceded with a shrug of his hands. "Yeah, anyway, why don't you come on down with us..."

"No."

"Are you dumping me as a friend just because I..."

"No. I'm not going to the meeting. Nothing to do with you. Stay here and talk if you want. Help yourself to whatever's in there. I'm not sure and I don't have the energy to check."

Steve pressed a hand against her forehead. "You are pretty warm."

"No, I'm not. The fever's gone..."

"I'd say it's not." He moved it to her neck. "Definitely it's not." Steve got up and headed to the kitchen. Greg told her to lie down. She refused. Not with company. Definitely not with Nathan there. Warm again. She needed to get up and get something to drink. Rehydrate. Cool down before Evan came back and called Doc again.

Before she could, Steve returned with a glass. "Ice water." He grabbed a blanket from the couch and draped it over her. "Forget downstairs..."

The door interrupted and Laura came in. Great. She'd tell Evan.

Suddenly Susie didn't care if she did, if he knew, about her fever, about Nathan being there, about whether he called Doc. She was tired. She asked Laura to watch Nella and made her way back to her room, closed the door, set the water on her bed stand, and covered up. She was cold. With a fever. Great.

Thoughts of Blue River ran through her head. Meeting them during Raucous's first big tour. Greg hitting on her in front of Duncan while they were dating, competing with him. Susie commenting to Greg about how she loved his primal dancing on stage, which he repeated to Duncan. Her boyfriend blowing it off as though he had no concern about the competition. She learned only later that he was, often; he had often been concerned she'd find someone better. She couldn't imagine. Then. Or now. No. He was her heart from the time they met. He always would be.

She wanted him home. Wanted him at her side helping her get better, taking care of her, holding her. She wanted him home.

Damn she hurt. Physically. Emotionally. To her core, she hurt. "Oh Duncan, come home now." She clenched his pillow into her arms. "Come home now. I need you." Tears flowed but she didn't care about that, either. She smelled him. Saw him. Felt him. And regardless of how crazy they thought she was, she heard him.

She heard him, his voice. Strong enough she turned to the door to see...

Danny came in. "Laura said y' were hot again." He moved closer, to her side, felt her head.

No. It was his voice. Not his brother's. It was his voice. Calling her name. Susie knew it was.

"Suse?"

She stared up at him. Not Duncan. Danny.

"Le' me go an' ge' someone t' call your doctor."

"No." She grabbed his shirt as he started to move away. "Don't leave."

"I will be righ' back."

"No. I..."

He sat on the bed, brushed moisture from her face. Her tears strengthened. He pulled her up to sitting and held her. Tight. Moved positions, but held on. Gave her tissue. Stayed quiet and just held her. Until she got too tired. Until the fatigue made her dizzy, slowed the tears, turned them to light gasping sobs. And he helped her lie down again, covered her, stroked her hair...

"Y' are going t' be alrigh', Sis. I promise y'."

So like Duncan's voice. Soothing. Beautiful. Calm...

Evan checked on her for the fifth time. The fever shouldn't keep returning. He called Doc and was told to watch her and keep checking it, not to worry if it didn't go higher than 100. It was exhaustion, Doc expected. And nerves. Not eating well.

She was still asleep. A good thing. She needed sleep. She looked comfortable. Didn't feel any hotter.

He rubbed his eyes. It was just as well she hadn't come down for the meeting. Adam thought she should know the latest, that it had been leaked she thought Duncan was still coming home and there'd been a rumor about trying to get to Danielle, a threat to get her away from her "crazy" mother before she took Duncan McGuire's only child out of the States forever. Adam didn't think it was more than some bereaved fan talking, but he'd been in touch with Chief Carr, privately, and their guards were on alert. Adam thought she should know. Evan thought it was best she didn't; she was too fragile right now, enough she couldn't even get over a simple virus.

And he would never let it happen. If he had to take them away somewhere himself, he would do that. No one was getting to Danielle. He stretched his neck and shoved a hand through his hair. Whatever he had to do...

"Go get some sleep."

He started at John's voice at the doorway.

"It's after midnight. And I hear you missed your date."

"What?"

"Stephanie was here."

Stephanie. Yes, she'd been there. Danny told him to go on ahead next door to talk to her. Evan couldn't do it. She was hot again. She shouldn't keep getting hot after this much time.

John set a hand on his arm. "Go on home. Call her. And then get some sleep."

"Doc said to watch her."

"I know. I'll take this shift. Go on."

He started to argue but John nudged him away, toward the door. And he was tired. The meeting hadn't gone well even beyond the threat. Roy ranted and raved when they refused to do promo. Again when they refused to let him look for another guitarist, or better, a bassist in order to put Evan back on guitar. They couldn't think of a replacement yet. None of them could. They told him to back off. He ranted more. Adam tried to back him down. Mike yelled back.

Evan couldn't even answer. He was glad Susie wasn't there to hear it. He did need sleep.

22 July

Doug pushed past the crowd on the sidewalk without answering any of the comments. Adam suggested they say nothing. Doug wasn't sure it was a good idea to ignore their fans, although he had no problem ignoring those who threw criticism. They needed to tell them something, though, about the band's plans. The problem was: they didn't know their plans.

The album didn't need promo, regardless of Roy's unending, unnecessary rant. It was selling fast. They all knew it was because it was their last with Duncan, so regardless of whatever else they did, it would sell. Collector's item. Even non-fans were buying it for future sales potential, he figured. The idea didn't bother him like it did Stu. His friend ranted against the money-grubbing vultures nearly worse than Roy did about their refusal to make appearances. That was the way it worked; no point fighting it. Proceeds would help insure Susie and Danielle's economic support for many years to come, possibly the rest of Susie's life, considering how thrifty she was, and considering

Duncan's producing status on the album. He was half producer on this one. He would have had a heck of a career in production. He was good at it, exceptional.

At a sharp pain on the back of his arm, he yanked away from the gripping fingers and started to tell her not to touch him again...

"Tell her we want a memorial stone."

Doug stared at the wide eyes, the vulgar way she grabbed him again, on the stomach this time, gripping his shirt. The desperation in her face, in her manner. Others joined in, grabbing any part of him they could reach.

He was in front of the café, Ali's parents' café. He'd been lightly accosted there before, but only enough to try to talk, never so outrageous. He tried to free himself as he crept toward the entrance, cringed at a pain in his side, a scratch, fingernails, at pulled hair along his neck. Adam had warned him, told him to take security anywhere he went for a while. He didn't figure he needed it there.

The cries and commotion were deafening. There were too many to free himself. He couldn't go in even if he did. They'd swarm the place, put Ali's family in danger.

"*Back* up. Get on out of here. *Move.*"

Doug recognized the voice. Her cousin. The large male cousin. And her father's. Along with others he recognized. Employees of neighboring stores who ate at the café at a discount during their lunch hours. He'd talked to them often. They managed to push the crowd away just enough to pull Doug along with them, inside the door. And someone locked it.

Ali threw her arms around him. "Are you all right?"

"Other than annoyed? I think so." He looked over at her father. "I'm sorry about this. I didn't expect it. And I wasn't paying attention, didn't even notice them..."

"You have no reason to be sorry. The police have been called. We'll keep the door locked until then."

Ali's hand rubbed over a sore spot and he flinched. Doug raised his shirt just enough to survey a large red mark on his stomach, just above his jeans. There were touches of blood.

Ali took his hand. "Let's get that cleaned up. Are there more?"

"Might be." He felt a spot on his back and maybe another on his side.

"The pigs. I wish I knew which one did this. I'd sure go give her a good piece of my mind."

"Stay away from them." Doug touched her face. "You keep yourself out of the way, whatever happens. Stay away from it."

"I will not." She raised her chin, crept closer. "Doug Lawrence, we're in this together. I will not leave you stranded to those pigs. And I'm German, you know. I can handle myself. Next time, I'll knock out whoever puts their hands on you that way."

Her cousin was lowering the blinds. The closed sign was out. Customers already in the café asked if they could help. He figured some of them already had. Doug again apologized for the commotion and offered to leave out the back door so they could reopen.

Her dad set a hand on his shoulder. "You'll stay right here until they're cleared away. Go on and let Alison clean you up. Get that tincture from your mother. Never know how dirty that girl's fingernails might have been. I've seen some terrible dirty nails in here. Pigs is right."

Doug couldn't help but be amused. Her father always amused him, with as outright and blustery as he always was. So opposite his own quiet father. Doug enjoyed their loud conversation, the way they joked with each other, even as vulgar as it often was. His family never said such things in public, or in private. They were reserved. Mannered. Sharp at times, but quietly. They kept most of their thoughts to themselves. He liked that the Luchners didn't, that they were open and welcoming.

Mrs. Luchner insisted on checking the scratch herself, which made Doug slightly uncomfortable, but she brushed off his concern with a German phrase he hadn't yet learned. Something about being a mom, as far as he could catch. Ali blushed, took the cream, and led Doug back to the sink.

"What did she say?"

Ali caught his eyes. "You didn't understand? Good. Just as well. Here, let me clean it first." She got a rag wet, added a touch of soap, and ran it across the scratch. "Does that hurt? I'm trying to be easy."

He took it and did it himself, harder, to be sure it was clean, and let her put a couple of bandages on it. Hesitating at her request to take his shirt off so she could check the rest of him, Doug figured her family would give them space. They often did when he was there. So he gave in and she checked his stomach and his back, cleaned another spot and put cream on it. He pointed out the one on his side that didn't actually need attention.

"I think you're enjoying this too much."

"It's hard not to the way you're doing it." With her hands all over him. Gently. With light kisses on his bare shoulders as a kind of apology for "hurting" him, although it didn't.

When she finished, he took her hands. "What did your mom say?"

"You don't want to know. It doesn't matter..."

Doug leaned in to brush her lips, felt her hands pull from his and rest on his stomach. "What did she say?"

"She said ... nothing."

"Alison." He held her eyes. The round hazel eyes.

"She said she was nearly your mother and not to be embarrassed in front of her." She blushed. "Sorry. They're being presumptuous. I haven't said anything as though... I haven't. I'll tell them to behave."

Doug caught her up with an arm around her back, pulling her body against his. He caressed her forehead, down alongside her ear, under her chin. "I don't think they're presumptuous. Don't worry about it."

"No?"

"No." He kissed her, only lightly since her family could always need something from the back. "And you know it. You've known from the first time." He grinned when she blushed again. But she knew. He was her first, her only. He planned to stay her only and she knew he did. She made the kiss stronger, gripped the back of his neck, pulled him closer.

Noise at the front pulled him away. Someone called his name. Their security team.

"Hey." Ali pulled his face to hers as soon as he had his shirt back on. "I meant it. I am in this with you, and I'll do whatever you need. You know that, right?"

"I was hoping it wouldn't bother you. I've stayed out of the limelight as much as I can in hopes they'd leave you alone. I think Susie's at about the end of what she can take. The crowd hasn't left our building yet. I didn't want them here."

"I know."

"They may not leave now. They may keep hovering around the door."

"I know. It's okay."

"It's not okay."

She shrugged. "I'll start meeting you somewhere else instead if needed."

"I'm not sure I want you out on your own for a while. Is it possible..."

"Doug, you've done a good job keeping me out of the limelight. They followed you, only because of... Well, it'll stop again. Don't worry."

"If this hurts you, or your family..."

"It won't." She touched his lips. Briefly. "And I won't let them force us apart. I won't let that happen. I'll be careful, but don't worry."

One of the security guys called his name again and appeared, told him they were getting him out of there. There were three of them, and a police officer. The officer said there were more outside clearing the area and asked if he wanted to file a report for assault. He refused. It would look bad for Raucous and he wouldn't make an issue of a couple of scratches.

As the officer left, the older of the guards stepped forward. "We'll get you back home."

"That's not necessary. They're clearing the crowd out."

"I'm afraid it is. There's a hell of a mess in front of your building. Can't let you get through that on your own. We'll come back for your car."

A mess? "There wasn't. I just left there a half hour ago. It wasn't worse than it has been."

"Seems someone let it slip that the McGuires are behind the reason there's no memorial, that they insist it only be done in Scotland, and they're trying to take his daughter back home with them."

"That's nowhere close to true. Are they all right? The McGuires?"

"They're at the apartment now, barely got in without a fight. We have the apartment covered well and we need to get you back before the crowd here gets worse."

"I'm going with you."

"Alison, no." Her father stepped in. "You should keep clear. Maybe a few days. Let this simmer down."

"No. I'm going."

Doug met her eyes. "How about I pick you up later? Go to New

Hampshire with me for a while. That's what I came to ask, although I meant in a week or so. Now might be better. I'll leave and draw them off. When it's clear, go pack a few things. If you'll come."

"Yes."

"Are you sure? I meant to give you more time."

"It doesn't matter. Yes."

He touched her face. "Wait here till I send one of the guards back for you."

"No, they need to stay with you. I'm fine. You just be careful."

"Ali..."

Her cousin took her side, the big one who pushed the crowd away. "I'll stay with her until you come. No one's gonna get through me."

With some hesitation, Doug gave her a hug and light kiss, assured her he would be fine, and left through the front door, flanked by his guards, to be sure anyone still around would see he was leaving. He'd call his parents as soon as he got to the apartment, give them as much warning as possible, tell them not to let anyone know they'd be there, and that there may be four of them instead of two.

"Come with us, Suse."

Evan glanced at Doug, then to where Susie stood looking out at the growing crowd. The signs. Now protesting not only her but Duncan's family.

Doug walked over and blocked her view. "You should get away from here. Let it pass. Get Nella away from it. We have a big yard. It's in the middle of nowhere. No one will dare come on the property with Dad's shotgun sitting by the door. They all know it does. He's an expert marksman. They know that, too. And they'll be sure any intruders who come to town asking directions know." He set a hand on her lower arm. "Come with us and get away from this."

Susie didn't answer. She didn't even change positions. He appreciated Doug's offer and except for one issue, Evan would push her to accept. She couldn't. He didn't want to say why she couldn't. Where was Adam?

Ali took his side. "Help him convince her, Evan. She might listen to you. It's nice there. Quiet. She and Nella will be fine."

"Adam will be here in a few minutes. There are plans in the works. We'll have to see what she thinks about it all before anything else."

"Plans?"

"I don't want to say until we're all here." He saw Ali shake her head when Doug looked back at her. Watched him rub Susie's shoulder a second while she returned her gaze out the window.

Luckily, Nella was asleep. It was late. Doug and Ali were waiting until the early hours when the crowd would thin, or fall asleep, before they crept out. He had planned to pick her up at her place and leave from there, but Adam asked them to all wait and be at the apartment. Including the McGuires and John. Not Roy. Roy would know nothing about it until too late, and even then only part of it.

The knock at the door sent John to answer.

Adam swept in, his briefcase under his arm, his expression harried. "Sorry I'm late. Things got crazy." He glanced around the room. "Glad everyone's here. And Danielle's asleep?"

At her daughter's name, Susie turned and gave him a nod.

"Good. I'll try to make this quick. I've been at meetings with Axis. They only know part of what I want to discuss tonight. The rest I want to go no further than anyone in this room. That includes friends, family members, anyone who doesn't have to know. Including Roy. And I didn't just say that." He accepted an offered chair and thanked John.

"Do you want to sit down?" Adam paused long enough to realize Susie was on her feet, at a distance, still close to the window but not close enough anyone could see her from the sidewalk.

She shook her head. Refused a couple of offers to give her their place.

"Okay. Well." Adam grabbed a folder from his case and pulled out a sheet of paper. "First, as far as promo, I think there's no point in discussion. Axis agreed this time. Album sales are flying without our help. They've even stopped putting money into advertisement. It's unnecessary."

Evan watched Susie's face, as did most of the room. She knew why. Duncan's last album. She didn't show what she was thinking.

"Second, a statement from the band. I have to admit I agreed with this. They think at least a couple of you should go on record with some kind of public acknowledgment, grant a short interview to discuss his ... sorry, but discuss his life and his work. They think it would look better. Of course, they wanted it done yesterday. I argued that, said it would wait. I'm not horribly popular at Axis at the moment, but what's new?

Anyway, I do want your feedback. They'll do it anyway. Several TV stations and magazines are working on features, interviewing whoever they can reach. They all want you, as many of you as they can talk to." He took a breath and looked at Susie, lowered his voice. "They especially want to talk to his wife."

She met his eyes. "No."

"That's what I said. Our answer on that is strictly a negative. The rest of you, I said I'd talk with." He cast his gaze around at them, put them back on her. "Of course, I want your input on that, also, if you want the rest of us to talk."

Susie stared at him. Silent.

"Is that a no for that, as well?"

She turned away, looked back out the window. Laura went to her and wrapped an arm around her shoulder. Susie looked so tiny next to her sister, her sister-in-law. So frail. Laura was only about three inches taller, but she was Scot-sturdy. And she luckily hadn't had Susie's health issues that made her smaller than Evan figured she should have been.

He knew he was distracting his thoughts.

"Okay." Adam sighed. "How about the rest of you? Thoughts? And I'm not only asking the band, but family members, as well. They will be calling if they haven't already."

Silence invaded. Evan agreed they should, but he didn't want to say it. Everyone either agreed or didn't want to say they didn't. At Adam's prompting, Stu looked up from his glare at the floor. "I vote we tell them all to fuck off and leave us alone."

Evan jumped in. "We can't say that."

Stu swiveled toward him. "Why? They don't give a shit about how we feel, as long as they get their stories..."

"That's not fully true." Adam played interference. "A lot of them are your fans, also. And Duncan's fans. If we're careful to weed out those who will do it well, talk to those we believe will do a nice job and ignore the rest, I think it could be helpful to get the story straight. Quench some of the rumors right off the bat."

"Not that they'll believe us." Mike. Switching his gaze between Adam and Susie and his band mates. "They haven't yet. Why would they now?"

"Because now..." Adam hesitated, then continued. "Now they're in 'play nice' mode. They'll give us the benefit of the doubt for a while.

That won't last. We might want to take advantage of it while we can."

Susie looked over at him.

"And I mean for his benefit, Suse." Adam noticed. "Clear his name now while people are listening."

Stu jumped up. "His name doesn't need clearing. We answer the bullshit and it's like we have to defend him for something. Nothing he's done needs defense. To hell with the idiots. Don't play their game."

Doug stood beside him, pulled him back down. "He makes sense, Stu. We know he shouldn't need defending, and I think it wouldn't hurt to say so, to mention how sad it is that false rumors have abounded. To try to ... keep the facts straighter, since facts will now be set in stone, so to speak. They should at least be set straight."

Evan nodded. Adam looked up at him. "You agree."

"I'd rather people knew the truth, or at least be told the truth. We go on record with it and at least there's that. You can't convince everyone, but there should be at least that negation from those who know."

"Yes, that's my thought." Adam looked over at her again. "Suse? Input?" When she didn't answer, or even acknowledge that he spoke to her, he went to her, stepped in front. "I know you don't want to think about this, and I am sorry to have to push it, but I've put it off as long as I can. We have to decide one way or the other. I'd rather know your thoughts, what you want, before we do anything."

She stared at him a while, then walked away. John started after her. Evan cut him off, said he needed to talk with her. He found her sitting on her bed playing with her wedding ring. "Can I come in?" When she didn't answer, he took her side. "What do you want us to do, Suse?" At her continued silence, he grasped her hand. "I'm going to get you away from this, but first, I have to know what you want us to do."

She sniffed, held her breath, bit her lip.

"Don't do that. Breathe, Angel. Come on." He set a hand along her face and drew her eyes to his. "I know. It's not fair to have to deal with all of this on top of... I know it's not fair. And I'm going to get you out of here for a while to let you have time to recover. Just come back in with me and do this first. Get it over with. And I'll get you away from it."

"How can I think about it? I can barely make myself get up in the morning, can barely make myself just keep breathing. I can't... I can't,

Lee."

He held her in. Cuddled her close. Felt her ragged forced breaths. "Do you want me to decide? To answer for you?"

She nodded against his shoulder.

"You're sure? If I do, I want you to at least come out with me so you can stop me if you disagree. Okay? Just come back out."

She hesitated, then nodded again.

He unwrapped her from his arms and stood, pulled her to her feet, let her hold him for a minute, and led her back to the living room, to her favorite place on the love seat. Lowering beside her, he grasped her fingers and she dropped her head against his shoulder. He had to pull himself together enough to address the group. His nerves kicked in. It was only his friends, he told himself, their families.

John brought them both a glass of wine. Susie wouldn't take hers.

Evan took a swallow and set it aside. "Adam, contact those you most trust. Tell them we'll grant interviews in a few weeks, maybe at the one month point. Not before. I think we should all do the interviews together, at least the whole band. Beyond that, it should be at your discretion." He focused on the McGuires, on Gene. "It's not our place to suggest who you talk to, but if you want information about which journalists over here Adam would recommend, ask him. Or refuse if you'd rather. It's your call."

"We do want t' know what would be better for your band, for its continuance, so le' us know that much."

Adam took over. "I can't imagine it will matter. As long as you don't go on record saying we were unfair to him or anything of that nature."

"Of course we wouldnae." Laura. "Because y' werenae. He loved all o' you. We all know he did."

Stu shoved a hand through his hair. Looked away.

Adam took control back. "And it was mutual. I'll give you any sources you want or check into anyone who contacts you if you'd like. Is everyone else okay with the one month date? Are you going to do it if I say you will?" He waited through hesitant nods from Mike and Doug. "Stu?"

"Yeah." He was quiet, his head still down.

"Is that a yes you're listening or yes you'll do an interview?"

He looked up. "If they're respectable enough. If not, I won't be, either. Just a warning."

"Understood. I'll be careful who I let you talk to." Adam gave him a light grin and wrote some notes.

Evan thought about letting him know he meant respectful, not respectable, but it didn't matter. And maybe Stu very well meant it the way he said it. He asked Susie if she agreed so far, felt her nod, and saw Adam catch it. So did Gene.

"So. Third. And this is what goes no further than this room. I'd like all of you to scatter. By that, I mean go home. Everyone. Take time off. Separate. All at once. Now."

"Go home?" Mike raised his eyebrows. "I feel no need to go home. This is home."

"Okay, then find somewhere else to be. I will send guards with all of you and I have them ready, but I want you to be as discrete as possible..."

"You want us to hide."

Adam gave a light shrug with his head. "If you want to put it that way. Take a vacation. Somewhere small, fairly unpopulated. Make it easy on your guards."

"I don't need a damn guard." Mike glanced at Beau at the door standing stiff and serious like a Palace Guard, except in jeans and T-shirt. "No offense."

"You all get guards, at least nearby. They don't have to be right on top of you. No vote on that. No objection." Adam seemed to be waiting for Mike to argue.

"And I have until tomorrow to find somewhere to go? I'm sure as hell not running back to my family for *protection*. That's all I need. Talk about 'I told you so.' No way in hell. I'll stay here and risk it, whatever it is I'd be risking."

"You can stay with us." Stu shrugged. "They'd love that."

"Or y' can all come back and stay with us. Travel as you wish. Use the house as a home base." Gene extended the offer to all of them but focused on Susie. "And I expect he migh' mean you and Danielle in particular. Coming home with us."

Adam fidgeted with his paperwork. "Actually, if you'll agree to help out, I want it to look like she and Danielle went home with you, but..."

"Her home is here in the States." Stu straightened his shoulders. "In Pennsylvania, where she grew up. You mean for them to go back there with Ev, right?"

"No." Adam waited to see if Evan wanted to jump in, and continued when he didn't. "We have other plans. Like I said, I want it to look like they're in Scotland, which will take some fast planning on our part and yours. We already have it in progress." He looked at Gene again. "We only need to know if you're willing."

Linda took her husband's hand. "We will do anythin' we can. Wha' is it y' need?"

"We have a night departure planned out for tomorrow, a private plane from Boston to New York then transfer to a commercial jet with a private first class area. A daytime arrival where three people in disguise will appear to be Susie and Danielle, and Danny, if he agrees, so it looks like they are with you. Kate helped us find actors she trusted who should look similar enough. We'll have planned photos, an *accidental* media leak. I have that in the works already. Of course, it depends on agreement..."

Laura tilted her head. "Why woul' Danny need a disguise?"

"No, Danny would stay here, but it needs to look like he's there with you."

"Why woul' he?"

Evan took over. "I want to keep him here, to go with Susie and Danielle." He caught her eyes. "To Greenville. I've talked with Joe and Mel. They'd love to have the three of you come stay and will do their best to help disguise you. You'll just look like a young couple with a child, no more than that. No one will expect you to be there. It should work."

"Greenville?" Her eyes watered. "Where you met him?"

He nodded. "Seemed the safest option to get you away from it all. We don't want you to go to Scotland right now because of the rumors. We want, later, to be able to say you didn't, but if they think you are now, no one should be looking for you here."

Evan asked Gene, said it meant there may be fans at their gate, following them. Gene assured him they could deal with the situation if there was one, but harassing an ambassador's family was strongly frowned upon. Not many would take the risk.

"You're going to dump us off there alone? I barely know them."

"Oh Suse, I'm not dumping you anywhere. And not alone. I'll go with you to get you settled, then head back to Glenn Heights so people will see me there and know I am."

"Why?"

He couldn't answer. She was going to argue; Evan could see it.

"We're trying to put out a message that we need space, that we're not working right now, an off limits kind of thing until it settles some."

She barely acknowledged Adam before meeting his eyes again. "Why don't we just go home with you, like Stu said?"

"I think it would be better if you didn't. I can't say more than that." He wouldn't tell her people were talking about the two of them. She didn't need to know. He'd heard it. Duncan had heard it. They both chose to ignore it and not bother her with it. But he wouldn't feed it, either.

"Then I'll go with Doug and Ali, as they offered."

"Not a good idea, either."

"Why? What are you hiding?"

He grabbed a deep breath. He couldn't say it. To her. Or to Stu. When she pushed, Adam jumped in. "Because Stu will be there."

"So?"

Stu raised his hands in a shrugged protest. "Yeah. So?"

"Forget the rumors already? Your being on her 'list' and such?"

He rolled his eyes. "You have to be fucking crazy. So what?"

"So, it matters. Right now it does." Adam stopped the coming protest. "Look, there is more to this than you realize. Where she goes and what she does right now matters more than you realize. If it looks like she's in Scotland with his family, that makes sense and they don't try to find her here. If we say later, after we're all back, that she was actually staying with Duncan's friends, an older married couple, not with any of you, that still looks better for her."

"Are you worried about me or the band?" She eyed Adam directly. "Both."

"Well, you know what would be best for the band. You do know that. Just say it. Ask me."

"Ask you what?"

"To resign now. To keep my distance. That's what would look best for the band. If you want that, say so."

"No." Stu jumped up again. "Hell no." He looked at Adam. "That better not be what you're suggesting, because if it is, you can fuck that. She's one of us, doesn't matter how it looks or what they say. We already lost one of them. We're not losing all three. No."

"Stu, relax."

Adam's calm voice didn't calm him. He turned to Evan. "You can't want that. Tell me you don't want her to be part of this. I know better."

"You're right. I don't want that." Evan rubbed Susie's hand. "That's why we're doing all of this, to calm things, to quench rumors. It's why we're making it so complicated. You think I want to leave her in Greenville when I'm not there? I don't. I tried to think of any better option, where I could... I can't. Neither can Adam. That's why I'm asking Danny to go, to stay with her. It's the only way I can do it. We're trying to pull focus off her so it won't be such an issue when she stays, when she comes back to work for us as she has been."

"It's not going to be an issue." Her voice was quiet. She touched his eyes. "You're going to too much trouble for no reason."

Evan didn't want her to say it. Not in front of everyone. He didn't want her to say again he was coming home. "No, I don't think we are. The only question is whether you'll go along with it. You and Danny."

She stared at him. Silent. Pondering. Then she looked at Adam. "You're staying here? By the phone? Keeping up with everything?"

"Yes. And I'll stay in touch."

She turned to Danny. "What are you thinking?"

"Me? I am honored tha' your friend is askin' me to be the one t' stay with you. I wouldnae 'ave expected it."

"But, your job. And ... a place you don't know. You have better things to do than be my bodyguard. I can ask Beau." She looked over at her faithful guard.

"We thought about that, too." Adam glanced back at him. "But people know his face, his size, and you'll look more comfortable with someone you know well, someone closer..."

Mike leaned forward, elbows resting on his knees, hands clasped in front. "Hell, I could do that. I have nowhere else to be. I can take Keith since he and Nella are like siblings already and ... no offense to Danny, but I sound American and I have no other job to worry about."

Adam shook his head. "I need you to be seen elsewhere. Briefly. Take Kate and Keith with you, if they will. Go vacation somewhere."

"What else is going on that we don't realize?" Mike eyed him. "Why all the cloak and dagger?"

"Nothing more I'm going to say, but as Evan said, I have your best interests at heart. I do hope you realize that by now. So let's just go with this if all are willing and be sure I can reach you wherever you are. We'll all take a break from the whole thing and come back at the right time, say a few days before the sixteenth unless I tell you otherwise. Agreed?"

Evan wasn't sure if they all agreed because they agreed or because they were all too tired and overwhelmed to argue. Especially Susie. She didn't actually answer. She leaned her head back against his shoulder and closed her eyes. Laura fussed. She wanted to stay with Susie. Adam convinced her another time would be better. Danny agreed to work hard on softening his accent.

It brought to mind how Duncan worked at that, how it bothered him that it didn't work well, except when he sang. He never sang with an accent. Danny might have better luck. He already imitated Stu fairly well when he tried, better than Stu imitated Danny, or Duncan. Evan was glad Stu would be nearly next door to Doug and Ali. He didn't want him anywhere alone for a while.

Evan felt bad for hustling Susie and Danielle out away from the McGuires with so little notice, but the crowd was thin at two a.m. and those still in front of the building were asleep or out of it enough they didn't realize the three people leaving were not the same three as had come in earlier that night: the actors Kate found. They would leave with the McGuires that night. Danny carried Danielle with a blanket over her head as he and Beau shielded them on the way to the cars. Evan had shaved the back of his hair enough to help disguise himself as a guard. It worked as he hoped. They pulled away from Lakewood en route to Greenville without being followed.

On the other hand, it might have been far easier to do a quick hurried goodbye to his family than it would have been if they had more time to think about it. Danielle woke only enough for hugs and cuddled willingly into Danny's arms. Susie was too tired to say much, or to react much. She didn't. Except to tell him she hated his hair like that.

23 July

Susie rubbed her eyes and looked at the clock on the hotel night stand when Nella pushed at her to wake up. Just after seven. Seven-o-nine. The twenty-third. Exactly one week from when Evan pounded on her door to tell her.

No word yet. A whole week with no word from him. It meant he was somewhere without a phone. Or ... no, she wouldn't let herself consider other options. He couldn't get to a phone. He would.

"*Mummy*." Nella pushed her arm as she talked in a loud whisper. "We go and eat now. Yes. I *starving*."

Starving? At seven a.m.? They hadn't stopped for the "night" until five: two hours ago. Evan kept telling her to sleep as he drove. She couldn't. Nella slept in the back seat. Danny said he dozed in Beau's car. Susie couldn't sleep. She kept telling herself she should stay home, to be there when he called. Even getting to the hotel, the gorgeous hotel where in some other situation she'd enjoy the old look mixed with new elegance and antique gold accents and wish to stay several days just to enjoy it, she couldn't sleep. She and Danielle shared a suite with Danny; Evan didn't want them alone although Susie couldn't imagine why it mattered there. A sliding door between the bed she and Nella shared and Danny's allowed some privacy, even though it was only partly closed. Danny didn't want them too alone, either. She hadn't cared one way or another. He could have left it open.

Susie finally slept, about an hour after settling onto the plush bed. About an hour ago.

"*Mummy*, we eat now. *Please?*"

"Oh Danielle, it's early."

"Not early. No. Sunshine 'wake already. See?" The child hopped down off the bed and ran to pull the curtain back.

Susie clenched her eyes at the sudden bright light. Starving. "Baby, check your bag. Didn't Grandma pack some snack things in there for you?"

"No. I not want snack things. I want eggies and ham and ... and green eggies and ... and toast with lots and lots of butter."

Susie's stomach turned.

"Safe?" Danny. She told him it was, but it wouldn't be for Nella much longer if she didn't let her sleep for at least another hour. He came in and swooped the girl into his arms the way Duncan always did. "Come Nella bird, before y' ge' your li'l wings clipped. Let your mum sleep. I will take her t' find her eggies an' ham. My guess is they should migh' even make them green for her in a place like this."

"You don't need to. She has snacks. She'll wait."

"Aye right. A Sco'ish lass needs more than tha' t' start the day. An' I wouldnae mind a big American breakfast abou' now. Can we bring y' something?"

"She's not dressed."

"Aye well she will be soon enough. Do y' want me to wake Beau and le' him know I will be ou' a bit?"

"No. Just keep a grip on her."

"Donae worry, Sis. Li'l hummin'bird willnae leave my side. Go back t' sleep. After we eat, we will wander the hotel and look around."

She nodded and closed her eyes. Opened them again and sat up. "Danny."

He sent Nella to the bathroom to get dressed and sat next to Susie. "Donae worry. I amnae as strong as my brother, y' ken, bu' I know defense well enough if needed. She will be safe. I promise y'."

Susie felt her eyes water. She hated having to worry so. She hated to let Nella out of her sight. But she'd promised herself she wouldn't clip her child's wings only due to her own fear. And Danny would protect her with all he had, better than she could if it ever came to that.

"Go back to sleep, Suse. All will be alright. How is that for an American accent?" He grinned.

"Gud enough." She teased back and gave Nella a hug when she came out, told her to be good and to stay quiet in the halls. At the click of the door, she lay down again, closed her eyes, opened them and turned to the window. The curtain was closed. Danny had fixed it to help her be able to sleep. She didn't want to sleep. She wanted to go home.

She was too calm about it.

Maybe she was only exhausted. She wouldn't sleep in the car, either before or after they stopped at the hotel. She'd greeted Mel and Joe quietly, with no emotion, nodded when they asked if the small room would work well enough for her and Danielle, let Danny walk with Nella when Joe offered to show her the tire swing in the yard he'd put up for her, after cleaning the tire real good, as he said, so she wouldn't *get nothin' on her clothes.* They even had a tricycle that looked well used they'd borrowed from a neighbor whose *young'uns didn't need it no more.* Nella was excited. Susie glanced at her when she asked if she could really play outside in the yard *every day and every day*.

But Susie looked like a robot, other than being so graceful. Evan sighed as she sat on the steps of the back porch that overlooked the parking area. He couldn't call it a driveway. It was sparse gravel, with plenty of weeds shooting up through, and not well defined. Cars obviously parked in the grass beside the gravel, as well. There was a car-sized brown spot nearby that showed one had sat there for some time and recently moved. Joe had noticed him noticing and explained about a classic he used to work on now and then but gave up and finally sold it cheap to a kid in town.

Susie refused a snack before dinner when Mel asked. Evan tried to change her mind. She'd barely eaten anything. Said she was too tired. She hardly said a word since they'd arrived, or on the drive there.

And he had to leave. It was too risky to stay overnight, or until the bar crowd started to arrive. He had to get out before he was seen and recognized. Lowering next to her, he told her as much. She nodded.

He got up again to gather Nella in for a hug, told her to be good for her mom and have fun playing with Uncle Danny. When she pouted about him leaving, he reminded her Joe and Mel were friends of her daddy's and she would have a good time getting to know them. It worked well enough, though she still pouted. He took Danny's hand and quietly asked him to take good care of them and call if he needed, and to especially keep an eye on Danielle, on where she was. Evan had admitted the kidnap threat to Danny; he needed to know.

With thanks to Joe and Mel and making sure they had Adam's private number along with his mom's, Evan went back to Susie. "Take care of yourself, Angel."

She glanced at him and dropped her gaze back to where she followed the slow path of an ant carrying a very large white crumb.

"Are you going to be all right?"

She nodded, her eyes on the ant. Carrying a load far heavier than itself.

"Okay. I'll call you when I get there. Call whenever you want. Beau will be close by, paying attention, though you won't see him." He crouched to try to steal her attention from the insect. "Sure you're going to be all right?"

"Of course. I have Nella."

Evan watched her a moment, then got up and ran a hand over her back in a hug of sorts, since she didn't get up, and went to the car. Nella attached herself to his side until he picked her up for another long hug, kissed her cheek, and told her to look after her mom, to try to make her laugh now and then. The girl looked doubtful, but she nodded.

He looked back at Susie. She was in her disguise: a light brown wavy wig covered her own hair, baggy jeans and a too-large navy shirt hid her size, and instead of her sandals or flats, she wore tennis shoes. He didn't like the look anymore than she liked his haircut, but he figured it should work well. Danny had gone back to his older punkier style, no wig since he refused, but he pushed his bangs back down into his face and had added highlighted streaks with peroxide. Along with a large obnoxious earring dangling from one ear that he borrowed from Kate and the sleeves torn off his tee, he looked the way Susie had described him on the day they'd met. The look amused Evan, reminded him of the way Duncan used to talk about his brother's wild spirit.

A car pulled in around the corner headed to the bar. He had to go.

He kissed Nella's cheek again and tried to set her down. She gripped his neck. "No, you nae go 'way."

"It'll be all right, little one. I'll call you every day. Promise."

"No, you no' go too. My daddy go an' no' come home now. You no' go too."

Evan cringed. He thought of changing the plan, of staying there. Disguising himself and staying. But that would blow the whole thing. He couldn't do it to them. "Nella, listen to me. I will come back to get you. I will. It will only be a little while. And I'll call you every morning to say hello. Don't worry, baby. I will see you again very soon."

She frowned and looked over toward Susie. "And my mummy. Yes. You ge' us two of us. You no' go away long. I nae be here 'lone."

Danny stepped in. "Hey, and what am I? Rotten potatoes? Come here, Nella bird. Evan will come back again. Y' can spend time with me a while."

She frowned again, but she went to him.

Susie still sat unmoving on the porch step, now looking at the sky, the gray clouds. It would be nice for her to be out in nature again, to be able to wander around the yard, sit on the porch. He told himself it would be good for her. Yet his stomach churned. Danny told him she'd be fine. Evan nodded and went to his car, not his car, the rental. He'd pick his car up again on the way back from where he'd stashed it. No one could see that it was in Greenville.

Evan hesitated as he opened his door. Maybe this wasn't right. Maybe he shouldn't leave her now. But with the rumors, it would look better for her if he kept distance as he could, if it looked like Duncan's family and friends were there for her more than he was. He hated it. The whole thing. There was no reason he shouldn't be able to stay beside her as he always had. He *always had.* People should mind their own business.

But it was part of the job. Dwelling over it wouldn't change anything. And it wasn't for the band's good as he let her believe. It wasn't even for his, since he couldn't care less what people thought of him. It was for her. He had to go.

"Evan."

He turned at her voice, waited as she came to him. Slowly. As though she might not come the whole distance. But she did. And she threw her arms around him, around his neck, the way Nella had, with just as firm a grip. On her toes to reach him better.

"Be careful." She spoke into his ear, her face tilted up. "I can't have anything happen to you, too. I can't deal with that."

He held her, smelled her scent, her own, no cologne. She didn't need it. He often considered telling her she didn't. "Don't worry, Angel. I'll come back soon."

"You better. I don't want to be here alone, either."

"You're not alone. Danny's here. Nella..."

She found his eyes, stared.

He sighed. "You're not alone. I'll call every morning. You can call whenever you want. I'm here, Suse. Always." He saw her bite her lip, trying to prevent tears, and held her in close, caressed her back. "Trust me, Angel. Relax. Take care of yourself. Enjoy the quiet and being outside as you wish. It'll all be fine."

She released him, touched his eyes, and backed away.

As he left, he tried to decide what the look meant. Was she angry with him for leaving her there? Or had he gotten too close, caressed her too much? No. She would know he only meant to comfort her. He hoped she would. He shouldn't have said it would be fine. Of course it wouldn't. It would never be truly fine for her again. He knew that without doubt.

Susie went back inside to her room. It was rude. She knew it was. But she didn't want to talk to anyone. He had left her there. She hated knowing how easy it was for him to just walk away from her when she was so miserable, so worried. She hated that he would.

Enjoy the quiet. She gulped air, moist air, about to rain air. Let it. Let it pour every day. What difference did it make?

She flopped onto the bed. It didn't matter. She was only going through the motions, anyway. Every day was just a matter of getting through it, waiting. While everyone was trying to move on. It was all a haze by now. Waking up. Getting through the day. Going to bed and not sleeping but off and on. Just a haze. It wouldn't matter after he came home.

25 July

Susie woke with a start at a touch on her shoulder. Danny apologized, asked if she was coming out for breakfast. Nella was already eating. Susie shook her head and turned away from him. He tried harder. She didn't answer so he left her alone. As she wanted.

She could hear her baby's laughter in the kitchen through the door Danny didn't close all the way. Nella was enjoying herself, perfectly at home already. The child had a gift. Like her father. She fit in anywhere.

Refusing tears she told herself she would no longer allow, Susie crunched her body up, trying to collapse that huge hole, the huge gaping hole she felt non-stop, the one that threatened to stop her airflow, her heart beat, and made her not sure she would care if it did. Except for Danielle. Her Nella needed her. Like Susie needed her dad after... But he'd left, went away to work. She didn't blame him. He had to do it for himself. She understood that. Maybe. But she'd never do it to her daughter. She would never leave her now. Ever. Especially not now.

At least Danielle hadn't had to see anything that would haunt her forever. Susie could still see her mom lying there. So pale. Motionless. And not there. She wasn't there. Even at seven years old, Susie had known that she wasn't really there. Her dad gave in to let her see her mom, but maybe he shouldn't have. Then again, it did give her finality. At least she had that.

She swallowed hard several times, forced air into her lungs, and gripped the pillow Danielle was using in against her chest. She wouldn't cry. It helped nothing. It made her feel weak. And she felt weak enough already. They'd been in Greenville only a day and a half, without any of her band, without Evan, and she could hardly make herself function. Kate was right. Maybe Evan hadn't done her any favors by always being there. Even if she wanted him to be. Especially now.

Danny told Nella her mom was tired today from travel and fighting her cold. He knew it was more than that. It was past two and she wouldn't get up. She did talk to Evan when he called, only for a couple of minutes before she handed the phone back to Nella. Otherwise, she was silent. And she wouldn't get up.

He would allow her one day. He often felt like doing the same. Once he got back to Scotland where he wasn't needed as much, he might. He might even take two days, or three or four, and just refuse to get up more than for the necessaries.

He sent Nella in to give her hugs now and then and Susie pulled the child against her close and kissed her face. If she didn't get up by herself willingly in the morning, Danny would tell Nella to insist, to pull at her until she did. Or he would do it. Either way, Susie was damned sure going to get up and keep moving forward. DJ would make her do it. As much as Danny could, within bounds of her being his sister, he was going to fill in for his brother. He would make damned sure DJ would be proud of the way he did, the way he looked over his wife as he would expect.

Leaving Nella inside with Mel, who doted over the child as though she was her own grandchild, Danny went out in the yard, out into the trees, over fallen branches, toadstools, past an awkward stringy shrub that scratched at his arm. He made his way back to where he could see no sign of the house, no sign of people, and found himself on the top of a hill looking down toward a burn. Stream. It was called stream in America and he needed to remember that, needed to come off as American. For the safety of his sister, his niece. DJ would be ranting about the kidnap threat. How dare anyone think it? What in the hell was wrong with people to harass the family of someone they said they admired, cared for? How did harassing his family show anything but disrespect?

He leaned back against one of the sturdier trees. "Damn it to hell, DJ. *Why* did you come without them? Why did you nae *stay* with your family? I would 'ave waited. Y' *shouldnae* 'ave tried t' come. Y' should *be* here." He let himself sink to crouching, his back supported by the rough tree bark. The ground was wet. He wouldn't care if his jeans got wet or muddy, but Nella would ask. She noticed everything. The girl noticed *everything*, just like her father had.

He swallowed hard. Shoved his hands against his face. Shut everything out but the pounding of his heart.

And images of his brother: showing him the right way to chop firewood; teaching him to swim in that damn cold loch ... lake, it was a lake in America ... even through Danny throwing a fit; the endless patience, nearly endless, until Danny went too far and DJ knocked him upside the skull, and rightly so; the way he'd so often stepped in to save his ass when he had a good clout coming from a brawny scunner Danny pushed too far; teaching him Rugby, then stepping out of the way and giving his earned place to Danny, because he wanted it and could only get it if DJ or Collin left the team since he was number three and they were one and two (he'd wanted Collin to step down since his place was less earned than bought and then he and Deej could be co-captains – he'd never wanted DJ to quit); the too many times DJ stepped between him and their father ... Danny's father, not DJ's; their long walks up in the hills where they talked of everything; swimming together, after Danny had learned well enough to enjoy it, competing with him, never able to beat his brother and glad DJ never let him win, always said if he wanted to win, he had to work hard enough to win. Others resented him for that. Danny respected the hell out of him. He didn't want to be degraded that way. He could never have respected his brother if DJ had degraded him by letting him win when he didn't earn the win.

Swimming. In Loch Ness. In July. When they'd escaped for a bank holiday, the two of them, on the train. DJ took him to Loch Ness, to a remote area away from tourists and fishermen, and they stripped bare to swim and float and then sunbathed on the rocks with nothing around them but trees. Bare nature, Deej had said. They'd talked mainly of girls, of sex, the truths of it, the risks. Danny had just turned fifteen. His brother wanted to be sure he knew the facts. On their way home, he gave Danny protection and told him not to need it for a couple of years or so.

And he'd been railed on for the trip. DJ had. Again, he blocked Tom from taking it out on Danny, took all the fault on himself.

"Deej, I'm so fucking sorry for all the hell I was t' you." He whispered into the trees. "For the way I treated your wife when we met. For the stupid things I said t' you. I am sorry, bro. I love y' to no end. And I will make it up t' you the best I can. I will try t' be what it was you tried t' help me become. I will make y' proud." Eyes closed, he dropped his head back against the bark. He could feel the splashes of water his brother threw on him to convince him it was warm enough to swim, safe enough since he was right there at his side. He was always safe at DJ's side. And he could feel the water splashing him, reminding him, as he sat on that rock fully naked and fully safe...

A drop hit his forehead. He opened his eyes.

Eventually it came back. Not Loch Ness. Pennsylvania. Sounds of insects, fishing crickets as Joe called them the night before, ugly brown things that made a lot of noise as they jumped away. Fish loved them, Joe said. The few times he'd gone fishing with his brother, Danny didn't remember them ever using crickets.

A drop of water fell on his arm. He looked up at the bright green leaves. A maple, Susie told him. She loved the maples. Out farther in the short distance he could see rain. Again. Soft. Barely visible. But enough to gather on the leaves and get heavy enough to spot his skin and his clothes. He didn't care. It was warm. He was safe.

"It was my turn, Deej. You should have stayed back this time. Y' should have let me take the fall. It was my turn, not yours." And maybe they had named Evan Nella's guardian if needed, but she was his niece. Susie was his sister. It was his place. It was time he put himself in a place his sister would be comfortable if he ever had to be a guardian for his niece.

As he treaded back toward the little house, Danny eyed the ugly brown crickets when they jumped from his path. Maybe he would take Danielle fishing. They could catch some of the crickets, or at least entertain themselves trying to catch the things. He wondered if she would throw a fit at the idea of hooking one to use as bait, and he'd have to ask Joe just how you did that. Danny wasn't much of a fisherman. The last time DJ took him, forced him to go, he sat on the shore and slept. Disappointed his brother. Again. He could learn to fish and be sure Deej's daughter got to do it. Evan didn't like to fish. Danny remembered Susie say as much. He would take Danielle. Today. They could do it in the rain if it stayed light. It was warm. Nella liked the rain. Like her father.

27 July

Doug started to knock but Mrs. Lowe pulled it open before he had the chance.

"Oh Dougie, I'm glad you came by. And Alison." She reached out and gave Ali a hug, then Doug. "Come in."

He truly wished she wouldn't call him that, but he let it go, again, since saying so never made a difference. "What's he doing?" He held Alison's chair at the circular wood table Mr. Lowe had made years ago. It was almost a circle, anyway.

"He's out with the cows. Can't get him to come in for lunch. He's barely eaten a thing." Mrs. Lowe shoved a plate of rolls into the center of the table. The smell of her pulled pork filled the kitchen.

"Don't tell me he's sitting in the middle of the field."

"He is; of course he is. What else? Scares me to death the way he's hunched down so low. But Daisy's out there with him, barking her fool head off if any of them cows get too close. So I spose it's safe enough."

Doug sighed. Stu had always gone out to sit in the middle of the cow field at his lowest times. He touched Ali's hand. "I'm going to go talk to him. Mind staying here?"

Mrs. Lowe jumped in. "Oh go on ahead. Alison and I will be fine. We've barely been able to talk. It'll be nice."

He hated to do it to her, although she said it was fine and to drag Stu back in so she could see him. Doug made his way through the house he'd half grown up in to the back door. It wasn't much of a cow field. The Lowes were in town, or at least at the edge of town, and didn't have a lot of land, but she liked fresh milk and so kept a couple of milk cows and milked them herself. And she added a couple of bulls so they'd have "friends" as she called them. Her husband tried to tell her one friend would be enough since they weren't so particular as human folk, but she insisted. And Stu was sitting in the middle of them.

Doug stood at the fence and watched him stroke Daisy's head. Mrs. Lowe was right. If a bull got even slightly close, Daisy, a small mutt with curly hair and a constantly wagging tail, jumped up and scared it away with a bark that belied her friendly look. And Stu called her back. She belonged to him, and she was getting old for a dog. Doug hoped she'd hang on at least a while longer, although she didn't seem to have signs of slowing.

He also hoped Daisy would be that loyal to him, as well, as he climbed through the fence and made his way over. Slowly. Watching to be sure he wouldn't instigate the bulls. The cows couldn't care less; they raised their head toward him and went on chewing weeds.

Doug crouched in front of his friend and gave Daisy a pat. "Your mom wants you to come in and eat." When Stu shrugged, he tried a different approach. "Ali wants you to come in for a hug. I think she misses you flirting with her."

"Right. So they can make a fucking big deal out of that, too, so she's not allowed around me if she ever needs me?" He plucked a purple clover from beside him and pulled it apart.

"Stu, don't let them get to you."

He looked up. "Are you serious? She's over there alone because she can't come here because some asshole thinks I might actually..."

"She's not alone. Danny's with her. And there's more to it than that."

"Right. Same reason Evan's not with her. He should be. And yeah, I know why he's not. Same reason. It's stupid. It's more than stupid. It's..."

"I know."

"Duncan would be having a shit fit about now if he knew we all abandoned her just because of stupid rumors."

"We haven't abandoned her."

"Yeah we have." He pushed up to his feet and started toward the house.

Doug kept an eye on the bull closing in, watching them, as Daisy barked at it. Relieved to get on the other side of the fence, he grabbed Stu's arm. "Hey. We haven't abandoned her. Evan's calling every morning and I think every night. I talked to her before I came over..."

"Yeah? How's she doing?"

"Call her. You have the number."

Stu shook his head. "And say what?"

Doug tried to figure how to answer. Say what? He was right. What was there to say? He'd asked about Danielle and if she was comfortable enough there. The answers she gave him sounded rehearsed. Danielle sounded bouncy as always when she took the phone from her mom. Susie sounded like she was only ... there. Existing. It was hard to talk to her. He couldn't make himself push Stu to do it. He told his friend they were doing all right, and then forced him inside to eat.

Nella fished like a pro. Susie hadn't allowed Nella to fish in the rain, so Danny waited for clear enough skies. Joe had found her a small pole, again borrowed from a neighbor, and taught them both how to hook both crickets and worms. Nella started to object until Joe explained that all creatures feed off other creatures in nature; it was the way they were made and kept the world turning. She frowned at the turning bit but then shrugged it off and helped hold the crickets and worms. Danny wouldn't let her put them on the hook. He could imagine Susie's reaction if the girl cut her finger on the dirty thing. But she watched closely. And she looked every bit the serious fisherman as she held her line in the water and tugged now and then.

When they returned, she showed her mom the bucket with three little fish she caught. They were too little to keep. They'd go throw them back in the lake after lunch. Danny had caught a nice trout. Joe took it to Mel to "fix up" for them and Nella wanted to watch that, also. Danny had never been able to stomach cleaning fish, so he sat next to Susie on the porch. She'd talked to Doug. All was okay there. He and Ali were on their way to Stu's for lunch. Susie said nothing more about Stu, and Danny didn't have the heart to ask. The asshole should have called her by now.

29 July

Mike pulled into an overlook parking spot and told Keith he could undo his seatbelt. Kate had stopped bitching that Mike always made the boy wear it, since no one else ever did. As long as Keith was in his car, he would. And he wore his own to make a point. Kate wouldn't. He supposed it was her choice.

He led the way over to a row of large boulders that acted as a fence, making sure his son stayed at his side. He didn't have to worry much. Keith was a rule follower. And easy-going. So opposite Nella. He hoped the girl wasn't giving Susie too much trouble.

Kate took his other side. "Wow."

Mike gave her a grin and returned to stare out over the valley below and the mountains in the distance. The Blue Ridge Mountains. He hadn't had a clue where they would go when they left. Kate agreed to go and they just went. Opposite direction of New Hampshire. The one thing she'd liked about his home state were the mountains. When he saw the sign for the start of the Blue Ridge byway as they closed in on the western part of Virginia, he veered that direction. Adam had been pissed that he "lost" his bodyguard, but he said again he didn't need one. They stay in small areas and never one place long. They were simply out wandering. He liked the freedom of it. So far, so good. He wore his baseball cap low, as Duncan always had when he didn't want to be noticed, and it was working.

He rubbed Keith's head and let his hand rest on the boy's shoulder. "What do you think?"

"Nella would like this. She would draw it with her crayons."

Mike squatted to see his little face under the baseball cap he insisted on having in order to match. "Miss her already?" At his son's nod, Mike rubbed a hand down his back. "I bet she misses you, too. What about we call her tonight when we find a hotel?" Getting another soft nod, he stood again.

Kate gave the boy a hug and kissed his cheek. "And maybe you could draw her a picture of everything you're seeing so you can show her."

"I don't have crayons here."

"We'll stop and get some." Kate caught Mike's eyes and gave him a grin.

Amazingly, he and Kate were getting along well on the trip, better than maybe ever before. It was the lack of his job interference, he figured. Maybe she would actually stay with him if he got a more normal job. The thought was tempting. John's offer was still open to get him into his company. It would still be travelling, though, and maybe that still wouldn't be good enough.

Susie talked with Keith a good long time after barely saying hello to Kate and Mike. She missed him. Danny could see in her face how much she missed the kid. Eventually, he gave it back to what sounded from Susie's end as Mike, and then asked Danny if he'd take the phone.

It was Mike. He asked how Susie was, really, since all she would say is that she was fine and he knew better. She'd gone back to the front porch after handing over the phone. Danny admitted she hadn't done much at all but sit on the back porch and barely eat when they forced her. He had to wonder if she was sitting there waiting for Evan to come back and get her. Mike told him he'd check in more often and they could swing by if needed, to let him know. Danny agreed. He figured it would be safe enough. As far as he knew, there were no rumors to worry with about Mike.

31 July

"Wake up, my luv."

Susie turned and clenched her eyes. She'd barely fallen asleep. She'd seen two o'clock roll in. And three. And...

A soft touch to her head gave her a shiver. And his lips on her face. Warm ... not warm. Cold. Wet.

She turned back to him and opened her eyes. His hair was wet. She reached for him. "Duncan. You're..."

"Donae worry so. I will never leave you, my luv."

She touched his face. Or tried. He felt cold. Wet. And then she didn't feel him. Her hand shook. His face disappeared.

She bolted upright. "No." Looked around the dark room. Not hers. Small. And ... and not hers. He wasn't there. She wasn't home. Greenville. Mel and Joe's. A dream. No. His voice was too real. "Duncan." Her voice was a whisper through the dark. She brushed at moisture on her face. From his lips. From the water dripping off his hair. No.

Susie threw the covers off and stopped, remembering Danielle was beside her. At Mel and Joe's. In Greenville. It was only a dream. Her daughter stirred but didn't wake.

Her stomach hurt. She brushed at more tears. Then she kissed Danielle on the warm, soft little cheek and went out to the living room where Danny was asleep on the couch. Quietly so she wouldn't wake him, she slipped her sweater over her shoulders and went out to the porch, lowered onto the old wooden swing. Stared out at the moonlit yard, the trees with moss growing up their sides from the near constant rain, the weather-worn bird feeders nearly empty again although Mel had just filled them two days before so Nella could watch the birdies fly about.

She wondered if Evan was asleep. Since it was early enough to still be dark, she figured he was. Or should be. She hoped he was. And part of her hoped he wasn't, that it bothered him enough to have abandoned her in Greenville that he couldn't sleep any better than she did. Why here? He couldn't have found somewhere there weren't memories of Duncan, of how only a few years ago he'd stayed in the room she and Danielle were using now? Why here? And without him.

With a shiver, she pulled her legs up and wrapped her arms around them. Listened to the crickets. Heard a rustle of some small animal in the trees. A light rain started. Again. She watched it as the sky began to lighten in the east. Only a bare glimpse of deep blue behind the trees. She shivered again. He loved the rain. Susie wondered if he'd ever come out on the porch just before daybreak, on this porch, in this town, to watch the rain. Or to go out in it. She considered doing that, stepping off the porch in her bare feet and letting the rain wash over her. But her virus was barely gone. Her immune system too weak.

Danielle needed her well.

2 August

Evan hung up with Stephanie, stretched his arm which had stiffened during the eighty minute phone call, and stepped out into the back yard. The sky was a gorgeous pink striated with yellow. He wondered if it was as nice in Greenville. And he wondered if Susie would ever forgive him for leaving her there. She barely talked to him anymore when he called. Danny said she was functioning. She had started to help at the bar at night, against Mel's wishes since "the child needed rest," but her disguise was working. Danny made it clear she was there with him. Mostly the young college kids still filling Sam's Shack left her alone, and all of the locals did since Mel only had to make that clear to them once. Except one of Duncan's old band mates. They were still playing at the bar. The guitarist had already tried to talk to her a few times. Danny said she didn't answer him; she walked away. Evan wondered if the guy recognized her through the wig. It was possible. And maybe he could use that, even if he'd never liked the guy much. Danny was right there. And Mel. Mel was not a woman to trifle with.

Maybe they would shorten the time he'd allowed to give things time to settle down and take her home early. It had been barely over a week and he'd barely slept. He was starting to have a hard time eating. His stomach objected. Too much acid. He was near living on Rolaids. Not that it did much good.

He wanted to see her. And Nella. He wanted to take them home.

Stephanie had again offered to come visit. Evan nearly took her up on it, but he couldn't have her stay there at his mom's, not without a ring on her finger at least. He could go home early. If no one else was there ... if Susie wasn't there, what would it hurt? Possibly, he could stay at Steph's place instead, for a few days or a week. And if he led the hysteria to her door as Doug had to Ali? No, he didn't want that. She said she would wait. He hoped she would.

Or he could ask if she'd take off somewhere with him, like Mike and Kate; just go. He could take her ... hell, anywhere she wanted to go. To Ireland, maybe. She wanted to go to Ireland. Duncan had encouraged her to ask him that night, the night they met Steph, in between flirting. Duncan had flirted with her as soon as he noticed she was interested in Evan. No one else. He'd been careful, as much good as it had done to be so careful. But he flirted with Steph mercilessly. Evan knew it was part a test and part because he knew it was safe. Then she mentioned being part Irish and Duncan said she should ask Evan to take her to Ireland, that he'd been there and was part Irish himself and they should both go. The ass. Pushing. Doing his best to embarrass him. It hadn't worked. Steph took it well, teased back, and leaned more into Evan the more Duncan flirted. Exactly what his friend planned. The ass.

He pulled cool night air into his lungs. Maybe he would take her to Ireland. After things calmed. After Susie was doing all right.

It would have worked perfectly: he and Stephanie travelling with Duncan and Susie, not only to Ireland but everywhere any of them had interest in seeing. It would have worked. Evan would have been happy with that.

Maybe it would still work to an extent. Susie would have to find someone interested in travel. Eventually. It could still work to some extent. Never the same. And he wasn't sure he was interested anymore.

3 August

"Come on, Sis. We are goin' for a walk." Danny grabbed the rag from Susie's hand and set it on the counter. "Mel says y' have been working too much and she doesnae want y' to do so."

"I have to do something with my time. And your accent's pretty strong today."

He shrugged. "I amnae around anyone who doesnae know me. I will be careful while we are out." He tugged her hand. "Nella is putting her shoes on. Go an' fix yourself in your costume."

"Danny..."

"Donae conter me. Y' willnae win." He threw her a wink.

She felt her eyes water. It's what Duncan told Danny when he was straightening him up, pulling him off the drugs. And it worked. Danny had backed down.

"Nae, donae do that." Danny brushed fingers underneath her eyes. "It is a beautiful day. Lots of sun. A light breeze. You need to be outside. How was that?"

She grinned at his American accent. "Not bad. It might pass."

Mel pushed her to accept, to go out a while and get some vitamin D since she was too pale. Susie couldn't argue. Sun and breeze sounded good. Getting out of the bar with its stale smoke and alcohol odor sounded good. She especially couldn't argue when Nella nearly bounced into the room in her big straw hat that covered most of her head and was tied under her chin with an orange polka-dot scarf.

"You don't match very well."

Nella looked down at her clothes: a bright pink skirt and brown blouse that would have been fine without the orange added. "I like this. Yes. We go for walk in town by water. Not big water. Little water. And trees and birdies. Yes. Come." She grabbed her mom's hand.

"Okay, let me change." She tried to give Danny a scornful look at his 'I win' smirk as she headed back to the breezeway leading from the bar to the house. Sun and fresh air did sound good after the day-after-day rain they said was typical of western Pennsylvania until winter when it turned to day-after-day snow or freezing rain. At least it had given her a reason to stay in, to hide.

After changing into bulky clothes and old shoes, which Mel

recommended in case of likely mud, and adding her wig, she gave Evan a quick call to let him know they'd be out. No answer. She'd call when they got back.

Sam's Shack was on the north-west side of town, barely in town, what there was of the town. Greenville was hardly more than one long street and a road that led to the college, but Mel told them to take the car in. She used Nella as an excuse, but Danny figured Nella would be just fine walking it. The girl was always on her feet. Susie didn't even argue about not walking the whole way, but she didn't want to drive as she didn't know where she was going. Danny hadn't seen reason to get an international license, but then he didn't expect Evan to send him to be Susie and Nella's main keeper. He'd never been that, or been asked to be that, for anyone. He supposed some would say he wasn't now, either, since it wasn't his place they were in, he wasn't financially supporting them. They didn't need financial support. What she needed most is what he was there for, and he could see in her eyes that it was him, not Joe and Mel, she counted on for it. Now and then she looked over at him, in a way he finally figured out was a plea for rescue of some sort. He'd go sit next to her or get her away from Mel's chatter – the woman could talk the hind legs off a donkey, worse than Laura, even – or take her side when Nella tried to play Joe's goodwill against Susie's parenting. Other than that, she trusted him to help her keep Nella safe. She was worried about Nella. As far as Danny knew, Susie heard nothing of the threat, but she worried all the same.

Joe tried to tell him he'd be alright just driving uptown and back. But the last thing they needed was to get stopped because he drove on the wrong side of the road, or the right side, as far as he was concerned, and have some local bobby make a ruckus. Danny refused, so Mel dropped them off. She said she had an errand to run anyway.

They ambled along the sidewalk on Main Street and stopped at several of the little businesses that lined the road. Susie enjoyed the quaint architecture that looked almost like one long building on each side that separated into different businesses with different but compatible fronts, all with a vintage look that made her feel comfortable regardless how far away from home she was. She stopped to admire a large building with many arched brick windows across the top. A beautiful thing. She vaguely remembered spotting an old brownstone as Evan was driving them into town, but she couldn't remember where it was. It reminded her of Doc's.

Susie also loved the friendliness of the locals. Many of them said hello. None of them realized who she was or interfered with their browsing, other than to chat with her overly-friendly daughter now and then. Susie jumped in when they asked the girl's name, said it was Lynne. She'd explained to Nella again before they went out that they were playing a pretend game and she was to use her middle name instead, but Susie wasn't sure her daughter would remember. She was going by her middle name, as well, although no one asked. Danny pretty much stayed quiet and acted unfriendly so they wouldn't talk to him.

It worked. And she could understand why Duncan had stayed there so long, until he became wary of the guy he figured was INS and took off. She had to wonder what would have happened if he'd known it was a guy Gene hired to find him, to tell him it was safe to go home. Would he have? Would he never have gone to Lakewood to take Evan's offered respite when he needed one? Would she not have met him? She figured she might have anyway, since he was friends with Evan before then, since the friendship mattered to him.

"Wha' say we get the girl a pokey hat?" Danny tugged the back of Nella's shirt as she lagged at a window, and nodded across the road at a little diner.

"A what? That's a restaurant."

"Right an' where else would y' find it?"

"A hat? She has enough hats."

Danny chuckled and slipped an arm over her shoulders. "A pokey hat, luv, is an ice cream cone. I' is pokey at the end, y' ken."

Pokey. Susie couldn't help but laugh. A pokey hat. Because the end was pokey. She laughed enough she had to wipe moisture from her eyes and Nella tilted her little face up, confused. A couple of people turned to look. An older man commented how nice it was to see a young family laughing together. Danny used his best American accent as he swooped Nella up to ask if she wanted an ice cream cone. She looked every bit his daughter, especially with the big hug around his neck.

"I hate t' tell you, Sis, but mum would say it came from Italian lads in Scotland yelling something about *poco* as they sold them. Still, I like my story better. Yes?"

Poco. Little. Susie knew that from Nathan. But she agreed with Danny; his version was funnier.

Susie insisted they eat lunch first. She was starving. Suddenly. She even let herself get a burger and fries instead of something smaller and less greasy, and she enjoyed every bite of it. They did too much shopping afterward, and then had to carry the bags on their way to Thiel College. Susie told Danny the story of Brother Martin's walk and how a kiss at the end after a couple walked all the way through it meant they would marry. He scoffed at the story even though it worked for her and Duncan and he joked about grabbing some pretty redhead and walking with her through it to see if it would work.

"And what about Amy?"

He shrugged and called to Nella to stop and wait. "We are off and on. She isnae sure enough of me yet. Or sure enough of herself. I donae know which."

"She's afraid she'll embarrass you."

"Yea, maybe, no' like I havenae told her she needn't worry. But I think it is more her family doesnae approve. They do not trust me yet. I am sure they have a point."

Susie couldn't quite blame them if they didn't. Danny's stormy past would make her leery as a parent, as well. Not to mention the fact he still had tendencies toward that lifestyle. Still, he was a beautiful person inside, and trustworthy when he needed to be. "Well, if it matters, I do. And if there was ever a reason Evan couldn't care for Danielle if he ever had to have custody of her, I'd want her to go to you. That's in writing." She caught his surprised expression in between again telling Nella to slow down. "Duncan wanted to wait to tell you ... well, I think he didn't want to pressure you at all, toward anything, while you're still trying to find where you want to be, but ... I want you to know. In case you need to."

Danny caught her in a tight hug. "I will never need to. Y' are going t' stick around and raise your daughter and I will be glad t' help you as you need. Bu' thank you." He found her eyes. "I am honored, and it means more t' me than their opinion, even if she never goes against their wishes t' settle with me." He backed up and shrugged again. "There are a lo' of bonny an' fiery lasses out there who might nae be so particular." Without giving her time to respond, he jogged away to catch up with Danielle.

She was tired and her feet ached by the time they reached Riverside Park, so she planted herself on one of the stone steps of the amphitheater, on a middle row half way up where no one would approach without giving her plenty of warning, and let Danny take Nella to see the "little water" that was one of the branches of the Shenango River. It split off in the middle of Greenville, became more of a stream that went through the park in one direction and off east in the other.

Susie had heard more history of the area than she could possibly remember during quiet evenings before the bar got busy while Joe rambled about his town. It was *his* town, as far as he was concerned, since he was born and raised there, as were his 'pappy and grandpappy,' and they helped build up the little steel-mill-and-foundry turned college town. If she and Danny had any trouble while they were out, he told them, *just tell 'em you're a guest of Joe's and they'll back off.* She chuckled at the thought. She also had to wonder if Duncan had listened to the same stories when he stayed with Joe and Mel.

With a sigh, she pulled her knees up and laid her arms and head atop. Two and a half weeks now. Where was he?

"Your mum isnae going t' be happy, li'l dove. Look at your clothes."

Nella bowed her head deep down to study the mud on her outfit, brushed at it with muddy hands, and looked up with those bright blue eyes – Duncan blue, as Susie called them – and shrugged. "I' can wash, yes. I wash them in the sink so mum no' worry."

He smiled at her accent. Such a lovely cross between Susie's and ... and his own. She'd picked up some of his since he'd been there. "Aye, right. An' then she will 'ave a water mess on the sink and floor, as well. Y' better le' that thought go, my Nella bird."

"No, I no' make water mess. Water no' messy. It is wet. And it ge' dry and no' wet more."

"Any more, and you better talk like the American y' are before your mum keeps y' away from me."

She frowned and shook her head. "My mum no' keep you 'way. No. I Sco'ish, too. Yes. Like you an' G'pa Gene an' my daddy. Yes."

Danny tried not to laugh at her scornful frown. And the way he used to be afraid Susie would take his brother away from his roots, would separate him and his children from his background, his family. A pure git he used to be. Susie had done everything she could to make Danielle feel Scotland was her home, as well, half her culture. Much of him wished Gene would eventually talk Susie into moving there, in being with her family, to let them help support her and Nella in Duncan's place.

The thought made his eyes moist and he pushed it aside, grabbed Nella's hand. "Yes, my dove. Y' are a true li'l Sco'ish-American lass, a beautiful mix of your mum and your Aunt Laura." Dirt and all, he knelt and hugged her close. "And y' know I will always be here for you. Yes? Even when I go back t' Scotland to work. I will be here for you. Anytime y' need." He felt her nod against his shoulder and again fought moisture in his eyes and the pit in his stomach that had been there for nearly three weeks now. Three very long weeks. He would also do everything he could to help her remember her father.

"Come. I' is getting late. We should find your mum and ge' back t' wash for dinner." He checked his watch as he stood. Nearly the time Mel said she'd be there to pick them up.

They went through the grass, the shortest way back to the amphitheatre, and he stopped at the bottom. Susie sat with her head on her arms. She'd said she would sit and read the new book she picked up while they played. He wondered if she tired of it already or hadn't bothered.

Nella took off to the gazebo and twirled a circle, arms overhead, fully graceful, in the middle of it. Danny told her to stay right there and keep dancing to whatever music was in her little head, and went up the stone steps. Susie jumped when he sat beside her. "Sorry, were y' asleep?"

"No." She looked around to find her daughter and chuckled lightly.

"She is a natural performer, tha' one. Maybe she will be a big-name musician like her dad."

"I don't want her to go into music. Not like that, anyway. A concert musician maybe, in an orchestra or something. Sure. But not..." She shook her head.

Danny eyed her, Duncan's wife, who supported his career so fully and yet hated it, also. She never admitted it, but he knew she did. "Well, maybe now y' can both go back t' something more normal."

She flashed him a questioning gaze.

"There is no reason y' cannae. Move away from the band, Suse. Ge' your own life back as y' want it."

Her jaw clenched. She turned away.

"It is nice here. Maybe stay a while. Look for an apartment or..."

"I'm not moving. I'm going home."

"For what?"

She jerked back to him. Started to talk. Stopped. Stood abruptly and headed down the stairs.

Danny caught up and took her arm. "Hey. Maybe it is too soon, but y' should think about it. This is nice for y' both, to walk around town and not be hassled. Yes? Nella is lovin' it. I think you will once you ... in a while. When y' feel better than y' do now."

Her glare said he was pushing too far, but it would be good for her. She'd earned it. She had the funds to do as she pleased, to live where she pleased. It was her turn to be able. Before she could answer, Nella called up to her to come down. Susie gave Danny one more glance and went to her daughter.

So she was mad at him again. She'd get over it. He had to speak his thoughts. She hated the crowds. He knew she did, had always known. And she needed to back away from the band members, or at least away from one of them. He wouldn't say that. That, she might not get over if he dared say it.

He kept an eye on her through the night while she floated around the bar, sometimes helping behind it, pouring sodas or grabbing orders from the back for chicken wings or other fried things she wouldn't eat herself. A teenager Mel fully trusted was sitting with Nella, playing *Go Fish* when he last checked, as he did often, in between Susie checking on her.

Susie talked with people more than she had been, and she stopped to watch the band at times. Danny could see what was in her thoughts, but she kept it in, acted like it was just a local band of no particular importance. Except it wasn't. They were Duncan's old band mates. She avoided them when they took a break, watched from a distance. Finally spoke to the one guitarist when he approached again, then backed away from him. And she showed nothing.

Danny wanted to talk with them, to let on who he was. He didn't dare. And he didn't dare get close enough they might see the resemblance, or hear his voice. The last thing he wanted was to ruin the plan that was working so well, that was giving Susie and Danielle time to recover.

Susie nodded at the thank you as she set drinks on the little table and ignored the young male's flirtatious comment. Too young. He'd been eyeing her for some time. Even Danny noticed. He asked if he should "have a blether with the lad." She didn't see any point, and she didn't want the attention. She did wonder, though, if the insinuation she and Danny were together wasn't working. Susie wouldn't be at all surprised if it wasn't. Danny was even worse at playing her date than Evan always had been.

Maybe she'd played waitress long enough. She was tired after the long walk around town and ... and trying hard not to acknowledge how the band affected her. Duncan's old friends. Not friends, so much, but band mates. Her wig kept her hidden; they hadn't recognized her, thankfully. She told Mel she was taking a break.

Mel gave her a grin and set a hand on her arm. "About time you did. Go have a seat and relax. No need to wear yourself out."

Susie didn't argue, not out loud. She did need to wear herself out. It was the only way she even half slept at night. As she headed toward the back door, to go check on Nella and decide whether or not to return to the bar, she stopped. The first strains of *Let It Rain* began. The one Duncan played with them the first time she visited Sam's Shack, when they were still dating, when she was still so unsure of him and whether he'd stay with her.

Trying to force herself through the door and away from it, Susie couldn't do it. She turned back, ambled into the main room, out from behind the bar, and stood watching. The guitarist did okay. He didn't do it with even half the quality Duncan did. Yet she stared at him, remembering how they'd joked with each other afterward, how this guy gave so much grudging respect to her husband.

He looked at her. Directly. Curiously.

Susie backed away a couple of steps and pivoted, out the back door to the little porch area where some of the patrons went to talk in between listening to the music, or to ... she pulled her eyes from a couple making out nearby, barely under the roof extension. It was raining again, a soft gentle rain that played its own music against the grass. The kind of rain Duncan loved to walk in.

She bit her lip, forced back the tears.

And she walked out in the rain, wishing she could take the stupid wig off so she could feel the water on her head. It began to soak her arms through her too-big shirt, pressed it to her skin. She closed her eyes and let it drench her. The remnants of Clapton's song drifted through the open windows. But it was softened by the rain. By her pounding emotions.

She wanted to go home. *For what?* Danny's question ran through her mind. To be home. Where she belonged. To wait for him.

"Wha' are y' doin'?" Danny's voice startled her.

She opened her eyes as he was wrapping his jacket over her shoulders. Susie pushed it off again. "No."

"Y' will get sick ou' here. It isnae warm enough t' be..."

"He loves the rain. You know that, right? He would walk in it..."

"Suse, come in now." Danny wrapped the jacket around again, held it on.

She shook her head. Heard thunder, saw lightning flash in the distance.

"I know he walked in the rain, yea, bu' he didnae tend t' ge' sick when he did. He wouldnae want y' t' get sick bein' so stubborn. Come in before y' catch the lurgie."

"I'm not cold."

"And I donae want y' t' be. Evan trusted me t' take care of y', y' ken. Donae make me call and tell 'im I couldnae keep y' well because y' wouldnae listen."

"Think that would surprise him?" She watched another streak of light pierce the sky and highlight the tops of nearby trees. She hadn't even jumped. The rain was getting heavy. She shivered. But she didn't want to go in. He was maybe out in it, also. Would it be raining where he was? Maybe not. But maybe he was still wet. Cold. Alone. If this was as close as she could get to being with him, then it was what she wanted.

The rain stopped. No. It was still raining ... an umbrella blocked it. A man stepped in front of her. The guitarist. Staring again. She tried to move away.

He took her arm. "I know who you are."

Susie felt her eyes widen. She felt Danny move closer.

"It's all right. I won't tell anyone." His sharp features were outlined in the glow from the porch light. "I've known since I first saw you here. Figured you needed time to be left alone." His head dipped closer. "If there's anything I can do, let me know. He was a good man..."

Her eyes watered and she turned away, hurried back up the porch and into the bar, through patrons staring at her for being soaked to the skin, back to the door connecting the house. She went in quietly, avoided letting Danielle see her, and disappeared into the little room they shared.

Susie shivered. She still had Danny's jacket over her shoulders. Starting to take it off, she changed her mind and pulled it tighter, ignored a knock, ignored the door that opened anyway. Danny came in and wrapped her in his arms. She let the tears go. Let him hold her in. Felt herself dissolve against him.

He pulled the sopping wig off and dropped it somewhere. "Alrigh', Sis. I' is goin' t' be alright. Go on and take a hot shower and warm yourself again. Y' will feel better."

She shook her head.

"Then if y' willnae shower an' warm up, ge' changed an' under the covers."

She shook her head again.

"Alrigh' then, change an' come on out and we will sit and ge' pissed tonight once Nella is in bed. How is that? That should warm y' right up again."

She chuckled. Bit her lip.

He stepped back to see her face, raised it to his. "I miss him, too. I know it hurts like hell. Bu' y' will, sometime again, feel okay. I will make sure of it." He released her. "Change now. I will be back in a few minutes."

Susie felt a deep heavy breath surge through her body. And her body felt horribly heavy all at once. Fatigued to the core. Knackered, as he would say. She stripped out of the wet clothes, hung them over the hamper, and pulled into some big sweats and one of Duncan's tees. It still smelled like him.

Biting her lip harder, she forced the tears to stop, went to wash her face and put Visine in her eyes to clear the redness, then joined Danny where he was convincing Danielle it was time for bed. Motion at the side door that led to the bar caught her attention. Mel. And the guitarist. Staring at her again.

Mel looked between them. "He said you know he recognizes you, asked only to say hello. I hoped it was okay."

The guitarist whose name Susie couldn't remember approached, ran his eyes over her, shook his head. Danny stepped up beside her. The guy turned to him and extended his hand. "You have to be the brother he talked so much about. Good to meet you. You look like him. Eerie, actually, how much you look like him."

Danny accepted the handshake but barely. "Wha' do y' want?"

"Only to say hello, as I told Mel. We ... all of us in the band feel..."

"Don't." Susie went to Nella. "Come on baby, it's bedtime." She picked the girl up and held her close, headed toward their room.

But he came up to them. "This is his daughter. Beautiful child."

"Thank you." Susie pulled away and closed the door behind her.

"I not like him, my mummy. No."

She was too tense. Nella could feel it. Susie stroked her hair. "It's okay, baby. Want me to read a book before bed?" With her daughter's nod, Susie helped her change into her pajamas and brush her teeth, then chose one of the longer books they'd borrowed from the library, with Mel's card. Maybe the guitarist would be gone by the time she went back out. And she had to call Evan. She'd promised she would since she told him Danny talked her into spending the evening at the bar.

It was late by the time she got Nella to sleep and then got off the phone. Evan asked repeatedly what was wrong. She didn't want to say. She didn't admit to standing in the rain. She did say the guitarist, Frank as he reminded her, recognized her and said he'd stay quiet. Evan figured he probably would and told her not to worry. She'd judged him too harshly, took her mourning out on him ... not mourning, missing. She missed Duncan. She had no reason to mourn, only worry, and miss him.

Evan calmed her about it enough to let her sleep.

Danny knocked softly. Light crept under her door but she didn't answer. It took him a while to get the guy out of Susie's way, but she didn't come back out, so he had to check on her before he could settle in.

He opened the door with an effort not to make noise. The bedside lamp was on, but they were both asleep, cuddled together, with Susie's hand holding Nella's little arm. He crept over to her side of the bed, pulled the covers up farther, and touched Susie's head. He wanted, as much as Gene did, for them to come home with him, back to Scotland, where he could continue to look after them. Duncan would want it, wouldn't he? They were family. They belonged ... they belonged in Lakewood. With the band. Her friends. It's why his brother stayed when Danny knew Scotland pulled at him.

A deep sigh invaded. So he'd come back often, make sure they were doing well. For his brother. For the two people who meant enough to Duncan he would have given up anything for them. If he ever thought Susie needed it, Danny would do the same. He'd give up his home and move closer to them. And it was tempting already. Nella needed a father. If she couldn't have that, she should at least have someone willing to be there as her father would have been. But Stu would be around. Mike. Doug. And Evan: her godfather of sorts.

With the thought swimming in his head, Danny switched off the lamp and closed the door behind him. That could be dangerous ground, he feared. Susie was too close to Evan already, too dependent on him. Letting him become like Nella's father was too dangerous.

5 August

Susie woke to the crash of thunder. She checked her daughter. Still asleep. Like her father, she slept well during storms.

Pulling the blanket up farther over the little shoulders, Susie leaned back onto her pillow and listened to the storm, watching it as well as she could through the small curtained window. It moved quickly, away to where it was only a light rumble in the distance, and she rolled over to grab the phone. She'd owe Joe and Mel a large phone bill if she didn't stop calling him so often. So what if she did?

Waiting through the rings, she took a deep breath at Evan's voice. "Did I wake you?"

"No. I'm lying here listening to a storm move in."

"Are you? I'm lying here listening to a storm move out. It woke me up."

"If it's moving out, you should try to get back to sleep. It's early."

"Is that a nice way of saying I shouldn't call you so early?"

"Oh Angel, of course not. Call any time. You know that. Are you okay?"

She grabbed another deep breath. "I want to go home." Silence came from the other end. "Evan? It's been long enough, hasn't it?"

"I thought you were doing well there. When I ask Danny or Mel, they say you are."

She bit her lip. Apparently her act was better than she expected. "Suse?"

"I need you here. Or I need to be there with you. I can't... Danny's great. So are Mel and Joe, but I ... I need my best friend. I need to be with you through this. Come here. Or I'll go there..."

"Okay."

At the one word, she relaxed, let the tears fall. "Should I go there or home? Where will you be today?"

"Today?"

"Yes. I can't do this anymore."

"Suse, hang on. I'll make arrangements. Stay put until I let you know..."

"Evan..."

"Trust me, Angel." He paused while she stayed silent, as she wondered how long he meant, how many more days. "And hey, I'm glad to know you want me around."

"You know I do. You've always known I do."

"It was a joke, like you asking if you shouldn't call." A pause. "I'll see you soon. Just hang on."

She nodded, biting her lip.

"And yes, I've always known. Go back to sleep, Suse, now that the storm's over."

Susie hung up with a hard swallow. She should have pressed more, insisted on knowing when he meant, but it was too hard to talk and she didn't want him to know how hard it was, how badly she was fighting tears.

When Nella stirred, Susie wiped her eyes, pulled herself together, and turned to find the beautiful trusting little face looking at her. "Morning my mummy. My daddy on phone call? I talk too, yes. I not talk my daddy in long long time."

"Oh baby, I know." Susie scooped her into a hug. "It was Evan."

"I talk my Evan Lee too. Yes." She nearly jumped out of bed and around to the phone to pick it up. "You call back 'gain."

Susie couldn't refuse. At least it distracted her from the daddy conversation. As Nella jabbered into the phone, Susie kissed her head and went out to see if Mel was up and making breakfast so she could offer help she knew would be refused.

Frank was there, at the table, head in hand, nursing a cup of coffee. He looked over and winced and grinned at the same time.

Mel gave her a smile. "Well good morning. You're up early. I would've warned you about the company but ya snuck up on me." She poured a cup of coffee, added a hint of sugar, and brought it over with a nod toward Frank. "Stayed up too late with your brother-in-law sipping Scotch Whisky waiting for you to come back, so we refused to let him leave."

"Oh? So Danny probably isn't feeling well, either?" Susie wished she'd gotten dressed instead of going out in her robe.

"He should be okay." Frank interrupted. "Looked okay last night even if he did out drink me. Embarrassing, if you want to know."

Susie thought about Evan's words, how Frank would probably stay quiet and not to worry, and decided she was being silly to avoid him. She took her coffee over to the stove and asked if she could help. Of course Mel said no. She always said no; she was used to doing it herself and preferred it that way.

"Joe's already up and out, playing outside as though he's taking care of those weeds like he always says he does, never mind I can't never tell he does." Mel shook her head. "Sit down, dear. You look tired still. Storm keep you up?"

"Yes." Susie accepted and sat at the place farthest from the guitarist.

"So what are your plans today?" Frank eyed her with amusement. "How about a jaunt up to Jamestown to see the Deer Park?"

"Deer Park?"

"Like a mini zoo. Not much of one but your little girl might like it. She can pet the goats."

"Oh. I don't know. I might have plans." She sipped her coffee and tried to tell herself he wasn't looking at her in *that* way.

"Might have?" He laughed. "If you're worried about the rain, it's supposed to stop soon. Just wear shoes that can handle mud."

"No, I...." Susie looked out the window. Stop soon? It was gray and windy. It didn't look like it would stop soon. And she wasn't going out with him. Not even to the zoo for her daughter. "I'm waiting for a call. I need to be here."

He nodded. "Well, tomorrow then? Should be even nicer if it's true to what they say."

"Yunz go on ahead." Mel refilled Frank's coffee. "Would do you good to get out. I can take a message for your call."

"No, thank you. I'm tired from yesterday and from not sleeping well. I'd rather stay around the house." She felt Frank studying her but didn't acknowledge his gaze. Nella didn't like him. Susie wasn't sure she did, either.

6 August

When Mel called her to the phone, Susie looked up from where she and Nella were coloring side by side pages of a coloring book, but her daughter beat her to the phone and grabbed it.

Mel started to object, with a look at Susie. "It's not Evan. It's..."

"*My Stuey!*" Nella nearly yelled half into the phone and half at Susie.

Stu. She hadn't talked to him since she'd been there. He had the number. They all had it. Ali and Doug had called a couple of times. Mike called once so Keith could talk to Nella. Adam called three times so far, to make sure she wasn't bothered by anyone, he said. Her dad called a few times. Stu had been silent.

Nella bounced, literally, while she told him about coloring, about the little water at the park, about the rain that never, ever stopped, about Uncle Danny making mud cakes with her ... and then she nodded and gave the phone to Susie.

"Damn it's good to hear your voice. Thought about calling about a million times."

She sank onto a hard wooden chair. "Why didn't you?"

"Didn't want to be a pain in the ass." His voice calmed. "Doing okay?"

"I enjoy you being a pain in the ass." She felt her eyes water and turned away from Nella.

"You don't sound too okay."

"Hey, hold on a sec." Susie asked Mel to take it and hang it up so she could move to the bedroom. "Okay, sorry. Wanted privacy."

"Yeah? I'm flattered."

"Don't be. I'm just trying to hide from my daughter so I can talk easier." She swallowed hard to try to calm herself. "And things are okay here."

"Sounds like it." The sarcasm shined through well. "What can I do?"

"Come take me home." Silence came from the other end. "You're still in New Hampshire though, right?"

"Yes. Did you mean here? You can come up. I'll come and get you or..."

"No, I'm kidding. And I meant home. My home. But Evan's making arrangements, I guess. I'm waiting to hear."

"This was a stupid idea. We never should have agreed to it. Hell, you need us now more than ever, right? That's what I told them. I argued..."

"Yes." She grabbed a deep breath. "I feel like I'm being punished."

"For what?"

"For ... I don't know ... letting him go. Telling him to go. If I hadn't..."

"Stop there."

"It's only fair I got exiled, right? For making such a bad judgment call? But I meant well. He needed time with Danny and..."

"You're not exiled."

"Yes, I am. Evan doesn't even want to stay in the same place with me. How is that not exile?" She sniffed, grabbed a tissue. "Sorry. Guess you were smart not to call just to hear this."

"Danny's still there with you, right?"

"Yes. He's ... out helping to build or fix something. He's been a lot of help to Joe, in exchange for letting us stay. I try, but they keep telling me to relax and ... and I need to be home."

"I'll get you there."

"What?" She wiped her nose again. "No, I'm just... Evan's making arrangements..."

"For when?"

"I don't know. He wouldn't say. A few days, maybe. I don't know. Sorry you called yet?"

"No. I'm damned glad I called. Should have sooner."

"I miss you guys. This... I can't do this. It's too hard."

"Hey, we miss you, too. About every other thing Ali says is about you. And this was a stupid idea. They should have listened to me. They never listen to me, like I'm some kind of moron or something."

"You're not. And I listen to you."

"Yeah. You're the smartest of the bunch."

Susie bit her lip. Took a breath. "So, now that I've bitched enough, what have you been up to? Just talk to me. Fill me in." She wiped her eyes often enough to empty the tissue box as he talked, about his family's farm, his siblings and parents, Mike's family he ran into and how they mentioned they were sorry about his friend's loss and asked where Mike was. He told them Mike was probably putzing around the world showing off his son and girlfriend and doing it in every gorgeous spot they could find, which ticked them off, which made Stu smirk. How Mike's youngest sister flirted with Stu in front of them, which ticked them off even more, so he asked her out. As a joke. She'd accepted so he took her to a movie, just for the movie and she seriously hit on him until he had to back her off.

"Worried that Mike will break your legs?"

"Nah. From what I gather, I don't think he'd care."

"Oh? Then she's not your type?"

"Don't know, Suse. Maybe she could be, but I don't want attachments to her parents. No way in hell. Not worth it."

Susie chuckled. And she saw Mel in the door, knocking to tell her dinner was ready. Had she been on the phone that long? Then Danny was behind Mel, dirt smeared on his face and clothes.

"Want to say hello to Stu?"

Danny raised his eyebrows. "He decided t' pull 'is head out of his arse, did he?"

Susie gave him a grin and said her goodbyes to her friend, handing it off to her brother-in-law. She followed Mel out to get Nella's hands washed and see again if she could help while Danny talked and cleaned up.

"Nice to see ya smiling. He's a special one to you, the one you've been talking to for an hour now?"

"Yes." She noted Mel's raised eyebrows. "They all are. The band. He's our keyboardist." Susie brushed off the not-so-sure nod and remembered the recent rumors about her and Stu, that she was on his list, that she gave him *special* attention on tour when he was sick. Surely, Mel didn't believe it.

Frank came over after dinner and asked if she wanted to go to the local drive in. She and Nella both, of course. He figured the kid might watch the first movie then could sleep in the back during the second. Susie's stomach turned. He was hitting on her. She'd tried to deny it but the look in his eyes, and the way he asked when Danny wasn't close enough to hear, when Joe and Mel were out enjoying their Sunday night, the one night the bar was closed, playing cards with friends ... no, she would not go out with him. She said it would blow her cover if she was seen with another man since she and Danny were supposed to be together. He said that's why he chose the drive-in. No one would see her.

She refused and sent him away.

He was hitting on her. Three weeks and the creep was hitting on her. It made her shiver.

Nella looked up at her curiously. "Not cold here. No."

"No, sweetie, I'm not cold. How about I make graham cracker cookies? I think there's frosting left. Want one?"

"*Yes*. I help." She jumped up and ran to the kitchen.

Susie was quite happy enough alone with Nella and Danny enjoying graham cracker and frosting cookies and watching television. When Duncan came home, he'd take her out when she wanted to go. Or they could stay home, which was just as well, or better.

7 August

Sam's had a small Monday brunch crowd – Mel said it helped defeat the Monday blahs – and Susie refused to sit and do nothing while Mel and Joe worked to serve their customers. She hated the wig, though. And she hated being stuck in exile. No matter what Stu said, she was stuck in exile. Evan couldn't say yet when he'd get her out of there, but she considered leaving on her own. If not for Nella and the threat they'd be discovered, she would.

Maybe she would, anyway. Beau was nearby, so she was told. Susie hadn't seen or heard from him. But she could call Adam and find out how to reach him and tell him she was leaving. He'd follow, or drive.

Susie knew he would.

"Want to watch what you're doing?"

The customer's rude tone brought her back to where she was. A drop of coffee ran down the cup onto the table. Not enough to get irate about. Still, she apologized.

"Stop daydreaming and do what you're paid to do." The gruff old woman sopped up the little spill with a napkin and nearly threw it at Susie.

"Don't talk to her that way." Frank. Standing beside her now.

"Frank Airdale, don't you give me any of your lip. I'll let your mother know..."

"Go ahead, Mrs. Crowder. Let my mother know. But don't talk to her that way again. You don't know who you're talking to."

Susie threw him a warning glance and cut in. "Never mind. I'll get you a fresh napkin."

Frank took her hand to stop her. "No, you won't. Come on. You shouldn't be doing this at all. She's not getting paid, if you need to know. She's only..."

"Don't." Susie pulled away, headed back to the kitchen. He followed as she expected. "You can't do that. You'll blow my cover and..."

"I'm supposed to blow your cover."

"What?"

"Talked to Evan this morning. Part of the plan." He moved closer. "I wouldn't do anything to hurt you, or your daughter. And I do hope, when things calm down, you might consider coming back. To visit. Or to stay." He took her hand again. "I told him he was damned lucky to have caught you. You are beautiful, you know, sexy even in those baggy clothes, charming ... and in time, maybe..."

She pulled back. Stared a second. And pivoted, back to the bar guised now as a café. The nerve of him. No, she didn't like him, not any more than her daughter did. The girl had good intuition. Nella liked most everyone, but not him.

"Hey, I'm sorry."

Susie looked back at where he followed her, his hands raised in a shrug.

He moved closer, although she'd weaved between tables, went to clear dishes from one that was empty. "I was trying to help. For an old friend, you know."

Was he telling the truth? Did Evan want her cover blown? If so, why didn't he tell her?

"You can take the wig off. Your natural hair is so much nicer."

She backed away from him again.

"Susie. Come on. I'm trying to help." His voice was too loud. He had the attention of everyone in the place. And he moved in closer. "He was my friend. If there's anything I can do..."

"Just stop." Before Nella saw him, he had to stop, to back off. She wasn't sure enough that Evan okayed it, and even if he did, she didn't. Not like this.

"Hey man." A guy around his age came to his side, threw him a curious look. "Who was your friend? What's up?"

"You don't recognize her?" Frank grinned. "Mel and Joe have been hosting a celebrity right under our noses."

She tried to back away but he caught her hand. "Let go."

"Celebrity?" The guy frowned and studied her. "Doesn't look familiar."

"It's the wig."

Suddenly, Danny pushed between and took her in his arms. "Come on. Someone found out. You have t' ge' out of here."

Susie felt herself pushed through the bar and into the back room while Danny said he'd take her and Nella somewhere else and come back for their things. She was in Mel's house before she found her wits. Frank was there, too. And Beau, talking with Nella.

Danny spoke into her ear. "I' is alrigh', Suse. Just go along with it an' I will explain la'er."

"I'm not going anywhere with him."

"Beau?"

"No." She glanced at Frank.

"He is part of the plan. Donae worry."

No. Maybe he was. But there was more. The way he looked at her...

"My mummy, we go home again now. Yes. Mr. Beau say we go now to our home."

Susie picked her up and held her close. "Okay, baby. Let's go pack a few things..."

"No time." Beau tried to take Nella. "I'll come back for it."

"I'm not leaving my..." She stopped. It wasn't anyone's business what she couldn't leave.

"Grab whatever is that important. Leave the rest."

She bristled at Beau's order. It wasn't his job to order her. It wasn't Evan's job to set this up without telling her. She didn't have to do it if she decided not to. Maybe she'd ... take off somewhere else, just her and Nella and ... and not if there was a crowd gathering as she just heard someone say.

"*Wha'* in the fuck are you *doin'* here?"

Susie turned to see who Danny was yelling at. Stu cut through the crowd. Nella jumped at him and he caught her in a big hug. "I came to take you both home where you belong. Just in time, from the looks of it."

A couple of their guards were there. Susie wasn't sure if Beau called them or if Stu brought them, but she fell in against him and gripped the back of his shirt. "Thank you." He smelled like faded aftershave and sweat. She buried her face in closer.

His arm tightened around her. "Took three planes and a couple of cabs plus a rental since cabs don't come out this far, not to mention getting lost in the woods twice. Would've been here sooner if it wasn't in the middle of nowhere."

"Y' arenae supposed t' be here. Ge' out before anyone sees y'."

Susie looked at her brother-in-law. "No. I don't know what's going on or what plans have been made, but we're going home with Stu." A flash hit her face. A cameraman. Inside Mel's house? No, at the door, where Frank pushed him out again.

Beau went to peer out the window. "Change of plans. Can't go out there now." He shook his head at Stu. "You bring them all with you?"

"No, they were pulling up as I did, or were here already. Why? I thought they were undercover." He set Nella down but kept a hand on her shoulder.

"They were. Until today. It was part of the plan and you aren't supposed to be here. Does Adam know...?"

"No. She said she wanted me to take her home and Evan couldn't give me a timeline so I came to get them. They're coming home with me. Make it work however you have to."

Danny pulled Susie's attention. "You told him to come get you?"

"No. Well, yes. But I was..."

"I wouldnae le' anything happen t' you. Y' know I wouldnae."

"I know. But I want to be home. I told you I did."

"I amnae runnin' the show. I only..."

"I'm running the show. At least as far as where my daughter and I go. It's my choice."

"Evan 'ad it planned ou' for y'..."

"I don't care." She turned to Beau. "Make it work, like Stu said. We're going home."

"No one else is there yet." Their young guard looked flustered.

"Stu will be, and I suppose Danny is coming..."

"Y' are damned right I am."

"Then it's good enough." She stared at the large man Duncan had assigned to her and Danielle. She wouldn't back down. To hell with Adam's plan, or Evan's plan, or whoever had been calling the shots. She was calling her own from now on.

Frank sidled around Beau and in front of her. He set a hand on her arm. "I think it would be better to follow the plan. We can get Stuart out of here again... Nice to meet you, by the way." He gave Stu a nod and put his focus back on Susie. "Let things calm down and I'll stay right here, to help watch the door or whatever." He stepped closer yet, slid the hand up her arm.

Susie stepped back. "Don't."

"Susie, let me help. Follow the course." He tried to touch her face.

As she pulled back, Stu shoved a hand against his chest. "*Back* the hell *off*. What is *wrong* with you? Hitting on her when she's only been widowed three weeks? Who the hell *are you*, anyway?"

He introduced himself as Duncan's old band mate and insisted he wasn't...

Susie picked Nella up and headed to their room, closing the door behind. She couldn't hear that. Her daughter could not hear the fight about whether he was or wasn't hitting on her. But at least she wasn't crazy. Stu saw it.

"My *mummy*." Nella tugged at her when Susie set her down. "We go with my Stuey now. Yes. To our home."

"Yes, baby." Susie knelt to pull her into a hug. "Yes, we're going home with Stu. Don't worry. Everything's okay. Come on, let's start putting our clothes in our suitcases so we'll be ready to go." The first thing she grabbed was her notebook, the journal she was keeping for Nella, to explain things to her she couldn't now, plus notes about her life with Duncan, things he said and did, things people said about him she should know, the truths behind the rumors, the real story. Just in case.

No matter how he liked Stu, Danny wished he had stayed out of it.

He understood what Evan was doing. It made him respect his brother's friend more than he ever had. It was for Susie's good, and for Danielle's … and for Duncan's name. She was sent to stay with Duncan's old friends instead of with any of the band for a reason. A damned good reason. And Stu just blew it. Yet he couldn't be angry with him. Susie had calmed since he came, since he promised to take her home within hours, not days. They would leave during the night, late into the night, after the crowds had gone home to bed.

He looked across the room from where he played cards with Nella at Susie and Stu, sitting close, talking alone. She trusted Stu. And as Duncan had told him more than once, she adored him. Only a buddy, he said, like him and Ev. The way she was cuddled next to him, though, Danny could easily see them being more than that. Eventually. In a couple of years or so when she decided it was time to start again.

Despite the cringe in his stomach, he wanted her to do it. Eventually. When it had been long enough. Maybe even with Stu. Danny could be comfortable with that. Eventually.

"Uncle Danny. *Look.* You the old maid." Nella laughed.

"Nae, I cannae be an old maid. Maids are lasses, no' lads."

"But you lost and I won. Yes. *See?* You the old maid 'cause you lost."

"Nella." Susie called over to her. "Be a nice winner. Don't be rude."

"I no' rude, my mummy. Uncle Danny is too the old maid. We play cards only. Mine all ou' first."

Stu laughed and joined them at the table with a hand on Danny's shoulder. "Hey, I can easily see you as an old maid. Who's gonna want to stay with your ass long term?"

"Watch the language in front of her, please."

Stu shrugged at Susie. "You know she's going to hear it. With as much as she's been around him, I'm surprised she's not saying worse already."

"He's careful in front of her."

Stu lowered his voice. "Bet you had a hard time saying much of anything without your favorite word thrown in."

"And you are one to talk. Nella bird, are y' all packed t' go home?"

"Yes." She nodded hard. "I put all my clothes in my bag and I take it back home again. Yes. And my daddy be home again, too. Stuey take us and we go see my daddy."

Danny stared at her. No one had told her that. No one had even mentioned him to her.

Susie came over and interrupted before he could think how to answer. She hugged her daughter and kissed her head. "No, baby. Your daddy isn't home. I'm so sorry. I know you miss him."

Nella pulled back and frowned again. "He gone too long now. Yes. You call and say come home now. His Dani-nella want him home again. Yes. You say so."

"Oh baby. I know. And I'm sorry. I want him home, too. But Stu will be there with us, and Evan and Mike and Doug and Ali and Kate and Keith. They might not be there yet but they will be soon. Okay? Maybe Keith will come up and stay with us a couple of days. What do you think?"

Nella frowned again but let it go to pick up her miniature cards and shuffle them. Blocking it out. Susie was going to have to tell her. Danny saw it leading to too many problems if she didn't, and soon.

8 August

Susie rubbed her eyes and stared out at the edge of Glenn Heights. Beau had orders to go straight to Lakewood, but Susie overruled him. Evan was in Glenn Heights. It was nearly straight on their route. They could go the rest of the way home together. Besides, it was a six hour drive from Greenville to the eastern side of Pennsylvania and so a good stop and rest point. Beau suggested a hotel. Susie didn't want a hotel. She wanted to be home, but Beau and the other guards had driven through the night. They needed sleep before driving the final four hours to Lakewood.

Other than not wanting to go to a hotel, Susie wanted to see Evan. She'd refused to talk to him the night before when he called. Her anger got the best of her. He should have told her of the plan to be sure she was seen at Joe and Mel's before she came home so people would know that's where she'd been. He was her friend, not her father; he had no right to make those decisions without asking her. Even her father didn't do that anymore and hadn't since she was about ten or so. He always talked to her first, asked her thoughts.

Still, she missed him. As much as she didn't like Glenn Heights, if he was there, it was fine. It had always been okay as long as he was there. Only after he moved away had it been...

"So this is where you and Evan spent your childhood." Stu peered out at the small town, the well-kept houses in various styles, many either redone Victorians or Cape Cods, others Ranch style or two-story brick houses she didn't know what to call. "Suits him better than you."

Susie considered saying something smartass in the vein of no shit, it *was* Evan's town, not hers, and he already knew damn well she hadn't fit there, but just because she was annoyed with Evan, she wouldn't take it out on Stu. With a sigh, she stroked a hand over Nella's head. "Wake up, baby. We're nearly at..." She almost said they were at grandma's. "Diane's. It's morning. The sun's out."

Nella raised her head from Susie's lap and rubbed her eyes, then sat up and looked around. "We at Evan Lee's home. Yes. I know that." She pointed at the little park where Susie, Evan, and Jeremy used to swing. "My Evan Lee take me to swing, my mummy?"

Surprised she remembered, as long as it had been, Susie told her they'd have to see and maybe he would, and gave Beau the final directions to the house. No crowd. Relief drained into her tired body. She'd drifted to sleep now and then through the night drive but not often. Her dad's car was there. Evan's wasn't. Maybe he was out at the store or something. He still did that, she knew, when he was home. The locals didn't bother him much. They respected his space. He could still be human at home. Susie hoped it would work for her and Nella, as well.

Although they weren't staying. It was a one day stop through. They'd rest and let the drivers sleep and then take off again late at night. Maybe. If they were left alone enough, there was no reason they couldn't leave in the morning like normal people.

The front door opened as they pulled in and her dad and Diane stepped out. Nella nearly stomped all over Susie while she pulled out of her seat belt and pushed out the car door to run to her grandpa's arms. By the time Susie got there, Diane had her distracted with the promise of chocolate chip pancakes and the girl ran inside to wash up, dragging Stu and Danny along with her. Diane introduced herself to the guards she hadn't met and invited them in. They called her ma'am and said they could go to a local hotel. She let them know it was already arranged for them to stay at the house. Evan had insisted.

Susie knew Beau was waiting to see if she would contradict Evan again. She didn't. It didn't matter if they were there. When her dad asked how she was doing, Susie fell into his arms and closed her eyes. He kissed her head as her fingers tightened around him. She heard Beau tell him she'd barely slept and that Danny, in the front with him, didn't sleep at all but kept him company instead. She heard her dad tell them to go on inside and have breakfast before they lay down. But she kept hold.

"Come inside, sweetheart. You need to eat and rest."

"Where's Evan?"

"He went back to Lakewood."

"What?" Susie raised her face to his.

"He said it would be better if you went the rest of the way with Beau and Danny, and Stu since he tagged along."

Better? He'd left, knowing she would be there?

"My *mummy*." Nella came back and grabbed at her arm. "My Evan Lee not here. No."

John picked her up. "Miss Nella, did you wash for breakfast?"

"Yes. I wash with water and soap too. But my Evan Lee not here to swing me. I go to swings and play after pancakes with choc'late chips and lots and lots of syrup."

John chuckled. "How about I take you? Will that work?"

Nella took her grandpa's face in her little hands. "Yes. You swing me high. Like the birdies."

"We'll see about that." He set her down again. "Go on and eat. We'll be right there."

Susie walked over to the porch swing and plopped onto it. He hadn't waited for her. He knew they were headed to Glenn Heights. She knew he did. Was he mad that she wouldn't talk the night before? Still, he could have waited a few hours or... "When did he go?"

"This morning, after Beau let us know you were headed this direction instead of home. I was about to head there to meet you but he had to change plans so he asked if I'd stay and see you home.

Sweetheart, you should have done things the way he asked."

"He didn't ask. He *didn't* ask me. He just..."

"He has reasons."

She nodded, biting her lip. Reasons. And her dad would never take her side on it. Overprotective. Kate was right. Overprotective to the point he wouldn't even ask her opinion; he just planned around her and expected her to listen, to do as she was told. That wasn't very fucking likely, not anymore.

She'd told him she needed him, that she wanted to be with him through this, that ... and he left when he knew she would be there. Why?

"So how was Greenville? You didn't say much over the phone."

"Lonely." As she said it, she wished she could take it back.

He wrapped an arm over her shoulders. "I suppose I don't have to say how unfair it is for you to have to go through this, also."

"You don't believe fair exists. Isn't that what you said? Just like Evan. Neither of you believe it. Why should I?"

"And I was right, because this isn't." He squeezed her shoulder. "Have you told Nella yet?"

Susie shook her head.

"Sweetheart, you have to tell her. She needs to know."

"Why? It didn't make me feel better. It didn't hurt any less knowing for sure I'd never see Mom again. At least she ... she has a maybe, anyway."

He pivoted to face her better. "No, she doesn't have a maybe. Susan..." He rested a hand alongside her head. "I know it hurt you. I know it'll hurt Danielle. But would you rather I had lied and told you she went away and maybe she'll come back when I knew she never would? Would that have helped you?"

"I'm not lying to her."

"Not telling her is the same."

"No, it isn't. It *isn't*. Because I *don't* know."

He stood, stared. Turned and walked a few steps away and came back. "I think you should talk to someone when you get home. Someone to help you get through this."

Susie got up and went into the house. Talk to someone. No. She had plenty of people to talk to. She had Danny and Stu and ... and Evan. She wanted him there. She wanted to punch him in the stomach, but she wanted him there.

Diane found her as she was heading upstairs to wash her face and hands and change clothes. "There you are. Evan's on the phone, checking to see that you got here all right. Do you want to talk a minute?"

"No. Tell him we're fine." She continued up to her room, the room that she grew up in, that had been her ... her exile after losing her mom. No, it wasn't the same. She wasn't lying to her daughter. She was not. It was still a maybe.

Not a maybe. He was coming home. And he could punch Evan in the stomach for her. But he wouldn't. He'd try to understand it from his friend's viewpoint. She couldn't. She was too totally pissed off to even try.

She should have talked to him. His mom let it "slip" that he hadn't been home yet when he called. He'd stopped for gas and to use the phone to check on her and had to cut the call short because he'd been recognized. He had no guards with him. After Adam's lecture about them all having guards, Evan didn't. He hadn't called back yet. He should have been in.

Susie paced around the house and then went out to the front porch and paced along the porch. He should have called. Where was he? Danny followed her out, told her he would be fine, she should rest. She couldn't answer. She should have talked to him.

Biting her lip hard, she lowered to the steps and looked out over the flower gardens she used to help Diane with. They were scarce this year. Weeds were trying to overtake the few flowers, all bulbs and perennials, no annuals as filler the way Susie had always done. She got up again to pull weeds. At least she could keep her hands busy while she waited.

A car slowed in front of the house. Susie heard it, decided to ignore it. Her back was turned, her hair pulled up. She was weeding. No one would expect her out there pulling weeds.

"Sis, y' might want t' come inside."

She didn't want to be inside. She wanted to clean up the flower beds, maybe go see if the local nursery had a few annuals left. Even if they were the last of the season's offerings, it would make the beds look nicer.

A car door slammed. She turned. Two reporters headed her direction, called her name as though it was a question. As she stood, Danny reached her side and put an arm around her, escorted her in, and locked the door. More cars pulled up. The phone rang.

"Where's Nella?"

"In the back with Stu."

Susie ran through the house but by the time she got there, her dad had Nella in his arms and Stu followed them in. He locked the door. Susie took her daughter, told her it was fine, they couldn't get in. There would be no going to the park after lunch, not even with their guards. The phone rang again. Diane answered, told someone she had no comment and not to call back. It rang nearly as soon as she hung up.

"We have to leave." Susie looked at Stu. He nodded.

Her dad said they should wait it out, let them go away and leave during the night as planned. She went back to the front window. More cars. People on foot. Cameras. "No. It'll get worse." She went to grab the ringing phone, heard a strange voice, clicked the bar to disconnect and called Evan's apartment. Five rings. Then voicemail. He should have been there. She tried Adam.

Robin answered, said yes they heard from him and he's fine but they were holding him up outside of town until they could get the streets cleared enough. Someone heard they were coming back today. The town was packed. Adam wanted her to stay where she was.

In exile. Again. But Evan was okay. She agreed for the moment and talked Nella into watching a movie with her. Beau was up; the phone woke him. He woke Vasquez to stand watch at the back door as he watched the front and let Clemens sleep so he'd be able to drive all night. Susie told him he should sleep, also. Her dad was there. Danny. Stu. No one would get in. He said he was on the job and he'd sleep when he wasn't needed. She went to make him and Vasquez – she didn't know his first name – fresh coffee. Susie tried to ask his first name when she took it to him. He preferred his last. She was uncomfortable calling him that, so she just thanked him for the help and Nella handed him cookies she'd found in Diane's jar. They were store bought since Diane rarely baked, but it was a nice gesture and got a grin from the large man.

They should have gone straight to Lakewood, as Evan suggested.

9 August

Evan paced around the apartment. They should have been home by now. He should have waited and driven back with them. But they were being watched too closely. A couple of people in Glenn Heights who knew him even mentioned the rumors about the two of them. He and Susie. He flatly denied it. The ones about her and Stu were harder to deny, especially since Stu had been stupid enough to go to Greenville to meet her. Susie could say all she wanted that it didn't matter, that she didn't care what people thought, but it did matter. For too many reasons.

And they should have been home by now.

Unable to stay put and just wait, he went down to the front door, peered out at the huge crowd, grabbed a deep breath, and went up again. Mike wasn't back yet. Adam hadn't reached him that Evan knew of. Doug would be back in a couple of days. He wanted to wait until Susie was home and resettled before bringing Ali into the mess.

It was still a mess. Fans surrounded the building. Adam said they'd been there since they heard the band was coming home. Evan didn't mind that. Most of them were respectful. What he minded were the damned vultures with cameras trying to get a story to sell to make a buck or two off of them. It was all well and fine when they were on the road working, but at their home day and night was too much.

He had to wonder if that "couple of days" might turn into more for Doug, if he was waiting to see if it was too much hassle to be worth it. After all, what were they doing now? They'd given up on album promotion. He and Adam agreed there was no real point since Duncan had done all of that for them unintentionally. What next? Without their lead guitarist, they wouldn't be doing anything. Unless they replaced him.

The thought made him start to shake again, as he had too often while he was at home after talking with Susie. Fatigue. Nerves. He had to pull himself together. He paced to relieve tension. Being away from her now was hard as hell. Still, it was better. She couldn't know how hard a time he was having with it himself. And that had to stop. He had to be there for her. For Danielle.

Danielle. Evan stopped pacing and crouched, hands locked behind his head. Danielle, who was so fully attached to her dad, would need him. For as much as he could do for her. He felt his eyes water and pushed himself up again, went to the kitchen, and grabbed a beer. He put it back. No. He wouldn't do that. He would have one occasionally when socializing, but not for emotional reasons. Never for that. He'd seen where that led.

Instead, he turned on a burner and filled a pan halfway with water, adding several tea bags. He'd already made a pitcher of tea at Susie's so it would be ready for her. He had a few groceries in her apartment, fresh vegetables, and plenty of bananas for Nella, with help from the store. He didn't dare go himself, not until things calmed. They were happy to deliver. He'd opened windows to air the apartment, checked to make sure all was as it should be. Stopped in the little hallway between the bedrooms and main rooms where she had several photos framed. Their wedding photo. Nella's baby photo and one from each birthday so far. A few of the three of them together. A nice one of the band. One from Scotland of Duncan with his brother and sister. And one of him and Duncan together. She'd caught them at the perfect time, both with grins, with their guitars.

Evan leaned back against the counter for support. He felt half empty. He couldn't imagine feeling any other way for some time to come, possibly ever. Thank the Lord Nella had been sick so he still had them.

And they should have been back by now.

The doorbell made him jump. Evan went to check. Adam asked if he'd heard from them yet. "No. Hoped you did." He went back to the kitchen and pulled a package of hamburger from the refrigerator. He could go ahead and make the patties, maybe throw the fries on a baking sheet to put in the oven as soon as they got home. He'd promised Nella burgers and fries with plenty of ketchup.

"They probably left later than expected."

He nodded. Except they didn't. His mom let him know the minute they left, much later than they should have. They should have left early that morning as planned. Why she kept changing everything on him, even if she was annoyed, he couldn't understand. It would have worked better. There would have been fewer people outside to get through. She hadn't even told him herself. She let John tell him. Infuriating. She was so ... damned infuriating, and damn did he miss her.

"So it worked well, even if Stu did change the plan for us." Adam made himself at home, lowering onto a kitchen chair.

"Did it?" Evan opened the hamburger and dumped it into a bowl.

"It's pretty well known by now where she's been, and Doug helped out by spreading it around in New Hampshire that Stu's been up there. I hear Mike's little sister helped with that, too, although I'm not sure Mike will be thrilled considering how she's saying she knew Stu was there."

Evan washed his hands well. "He won't care."

"No? You know what she was saying?"

"I can guess, and it doesn't matter. He won't care." He grabbed several seasoning bottles.

"Good. So overall, it worked fine. You don't seem relieved."

"They should be here by now." He dashed a bunch of seasoning into the meat and returned the jars to the shelf.

"They're fine. I'm sure of it."

"Are you? How?" He stopped mixing it together long enough to eye their producer.

"I haven't heard otherwise."

Evan gritted his teeth and turned back. He was probably right. That kind of news would travel fast. As they well knew.

Susie peered out the car window, keeping Nella's head low with an arm holding her close, at the row of police cars, their lights flashing. A blockade. For what? Just outside Lakewood? Could anything else go wrong on the trip? They were so close. She was still shaky from being up all night running back and forth to the bathroom. Her stomach was still touchy. At least she'd been able to keep water down for the past couple of hours. The tuna sandwich. It had to be. Evan had left instructions for dinner to be delivered and had paid it already. She chose tuna. So did Clemens. They were both up all night. At least Nella had turned her nose up at the thought of tuna. Her macaroni and cheese was apparently just fine.

The thought of it turned her stomach again and she held Nella closer when her dad rolled down the window at an officer's request. He looked in the back seat, directly at her, and waved someone else over. Her stomach twisted. Evan. He was the only one in town. Something happened.

She needed to get out, find a toilet.

"About time, John. What took you so long?" Chief Carr's friendly voice drifted through the car.

"What's going on?" Her dad asked. Susie didn't dare speak.

The chief gave her a nod. "Huge crowd around her place. And yours. Word got out they were coming in today. Adam says we should guide you to his place instead."

Huge crowd. She swallowed hard. "Where's Evan?"

"At the apartment. Wasn't as bad when he came in. Pull on over here and let us let these people around and out of the way. How many are with you?"

Her dad said just the car behind them, with Danny and Stu. They both veered into the parking lot off the road, far enough those on the road couldn't see them well. But they would know. Officers flagged them to keep going, to move along.

Her dad got out when they stopped. Nella tried. Susie held onto her, told her not to push on her stomach. She rolled the window down just enough to hear. *To Adam's...*

"No. Take me home." She got argument as she expected, but she wouldn't back down. Beau would take her where she demanded, with or without police escort, and they didn't need it, they had their guards. Since she wouldn't give in, they did.

It was odd having their car fronted and backed by squad cars plus the chief in lead. Her dad repeated what the chief told him: they'd followed Evan in or heard that he had returned and figured Susie would be with him. There were rumors that they'd found Duncan and were bringing him home.

Susie distracted Nella so she wouldn't hear and gritted her teeth. That explained it. The crowd. For him, not for her. Evan kept saying they wanted to see her and Danielle. He was wrong. They thought he had come home.

A heck of a homecoming it would be for him when he did. She pressed an arm against her stomach. Beau noticed through the rear-view mirror, asked if she had to stop. No, she'd hold on. She was almost home. Evan was there. And if he'd waited and gone in with them, there wouldn't have been such a crowd. He should have waited.

She gaped at the scene on their road. It took forever to clear people and cars away so they could creep through and into the parking area. Beau told her not to get out, as though he had to say it. Nella clung to her, wide-eyed. More of their guards were there. The officers got out and started moving people away, threatening arrest since they were on private property. It took forever. Susie tried to keep herself calm as she told Danielle it was all right, not to worry.

Finally, Chief Carr opened her door, asked Nella to go to him. The girl shook her head, clung to Susie.

"No, she stays with me."

"Susan, let me carry her inside the building and I'll give her right back. Your guard will stay at your side..."

"No." She hated to argue with her dad's friend, and she understood, but...

He squatted beside the car door. "No one will dare try to pull her from me if they get through my men. They know who I am."

Right, and he was six foot something, big shouldered, heavy muscled. She understood that. But she couldn't let go of her baby. "No one will get her out of my arms, either. I will guarantee that." Susie set her jaw, looked him in the eyes.

He chuckled. "I'm sure you're right. Come on then."

Danny tried to take Nella, also. Susie refused. No matter how bad she felt, she was keeping hold of her baby.

No one got close enough to worry about, not with Chief Carr on one side of her and Beau on the other, plus their guards surrounding them and Stu and Danny and her dad. She didn't have to worry about photos of Nella's face. Her baby kept it buried against Susie's neck, her little arms tight around her shoulders.

"It's all right, now, Angel. Let me take her."

At Evan's voice, Nella jumped at him. They were inside. The front door. Susie grabbed at the arm next to her. Danny. Eying her. Asking if she was okay. She shook her head. Looked around. They were all inside. Including the chief and a couple of his men. She had to... She found Stu, looked at his door. "Let me in."

He got it unlocked, helped her inside and to the hall. She shut them out on the other side of the bathroom door. She shook. And nearly collapsed against the sink while washing her mouth, her hands, her face...

She woke up in her own bed.

Susie had no idea how she got from ... from Stu's bathroom to her room, but she had a sore shoulder and a sore wrist. She sat up, heard voices. Nella's. And...

She was dizzy when she tried to stand and sat down again, gave herself more time, then made her way to her own bathroom and washed her face. She needed a shower. Why was she sore? Twisting her hand, she decided the wrist wasn't bad. Maybe she'd strained herself more than she thought while carrying Danielle.

Drying her face, she carefully made her way to the living room. Nella ran at her, said something about hamburgers and fries and... Susie's stomach twinged. Danny captured the child. Asked how she felt. When she just looked at him, her dad took her arm and led her to the couch and told her she'd passed out.

"Guess that explains my shoulder."

Doc was there. Sat next to her. Pressed his thumbs into where it hurt and she cringed again. He apologized. She didn't dare mention the wrist. She looked around. The chief was still there. Off duty, he said, hanging out.

Evan wasn't there. Again, he wasn't there. She lay down against the arm of the couch, heard a question about soup, closed her eyes.

He heard Adam ask if he was all right. It was a stupid question. She'd passed out. Food poisoning, on top of everything. And he hadn't been there. Maybe Duncan was right. Maybe they should all just say fuck the rumors and go about their business; he could stay at her side where he should have been and let them think as they wish.

Easy for Duncan to say, though, since he wasn't being accused of inappropriate relations with his friend's wife. Affairs, yes. He had plenty of those accusations, but even if they had been true, that wasn't as bad as screwing over your best friend with his wife. And the real problem was Evan's feelings for her that he couldn't even deny. He felt guilty enough. It was too close for comfort.

Maybe he would call Steph, see if she'd come over after work. She'd offered to skip work, to be there with him today. He should have taken her up on it.

"Evan?" Adam moved in front of him, took the spatula from his hand, and flipped the burgers in the pan. "Let me do this while we talk."

They were nearly too done on one side. "No, I got it."

"You're exhausted."

He reclaimed the spatula, and made himself return to business. Roy could sit there and scowl all he wanted. It changed nothing. He was already keeping Evan next door, away from Susie, because he insisted on talking about what was next, where they were going ... and trying to force Evan to take lead guitar.

"So." Adam remained beside him, on his feet. "I have options for both lead guitar and bass, depending on what you decide. I do tend to agree with Roy that you should take lead, although I also understand your feelings about it and that does matter." He glanced at Roy. "It does. You don't want a lead guitarist who doesn't really *want* to be lead guitar. It'll show."

"He can *learn* to want to be."

"You can learn to *do* it; you can't learn to *want* to do it if you don't."

"Hell you can't. It's only because of that greaser he doesn't want to. He did before."

Evan clenched his jaw but refused to react. Roy was only trying to get to him. Wasn't going to happen. And he wasn't right. He didn't want to. He wanted Duncan there, just as he'd always wanted. He wouldn't mind having a bassist along with lead guitar so he could stay on acoustic which he preferred, but he'd never wanted to be lead.

Adam sat again. "Regardless of the reasons, and if that's true, it's as valid a reason as any other, if he doesn't want to..."

"This is a waste of time." Roy shoved himself up from the table, scratching the chair against the floor. "Might as well go out and tell them we're done. Finished. Tell them you're all just walking away from your fans just because you lost one freaking guitarist who could be replaced easy enough. Tell them to go screw themselves because the greaser matters to you more than *they* do."

Evan slammed the spatula down and found his fist around Roy's collar. "Shut the fuck up *now* before I take you out the way he wanted to, and should have, for being such a rude, obnoxious *asshole*. You *know* why you're still here. *I* can change that. *Don't* forget that for *one fucking second.*"

Adam pushed between them. Evan nearly didn't let him. He wanted to pound Roy's round soft scowling face into the wall. If he had a better option, could find someone willing to work the way he needed him to work, the asshole would be gone. It was too risky to try. At least for now.

"Come on, Evan. You're right. I know you're right, but don't do this." Adam pushed his chest, trying to add space.

Only because Roy was barely smart enough to keep his mouth shut did Evan release his grip with a shove. With every muscle in his body tensed, he forced deep breaths until he could return to the burgers, Nella's burgers, as he promised her.

When Adam asked, carefully, what he wanted him to do, to find a guitarist or bassist, Evan shook his head. "Neither."

"You're screwing over your fans and walking away? You can't do that..."

He shot a look at Roy. "It's not the fans you're worried about; it's your money, for doing next to nothing, by the way."

"Who in the hell got you all those shows when you were still *nothing?*"

Evan snickered. "Susie did. Most of them. Play it off all you want. I know better, even if she doesn't realize I know. I do know. There's very little I don't know." He moved the too-browned burgers to the plate and added more to the pan, stuck the plate in the oven to keep them warm. "You might remember that, too." Calming with his voice of authority, he dismissed Roy and spoke to Adam. "We're not quitting, and we're not replacing him. We'll manage with just the four of us." Before Roy could yell, Evan threw him a warning.

"So ... you're taking lead?"

"Depends. We'll talk. I will if I can't get Stu to do it."

"You'd lose keyboards."

He shrugged. "Not all bands have keyboards, at least not prominently. We can work around it, do it in the studio, not on stage, or hire a road musician and make it more background."

"Evan..."

"I can't do it." He swallowed hard, kept his eyes on the frying meat. "I can't bring someone else in. I'd rather walk away."

Adam set a hand on his shoulder. "All right. We'll make it work. And I do understand."

He nodded but continued making lunch. Roy left. Pissed. As though Evan gave an ounce of concern to whether he was pissed. He wasn't going anywhere, not until Evan decided things had to change. He'd take lead guitar if necessary. He would not let things change more than that, not yet.

Susie had managed to drink some tea and she'd nibbled on crackers. It was at least enough she felt okay to sit up and to walk around to some extent. She watched, amused, as her daughter piled Dominoes on Chief Carr's outstretched arm to see how many she could get to stay. He was amused, also. His kids were older, both married, neither with kids yet. He said he missed that age and envied John his granddaughter. So he held still and let her pile up the Dominoes.

Susie wasn't sure if he was still there to play with Danielle, to talk with her dad, or because he thought he needed to be for safety reasons. Her guards had been sent to sleep, but she was sure at least a couple of them were still hovering around the building since it was still a madhouse out there.

A knock sent Nella flying to the door, scattering the Dominoes, and her grandpa caught her before she could open it. *"My Evan Lee."*

He picked her up and accepted a big hug. "Hey, little one. Are you getting hungry?" As Nella nodded hard, although she'd just snacked on pretzels and cheese, Evan looked over at Susie. "How do you feel? Think you can eat? I have hamburgers and fries ready, but I can do a quick soup..."

"We're fine. I'll cook for her. I have pork chops defrosting."

Her dad jumped on that, said she didn't need to be cooking.

"No, I have burgers and fries, my mummy. I not like bro'kees an' chops. No." She shook her head.

"I have it ready, Suse..."

"Maybe you should have asked me first. She's my daughter. You don't make decisions for her without asking, or for me, either." Maybe it was rude to say it in front of company, but she couldn't care. She got up and went to the kitchen. She could take care of her daughter on her own, no matter what. She could.

He followed but didn't bother to say anything. He just stood there like some ... some bodyguard or ... prison guard. It wasn't bad enough she felt exiled in Greenville; now she felt imprisoned in her own home, by the crowd out front, by feeling like total hell, by ... the one who was supposed to be her friend. Her friend, not her guardian. Not her guard or...

She gave up on the pork chops. Still too frozen. She still had no strength. He stepped closer and she turned to him. "I don't know *what* you were thinking, setting me up like that without even bothering to ask if it was okay, but it wasn't. Was he supposed to hit on me, too? Because it wasn't funny, and it wasn't okay. And if you weren't going to be in Glenn Heights, you should have let me know so Nella wouldn't have expected you to be. She's dealing with enough and she wanted to see you and..." And so did she.

"Have you told her?"

"Told her what?"

"Suse, you know what."

"That's not your business. But I guess I'll have to let her have hamburgers with you tonight since you said she could. Next time, *ask* me." She gripped the counter for support. She needed to sit.

"Fine. I apologize. For the hamburgers without permission. If you'd rather, I'll bring them over and leave again so she can still have them."

"Don't be an ass. I'm not in the mood."

His shoulders pulled back. "What do you want from me, Suse?"

She started to speak and stopped. Shook her head. Then looked at him. He hadn't shaved. For at least a couple of days. It was nice, really. Rugged. The hair he had cut too short in the back was growing in – his hair always grew so fast. It looked better. It looked more like him. Except for the short beard and the lines under his eyes, the redness of his pupils. Red. Fatigue, she hoped.

He moved in and took her hand. "How about you be mad at me later? You need to sit down. I can see..."

"Don't screw with me."

He was taken aback by her language. Susie supposed it was good she didn't say what she nearly had. "Okay. Did you hurt yourself when passed out? Can I at least ask that much?"

"You know I did?"

"Are you kidding? I brought you upstairs. Figured you'd rather be in your own bed than Stu's. Did you hurt yourself? We checked your head. Doc said you seemed okay."

Brought. Carried, he meant. He'd carried her upstairs so she'd be where he knew she'd rather be. She felt her eyes try to water and pulled from him, forced the tears back; she wasn't doing that anymore. "I'm fine. Bruised my shoulder. It's not bad."

"Good. Would you come sit down? Wait. Who hit on you?"

She met his gaze. "The guitarist. Frank. Your idea, too?"

"He didn't..."

From his expression, she knew it wasn't his idea, and he wasn't any happier about it than she was. "Don't worry; Stu shoved him and told him to back the hell off."

His chest filled and released. His face was hard. "I never liked that asshole. He assured me I could trust him."

"Yeah well..." A wave of dizziness hit her.

Evan's arm went around her. He helped her to the couch. She lay down, told Nella not to worry, to go next door and have hamburgers and she'd come later.

She was overruled. He wasn't leaving her. If she had the energy, she would have laughed at the absurdity. He could leave her in Greenville for two weeks during one of the lowest times in her life, but he wouldn't go across the hall when she was home and her dad was there with her? He brought the food to her place. At least he was smart enough to let her dad try to get her to eat instead of doing it himself. Since she needed to build strength again, enough to take care of her daughter, Susie forced herself to eat as much as she could handle.

10 August

"My *Evan Lee*, Come. Look."

Evan opened his eyes to Nella tugging his hand and checked the clock. Six-forty. And he'd been awake far too late. "Why are you up already? You know what time it is?"

"No. I not tell time clock. I li'l still. Come." She tugged him harder. "My mummy here on couch. I put my b'anket on her 'cause she no' have one."

On the couch? Evan yawned and forced himself up. Why was Susie up already as late as she was awake? Mad at him or not, she'd let him stay when he and Nella took a hamburger and fries over to be sure she ate. She ate it with Nella's pushing, and her dad's. She wouldn't talk to him. She sat silent while Danielle talked about her visit to Greenville and the rain and the birdies that emptied the feeders so fast and the small water. Danny left early to head down to Stu's, as soon as he saw that Susie did eat and seemed okay. Evan played Candyland with Nella to get her to calm down, and after John and Chief Carr left for the night, he read a couple of books and got her ready for bed.

Still, Susie shut him out. She'd walked over to the window seat, dropped her head back against the wall, and stared out at the dark. Fans still lingered on the sidewalk. The chief had men patrolling regularly so they didn't come onto the property. Adam had two of their guards stationed inside the front door. Nella had insisted on making cookies and taking them down. Susie argued until both Evan and Chief Carr said they'd walk down with her.

He wondered if someone had told her about the kidnap threat, with the way she hovered over her daughter. As far as he could discern, no one had said anything, and she hadn't even touched a newspaper while in Greenville.

She'd gone to bed without saying a word to him. He cleaned up Nella's clutter and put the dishes away and went to check on Nella, saw her stirring, fighting a nightmare, and went it to calm her. She clung to him, begged him not to leave, so he took the child to his place and let her stay in Keith's room, with a note to Susie left on the refrigerator.

He understood why Duncan always hated how often his daughter had nightmares. His friend couldn't understand why she did. She never seemed bothered during the day, or almost never. She was happy and bouncy and not easily ruffled, but she often had nightmares. Danielle wouldn't even tell her dad what they were about. Ever.

"Come, my Evan Lee. Up. Yes."

He grinned and smoothed her unruly dark curls. They bounced right back up again, the same way she did. "Okay, little one. Let me get dressed."

She tilted her head and lifted the blanket from where it still half covered him. "You dressed 'nough. Boys not have t' wear shirts. No."

He was glad he'd left his shorts on, but then he knew better when she was there. Now and then she'd crawl in bed with him during the night when she stayed. Either way, he was at least pulling a shirt on if Susie was on the couch.

She was asleep, curled up tight, with Danielle's favorite blanket over top. He grinned when Nella put her finger to her lips to tell him to stay quiet, and picked her up to take her to the kitchen. "What should we make for breakfast?"

She frowned in thought, then her eyes lit. "G'avy an' biscuits. I have it at Mrs. Mel's home. I like g'avy and biscuits. Yes."

"You better let me make coffee first if I'm going to do all that."

Susie woke to the smell of coffee. And food. Sausage? Rolling over to stretch her aching muscles — why did they ache? — she nearly rolled right off the ... the couch. At Evan's. She sat up. Danielle's blanket. Voices in the kitchen. Her head ached worse than her muscles.

She sat still for a minute then made her way in to find them.

"My *mummy*. Look. Evan Lee made us g'avy an' biscuits. Yes. Like at Mrs. Mel's home. Come." Nella patted the chair beside her.

Evan got up. "Sleep okay?"

"No." And her muscles ached, along with her head.

He poured her coffee and set it in front of her as she lowered beside her daughter. "It didn't turn out too bad, even if it's not as good as Mel's." He gave Nella an amused grin. "Are you interested at all?"

"Actually, it sounds good. Thank you."

"Your stomach's better today, then."

"I think so. Guess we'll see." She pushed a hand against her head. "But I have a headache from..." Susie caught herself before she said it. Not that Nella hadn't heard the word, and often, but not from her that she could remember.

He set the plate in front of her, disappeared, and came back with pain reliever. She took it gratefully and listened to Nella chat with Evan as she picked at her food.

She still didn't talk to him more than to answer if he asked her something directly, but he attributed it to the way she felt, the headache she said was better but not gone. She moved in a way that looked as though she was in pain from more than her head. Monthly timing, maybe. He'd seen her move that way often. She hated to discuss it so he didn't ask.

When Danny and Stu came up, Evan went back to his place to call Doug to see when he planned to return. The one month mark was coming fast; they had an interview lined up and they all needed to be there for it. No matter how much he wished he hadn't agreed to do it.

Doug suggested he might meet them for the interview and return to New Hampshire, where he wanted to leave Ali. He asked if there was any reason, other than the interview, for him to be there.

Evan rubbed the back of his neck. "Think there's any chance Stu will take over lead guitar?"

After some silence, Doug's voice was quiet. "No. Not as long as you're in the band with us, since you're better and he knows it. Not a chance." He said something to someone there with him and came back. "So what are you going to do, Evan? We've all been wondering."

His stomach hurt. His hands shook. He lowered to a crouch position against the wall. *Better.* No. More experienced. Stu spent more time on the keyboards, on the piano, the bass, on several other instruments including the drums. He didn't specialize on lead guitar. He could.

"Evan? I know this is tough and we don't have to do anything right away. We can spare some time off. Give you time to adjust. To heal. We're more than willing to work with you. But we do hope you'll stick around. That's all we need to know, if you'll even consider it."

Stick around. Hell, what else was he going to do? And Susie needed it. No matter how hard it would be for her, she needed the band to keep going. "Yeah." He rubbed his neck again, took a hard swallow. "Already told Adam I'd take lead if Stu won't. I'd rather leave it just the four of us instead of..."

"Agreed. We'll make it work."

"Right." He dropped his head back against the wall.

"You all right?"

"No. Not even close."

"Sorry, stupid question. Ali's right here. She wants to say hello if you don't mind."

He couldn't refuse and it was nice to hear her voice. She asked about Susie and Danielle, asked if he was alone and told him to call Stephanie and let her hang out, let her help him through it, teased about having the place to himself.

But he wanted off the phone. The pain in his stomach turned to nausea. Lead guitar. In place of his friend. And on stage. He told Ali he had to go and would see her soon, and rushed to the bathroom.

Then he called Stephanie.

Before he left to see his girlfriend, Evan had to check in with Susie, despite his head telling him to let her be since she wouldn't talk to him. He couldn't do it.

Stu answered and stopped him barely inside the door. "Careful. She's in a mood."

As though he didn't know? He nodded and tried to move past.

"Hey, I didn't mean to mess anything up. By going to Greenville, you know. I just..."

"You should have stayed in New Hampshire as Adam told you."

"Yeah well, she sounded like she needed ... something, to be home, or whatever. What did you want me to do when she practically begged me to come take her home? Say no?"

"Yes." And he wasn't in the mood to discuss it.

"Because you could, right? You could tell her no?" Stu paused. "I guess you could, since you did, but I couldn't, not as upset as she was. I don't care what anyone says."

"And that's why I could. Because I do care. You should have stuck to the arrangements and stayed in New Hampshire."

"Don't fuss at him." Susie, from behind. "Leave him alone." She told Stu that Nella wanted him to finger paint with her and Danny, and he shot Evan a hesitant look and headed to the kitchen.

"Suse..."

"I'm going to take a shower while she's busy. Come in if you want." She started away.

Evan caught her arm and moved in close, forcing her attention. "Don't do this."

"Do what?"

"Suse, yell at me if you're mad. I know you are. But don't stop talking to me. This isn't the time..."

"I don't have the energy to yell, and it wouldn't do any good. Nothing I say makes any difference to anyone. Why bother?"

"That's not true."

"Isn't it?"

"Not at all. Hell, Stu hustled all the way over to Greenville because you said you were ready to be home, never mind I was already making plans and told him that."

"I didn't expect him to come."

"I figured you didn't."

Her eyes pierced his. "But it was nice. I told *you* I needed you and you gave me the run-around. I told *him* and he was there."

"Suse..."

"Forget it. I'm going to take a hot shower and read for a while. My headache's not gone and I just..."

"*Don't* think what you want or what you need matters more to him than it does to me. You know that's not true."

"I can't talk about this now." She pulled her arm away and headed to the back of her apartment.

A pain shot through his stomach. *Gave her the run-around.* He wasn't giving her the run-around. He was trying to protect her, as always. As she'd told him over and over not to do, but how could he not? It mattered too damned much.

He went in to let Danny know he'd be at Stephanie's and wrote the number down, in case Susie actually needed him. Nella was plenty happy making a big mess, so he gave her a kiss atop her head and told her he'd see her in the morning.

Stopping at his place to grab his bag, and his acoustic since she'd asked if he would, Evan couldn't stop hearing her words. *I told him and he was there.* He was there. He damn well wasn't *supposed* to be there. They were already jumping on her for *going away with* Stu, wondering if he'd actually been there the whole time and Doug was only covering for him in New Hampshire. The fact that people had seen him didn't matter in the slightest. What in the hell use were *facts* when there was a better story to spread around?

He grabbed the closest thing off the top of his dresser and slammed it against the wall. It didn't shatter. He could only wish it had. It did dent the drywall; not good enough, but enough he'd have to fix it. Later. The hell with what she thought. She could get over herself.

Stephanie was waiting, anxious to see him.

By the time he got through the damned crowd and ditched a couple of cars following him, one being a guard he didn't want, Evan was ready to escape into Steph's arms.

And she was more than ready for him. She opened the door in a cream-colored lace robe barely concealing the little she wore underneath. "Oh, you look tense." She closed the door and locked it, then took his bag and dropped it to the floor as he set his guitar case against the wall. "What's wrong, baby?" She slid a hand up the jaw he shaved just before he left, along his face, into his hair.

Evan felt his head shake, not to say nothing was wrong because everything was wrong, but he didn't want to talk about it.

"Want a beer? Or wine? I have..."

"No." He kissed her and pulled her warm body against his, her warm soft curvy willing body.

"Okay. Got it." She grinned and began to unbutton his shirt.

Evan raised her eyes back to his with his hands aside her face. It wasn't right. Not exactly. But it was damned sure right enough.

"What is it, Evan? What happened?"

"Why are you dating me?"

"What?"

"Why, Steph? Is it my job? Be honest. I can deal with it..."

"Your job attracted me. Yes. You know I'm a fan, but..."

"If I was nothing but ... a businessman trying to make enough to survive? Would you still want me here right now?"

"You have to ask?" She backed away, paced a few steps, turned to look at him. "It's because you're incredibly sexy and rugged and gorgeous all together. That's it. There's nothing more. It's not your job. It's not even you. It's pure lust. Same reason you're here right now, isn't it? Because you can't resist my body?" She returned, stood close in front of him. "And I'm going to humor myself and pretend there aren't two hundred other women with better bodies who'd be glad for the chance to sleep with such a sexy rock star. So play along with me."

"Only two hundred?" He stroked a finger along her bare arm.

"Hm, okay hot shot, two hundred and twenty. Inquisition over? Because I really did miss you while you were away and you really are tense tonight. I want to talk about why, only because your voice is sexy, too, and not that I'll listen to the words, but..."

Evan met her lips, swept her back in against him. A perfect answer. Teasing. Brushing it off as though it didn't need to be asked. She was never easily rattled. He loved that. She was so easy to be around, undemanding except in the right ways and unbothered by his moods. She tasted like fresh mouthwash. Ready for him.

11 August

"What should we have for dinner? Suggestions?" Steph traced a finger across and down his chest above his guitar, outlining the instrument on his bare skin.

"Tired of my playing?"

"Oh no, you can play for me all night if you want. And you can take that as you want." She grinned and raised her hand to trace his hairline, forehead to around his ear. "But it is nearly six. Thought you might be hungry, and thought I'd offer to help you with that."

Evan caught the spark in her eyes that again said to take it as he wanted. "Nearly six?"

"Mm, yes, so ... how about a quick meal and then we can continue this? I'm good with Italian. Fettuccini sound okay? I make a wicked Alfredo sauce I haven't tried on you yet."

Nearly six. He'd been there twenty-four hours. "Steph, I should..."

"No. Don't say it." She took the guitar and propped it against the coffee table. "I took the day off for you. You can at least spend the rest of it with me, and the weekend if you'd like, or if you can." Moving in, she kissed his shoulder, and his chest, avoiding the small amount of hair she'd asked if he would consider shaving. He wouldn't consider it; he was as he was and it had to be good enough. And it didn't deter her. She'd said okay and let it go.

There was no reason he couldn't stay the weekend. Fettuccini Alfredo sounded good, particularly if he didn't have to make it, and the idea of her fingers continuing their path sounded better.

She'd made him talk in the late hours of the night when he was more relaxed and yet not relaxed enough. He focused it on media interference, on rumors that interfered with their lives. She said the same thing Duncan always said: ignore it, don't let it interfere. Maybe. But he'd had "reputation" drummed into his head from the time he was little and it was hard to dismiss. Hers. Not his. He couldn't care one iota what they, whoever they were, thought of him. Her reputation mattered. He knew it did. Something inside him nagged and poked whenever he considered taking their advice to ignore it. Some day she needed to go back to her dancing, her teaching. It would matter then.

He couldn't ignore it.

"You're getting tense again." Steph caressed his shoulder, moved so she could reach both. "If the thought of staying makes you tense, then say so, Evan. I don't want to add to..."

"No." He ran a hand up her hip to her side. "It's the thought of leaving, of going back to ... everything."

She gave him a soft grin. "Then don't." Her lips brushed his.

"Stay." Pressed in. "As long as you can." Moved against him as she spoke. "Let me help you unwind."

"Steph…" He slid his hands underneath the skimpy tank top. She never wore a bra around the house. He loved that she didn't; he also loved that she was well covered when outside the house. A good balance. "Come here."

She chuckled. "How much closer do you want me?"

Evan gripped the bottom of her tank; she raised her arms so he could pull it over her head. "All the way."

"Oh, careful, baby. I'll take that the way you don't mean it."

He wasn't sure he didn't.

12 August

She had to get back to her workouts. Duncan wouldn't be happy if she let herself go so far she was always sick again. She needed to be in shape when … when he was home again and needed her care.

Calling to Danielle, Susie grinned when the girl came running and couldn't even scold her for running in the house. "Hey, how about we go downstairs and work on our dancing?"

"*Yes.* I get my dancing clothes on. Yes." Nella hustled back the way she'd just come.

Susie wished she could feel as excited about it. She didn't want to dance. She wanted to stay in bed until he was home. But he'd told her to take care of herself.

The phone interrupted: Adam, looking for Evan. She gave him Stephanie's number in case it was important and said not to bother him if it wasn't.

"I can wait till later. Know what time he'll be back?"

"No, and he might not be. Not tonight, I mean. I have no idea." The silence from the other end told her he didn't know how to answer. "If it's important, call him. She won't mind."

"Maybe you can answer me instead."

"No." Band business. "I can't. Call him." He tried to say more but she told him Nella was waiting for her and she had to go. She wasn't doing band business. Evan could handle it. It was his band, not hers.

Evan pushed back through the crowd to get into the building. He hadn't missed fighting the crowd just to go home, or to go out. Steph had asked him to stay through Sunday night, but it was Saturday night and he'd been out since Thursday. He needed to check in on Nella.

Music from the basement pulled him that direction. Why was there no guard at the front door? He'd left instructions for one to always be there, to change shifts often, but to have someone always there. Maybe he was downstairs instead. With Susie?

With a frown, he made his way through the dim light of the basement entrance. Susie and Nella were there. Nella was dancing away, sometimes with actual dance steps and sometimes with whatever she made up, which she often did. Susie sat on a mat nearby, her knees up and arms crossed over top, her head on her knees. The anger drained from him, in that instant. She was hurt and trying to protect herself. He knew that's what she was doing; getting angry at her was ... selfish. He felt like shit for allowing himself to be that selfish when she hurt so badly, for staying with his girlfriend and hiding away when she...

"My *Evan Lee*!" Nella spotted him and ran his direction, jumping into his arms when he held them out. "I not see you today. No. Or 'nother day."

"You are seeing me today. I'm right here. Having fun?" With his attention mainly on Danielle, he caught Susie raise her head. Otherwise she didn't move.

"I dance and dancing. My mum dancing bu' nae now. She tired. I nae get tired. I have beans jumping in my little legs, my Stuey say so."

Jumping beans. Nella had no idea what Stu meant half the time but she was always amused by his expressions and always found a way to repeat them. Susie was dancing? When Nella said so, Susie got up and went to turn the music off.

"No my mummy I nae done."

"Sorry baby, maybe we can do more tomorrow. How about some dinner?" She didn't even look at Evan as Nella argued she wasn't hungry.

He offered to cook, not that he wanted to cook. She refused, said she had something in the slow cooker, and didn't invite him over. Whether she wanted him to or not, he walked up with them. Nella chattered. Susie stayed quiet. Evan tried to figure how to break through, to get her to say anything to him, to let her know he understood and it was fine.

When Nella ran up ahead toward the top, Susie broke the ice. "How is Stephanie?"

"She's good." Maybe not the right choice of words...

Susie flicked her gaze at him. "Good. I'm glad."

He wasn't sure if the repeated word was on purpose or coincidental, but he knew from her look how she took it. Fine. Doing well. Anything more general would have been far better.

"Suse." He stopped her as she opened her door but then didn't have any idea what to say. "Adam called. The interview is set up for the sixteenth."

Wrong thing to say. She nodded and went inside, shut the door. He sighed and went to his own apartment. It was quiet. He checked the machine to see if Mike had called in but found only a bunch of garbage so he deleted them all.

Susie sighed as she closed the door. She should have invited him for dinner. It was rude not to, especially after he offered to cook, but ... but she wanted him there too much and she couldn't let him know that. He had a right to be with his girlfriend. It was good that he had her through this, and she was good for him. He deserved that. Danny and Stu would be there soon. She'd be fine.

Nella frowned and asked where he was. Susie sent her to change clothes and clean up, distracting her with the reminder her uncle would be over soon. It worked well enough. It worked for her, also, pretty well, while she changed and wished he'd come back over and just sit with her, tell her he believed her, or even if he didn't believe her that he trusted her and wouldn't look at her like she was crazy. She pushed a couple of tears away, gritted her teeth, and told herself to stop it. Danny would be there soon. He'd sit with her and at least try to look at her like he didn't think she was crazy, and if she was, he didn't care. She'd be fine. Everything would be fine. Despite the stupid interview on the sixteenth to finalize things, to prove at least the band all believed it was final.

Inhaling as deeply as she could, Susie gritted her teeth again and went back out to get dinner.

Danny got there first, said Stu would be there in a couple of minutes. He teased his niece about the strange outfit she'd put on: green shorts with yellow flowers, a long sleeved T-shirt in red and white stripes, and a braided belt tied more like a tie than like a belt. Susie shook her head and let it go.

"So." Danny sidled up next to her as she pulled out plates. "Hate to say it, but the paper wants me back. I tried t' push it off more, but I cannae bitch since it has been a while."

She gritted her teeth and set the plates around the table. Four. Maybe she should go invite Evan and add another.

"Sis, are y' going t' be alright? I can beg them more if y' want..."

"No, it's fine." She gave him a light hug and went for the silverware. "Thank you for staying so long. You shouldn't have."

"Your other friends will be comin' back soon, yes? So you will have more company than y' want again and it will be just as well..."

"You're not company. But yes, it's fine, Danny. You should go back to work." She set the silverware around the plates and grabbed a big platter for the roast and potatoes and carrots. "When are you leaving?"

"Tonight."

Susie turned to him.

"Last minute. Sorry, bu' Adam thought it would be better nae t' schedule farther out than I had to, easier t' keep people from knowing. All those times I harassed Stu for havin' all the attention, you know? Now tha' I have it, I cannae say I want it."

She nodded and turned back to the roast. "You have time for dinner?"

"Yea' and I wouldnae miss it." He hugged her from behind. "Stu has been warned t' help look ou' for you in my place. Le' him know if y' need anything. He will be glad..."

"We'll be fine. Thanks." She half listened to him say he had a couple of hours as she finished moving everything to the table and he told Danielle, through her major pouting, that he had to go home. Stu came, and as she started to tell them all to sit, Susie went to the door. She was inviting Evan. She couldn't have him over there alone.

He opened the door before she knocked.

"Hey I um ... I have roast ready if you want to come over..."

"Thanks. I have plans."

She nearly didn't want to ask, but he smelled nice.

"I'm heading to Stephanie's. I'll be back Sunday night. Doug should be in by then, if all goes well."

"Oh, you just... I thought that's where you just came from."

"I did, but I'm not needed here with nothing going on, so I might as well be there."

Not needed? "Okay. Tell her hello and if she can handle this madhouse, she's welcome any time."

He agreed and headed down the stairs.

"Evan?" She waited until he turned to her, at least half way. "You're always needed here. Nella ... she..."

His shoulders straightened. "I'm sure Stu will be there for *her*, too."

She stared as though he'd just stuck a hand in her guts and twisted them, on purpose. She could say nothing as he continued down the stairs and out the door, to his girlfriend, who was just fine and dandy and yet apparently needed his attention more. Maybe he was mad at her for pushing Duncan to go. If she hadn't, his best friend would still be here. But there was no way in hell it hurt him more, not even nearly as much. Except Evan was convinced it was final, that he wouldn't be back, so maybe he did hurt more.

Still ... still, it was ... mean. It was a mean thing to throw back in her face. He *hadn't* been there. He *hadn't* come when she asked. Stu *had*. What right did *he* have to be mad? He could screw his attitude. She had company ... not company, her friends, her family. Evan had said often enough he wasn't her family. He was right; he wasn't. He'd just made that glaringly obvious.

Swallowing back her anger, she breathed deeply until she could act like all was okay.

After a long hug, Susie let Danny loose and made him promise to be careful, and that if there were any delays at all, he would come back and try later. The thought of him getting on the plane alone made her sick. She thought about going with him. She and Nella could go for a while, get away from everything, let the band get back to work, and Evan could go screw himself if he didn't want to bother with her and Nella. Fine. She could go...

"Are y' alright, Sis?" Danny set a hand on her face.

"Fine. Thank you, again. I couldn't have ... if you weren't here..."

He grinned and gave her another hug. "Y' could have, bu' I was glad t' have the time with y' both. Come and visit soon. Take a boat if y' need."

"I might." She wasn't even sure which she meant, visit or take a boat. With Danielle so upset that he was leaving, Susie had to push her own thoughts aside. "And it might be soon if this one is going to make a federal case of it for very long."

Nella frowned at her and Stu whisked her away for a minute to let Danny out the door.

"Suse, do y' remember when y' told me you wished y' could have seen DJ when he was little, to know him back then?"

She nodded. He couldn't do this now. It was too hard already.

"Y' are seeing him when he was li'l every time y' look at her. I know it is hard for y' to believe he used t' be as full of piss and vinegar as Nella, bu' he was, before so much happened t' calm him down. She is DJ in female form, near exact. Except prettier, which she go' from you, thank the Lord."

She brushed at her eyes and held him again. "Take care of yourself, Danny. It might not be long before we come over and bother you."

He called out to Nella to be as good as she could be and gave his niece another hug. Stu was walking downstairs with him. Susie couldn't do it. She left the door open so Stu could get back in.

Straightening the house as a way to normalize, to show her daughter all was okay, she fought an intense desire to stop him, to tell him to take them, too. To his family. To Duncan's family. Closer to where her husband was. She should go. It was her chance. She could just say she was going to stay with his family and then ... then what? Go where?

A deep sob tried to overtake her and she choked it back until Stu returned and she asked him to watch Nella so she could shower. Escaping, she closed her door, leaned against it, and stopped fighting. Her legs collapsed. Her body shivered. Her insides hurt all the way through. But she couldn't cry. She couldn't allow it.

Evan stared out the window and into the dark yards of the town homes across from Stephanie's. They weren't much for yards with one running into another and only slightly different landscaping but they were nice and well kept. And there was no crowd on her sidewalk. She had taken to leaving her car on the street so he could park in the small garage beneath her side of the house in order to hide that he was there. Some of the neighbors knew he visited, or stayed, now and then, but they didn't spread it around. In return, he left personally signed items from the band for Steph to give them.

He shouldn't have said it. The way Susie looked at him hadn't left his thoughts since. She had to know he didn't mean it; he would always be there for her, for Nella, when she wanted him to be there. She had to know. Even if it had taken him longer than she wanted when she asked him to come, he was working on it. He...

"Evan?" Soft fingers slid up his back. "Ready to tell me what's wrong?"

"Everything is wrong." When she stopped the caress, he figured that was also the wrong thing to say. Not everything. She wasn't. He turned. "I'm sorry. That's not what I meant."

"I know. Don't worry so much about everything you say. You know you don't have to. You know I understand what you mean even when it doesn't sound like..."

"Teach Susie how to do that." He snickered, shook his head.

"Is she upset with you? Is that what this is all about?"

"Understatement."

"Then why are you here?" Steph ran her fingers back through his hair. "She's hurting, Evan. I know you are, too. I understand. And I know you're being this tough guy and all for her sake, and that's hard on you when you miss him so, but it's different. He was her husband. She..."

"I know that. Steph..."

"Then why are you here? Not that I don't want you here. I do want you here." She leaned in to kiss him. "I love having you here. I love having you." Her lips teased. "But you should go talk to her, explain whatever it was, and I'll still be here. Or I'll go with you. I'll wait at your place, in your room, even in that nightie you like so well, or in nothing. Your choice." She wrapped in tight as she tasted him, teased, meshed with his mouth.

She was right. He needed to go talk to Susie.

He set his hands on her hips, over the tight jeans, to move himself away, to go... because she was right. And she was beautiful. And he didn't want to leave, to go back to ... be ignored, or be yelled at, or ... to be surrounded by Susie's overbearing grief on top of his own.

Selfish. He knew it was. Protecting himself in Stephanie's arms. But they were beautiful arms. Soft. Warm. Kind. Instead of moving himself away, he moved his hands to the top of the jeans that barely covered her hips, slid them around to the front to find the snap, and the zipper.

"You should go talk to Susie." Steph kissed under his ear.

"Saying no?"

She groaned at his caress. "Oh no. Not at all. I can't imagine saying no to you." She kissed his neck. "Talk to her … later, Evan. Talk to her." She arched her back, her eyes closed, her chest rising and falling hard and fast. "Later."

Stu was there with Susie. Evan knew he was. And Danny. Maybe her dad. She wasn't alone. And he didn't want to be.

13 August

Shoving two pills in her mouth and swallowing them with water, Susie crept out to the couch and lowered carefully, a hand pressed hard against her head. She'd have to yell at Stu for putting too much Jack in her Coke. Although, she figured it was more from lack of sleep. She'd tossed and turned all night, often with Evan's words ringing through her aching ears. *Stu will be there for her, too.*

The ass. Hopefully he'd stay at Stephanie's for two or three more days so she wouldn't have to see him.

She cringed when Nella yelled at a knock on the door, said it was her Evan Lee. Guessing it was. Susie figured she was wrong, and hoped she was wrong. Carefully, trying not to jar her head more than necessary, she checked first. Holy hell. Maybe she could pretend not to be home. But Nella was making too much noise and her dad would freak out if he didn't know where she was, so she let him in, with Diane.

With a hell of a lot of forced control, Susie made herself not snap at him when he asked if she had a headache. As though it wasn't obvious. She crept back to the couch and closed her eyes, said yes she took something and no she didn't want to go lie down. She wanted to not move. And she wanted Nella to stop yelling.

Diane asked where Evan was. Susie very much wanted to tell her he was shacked up at his girlfriend's house where he'd been for days on end. She couldn't quite make herself do it. She only said she hadn't seen him yet that morning.

Nella had cereal already but she jumped at Diane's offer of

scrambled eggs and bacon. Susie told her she didn't have either one, or too much of anything else since she couldn't make herself go out through the crowd to get groceries. Her dad fussed about not having someone do it for her, or not calling him, and she said they were fine, not starving, and cereal was good enough. He left again, to get groceries, but he left Diane there to help with Nella. Susie again used her well-taught control and manners to keep herself from saying it would help more not to have Diane in her house.

She tried hard not to hear the little remarks meant to be helpful, but with an edge that spoke huge disapproval. Diane told Nella she always made breakfast for her boys,. and for Susie when she moved in, because breakfast was so important...

For a minute or two, Susie couldn't even blame Diane's husband for taking off and getting away from her yammering.

But that was unfair. She was just grouchy. Tired. Frustrated. And Danny hadn't checked in at all as he was supposed to. She considered calling the McGuires to ask if he checked in with them, but if he hadn't, she didn't want to cause them unnecessary worry. What was anyone going to do about it, anyway? Nothing, apparently. No one did anything about it when something went wrong. They just let it go, left it to someone else.

Why did she have to deal with Evan's mother this morning, when she was mad enough at him already?

Duncan... Where are you? I need you here to help me deal with this. Come home.

A voice in her head said she didn't have to deal with her. She asked if Diane would look after Nella until her dad got back and went to her room to lie down.

Evan turned from where he'd been staring out the bedroom window to study his girlfriend. He didn't want to go home today. He wanted to stay with her and just ... lose himself in her, forget everything else, leave Stu to...

Stu. Hell. He'd thought about calling Susie last night, to apologize, but it was late and he hoped she was asleep. He could call now. After eight. She'd be up. Nella would have her up. Calling wasn't good enough; he had to go home.

With a sigh, he returned to where Stephanie was sleeping, her shoulders and feet uncovered as always, and sat next to her, gave her a soft kiss above her ear. "Steph."

She reached up to him, eyes still closed, pulled him closer. "Come back to bed, baby."

With a soft touch of her lips, Evan nearly gave in. "I have to go."

Her eyes opened, questioning, and she looked over at the clock. "It's early. What's up? Something happen?"

"No. I've ... it's time."

As she sat up, she let the sheet fall away. "Evan..."

He could see her want to argue, want to ask. He didn't want her to ask. Giving in to himself, to his own needs, for just a moment longer before heading back to work, to responsibility, Evan kissed her gently, caressed her back, the soft bare skin that felt like flower petals. Maybe she was right; there was no big rush to leave. It was Sunday morning. No work. Doug and Mike weren't even home. He could stay...

A pit inside punched a hole in his thoughts. He couldn't stay. He'd walked out on her when she most needed him. Twice. He had to go home and deal with the fallout. He had to be there.

Stephanie's pull was too strong. Or it was the pull of pleasure away from work, away from ... everything. An escape. "I can't do this." He heard it come out, as hardly more than a whisper.

She pulled back. "Can't do what? Can't leave? You don't need to leave yet. It's early. Stay a while."

His head shook. She knew.

"Oh Evan, don't do this. I see it in your eyes. Don't do this. You're upset. You just..."

He got up and grabbed his jeans. She stood next to him, fully naked, unconcerned about it either way. Her fingers traced through his hair and her look said he was crazy, he couldn't walk away from this. But he had no choice. "Steph, I need ... I have to have some time..."

"Of course. Whatever time you need. Just tell me..."

He met her lips to stop the request. He couldn't promise anything. Shades of the way he broke up with Myra flirted around his brain but it was different. He didn't break up with her. She did it. Because of Susie. And this was because of her, also, but not in the same way. Because he was finding it too easy to not want to be around her, to escape from her pain, from his own.

Her shoulders quivered when he slid his hands down, slowly,

gently, his gaze on hers. "Tell me this is temporary, Evan."

He gave her a light grin and a light kiss. "I'll call you when I can, when I can think again. I'm sorry. I'm using you to run away and I can't. I have to be there. I have to deal with this."

"Of course, but I can be there to help you, at least now and then. I'll come to you. Just call me. Okay? Let's leave it at that for now. When you want company, call and I'll come see you and I won't push for more. I won't call." She ran her hands down his chest to his stomach. "And I'll be fine, so don't worry about me. But ... leave it there for now. No finality, okay? Get your head together and then let me know where we stand."

"I can't ask you to sit around and wait. It's not fair to you."

"No." Her fingers wrapped around his back. "You're not asking, and if I decide not to, I won't. Don't worry. We'll see where we are ... when you call."

With a nod, he finished dressing as she put her robe on and barely tied it and walked him to the door. He paused there. It was too much like a hit and run with her not even dressed and them barely out of bed. "How about breakfast before I go? Can I take you out?"

She grinned with a small laugh. "You are the most unusual man I've ever met. I know you're not going to call. I'm giving you the easy way out. And you ask me to breakfast before you dump me?"

"I'm not dumping you." Evan cupped her face in his palm. "I will call. And I'd love to take you to breakfast, if you can handle a crowd since there could be one if I'm spotted."

"I don't care if you don't. But are you sure you want to hook yourself to me in public view before you walk away? Because no matter what you say right now, I know you are."

"Steph, it could bring people to your door, reporters..."

"I'll risk it. Just let me change." As she walked away, she looked back. "And don't worry, I'm good at self protection."

He half thought about telling her to teach Susie that, too. Although Duncan had, to an extent. She didn't have the personality to be as fully self protective as Steph was, and he knew Steph was. The perfect rock star wife. He knew she could be. If Duncan was around to be his best man, to return the favor, Evan might even consider it.

She put Clapton on the record player and sat again to ignore the voices in the kitchen. Groceries were put away. Breakfast was eaten. Now clean up. Diane and Nella did it, with her dad's supervision; Diane insisted Nella was old enough to learn to start cleaning up. Susie wondered if that's when Evan started helping with the house, when he wasn't even three years old. Picking up her own toys was well and fine, but ... but it was keeping Nella busy, Susie supposed. There was no point in taking her anger at Evan out on his mom.

And she was too angry at him for no real good reason. Too emotional. Too tired. He hadn't done anything, not really. She could have said no when he talked about leaving her in Greenville and she didn't, so it was her own fault. She shouldn't have said Stu was there for her when he wasn't. It was wrong. Evan didn't have to jump the minute she called him; he didn't, and he shouldn't.

Her eyes started to water again, for the millionth time in the past couple of days, and again, she pushed it back, focused on Eric Clapton, on Duncan's favorite guitarist, his favorite music ... along with ... Buddy Holly, Chuck Berry, Zeppelin, ... Chicago. She heard his voice from their first date when she mentioned she liked Jim Croce, expecting it was too light for him but he liked it, too, along with...

He'd sung part of *Maybe Baby* to her as they danced. She knew then she loved him, on their first date, when he was so ... so everything. So beautiful, giving, strong, gentle ... everything.

Evan showered before he headed to Susie's, and he rubbed his hair in front of his fan on high to help it dry so it wasn't obvious he'd just showered.

He ran into Stu leaving her apartment.

"Hey man, the girlfriend's keeping you busy these days, isn't she?" He smirked. "Can't blame you. Damn she's hot. When are you bringing her back this way instead of keeping her to yourself?"

"How's Susie today?"

Stu shrugged. "Bitchy. Fair warning. But the headache's better by now. Wish I'd got the hangover instead since she didn't need that on top of everything, but she's a damn cute drunk."

"She's what?"

He shrugged again. "Guess you know that. Or do you? Maybe she doesn't in front of you with your... Anyway, she was in a better mood last night."

Evan held his breath long enough to hold his tongue. "Who all was here last night?"

"Just Danny and me and then just me. Well, Nella, but she was in bed early after being such a hot potato all day long. Wore herself out."

It wasn't his business. She was an adult. If she wanted to get drunk with Stu, it was her business. He just nodded and continued across the hall.

"Hey, you know I didn't mean to screw things up, right?"

Evan turned to him with raised eyebrows, wondering just what in the hell happened while they were drunk together.

"By going to Greenville. People should really mind their own fucking business but it's not like I was trying to..."

"Forget it." *Should* didn't matter; they didn't, and Stuart knew they didn't.

"She's not really pissed at you. She's only..."

"Glad you were there when I wasn't. Thanks for that." Evan knew it was pissy and he shouldn't have said it. He knocked and the door opened before Stu could answer him. His mom. Why in the hell was she there? He made himself greet her, and John, and picked Nella up when she ran at him talking about sand and birdies and colors and...

Susie stepped in from the kitchen, glanced at him, and went to flip an album on her stereo. Clapton. From 1970. The one Duncan and Susie had talked about the day they met.

John said something about her having a headache, an excuse for her ignoring him. His mom asked if he'd been out on business and asked what the band was doing. Susie sat on the couch in the spot closest to the stereo and closed her eyes. She didn't want them there. They were ignoring the signs. Evan said only that Doug and Mike would be back within a couple of days and suggested his mom come over to his place. Maybe John would follow, or at least having John there wouldn't annoy her so much.

His mom suggested they all go to Ben's where there was more space and where Danielle could go outside as she wanted.

"I already said no. I'm not going out." Susie didn't even open her eyes.

Her dad suggested he and Diane could take Nella to Ben's and let Susie rest better. She said no to that, also. He looked to Evan for help. His first thought was that he should have stayed at Stephanie's, or brought her back with him. Unsure what to say that wouldn't piss her off, he opted for the easier path and sat next to her. "Water might help your head. Can I get you a glass?"

"I already took something."

"Okay, but that's not what I said. It may be dehydration..."

She looked at him. "Why?"

He leaned in to prevent their parents from overhearing. "Stu says you're a cute drunk. Have a nice evening, did you?"

She shoved herself off the couch, then cringed and put a hand on her head. "You know, you don't have to whisper. Dad already knows but it's not from that, it's from not sleeping, and I wasn't ... it's not from that, and if it was, it's not your business, and you can keep your insinuations to yourself, by the way."

"Suse, I wasn't..."

"I don't care what you think. I don't care what they think. I *don't* care. Do you get it yet?" She pressed harder against her head.

"You're making it worse. Relax. I didn't mean..."

"Don't tell me to relax. Don't tell me where I should go or what I should think or ... that I'm wrong, or crazy, because I'm *not*. I'm tired and I'm frustrated and I'm ... I don't need your comments making everything worse and I *don't* need you hiding me somewhere again or acting like I'm some little kid you need to take care of because I'm *not* anymore. I'm *not*."

Nella peeked around the couch, staring at her mom. Susie didn't see her. John did. He went to pick her up, handed her to Diane, and suggested they go next door.

"No." Susie calmed and went to take her daughter. "It's fine. We're fine." She settled the girl against her hip and stroked her hair. "It's fine, baby. Come on, let's go read a book, okay?"

Nella cuddled against her with a look back at Evan. Her frown seemed to be scolding him for upsetting her mom.

Lovin' You Lovin' Me came on and Evan couldn't help think of the irony of it. It was one the band used to play at clubs now and then, only because Susie thought it would sound good with him singing it, so he did, because she asked.

And only you can love me more... Then she turned around and started telling Duncan, when he said he loved her, that she loved him more. It felt like a betrayal, even if it wasn't.

He heard his mom ask what she meant by insinuations and thinking she was crazy and told her it was nothing, a misunderstanding. Asking if they would wait there, Evan went back to Nella's room and stood at the door as Susie finished reading a book. She saw him. She didn't stop. He supposed it was a good sign. When the book was done, Nella hopped up and came to him, looked back at her mom, and up at him.

He crouched and took her hands. "It's all right, Danielle. Go talk with your grandpa a minute and we'll be right behind you." Evan expected Susie might argue but she didn't. She told Nella to go ahead but then stood and told Evan he could take his mom and go home, she didn't want company.

Company. He grasped her arm as she tried to pass him.

"Let go of me." She yanked it away.

"Suse, stop this. I'm sorry. I shouldn't have thrown that back at you, about Stu, and I didn't..."

"Doesn't matter. You're right. You don't have to be here."

"That's not what I said."

"Isn't it?"

He stopped her again when she started away. "It's not what I said, and you know better."

"Do I? It's kind of obvious, Evan, and I don't blame you. It's fine. Really. Nella and I can take care of ourselves."

"Suse. She'll hear you. She's in the living room with..."

"So what if she does? You keep saying she should know the truth, so fine, the truth is I can take care of my daughter on my own until her dad comes back and she needs to know I can, and apparently you know I can since I haven't seen you but a couple of times since you dumped us there alone." She shrugged. "But it's fine."

"You weren't alone, Suse, and you haven't been. Danny was with you. I'm surprised he isn't here now since he has been..."

"He went home." Susie pulled from him and went to the living room. They weren't there.

Next door, he figured. Just as well. "He went home?"

"Last night. And I haven't heard from him. I should have by now. Nothing. No word. And I *told* them I wanted my daughter to stay *here*." She headed to the door.

He stopped her. Held both arms. "Stop running and just talk to me."

"Running? Look who's talking, Evan. Who has been running from whom? I've been here. I asked you to... It doesn't matter. Just let it go."

"I know, Suse. I know you asked me to come to you and it was hard as hell not to get in the car and go..."

She yanked away. "Don't. Just don't. Because it obviously wasn't that hard, but you know, I shouldn't have asked. I should have just gone home by myself, or I should have refused to go. It was my fault, not yours. Forget it. And quit blocking the door so I can go get my daughter."

It *obviously wasn't*. Never mind how sick he'd been the whole time, how he'd been on something for his stomach, because he was so worried about her, about them, because he wanted to be at her side.

"Move."

"No." He tried to touch her. She backed away, threw a fiery piercing stare. He sighed. "I know what you're doing. It's not going to help. I know. I did it with Jeremy, turned the pain into anger, took it out on everyone..."

"No you didn't. I was there."

"Everyone but you. I didn't take it out on you because you..."

"Because I'm a weak little girl, right? You had to protect me. You always have to fucking *protect* me. Right? I'm still that weak little girl to you..."

"Because you were in pain, too, as much as I was." He barely got it out. Hearing her say that word he could never imagine her saying shocked him. Too much time with Danny and Stu... or just too much anger, too much pain. "And you might want to remember that losing Duncan hurts me, also. It hurts like hell, and I'm not afraid to admit it. Take it out on me if you have to, but don't forget he was to me what Jeremy was to you. Yell if you need. Cry. Let it out..."

"I'm doing the best I can." Her face was resolute, steeled, controlling the tears from her moist eyes.

"No you're not. You're hiding from it. You know damned well he's not coming back and yet you're still..."

"Go." She backed up. "Just *go*."

"Suse, you have to..."

"I don't *have* to do anything. Just get out. Tell my father to bring Danielle back here where she's *supposed* to be..."

"I won't tell him any such thing. If you want her, come over and get her." Evan opened the door. She'd have to come to his place and tell her father herself. He wasn't her errand boy.

"By the way..." He had to tell her. She didn't want to be protected? Fine. "I left Glenn Heights when you decided to go there in order to draw off the crowd, to hope they'd follow me and leave you the hell alone, and I left early that morning after sleeping maybe two hours at best because I was so damned worried about you, but yes, it was for you, to try to keep them away from you, to keep whoever sent that damn kidnapping threat away from you if possible. That's why I set it up so they'd think you were overseas, so they wouldn't look for you..."

"Kidnapping?" At least her voice had calmed. She wasn't screaming at him. "That's not true. No one would care about kidnapping me. Why would they?"

"Not you. Danielle. There was a threat to kidnap Danielle."

Her face went white, even more than normal. He was nearly sorry he told her. "Adam's sure it was nothing, just an angry, mentally disturbed fan who didn't want his daughter to leave the States. Still, I wasn't taking chances. It was all to protect you, to protect Danielle. If I'd been there with you, Suse, they would have found you, so I made sure they knew where I was and then I had them at Mom's doorstep constantly. I did it for you. She put up with it for you. The *last* damned thing I wanted was to be away from both of you, to worry about you *every* damned second of *every* damned day. But you'll have to forgive me for wanting to *protect* you and your daughter. Or don't. It wasn't your call. Duncan told me to take care of you. It was *his* call. I wasn't about to let him down. I wasn't about to risk some deranged asshole finding his daughter."

She was quiet. Staring. Still in control. Better than he was. He had to get out. Turning to go check on Nella, he ran into Doug and Ali. He imagined they heard enough. They could talk to her about it. He went home.

Doug followed him, felt that he was shaking, gave Nella a hug when she saw Doug and ran to him, and asked her if she would get Evan a glass of water. He walked with him to the couch, told him to take a deep breath and let himself relax.

His mom hovered. Doug asked her to help Nella although John already was. Did he want to talk? No. He closed his eyes, head in his hands, elbows on his knees, hoping they'd keep Danielle away for a few minutes. John came back with his water. Not his mom, or Danielle.

Straightening enough to sip at it, Evan felt his body untense just enough to stop shaking. He shouldn't have told her. She didn't need to worry about it, and now she would, but she didn't want to be protected...

"She's hyperventilating and I can't get her to calm down." Ali. At the doorway.

John rushed out. Evan followed. Doug stayed at his side. His mom was with Nella.

Susie was on the floor in front of her stereo, tucked into herself, breathing hard and fast. Clapton sang *Let It Rain*. Perfect. John was doing his best to calm her. It wasn't working. He got her to look up by stroking her head. She caught Evan's eyes and held them. Hers watered. She tried to catch her breath and failed. Evan stood there, in the middle of her living room, unable to move his feet.

She got up, with her dad's help, and came to him, wrapped her arms around him, dropped her head against his chest.

Evan clenched his eyes and held onto her. Her body shook, breathing changed. He felt moisture through his T-shirt, her tears. He stroked her hair, her face, held her close to him. "Okay, Angel. It's okay, and I'm sorry. I'm so sorry." He dropped his head against hers. "You're right. I was running from you. It hurt... I'm sorry. I won't again."

She held tighter, sobbed harder. He asked everyone to leave and waited for the door to close. He got her over to the couch and held her in, cried with her. Promised her no one would ever get to Danielle, ever. Told her how much security he'd had in Greenville, to include some of the patrons, that they'd been well protected.

John came back just long enough to say Laura had called in. Danny had tried to call Susie but got no answer so she called Evan. Her brother was home safe. Susie slumped against him, the relief draining her.

Before long, she fell asleep in his arms. She was so exhausted. So was he, but maybe he would sleep tonight.

Until her daddy comes home. She'd said it as though she believed it. She still believed it. He shuddered. She was going to have to talk to someone.

14 August

Evan left Susie on the phone with Laura and went back to his own apartment to meet with Doug, Stu and Adam. Ali greeted him with a long hug, ran a hand over Doug's shoulder, and said she was going to go entertain Danielle while they talked.

They asked him when Mike was coming back and he said he wasn't sure, he figured he would have been there already knowing the interview was in two days, in New York. Getting up for the phone, expecting to hang it right back up again, Evan heard his friend's voice. "Hey. Speaking of."

"Talking about me when I'm not there to defend myself?" Mike at least sounded in a decent mood.

"Wondering if you're headed this way any time soon."

"Yeah, I don't know. It's been nice out here. But yeah, I figured you might be wondering. I'm headed in tonight. Late. Sometime after dark."

"I'll watch for you. Call if you need anything. Crowd has thinned some."

"Not worried about it. Hey, Keith is bugging the shit out of me to talk to Nella. Is she there?"

"Next door. I can get her."

"Nah, it's all right. He'll see her tomorrow." He mumbled something away from the phone. "So how is she doing? You know who I mean."

He didn't want to say over the phone. "We'll talk when you're back."

"Kinda what I figured. So I gotta ask, other than this interview, will there be much reason for me to be there?"

Evan hesitated. But he'd already agreed. "I'm taking lead. The rest we'll discuss when you get here." He ended it with a request to drive safe. He was surprised at how much he was ready for Mike and Keith to be home.

The others were watching him, reading his hesitation. Stu raised his head from where he was slumped on his elbows. "You going to be okay with that?"

His breath drew in sharply. He raised his eyes to the ceiling.

"Yeah. Thought you might not be. And I think you're getting

pushed into this." Stu leaned back against his chair, kicked an ankle over his knee where his elbow had just been. "What do you actually want to do?"

"What do I want to do? Go after him, like Susie keeps telling me I should. Prove either she's wrong or I am. I can't even say I'm sure she's wrong since she's so adamant about it, so one of us must be at least edging on crazy: her for thinking it's possible or me for not turning over heaven and earth to find out."

"She still thinks he's coming back?"

"She's still positive he is, and she's pissed off at me to no end since I won't go, or take her, or even let her go. Go where, I can't imagine. To the middle of the Atlantic? For what? They've been there. Twice. Professional rescue searchers." He stood. "Maybe I should just go to Scotland and..."

Doug took his side and his arm. "Evan, you know there's no point in that. She's only fighting it. She needs to talk to someone."

"Yeah, but tell her that. I have. So has her dad. She just gets more pissed. Maybe I should take her to Scotland or Ireland or wherever she thinks he might be. And I would, but she won't leave Danielle and I can't..."

"No. You can't. The child is confused enough already. Don't let Susie get to you. You know she's only grieving. It'll take time."

"Time." He nodded, his jaw tense. "And in the meantime, she'll barely talk to me, as though I don't care enough." He grabbed a breath. Held it. Pushed his emotions back.

"My guess?" Doug moved his hand to Evan's shoulder. "She knows darn well how much you do and she knows she can't keep holding out if you don't give in to her. And you can't give in to her."

"I don't know. Maybe I can. We can take Danielle to visit her grandparents and leave her there while..." He shook his head. He knew, as he said it, he couldn't do it. He couldn't give Susie false hope. But damn he wanted her to be right.

"I think..." Adam came to join them. "This interview might be good closure for her, for everyone. Since she wouldn't go to the service and won't have a memorial, this might be what she needs. Can you get her to come?"

"I doubt it, but I'll try."

15 August

Stu tried to keep his mind on preparing for the interview he didn't want to do, but the contrast of Nella staying right on top of Keith to show how she'd missed him and Susie avoiding Evan to show him the same was too distracting. And he didn't want to do the interview. He didn't want closure any more than she did. He had to think Evan knew she avoided him because she'd missed him; he had to know. It was the best she could do right now, but it would change. She'd go back to seeking him out the way she had when she first moved to Lakewood with him. Constantly. He was her ground. They'd all seen it.

Even when it looked like she ignored him all day, she didn't. Stu often saw her look over at Ev, just to see where he was or at something he said or when he got up to leave the room or when he came back. She was careful about it. Hell, maybe he didn't know. But it would change.

One of these years, it would change big time. He'd always seen it coming. Until Duncan. With a shudder he wouldn't let show, he bounced it out through his heel against the chair.

Of course she wouldn't go with them to the interview; if she didn't think it was final, why would she go to a memorial interview? He'd thought about Evan's comments from the night before, how he nearly believed her or wasn't sure she wasn't right. It had been a month. No way would Duncan stay away willingly. No way in hell.

"Are you paying attention at all?" Mike whacked his arm.

"What? No."

"Come on, Stu, none of us really want to do this..."

"Then why are we?"

Adam looked at Evan but decided to answer himself. "As I said, to clear the rumors."

"Which won't do any good. Like you also said."

"I don't think I said that, and it might not do much good right now, but in the long run, I think it will, I think people will listen later."

"What in the hell good does that do?"

Evan looked over at Susie, at a distance, there but not taking part, and spoke quietly. "For them. Because it will matter to Susie and Danielle, maybe to Danielle the most. It will matter to her."

Stu supposed he was right. He set his mind to paying attention.

16 August

Kate gave Susie a hug and coerced Nella downstairs with the promise of making chocolate chip oatmeal cookies. Her friend nearly refused to leave her alone to watch the interview, but Susie had to watch it and Nella couldn't. She promised she'd be fine, and *fine* was a subjective enough word she figured it was fair enough, as Duncan would say.

With a deep breath, she turned the television on and cuddled into a pillow on her couch. Maybe she should have gone as they asked. She couldn't do it. Her stomach hurt bad enough just at the idea of watching it from home. She wished Danny was still there.

Or maybe she didn't.

One month today. "Where are you?" She spoke to the ceiling. Not to the ceiling although it would have looked like she was if anyone was there. "Come home to me." She felt her eyes water and fought it back.

Getting up, she searched the pantry, hoping she still had a bottle of wine back in there somewhere. Yes. One. Not her favorite. One of his favorites. She put it back. It would wait for when he was home.

At a knock, she wavered between answering and ignoring it. She figured she could at least check. Her dad. He studied her face as he came in and gave her a hug, said he meant to be earlier, said he couldn't let her be alone for this. He sat where Evan usually sat. Close but not right next to her in her husband's spot. She clenched her jaw.

The show started. Mentioned the "very special" interview. She bit her lip. The tears tried again as soon as she saw them. Her band. Her friends. She should have at least gone to New York with them, stayed in the hotel to watch so she'd be there when they got back. Her stomach tightened. She held her breath until the moisture dried.

Susie tried to put herself in management mode, to listen to how they answered questions from a professional standpoint. It didn't work well once Stu dropped his head as they were questioned about their individual relationships with their former lead guitarist. He managed to answer. She could see his body shake from the foot she knew he was bouncing under the table. But he did well.

Evan didn't do as well. He was the last one asked and he stopped several times, looked away, held his breath, swallowed hard.

"I should have gone." She brushed moisture from her face. It hurt him too much. He shouldn't have done it.

"No, I think you did exactly as you should have." Her dad moved to her side and stroked her hair the way Duncan so often stroked Danielle's. "This is hard enough."

"But he..." He stopped again mid-sentence. Doug took over, helped to change the subject. It moved to rumors. About Duncan's *affairs*. They denied all of it, said it couldn't be further from the truth. It was obvious the woman interviewing them didn't believe it, but it led to questions about Susie ... about her relationship with Duncan, about his relationship with his daughter. Mike answered most of it, with Doug and Stu chiming in. Evan dropped his head, pushed a hand through his hair, rubbed his neck.

Susie couldn't hold her tears back. And she couldn't take her eyes off him. She should have gone. She'd hardly spoken to him in days and ... and he hurt so much. She should have gone.

She was glad when it turned to music, his guitar work, his songs, the band's plans. Evan was taking lead back. He managed to say so. She didn't know he'd decided yet that he could, or would, but she expected it. It was right. It was his place, until Duncan came back. And then all of this would be for nothing.

It lasted an hour minus the commercial breaks. She wished she was there backstage waiting for them. For Evan.

"They did a nice job." Her dad rubbed her back. "Are you all right?"

"Yes. I should go get Nella."

"I think she'll wait a little while longer. Relax first."

"No, I want ... I want my baby. I need to be with her right now."

17 August

Evan trudged up the apartment stairs, vaguely aware of Mike talking to him, trying to counter Evan's statement that he'd looked like an idiot during the interview, and sounded like one. He'd been fine. He'd felt calm and controlled going into the studio, but the lights and cameras and the fact he'd have to talk instead of play and sing slammed into him full force. And then she had to start by asking about their personal relationships with Duncan instead of starting with the music as they should have. If it had started with the music, he would have come through that looking at least half intelligent, but by the time it went that direction, he was already too flustered. His personal relationship with Duncan. How in the hell did he explain it? He remembered saying something about a brother and how their differences worked together well and even that wasn't enough; it wasn't close to enough, but he couldn't say more. His voice kept giving way. He'd sounded like an idiot.

Mike had been great at taking up the conversational slack, even without the help he usually got from Stu. Evan knew their lead had expected it, had prepared for that, and Doug jumped in better than normal. He'd expected it, as well.

Within an hour of getting out of the interview, Evan was in the hotel suite on the phone with Nella since John answered and Susie wouldn't come to the phone. Mike and Stu were enjoying the mini bar. Stu enjoyed it far too much and spent the rest of the afternoon passed out. He had to stop that before it hurt him, and he had to be careful not to pull Susie that direction.

A cute drunk. Stu's words still bothered him. Evan had never seen her even close to that. She'd always been so careful. She had to be careful. Even coffee upset her system if she had just a little too much.

She could have at least come to the damn phone yesterday if she couldn't make herself go with them, as she should have. Mike said he was going to Susie's to get Keith and asked if he was coming. No. She couldn't even pick up the phone; he didn't need to go to her place.

As he unlocked his own door, Susie opened hers, greeted Mike with a soft hug, and met Evan's eyes. She bit her lip and came to him, stepped between him and the doorway. For a moment, she only stood there as he couldn't figure out what to say to her. She'd at least watched it; he could see in her eyes she'd watched it. As band management, she should have been fussing at him about how badly he did, just as Roy had done and had the right to do, more or less.

She set a hand alongside his face. The kids were in the hall now, also, with the open door and Mike asking Keith if he'd behaved well and Kate saying ... something back, kindly, gently.

"Are you okay?" Susie's eyes were still locked on his. They were moist, concerned. Her voice was the same. Her fingertips slipped back slightly, enough to remind him her hand was on his face.

He couldn't answer. He held the gaze, tried to remind himself he was pissed off at her, that she was pissed at him...

A tear ran down her cheek and she wrapped around him, arms over his shoulders, squeezing tight, on her toes to reach better, face against his shoulder and his neck. Evan put his arms around her, felt her strength through her smallness, felt her giving comfort, not asking for it.

Mike slid past them through their door, with Kate and both kids, set a hand on Evan's back a moment, and closed the door most of the way. Left them in the hall alone. Susie held on for the longest time, until she lowered back to her heels and barely separated from him.

"Lee, I'm..." Her head shook softly, her arms lowered to circle his back instead of his shoulders. "I'm sorry I wasn't there with you. I couldn't do it. But I should have, at least..."

He kissed her head. "It's all right, Angel."

"It's not all right. It isn't." She looked up, her blue eyes sparkling with the moisture. "I don't know how to deal with this and I'm doing it wrong but I ... I'm taking it out on you and I shouldn't, but I want you to tell me you believe me, at least believe I could be right, and I know you don't and it's frustrating..."

"Suse, I wish to hell you were." He raised a hand to stroke her face. I just think..."

"Don't say it. I don't want to be mad at you anymore. I don't have the energy, and Dad is already pushing it. I know, talk to someone, it's only grief and non-acceptance. I've heard it all, but he's wrong. So are you. And I can't..." She bit her lip and looked away.

"What do you want me to do?" Evan couldn't help but ask, even if he couldn't encourage her.

Her head shook again. "I don't know." Her voice was nearly a whisper. "I just know ... I'm not crazy, and ... and I need to not be mad at you. So I won't be. But..."

Evan held her in again. "I want to believe you. And I respect how you're holding on, that you have to. I understand why you do. I just don't want you more hurt than you are already, but I know you will be, when you realize..." He couldn't quite say it. "I'm going to be here, Angel. I won't let the rumors or anything else pull me away again. Whatever happens. I'm sorry. I was trying... It was a mistake and I'm sorry."

Her fingers tightened against him, gripped his shirt. She held on some time longer, then agreed to go inside with him. He left her side only long enough to shower and change and they cooked together and talked with Nella together and she stayed at his place until too tired to keep her eyes open, then he walked them home and tucked them both in.

1 September 1978

Evan gave Nella a hug and asked about her day so far, listened to how Stu let her play on his "boards an 'tar," then handed her a bag of new coloring books and new crayons and sent her across the hall with Mike to go share them with Keith. As the door closed behind the little chatterbox, Evan turned his attention to her mom. September first. On what would have been their fourth anniversary.

Susie sat on the window seat, arms around her legs, staring out at fitful branches and fast-moving dark clouds. Thunder rumbled in the distance but it was moving away; they were only getting the edge of it. He'd wished for a beautiful, sunny day so she wouldn't have to have gray outside, as well. It had been beautiful on their wedding day, perfect weather for an outdoor ceremony. He supposed this was more appropriate this year.

With a sigh, he took her side and stood waiting for her to talk if she wanted to talk. She stayed quiet, didn't acknowledge he was there. "Come on, Suse. Let's go out. The storm is passing."

In her silence, he brushed hair behind her ear. She'd done nothing with it other than washing and brushing for the past month and a half. When she worked out, which wasn't often and only when Nella was driving her crazy with her energy, she put it in a simple ponytail, but otherwise it hung straight down, sometimes partly in her face which she didn't seem to notice. It was beautiful just as it was, near black and shiny, although it had lost some sheen recently; she wasn't eating well enough and it showed on more than her hair, but she never braided it or styled it in any way. She let it hang.

Six weeks. It was time to pick herself up. "Suse, I think you should keep honoring your anniversary. Go change and I'll take you out, anywhere you want." As always these days, she was in old sweats and a big tee, often one of Duncan's, including today. The old red one he was wearing when she met him, the one that had stuck to his body just enough to draw her eyes to the outline of his build. The one she was wearing when they were mugged in the park; it had been covered in his blood. She hadn't worn it since; neither had he. Evan figured she got rid of it.

"Angel." He lowered to the seat and touched her arm. "You need to get out of this apartment. How about we go look at furniture for your house? It needs more than a couple of beds and a table. We'll go look, then have dinner while you think about what you want to do with it."

She shook her head.

"It's ready to move in, Suse. You should do that."

"Not until he's home."

Until he's home. She hadn't said it in at least two weeks. Since their talk, she'd been at Evan's side most every day, most of the day, at her place or his, if he went down to work out or for a quick meeting with Adam, to practice when they bothered. Even when her dad was around, and he was around a lot, she didn't go long without at least touching base with him. In all that time, she hadn't mentioned Duncan coming home.

Evan stood again, grabbed a deep breath, paced to the far edge of the living room. What should he say? Not to do this? To tell her, again, he wasn't coming home, that she had to move on? Maybe not move on so much yet but at least accept that she would have to move on. Eventually. Not twenty years down the road as her dad did.

He decided to skirt the issue as he returned to her. "I think you shouldn't wait to move in. He'd want you to enjoy the house, to give Nella more room as he wanted her to have..." The telephone interfered and he went to check. John. Asking them to dinner at his place, to meet his date. He relayed the message. She shook her head.

Evan told him she wouldn't go, so John said he'd bring dinner to them. Evan warned him it wasn't a good night to bring a date, but he insisted, said she couldn't be alone on her anniversary, she needed to be distracted whether or not she wanted to be. They would be there in about an hour. He thought about not telling her since he wasn't sure she wouldn't bolt ... somewhere. To Stu's maybe. She didn't even answer.

He again suggested she start moving into her house and offered to help with whatever she needed, said Doug was a better handyman than he was if she needed one and she wouldn't be on her own with it. He might as well have been talking to the house itself.

At a loss as to what to do for the next hour, he went next door to grab the book he was reading – James Joyce, in his quest to brush up on Irish and Scottish literature – and returned. Just so she'd know he was there, he planted himself on the other end of the window bench.

She looked over at him, and at the book. "Since when do you read fiction?"

"I do now and then. Want it when I'm done?"

"I think that's over my head."

"Of course it isn't." He studied her as she returned her gaze to the clouds and blowing branches. "Suse..." But he'd lost her attention. Over her head? What she meant was she wasn't interested. Maybe he'd leave it when he was done. She could change her mind.

John greeted Evan and introduced him to his "date" although she wasn't a date in anything more than show. Brenda was a highly recommended grief therapist who had qualms about letting him disguise her as a date, until he filled her in on Susie's losses as a child and how she still clung to the belief her husband was coming back. She agreed to meet her casually, with the stipulation he would tell Susie who she was, and she would not charge for the night since she couldn't count it as work. John had the feeling the woman might be interested in more than work if he decided to make it that. She wasn't his type. She was nice enough, but he felt no attraction. And there was no need: she was only there to try to get Susie to talk.

He looked over at his daughter, on the window seat where she stared out at the hazy dusk left in the storm's wake. She'd been there for more than an hour, Evan said, maybe two.

John guided Brenda over. He figured they might as well jump right in. "Sweetheart, how are you doing today?" He gave her a hug as well as he could although she didn't move or acknowledge him. "This is a tough day for you. I remember well." He grasped her hands from where they bound her legs. "I want you to meet Brenda Hampton."

"I don't want company. I told Evan I don't want company."

"He told me. And I know you don't, but I'm your father and I don't care right now if you don't, so get up and use the manners you were taught."

She gave him a look he well understood. That didn't matter, either.

Brenda extended her hand. "It's nice to meet you. I'm sorry we're invading your privacy tonight."

She took Brenda's hand, only for a second, then started to get up and cringed at the movement.

"Stiff? Evan said you've been sitting here a couple of hours."

"Evan talks too much." She brushed past him, back to the back part of the apartment. If she stayed back there too long, he'd go after her. For now, John put his attention on Evan. "How are you holding up?"

"Better than she is." He glanced at Brenda. "Don't take it personally if she doesn't talk to you. She's not talking much to anyone."

"Oh I'm well used to that. Don't worry about it."

At his confusion, John glanced to be sure Susie wasn't within earshot and admitted who she was. Evan's shoulders stiffened, a sign he was about to argue. "This is my call, as her father. She needs to talk to someone and if I can't get her to go in, we'll do it this way."

"You plan to tell her."

"Think she'll talk if I do?"

He hesitated. "Probably not, but I don't think..."

"Then she leaves me no choice. I'll tell her after dinner. First, I want you to help me get her to talk, about anything, just..."

"This is not a good idea. I can't be part of this." Evan stepped backward.

John caught his arm. "It's been a month and a half and she still thinks he's coming home."

"I know how long it's been. I know she needs to acknowledge it. I know she needs to tell Danielle. But this ... with no offense to Dr. Hampton, this is not a good idea, John. You need to tell her. Let her wait until she's ready."

"In twenty years? I can't let her do it the way I did. I accepted it and it was still hard enough..."

"You had no choice but to accept it. You saw it. You had proof. She didn't, and doesn't."

"You think she's right?" Dr. Hampton eyed him.

"No. I don't think she's right. If I did, I'd be out there looking for him day and night until I found him and brought him back home. I know after this long there's no chance. I just think we should let her do it her way."

"He may be right, John. It hasn't been terribly long yet. You might give her more time. I'll still be available."

John shook his head and took a couple of steps away from them. Evan could easily tell Susie if he decided. He didn't want that. She would go hide in her room and refuse to come out if she knew. "Tell you what. Let's just keep this dinner and conversation and I won't ask you to help me push her to talk. Will you go that far?"

Evan rubbed his neck, about to argue, until Susie came back. She'd changed clothes. With a warning glance at Evan, he went to meet her. "I have dinner ordered. Should I call back and add wine to it or do you have something here you'd prefer?"

"Tea is fine for me and that's all I have I'm willing to open. Order something else if you want it."

To his relief, Evan said nothing to her through the evening about Brenda, but he also didn't push her to talk. A couple of times he changed the subject when Brenda asked questions about her husband, despite John's protest glances. Susie did talk about Danielle to an extent. It was the only time she seemed in the conversation instead of withdrawn from it. She refused to talk about Duncan. Not one word.

As he drove Brenda home, John asked her opinion and tried to insist on paying her for the evening, since it was work. She refused to take it. It was no more than dinner, as far as she was concerned. Her professional ethics wouldn't allow otherwise. She'd enjoyed the conversation and the company and her advice was to give Susie more time, to make sure she stayed busy, got out of the house, did things she normally did. She would let the truth sink in as normal life returned.

John hoped she was right. But Brenda had no idea just how stubborn the girl could be.

With Nella finally in bed and Evan finally back in his own apartment, Susie returned to the window seat and looked out at the darkness. Part of her wished the fans with candles and flashlights would come back. It had been so much less dark with them there. Less silent.

Less final.

Not final. But they'd given up. So had everyone else.

She wouldn't. Even if the papers were right. Maybe they were.

Maybe he had found somewhere else to be, used it as an excuse. Maybe she'd been too bitchy, about the adoption, about the fans and crowds, about ... how she wanted "her own" child. About the house, and insisting they keep it as much original as possible although it would have been faster and maybe less expensive to take it down and rebuild, or find something else. She didn't want something else. It had been within her grasp and ... and now she couldn't let herself move into it. Not without him.

Maybe he had left it all behind and found somewhere else to be, away from her. How could she blame him?

But not without Danielle. He would never, ever leave Danielle on purpose. Never.

Even if she did still feel him. Even if she knew he was still out there. He wouldn't leave his daughter.

7 September

Evan shook his head. He was never going to get it the way Duncan played it. It sounded like pure shit next to the original.

"Man, just remake it into your own style." Mike shrugged. "Your style was good enough for us before. It is now."

"With it so different on the album? That's what people are going to want to hear. And I can't do it. It's not going to happen. He's impossible to imitate. Better guitarists have tried; I haven't heard it happen yet."

"Then don't try."

"I agree, Evan." Doug set his sticks on his snare. "No one is going to expect you to play it the same. He had his own style. You have yours. Go with that."

"Fans will notice."

"Yes, but then they will anyway. They know he's not here. They're not going to hold that against you."

"Would you want to try to follow that?" He pulled the guitar off and set it on the stand. Rubbed the back of his neck.

"Why do I think that's not the real problem?" Mike came over to him. "It's just that he won't be on stage with you. You never wanted to go too big before and now you just want us to go back to small time shows since he's not here with you. Am I right?"

"No." Half right. Only half. He didn't want to hold them back from the big stage. He rubbed his neck again. "If you tried to take John Lennon's place on stage, think you could sing his songs when his audience expects, or at least wants, him? Could you do it?"

"Different." Their lead flipped his hair back from his face with a fast twitch of his head. "They aren't my band. This is your band. It's different. And you were lead before."

"Before anyone knew us. I didn't get us there. Wasn't good enough before; why in the hell do you think I will be now?"

"That's not true." Stu raised his head. "As Susie has told you, he's not ... wasn't better. Only different. You're just as good. So just do this with us. We can't lose you, too."

"I'm not sure that wouldn't be better. Reform the band. Grab a couple more guys who are good enough. Change the name. Go on. You'd be right back up there."

Stu threw his hands up and walked off stage. He didn't get far. Adam stopped him. "Sounds like a good time to interrupt."

"Interrupt what, exactly? Hell, not like we're doing anything." Stu threw Evan a look.

"Right." Adam glanced around at them. "Time to change that and get back out there. We have a tour in the works, being reworked. Are you going to be ready?"

Stu snickered. "Because Evan talking about breaking up the band sounds like we're ready?"

"We'll talk about that later. I have news."

"What? Another attack on us for hiding? So what?" Stu ambled over to sit on the edge of the riser, dropping his head to his hands, elbows on his knees.

"Keith Moon died today."

Stu raised his head again. "Of *Who*? Are you serious?"

"It's on the news. Drug overdose."

"Shit. Rock stars dropping like flies." Stu stood again, paced.

"Hell, he should have just taken Duncan's place on the plane if he was looking to be done with it all. At least Duncan didn't do it to himself."

"Mike." Doug scolded as he got up and came around from behind his set. "What was he, my age?"

"A bit older. Thirty-one."

"Hell of a loss of talent."

"Don't say that in front of Susie." Mike rolled his eyes. "She'll take your head off for thinking about the talent instead of his family."

"I don't know his family. I know his drum technique."

Adam bypassed them and put his attention on Evan. "Guess you still can't get her to come downstairs? It's been a week now."

"No, and I'm not sure she will. I barely got her down here before and since her anniversary, she's hardly talking to me again."

"*That's* what it is." Stu stopped pacing and stared at him. "It's not that Duncan isn't here. It's that *she* isn't. That why you've lost interest?"

"I didn't say I've lost interest."

"Don't have to say it. Damn, that's easy enough. I'll go upstairs and tell her you won't play with us anymore unless she comes down and..."

"No, you won't." Evan heard the edge to his voice. Stu was not going to pressure her. "And I told you what it was."

"I heard what you said but I don't fucking believe you, alright? You know you can lead fine. So if it'll take her telling you to keep going..."

"Don't."

Stu stared a while, then walked away, out of the basement.

Evan started to follow. He couldn't let Stu...

"He won't do it." Doug stopped him. "My guess is he's right, but he won't do it. Maybe you should. Hang out at her place while you're supposed to be at practice. She'll know. Tell her you're waiting for her."

Waiting for her. No. He wasn't. They didn't get it. It wasn't about Susie. Not this time.

Mike pestered him about his suggestion to find another guitarist and regroup, said they didn't want that, it wouldn't be Raucous without him. Evan hardly thought it would be, anyway, without Duncan. He didn't say it; it would be unfair to his band mates. It would sound like he didn't believe in them, also, and that wasn't true. He did. They were good. They were damned good, and they deserved a lead guitarist of Duncan's calibre. Maybe he would start looking for one, while he stayed long enough to hold them together.

8 September

Getting away from the noise of Nella and Keith and Stu playing Dominoes, lining them up on the kitchen table into a chain and knocking them over, usually not on purpose, Susie headed next door. She wanted to go somewhere out of the way, somewhere Nella could go outside and run and yell without making Susie cringe. Evan would have an idea; he'd know where, and he'd help make arrangements.

Stephanie answered the door and greeted her with a wide smile. "Come on in. How are you? It's been forever."

"Am I interrupting? I can come back..."

"No, not at all." She grabbed Susie's hand and half pulled her inside. "Evan's in the shower but he should be out in a second."

"Oh, I should go. I didn't realize..."

"No, it's fine. Sit. Want some wine? He doesn't like it much. I guessed wrong. You can share it with me." Stephanie grabbed another glass and uncorked the bottle.

"Oh. No, thank you. I'm not staying. And that's too sweet for him. He likes it dry, and white usually, but always dry."

"Ah. Good to know." Stephanie poured herself more and sat back, crossing her legs. She was dressed nice, in a dark brown flowing pant suit that brought out the red in her hair and accented her figure. At least it hid the birthmark on her shoulder Duncan had told Susie about the night he and Evan met Stephanie. Duncan liked her. Susie wasn't sure she did, although she had.

She tried again to leave, but Evan came out, in khaki pants and nothing else. He stopped his approach when he saw her. "Sorry, I was just leaving." Susie took a couple of steps toward the door and told Stephanie it was nice to see her again.

"No, stay." She jumped up and came to her. "We're not leaving for dinner for nearly an hour. I haven't talked to you recently. He won't mind."

She was pretty sure Evan did mind, actually, but of course he said he didn't and disappeared down the hall. Giving in, only long enough not to be rude, Susie took the chair Duncan always had and nearly felt him sitting there with her as she wanted to escape. Stephanie again mentioned how long it had been and Susie had the feeling she meant with Evan, also. She hadn't even thought of it, but he'd been with her most all day every day for the past ... week or more and even before then, she hadn't seen Stephanie around.

"... I really didn't think he'd call again so it was a nice surprise. Usually when men say they need space and will call later, you know they won't, and I didn't expect he would..."

Evan told her he needed space? When?

"... told me I was an idiot for jumping when he finally called again, but you know, I never expected this to be permanent..."

Permanent? No. She heard Stephanie ramble about how she was fine with whatever time he needed and it didn't bother her, and even when he came back out, this time with a shirt on, she kept rambling as though she was... Susie noticed the wine was more than half gone. Evan wouldn't have had much if any with as sweet as it was, one Susie liked a lot and had teased him about sharing ... when they were out together with Duncan, and Stephanie. It was the same wine. Stephanie didn't remember.

Evan offered coffee. He asked Susie but she understood why he offered.

"Thank you, no. I need to get back. I just ... I'll talk to you later."

He caught up with her at the door. "What's up, Angel?"

"Nothing. I ... nothing. Have fun tonight." She gave him a quick hug and rushed back to her own place.

The night they were all out together. The four of them. She shoved the memory aside and went back to the kids.

9 September

"Why did you send her home? Take her next door with you."

Evan glanced at Mike and grabbed his apartment key.

"Ev, she's not going to let you keep putting her off like this. The girl stays all night and you sleep on the couch and then send her home when it's time to go next door, when you know she enjoys talking with Susie?"

"I'm not taking a date next door. Not until she's back on her feet."

"Why? Maybe it'll help her normalize if we all normalize around her."

"Great, Mike. So John takes a date and I take a date? You don't think that would be throwing salt in a wound?"

"I don't know why. She was happily married for years while the rest of us have floundered with our own pathetic love lives. That seemed to be okay."

Evan stopped at the door and turned to stare at his friend. "Don't be an insensitive ass right now. Most times, I couldn't care less. Right now, I do."

"Uh huh. Maybe you shouldn't have slept on the couch."

"She was lit. I'm not into that."

Mike walked closer. "And maybe you don't want Susie to see you dating for the same reason you never used to want her to see you dating?"

Evan's stomach tightened. His whole body tightened. He considered throwing a fist into Mike's ribs for thinking it. "Not even close." He walked out, closed the door, too hard, then let himself breathe deeply for a minute before he went to knock on her door. The reason he didn't used to want her to see him date: because he'd wanted her to accept if he ever decided it was time to ask her out.

No.

Not even fucking minutely close.

After Stu broke up with Kara, Susie had been more careful about not hanging all over her husband in front of Stu. She'd done the same when Myra ... she'd done the same for him. He would not take a date to have dinner at her place. Not until her feet were under her. Stephanie could call it quits if she wished.

He heard her music before the door opened.

"Come on in." Susie turned before he could offer the wine he brought. Her favorite. Second favorite. Not the one Duncan always bought for her.

"Danielle, get those toys picked up *now*. Don't make me tell you again." She disappeared into the kitchen. There was no sign of Nella other than her mess. He followed Susie and found her scrubbing the wall. Crayon. A very large drawing. On the wall.

"She's been busy today, I see. Want help with that?"

Susie didn't look up. "No, but you can call Dad and tell him this isn't a good night to come."

"I could try, but I doubt he'd listen." Evan set the wine in the refrigerator and went to crouch beside her. "Let me deal with this. Go ahead and get ready for company, unless you are ready."

She flashed him an unamused look. He knew full well she wouldn't wear an old tank top and shorts to entertain her dad's date, or fake date, although Evan wasn't terribly sure anymore. "You could wear what you have on. Looks good to me."

She touched his eyes and paused. Caught the tease he hoped she would catch. "Thanks. But just because I let you see me at my worst, that doesn't mean I'll allow just anyone to."

"Your worst?" He raised his eyes and skimmed her. "Not hardly. This is much nicer than those baggy things you wore in Greenville."

"Right. And no use trying to make me not mad at the kid. I can't even tell you how mad I am right now. This is only the topper today. And I shouldn't ask, but I would be very grateful if you could get her to pick up that mess out there."

"Why shouldn't you ask?"

"She's my kid. I should make her do it."

"Suse, he asked me to look after you both, to help with her. Don't ever think you shouldn't."

"Yeah well, he meant for the week." She bit her lip and scrubbed harder.

Evan took the green scrubbing pad to set aside and grasped her hands. "You know as well as I do that he would darnn well expect it to be for as long as you need. And he wouldn't have had to ask. You and I have been friends too long for you to think you shouldn't ask."

Her eyes moistened but she swallowed it back and nodded. "I'm sorry. I've been..."

"Don't be." He stood and pulled her up with him. "Go unwind a bit and get ready. I'll take care of the little terror. And if this isn't done before they get here, it doesn't matter. Let it go for tonight. It'll be just as hard to clean tomorrow."

She gave him a half grin and a quick hug. He followed her back to where Nella sat on her floor ... with a broken ink pen. And ink on the light blue carpet.

"*Danielle Lynne.*"

The girl jumped. At least she had the decency to look ashamed. "I not mean to, my mummy."

"*How* did you not *mean* to?"

"I see inside. Yes. I not tell it to spill." She shook her head.

Evan grasped Susie's shoulders and led her out of Nella's room, to her own. "Go on. I'll deal with her."

"That won't ever come out. She already has nail polish under her throw rug, that she took out of my bathroom, by the way. I can't cover the whole carpet with rugs."

"So maybe we'll pull up the carpet and make the whole thing one big canvas. When she grows out of it, you can give her carpet again."

She shoved a hand through her hair.

"Relax, Angel. It's just a phase. She's only two." He kissed her forehead. "Take a hot shower. We'll get her mess cleaned up in the living room and I'll get the ink off her hands. We'll deal with the rest later." He saw her clench her jaw with the light nod and turn to go to the shower.

Evan closed her door behind him and went back to find the girl using a washcloth to try to get the stain out. One of Susie's good washcloths. "Oh Danielle, let me have that before your mom sees it."

"I clean it. Yes."

"It won't work that way, little one. Come on." He took her to the bathroom and turned the bathtub on to get it warm. "Stick your hands under here and scrub them good." As she did he handed her the soap.

"It not come off, my Evan Lee." She shook her head.

"Keep trying and stay there. I'll be right back." He went out to give his mom a call and told her quickly what happened. Of course she knew what to use. Jeremy had been just as bad. Thanking her, he returned to Danielle with an old kitchen rag, dried her hands, and rubbed toothpaste over them. Luckily, it worked. "Now don't play with your toothpaste like this. I don't want your mom mad at me for showing you."

"My mum no' ever mad at my Evan Lee. No. And my hands all clean 'gain. Look."

"Good thing. And Danielle..." He crouched to her level. "Yes, she gets mad at me, too. It's okay. Everyone gets mad. It's all right to be mad sometimes. But maybe you should only color on your paper from now on and don't play with pens. Can you do that for me?"

She frowned. "I make pretty, pretty pi'ture on wall for my mummy and she taking it off again. Wainbow and birdies and my daddy. Yes. I draw my daddy and she say *no, no*, and taking it off."

Her daddy. And a rainbow. Evan swept her into a hug. She smelled like little girl sweat. "I bet she didn't know it was a drawing of your daddy."

"No, she mad and yell *no, no*."

"Okay baby. I'll talk to your mom. How about you take a bath before your grandpa comes to dinner?"

"I not take bath. No." She backed up to show her hands. "I clean now."

"Your hands are clean. The rest of you smells like you've had a hard day harassing your mom. First, we better get your toys out of the living room. Can we do it quick so it's done before she gets out of the shower?"

Nella was clean and dressed with the living room picked up by the time Susie came back out. Evan handed her a glass of wine.

"Thought this was for dinner."

"Didn't know you even noticed I brought it."

"I noticed. And thank you." She took a sip and glanced around. "Did you tie her up somewhere?"

He chuckled. "No, but I'm guessing you had that thought at some point today."

"More than once. What is she doing?"

"Reading. On her bed."

"I should go talk to her. I got pretty mad..."

"Before you do, there's something you should know." He led her to the kitchen and pointed at the drawing. "What does it look like?"

"Crayon on my kitchen wall." She took another swallow.

"Okay, other than that."

"I don't know, Lee. I'm just... What is it? Did she tell you?"

"Look." He pointed out a stick-like figure with a fairly good reproduction of a guitar and traced it with a finger.

Susie shoved a hand through her bangs. "It's her dad."

He nodded. "And this, I assume, is the rainbow she mentioned. And her birdies. I think she was actually trying to make you feel better. She talks about how you're sad because her dad isn't here, so she brought him to you."

Susie fell against him, gripping him with her free hand.

"I wasn't trying to upset you, Suse. I just thought you should know her intention." He felt her nod. "So whatever's in the oven smells wonderful. Should I check on it?" He felt another nod. "Go ahead. Go talk to her, Angel."

With another swallow, a good swallow this time, of her wine, Susie set her glass down, took a deep breath, and went to find her daughter.

She was actually on her bed reading, stomach down, elbows propping her shoulders and head up, legs raising and lowering together as she kicked the bed with her toes. Her little body rocked with the rhythm of it. How she could concentrate on the pictures in the book while moving around like that, Susie didn't understand. "Danielle?"

The girl swiveled around and sat up; a worried frown emphasized her round cheeks. The most precious thing in the world, her daughter. And adorable even with the big frown, and even after the horrendous day.

Susie went to sit next to her and gave her a hug. "I'm sorry I yelled so much today."

Nella crawled up on her lap and held tight. "My daddy come home now? Yes. Want my daddy home now."

Susie clenched her teeth and squeezed her eyes closed. She'd promised herself no tears. No more crying. It did no good. Her baby needed her strong. She focused on the light scent of shampoo in the damp wavy hair, on the softness of fresh nearly-baby skin, on the intensity of Nella's hug, her little fingers gripping Susie's back. Her precious baby. Duncan's baby, so like him. Maybe he'd been right all those times he said he wasn't an easy child to raise. She'd never believed it, but he could be right. Or maybe he exaggerated and all of this was how Evan told her she had been as a child.

She chuckled and her daughter looked up at her curiously. With a deep breath, Susie combed fingers through Nella's bangs and down the side of her face. "Can I tell you a story?"

"Yes. I like stories. I get a book."

"No." Susie held her still. "This is a real story, about when I was your age. Do you want to hear?"

Nella nodded hard.

"When I was little one of my favorite things to do was to pull things off the shelves to ... well, to look at them, I guess. When my mom was busy, I would pull down all of the toys she kept on low shelves, spill them all over the floor, then find other things..."

"No. You not like mess."

"I don't like messes now. I did when I was little like you." She saw the curious expression again and gave her a kiss on the forehead. "One day when your grandpa came home – your grandpa is my daddy, remember? – well, I had my toys *aaalll* over the floor, and mixed in with them were the metal bowls from the kitchen I liked to bang together, and your grandpa's books, and my mommy's pretty things that weren't breakable, and her yarn. A lot of yarn in all colors. I had run through the house with one of each color in my hands pulling them all around the living room until it looked like a lot of rainbow spider webs wrapped around our furniture. It was such a big, big mess, your grandpa stopped at the door and just looked at me."

Danielle's eyes were wide. "My g'ampa yell loud and loud?"

"No. He didn't yell." Susie brushed fingers through her hair again. "He laughed. He laughed so hard, he nearly fell to the floor laughing." Her eyes moistened as she thought of her dad describing the scene when Evan mentioned it. He'd laughed again while telling her. "My mom didn't like messes, either. Usually, she didn't let me make that much mess. But she got tired of telling my dad how much trouble I could be when he didn't believe it, so she didn't stop me all day long. She just let me go so he could see just what she put up with from me all day every day."

Nella frowned. "You messy when you little too?"

"Yes. And it's okay to be messy. But Danielle, that's what happens when you make messes all day and don't stop between to clean it up now and then. It gets so bad you can't walk through the house."

"And my g'ampa laugh and laugh."

"Oh. Well he did that once. But after that, he helped Mom convince me I needed to pick up my messes. He didn't want her to be always tired. And I don't want to be always tired, either. Okay? I understand, baby. I know you're curious and you're busy and it's more fun just to do what you want, but sometimes you have to do what you don't want so someone else will feel better, too." Susie wasn't sure anything she said would get through. Maybe the child wasn't old enough yet.

Either way, she had the more important thing to talk about. "Evan said that's a picture of your dad on the wall."

Nella dropped her head against Susie's chest.

"Baby, I'm sorry. I didn't know. I know you miss your daddy and I'm so sorry you're sad. I wish he was home with us. It's okay to be sad. You can tell me you are. But Nella, you still have to follow the rules and you know you aren't supposed to color on anything but your color books and paper. Right?" She felt a light nod. "Okay. So how about we leave it there for tonight and you can show Grandpa. Tomorrow I'll take a picture of you standing next to your art, and then we can clean it off the wall? Okay? Then you'll still have it."

Nella's shoulders rose and fell and she climbed off Susie's lap and down from her bed. "I hungry now."

"John, let her know or I will." Evan knew he was pushing his luck, and his relationship with her father, but he couldn't go along with it.

"I think you're overstepping your bounds."

A warning. But what did it matter? She wasn't seventeen anymore. He couldn't pull her away from him. "Maybe. Maybe not. I'm her friend. She trusts me..."

"And she doesn't trust me?" His shoulders stiffened.

"That's not what I meant. You're her father. As mad as she might get, that won't ever change. She's barely over the fact that I left her in Greenville and I can't let her think..."

"It was for her own good. She knows that."

"Which doesn't matter, since she figures that's her call, not mine, and she's right. I told her she was right and it was a mistake and things are okay, but I can't let her think I agreed to this, to not telling her who Brenda is."

"This isn't your call. It's mine."

"You made me part of it by telling me. So tell her or..."

"*My G'ampa.*" Nella flew from the hallway into John's arms.

Evan gave him a glance to say he meant what he said and turned to tell Susie Brenda would be over soon, with another look at John. Her father said nothing other than to chat with Nella.

Susie was friendly enough when Brenda came. She sipped her wine as they chatted before dinner and added to it to have with her meal. Evan needed to warn her. She was relaxing too much, saying too much.

"Nella, stop. That's enough butter."

"No, not 'nough my mummy. I like lots and lots."

Evan chuckled. "Just like her dad."

Susie glanced at him with at least a partial grin and grabbed the butter knife from her daughter. "Danielle, I said enough. Your fish doesn't need to swim in the butter."

Nella paused from struggling for the knife and poked at the filet with her fork. "No. Fishie not swimming still. Fishie need wa'er to swim. Cough and cough and not breathe longer in no wa'er. And we eat the fishie. Yes. Not swim in butter." She poked it again. "All dead, see?"

"Oh Danielle." Susie shoved a hand through her hair and rolled her eyes toward the ceiling.

"Okay pumpkin." John moved the butter to the other side of the table. "Just eat now."

Evan tried hard not to laugh at the child and he was glad Susie didn't notice. He watched her as conversation continued and John took over with Nella. Susie poked at her own barely touched fish and set her fork down.

"Did she make your lose your appetite?" Brenda studied her, prodding.

"I guess. Sorry. I hope she didn't bother you."

"Not at all. My boyfriend and his sons say much worse..." She stopped when Susie looked at her dad.

Brenda shrugged. "It's not what you think."

Susie had started to eat her potatoes and again put her fork down.

"Finish eating, sweetheart. We'll talk after dinner."

She stared at him.

"And I know you're not that touchy, either. You need to eat. You're too thin again."

"Boyfriend?" She moved her stare to Brenda.

"She might as well know, John. It's time. I'm not actually his date. I'm a grief counselor. He thought..."

"What?" She pushed back from the table and turned her gaze to Evan. "Did you know?"

He tried to answer and wasn't sure how.

Brenda jumped back in. "They thought it might be more comfortable for you if you got to know me first..."

They? The accusation in Susie's eyes hurt his stomach. "Suse..."

She left the room.

Evan grabbed a deep breath, shook his head, and got up. "Did you have to make it sound like I approved of this?" He didn't care how rude it was. He told Nella to keep eating and followed her mom. Her door was closed. He knocked. No answer. Slowly, he went in. She was on her bed, legs crossed in front of her, her head leaned down over them. "Suse..."

"I don't want to talk to you." Her voice was muffled but terribly clear.

"It wasn't my idea."

Her head shot up. "But you knew? How long? Since tonight?"

He wanted to say yes, it was only since tonight, but he couldn't possibly lie to her. "No. From the first dinner. I argued with John…"

She nearly jumped off the bed and came toward him. "Since the *first* dinner? You knew? And you didn't *tell* me?"

"Your dad wanted…"

She shoved him. "Just get out. *Get out.* And tell them to get out, too."

"Suse. Listen to me a minute."

"Listen? Why? You won't listen to me. You think I'm nuts like everyone else does. Just get *out* and quit acting like my friend. Just get *out.*" She walked around him and out of the room.

Acting like her friend? Maybe she was nuts. Or bordering on it. He followed her out. She was grabbing the salt away from her daughter, yelled at her to just eat already and quit playing with the food. And she told Brenda to leave, not to come back.

Her dad tried to calm her. She pulled away, looked at where Danielle had shoved her plate away, and took her down off the chair. "Fine, you're done. Get ready for bed."

"No, I not done. I eat my 'tatoes."

"If you wanted to eat them, you would have by now. Go on. *Move* it."

"Sweetheart, don't take it out on her."

Susie pulled away from him again. "Take it out on her? Do you have any idea what she's been *doing* today? Did you look at my *wall?*"

Brenda moved in. "I understand you're upset and you have a right to be, but your father's concerned with good reason. Are you sleeping at all? Much of the time, lack of sleep makes the grief worse. I have an associate who can prescribe something to help you sleep…"

"Really? Is she going to lie about who she is, too? Leave. I don't want you in my house. And if you repeat anything to the press, I'll sue. Nella, go to your room."

"Susan." John gripped her arms. "You need to talk to Brenda…"

"No I *don't.* I just need *one* fucking person to *believe* me and to be *honest* with me. *That's* what I need. I need my *husband* back."

Evan picked Nella up and took her to her room.

"Evan Lee, my mummy not okay. No."

He set her on her bed and wiped her tears. "I know, baby. But don't worry. She will be better soon. I promise." He kissed her forehead. "Stay here and color a while and we'll get a snack later. Okay?"

"I not color. No. My crayons all gone now."

Gone. Susie took them away. He couldn't blame her for that. "Well then, how about you build something with your Legos?"

"No. My Keith not here."

"Tell you what. You start building and I'll see if Keith can come play. Is that all right?" Getting a reluctant nod, he closed her door behind him. Susie was still yelling.

As he went back into the kitchen, John suggested she go back to Pennsylvania if she wouldn't see a therapist in Lakewood where people might find out.

"And you'll find one who agrees with *you* again? Who'll *hide* who they are? I'm not going anywhere. This is *my* home. I want her *out* of it."

"Susan..."

"She's right, John." Evan risked moving up beside her. "I shouldn't have let this happen." He pulled Susie's face to his. "I'm sorry. And I don't think you're nuts."

She pushed away. "How am I supposed to trust you? You leave me in Greenville alone and set me up without telling me and ... and now this? How can I trust you?"

Evan wished she'd punched him in the stomach instead.

"Just go. All of you. Leave. I'm tired and I want to be left alone."

Her dad closed in. "I don't think that's a good idea. Evan, maybe you could see Brenda to her car. I'll stay..."

"No." Susie pulled away from him. "Just go. I don't need a babysitter."

"I'm not sure you don't, sweetheart. At least for Danielle. Maybe she could come stay with me a few days to give you a break."

Susie froze. Stared at him. Wrong thing to say. Evan had to interfere. "John. Don't do that."

"Now you think I can't handle my daughter? What? Do you plan to take her away from me if I don't..." She stopped again.

"I think, until you get yourself together and face reality, this isn't the best place for her."

Hell. Evan told him not to say it. He warned him.

"You think that, too?" Her eyes pierced through Evan as she moved directly in front of him. "Tell me. You think I'm not safe to keep her alone? Is that why you're always here or taking her over there? *Is it?*"

"No."

"No?" She bit her lip to prevent the moisture in her eyes from spilling over. "Are you being honest this time or only trying to make me feel better?"

"You're a wonderful mom." He touched her face. "I'm here all the time for *you*. Or I take her next door to give you a break. Nella's doing fine. I'm here for you. For *you*, Suse, not because I'm worried about if you can handle her, only to help."

"I'm not crazy." Her voice trembled.

"I know you're not."

"Don't let them do this." A tear fell down her cheek.

He brushed it off and pulled her in against him. "I won't. Danielle is not going anywhere. She needs you as much as you need her. I won't let anyone take her from you. I promise you I won't. And I am sorry."

Her body shook. She let him hold her but there was a distance. A tension there usually wasn't. She didn't quite believe him, or trust him. He looked at John. "I do mean anyone. Danielle stays here."

John cast his eyes over to Brenda. A pit grew in Evan's stomach. He knew they could if they thought they had reason. But it would be a huge mistake, all the way around. He repeated himself, sounding more sure than he was. "She stays here. If you need, I'll stay also, in the spare room."

Susie looked up at him, about to argue.

"Suse, for you. Because she is a huge handful and it's not fair to you to deal with it alone. He would want me to. You know he would."

Her tears strengthened and she dropped her head into his shoulder. Rubbing her back, he returned his gaze to John.

Her dad gave in. "Fine. If you stay. But neither of them are eating enough. Nella hardly touched her dinner."

"Nella eats all day long. She never eats much at dinner. She eats plenty during the day. Here. At my place. At Stu's. She eats plenty. Does she look unhealthy to you? Do you honestly think Susie wouldn't feed her enough?"

"Not normally..." He eyed his daughter as though she was some kind of exotic unknown animal.

"I take care of my baby fine." Susie raised her head and wiped her face as she met his gaze. "Ask her."

John's chest rose high and fell. "Susan, it's you I'm worried about."

"Me? You've barely even looked at other women in almost twenty years. And you're worried about *me*? Maybe *you* should be talking to Brenda. My husband has only been ... not even two months." She wiped her face again.

"Maybe I should." John dipped his head. Returned the gaze. "Maybe I'm worried I didn't take care of my baby well enough after she lost her mom and I'm afraid..."

"I'm not leaving her. I'm here."

John dropped his head again. Evan nearly felt sorry for him, but she had a point. How did he have the right to give parenting advice in the face of grief when he'd gone off and left her where she didn't want to be? Either way, he wanted that woman out of the house. He kissed Susie's head and told her he'd come back to help her clean up from dinner in a minute. Then he pulled them away from her, to the front door, out to the hall.

"Evan." John grabbed his arm. "Be careful with this. She's not as all right as she says. I understand you think she'll stay closer to you by taking her side, but be careful."

"John, you heard her. She needs one person she knows she can always trust to believe her. Not that I can believe her on that particular matter, but it's your job to be her father. It's mine to be her friend, to be that one person, since she lost the one who was always on her side through everything. If that's what she needs most..." He shrugged and heard music floating out from the apartment. Fleetwood Mac. *Heroes Are Hard To Find.* It nearly brought tears to his own eyes. Was that how she felt about him now? That whatever he said, she shouldn't believe him? That couldn't happen. He had to be that hero for her now that she needed it more than ever before.

He managed to get them to leave and returned to her. She didn't argue about his help and he didn't badger her with talk. They worked together as normal, putting leftovers in containers and doing the dishes, drying, putting them away.

When *Angel* started, Evan looked over at her, took the sponge out of her hand, set it down, and grasped her in a dance pose.

"Don't." She tried to pull away.

"It's been a while."

"I'm not in the mood."

"I know. That's why we should." He refused to release her and she gave in. Reluctantly. He didn't dare try to take her to the living room, closer to the music. They danced there in the kitchen and she relaxed more as the song went on. As it ended, she held him.

She would be okay. He would make sure she was. And as much as he hated playing matchmaker, he might, if she waited too long to date again. Two or three years or so. He wouldn't give her longer than that to try again, to date again. As she'd always told him, he also wouldn't ever let her settle with anyone not good enough, no matter how long it took to find.

Telling her of his idea to call Keith to come play, she agreed. Again with reluctance. The boy was more than glad to agree and was nearly as bouncy as Nella. Kate brought him up. Evan went in to help the kids with their "castle" for a while to give Susie and Kate space to talk.

Kate stayed longer than he expected. They stopped talking when he came back out and Kate looked at him, annoyed. Susie avoided his eyes.

"Do you want me to stay..."

"No." She got up and went to the kitchen.

Kate got up and moved close, stared him in the eyes. "Don't do this."

"Do what, Kate?"

"You know what."

"Do I?" He returned the stare. "Don't leave Keith with her tonight. She's not up to it."

"No shit, Sherlock. She's not up to fending you off, either."

Evan didn't even bother. He swerved around her, went to tell Nella he was leaving and got a hug, then told Susie he was, without a hug. Fend him off? Kate was an idiot. Fend him off. Susie had never in her life had to fend him off. She sure wouldn't have to now.

What had she said?

In his own apartment, he grabbed a beer, turned on the television, and let it warm up to see what was on whatever channel the thing was already tuned to. The new law student series he'd seen commercials for. *Paper Chase.* He supposed it could be interesting. He sank onto the couch and tried to keep his concentration on it.

What had Susie said to make Kate think she had to fend him off? Because he danced with her? It wasn't like he moved any closer than normal. He sure as hell didn't grope her. What had she said?

Telling himself to let it go, he had half the beer gone before the show was fifteen minutes over and went to change it. Not something he could get into. What else? *Miss America* pageant. Not likely. Stu was probably watching it. The game. He'd forgotten the third game of the Sox against the Yankees was on. And they were behind again. Four to zero.

With a shake of his head, he returned to the couch and absorbed himself in the game. Maybe he'd take her to another game in the spring when season started again. Maybe not a Chicago/Boston game, though. Too reminiscent of the one where Duncan had bet her dinner. The one where she thought Evan set her up with his friend.

Fend him off. Fend *what* off? His friendship? Wouldn't happen. He wouldn't allow it. He'd play matchmaker and find someone else who could make her happy again before he'd ever let that happen.

Kate could go screw herself.

12 September

"Why aren't you at practice?"

Stu tried to hide his victory. If Ev wouldn't do it, he would. He shrugged. "What practice? Hey Nella, look. I bet you can't get it this high." He stacked another Lego on its side in a straight tower on the kitchen floor. Danielle frowned at him and grabbed more blocks from the floor to add to her own.

"You were here all day yesterday, too. What's going on?"

"Nothing." He added another and held his hands close to it when the tower started to shake.

"Stu. Tell me."

He shrugged again. "I did tell you. Nothing. We're doing nothing. I'm here because I'm bored to all hell. Sorry. All heck. I'm suddenly downgraded from a rock star chasing off girls, or not chasing them off, to Lego builder with a two-year-old. Not that there's anything wrong with hanging out with a two-year-old, especially one so cute." He scuffed Nella's hair.

"*No.* You make it *fall.*" She pulled from him.

"Nella, don't yell." Susie moved closer, squatted beside him. "What do you mean, you're doing nothing? You should have an album tour in the works. You're not going to practice for it?"

"No tour in the works. It was. Seems to have been cancelled. Guess Evan figures this one doesn't need promotion since he won't go."

"What?"

He hadn't meant to say that. "Nothing. It's doing okay on its own. Just as well, I guess. Could be the last. This Lego thing might be my permanent gig now." He added another block. It shook. He steadied it.

Susie got up and moved away. Nella's tower fell. He teased her. With a frown, she pushed his to scatter them all over the floor.

"*Danielle.*"

Stu shrugged at Susie. "Doesn't matter. It's just Legos."

"That's not the point. Danielle, that was rude and you know better. Pick them up now and put them away."

"No, I not. I make tower higher and higher."

"Not now, you're not. Pick them up or I'll take them away." She continued her path out of the kitchen.

Stu wondered about the way she ignored what he said about Evan, and about the album being maybe their last. She didn't care? Or she didn't believe him. Or maybe she was headed to talk to Evan. He caught up. She was on the couch with a book open. He sat next to her. "Am I bothering you being here? You can tell me to go."

"Doesn't matter, but don't let her treat you like that. She's getting impossible."

"Probably as bored as I am, Suse. She's been inside the building for ... how many days straight now?"

"Evan takes her out back."

"Okay. In or at the building. Aren't you going crazy stuck in here by now?"

She threw him a glance. "Where am I supposed to go?"

"Anywhere. Hell, want me to go out with you somewhere? We can..."

"So people can jump all over me again, ask me why there's no marker, no headstone, no... No." She went back to her book.

"Come up to New Hampshire with me, then. No one will bother you there. If they start, I'll take care of it and that's it. Nella can play outside to her heart's content. There's a park not far away, even a little petting zoo."

"You know I can't."

"Why can't you?"

She met his eyes. "Because you're on my list."

Her list? Her list was ... it wasn't ... he wasn't...

"So they say. They'll make a big deal of it."

"Hell. So what? Let them." Stu wrapped an arm around her shoulder. "I don't mind. You'd be great for my reputation, someone as classy as you connected with me."

"You're Duncan's friend, too. It matters. And classy is about the last thing they think I am."

"Yeah so, you think *you* can ruin *my* reputation? Not damn likely. I've done a good enough job of that."

"It's not your reputation I'm worried about."

"Ah, nice. I think I'm insulted." He grinned. It didn't work. "So let me help ruin your reputation a bit. Easier to just do it and get it over with ... uh, and I mean letting them think what they want, than to keep worrying about it. And hell, Suse, most people like people better when they think they can look down on them. Makes them feel superior. They'll give you less grief that way. Human nature to want to knock down anyone on a pedestal."

"I'm not on a pedestal. And it's not mine I'm worried about, either."

"Heck you're not." Not hers? "Uh, if you're worried about Nella..."

"No." As though he bit her, she jumped up and dropped her book on the table. "Want to keep an eye on her while I shower? I haven't for two days because I don't know what she'll do and even at night I can't count on her to stay in bed."

"Sure. Any time. You don't have to deal with the little monster alone, you know." He saw her grit her chin with a light nod, stop at the kitchen to remind Nella to get them picked up, and head to her room.

You're Duncan's friend, too. Too? Not her own reputation that worried her? Evan. She'd often badgered Evan about his reputation. He'd barely been there the past two days. When he was, she barely spoke to him. Duncan's friend. Why did it matter? Evan wasn't even on her list, as far as the press...

Duncan's friend, too. But he'd been her friend first.

24 September

John knocked and walked in, as Evan told him he should. He would be there with Danielle. And he was. Helping Nella play the guitar. They were adorable, with Nella on his lap stroking the strings while Evan fingered chords. It reminded him of how Evan used to try to teach Susie. As a distraction. Maybe he should do it with her now. Evan said she hadn't been downstairs at all, not even to dance, not even as a workout.

Nella looked up and told him she was learning *'tar* with *Evan Lee.*

"Sounds good, pumpkin. Keep going. Where's your mom?"

Evan nodded behind him, to the window seat. Nella said her mum was reading. Not unless she had the book memorized, she wasn't. It was open, propped on her pulled up legs, but she was staring out the window. He looked back at Evan. Evan glanced at her, his chest rose and fell, and he continued with Danielle.

John rubbed his face and went to his daughter. "Book not very interesting?"

She didn't answer. Or move.

"Susan." He took it from her hands and sat in front of her. At least he got a flicker of a reaction. "Come to lunch with me."

She shook her head. Kept watching the window.

"You need to get out." When he lost Angela, what rescued him other than Susie was throwing himself into his work. "So how's the tour coming along?" She threw him a glance, only for a second. He knew it wasn't. Evan said he couldn't even talk about a tour until she was at least responsive. Until she would go is what he meant but didn't say. "Aren't you supposed to have a tour with an album release? It's been out three months now, right? Isn't it time?"

"Not up to me."

At least it was something. "Doesn't the assistant manager have something to do with the planning? You always have that I've seen."

She didn't answer. Evan was watching. John kept his attention on her. "So? Aren't you supposed to push them if they need it? Looks like they need it. I don't see them doing much."

"Duncan will get them out there again when he comes back."

John held his breath so he could force himself to hold his tongue. Still? After two and a half months? Brenda had stayed in touch with him, talked with him about her. And recently her office mate had joined the conversation. She was a child therapist. He wanted her opinion on Danielle, on how harmful it would be that Susie hadn't told her the full truth. Valerie didn't seem terribly concerned about Danielle. Young children don't understand the concept of death well, anyway, she said. *Away*, she understood, as well as she could. For now it was all right. She knew he was away and she couldn't see him. Her acting out was part of the grief process, so she was grieving.

Susie was still in denial. How did he get her to move past that?

Kate. She needed to hang out with girlfriends. Ali maybe. Evan's ... was Evan still dating Stephanie? John wasn't sure. Would she want to hang out with Evan's girlfriend? Maybe. She'd enjoyed Myra.

Giving up on trying to talk sense into his daughter for the moment, he went to interrupt Evan and Danielle. "Hey pumpkin, go tell your mom we're going to lunch. I'll take you to Minuteman Park and we'll have a picnic. What do you think?"

Nella jumped up as Evan grabbed her guitar to rescue it. "*Yes!* I see bridge and wa'er and I feed duckies." She ran over to Susie and pulled at her. "My mummy, *come*. G'ampa take us to minute park and duckies and picnic. *Yes.*"

Susie gave him a glare. He shrugged at her. "Better get ready."

She looked back out the window. Nella pulled at her more. With a sigh, she got up and went back to her room. As she went, John suggested she wear her wig to disguise herself. He supposed she would actually go. He asked Evan to supervise Danielle putting on something her mom would let her be seen in, even if no one knew who they were, and invited him to go.

"Oh, I don't know. She doesn't seem terribly interested in having me around. I might bow out this time."

John didn't argue. He went down to find Kate and invited her and Keith. And he asked for her help.

Evan was glad Doc agreed to go with them, since he hoped Susie would ask him to go herself and she didn't. Nella was just as hyper when she returned as she'd been when they left. As far as Evan could get out of her fast chatter, several ducks came upon them as they threw bread from the bridge and John and Doc had to pick the little ones up out of their reach. Kate rolled her eyes about it scaring Keith while Nella kept trying to lean back down to pet them.

Susie was just as quiet as before she left. She shuffled Nella home for a bath and said nothing else.

Evan stopped John in the hall as he was leaving. "Anyone bother you?"

"No. A few young men flirted with the girls. Kate encouraged them. Susie took the kids' hands and walked away. At least she was out, and she helped the kids tear bread for the ducks and talked to them. Ignored me the whole time. Mad, I suppose."

"I wouldn't be surprised."

"She'll get over it."

"I hope."

"Evan, get the band going. Pull her back into it. She needs to keep busy."

"I'm not sure she will."

"She can't if you're not doing anything."

26 September

It wasn't horrible, he supposed. With the album playing in the background, Evan forced himself to focus on Mike, Stu, and Doug and played lead along with it. It wasn't as good as his friend's version, but it might do. What choice did he have? He didn't want lead. He also didn't want to bring in a new lead. Stu was adjusting the songs to leave out keyboard on stage for most of them, taking bass or acoustic guitar, with Mike filling in on bass when needed. Evan had to take lead. Stu could if he would. He wouldn't.

As it faded, he sighed. Not nearly as good, no matter what his band mates said.

The record stopped and he looked over. Mike gave him a grin. "About time. Sounds not bad with the record. Gonna try it with us now?" They were all there. And Adam. He supposed he had no choice. It was time to move along. To pull her back into it. If she would.

Adam stayed a while and nodded his approval now and then. In the middle of a song that was particularly frustrating Evan, Adam left. He'd wanted to talk to him, but it could wait. At least he knew they were doing something again.

Susie gave in to Adam for one reason: she was sick of doing nothing but dealing with Nella, cleaning, and ... and moping. Two and a half months. On the way downstairs, she tried to tune into her husband. *Two and a half hell months already. Where are you?*

Where are you?

Maybe she was crazy. She hardly felt him anymore. But she did at times. Maybe he had found somewhere else to be, somewhere he wasn't trapped.

Come home, Duncan. Just come home. We'll move if you want. We'll join whatever band you want. I'll sing with you. I'll follow you anywhere in the world. Just come home.

"Suse?"

She pulled out of her one-sided silent conversation and looked at Adam. They were at the basement entrance. He was holding the door. She was glad Nella was at Kate's. Maybe she'd change her mind, go back upstairs, and ... and what?

Adam took her hand. "I know it'll be hard, but it'll be all right."

Would it? She heard voices. They were discussing. Not playing. She didn't even want to hear that. But she gave in, allowed Adam to pull her in, his fingers still locked around hers as though afraid she'd bolt. Maybe she would. She was suddenly nauseated. "I can't."

"Yes, you can." He held firm. Kept walking. "Come on, Suse. Don't make them think I'm dragging you here."

"You are."

"Okay, but they don't have to know that." He paused, met her eyes. "They need you."

"No, they don't."

"Don't they?" He nodded toward them. Back where they wouldn't see her yet, she made herself focus on them. Not discussing. Not even arguing. Giving up. Or trying to decide whether to give up.

They couldn't give up. Duncan would be back. He'd get them going again. Until then, they had to hang on. Even if she had to force them to hang on. Susie swallowed hard, grabbed a lung full of air, released Adam's hand, and went up to the front to grab a chair.

They all went silent.

"Well?" She shrugged her hands at them. "Are you working or did I come down for nothing?"

Stu glanced at Evan then jumped down and came to her. He threw his arms around her neck from behind the chair, kissed her head, and ran back up to the stage.

Adam chuckled. "Told you they did."

Susie pulled a foot up on the chair and wrapped her arms around her leg. It stabilized her. It's why she'd done it as a child at the hospital during the thunderstorm when her mom was having her sister and why she still did it often. She was glad to see them start to pull it together, although it took a while. They sounded almost like Raucous again. Evan was doing great on lead, as she expected, as he always had. She found herself focusing more on him than on the rest. He was hesitant, not enjoying himself as he used to.

Not that she could blame him. It wasn't the same.

Still, they were her band. They were hers before Duncan joined and they were still... She bit her lip. Put her focus back on Mike. And on the left side of the stage, her left. Evan stayed on the right. On the left, Mike's left, where he had been. Lead guitarist generally took the lead singer's right side. Easier for cues and such. But he didn't. He stayed in his normal position.

Refusing to take Duncan's place entirely.

She felt her eyes moisten and forced it to stop. She didn't do that anymore. He was coming back. She just had to hold on, to be strong as he would expect of her. She was. More or less. But his space was empty. As was his side of the bed. The apartment. Her heart.

Biting her lip hard, she put her attention on Stu. Incredible as always. Bouncy. And she'd been so rude to him all the time he'd spent helping to entertain Nella. She knew darn well that was only partly the reason. He was entertaining her. Checking on her.

She brushed at her eyes, tried to focus on the music and nothing else, closed them as she used to, let the music invade her senses, her soul. It made it worse. She grabbed for breath, pinched her lips tighter together, tilted her head up to make herself stop.

"Suse?" Adam touched her shoulder. And she lost it.

He held her in. The music stopped. She tried to make herself stop. But she missed him so. *Come home, Duncan. Just come home.*

Strong arms surrounded her. "Angel, it's okay."

She let him possess her, surround her, felt her body shudder with her fast breaths, felt her tears dampen his shirt. He stroked her hair, held tight. Someone pushed tissue into her hand. She wiped her nose, yanked at air, kept her forehead in against his shoulder, the strong shoulder that had supported her so often, and she'd been rude to him, as well. To everyone. "I'm sorry." It barely came out through her ragged breaths.

"Don't be. It's all right."

She felt her head shake. It wasn't. Nothing about it was right. Her body suddenly felt fatigued to the point of inability to hold herself up. Her breath slowed, she loosened her grip on his shirt. "I'm sorry."

"No, Angel. There's no reason to be. We're all glad you came down."

"I miss him. Evan, I ... I just want him back. With me. With you. Danielle." Her breaths grew faster again, her tears stronger.

Strong fingers raised her face, his brown deep eyes met hers. "I know. But you're going to get through it. This is a good step."

She felt herself snicker. "Is it? I'm..."

"Yes." He rubbed fingers along her face, pushed hair behind her ear. "It is, and you are going to be okay. We miss him, too, but we're all going to keep going. He would want that."

She gulped for air, dropped her head back against his shoulder.

"We haven't had a pizza party in a hell of a long time." Stu. His voice was strained. He was trying to make it sound not strained. "Think it's time."

"You're working."

"Yeah well, we got a start. Good enough for today. Tomorrow will be better. Right?"

She wiped her face again and nodded. Evan sat still and let her hold on until she decided she could maybe make herself get up. On her feet. It was time. Tomorrow would be better. Even if she did still hurt like holy hell.

27 September

Susie listened to her band but watched her daughter make her grandpa dance with her. Her dad was a good dancer; she used to love to watch him force her mom away from whatever household chore absorbed her and take her in his arms to slow dance. It was comforting, secure. If she thought back, Susie could remember, vaguely, that they did get annoyed with each other now and then, but mostly she remembered them dancing or talking or working together ... or the way he'd touch her rear and she'd push his hand away, teasing.

She also loved when he would teach Susie a few basic dance steps, his frame so elegant, his manner as though she was a lady dressed up in a ball gown. He was doing the same with Nella. Her daughter's face said she loved it just as much. At least she would still have that; her grandpa could do it for her if her dad couldn't.

A sharp pain poked her in the skull. He would. When he came back. Until then, she had her grandpa. And her Evan Lee. Susie looked up at him. He was watching Danielle, also, with a soft grin between harmonies. Evan would do dad things with her. She at least still had him.

And Uncle Danny. They'd talked to him the night before. Susie told him she went down to practice but couldn't stay long. He was glad she did and told her to keep going, to keep pushing them, that he wanted another Raucous album to add to his collection. He listened to them a lot, he said; it was comforting.

Yes. Susie returned her focus to them, the way they were when she first moved in except more mature, both physically and musically. She enjoyed Evan on lead guitar as he was before, except ... more musically mature. There was a difference in his playing, his technique, his attitude. He was far more ready to be lead guitar than he was back in 1974 when she first heard him with Mike, Doug, and Stu. He didn't believe he was up to it. He was wrong.

Once she pushed her own thoughts out of her way, Susie could easily see how wrong he was. He was definitely up to it. And he should have it. Roy was right. Susie flinched to think it, but he was. Evan deserved to be lead guitar. Had she really been so blinded by her husband that she didn't realize how much Evan had kept hidden?

29 September

Susie opened the door to Kate and Mike and returned to tell Nella to change her clothes.

"No. I like this."

"I'm glad you do, but you're not wearing it again until I wash it. Go change."

"No' dirty. No."

Susie rolled her eyes. "Danielle, you have food spilled down the front and dirt on the knees. It's dirty. Go change."

"Come on, little one." Evan came from the kitchen and swept the girl up by the back of her knees, letting her hang upside down. "We'll find something else you like for a couple of hours." He gave Susie a grin and carried her back to her room as Nella laughed and grabbed at the floor.

"That child needs a good whack upside her keister." Kate plopped on the couch.

"Where's Keith?"

Mike remained on his feet and rubbed Kate's shoulder. "Next door. I'm going right back. Kate has an invitation for you. Thought I'd listen in, just for the hell of it."

Susie braced herself, and nearly laughed at the invitation. Instead, she shook her head and went to the kitchen.

"Come on, Suse. It'll be fun. You need time away from the little maniac, and you need to start finding yourself again – you know, who you are underneath the whole mom thing."

"Never did that before. Why would I now?"

"Before? Hell, you were hardly old enough before the mom thing. You are now. It's about time. Tell her, Mike. Tell her it would be good for her."

He gave her an amused grin as Evan joined them. "I kinda think she's right. You should go. Sit and have some wine with the girls and look through all of that ... uh, stuff guys really do like even if we say we don't, and have a good time."

Susie explained to Evan. "She wants me to go to a lingerie party tonight." He didn't look shocked. Or annoyed. She put her attention back on Kate. "You know I'm not going. Anyone else want tea?"

"Why not? It'll be fun. Come on, I want you to go with me. We haven't done anything together in ... I don't even know when. Mike volunteered to keep Nella unless Evan does. Come with me."

"Kate, what in the world use would it be? Why do I need lingerie? It's not like..." She nearly let it embarrass her to talk about it in front of Evan, but it didn't. Why did it matter?

"For yourself. You know, it's not all negligees, Suse. There are some really cute bras and panties. You do still wear those, right?"

She set the pitcher back in the refrigerator. "And I have what I need. Thank you."

"So what? A girl can never have too many cute bras." Kate grinned at Mike. "Tell her."

He shrugged. "Gotta agree again. Go, Suse. Have fun."

"No." She went back to the living room and reclined onto her love seat.

"Why?" Kate sat on the couch facing her, her shapely model legs crossed, catching Mike's eye. Kate had reason to go to a lingerie party.

"What's the point? Seriously, Kate. Why would I?"

"Because you feel good when you pamper yourself." She leaned in closer. "Suse, you know it's true. It doesn't matter if anyone else sees it. You will. Come with me. Let your hair down and unwind a bit."

Let her hair down. Her hair had been constantly down for ... a long time, or in an easy ponytail out of her way.

Kate apparently figured she won. "We're leaving at seven. Don't fill up at dinner. She'll have plenty of goodies there, and of course the wine."

"Kate, I'm not going."

"Aw, come on. Evan, tell her she should go."

Susie nearly laughed. Evan? Kate wanted Evan to say she should go to a lingerie party? That was nearly as funny as...

"You should go, Suse."

She turned her head up to him. "What?"

"She's right. You should go. Even if you don't buy anything, although there's no reason you shouldn't. Go have fun with the girls."

"I..." Susie was too shocked to answer.

"Ali's going." Mike this time. "She really hopes you will. Doug's already teasing the hell out of her about it."

"Doug is?"

"As I said, we do like our girls in pretty decorations, even if we like them out of them, too." He winked.

"Yeah well, I don't... I have no reason to..."

"You're still a girl." Kate moved over next to her. "You should never think you don't have reason to feel like one."

"I don't."

Kate rubbed a hand over her hair. "Why don't you?"

"Are you kidding? Why should I? I don't have... Hell, Kate, I couldn't give my husband the second child we both wanted. Now I don't even have him. Why in the world does it matter if I feel like something that's not doing me any good?"

"Because you still are."

"I don't care."

Evan moved in, crouched in front of her, and took her hand. "That's why you should go. She's right. Go reclaim yourself, Suse. It does matter."

"To who?"

"To you."

"No it doesn't."

"Okay, but it should." He stood and pulled her up to her feet. "Go. Just let me get hold of Beau to accompany you..."

"We don't need a bodyguard tagging along. I'll take care of her fine."

"Kate..."

"Unless you want to call two of them, two good looking ones, built and all, and we'll make a night of it, take the bodyguards to dinner first and flirt as though they're our dates." She looked back at Mike. "Don't worry. No more than flirting. Just for fun. By all means, call a couple of them. Make them really hot hunks so we can really have fun. They can walk us to the door and let us introduce them, and see that we get home again, no matter how much wine we have. Sounds good to me. Say yes, Suse. The night just got a lot more fun."

"I better arrange for three if you're taking Ali."

Susie looked at Evan like he'd lost his mind. "You're agreeing to this?"

"Absolutely. Wear your wig. Flirt with the guards. I'll make sure they're ones I know I can trust to let you flirt."

"Fine, but make sure they aren't dogs."

Evan shook his head at Kate and touched Susie's back. "One will be Beau. It'll be fine. Go get ready."

"Evan..."

He leaned in to speak beside her ear, low and soft. "It matters to me, too, that you remember who you are. It does matter, Suse." With a quick catch of her eyes, he moved to the telephone.

She couldn't believe she was giving in to this. But she would not flirt with their guards, especially not with Beau.

30 September

She should not have gone.

Her head hurt as she got out of bed. It couldn't have been from the wine; she hadn't had that much. The tension. The girl talk, that had actually started out fun, turned too intimate. Most of them were Kate's model friends. Open. Not shy. Most not terribly exclusive with their relationships. She didn't fit in. Neither did Ali. But Ali didn't seem to care that she didn't. She ordered a couple of things for her 'hope chest' and giggled with the other girls about when she might show them off. Not until after she was married, she said. They didn't believe her. Susie did. Even if she wasn't engaged yet.

Susie didn't believe she and Doug hadn't slept together, and probably often, but she did believe Ali would make him wait to see what she ordered until things were finalized, at whatever point that happened.

She nearly didn't buy anything. There was no reason. But she felt guilty after the hostess put so much effort into the several appetizer platters and several different wines not to at least order something. So she'd gone low key, cute but normal enough to wear on a daily basis bras with matching panties that she might not bother to wear. They were skimpier than she liked, and there was no point.

At least not until he came home.

She'd realized halfway during the party that she let herself believe he wasn't coming back so she wouldn't need anything sexy. From then on, she just wanted to go home. To her pajamas and slippers and robe and television and ... and her best friend. To get away from the girls talking about their men or men they wanted or men they would gladly "do once." Home to her Evan.

To her baby. The one she did give her husband.

She'd also been the youngest at the party. Physically. Twenty-four. She felt like thirty-four. At least this morning with her head pounding. And she'd acted like the oldest, like a stodgy old woman who wouldn't let herself buy anything too sexy.

Hand against her head, Susie shuffled out to find something to relieve it. And maybe the nerve pills she still had that Doc left for her after... No. It made her too tired. She wouldn't be able to deal with Danielle if she was that tired.

"Mummy." The little body jumped from the chair and pounced into her.

"Danielle, easy."

"Good morning." Evan studied her.

"Why are you here?" She reached for the pain reliever she kept on a high kitchen shelf.

"As late as you were, I expected you wouldn't be up for a while. Here, let me." He took the bottle she fumbled with and opened it, held two in his palm.

"Thank you."

He poured her a cup of coffee. "Have fun?"

"Not as much as it looks like." She ambled over and sat next to Nella. "Were you good last night?" Susie tried to listen to the litany of what Nella and Keith did during the evening, but the girl was loud and it hurt her head. "Okay baby, tell me more later, okay?" Susie kissed her cheek and got up. "I need to lie down. Do you mind..."

"Go ahead. Nella, finish eating. I'll be right back." He walked back to her room with her and helped her pull the blanket around her shoulders.

"It's not from the wine, if you're wondering. I didn't have that much."

"No, I know. What happened, Suse? Kate said you were having a nice time and then in the matter of about two seconds, you weren't."

She clenched her eyes together. Damn her head hurt. Like it had that day she'd gone wedding shopping with Janet and told Janet she could tell her what kind of underwear Evan liked.

"Angel?"

"You're not going anywhere, right? Ever? You won't leave me alone?"

He ran fingers over her head. "Never. I'm sorry I pushed you to go."

"No, you're right. I do need to ... do something, with friends. I know. But I ... I couldn't relate to them. I couldn't... I just want to go back to being Duncan's wife. I can't even ... the thought of dating a stranger ... I can't even think of it and it's fine, Nella and I will be just fine, but..."

"Then don't. Not yet, Suse. It's far too soon. I shouldn't have pushed you to go. I hoped... It doesn't matter. I'm sorry."

"Ali had a lot of fun. I hope she doesn't ever lose Doug."

"I don't see that happening."

"No. I just... I wanted to..." She wiped tears trying to start.

"To have fun like Ali was."

She nodded.

He leaned down to kiss her head. "You will. Rest now. Nella and I will have pancakes ready for you when you want them."

"I really thought it would be good for her."

Evan checked the clock. Nearly two hours. She needed to be up so she could eat. He heard John answer Kate, said it was good that she got out however it turned out in the end. Evan wasn't sure that was true. Maybe it was. John asked Kate to keep trying, to take her somewhere else, anywhere, to keep her moving.

"She's been coming to practice. She doesn't stay long, but she comes down. It'll be fine, John. It hasn't been long yet."

John started to answer and looked over at the hallway. "Hey sweetheart. How's your head?"

"Attached." Susie shuffled over and sat next to Evan, leaned in against his shoulder and held his arm.

"Hungry yet?" He ignored Kate's look.

"Starving. I'll get it in a minute. Where's Nella?"

"Downstairs. She and Keith are entertaining Stu in the form of begging for music lessons."

"Hm. The girl doesn't even know her alphabet yet and she's trying to learn chords."

He chuckled. "She seems more interested in the chords."

"Wonderful." She straightened, released his arm. "Why are you all here?"

"He wouldn't leave you here alone." Kate rolled her eyes. "Never mind you were asleep. So we stayed to talk. Sorry you had a lousy time. I hoped you'd enjoy it once you got out."

"It was fine." She started to get up.

Evan stopped her. "Sit still. I'll make a pancake unless you want something else."

"I can do it. Have to get more aspirin, anyway."

"It's only been two hours, Suse. You took two."

"But my head's going to explode."

"Let's try food first." He got up.

"And coffee. Please."

"Of course." He turned the burner back on and got her coffee while it warmed. She gave him a light smile. Kate and John both gave him curious looks when she touched his hand for a second. He was glad they were in the kitchen so he could cook and listen at the same time.

"So, did you send your girlfriend with them last night?"

He turned back to John. "Girlfriend?"

"Stephanie? Isn't that her name?"

"We aren't dating any longer."

Susie looked at him. "Stephanie. I forgot. Why?"

"Didn't work. Not a big deal."

"I'm sorry, I should have at least noticed."

"Why? It wasn't at the point of asking for your approval." He teased as he poured the mix into the pan.

"Good. I'm not sure I would have."

"No? Thought you liked her okay."

"Yes, but she wasn't good enough. Try again."

Kate got up to refill her coffee. "Like you'll think anyone's good enough for him. Wow, Suse, I feel sorry for Nella if you're this bad about Evan's dates."

"Oh. Don't talk to me about Nella dating. I can't think of it."

"The girl will be thirty and you'll still be telling her no, not good enough."

"Right, because she'll listen to me that well. Not likely, which is why I can't think about it. Her dad will have to..." She stopped, set her cup down.

Evan moved to set a hand on her shoulder. "Don't worry. I'll help you chase them off when needed."

She met his eyes and pulled away again to sip her coffee.

"Or her stepfather will. My guess is she'll have one long before then. It'll be his job."

Susie flicked her gaze to Kate and down again. Evan handed her a pancake and she thanked him and ate in silence although conversation changed and swirled around her.

She was accepting it. Evan could see in her face and in what she said, she was finally moving to acceptance. It was good. He knew it was good. So why did it bother him to know she was?

4 October

Susie pulled her sweater tighter around her front. It was chilly in the basement. Nella kept pulling her sweater off as she played on the mats doing, or trying to do, somersaults to imitate Keith. Susie gave up. The child was too active to be too cold just because she was. She hadn't done anything active in ... longer than she could remember.

She listened to the guys discuss a possible short tour. None of them were too enthused about the idea. They weren't ready, they said. Still trying to adjust. Adam asked what she thought. She shrugged and said if they weren't ready, it would be a mistake. She also told them it was about time to get it together and be ready, though.

They decided to start again slower. A few shows here and there. Now and then. Just to start making some kind of appearance again. Adam figured it would be good enough for now and he'd work on it. She agreed to help as needed. And she went back to watching Nella and Keith.

Her daughter had asked about Duncan again before they came down. Susie nearly told her. Nearly said he wasn't coming back. But she couldn't. She wasn't sure anymore if she fully believed he was. She still couldn't tell Danielle. Not while she had doubt. Not while it would hurt too damned much to see the pain in her baby's eyes. As though that would ever change.

The guys finally went to the stage and tuned. Adam tried to ask her about locations. Times. How many shows she thought. And she tried to answer, tried to think about it. But she kept seeing that empty spot at the left of the stage. He gave up. For the moment. Susie knew he'd try again.

She focused on the music. Shivered. Thought about going up for a warmer sweatshirt, maybe one of Duncan's. No. She didn't need warmer clothes. She needed motion. Better metabolism. From activity. She needed to start working out again. Both cardio and ... and weight training. Duncan told her muscle mass would help her stay warmer, get sick less. Maybe Evan would work with her. With the weights. The cardio she could do herself.

After practice.

They stopped. Argued. Started again. Stopped again. It was one of the songs with a harder lead guitar part. Evan was resisting still. Mike was getting annoyed with him. Doug said to start again from the beginning and just keep going no matter how it sounded. They agreed to at least try. How they were talking about setting up shows when they were still having such trouble, she didn't know. Or maybe having shows set up would push them to settle their differences.

She cringed at a bad chord. Evan nearly stopped. Doug told him to keep going. He shook his head but obeyed. He didn't get it. It was good. She knew it was. Doug, Stu, and Mike knew it was. Evan thought it was garbage only because it was different than Duncan's version. It wasn't. It was good. Actually, it was … very sexy, sensual. In a softer way. She'd always loved his style.

Maybe she'd encourage that.

Getting up, she moved away from the chairs, to open space, and began to stretch in time with the music. She immediately felt how out of shape she was. It didn't matter. She just needed to move. And to encourage Evan. When it ended and he complained about it not being right, she looked up at him. "It sounds nice, Lee. Really, it does. Stop hesitating and just play it."

Mike looked at her, then suggested they start again. From the beginning.

This time, she moved into actual dance. Focusing on his guitar, his style, as she had done with Duncan whenever she worked out during their practice. She tuned into him especially. He'd said he noticed. He'd loved it.

She nearly stopped. But she couldn't. It was sounding better. More relaxed, natural, in sync. And the movement felt incredible. They continued with another song and she continued her workout. As she got too warm, she took the sweater off, blocked out everything from her mind except the music and her movement. It didn't even matter that she stepped out of a few poses, didn't land quite right on a couple of turns. It still felt incredible.

I want you to keep dancing.

Susie heard his voice. Duncan. From the night they got mugged, when he nearly got himself killed protecting her. She heard it again as though he was beside her. He'd thought he wouldn't make it out alive that night. She knew at the time that's what he meant. And yet he wanted her to keep going. To keep dancing.

She brushed moisture from her eyes and paused, stood watching her band. They were still her band. He would want them to keep going, also. At Evan's gaze, she gave him a light grin, and moved back into her workout.

"Wow it was nice to see that again." Stu gave her a hug.

"I'm sweaty."

"Yeah, like I care."

"Well, I do. I'm going up to shower." She looked over at Evan but addressed all of them. "Anyone want to come for dinner in ... about an hour and a half? We can discuss the shows. Bring Ali if she's free."

"Sounds good." Doug gave her a grin and the rest agreed.

"Evan and I will keep the kids until then. We can take turns showering and supervising." Mike set a hand on her shoulder. "It *was* nice to see again."

"Hm, it was bad, really. I'm so out of shape."

"Yeah so are we. But we'll both pull it together."

Progression

8 October 1978

Evan pulled the album out of a bag as he followed Susie into her kitchen. He wouldn't tell her what a hassle it had been to pick the thing up. He'd been recognized in the music store and was stuck there for over an hour signing albums and anything else patrons had on them to sign. It turned out well, though. The store sold out of Raucous LPs while he was there and promised to order more as soon as possible. The manager told his patrons he would try hard but Axis was running low on stock so it could be some time. Evan promised to do what he could to help.

When they saw which LP he was buying, that one sold out of the store, as well. He didn't say Little River Band's *Sleeper Catcher* wasn't for himself although he did love a couple of songs from it, including one on the radio often: *Lady*. He'd been working on playing it acoustic. He wouldn't tell Susie that yet.

She put ice in her large plastic cup, added water, and snapped on a lid.

"I have something for you." He handed her the album. "Mike got this recently and he's been playing it a lot. Whenever I hear it, I think it would make nice dance music for your workouts."

"Thank you. I love that one. It's on the radio a lot. Are the rest as good?"

"Close."

She grinned. "I'll take it down with me now. Want to come? Maybe ... I've been thinking about asking if you'd do some weight training with me. I've lost too much muscle and it's getting cold and..."

"Of course. Nella's okay at Stu's?"

"I imagine. He knows I'm headed downstairs if he needs me."

Evan was gratified that she put the album on to use already. He thought she might want to listen to it first, to get a feel for the style. But she jumped right in, using half of the first song to stretch and then going with its rhythm. It was a quick tempo, nice to start with. The other one he liked a lot, *Reminiscing*, was slower and she did more ballet movements. He always enjoyed her spirited jazzy sensual dances, but he especially loved to watch her do ballet. She was so graceful, so elegant. Controlled and balanced but with a certain style of her own that tipped it from technique into art.

Red-Headed Wild Flower was fast tempo, upbeat. She pushed herself. Her stretch was incredible for as out of shape as she claimed to be. As it ended, she was breathing hard and paced around the area to keep her muscles moving but letting herself have time to rest. She came closer and talked with him about the music, the guitar in it, listened to his thoughts. She picked up the nuances of instrumentals better all the time as she listened to them, as she watched practices, as she paid attention whenever he worked with Nella. Susie had learned so fast when he started with her when she was young, and she picked it up again fast when she was pregnant and he helped keep her hands busy by teaching her while Duncan and Stu wrote together. But as far as he knew, she hadn't touched it since Nella was born. Maybe she would again.

When *Lady* started, she offered her hand and danced with him. As they used to. Comfortably. It was nice. He saw a touch of a spark in her eyes, which was as nice to see as her dancing. When it ended, she suggested they move to the weights.

13 October

Susie knew Duncan's family had actually come to check on her, although they used Evan's birthday as an excuse, and she did her best to convince them she was fine. They'd asked her several times to visit Edinburgh. She couldn't do it. She couldn't go without him.

Offering Gene more coffee, she barely waited for his agreement before she went to refill his cup. The man nearly lived on coffee from what she could see, more than she noticed before. Everyone carefully avoided mention of Duncan, but it was in their eyes. Every time they looked at her, she saw it, wondering, watching over her. So she barely met anyone's eyes.

Only Evan. He didn't baby her like everyone else. He still talked to her the same. He still argued with her when he felt the need. And he was always there. Even when she told him not to be.

"Here." Evan pushed his plate at her as she handed Gene his cup.

"This was way too much. I separated it. I didn't eat off it." His cake, with lots of frosting. He had eaten only half a piece and much of the frosting from that was set aside.

"Like I would worry about your germs?"

"You worry about everyone's germs."

"No. Not everyone." She caught his eyes, knowing he would understand. She didn't eat after Danielle. The girl was too often fighting something and it was hard enough to try to avoid it. She wouldn't share a drink with anyone, not even her dad or Stu or Kate or ... anyone but Duncan. Or Evan. She loved how they could mention him to each other and no one would know they were. Inside stories and secrets only Evan knew made it easy to throw a simple hint and know he understood.

Her feet were tired from playing hostess and she moved, plate in hand, to a free spot on the floor, with her back against the wall. He'd gotten a clean fork before he handed her his plate. She couldn't help being amused.

"Suse, come sit here. I'll move."

She grinned at Doug and shook her head. "I'm fine."

Stu plopped beside her. "Leaves room for me this way." He nudged into her arm. "Eating again? Careful. You might gain half an ounce."

"Funny." She savored a bite of the cake, white instead of chocolate since that's what Evan liked best. Still, it was sweet and decadent and she didn't bother to brush part of the frosting aside. She wanted sweet and decadent. If there was more left when everyone cleared out later, she might even grab another piece.

Commotion turned her head toward the hallway where she caught glimpse of a little body moving fast. "Danielle, don't run in the house."

"I not running. I playing. Uncle Danny no' catch me. No. I too fast."

Susie threw her brother-in-law a look.

He shrugged. "She is nae runnin'. She is playin'."

"*Danielle.* Stop *now.*" Her words ignored as usual, Susie started to get up, but Laura grabbed Nella, wrapped her in a huge hug, and scolded her brother for getting her niece in trouble.

Evan went to answer a knock and let her dad in. He greeted the McGuires and made his way over to her as she finished the cake. She wanted more but she didn't bother to get up. She was tired. He leaned down to kiss the top of her head. "Let me take that since I'm up." He accepted the plate without her resistance. "Sorry I'm so late. I wasn't sure I'd get off on time."

"It's Evan's party, not mine. But I'm glad you made it."

Eyeing her too long, he gave in to Diane's offer of cake and ice cream, easy on the cake, heavy on the ice cream, as always. They went to the kitchen together. Susie decided to let Diane play hostess for a while as she'd been trying to do. It was her son's birthday. His twenty-ninth; Susie couldn't believe he was that old already. And they were in his apartment, not hers.

"Hey." Stu pushed at her again. "Want more? There's still plenty. Unless Nella's been at it again."

"She better not have. She'll already be wound up for three days. I may be sending her to you."

Stu chuckled. "Okay by me. We'll work more on the keyboards. She's actually learning pretty well. I'm surprised."

"As much as you give in to her and help her with it? You shouldn't be."

"Music is good for a kid. Only thing that kept me going at times. You know?"

"Yeah, and I appreciate it. Really. More than I probably say, and not only the music..."

He slid an arm around her shoulder. "You don't need to. She's a great kid. I enjoy having her around. And I'm always here."

"She's a terror. You just have incredible patience."

"Ah well, I suppose it's my turn. I was a terror as a kid, too. Yeah, I know, still am at times. Probably always will be."

"That's encouraging."

He chuckled. "I'm sure Mom wouldn't mind chatting with you about what worked and what didn't, not that much really worked. She just kinda let me live and then sent me out to annoy someone else for a change."

"I'm not sure I have her strength." Susie watched her daughter egg Danny on, pushing at him. "I was never the one to get her to listen well. Or to get her to sleep at night. Or calm her when she was too wound up. I could never do it, and now I have to, and it isn't working."

"Suse, she's all right, only energetic and curious and creative. It's tiring, but she's a good kid."

"Yes." She shoved a hand through her hair when Danielle took off running again. "But I expected to be able to do better than this. I thought I knew what I was doing with kids."

"You do. If you didn't, she would be completely out of control by now instead of only partly." He threw a wink. "Seriously, she just lost her dad recently. She's trying to adjust. You're doing fine considering everything."

Before she could thank him, her dad interrupted and lowered next to her, adjacent, so he was facing the room in general. He handed her a plate of various snacks. "Diane says you didn't eat much. Thought you might want more than cake."

She didn't have the energy to argue or worry about the interference, or annoyance. Setting it in front of her crossed legs, she picked at it while she listened to conversations here and there. She was ready to go home, but she couldn't leave Evan's party. Especially since her dad had just arrived.

Pulling her attention away from the talk about Sid Vicious and his arrest for murdering his girlfriend, which Susie did not want to hear about, she got up and went to the kitchen. She could start straightening, clean up the few dishes in the sink, wipe counters, anything to keep her hands busy. Mike and Kate were there, and a girl Stu brought he'd just started seeing but who spent more time flirting with Evan. Susie did her best to ignore the girl since she had adopted Miss Piggy's "moi" as many others had. Susie was completely annoyed by the stupidity of echoing a Muppet. And the most annoying Muppet. Nella liked Kermit but especially the bear, whatever his name was. Susie could hardly stand to have it on in the house. Stu usually took Nella downstairs when it was on. She supposed it gave him an excuse to watch it without looking like he actually wanted to watch it.

"I'll get those, Angel. Leave them." Evan leaned in against her to turn off the water.

"I don't mind. I'm not doing anything else."

"You're not supposed to be doing anything else. Come visit while your in-laws are here."

"You know I can't sit and do nothing for very long."

He leaned closer. "Suse, I know it's hard to talk with them, but they're still your family and they came to see you and Nella, not me. You can't keep avoiding it."

"I can't stand that look. The pity thing. They lost him, too. Why do they look at me like that?"

"Because they know he was part of your everyday life, always at your side, and it's a huge adjustment for you along with how you miss him. Of course they do, too, and they still hurt as much, but they were used to seeing him only occasionally..."

"Oh I don't know. He was on the phone with them a lot. More than you knew. Not with his dad so much but..."

"Yes, but Angel, even though he was also part of my daily life and with as much as I miss him, I know it can't come close to comparison of what you're dealing with. You expected forever, old age, side by side through everything. Raising your child together..."

She grasped air, deeply, and nodded.

"It's not pity, Suse. It's concern. They're worried about you."

She nodded again. "Guess I better show them I'm okay, right?"

Stu's date came in and asked if they needed help with the dishes. She brushed against Evan's arm. For some reason, Susie wanted to belt her. She knew why. Stu brought the girl. She had no right to flirt with Evan, or with anyone other than Stu.

He refused politely and guided Susie with a hand on her elbow out to the living room. He accepted Doug's repeat offer of the space on the couch and sat on the arm next to her. It was okay. If he was sitting with her, she would be okay with conversation. He was great at redirecting whenever she needed him to redirect, and to answer for her when she didn't want to, but she did her best to answer, to put herself inside, to make them more comfortable. She even pretended she would consider going to Scotland without her husband.

"Nella. Get off that." With a flash of curls, her daughter looked at her long enough to show she heard and swirled back to put her foot on the lowest ledge of the book case, trying to grab a candy dish on top. "*Danielle.*" She shoved herself off the couch. Mike stopped her, but Susie was fed up. She grabbed the child's hand. "I said get off. *Don't* ignore me."

"I have candy. Stuey say yes."

"Whoa, no I didn't." Stu argued from across the room. "Don't get me in trouble, Miss Nella. I said to ask your mom."

"Stay down. No more candy." Susie ignored the pout. "And don't lie. It's not nice. Go play with Keith."

"Keith reading."

"Then go read with Keith."

"*No.* I *not* read."

Gritting her teeth, Susie took a deep breath and looked over at Evan. "I'm sorry. We have to go. I can't..."

"It's all right." He came to meet her. "Want me to walk over with you?"

"No. It's your birthday. Stay. I'm going to put her in the bath and..."

"*No* bath! I *not* go." Danielle pulled out of Susie's grasp and ran across the room.

Danny got up and grabbed her, holding her in one arm while she struggled. "C'mon, little Nella bird. Be nice t' your mum. G' and take your bath an' I will come bother y' later, yes?"

"No." She pushed at him. "*No.* You not my daddy. Let *GO.*"

"*Danielle.*" Mortified, Susie went to try to take her, but the child pushed at her too, until her dad came over, grabbed Nella under the arms and turned her to face him. "Enough." He calmed her instantly. She never argued with her grandpa. "Time for you to settle down."

Susie had to hold back her frustrated tears while her dad managed her child better than she did. She followed them next door, glad it was just the three of them, that she was away from the crowd. "I'm going to go run her bath." She started away where he wouldn't see how hard she was trying to control herself.

"Sweetheart." His hand on her shoulder stopped her and he set Nella down and told her to go to her room and find pajamas for after her bath. And he wrapped Susie in a hug. "Don't worry. It's her age. She knows how tired you are and she's taking advantage of it."

"I can't do this. It's not working. She won't listen. She ... she's so angry at me and I don't know what to do about it."

"She's not angry at you. She's only angry in general. You're her easiest target. Don't let it get to you, honey. She'll be all right."

"Will she? It was hard ... hard enough on me and I was ... seven ... older."

"I think it was harder on you because you were older." He stroked her hair. "And because I still had to be away at work too often. She's lucky you're here with her always. But you need to give yourself a break more often. Leave her with Evan and get out, or leave her with Kate or the guys and let Evan take you out. Anywhere...”

"I can't." She grabbed a deep gasp. "Anytime I'm out, I'm surrounded by fans, reporters, someone. And talk about angry; they *are* angry with me. They keep... I can't. I can't deal with it."

"Then go to Scotland for a while. You said that doesn't happen there. Go visit as they asked..."

She shook her head. "Not without him. I can't go without him."

"Sweetheart..."

"I can't." Shoving moisture from her eyes, she tried to calm herself. "I have to start her bath."

"Go shower." Her dad stopped her again. "I'll take care of her. Go take a hot shower and calm down." He sensed her hesitation. "Or go back and read in your room, close the door for privacy, and I'll put her in the bath."

"She'll be easier for you if she takes a bath. It's hard to get her in but she loves it and stays forever when she's there. Getting her out again can be hard..."

"I'm not concerned about how hard she is to deal with. Trust me, I've been well broken in." He gave her a light grin. "And she knows I'm not tired enough to be pushed. Do whichever you want to do. We'll work around you for a change."

The phrase started her tears again. Work around her. It would be a change. Nothing worked around her anymore. Everything was around Danielle. Around the band that was still hesitant. Talking about promoting, playing short tours or single shows, something so they didn't just stop. They wanted Susie's opinion. She didn't have one. She couldn't think about it, about the band playing ... without him. About watching them, sitting and facing the stage knowing he should be up there showing off guitar licks and... Her body protested her thoughts, and she let her dad pull her in again.

"Go shower, Susan." He kissed the side of her head. "It'll help you relax. And do what you want the rest of the night. I'll keep Danielle. You can visit in peace or I'll tell them you're resting. Whatever you want."

"They're only here a few days. Except Laura is staying a while."

"They'll understand."

She shook her head. "I'm going to shower, just real quick, and ... and I'll be fine to visit. Just them, not the whole group." Convincing herself she would be, Susie headed back. She refused to even look into her daughter's room. Danielle would see she was upset. She didn't want that. She was the parent. She had to be the strong one. Somehow.

She took longer than intended in the shower, but she did feel more relaxed. Her eyes were a bit swollen and the cold washcloth she pressed against them didn't help. With a sigh, she went out to find Laura in with Danielle, talking with her while she bathed and played with her toy boats, making tooting sounds for the whistles.

"Want me to take over?"

Laura turned. "Nae, we are makin' a story for the boatmen. She will 'ave t' get ou' soon, though. The water is gettin' cold."

Danielle objected and Laura teased her and told Susie to go ahead and not worry about them.

Her dad was still there with the rest of the McGuire clan. A gorgeous smell emanated from the kitchen. Linda smiled at her from the stove.

"We decided t' treat you tonight. It has been some time since y' had a Scottish meal, has it no'?

She nodded, avoiding Gene's and Danny's stares as she looked into the sizzling and steaming pans.

"Bangers and mash." Linda explained although she wouldn't have needed to. Sausage and mashed potatoes with peas and gravy. One of Susie's favorites, even though she had trouble with sausage. It made her suddenly wish to be in Scotland, in a little pub listening the gorgeous accents and enjoying the friendly warm eyes and square dignified faces.

Her dad joked about them getting her so absorbed into Scottish culture he would have to fight to keep her in the States. Danny joked back that he'd tried hard enough to get them to move.

And Susie left the room. Three months. It had been three months.

"Having us here is makin' it harder for you."

She turned to Gene's voice. He was the only one who had followed. "No. I'm sorry. You know I'm glad you're here."

He gave her a smile and moved closer. "I didnae mean t' suggest y' were not. Bu' it is harder."

She couldn't argue. Yes, it was harder. She could feel their loss, their grief, on top of her own. She knew how hard it had been the five years they hadn't known where he was and how relieved they were to find him, how often they called just to hear his voice. How much like his father he was.

"Y' donae have t' try t' make us feel better, t' worry about upsetting us, as I think y' are. We are worried about y', my dear one. Are y' taking care o' yourself?"

Fighting her emotions again, she looked down at the floor, concentrated on the mixture of Danielle's and Laura's voices as they moved out of the bathroom and into Nella's, still talking about boatmen ... and the Forth River.

Gene moved in and rubbed a hand over her arm. "I wish we could be here t' help y' more."

"Oh. The guys are always here. Evan..."

"He is a nice help t' you. Our son would be glad t' know his friend is here helping t' care for you, and for Danielle. It is nice for Evan, as well, t' be able. I know it makes him feel better t' be useful t' you."

She frowned at the term. Useful. Evan wasn't useful. He was ... her sanity saver. She supposed she wouldn't say that. It would only make Gene worry more to know she was concerned about her sanity. She wasn't, actually, but she would be, if not for the ton of help she did get from Evan, from the guys. Even Kate had become helpful instead of a constant worry and drain.

"Susie." Gene slid his hand around her shoulders. "Donae be afraid t' do what y' need t' do. We are your family. Still. Always. We want y' to move ahead, t' do what y' need to be all right. If y' want t' come visit, we would love t' have you, bu' donae push yourself until y' are ready. We will come t' you as long as we are not intruding too much. Say so if we are."

"No. You're not." Intruding? She wanted them there. Much of her wanted to go back to Scotland with them, to escape into Duncan's family and get away from the home that used to be theirs. That was back to being hers. But she couldn't leave it, any more than she could sell the Victorian next door. She veered around the subject with talk of the band, tour planning, and how she had to be there to help them. He mentioned the album was popular in the UK, as well, and she worried that it was only selling because of him, because of ... it being his last, and she felt it was wrong...

He hugged her. "Donae think of it that way, my dear one. It is respect. They respect his work and want t' be sure t' have it. If it didnae have such good quality, being his last wouldnae mean anything. Think of it as respect of the band's talent. Tha' is wha' it is."

Relaxing with his strong arms around her, she calmed. Respect. She hadn't thought of it that way. She supposed it was true. Some third rate band wouldn't necessarily boom in sales only because they lost one of their members.

"I think Linda 'as dinner abou' ready for us. Smells incredible, does it not?"

She nodded, realized her fingers were clenched in his shirt, and released them.

Nella started to throw a fit about the food being mixed together, which she hated, and her grandpa grabbed her again, told Susie they would go bother Evan and Diane for dinner instead.

She felt guilty at the relief of having the child out of the house instead of fighting with her through dinner. She knew Evan was worried about her losing weight again, but it was just too hard to take the time to eat much in between the arguing, trying to get Nella to sit still, to try whatever she'd made. Even when it was something the child had enjoyed before, she often tried to refuse. Everything was a battle.

Yes, she was tired, as her dad said. She was more than tired. She wanted to go to bed and just stay there for days.

When Gene and Linda headed next door to the Victorian, Susie told Laura she was headed over to grab Danielle for bed. Danny had taken off downstairs with Stu. It was nice to see them together. Nice for both of them to have each other. She wished Danny got along with Evan that well.

With a sigh, she knocked and let herself in. His mom was still there. And her dad. Doc. "I just came to get Nella."

Her daughter began a little fit. Evan picked her up and brought her to the door. Susie let him carry her over. It was a good excuse. She needed him to come over for a few minutes.

Laura took over with the child and Susie stopped him from leaving. "Hold on. I have something for you." She went back to her room and returned with a package.

"Suse..."

"I know. You told everyone no gifts. But like usual, I didn't listen to you." She gave him a teasing grin. "Actually, it's from both of us. I mean ... well, open it." She waited until he had the framed print unwrapped to see what it was. "I've been doing some research since we were in Ireland and you mentioned how you felt more at home in Scotland. Duncan helped me, with assistance from one of his friends, to search the Scott family name. And you're right. You should feel more at home there. Scott literally means from Scotland. The clan is from the borderland of Scotland and England. Supposedly, they're related to a brother of one of the Scottish kings. The material behind the crest is Scott clan tartan."

He rubbed fingers over the glass. "Amo."

From the crest, a golden belt wrapped in a circle with a proud buck in the middle and the word *Amo*. "It means I Love." He caught her eyes and she shrugged. "Many of them did move to Ireland so it makes sense you're also Irish but your roots..."

"Are Scottish."

"Yes. So I guess Nella is right when she calls you her Heavenly Scott."

"Suse, this ... this is incredible. Thank you."

"Like I said, it's from both of us. Duncan was amused that your roots are more Scottish than his. He looked forward to..." She bit her lip.

"I wish we'd had the chance to hike in the Highlands as he wanted."

She nodded. "Me too. He looked forward to that, also. He wanted so much to take you there." She forced her thoughts back. It was Evan's birthday. She didn't want to upset him. "I have something else, too." She pulled a chain out of her sweatshirt pocket: a heavy silver chain with his clan crest dangling from it. "Laura found this for me."

He studied it a second, then put it around his neck and gave her a hug. "You are the most beautiful person I have ever known. Thank you. For going to so much trouble."

Susie pulled back and shook her head. "It was..."

"I know." He kissed her forehead. "And I'd like to go back with you someday when you're ready. We'll take Danielle. She should go often enough to maintain the other half of her roots."

"Yes. And I may need you to go with me. I'm not sure I can do it alone."

"Whenever you decide you want to go, I'll be there."

"Happy Birthday, Lee." Susie gave him a warm hug. "I can't

imagine what I ever would have done through the years without you."

24 October

Susie wished she could go to the airport with them, just to have them that much longer. At least Laura was staying. Susie gave Linda a hug, then Gene. When Laura released Danny, he turned to her. "Donae le' her annoy y' too much. If she does, give me a call an' I will speak t' her about it."

Susie chuckled as Laura bopped him upside the head. Then she gave Danny a hug, held him tight. Bit her lip. She didn't want him to go.

She heard Adam say it was time. He had security driving them to the airport and staying with them. Too many knew who they were by now. She made herself release Danny and told them all to have a safe flight. The idea of the flight hurt her stomach. She forced her thoughts away from it.

As he walked away, she wiped at her eyes. Laura rubbed a hand over her back. It only made it worse. Danny noticed. He stared a second, and returned to her. "Y' know if you do this, I will 'ave t' just take you and Nella back with me t' Scotland."

Nella was in Evan's arms. Susie glanced over at her as Linda gave her another hug and told her to be good.

"I am serious, Sis. Are y' sure y' donae want t' come? They can go on and I will wait a day or two and take y' back."

She shook her head. "I can't. I have work to do here. I can't leave right now." At least it was an excuse. She told herself the band had to have her while they struggled to return to the stage.

He hugged her again, for the longest time, until Adam got more insistent. "Are y' going t' be alright?"

She nodded. Swallowed hard. Tried to give him a grin. "Call me as soon as you get there. And ... maybe now and then. More often. I've missed you."

He tilted his head. "And tha' is a fair turn of events, is it nae? I am flattered."

"Donae be." Laura pushed at him. "It is only because y' kept Nella ou' of her hair and I will do tha' now. So go on before y' miss your flight."

Susie gave him another grin. "Better listen before she bops you again."

"Aye right, 'cause I need another ding on the skull." He teased Laura's hair and backed away. "Call me anytime, Sis. Either o' y. Love you."

Susie wiped her eyes again as he got into the car. She didn't want him to leave. Laura went to claim Danielle and took her back into the building. Evan wrapped Susie in his arms. He let her stand there a while, until Adam mentioned there were people stopping their cars nearby, on the road, staring, and he guided her inside.

31 October

"I don't know what to do with it." Susie held the black cat mask and waited for Danielle to go get her bucket for Trick-or-Treating. She was hesitant about letting her go, even if she would be disguised. Her own disguise should work well enough, she supposed, if they could get over to her dad's building without being noticed. She was a witch, with a big flowing robe that hid her shape, a long stringy grey-black wig, and a partial mask that gave her a long crooked nose and square chin. With makeup on her eyes and fake eyebrows, she was unlikely to be recognized. No matter how appropriate her costume was, as Stu had joked.

He was right. She had been pretty witchy. That would have to stop. Her daughter was excited about Halloween, about walking around outside as other kids always were able to do. Danielle promised she would leave the mask on with Susie's warning they would go right back to Grandpa's apartment and stay there if she took it off. They'd even come up with fake names, in case anyone asked, playing like they were new to the area. She hoped it would work. Her daughter deserved one night of fun where she didn't have to worry about hiding from cameras or fans or reporters.

"Suse?"

She looked back at Doug. "Sorry. What?"

"How about renting it to me?"

Puzzled, she shifted her thoughts back to the conversation. The house. "Renting it?"

"I have the feeling you don't want to sell."

"No. Come here, Nella. Let's finish getting ready."

"Are you thinking about moving in?"

"No." She shook her head. "There's no point now."

"It would still give you more space. Nella could have room to play without being on top of you."

"I can't. Doug, I can't do it." Her daughter nearly jumped on her lap to wait for Susie to pull her costume over her warm clothes.

"Then rent it to me. It can't sit empty."

"You want a big house to live in by yourself? Not that I ... I mean..." She sighed as Nella ran off again only half done.

"Not by myself."

She found his eyes. "You're asking Ali to move in with you."

"Not exactly. When she graduates in December, I plan to propose."

"Doug! That's wonderful!" She turned to give him a hug.

"No one else knows and I'm not telling anyone else. But I don't want us to live here in the building. No offense. I know you did, but I can't ask Stu to move out and..."

"That would be perfect." She couldn't even think about being offended. "The house. Yes. Of course. That way I don't have to sell it or worry about how to take care of it on my own and ... are you sure? You're not just trying to help me out?"

He grinned. "It's a gorgeous place. And being next door will be handy. That way, you can go ahead with plans to fence in the back yard completely and put stuff out there for Nella as you were going to. It's still her back yard. We'll just look after it."

"Thank you. I'd like that. I already promised her ... before..."

"Eventually, maybe Ali and I can help put the kid stuff to use, also."

Susie smiled. "Yes. I hope so. You'll both be great parents. And I am so happy for you."

"She hasn't agreed yet."

"She will."

Laura came from the guest room in her zombie costume, minus the mask in her hand, with Danielle in tow. "I need t' come every year this time. This is the grea'est fun."

Susie grinned at her. "It hasn't started yet."

"Aye and it has for me. It isnae everyday I try t' look ghastly. D' y' think I am more so than Stu will be?"

"I don't know. He gets really into this."

Doug rolled his eyes. "He's been getting ready all day, like a teenager."

Susie knew Stu had decided to be a zombie twin with Laura. Evan was going, also, but she didn't know as what. Something that would cover his face. And they were taking Keith. The six of them would look like two couples with a kid each. Laura had already claimed Nella and Stu. Susie had to appreciate her energy for wanting both of them.

1 November

With a lightness of spirit she hadn't felt in ... since July, Susie bagged up the excess candy and stuck it on a high shelf. Danielle and Keith had an incredible time gathering it. Susie wasn't sure Laura and Stu didn't have even more fun, though. They took charge of both kids, leaving Susie and Evan to walk along behind and just enjoy being out and about and unbothered. Evan dressed as a warlock to match her witch costume. Nella had laughed to no end about his big nose and black stringy hair. Luckily, it worked well and Nella even talked to kids her age and older. She loved it. It made Susie feel a bit guilty that her daughter couldn't just go play with other kids on a normal basis. Maybe she'd have to figure out how to let her. Keith had no interest. He only went up to the houses because Nella pulled at him.

Beau and another guard had stood in front of their building handing out candy along with guitar picks that said *Raucous*. Adam's idea. He'd ordered a heck of a lot of the things and they still ran out fast. Especially since Doug and Mike made brief appearances at the door now and then to talk with parents and teenage siblings of the Trick-or-Treaters.

Sweeping up the crumbs and bits of paper she hadn't bothered with the night before after pulling the candy away from her daughter's fingers and getting her settled down, reading to her until she could sleep, Susie thought of Doug's offer to rent the house. She was glad the Victorian would be put to good use and considered what to do with the yard. She wanted a nice big play area for Nella and Keith, and for Doug's kids when he had them, but she also wanted space to entertain outdoors, closed in from neighbor intrusions but somehow without blocking it off from the band's building. Doug and Ali would work with her, she knew. She'd talk to them about it after the proposal. Since they were on a very large lot, both her house and the building, they should have no trouble using the space for both, especially if they combined the yards, at least mostly, and put some kind of fencing around them together, up to the sides of each building maybe.

A knock took her to the door. Stu returning Danielle, she supposed, though it hadn't been long. Sometimes not long was long enough with the nearly three year old, though. She checked the peep hole and rolled her eyes as she opened the door

"Hey, Suse. Guess Stu didn't tell you I was coming." Nathan was unnaturally subdued. He didn't make a move closer to the door.

"Why are you here?"

"Checking on you. How are you by now?"

"I have family and friends for that. Why are you here?"

"Roy asked me to come. He's been calling to ask if I'm still interested in playing bass with Raucous."

Play with Raucous? Why hadn't she heard of it? No way had Mike agreed... or Evan. "Mike and Stu are playing bass. We already said no to you."

"That's what I said."

"Really? Did you? And yet, you're here. Trying to jump in now that they're a big name and there's a space available?"

"No."

"No?" She almost laughed.

"Suse, I came to let you know what he was doing, to tell him, in front of everyone, that I'm not willing to try to push in where I'm not wanted, that I respect you too much for that."

"Oh come on, Nathan. I know you want back in. I know you do."

"Suse." His voice lowered, a strained look on his face. "Seriously. I know you have no reason to believe me. I understand. But I'm not that kid anymore. And I do have an awful lot of respect for you, for the band. Even for your bodyguard ... sorry, for Evan. I may not like him a lot, but I do respect him and what he's done with the band. I'm not trying to push in. I want to let them know if they want any backup support temporarily, I'm willing..."

"Of course you are. Hoping it'll become permanent. Was this Roy's idea, too? Because you know, I don't put up with crap from him anymore and I'll go tell him to stay the hell out of it if this is his idea.

He's only still hanging on out of the guys being too nice to dump him after his contacts have helped us out. That can be fixed, though."

"Hey. Okay." Nathan stepped forward, ducking his head as though in surrender. "I don't want to cause you more stress..."

"Then you shouldn't be here."

He nodded, grabbing a breath to try to regroup. She almost felt sorry about being so nasty. But not quite. "I'll go tell him not to call me again. I'll change my number if I have to. Suse, I really am sorry ... about what happened with us, about ... your husband. I am sorry. You don't deserve to have to go through this."

She couldn't answer. Deserve didn't seem to matter. Duncan didn't deserve it. Danielle sure didn't deserve to lose her daddy. Susie didn't think she did, either, but it was all besides the point.

"I'm..." Nathan backed away. "I am going to check in with Stu while I'm here. He actually didn't know I was coming. It was last minute on my part. I did really want to see you, to see if you were okay, but I understand if you avoid Stu's tonight. I won't come back up here. Don't worry."

Susie watched him turn to go. As he reached the top step, she opened the door a bit farther. "Nathan." She waited until he gave her his eyes. "If you want to ask the guys about temporary backup, it's up to you. It's their decision. Just keep some distance. Because there's still part of me, when I see you and I'm here alone, that gets nervous. Even if I know I shouldn't..."

"Understood, and I'm sorry. I'm truly sorry. I hope I'll eventually be able to prove you don't have to be. I would never hurt you again. It was the biggest mistake of my life. I haven't... I actually went into rehab and got help when I left here, which is why I couldn't contact you, to explain. I was... It doesn't matter. But I want you to know I've never been that drunk since. I haven't used anything illegal since. And I won't. I won't again risk hurting someone that way, especially someone I care so much about."

He continued down the stairs and Susie stood there, stunned. Rehab? Anything illegal? He hadn't only been drunk the night he tried to force himself on her. He was on something. With a deep breath, she realized Laura was at Stu's, where Nathan was headed. Laura had stayed up late with Stu watching some horror movie. She'd risen late, lounged in her robe a while, then finally decided to shower and said it was her turn to take over with Nella. Susie and Nella had been up for three hours by then. Susie was already tired again and Nella was bouncing off the walls, near enough. Laura was so different than her brother. Both brothers. Except similar in that she would deal with Nathan just fine if she had to, which Susie doubted. Duncan's sister? Not likely. And Stu would likely knock him flat out.

Evan eyed her. Let Nathan join? Even temporarily? He couldn't figure why she would ever agree to that.

"I know what you're thinking. You're probably right. But it was a long time ago. He's older. So am I. I'm not so gullible. I'm... I'm not young and single and unencumbered so I'm not his type anymore even if..."

"I wouldn't count on that, Suse. He's still pretty hooked on you. I know I never approved but I always knew he was truly..."

"I know." She shrugged. "But everything's different now. And I'm not saying you should agree, that the band should agree. I just don't want you not to agree because of me."

"Fat chance we won't." He shifted to face her more directly. "After how much he bothered you, you think we want anything to do with him?"

"It was a long time ago. Things have changed. I guess I just can't shut out the friendship we used to have. Even if it can't be the same, it was there. Maybe ... maybe part of it was my fault. Maybe he needed better friendship than I gave him…"

"That's not true."

"Isn't it? I'm not sure anymore."

There was something she wasn't telling him, something she was holding in. She was single now and just starting to come around and find herself again. It was the wrong time for Nathan to be around. Maybe she wasn't so gullible anymore, but she was vulnerable. He would take advantage if she allowed. Evan knew he would. Nathan wasn't only interested; he was obsessed with her. He always had been.

"Well." He decided to change course. "I think for now, we should stay with the four of us. It's working all right. We likely won't be doing many shows for the album that has heavy keyboard and the next one will have less emphasis on keyboards to leave Stu free for bass, or for guitar while I'm on bass. It's not ever going to be as good; it won't ever sound as good as what they're used to, but some fans will stay."

"Of course it will." She moved closer to him. "Evan, you are an incredible guitarist. You can use backup musicians for tours, for either bass or keyboard, and while recording just do it in tracks. You and Stu can both double on albums. It'll still sound incredible. It sounded incredible before. It will again."

He touched the side of her face. "It's nice to have you back." Her reaction said maybe it was the wrong thing to say. "Suse, I mean in band business, throwing that unwavering support."

"Is that what you meant?" She stared into his eyes, knowing better.

"Partially. I thought I shouldn't infer more than that."

"Don't start that again."

"Start what?" His hand slid down to her arm.

"Being safe. Don't pander to me. You were the only one who didn't right after... I got mad, I know, but I loved you for that. You got me through by being straight, not tip-toeing around me. So don't do it now. I'm not really as *back* as I'm trying to look."

Loved him for it. She loved him for it. Evan knew she couldn't understand what that meant to him, although she didn't mean it more than casually, like a friend, a best friend. Still, he was glad to know he'd made the right choice. He nodded, considering his words. "I mean, I'm starting to see *you* again, to see a touch of fire return to your eyes. It's nice."

"I still hurt like hell." Her eyes watered.

"I know." He moved his fingers back up to brush the moisture away. "So do I." Lowering his eyes a moment to compose himself, he grabbed a deep breath. "You haven't done much dancing recently. You should. The band ... playing again, it helps me. You need to let yourself go back to your dancing."

She rolled her eyes. "I'm so out of shape by now, it's hard."

"Tell me about it. Being nearly thirty is starting to show." He grabbed his stomach to emphasize the extra he didn't use to have when he and Duncan ran so often, worked out together. At least she grinned. That grin was worth having the flab.

"Guess we didn't get far on the workout thing, did we?" She tilted her head in thought. "We should try to do better. I really feel like nothing but ... mush and fatigue. Attractive combination, isn't it?"

"You're still beautiful. But maybe we can help the fatigue."

She chuckled with another roll of the eyes. "Maybe we should get Nella to work out, too. It might help her get to sleep faster, which would help my fatigue."

"She's still fighting you every night?" Getting a nod, he felt horrible that he didn't know she was. He could help with that, also, stay at night until the child went to sleep, fight with her himself instead of leaving it to Susie. She was right. She was much too fatigued, too constantly.

Standing, she grasped his hand. "So come with me. We'll ask Stu if he can keep her that long. Or Laura will."

"Didn't you say Nathan's at Stu's now?"

"Yes. I want to talk to him a minute, also. But I want you close."

"Of course. Let me change if we're going to work out." Heading to his room, to change from jeans to ... to what? Sweats or shorts? It was warm for October, at least it would be while he was working out, but he always tried to stay more covered in front of her, as a gentleman ... which was ridiculous. She wasn't a young girl anymore. She was a mom, a widow. His wearing shorts instead of sweats didn't matter. She was in capris, stretch capris, covered by a long shirt. Her round dancer's calves showing, softer now with the lack of constant exercise. No. Sweats were better. For his own sake. He didn't want his head going that direction.

She was at the window when he returned. He touched her back to get her attention, and a soft smile. "Three months and they're still coming."

He looked out where she nodded. A couple of fans with a bouquet of flowers sat on the sidewalk in front of the building. He didn't recognize them. They were likely more from out of town who still filtered in from time to time. At least it didn't upset her anymore.

He still had a supply of signed photos, signed by the whole band. There were only two of them out there. They may have come from some distance. Evan grabbed two photos, told Susie to stay inside as they got to the entrance, and went out to hand them to the girls. He got huge hugs in thanks and he assured them Raucous would be out and about again.

"I damn sure didn't expect you down here. Would've brought your kid up if you wanted her." Stu glanced at Nathan.

Susie explained, and asked if it wouldn't be too much trouble if he kept Nella longer.

"Hell, she's never trouble for me."

"And when she starts talking like you, I'll know she's been down here too often."

"Sorry. I do try."

With a light chuckle, Susie figured it was pointless. Growing up around the guys meant Danielle would have to adjust to their language, among other things. Evan never used it around her, so at least she had him as an example, and she didn't either, although her language had deteriorated recently. Not around her daughter.

Gathering her thoughts, she looked at Nathan. He was staring at her. "Can I talk to you a minute?" She led him to the kitchen. Evan gave him a quick warning glance and went to talk with Nella.

"I um..." Susie leaned back against the counter. "I didn't know you were having trouble and maybe I should have."

"It's not your fault."

"You could have told me. We were friends. We started as friends."

"As much as you objected to it? As much as you complained about so much drug use and how disgusting it was? I was supposed to tell you?"

"Nathan..." She dropped her eyes and raised them again. "I knew a lot I didn't really know. I mean, I thought I knew a lot that I didn't. I thought parenting was going to be pretty easy, too, with as much practice as I had, all the babysitting I did. And it's not. I don't know anything about it. I can't even control my own kid." She shrugged. "I'm sorry."

"Suse, you don't have to..."

"I do. I shouldn't have made you think you couldn't talk to me. I wasn't really much of a friend like I thought I was. I was too full of what I thought was right and..."

"And you were right." He shifted, moving closer, still not too close. "Everything you said about it was right. I knew it was. It wasn't you, Suse. It was because you were right and because I wouldn't have had a leg to stand on if I argued with you and I didn't know how to stop. Any time I was with you, I wanted to never touch it again. I was fine when we were out together, or in together. It was those times in between, when I was out on my own, with friends who weren't really friends, that made me keep going back to it."

"Then why didn't you stay away from them?"

He shrugged. "I was so damn guilty about hiding it from you. And I couldn't make myself tell you. But I never meant... I didn't expect you to be downstairs that night, dancing, looking so incredibly sexy and..."

"Don't." She pulled back when he stepped closer.

"I'm sorry, Suse. I can't tell you enough how sorry I am."

"What made you go to rehab after you left here? Why didn't you go before? I would have helped as I could. I would have understood."

"No you wouldn't." He grinned. "You're the proverbial good girl, one of the few that actually exists who would never do something so incredibly stupid, who hangs out with the captain of the football team and straight A college grad who hardly ever even has a beer. You wouldn't understand, even if you'd tried."

She walked across to the other side of the kitchen.

"I never would have even considered admitting myself if not for you, if not for knowing what I almost did. It was either that or completely give in to it because I couldn't live with myself as I was. And I've been sorry every day since. Not that it helps."

She met his eyes. "Yes. It does." With a deep breath, she moved closer. "I wish you would have told me. I spent a lot of time feeling betrayed, worried that I didn't dare trust again, afraid you would come back, afraid that since I had misjudged you so badly I couldn't trust myself."

"But you did. It wasn't that long until you started dating Duncan."

"He had a hard time getting me just to go on a date. And I wouldn't have, if Evan didn't trust him. I wouldn't have otherwise."

"Yeah, you would've. Maybe it would've taken longer, but you would have." Nathan studied her eyes. "He was what you needed. It didn't matter if I messed up or not because you woulda dumped me after he came, anyway. I couldn't have competed with that."

"No."

He chuckled. "Thanks. You could've argued."

She dropped her eyes. No, she couldn't argue. She would have dumped anyone for him, almost anyone, maybe anyone.

Nathan cautiously touched her arm. "I really am sorry. About you losing him. If there's anything I can do, ever, let me know, okay? I have making up to do, if you'll allow, not that you don't have plenty of help, but..." He reached into his wallet and pulled out a card to hand her.

"My new number. If you ever need anything."

Looking at it, she had to question him. "Guitar tech? Since when?"

"Since you asked if I'd ever had a real job. Pissed me off royally, but of course... Stu helped me get it, a different branch of his store."

"Full time?"

"Full time. Sometimes more than full time. And there's something else I'm working on in between, another direction. We'll see how that pans out. In the meantime, I'm working steady. Yeah, hard to believe, I know. I like it, though. It's a good show off job, and I've had to practice more regularly so I don't get shown up by some kid just learning."

She couldn't help a light grin. "I'm glad to hear it. I knew you could."

"You were the only one." He ducked his head closer. "He was a lucky man, Suse, to have had your heart so thoroughly, even for such a short time. I will always be jealous of that."

"Thank you." Susie refused tears. She would not do that in front of Nathan. "But Evan's waiting, so I should go." With a couple of steps, she looked back. "Did Stu know? About rehab. Did he know?"

"Only after I got out. If it didn't work, I didn't want him to know it didn't."

Nodding, she turned to leave, to go back to Evan, to go work out. Stu knew why he'd been so horrible. Susie had never understood why he kept inviting Nathan back when he knew how she felt. Now she did. She was glad at least one of Nathan's friends had been there for him.

Nella ran up and grabbed her legs. "My mummy, I dance, *too.*"

Evan moved closer. "Stu was talking about you dancing again."

Dance again. She hadn't said that. She only meant to work out. But her daughter looked up at her with so much expectation and excitement, Susie couldn't turn her down. "Okay." She rubbed her head. "I tell you what. Ask Stu if he'll bring you downstairs in half an hour."

"And we dance in half an hour? Two of us?"

"Yes, sweetie. We'll start working on it again if you want."

The child bounded over to Stu. "Half hour. Mum say half hour. You take me down'tairs?"

"Yes, I'll take you downstairs, little monster. Let mommy go warm up her muscles first."

"I warm mu'cles, too."

Stu tickled her. "I'll warm your muscles, like your muscles aren't always warmed up, silly girl."

Through Danielle's laughing, Susie went over and gave Stu a long hug. She didn't bother to explain, but she caught Nathan's eyes on the way out.

Evan watched Susie and Danielle work on relearning simple dance steps. He knew Susie wasn't quite ready, or didn't think she was, but it would be good for her. It would help her move on. She gave up her teaching for Duncan, to wander the country with him on tours, to help the band. It was time for her to go on with her career. Although Evan wasn't sure how she would do it now, since the band's popularity made almost everything normal impossible. Maybe she could hand pick a few of her old students who might still be interested, refuse to take in anyone she didn't know, keep the risk of girls signing up just to get glimpses of the band low. Not that they cared much, but it bothered her.

It bothered him to see her lean toward trusting Nathan again. He didn't like it. Maybe Nathan did act more adult than he used to. Maybe he was safe enough, technically. But the glance she gave him as they left Stu's apartment was disquieting. There was too much in it.

He couldn't help but be amused when Stu pulled Laura out to dance, and even more when Nathan tried to cut in and Stu shoved him away, said Duncan's sister was off limits.

"Evan Lee. *Look*." Nella called to him and then did a turn, her hands held nicely rounded above her head.

"Wonderful, Miss Nella. You're going to be a good dancer like your mom."

She beamed, nodding. "Yes. I be dancer like my mum and I play 'tar like my daddy and boards like Stuey."

Stu shook his head. "Is there anything you're not going to do? What about drums? Doug can teach you drums."

"No." She shook her soft dark curls.

"No?"

"They loud and big and I not big yet. I not reach."

"You will be." Stu grabbed her and swung her in a circle. "And I can't believe you would have trouble with the noise."

"Noise hurt my sore ear." She frowned and set her hand against the side of her head.

Susie went over. "Your ear hurts again?"

"No. Not hurt now. Drum noise hurt my sore ear."

"You tell me if it starts to hurt again. Don't let it get bad first. Okay?"

Nella wrapped her arms around Susie's neck and kissed her cheek. "I okay, my mummy. We dance more."

Evan went to interfere. "Come, Miss Nella. I think your mom's tired enough for today. How about another time?" He ignored her pout and took her hand.

"Hey." Stu nudged his arm. "I'll take her upstairs. You two stay and unwind."

Starting to protest, figuring Susie would want to shower anyway, he turned enough to see her sitting on the mat, stretching her arms over one leg. Looking every bit the professional dancer, although she didn't bend as low as she used to. That would return with time. He told Danielle they'd be up soon and heard Nathan ask Susie if she wanted to dance, as they used to.

She refused. No excuse. Just a simple no. Evan was relieved to hear it. And Stu yelled at Nathan to catch up.

Evan sat at the edge of the mat where she continued her stretch. Silent. Allowing her space to be absorbed into what she was doing. Maybe he didn't need to worry about Nathan. Stu seemed to have an eye on him. Evan would just as soon let him run interference instead of doing it himself.

4 November

Adam supported their decision not to add another band member, not even a temporary one. Evan considered trying to convince them Nathan would be okay as a fill in, because he knew Susie thought it would be okay, but he couldn't. He didn't want him to stay around.

Susie still hadn't decided whether or not to go to their first show of a series of smaller events Adam had found for them. It wasn't only a show. It was more a party, with several bands Axis represented playing a couple of songs in between piped music. Most were newer bands, an introduction of sort, with plenty of celebrity reporters invited.

Mike had a date lined up already. Ali agreed to go with Doug. Stu would have a date if he didn't have yet. Evan didn't want one. He wanted to convince Susie to go, to be part of the band as she should be. And he couldn't take a date and leave her the only one without one. Laura wasn't staying that long, so Evan needed to be available.

Stu offered to find a guy for her. She walked away. He was teasing, but it was too soon. Nathan jumped in to offer. She only threw him a glance. She didn't want a date. She didn't want to go.

"Why don't you come over for dinner?" Evan took her side as they left the meeting. "Mike's girlfriend will be there. Maybe Laura could keep Danielle so you can just be part of the conversation and get to know her."

Susie looked around him. "Should I meet her?"

Mike half-shrugged. "It would be nice to have you there. Keep Evan from feeling in the way."

"In other words, you're at least kinda serious about this one." Susie grinned.

"Maybe. Not sure yet."

"Sure you wouldn't rather send Evan over to my place so we're all out of your way?"

"Nah, I promised her dinner and I don't cook worth anything."

She chuckled. "Oh, that's nice."

"Hey, it was his idea."

When Susie looked up at him, Evan changed tracks. "She'll be at the party. I thought it would be nice if you would meet first, have more people there you know."

"Lee, I just don't know if I can. You should find a date. Maybe Mike's girlfriend knows someone nice."

"I don't want to take a date, Suse. I want you to go with me. You should be there."

Pausing in their trek up the stairs, she stared at the floor a moment. "And you can't keep revolving everything around me. I'm okay. And I don't want to interfere. Find a date. I'll still go if I decide to. I just don't know if I can." Starting up again, she didn't bother to notice he didn't, or she didn't worry that he didn't.

Mike spoke quietly beside him. "She's right. That's what you need to do, Ev. Find a date."

Find a date. She wanted him to find a date. He supposed it would be for the best.

She did come for dinner, without Danielle. Mike's date, Kelly, was a charming girl, slightly star struck maybe, but soft-spoken and intelligent, and she flirted only with Mike and it was subtle. A glance. A light touch of his arm from time to time. Paying more attention to him than to anyone else. Evan liked her. She would be good for his friend. Much better for him than Kate, who had gone off somewhere again. Keith was spending the weekend with his grandpa just for a change of scenery, so Doc said. Evan knew he absolutely doted on the boy and enjoyed him more as he got older and could talk better.

Susie didn't say much other than when spoken to directly. It was a nice evening, though. Evan was glad she decided to come early and help him cook, not that he was doing anything complicated, a fairly simple beef wellington, but he enjoyed her company. No one worked in the kitchen beside him as easily as she did, as she always had. It was their thing. Duncan had often left them alone in the kitchen while he messed with the guitar or entertained his daughter. He understood how they enjoyed the time.

Mike and Kelly sometimes came in and chatted with them and sometimes stayed in the living room alone. Evan didn't mind either way.

Dinner was relaxed and easy and they sipped on a glass of wine afterward. Evan wasn't sure whether or not Mike had warned against it, but although Kelly seemed interested in talking with Susie, she didn't push. She did ask about her daughter, about how she dealt with a little one while travelling, saying she'd vacationed once with her sister's young children and it about drove her insane, but then, there were three of them. Susie shrugged it off, said she relied on the guys a lot and there was always help around.

She was throwing off more credit than she should, though. She didn't hire a nanny as most moms on the road did, although the nanny Mike hired tended to help with Nella at times. She didn't have people running errands for everything she needed. Susie still did most everything herself. The help she got from the guys was minimal, background support. Duncan of course did a lot of it, also, but with his job, he couldn't do as much as he wanted. She did it. And now she felt like a failure as a mother only because Danielle didn't listen to her well. Evan knew she did, no matter how he tried to convince her otherwise.

As conversation quieted, Susie said she should go get Danielle settled in for bed. He was glad she agreed to let him walk with her.

After Nella was bathed and calmed down and tucked in to sleep and Laura headed down to watch something with Stu, Susie held him there, asked if he wanted coffee, decaf, and to watch something with her. She used the excuse of leaving Mike and Kelly alone. He had the feeling it was more because she wanted the company.

13 November

Laura wrapped her arms around Stu's shoulders and gave him a tight hug. "You take care of her for me. She is not okay yet."

"I know. And I will." He rubbed her back. As soon as she left, he would call Danny and tell him the same about Laura, that she wasn't as okay as she was acting, that she'd spent a lot of time with him to try to hide from Susie how upset she was, how it bothered her to see Susie only kind of here with them. Because she wasn't, really. She was functioning. Laura could see it.

It had been hard on her to stay for the month. Stu knew at times she thought of leaving early because it was hard, just to get away from it, but she couldn't. Instead, she hung out with him.

He would tell Danny to be sure to check in with Laura often, even if his work hours were intense right now. His sister needed him.

She needed a boyfriend, also.

As Laura went to hug Evan, Stu thought of her words, when he teased her about not dating. She was afraid of it. She blamed Danny for chasing them off, but truth was she rarely saw Danny anymore. He was busy. And her mom wasn't back to herself yet, either. She was ... only functioning. Part vacant. Aunt Loretta drew her out at times and hovered to be sure she was alright. Gene was busy a lot, too. Gone a lot. He and Linda were barely talking to each other. It worried Laura, and she couldn't tell Susie.

She had her friends, but she often didn't want to be with them. They were still the giggly upbeat carefree girls she had been before and now she wasn't and she just couldn't deal with them. She was alone too much. Stu warned her against it, said to date, but date carefully.

Laura was afraid of it, afraid of getting hurt, that any guy interested would probably only be interested because her dad was an ambassador or because she had money and not because of her since she was heavier than she should be and ... and Stu argued every time. She was beautiful and sweet and smart and any guy would be lucky to have her and she needed to remember that.

But she wouldn't. He knew she wouldn't. He wished she would stay so he could play brother to her for Duncan, to watch out for her.

She told Nella to be good and to send her drawings, and then held Susie a long time before releasing her to go to the airport. Beau was accompanying her, on Susie's request. Susie told her to take care of herself and to come back anytime and to call...

Stu walked with her to the car and opened her door. Then he took her face in his hands. "Hey. Remember what I told you. Date. Don't be alone. But don't get serious with anyone your brother wouldn't approve of. Right?"

She gave him a light nod. And she got in the car.

16 November

Yawning, Susie pushed hair out of her face. She'd stayed up too late. Nella woke too early, always too early. Trying to come to life enough to consider making breakfast, she decided the child could have Cheerios this time. She would make up for it later with lunch. Susie missed Laura already. She'd only left three days before, but the apartment was so much quieter without her.

"Mummy. Where is my daddy?" Danielle tugged on her arm.

With a fair amount of surprise, Susie stared while the question was repeated. It had been a long time since she'd asked.

"Mommyyyy ... I want my daddyyy."

"Did you have a bad dream again?" She sighed at Nella's nod. "Baby, I know. I want him here, too." Squatting down to see her face, Susie rubbed fingers along under her chin, studying the gorgeous Duncan-blue eyes and more feminine version of his jaw line and hair that was nearly the same color now that it had lightened. It used to be as dark as Susie's. Now it was a deep mocha brown with a touch of red and had a nice wave at the ends. So like her father. It was amazing how she looked more like him the older she got. "He would be here with you if he could. You know that, right? You know how much your daddy loves you."

She nodded again; her frown deepened.

"I know, baby. I'm sorry he's not."

"The trip toooo long. His Dani-nella want her daddy here now."

Susie pulled her daughter in against her. "I know, baby. I know. I wish I could go get him for you." Four months today. Far, far too long. After a minute, she grabbed a deep breath and stood again. "How about we have cookies for breakfast today? We'll eat real food later. What do you think?"

"Yes." She nodded again, solemnly, but showed expectation in her eyes.

Having cookies for breakfast was a special treat. Duncan decided it was okay, now and then, to grab a handful of them and a glass of milk and sit on the living room floor watching cartoons while dunking them in the milk. Susie had large trays for the occasion. She didn't want squooshed wet cookies in her carpet. And she was a poor substitute for Duncan, especially since she didn't like cartoons terribly well, but she tried.

Getting her daughter to add a bowl of cereal to her earlier milk and cookies, Susie sighed at the doorbell. She hadn't bothered to change out of her pajamas and robe, but it was likely her dad or one of the guys or Kate or Ali and it didn't matter. She hadn't seen Ali much and would welcome a visit, although Susie knew how busy she was with her finals coming up and with as many hours as she could manage at her parents' restaurant.

Checking the peep hole and finding Stu, she opened the door as she told Nella to stay at the table until she finished ... and it wasn't only Stu.

"Hey Beautiful." Greg threw her a grin and walked up to engulf her in a big hug.

She wished she'd dressed. It was nice to see him though, with Lisa and her kids.

"Susie, how are you?" Lisa gave her a hug and studied her with a sympathetic look she didn't want.

"I'm okay. Is Tony here, too?"

With a glance at Greg, she shook her head. "He's ... busy. You know, he's always busy, and when the band isn't out running, he wants to stay put. But I had to see you. It's been almost four months since the service. Are you doing all right?" Joshua fidgeted in her arms, wanting down.

"Yes." She grinned at Tonia who clung to her mom. "Honey, Nella's in the kitchen finishing breakfast. Do you want anything?" Leading them into the apartment, she took the boy from his mom. He was almost two, in a couple of weeks. "Mr. Joshua, how about you? Are you hungry?"

He nodded while his mom said he'd already eaten.

"He's a growing boy. Always room for more, yes, sweetie?" With another nod, Susie carried him into the kitchen and gave Nella time to greet them in her excited way before reminding her to finish. "Cheerios okay? I didn't bother to cook this morning."

Lisa was still eyeing her. "Oh, just put a few in a bowl, no milk. He'll spill it. And he likes it that way."

Tonia said no thank you and sat quietly beside Nella so she would stay still to finish. Figuring they would be all right alone, Susie took her friends back to the couch. She didn't like that Lisa travelled with the lead singer of her husband's band. It didn't look good. Usually Steve was with them also, which was better.

Greg sat next to her. "I've been keeping up with Stu. He's had a hell of a time with this, also. But he's been here a lot, he says."

"Yes. He and Danielle do great together."

"He's been worried about you."

Susie pulled her legs up beside her. "I'm okay. Really." Then she unwrapped herself again. "I'm sorry. I have coffee made. Do you want any?" With one acceptance and one refusal, she went to get the new cup and refilled hers. The kids were laughing together. Good timing. Nella needed the distraction today. And Susie didn't want sympathy conversation. She wanted to drag Evan over to help avoid it.

She handed Greg his cup and switched topics. "So what is Blue River up to recently? I haven't kept track well."

"Of course you haven't." Lisa cocked her head. "And we're rather surprised to hear Raucous will be at this party coming up. We're glad they are, of course. We'll all be there."

"But I hear you refuse to go to the party with them."

"Did you?" Susie glanced at Greg but distracted herself with her coffee, staring at the rising steam, focusing on the warmth of the cup against her fingers, on the strong aroma. She was making it stronger than she used to.

"Does that mean you're not? Or you are?" He smelled of something smooth and elegant, likely expensive. It opposed his big untucked shirt, faded jeans, and old sandals. As interesting a combination as Greg himself.

"I haven't decided." Too-loud laughter from the kitchen sent her in to check. Nella had apparently finished her cereal and was balancing the bowl on her head, making Joshua howl and Tonia giggle. "Okay. I think you're done." Susie took it from her and pulled her down from the chair. "How about you go play in your room?"

She told Greg and Lisa she'd be back in a minute and went to find clothes, something loose and comfortable. Susie rifled through her drawers but didn't find anything she wanted to wear, so she went to Duncan's dresser. She pulled out one of his bigger T-shirts, held it to her face, breathed his scent embedded in the fabric, and closed her eyes. She could see him in it, see it accenting his strong figure, his gentle muscles and graceful movements. She could see places he'd worn it, his smile, his eyes when he looked at hers. With a deep breath, she pulled it over her head. It made her feel even smaller with its largeness enveloping her. She wanted him there. Wanted his arms around her, his breath on her neck, his soft voice in her ear telling her everything was alright.

By the time she washed her face and brushed her hair into a loose ponytail, Evan was there. And Mike. She supposed Greg went and knocked on their door. It didn't matter why they were there; she was glad they were, and she sat next to Evan on the couch instead of beside Greg. He teased about avoiding him.

Before long, Stu and Doug were there also, and Kate. Susie melted into the background. She checked on the kids now and then and pulled out snacks and drinks for her guests, but unless someone spoke to her specifically, she didn't bother with conversation. Keith had come with Kate and gave Susie a big hug, then kept up with the others, back and forth from Nella's room. Several times, Susie saw him try to talk to Tonia but the girl wanted nothing to do with him, or with her own brother. She talked only to Nella. Lisa apologized, said she was at the age boys had cooties. At five and a half, Tonia was young for that, Susie thought, but she hugged Keith again and told him to never mind, some day he would be so handsome and so smart and such a gentlemen that girls like Tonia would be begging for his attention. Only Mike heard her and he rolled his eyes. He told the boy not to worry about what anyone else thought, and to ignore her right back.

It all sounded so festive, party-like, happy. Like it had been, when Duncan was still there. When there were always people around. When she could walk past him and touch his arm or his back or his fingers, or steal a few moments for a kiss. Or stand and hold onto him while she ignored the crowd, just hold him and breathe his scent and feel his warmth, his security, his love.

She got up and went to the kitchen, just to escape for a minute. Maybe she'd make a dessert of some kind. What did she have? A glance through her pantry showed she didn't have anything quick, but she had flour, eggs, sugar ... she could make something from scratch. It would take longer but that was fine. Quick rise rolls, maybe. If she had yeast. With a check of her refrigerator, she ruled out that idea. No yeast. Cookies would do, she supposed. Or ... pecan pie. She had pecans and corn syrup. His favorite. When had she last bothered to make it for him? Too long ago. She should...

Her eyes watered. She forced it back. She'd make it when he came home. Every day if he wanted. But he wouldn't want that; he'd tease about trying to make him fat and then she wouldn't be attracted to him and she wouldn't ... always ... be so interested, so willing. She'd argued, said it wasn't...

Pushing at tears again, her legs crumpled and she lowered, her back against the cabinet, hands in front of her eyes, trying to stop the tears, the pain. Four months. He'd been gone four months. It was nearly impossible to hang on to the thought he'd come back. After four months. And she hurt. Inside out, an encompassing constant ache that most often now she could shove to the back of her mind, but she wanted pecan pie. And coffee. Her first cup of coffee had been with her husband, the night he...

She thought someone came in but couldn't move her hands to check. She wanted to be left alone. They went out again. Maybe they would leave, just go away and take the laughter somewhere else. She couldn't deal with it. It hurt too much. It hurt more when those around her seemed just fine and dandy and acted like she should be, too. How? With such a huge hole...

"Angel." Evan crouched in front of her and grasped her fingers, trying to see her face. "What is it? What happened?"

She shook her head. Nothing. Nothing happened. She wanted her husband. She didn't want this crowd trying to make her feel better, trying to make her laugh, while looking at her with that damned sympathy in their eyes. She didn't want to see that anymore.

He pulled her into his chest and held tight. Let her release her sadness, her frustration, her anger. She was so angry. He'd promised he would come back, that he would leave early if he could, if she wanted, that it would only be a short time, a few days. She was so angry at him for leaving her, for not being there with her, for his daughter who adored him, for ... for the years, the many years she wanted to have with him, for not staying so she could see him at sixty, at seventy... She was so angry, maybe more than she had ever been in her life. And she was guilty about being angry. But she wanted him. And she'd believed so hard he would be home again. She'd told everyone he would be home again. And he wasn't. And it had been four months.

"Shh, it's all right. Angel, relax now. Breath. Slow it down."

Her breathing. She hadn't realized it had increased so. It was making her dizzy and she hadn't noticed.

"Suse, slow it down. Here."

She grasped the tissues stuck close to her face. Kate. Sitting on the floor next to them. She was making a scene. She didn't want to make a scene. She'd tried so hard not to make a scene. She'd tried so hard to make everyone else feel okay, because they wouldn't if they didn't think she was. She'd tried. And she was. Mostly. But she couldn't deal with the laughter. She couldn't laugh when every part of her wanted to scream and rant.

Evan ran fingers along her head, stroked the side of her face, talked calmly, soothed her. She took deep breaths, tried to hold them long enough to slow down, and rested her head on his shoulder.

"Danielle." Susie sniffed, wiping at her face and nose. "I don't want..."

"They're downstairs. Stu took all of the kids down to the basement to run off energy. Greg is there with them, too. And Doug and Lisa. Ali's here."

"Can I do anything for you?" Ali was nearby, but not on the floor.

Susie shook her head, felt the tears explode again, and gripped Evan's shirt, her face pressed into him.

"Come on, Angel. Let's go back to the couch."

She allowed him to help her up, accepted more tissue from Kate, and was glad for his strength when her knees tried to give. Settled against him, holding his arm, her head propped against his shoulder, she felt herself calm, felt the quick gasps of air trying to recover to normal. "Danielle. She had another nightmare. Asked ... where Daddy was. Said ... she wanted ... wanted him to come home. I can't tell her. I can't tell her he isn't. I can't."

He stroked her head again. "Do you want me to talk to her?"

"No."

"Suse..."

"No. I ... I don't know. I just..."

He pulled her back in when her lungs started yanking in air too fast. "Okay, don't think about it right now. Just relax. Deep breaths, Suse."

Listening to his voice, concentrating on his fingers caressing her, soothing her, on his musky aftershave that smelled so strong and masculine, with a hint of ... something else she couldn't decide, she calmed. Felt his strength. Felt him holding her in, surrounding her.

Kate brought a cold damp washcloth for her face.

"I'm sorry." She shoved a hand through her bangs.

"Oh Suse, you have no reason to be sorry." Ali. Grasping her lower arm.

"I had company. I don't do this. I don't anymore. I just..."

"You should if you need to. We all understand. It's all right." Ali squeezed her fingers. "Hey, Doug and I were talking yesterday and he wants to go up to New Hampshire soon, just to visit. We wondered if you wanted to come with, you and Danielle, just to get away from this a while. His parents have space and Nella might really enjoy seeing the animals. If it's okay with Mike, we can take Keith, too. They'd both love it."

New Hampshire. A farm in the middle of nowhere, from what Susie knew. No fans crowding. Her and Danielle. Maybe Keith. She wondered if Ali realized she'd talked of asking Mike in front of Kate, but not Kate. She couldn't worry about it. Duncan would say it was fair enough, considering.

"Interested at all? His parents would love to see you again. And of course Stu's mom would drop in a lot. She still talks about you all the time."

"Is Stu going?"

"Oh, I don't know. I think Doug hoped to get some space from him. But if you'd rather..."

"No, I don't want to change Doug's plans. But wouldn't he just as soon get away from ... all of us for a while?"

"Not from you. It was his idea, Suse."

A couple more tears fell and she wiped them away. "Maybe. I'll..." She looked at Evan. Ali hadn't invited him, either. "I'll think about it. Let me know when you mean. Nella would probably love it. I hate not letting her run around in the yard."

Evan touched her back. "I'll take you to Glenn Heights anytime you want, also. You know that. She likes playing in the yard there. And I don't mean to interfere with Doug, only in addition, whenever you want."

She nodded. It would be better in the spring. In the spring, after Doug had proposed and she could talk about it, she would have the yard around the house fenced well so Danielle and Keith could play there, also.

As soon as she felt herself again, or as close to that as she ever felt anymore, they went down to join the others. She tried to apologize but both Greg and Lisa brushed it away. Lisa also offered her a place to stay if she ever wanted it. Susie couldn't imagine. Tony didn't like them much, or at least he didn't like Duncan, not that it mattered, except it did. She could never spend much time with anyone who didn't respect her husband for who he was. Or with a couple that didn't respect their marriage well enough.

The guys practiced a while, asked Greg for comments, let him play with them for a couple of songs just messing around, and Susie talked with Lisa, or sat quietly with her and enjoyed the music. Ali had to go back to work but would return later. Kate said she'd be back in a while, if it was okay to leave, or she'd stay if Susie needed her to stay.

She sent Kate along. Lisa was there. And Evan was. Even if he was on stage, he was there.

By the time they went upstairs, Stu was talking about food and ordering out and Nella had Susie on her last nerve. Showing off for her company. She kept taking things from Joshua because she wanted them, no matter how often Susie told her to stop, until she made the girl sit next to her and do nothing. It annoyed Nella but thoroughly frustrated Susie when she had to keep grabbing her to make her stay.

As she settled on Evan's couch, Mike handed her a coffee cup. It was cold to the touch and she looked inside. Not coffee. Deep red. Raising it to her nose, she inhaled the fruity-sweet scent of her favorite wine. He threw her a wink and went to harass his son. It did help her relax. When she finished it, he took it from her fingers and brought it back refilled.

"No, that was too much already." She could feel its effects, the fuzziness barely setting in, her muscles beginning to droop.

"Nella is staying with us tonight. We're having an indoor campout with Joshua and Tonia. So, no mom duty. Just head over to your place when you're ready and kick back and relax with the other girls."

"Indoor campout? You're not lighting anything on fire?"

He laughed. "No more than a candle or two so we can tell spooky stories in the dark."

"No. Mike, no. She already has nightmares. And Joshua is way too young..."

"Hey, I mean play scary, not real scary." He set an arm around her shoulders. "I would never scare her, Suse."

She grabbed a breath. "I know. I didn't mean..."

"She's going to be fine. I know you worry about that, but she will be. She has tons of family around. We'll always be there for her if she needs."

Susie sipped her wine slowly while chatter continued around her. Kate returned, and Mike's girlfriend, and finally Ali. Pizza was delivered and devoured. Greg started flirting with her again. Evan kept an eye on him nearly as much as Duncan had, or more. And Stu took her hand and pulled her to her feet.

"Why don't you girls go on over to Susie's and do whatever girls do when they're on their own? We kids are going to put on some music and get noisy."

Kate pushed an arm through hers and pulled her toward the door. Lisa, Ali, and Kelly caught up with them.

"Wait." Susie pulled away.

"Come on, they're fine." Kate tugged at her sleeve.

"I know, I just need to say goodnight to her." Handing her friend the cup that Mike had again filled to send with her, along with an unopened bottle he gave Ali, Susie went to Danielle and pulled her in for a hug. "Hey. You tell them if you need me, okay? I'm at home."

"We having camper party. No mommies. Mike say so."

"I know and I want you to have fun, but you know whatever anyone in the world ever says, you can come home to me. Any time. You know that, right? Just tell him."

"Yes. I not scared, my mummy. I a big girl now. I 'most three old now." Nella held up her fingers to show how old she nearly was.

Susie ran fingers down her baby's hair. "Yes, you're a big girl. I love you, my Danielle. You have fun, but be good. Okay?"

"Have fun, too. Yes. No mum work 'night."

"But mom work is fun. Mostly." With another hug and a kiss on the cheek, she made herself return to the girls. She was being ridiculous. They were in the same building. Next door. With Evan. It was fine. And Nella would love it.

"Hey Beautiful."

Susie looked up at Greg as he plopped down beside her. "You're not supposed to be here. Girls only."

"Well hellfire, why do you think I'm over here? Let's see." He held out his hands like scales balancing. "Guys and kids, or girls drinking wine? Hell, I'm no idiot."

"Sorry." Kate shrugged. "He was too persuasive. I couldn't say no."

Greg shifted his eyes up at her. "I like girls who can't say no. Especially when they're hotter than hell."

Susie shoved an elbow into his arm. "Don't hit on her. The answer is no."

"Why? Thought she was free and easy ... I mean, single." He winked.

"I am single and I can answer on my own, thank you." Kate tossed her head, using the red-brown wavy hair to all its advantage.

"Oh... and that answer?" Greg pressed against Susie while staring at Kate.

"Not a chance." She laughed and swallowed more wine.

"And why not? I got lots of girls who would give anything just to have the offer."

"Yeah, and that's why not. No band guys. No way. Not for me. Been there. Doesn't work so well."

Greg laughed. "And you're saying that in front of three band girls. Careful, they'll dump the rest of their wine on you."

"Not band girls." Susie shifted, pulling back. "That makes us sound sleazy. We're not that. We don't jump from one musician to another like some of them..."

"No?" He tried to hide a sly grin. "I don't know. They say once you've had a musician, you can't have anything else. Think you could, do you?"

"I don't want anything else." She got suddenly ticked off at his smug look. "I mean, I don't want anyone else."

"Never? Come on, I can't see you being alone for too damned long. And you and Stu were looking kinda cozy over there. Make a good couple, I think, unless you wanna push me back to the top of your list. I'm still willing."

"Get out." She shoved herself off the couch and headed to the kitchen, refusing to hear his thrown apology. "Just get out, Greg. You're not supposed to be here." She'd overreacted. Standing against the counter, she knew she overreacted. He was teasing. She pushed it in the wrong direction. It shouldn't have gone there. She made it go there when she should have stayed quiet. Kate could handle herself. It wasn't like he actually would, anyway, not knowing she was Mike's ex, that Mike ... had likely warned him. Even if they weren't still together, Mike would not accept Greg getting with Kate. Susie wondered if Lisa would.

"Suse, come on." Kate took her side. "He was joking."

"I know. It's ... the wine. I'm not myself. Tell him I'm sorry but I just don't want him here right now."

"Been too long, huh?"

"What?"

"After four months of ... being on your own, it's kinda hard to avoid thoughts that come up when a guy hits on you, isn't it?"

"No."

"No?" She shifted directly in front of her. "Come on, Suse. It's me. The one who used to be the one you told everything to. We could try that again. I do keep things to myself."

"I know. Kate, I know. And I guess I haven't... We haven't really kept up with each other well, have we?"

"You had someone much more interesting to do pillow talk with. And I wish you still did, Suse, but I make a good fall back. Ask Mike."

"He doesn't think of you that way."

"Well, whatever. But I do think... I know Stu would be about the last one, but Nathan's been around again. I hear you're talking to him. Getting close?"

"No."

She shrugged. "He's grown up some. Might not be so bad."

"Never. That's never going to happen. And I don't want anyone else. I want... All of those thoughts are for my husband. No one else."

"Okay."

"I don't want to do this. This is supposed to be girls' night. Just chatting and ... and nothing serious. No men here hitting on us or..."

"He left. Lisa kicked him out as she yelled at him for being a pretentious pig. I uh, I think she got kinda jealous about him flirting with me."

"She's married. It's not place..."

"Yeah, so not all married women are as devoted as you. They don't all have what you had, either, to want to be so damn devoted. Hell, if all men were like him, maybe we all would be."

"She should find someone she can be devoted to, then. Instead of staying. It's her choice."

"Not our call." Kate grabbed her arm. "Come on. No serious stuff tonight. Just girl talk. How about we play a good old fashioned game of quarters?"

"I think I've had about enough without that." Her head was far too fuzzy. She was far too relaxed, physically.

"Without what?" Ali looked up as they went back into the living room. She also refused the quarters idea.

Kate laughed when Susie steadied herself on the couch. "I should really go over and tell Evan his 'angel' here is about drunk off her feet. He won't believe it, but I'd love to go tell him."

"I am not." Even while saying it, Susie could barely argue.

Kelly looked at her. "*His* angel?"

"Evan. He calls me that. My middle name. Well, kind of my middle name."

"I know. Mike told me. But, *his* angel? Something I should know?"

Lisa nudged her. "She thinks it sounds like something's going on with you and Evan. I kinda wondered, too, but didn't think I should ask."

"What?" She shook her head, deciding she maybe shouldn't do that again, as she had to rebalance herself. "Why?"

"The way he pushed Greg away from you earlier. The way he watches you. And you constantly seek him out, more than anyone else."

"He's... I always have. We're friends. Forever. It's not ... he doesn't watch me. I mean, he watches over me, like always. He always did. It's not like that. It never was." She was saying too much, protesting too much. The wine was impairing her judgment.

"Except he broke up with his girlfriend, again, to stay with you." Kate eyed her.

"No he didn't." She needed to go to bed, to sleep it off, to stop talking.

"Yeah, he did. Mike told him he was crazy, that the girl was really great and he was crazy..."

Susie didn't hear the rest. She got up and made her way back to the kitchen. She needed coffee. Water. Something to help her wake up, to stop answering them. He didn't. He never had. And all of those thoughts were for her husband. Finding chips and pretzels and dip, she took them out. It would help absorb it. Her glass was refilled. Or she thought it was; she thought it had been nearly gone.

They talked about the guys, all of their guys, their builds, their good points and bad ... their builds. Kelly thought Evan was really sexy and loved how quiet he was, a turn-on, she said, but not her type. Kate talked about his football days, and baseball, and the girls following him he didn't notice, except this one girl who wouldn't give him the time of day, an elitist bitch, Kate said, and stupid, on the honor roll through cheating and sweet-talking her teachers. Why he liked her, Kate didn't know, except for her body, her long blonde hair; she figured it was only that.

Long blonde hair. Duncan said Evan liked blondes. Then why did he usually date brunettes? Susie had to wonder. She'd never met the blonde girl Kate talked of but she vaguely remembered her, in Evan's class, graduated when he did. But he was number three in his class. She was ... she'd scraped into number ten, Kate said. And she was only half as smart as Kate. Susie wanted to ask why Kate didn't bother to try harder, then, if she was so smart, but it didn't matter now.

They talked about their first crushes. Susie chuckled at some of the descriptions and the eye rolling. They asked her. It nearly slipped. Evan was her first crush. She nearly said it. But she wouldn't.

Evan was her first kiss, too. She knew it was unfair for them all to disclose their own and to refuse, but she couldn't. With them talking of how Evan watched her so close, how she always seeked him out, she couldn't. They would take it wrong. Kate rescued her, said it was some geeky guy and she didn't want to admit it. She made up some story. Told them she knew Susie's crush and her first kiss and it was too embarassing to say. Susie supposed Kate was partly right. Not geeky. Nothing at all geeky about him, and he was sexy, he did have a nice build. She couldn't say as much.

But she was tempted, just to get their reactions. It was time for bed...

17 November

"How do you feel?" Kate didn't wait for an answer as Susie made her way into the living room. "Aspirin's on the counter. With water."

"You're up early. Did Ali stay?"

"Early? It's nearly ten. And no, Doug took her home, or at least downstairs, just after you passed out."

"I didn't pass out. I was tired."

"Okay. Whatever you want to call it." She followed into the kitchen.

Susie swallowed the pill and poured a cup of coffee. "Nearly ten?"

"Yeah, guess you needed to catch up. Danielle is on the couch beside Evan watching cartoons. She's fine. I think he's a bit worried."

"Well, if you hadn't told Mike to stretch the truth that way, he wouldn't be. I heard you tell him to tell Evan."

"Was I really stretching the truth?" She threw an amused look. "Hey, it's about time you let your hair down a touch. You need it. It's good for you."

"I feel horrible." She sank into a chair and lowered her head onto her hands. "It was stupid."

"No. It was human. And you are human, you know."

Dropping her hands to let her arms lie on the table, Susie lay her head over top.

"Go back to bed, Suse."

"I need to go check on Nella."

"No you don't. She's fine. She's with Evan."

"He's not really ... watching me." She looked back up at Kate. "I mean, not more than he ever did. Other than, I know he's worried. If he saw me like this, he would worry more."

"Don't do that, Suse."

"What?"

"Not Evan. If you get tired of being alone, then by all means date, or just have a fling, but not Evan. You'll regret that."

"I don't want a fling, Kate. I told you..."

"I know what you told me. I also know you hate to be alone. You need that bond. You always have. Even if it's temporary..."

"Stop." She dropped her head again. "I can't. You don't understand. I can't." Closing her eyes, she concentrated on trying to force her stomach to settle, her head to stop pounding. She should have stayed in bed longer. At this point, she didn't want to move again.

She heard Kate walk around, heard her say to go back to bed, thought about sipping her coffee but didn't even want to move that much. She could just doze there a few minutes and then go back to bed. Kate told her again to go lie down. She couldn't risk it and told Kate she was fine there. Her stomach... It was stupid, no matter what Kate said. Susie had always thought it was stupid when she saw Stu or Mike that way in the morning, when they were late for practice or nearly. She couldn't imagine why they'd do that to themselves, and she didn't know why she had, but she didn't think she had...

"Come on, Angel."

Opening her eyes to Evan's voice, she wondered why he was there, how he wasn't there one second and there the next. He tried to help her up.

"No. I don't want to move. You can't be here. I don't want you to..."

"Don't want me to what? See you like this?" He rubbed a hand lightly over her head. "You need to lie down. Kate said you weren't feeling well."

"I'm... It was so stupid. I didn't mean to..."

"I know. It happens." He raised her arm to slide his underneath and around her back. "Come lie down. Just take it easy today. You'll be fine by this evening."

"I feel like an idiot. I don't do this."

"We're all allowed at least once. And you were safe at home, with friends. We all do it, some of us in stupid conditions. At least you didn't do that. Give yourself a break."

"You don't. You've never..." Her stomach twisted with her movement.

"What makes you think I haven't?"

"Because you don't."

"Not in general. I have. I do try not to, but I have."

She stopped arguing as she focused on getting up with his support. He'd been drunk? Evan? She couldn't quite believe it. He wasn't a drinker. He didn't approve of ... but neither did she. Her mind was too confused to pay attention to what her feet were trying to do, or supposed to do, and her stomach hurt... He lifted her in his arms and took her back to her room. She managed to get under the covers, and he pulled the blankets over her and kissed her forehead.

"Sleep a while. I'll make something to help settle your stomach when you get up."

"Danielle..."

"She's still enjoying the campout with the other kids. Rest, Suse. Your dad called. He and Mom will be in town tonight."

"Dad?" She pushed a hand through her bangs. "Don't tell him. He'll worry."

Evan sat on the edge of the bed next to her. "I wouldn't do that, but relax." He stroked the side of her face. "It's fine. Don't berate yourself for allowing a night of fun with the girls. Ali said it was nice to see you laugh again, that you're a wonderful drunk."

Susie scrunched her face and dropped a hand over it.

"Doug had to help her downstairs, by the way. And Kelly was passed out earlier than Mike appreciated. So don't think you were the only one."

"Ali?" She dared a peek at him through her fingers.

He grinned. "She really is a charming drunk. Kept flirting with me. And with Mike."

"That would have been funny to see."

"Yeah, I'm just as glad it was girls only over here. I'm quite sure you were charming, also." He leaned in to take her hand away from her face and kissed her forehead. "Get some sleep."

Watching him leave and close the door behind him, Susie thought of his words. He was sure she was quite charming. Ali was charming while she flirted. She'd flirted with Evan. He thought it was funny. Glad it was girls only. Did he think she would have been flirting with any guy around? Did it worry him?

Pushing it from her thoughts, she turned to her other side, facing Duncan's side of the bed. She ran her hand across his pillow and pulled it in. No. She wouldn't flirt with anyone else. She wanted her husband. Only. Forever. She'd told him forever. She would wait for him. Forever.

Evan watched Greg sidle up beside Susie, talking about the show Raucous was playing and Blue River was attending since Axis wanted to pull them in, away from their label. Greg asked her to go with him, as his date. As his "date that isn't a real date" as he said. Evan wanted to tell Greg to back off, but she didn't seem bothered yet.

"Damn, so just go tell him already." Mike spoke into his ear.

"Tell him what?"

"To keep his hands off."

Evan eyed his friend. Waiting for an explanation.

"Hell Ev, you know they were talking about it last night. The girls. The way you watch her. They all know. Just go over there and tell him that if she's going with anyone, it'll be with you."

"Don't start that. It's only been four months, and she's Duncan's wife."

"She was. Now she's widowed. And eventually, there will be someone."

Evan walked away, but not over to Susie and Greg. She could handle herself. Her dad was right there. And she was Duncan's wife. He was looking out for her as he asked. Taking care of her and Danielle as his friend had asked. Nothing more. Well, he adored them both and wouldn't have had to be asked, but nothing more than that. It couldn't be. No matter how long it had been, she was Duncan's wife. Duncan's widow. Either way, she was Duncan's. That meant it wouldn't happen, regardless of whatever she might feel at some point, which likely would be no more than she ever had.

He needed to date again. If she refused to go to the show, he would find a date.

As he talked with Ali about school and how her finals were going, he felt a hand on his arm, a soft hand, and knew it was her without looking.

"Hey." She leaned against him. "Greg thinks I should go to that party or show or whatever they're calling it because it would look better for you guys. I don't know if that's true, but he says…"

"You're going with him?" It came out. Evan was pissed at himself that it did, and how it sounded, and for the way she looked at him, surprised.

"No. You asked me first. Unless you have a date by now or were thinking of asking someone. Because you should…"

"I don't have a date and there's no one I have in mind to ask. You're sure you want to go?"

"Not at all." She squeezed his arm. "But I promised Stu I wouldn't abandon you guys and … I guess it would look like I was if I didn't go. I can't hide out forever. We've pretended to be dates before. Guess we can again, right?"

Her smile said she was teasing. Pretended to be dates. A hell of a long time ago. "Of course. We'll have to find a sitter. I think Keith is staying with his grandpa."

"Already did. Nella's staying with her grandpa, too. I won't be surprised if he takes her over so they can let the kids entertain each other so it's less trouble."

He touched the hand she had wrapped around his arm. "I'm glad you're going, Suse." Even if it was just for the band, for the way it would look. He was still glad she would be there.

She stayed and talked with them a while, with him and Ali and Doug, and then rubbed the back of his shoulder lightly and went over to talk with Lisa. She'd pulled together well after dragging much of the day. Forcing herself to look like she was "back" as she'd told him.

"Evan." Ali's soft voice pulled his attention. "You know you're the only one she actually smiles at anymore. I mean a real smile, not the forced smile she usually has now. I could be wrong, I guess, since I'm not here much, but I've never seen her fully herself except when she talks to you."

Doug eyed his girlfriend as though not sure she should say such a thing and Evan waited for his reaction, for an arguement. Doug had been around Susie quite a bit, more than before. He nodded. Barely. And he looked Evan in the eye. "She's right. I've noticed, too. She gives the rest of us an appreciative kind of smile, and she teases Stu, of course, but be careful, Evan." He paid no attention to Ali's surprise. "I'm not sure she's fully convinced yet that Duncan isn't coming back. She doesn't say it anymore, but I think in the back of her mind, part of her still thinks he might. And that's making it very hard for her to recover."

A knot formed in Evan's stomach. He'd had the same feeling, but he tried to tell himself he was being ridiculous. If Doug noticed, it meant he wasn't. "I don't think she's convinced, either. And I can't tell you how much I wish she was right. That it was possible. I know; it's been far too long and I know it's not, but damn, this time I truly wish she was right. And that makes it hard for me to approach it with her, to try to convince her..." He dropped his eyes. "She's even letting Danielle think he might, and that's not good, either. I can't go against her wishes and tell her what happened. But she's going to have to know."

"You shouldn't be the one to do it. Talk to her dad. Tell him. It would be better coming from him than from you."

"She'll just draw away. She won't listen to him."

"That has to be her choice, but if he decides to talk to his granddaughter over her wishes, that's his choice. You can't."

"No, I can't. And I won't. Even if I know she has to know, I won't go against Susie."

Ali shook her head. "No. She depends on you too much. Doug's right. Let her dad talk to her and do what he thinks he should do. If she pulls away from him for a while, she still has you. You're the one who's always here."

He had to stop the discussion before it got to him too much and she noticed. Evan walked away, over to her. She gave him a grin, a real smile, when he set a hand on her back. No, he would never go against her.

23 November

Susie thanked Danny and Laura for calling her on Thanksgiving, at Diane's, and hung up. Since she had a moment to herself, she decided to make the most of it. Slipping to the front door unnoticed, she wrapped her heavy sweater over her shoulders and stepped onto the porch. The old swing creaked as she sat down. The cool breeze made her shiver. She buttoned her sweater and stared out at the yellowing grass and leaves scattered over the yard. A few were still bright yellow and red and orange, but most had browned and shriveled in the Pennsylvania cold. Danielle had a wonderful time raking up a big pile in the back yard earlier and jumping in them, just to ask Evan to rake them up again. He had such incredible patience with her.

He should have his own. She should tell him to start dating, to stop worrying so much about her. There was no point in both of them being alone. If Duncan was there, he'd take Evan out and help him find a girl. The matchmaking thing didn't bother Duncan. He figured if it was supposed to work, it would. If it wasn't, it wouldn't. Not a big deal. And Evan was nearly thirty. He should have his own kids. Maybe she'd have to stop letting him take care of Nella so often. Stop ... stop being his wall as Duncan had warned her once.

"Come home." She whispered into the wind. Her dream the night before had been so vivid, so real. She'd heard his voice. Felt his fingers on her face. And woke up without him. Again. "Duncan, come home to me. I know you're there. I know." She clenched her eyes. The cold breeze made the moisture underneath even colder. She wiped it away.

The door closed. She looked over to find her dad.

"The first holidays are the hardest." He came to sit next to her.

She stared back out at the yard. Leftover weeds bent over with cold's grip made the flower garden in front of the porch look messy. They should be pulled before winter, to help deter their regrowth in spring. Maybe she would do that for Diane while she was there, as she used to, as she'd tried the last time she was there before the crowd interfered.

"I ate too much. How about a walk around town to work some of it off?"

She heard him, but in a haze. Maybe she'd ask Diane about separating some of the iris bulbs and taking a few home with her. Susie had asked for them, way back when. She'd planted them, cared for them. Diane surely wouldn't mind...

"Susan?"

"Guess it would be easier to just get new ones."

"What? Get new what?"

She realized she'd mixed her thoughts with the conversation. "Oh. Sorry. Iris bulbs. I thought... Nothing."

He gripped her hand. "Who were you talking to when I came out?"

Talking to? She shook her head. No way could she tell him.

"Susan?"

"You know many of the native Irish do actually believe in fairies and leprechauns in some form. Someone told me that when we were there. Maybe Nella and I will make a fairy house around one of the trees in the back. At home. Not here. She'd enjoy that." They kept evil spirits away, so the guy had said.

"Come walk with me. I'll let them know and be right back."

She sat and considered the fairy house. They could do a circle around the tree, edge it with some kind of pretty brick. Or stone. Stone would look more like Ireland. Natural. Earthy. Fill it with ... asters for fall and pansies in spring, maybe clover as a fill-in. Or Scottish moss. Maybe she could find that. A garden center should be able to find it for her.

"Come on, sweetheart. Nella's watching the game with Evan. We're free to wander as long as you'd like."

She nodded and got up, tucked her cold hands into her sweater pockets. As they walked, she focused on the yards, decorations, landscaping, at pretty bright yellow mums and deep red mums. She should add some to the front of the building. It looked ... dead by now. She'd paid too much attention to putting in spring bulbs and summer plants and she didn't have anything growing for fall. The guys wouldn't care what she planted. Something to go with her lavender. At least her lavender was still pretty. Even without its purple blooms, it was pretty. She could put mums in front of it.

Maybe she would landscape the Victorian's yard, get it ready for Doug and Ali. Much of the yard had been torn up during restoration. The grass was coming back in well, but it needed more. Something to match. Hollyhocks maybe. Hollyhooks looked old-fashioned; they would match the house.

"Evan says you're going to the show with them. It's a big thing, right? With other musicians and journalists?"

"Not terribly big, from what I know. And not really journalists. Just entertainment reporters."

"What's the difference?"

She watched a squirrel dart away from them. It reminded her of when she and Duncan had walked through the little park in Lakewood.

Before they got mugged. When her dad didn't approve of him, told her to rethink their relationship.

"Susan?"

The difference. "Oh. Well, journalists generally report the truth, the facts. Entertainment reporters don't seem to care much about the truth." At least he'd changed his mind. Her dad adored Duncan. Trusted him fully.

"What are you so engrossed in that you barely hear me?" He stopped in front of her.

"Just ... watching the squirrels, thinking about planting mums. They would be pretty in front of the lavender, don't you think? If I can plant them without disturbing the daffodils and tulips and..."

"Susan." He gripped her hands. "You can admit it's hard. Thanksgiving. Without him. There's no shame in admitting it."

She felt numb. She couldn't even answer. Admit it, why? What good did it do? If she admitted she still felt him, knew he was out there, he'd likely have her locked up and take Danielle away to live with someone sane. If she still felt him, he wasn't gone. He was there with her.

"I am truly concerned about you."

"There's no need to be. I'm fine. Yes, I'm going to the show with the band, as I should. I'm working, as you said I should. I'm dancing again. Not well, but enough to keep in shape. I'm even teaching Nella. I'm fine. What more do you want?"

He stared a long while, then turned again and continued walking.

Fairy houses. Mums and lavender. John couldn't express to her why he was so concerned. He didn't figure it would get in, anyway. She was blocking it out. He could see it. He'd done the same. For years. Many years. Too many. He remembered that empty, hollow, numb ache that came with acceptance. He still had it. Every day. For sixteen years. How did he keep her from doing the same? Fairy houses. He shook his head.

He'd planned to try to get her to stay in Glenn Heights a while, maybe return to work at the little studio that should be safe enough from reporters and cameras. He wasn't sure now. He'd done that. Escaped. Into work, but escape all the same. Maybe she needed to go back home and deal with the band, Duncan's band. Without him. She needed to face it. As he didn't.

They turned the corner and he hesitated. Mrs. Henry was in her yard, close to the sidewalk, pruning her shrubs for winter as she did every year on Thanksgiving, regardless of weather. Susie noticed her and kept walking, no hesitation.

The woman looked up, stared a second, and accosted them as they approached. "Well hello, John. Susan."

He forced himself to be civil. "Mrs. Henry. Are you having a nice day with your grandchildren?"

"Oh indeed I am. They're such lovely little things, all five of them. I have a sixth on the way you know, from my youngest."

"Congratulations." He wanted to ask why he would know, as little as he was in town and as little as he cared.

She turned her attention to Susie. "And how are you, dear? We were all so sorry to hear of your loss."

Susie met her gaze but didn't answer.

John filled in. "Thank you. We're out enjoying the air. Nice that it's so mild today."

"Yes." The woman tried again. "Diane spoke well of your husband, despite what we read, at least those who bother to read those magazines. I never had occasion to meet him, as you know, you're in town so rarely. A shame."

He saw Susie's jaw clench. She turned to him, flat ignoring the woman. "I'm heading back."

"Well." Mrs. Henry puffed up.

John set a hand on Susie's arm as a sign to wait for him, and tried to appease the woman. "Diane is right. You'd do well to believe her over the magazines. I was terribly proud of my son-in-law. I still am." He caught Mrs. Henry's eyes as a warning.

"That is good to hear." Her voice said she didn't quite believe it. She again looked at Susie. "I'm sure you're still dealing with the shock. I hope you'll feel better soon."

Susie moved away, pulled out of John's light grip.

"A simple thank you isn't too much, even for a celebrity, is it?"

Susie turned back. "Celebrity has nothing to do with it, except it's the only reason you're speaking to me. You never would before. You acted like I didn't exist. Why should I talk to you now?"

"Susan." John wasn't sure whether to scold or applaud.

"I'm heading back. And don't apologize for me. Talk if you wish, although I don't know why you're bothering. I won't." At that, she made her way back in the direction they'd come.

John watched her a minute, listened to the woman complain, then gave her a shrug. "You know, she's right. She's not here much because too many treated her that way when she was here. Can you blame her? Would you want your grandchildren treated that way?" He didn't wait for a response.

They didn't talk on the way back. Maybe she was more all right than he knew. It's was Duncan's influence. John saw it all over her, his gritted jaw, his stance, even some of his accent as she told the woman what she needed to hear. He'd been so good for her.

When she took Nella up for a bath, he related the incident to Diane and Evan. Diane looked appalled, said she would talk to Mrs. Henry...

"No you won't." Evan took a sip of his coffee, his gaze over his cup. "Good for her. The old biddy had it coming. She was one of the ring leaders in getting the town to reject Susie. And John, too. Don't apologize for her. Back her up. If that woman dares say anything to you, I expect you to back Susie up, be on her side."

"Of course I'm on her side, but there are things you don't do..."

"Like reject a little girl grieving her mother, your friend by the way, because of her race? Right. That should never have happened."

"Oh Evan, I understand that and I have said as much..."

He stood. "Don't apologize for her. I'm glad she did it. I'd prefer you didn't speak to that old biddy, but if you have to, at least don't apologize for Susie." He walked away, out of the kitchen.

"He's right, Diane." John stared at the table, his voice soft, but he had to agree. "And I told Mrs. Henry she was right. Proprieties can't take priority over friendship. I don't care for myself. I do care for my daughter." He didn't give her a chance to answer, either. Diane's rules for public behavior annoyed him often. Many times she was right. He was glad she helped teach Susie how to be a lady, not to always speak her mind when it was sometimes better not to, how to keep herself at a higher level than those who looked down on her and never be vulgar when she did speak up. He respected that. But sometimes, it went too far. He hoped to hell Diane would not apologize for Susie, or for him.

27 November

She was exhausted, but at least this time it was a good exhausted, or at least mostly good. She was still so out of shape. Trying to keep up with Evan, even on lower settings and with less weight, made her feel more pathetic than she did when she worked out alone. But as he told her, she was working out, not couch sitting, and that put her well ahead of many; she should be happy with that and with where she was at the moment.

She wasn't. Susie hated to get so tired so fast.

"Ready to move up to fifteen pounds?"

"Do I look like I am?"

"You'll advance faster if you push more."

"Yeah, I know. You don't have to remind me I'm so far behind."

"Just a couple of reps with these and then drop back. That'll help you build up..."

"I know, okay? But I can hardly handle ten pounds and yes I know that's pathetic and I don't need it rubbed in."

"Okay." He set them down and walked away, to his weight bench that was loaded with huge-ass weights no normal human should be able to lift.

"You need a spotter for that and you know I can't do it."

"I'm fine." He lay back and positioned his hands.

"Don't be stupid just because you're mad at me."

He sat up again. Stared. Waited.

She was bitchy. She knew she was. And she had been the whole time they'd been downstairs, after she asked if he would go with her. With a deep breath, Susie apologized for taking it out on him; she was only frustrated.

"Don't worry about it." He lay back again.

She went to him. "Evan, don't do that. I'll get Stu if you want..."

"I'm fine. It's not that heavy."

"Are you kidding? Even if you are He-man, that's a lot of weight." The wrong thing to say. Stu always called Duncan that, never mind Evan was bigger, stronger. She supposed he called him that because Duncan was smaller and yet damn strong for his size, more than people would expect.

Evan checked his grip and pushed it up, lowered it slowly, lifted again. It was a lot of weight. His arms showed the strain of it.

"Lee." She waited until he set it back on the bar. "I'm sorry, okay? I didn't mean to take it out on you..."

"You've always taken it out on me, Suse. I'm used to it. Not a big deal." He picked the bar up again.

She wasn't sure whether to punch him in the jaw or to apologize again. He was right. She knew he was right. Again. But still... She walked away, went up to get Stu and send him down just in case, not that Stu could pick the thing up on his own if he had to, but he could help Evan pick it up if he had to. She walked back with him just long enough to be sure Evan was still okay and went on upstairs. Kate would bring Nella and Keith up soon. She wanted to shower first.

Stu wandered closer, though he was pretty sure Ev wouldn't appreciate him babysitting at the weight bench only because Susie said he should. The look he got verified it wasn't appreciated. But she was right; it was a fucking lot of weight and he did need a spotter.

Ev paused and told him he didn't need to be there. Stu shrugged and said he was bored anyway and talked about a song he was working on that wasn't coming out right since he had an idea about the lyrics but couldn't write them worth crap the way Doug could. And the way Ev could. Toying with the idea, he figured he might as well suggest it.

Ev paused again.

"What do you think? I can give you the gist and show you what I have music-wise. Think you can put some words in the right order to make it work?"

"Never tried to do it that way."

"First time for everything." Stu shrugged. "I know you do the words first, but hell, I can change the music around if it needs." He sang some of the music as Evan went back to lifting. Until he'd had enough, strained himself enough, and sat up to stretch his arms.

"She's only worried about this party coming up."

"Yeah. Maybe I shouldn't have pushed her to go."

Stu jumped up and started to remove some of the weights. "You're gonna have to push her. She'll get over it, just don't let it get to you."

"Easy for you to say." Evan pulled them from the other side of the bar to keep it balanced, down to an amount Stu could handle. "She doesn't get pissed at you at the drop of a hat."

"Nah, 'cause it doesn't matter as much. I'm just her buddy. She brushes me off. You ... she depends on you more than anyone. It matters more. And she knows she can piss you off and you'll get over it." Stu locked the weights on his side of the bar and moved to take his turn at the things as Evan spotted him.

It didn't take long to have enough of it since he wouldn't risk making his arms too sore to play. Wasn't worth it. He was only trying to fill in, anyway, not compete with Evan as Duncan had. A big part of their friendship was pushing each other harder than they would have pushed themselves. He couldn't keep up with the weights, the running, the swimming, or anything else physical, but he could push music-wise, and Ev needed it.

He got up again. "So help me work on this song, and then I'll try to go joke her out of her mood for you."

2 December

She was playing the album he'd given her. Again.

Evan greeted John and assured him he didn't expect Susie to be ready yet; he'd come early in case she needed help with Nella while she got ready for the party she didn't want to attend.

John closed the door behind him. "And she probably would. The girl is on a roll today. Speaking of, let me go find her since it's too quiet for my liking."

Evan wandered the living room as John headed to the back of the apartment and picked up a drawing. Lines. Circles. Scribbles. Undecipherable.

"My *Evan Lee*." Nella ran at him and grabbed his leg.

He set the drawing down and picked her up. "What have you been up to today, little one?"

"I go work with mum anight. Yes. You say yes." She nodded hard.

"Sorry. Not tonight. This one's only for grown-ups."

She frowned. "No I go work too."

"Oh Nella, you'll have plenty of years ahead to work. Enjoy not having to work right now while you can."

"My guess is she'll be much happier when she can work."

He turned to Susie's half amused half irritated voice. She was in a skirt, a flowing long dark gray skirt, with an aqua-colored blouse tucked in, emphasizing her small waist, her curves. "You're probably right. And you look great, Suse. You know this isn't a dressy event." He was in jeans and a plain shirt, dark green. They looked like they could have planned to match.

"I know, but other management won't be in jeans just because their artists are. I suppose I shouldn't be, either."

He grinned. *Their artists.* It was adorable.

"What?" She gave him a curious look.

"Nothing. You're probably right again."

"Hm. I better write this down somewhere. I get to be right twice in a row? Nella, pick up your crayons if you're done with them."

"I rarely think you aren't." He set Nella down and caught her eyes, for a second, then she repeated the order. Her hair was in a soft bun at the nape of her neck, a loose bun that looked fully sexy rather than pulled-tight stuffy, with a few tendrils of hair falling along her face. She looked the part of band management: professional, sophisticated, and still ... sexy, especially with the dangling diamond earrings and the matching necklace that curved along her chest nearly to her almost-showing cleavage. Another just-because gift from her husband. He loved to see her wear it. Evan remembered Duncan saying so, remembered him tracing a finger down the chain of the necklace. Teasing. Until she'd grabbed his fingers and held them, with that look in her eyes: the *yes, later* look she'd had so often.

"Danielle, I told you to pick them up. Let's go." At the moment, her look was of nerves and exasperation. Evan wished her husband was there to change it.

"You're off duty." John took over. "We'll clean up before we head to Ben's. Don't worry about anything. Have a good time."

She gave in. Nerves. She had enough on her mind. He gave Nella a hug and told her to be good and waited for Susie to do the same, with an *I love you* thrown in and a kiss on her cheek.

He took her coat to carry with his down to Doug's and as the door was closed, she set a hand on his stomach. "You look nice, too, by the way. The workouts are showing."

He managed to thank her although it was a bit of a shock that she touched his stomach. She never touched his stomach. His arm. His back. His shoulders. Sometimes his face. Never his stomach. He'd noticed he lost some of the extra weight off his abs. It surprised him, though, that she did and would point it out.

The Boston hotel hosting the event overlooked the harbor. Evan figured Adam had some influence on it being held in Massachusetts, within driving distance for Raucous, instead of in New York. Evan much preferred Boston, regardless of travel. It was a quaint city, still active and expansive as far as opportunities and recreation, but its history was everywhere and it still held the atmosphere from earlier times when it played such a part in America's formation.

Susie played the management part well. She was calm and in control, gracious to all who spoke to her and offered sympathy, encouraging of the band's future, remaining a part of them, their friend, and yet distinctly on the management side. She didn't even show hostility toward Roy when he cut her off as she spoke of band business. She allowed it, and filled in as needed.

Evan had second-guessed himself about not taking a date, about he and Susie being the only two without dates and so too *together*, but it was unfounded. Stu and Mike both declined to bring dates. Ali had come with Doug and Robin with Adam. Otherwise, they were all on their own. It looked better. He knew they'd done it purposely.

She spent as much time, or more, talking to everyone else than she did with him, to include Greg and Steve. Lisa was there with Tony but barely had time with Susie. Tony stuck to her, or rather, made her stick to him. Evan could hardly blame him, considering. It looked better.

Evan kept an eye on her and stayed close through their mutual but mostly separate socializing. It was harder on her than she allowed anyone to see. At times, he found her looking out through the dark windows to the water where lights floated on waves. Through the music and conversation and glasses clinking and laughter, her thoughts resounded into his soul. He knew where her mind was at those times: in the water, with her husband. She hadn't looked at water the same since … since she lost him to it. She hadn't let herself go swimming at Adam's. Danny said she avoided even the small river in the Greenville park. Now, she stared out at it through the noise and commotion.

He made his way over when he noticed she didn't hear one of the Axis execs trying to talk to her. She was too absorbed in the water, the darkness.

She did look at him when he set a hand on her back. Her eyes said all he needed to know, and he made an excuse of having to call to check on her daughter so she would stop worrying.

They did give John a quick call, and then he grabbed their coats and walked with her out to the hotel patio. It overlooked the harbor, closer than she could see it from the window, and she took a deep breath, propped her arms over the railing, and expelled a white mist. It reminded Evan of just after Danielle was born, while Susie was fighting to hang on, to stay with them, when he stepped outside to get away from it for a few minutes.

"You're doing great, Suse."

"I don't want to be here."

"I know. But I'm glad you are, that you did." He stood with his arm touching hers, their coat sleeves a buffer, looking out at the white icy edges that waves bounced up over.

"How cold do you think the water is?"

Evan felt a bolt through his stomach, but he decided to tease. "Too cold to swim. I'm sure the hotel pool is heated, though."

"I don't..." She bit her lip.

He moved closer and ran a hand over her back. A few people ambled around them, other party guests and no one else since the area was blocked off. "I know, Suse. And it's far colder than it would have been in July."

She met his eyes. Grabbed a deep breath. Looked back out at the water. "He doesn't get cold easily, but still, even in July..."

"Don't think about it."

She looked back. "Don't you?"

"Yes. But I try not to. Still, I think ... he probably wouldn't have felt anything. You should tell yourself that."

Her eyes watered, shimmering in the light of the patio just as the harbor shimmered with the lights of surrounding buildings. "I know better."

She shivered and he wrapped his arms around her to share his body heat, as he had on the cliffs in Ireland. Her head dropped to his chest, arms tucked in against his sides. He knew they were being watched, but she didn't seem to notice or didn't care.

She knew better? Why? Something she'd read about how it happened? He tried not to let her see any of it. He knew better, also; he knew from the reports that many of them could have had at least an hour of fighting death before it came. Duncan was a fighter. He would have tried...

She shivered again.

"You need to go in." He spoke next to her ear and felt her soft shake of the head. She didn't release him. So he held her and rubbed his hands up and down her back to try to keep her warm.

"Evan." Adam stepped up beside them. "You need to get set up. Sorry to interrupt. Aren't you freezing out here, Suse?"

She said she wasn't, but she stepped back since she understood his hint. She was in control again. Management. Calm. Professional. He saw people stare, whispering to each other as they watched him and Susie. So did she. He told her to ignore it, asked if she wanted a drink. She told him to go on to work, she'd fend for herself. He refused and signaled a waiter, then led her to their reserved table. Ali and Robin were there. Adam. Roy was wandering, thankfully. Susie told him again to go ahead.

He kissed her head, despite who might notice, before he left. This would be hard for her. It would be hard for all of them, their first public appearance without their lead guitarist. Which was now his job. It was hard for him, also. But he couldn't let it show. She was watching too close. She knew it was hard for him. She always knew. And she was counting on his strength to get through it, so she could. Evan wondered if she had any idea that he counted on hers just as much.

It went better than he expected. He did a reasonable job with the guitar solos Duncan had written: not as good, but reasonable. There was no eye rolling as far as he could tell, no snickers. Although he mainly focused on her if he looked at anyone. He'd trained himself to look at the tops of heads, not at faces. It was easier, less nerve-wracking that way. Another thing his friend had taught him. There was so much. Evan felt his influence constantly.

He had to pull himself out of those thoughts when the emcee came up and thanked them and repeated how sorry everyone was for their loss and wished them well. It was nice, Evan supposed, but he wanted off the stage. Susie wiped a tear from beneath one eye and lowered her face. There were only a few press members allowed but the photographers all aimed at her as she wiped another tear. Still, the guy rambled. Evan tried not to look like he wanted him to just shut the hell up now and leave it alone.

Stu left the stage, brushed Roy off when he tried to stop him, and went to Susie. Adam tried to block the camera views but Stu did a better job when he hugged her. She was seated. He was on his feet, with his arms giving her shelter. It drew more attention, but the emcee stopped talking.

Evan heard the loud applause as they left the stage and tried to act appreciative. He was appreciative, even if it was more for his friend who wasn't there than for their performance. He was stopped by well-wishers, congratulated on his lead guitar work, tried not to be annoyed by those who were surprised he actually pulled it off, and made slow progress back to their table. By that time, too many were trying to comfort her, which only made it worse. Stu told them thank you but asked them to give her space. She got up, tried to get through them. Evan cut through with more insistence. She wrapped into his arms.

"Okay. It's okay. Let's go back outside for a minute."

She shook her head.

Mike called out for a beer or two or three or four with a whiskey chaser, and Greg chimed in, calling for two or three or four whiskey chasers. Evan figured they were bound to have a lot more of both than they wanted within minutes, but it worked. Music kicked back in. Voices waved over the room turning from whispers to a continual hum.

Evan didn't want to let her go, but he didn't want to keep standing there just holding her. "Dance with me." He caught her eyes. She wanted to refuse. "Suse, we'll go soon. Just let things settle first." She didn't quite agree but she let him take her to the dance floor.

She pulled together well, and fast, and refused when some guy tried to cut in. She knew as well as he did that photos were being taken, but she kept him out for a second song. She couldn't quite refuse when Adam cut in. And then Stu did when the music got faster. They were always fun to watch, since Stu did his best to keep up with her trained movements. Doug and Ali cut in on them when it slowed again and Stu made a show of dipping Alison where Doug could see him.

"Excuse me." A woman Evan half recognized stepped in front of him. "We met some time ago at one of your shows. I'm sure you don't remember, but I wanted to tell you how good you were tonight."

"Thank you, and I'll admit you look familiar but I can't place when we met."

She grinned. "I'm flattered, even if you're only trying to make me feel good. With as many women, people, as you meet..."

"No, I do. Your name?"

"Tabby. Well, Tabatha, which..."

"Which you don't like ... because everyone relates it to *Bewitched*, and you don't like Tabby because..."

"Because everyone relates it to a cat and ... you do remember. I am very flattered."

Evan wished he could remember more, such as how long he made her acquaintance and just how acquainted they got.

"Would it be too forward to ask you to dance?"

He figured they must not have been too awfully acquainted if she was worried about being forward. He glanced over at Susie. Dancing with Greg. He offered Tabby his arm and took her close enough he could keep an eye on Greg.

She was a talker. Luckily, she didn't mind if he didn't answer much. Related to one of their opening band members, also how she was able to get into the party, with, apparently, the sole purpose of hoping to run into him. She got closer as they danced, suggesting, with a mention of how she came with a girlfriend who had found someone more interesting to go home with. He tried to hint that they wouldn't get that acquainted tonight, either, as he saw Susie edge back from some guy trying to cut in. The guy didn't take the hint any better than Tabby was taking a hint, and Greg let him take over.

"Have you met Greg Harmon?"

"No. You mean Blue River's lead, right? Oh that's right. Your bands are friends."

"Would you like to?" With her agreement, Evan led her that direction, made a quick introduction, and skimmed out of there to step between Susie and the guy whose breath was so full of alcohol it made Evan cringe. The guy argued, but not for long.

Susie gave him a grateful smile and danced closer than the last time. "I know her from somewhere." She nodded toward Tabby and Evan explained as well as the girl had reminded him.

"Oh, right. I remember her." She chuckled.

"Want to fill me in?"

"You don't remember?"

"Not much."

"That drummer's sister who kept hanging on you all night talking about several bass players she'd *had*, with help of her brother's introductions. Disturbing, really. She never wants anyone but the bassist, something about the resonance of the strings. I'm surprised she's bothering with you tonight since you're on lead guitar now, and she had to have seen that."

"Maybe she's gone through enough bassists and had to change her quest."

She chuckled again. "And you had to give up the chance in order to come rescue me. Sorry. I'll go..."

"No, I appreciated the escape."

"Yeah? She's not bad looking."

"I need more than that."

Susie pressed in, tilted her head up to speak close to his ear. "I surely hope so, because you deserve a heck of a lot more than that."

With a light grin, he gave up on the formality of dancing one hand on hip one hand in hers and set his arms around her waist. She returned the grin and wrapped her arms loosely behind his arms, hands on his shoulders. Evan noticed the girl now talking to Tony, Blue River's bassist, and wondered where Lisa had gone. Maybe she hadn't changed her quest. He figured it might work with Tony.

After the song, they went to their table and he ordered her a fresh glass of wine. She talked with Robin mainly, and was polite to anyone who came over, but she was about ready to leave. He could see it. It was getting too hard to hear all of the condolences, as nice as it was.

Tabby came back. Evan refused another dance. She said something about finding Stu again instead, which Susie tried to block out, and Robin jumped in to interrupt the thought...

And the beginning notes of a too-familiar song filtered in between the barrage of words. *Just You 'N' Me*. Chicago. Their song. Susie and Duncan's. She was pressing her lips tight. Her eyes moistened but she fought against it. He could see the fight. Saw her sip wine in an attempt to hide her thoughts. Tabby kept talking about Stu. Susie kept trying not to hear, until their bassist/keyboardist came over and apparently didn't recognize the woman at all and she kept giving him hints and Susie got up.

Evan got up with her. "Ready to go?" He saw her nod, how hard she was biting her lip. He told them they were leaving. Doug and Ali were behind him. He said they'd find Mike and meet them out front. Evan told them they should stay, it would look better if some of them stayed longer. He had his own car; he'd expected she wouldn't want to stay the whole time. By that time, Stu had called Mike over and they agreed to stay longer but wanted to walk out with them.

Photos were taken of them as they walked together, as a band, through the crowd. They paused only enough to thank those who threw both compliments on the sound and more sympathy none of them wanted to hear. Susie kept herself in the middle of them. Evan kept his hand on her back so she would know, even if he trailed behind slightly, that he was right there.

Outside, away from the crowd, her tears started again and she apologized.

Stu hugged her. "Thank you for coming with us. This would have been harder if you hadn't. Don't apologize. You're incredible. We all know you're incredible." He stepped back enough to see her face. "Make him take you for dessert on the way home. Something chock full of sugar always helps me."

She chuckled as she wiped moisture from her eyes. "You're okay?"

He shrugged. "No, but I will be. So will you. And by the way, I recognize that girl, just didn't want her to know I did. Not one of my best moves." He looked at Evan. "Smart on your part to tell her to get lost that night. She's better at talking than at..." He stopped when Doug pushed his shoulder. "Well, anyway." He made a big show about handing Susie over to him. "Go get her something horribly sweet and some coffee to go with it. Or more wine. That would work, too. Maybe indulge in a couple of bites of pie yourself. It won't kill you, you know."

Roughly halfway between the event and home, Evan pulled off into a little settlement along the highway. Not too little; the lights made the sky glow orange and several signs advertised restaurants and such. She didn't question him. She stared out at the truck stop area, silent.

Searching for somewhere dark and decent, he pulled into the parking lot of a hotel that boasted a restaurant and lounge. A good place to unwind, he figured. Usually they weren't too full. She still said nothing. With an indiscernible sigh, he got out and went to her side of the car to open the door. "Is this okay? Say so if you'd rather not."

"We don't have to stop because Stu told you to."

"I know. You'd rather not?"

"They'll recognize you."

"I doubt it, since it's just me and not the whole band. And if they do, it's a small place, shouldn't be many in there."

"Maybe." She got out beside him but stood between the car and the open door.

"It's fine, Suse. You know I'm not one of the big draws of the band. Mike's not here. It should be safe." He worried more about her being recognized than himself.

"You know since you're taking lead, that will change, if it hasn't already, just because..." She bit her lip.

He'd thought about it, that lead guitarist generally got more attention than the bassist, which was part of why he enjoyed being on bass. "Not sure it will. I'm still the average boy next door type. Don't think I'll have to worry about it much when I'm out on my own. Are we going in?"

She finally met his eyes. "Are you kidding? That's how you see yourself?" She continued when he didn't answer. "Evan, you're ... you're wrong. You have every bit as much sex appeal as ... as anyone else in the band. You do. Don't think otherwise. And yes, actually, something chock full of sugar does sound good about now."

He was wrong? Hell, she'd been married to easily one of music's biggest sex symbols and he wasn't close to that. Next to Duncan, he was ... average. Even next to Mike, he was average. But he wouldn't argue with her tonight.

He set his hand over the fingers she wrapped around his arm. They were cold. She was always so cold in the fall and winter. She should consider moving somewhere warmer where she would be more comfortable.

As much sex appeal. Not close. She'd never looked at him the way she always looked at Duncan, from the day they met. Not even close.

He was right that there were few people in the dark restaurant/bar and he led her to a little table away from everything. She did get attention from a couple of men at the bar but they didn't appear to recognize her, or him. He ordered two glasses of wine, her favorite and something dryer for himself. She ordered cheesecake. He ordered a plate of fries covered in cheese. It would help counteract the wine, to keep it safe to drive. And he hadn't had much of an appetite at the party. Susie teased about his choice of *dessert.*

When she fidgeted with her napkin, he grasped her fingers, gave them something more substantial to hold onto. "Did you have any fun at all tonight, or was all of it an act? Which you did great with, by the way."

Her blue eyes touched his. "It was nice. Most of it."

"Honestly?"

"I always enjoy myself with you, with all of you. Okay, almost always." Her half grin showed she was teasing again. "But you spent too much of the night worrying about me. I'm sorry. It wasn't fair to you." She sipped her wine and checked out the room decorations, mainly area photos he assumed.

"I didn't spend too much of the night worrying about you. I spent the night glad you were there. As I always am."

She returned her gaze. "You should have taken a date. It would have been more fun for you."

"Not sure about that. With a real date, I always have to worry about what I'm saying that I shouldn't or what I should be saying that I'm not or if I'm too close or not close enough. That gets tiring. This pretend date was much easier." He tipped his glass to her as in a salute and got a nice grin in return.

John and Danielle weren't home when they arrived so Evan called Doc's. Danielle was asleep, tucked into one of Doc's spare rooms. John said he would keep her there if Susie didn't mind. Since it was nearly one in the morning, Susie couldn't argue although Evan thought she did mind.

He went to where she had pulled her feet up next to her on the love seat. "Guess that means you can sleep in tomorrow, or later today, without little hands pulling at you to get up."

"Yes, I hope I can."

"I'm going to get out of here and let you get to bed." He kissed the top of her head. "Good night, Angel. I'm glad you went with us."

"Stay a while."

"It's late."

"You're too tired? You don't look like you are."

"No."

"Then sit with me. It's too quiet in here. And I know you'll be awake until the guys get home so you know they're home."

"I would suppose that's true. Should be any time."

"So I'll keep you company." Susie stretched a hand out, asking him to agree. Despite his better judgment, Evan sat next to her and kept her hand in his.

7 December

Susie rifled through the mail that had piled up the past few days. Mostly junk. She'd sort it out later. Sometime. Unless her dad came over and decided to do it for her again. She didn't like to sort mail. Catching what she knew were bills, she set them aside for quicker attention.

She stopped at a letter from the adoption agency. Holding it in both hands, she stared at the envelope. They couldn't call them in now. Not while he was still away. She had to have him there. She couldn't ... but maybe it was only an update. The list was horribly long. It had to be only an update.

Danielle mumbled about something she wanted.

"You want what?" She tried to keep her voice from shaking.

"A 'nana. Mummy, I want a 'nana."

"Honey, I don't have any bananas. I told you yesterday. I'll get some, okay?"

"But I *want* a 'nana."

"You can't always have what you want. I think there are grapes in the fridge. Get some of those."

"No, mummyyyy." She stamped a foot.

"*Danielle.* Don't act like that. Get some grapes or pretzels and behave. I'll make supper in a few minutes."

"I not like grapes."

"Yes, you do." At a bigger temper tantrum, Susie set the envelope down and grabbed the child, carried her back to her room, and set her on the bed. "Sit there until you can behave." As she started to leave the room, she heard a small sniff.

"I sorry my mummy. I lonely. I want my daddy."

"Oh Nella, *don't* do this again. I know. Okay, I *know*. But you *can't* act like this. Daddy wouldn't want you to act like this." Tears welled in Danielle's eyes. With a sigh, Susie went back and sat beside her, wrapping her in her arms. "I'm sorry, sweetie." She kissed her head. "I know you're lonely for your daddy, and I'm sorry. How about we read a book?" Getting a very light nod of the head, Susie told her to go find one.

Her daughter's eyes were heavy by the time she got half through and Susie had her lie down to listen to the rest, glad she fell asleep before it was over. She was overtired. The storm the night before kept them both awake; Nella because she loved to watch it through her window and Susie because ... because her husband had kept her from being afraid of them, and now she had completely different thoughts whenever it stormed, thoughts she couldn't let herself have.

It was still cloudy, raining off and on. It would likely storm again overnight. She hoped it wouldn't, although part of her hoped it would.

Returning to the kitchen, she grabbed the envelope and sat staring at it. An update. Maybe the list was shorter now. Maybe the wait wouldn't feel quite forever. Tearing it open slowly, she felt herself hold her breath and forced its release. She scanned the bottom first. It was from their agent, the one who told them yes, they should be able to adopt. And then she went back to the top to start reading.

They'd been taken off the list. She'd been taken off the list. Due to ... her being a widow, to the state legally declaring Duncan... But he wasn't. She wanted to scream that he wasn't. And they couldn't take them off just to have to start again. It wasn't fair.

It wasn't fair.

She could do it on her own. She and Danielle, if they had to, could ... but of course they would never adopt a child to a single mother when they had so many whole couples waiting.

Dropping her head on her hands, she forced herself not to cry. She didn't do that anymore. She wouldn't. They would change their minds. When he came back, they would have to put them back on the list, move them up where they would have been. Duncan would insist. He would fix it. He fixed everything.

She felt herself start to hyperventilate and stood to walk around the table. It didn't help. She couldn't. She was there alone. With Danielle asleep. She had to pull it together.

In the living room, she sat on the floor and crossed her legs in front of her, closed her eyes, rested her hands palm-up on her knees. Concentrated on her breathing. Forced it to slow. She wouldn't give into it. They couldn't make Nella be an only child. She wouldn't allow it. She would fix it.

When she'd calmed enough, she got up and went to make coffee.

Only a small pot. Only enough to get through the rest of the night. And she would wake Nella soon so she would sleep at bedtime. They both only needed a good night's sleep.

Evan helped Susie with the dishes against only a minor protest. She was exhausted. He'd nearly checked on her the night before during the storm but decided against it, afraid a phone call would scare her at that time of night or that she might actually be asleep and he would wake her. He didn't want either. But she obviously hadn't slept well.

Danielle, on the other hand, was nearly bouncing. Susie said she'd taken a nap, too long a nap, since Susie was involved with dinner and forgot to wake her. She would have a hard time getting her to bed later. If Susie allowed, he would stay and help.

He'd come over to ask if they wanted to join him for dinner since Mike was out, but since she was already cooking she invited him. He'd brought over stuff he had to make a salad and did it there instead, along with a banana for Danielle.

Giving in to her fatigue after dinner dishes were cleaned up, Susie agreed when Nella asked to play the *Space Invaders* game Stu had given her to keep her busy and out of trouble. It didn't seem to bother the child that her game was always over almost as soon as she started. She simply kept starting over. He figured it was a good sign for her future.

"What's going on tonight, Suse?" He sat close to her on the love seat where she'd pulled a leg in front to wrap her arms around.

"What do you mean?"

He leaned closer. "Something's wrong." She shook her head. Hiding. He tried to decide whether to push or let it go. "Anything I can do?"

She stared a moment and shook her head again, then moved her focus to the television, to Nella's game.

He was at a loss as to what to say. It frustrated him to no end to want so badly to help, even just to listen, when she got into these quiet moods. Maybe he would go see if Stu was busy. He was a good distraction, never at a loss for something to talk about, even if it was nonsense. His nonsense was soothing to her. He'd been an incredible help during the past four months, nearly five now, just keeping her with them, involved, sometimes with a smile at his nonsense. The smiles were nice to see. He couldn't often manage it himself, even if Ali did insist she only gave real smiles to him. Not very often. He supposed it was his too serious nature that Susie had teased him about before. She both liked his calm and was frustrated by it. She wanted more of a reaction than she usually got, and he knew she did, but he couldn't, not with her. It wasn't in him to come back at her the way she wanted him to.

Duncan had, to just enough extent to back her off. Evan heard her now and then get snippy with him when she was irritated and he would raise his chin and come back with the same tone. And it was done. She backed off. He gave her what she wanted. It never went further because he never got mad and didn't let her rile herself into being too mad. But he did react.

Maybe he would take a cue from his friend. "Suse, come out here a minute." He stood and waited for her surprise to fade enough she followed him to the kitchen.

"Evan, what? I'm tired. I just…"

"Yes, but something's bothering you. What is it?"

"Nothing."

"That's not true."

"Nothing I want to talk about. It doesn't matter. And I could have told you that out there." She started away.

He took her hand. "Talk to me."

Tossing her head back as a sign she was getting annoyed, she pulled her hand from him. "I don't want to talk. It does no good. There's nothing I can say that makes any difference. Things are still as they are and I can't do anything about it and neither can you. Really. I just want… You should go. I want to settle Nella in and…"

"She's wide awake. Do you want me to help get her settled? I imagine it'll take a while."

"I can handle my own daughter."

That was the snippiness her husband knew how to handle so well. And he started to give it back. He couldn't. "I know. I didn't mean you couldn't."

"Are you dating anyone?"

Confused, he frowned. "No. Why?"

"Why aren't you?"

"Because I'm not. I don't always."

"Most of the time you do. You don't often go so long without dating. Why are you now? It's not like you don't have girls falling all over you waiting to be asked, or even just for a hint..."

"Suse." He moved in closer. "What is this about?"

"You should date. You don't have to hang around and babysit me every night. Really, Evan. You've been here every night for the past week and there's no need. I don't want to interfere with your life. I'll be fine. Nella and I will be fine. Go on with your life. It's time, you know. Thank you. For being here so much. I've needed you here. You know I have. But you have to get on with things."

"What makes you think I'm not? We're practicing again, doing shows."

"Your personal life, Lee. You're twenty-nine. You want a family. You have to get out there and date if..."

"Not right now, I don't." He backed up. A family. No. Not now.

"Why not?" Her eyes blazed into his, baiting him, trying to push for answers. "I know he asked you to look after us, but not to the extent you lose your own life. You can't do that to yourself. I won't let you."

"And you think I am? Being here with you and Danielle. You think that's some kind of loss for me?" He moved closer again, touched her face. "It isn't. There's no one whose company I enjoy more. This is my life, Suse. The two of you will always be..."

Susie walked away, back to the living room, and told Danielle to give Evan a good night hug. He looked like he might argue about getting kicked out, but it was time. The *two of you*. Two of you. As though he'd decided it would always be just the two of them, her and Nella, alone. No. She wouldn't accept it.

Making her daughter turn the game off, Susie grabbed a book she had nearly finished and told Nella to get a book also, or a quiet toy, something to help her wind down. The storm surged. It blew the top of her pear tree she could barely see in the glow of street lights and the building's security lights. She took her book to the window seat, which she never did during a storm, but she wanted to be close to it. She wanted it to surround her. She let the memories flood in: the way he loved to watch the lightning, the time he'd held her outside during a storm until she told him why she hated them, how he'd kissed here there in the rain amid the thunder outside the studio, how often he'd kissed her in the rain since, how he soothed her at night when it stormed, how he made her start to look forward to them. They fueled him, not that he needed the extra fuel. Still, it was...

"Mummy." Nella climbed up and cuddled against her legs.

Realizing she'd been staring out the window, her head propped against the glass, she wasn't sure how long she had been. The storm was closer, louder, brighter. She thought about going out in it and nearly laughed at herself. Of course she wouldn't. She was afraid of storms. She used to be afraid of storms. She didn't even know anymore if she was or wasn't. Maybe she was and it didn't matter. He was out there. Somewhere. In some kind of storm. Everything within told her he was. Or she was losing touch as they all thought. Maybe she was. Maybe she just didn't care that she was.

"My *mum*my."

"Yes sweetie. It's late. You should go to bed."

"No." She bounced her wavy hair with a hard shake of the head. "I look at the light'ing with you. Look." She pointed a chubby finger at a large jagged streak across the sky. "Big, *big* one. Yes."

"Yes." Susie brought her up on top of her lap and squeezed her in close, listening to her talk about the lightning. She never allowed her Nella close to a window during a storm, but she had no desire to move. She needed to hold her baby, Duncan's baby, and listen to her enjoy it the way he did. When Danielle sagged against her, Susie gathered her in her arms and carried her to her room.

"No' tired, my mummy. No."

"Okay." She pulled the covers up to her shoulders and stroked her hair, enjoying its soft shimmer with the reflection from the hall light. "Then I'll sit here and talk with you. How's that? Since you're not tired."

"Yes." But she closed her eyes as Susie caressed her head, her cheek. "I love you, my Danielle. You have sweet dreams tonight." She kissed her forehead and sat a few minutes to enjoy the peaceful expression, the beautiful baby features, the long lashes and round, soft jaw line. "Let it stop here." Her voice was nearly a whisper. "Please. Let it stop here. Don't let my baby have to do this, too. Let it stop here." Pushing moisture from her eyes, she gave Danielle another kiss and went to shut off lights, finding her way to her room in the dark with the help of night lights and lightning.

She didn't bother to get ready for bed other than to pull her bra from beneath her T-shirt. Sliding beneath the covers, Susie got up again to open her curtains so she could see the storm. She wouldn't sleep anyway. She might as well watch.

It got stronger, closer, with huge rain drops pelting the window; the wind's howl started to make her nervous. She wondered if she should scoop Nella up and take her down to Kate's on the ground floor. Or the basement. But it was cold down there. She could swear the building swayed in the wind. What would she do if...? She should at least go stay with Danielle so she would be right there.

She sat up, watched out the window, felt for the sway. Would she look like an idiot if she pounded on Kate's door because of the storm? Or Stu's. She didn't care if he thought she was an idiot; he wouldn't say so.

"Suse?"

She jumped at the voice in her doorway.

"Sorry. I didn't mean to scare you."

"Evan." Her heart barely started again. "What are you doing?"

"I was afraid the storm was bothering you. I thought about calling but I didn't want to wake Nella. Are you all right?"

"No. You scared the hell out of me. And the wind... It's bad. Should we...? I was thinking..."

He moved closer. "It'll be fine. Just a storm."

"How do you know?"

"No tornado warnings. A watch nearby like always but no warnings." He moved closer yet. "This is a strong building. It's fine. Relax."

"I don't like storms. I mean ... not like before. They don't bother me like before but this is..."

He closed the curtains and came to her, stood at the side of her bed. "I've noticed you've calmed quite a bit in bad weather."

"Yes. Usually." She looked over at the door. He'd left it open as she had it, so she could hear Danielle.

"Want me to go?"

"No." She pulled the blanket higher. "I mean ... you can. It's okay. You don't have to..." Grabbing a deep breath at a loud clap of thunder, she shoved a hand through her hair. "I'm sorry, about before. It's been a long day. I didn't sleep last night. And ... I didn't mean to be rude. I'm sorry."

He sat on the bed and grasped her fingers. "What's going on with you? Let me help, Suse. I'm not babysitting. I'm your friend, remember?"

"My best friend." She sniffed air into her lungs, trying to fight for composure.

"Your best friend. Always. So talk to me."

"I..." Another deep lungful of air interrupted. "I got a letter today. Or ... it may have been there a few days. I haven't looked at the mail. I was pulling out bills."

"What letter?"

"From the adoption agency."

Evan waited. It couldn't be good news, not as upset as she was. He'd forgotten about the adoption. He was ashamed he forgot. Of course she wouldn't have. But now, with Duncan gone...

"They took us off the list. They took me off the list. And I suppose ... I guess they had to. I guess... I'm having a hard enough time with Danielle, with trying... I guess it's good, but ... but I wanted this so badly. Evan, I wanted so much to have another, my own, but since I can't, I wanted... I don't want Nella to be an only child and ... and now, now she's an only child with a single parent and that's not okay with me. I did that. I had that. And I don't ... I don't mean it wasn't okay. It was, but I wanted..."

Evan pulled her in against him. "I'm sorry. I'm so sorry. You didn't need this. You didn't need that letter on top of everything." He cradled her head against his shoulder. He wished he had seen that damned letter, grabbed it and kept it out of her sight. It did no good for her to see it now, to have one more thing taken away from her. "I'm so sorry, Angel. There's time, you know. Later, when things are ... when you feel better, I'll go with you and we'll argue with them. You have plenty of help. You can manage two as well as one. I know you can. I'll help you argue."

It seemed to calm her. Her breathing slowed, her fingers relaxed. Or she was just exhausted. They sat quietly, holding on, her body pressed against his, relaxing more with time.

"Lie down, Suse. Get some sleep."

"I don't want you to leave. Just talk to me." Releasing him with one hand, she wiped at her face. "Wait until the storm starts to go away. I don't mind, except the wind. I don't mind the lightning anymore. Or the rain."

"I'll stay until it calms, but you should lie down."

"No."

He touched her face. "You're going to be all right. I promise." Still, she didn't budge. She turned her head toward the closed curtains at a loud howl. Talk to her. She wanted him to talk to her. To distract her. "So. Tell me how he did it."

"Did what?"

"Got you to stop being afraid of storms, at least not so much. I never could, although I tried. What did he say that helped so much?"

"Nothing."

"Nothing? Almost as soon as you met him, you relaxed about it, and more the longer you were together. He had to have said something or done something..."

"You don't want to know." She dropped her hand from his shoulder.

"Yes. I want to know."

Her eyes bore into his. Waiting. Pondering. "Are you sure? Because I think..."

"Suse, there are so many things he managed to help you through that I couldn't. And I don't mean to be competitive. Don't think that. But he got you on stage. He got you to show your voice when you never would to anyone but me. He got you to open up with your dancing." Evan hesitated when she pulled her eyes from him. But he wanted to know. She couldn't have felt safer with him. She had to know Evan would have kept her just as safe, that he would have...

"He made love to me." Her voice was soft and her eyes still hidden. "He loved storms. They... He said they made his urges stronger, that ... that he ... would help me get over the fear and help me love them the way he did. And every time it stormed, no matter what, he would ... we would find somewhere private if we were on the road or we would come back upstairs or ... and he made love to me. And it was so passionate, so intense, and..."

Evan felt himself draw back.

"I told you you didn't want to know."

Silence overtook the room while he tried to figure out how to answer. Nothing he had ever done would ever have compared to that.

He shouldn't have asked. He didn't want the image in his head. But he couldn't let her know it bothered him the way it did. "Well, I guess my sitting here talking to you pretty well pales in comparison. Sorry about that."

She laughed. Moving back in against him, her hand on the back of his shoulder, her head resting on the front, she laughed. More than he'd heard in ... forever. He supposed it was worth having to see that image just to hear her laugh, to know she still could. It made his own eyes moist. For so many reasons.

Then she calmed and raised her fingers to his face as though studying him for the first time. She tensed at another howl of wind and he instinctively pulled her closer, to comfort her.

She met his eyes. Caressed his cheek. And kissed him.

He froze, stunned. It wasn't like their first kiss when she was a young teenager and trying to figure out how it was done, so she said, or like the one on New Year's Eve when she was standing up to a challenge from Stu. It was soft, tender, like before but ... more ... and real. He felt himself give in to her ... and pulled back. "Suse." He couldn't find her eyes. She refused them, her face next to his, closing in again, her cheek rubbing his chin. His stomach tightened. "I need to go."

"Stay." Her fingers slid into his hair, caressed the bare skin of his nape. "Stay with me. Don't leave."

His eyes clenched as he fought himself, felt her lips return, grow stronger, bolder. And every part of him wanted to stay, to let her go as far as she wanted. Most every part. He pulled back again. "No." He grabbed a breath. "You don't want this. Suse, you don't want this. You're upset. It's late. You don't..."

"No. Lee, you don't understand. I do."

"No you don't." He pulled away farther, raised her face to his with his fingertips. "You don't want this. I understand. You hurt and you're lonely and ... I know. But you can't do this."

"Lee." She closed in again, rubbing her cheek against his, lowering her mouth to kiss his neck.

He wanted to give into her. Damn, he wanted to give into her. "No." He pulled away and gripped her hands. "Suse, I'm ... going to go now. I shouldn't have come. I'm sorry."

"Don't."

Blowing out the breath he'd been largely holding, he shook his head. "This... This would be a huge mistake."

Yanking her hands away, she turned and lay down, facing away from him, grabbing her blankets and pulling them to her chin.

He sat still a while, concentrated on his breathing, on the silence other than the wind howl which was softer, farther away. Unsure what to do or say, he remained still. He didn't want to leave, and he wanted to leave. To figure out why. Why she would have... She was lonely. She was such a nurturing person, needy in a sense, so needful of physical contact. They had touched each other constantly, she and Duncan: in public, with only the guys around, always. Grasping fingers or holding his arm or touching her back or her hair or her hand resting on his chest or his stomach. She needed that contact. And she no longer had it. It was nothing more. She was lonely. In a way he could do nothing about.

He needed to date. She said he needed to date. Maybe she'd been warning him that he was too close too often. Or she figured he would have to have that contact by now since she did.

How could he? How could he consider dating when she needed him as she did, especially now with that kiss. The most exquisite kiss he'd ever known. And he had to back off. Doug warned him. He saw it coming. He should have just said so. At least Evan would have been prepared.

"Go." Her voice was shaky, half hidden under the blankets.

"Are you all right?"

"No. And I can't even imagine ever being all right. But I'll get used to it. I'll ... I'll go find someone willing to be a fling if I have to, right? Why not? All of you do it. Why shouldn't I?"

"Suse." Shifting, he leaned closer. "Don't do that." She didn't answer. "Don't go find some stranger who will end up hurting you more. You can't do that to yourself." Still no answer.

No, he wouldn't allow that. Maybe the rest of them did. Maybe it was okay for the rest of them to find temporary companionship they knew would be temporary. It wasn't a big deal to any of them. Maybe it should be, but it wasn't. It would be to her. She wasn't Kate. It would only hurt her. She needed more than that.

Kicking his shoes off, he slowly lay down beside her, waited for an objection that didn't come. Cradling her in his arms, he kissed her shoulder. "You won't be alone forever. I promise. Just hold on. And remember I'm here. I'm always here for you, for whatever you need, whatever it takes to help you get through this. I'm here, Angel. Don't do anything that will hurt you more. I won't let you." He felt her shake softly and held her tight until she calmed again, her breath deeper. Asleep. He hoped she would sleep well.

A fling. Was she looking for that? With him? Would she actually have...? Evan couldn't let himself think she would. Granted, he would be more safe for her than anyone else, but ... no. It would hurt her. She was Duncan's wife. She still wanted him; more than anything, she wanted her husband.

8 December

Waking early, too early for as late as she was up the night before, Susie ran through the hot shower and tried not to think about what she'd done. She was an idiot. Why would she have hit on him? She didn't even want that. She wanted her husband. Why had she done such a stupid thing?

Upset wasn't a good enough reason. Now she didn't know how to face him. If he took it for more than it was ... although he sounded like he wouldn't ... but if he did, how did they go back to where they were? Friends. Best friends. That was all she needed, all she wanted from him.

Shoving her palms against her eyes to try to stop the tears she wanted no more to do with, she focused on the hot stream of water pounding her scalp, washing over her body. She wanted her husband back. Nothing more. She saw his face in her thoughts and grabbed onto that, let her eyes move down to his shoulders, his chest... No, she couldn't do that, either. Frustrated beyond rationality, she grabbed the soap and scrubbed herself clean, although she'd done nothing to make herself unclean, other than kiss her best friend. Damn. Why? Why did she insist on making everything more difficult than it had to be?

Giving up, she pushed the faucet off and scoured her hot wet skin with a towel, rubbing until she was red. How was she supposed to face him? Maybe she wouldn't. Maybe she just wouldn't let him in. He could go find some girl to date, some girl who had no reason not to kiss him.

At a cringe throughout her whole body, Susie forced deep breaths to calm herself while she pulled into her clothes.

She grabbed a book to take to the living room with a check on Danielle who was thankfully still asleep, and went to the kitchen to start coffee. Hit by the strong bitter sweet aroma of fresh grounds, she breathed it in.

At least he didn't stay. She'd waken during the night and noticed he'd gone back to his own apartment. She hoped he went back to his own apartment. Why did she hope that? Why shouldn't he go out and... Because it was late and storming and she didn't want him out in it. And she didn't want him to find another girl to kiss.

Damn.

Yelling inside her brain to stop it, she plopped on the couch, pulled the afghan over top of her legs, and delved into the book. It was too romantic. Maybe that was her problem. She needed to find something to read without romance. Something that wouldn't remind her of what she didn't have. Right. Like there was any chance of that.

Setting it down, she got up again, poured a cup of coffee and wandered over to her window. Luckily, the fans had stopped vigilantly standing out there in support, in mourning, whatever. She didn't want them there. She wanted ... she had no idea what she wanted. Maybe she would take Doug up on his offer to go to New Hampshire to his parents' place. He said they were never bothered there. It was remote. They minded their own business and left each other alone. She could go, distance herself from Evan ... except she didn't want to go without him.

"Mum, I hungry."

Her daughter's voice made her grin and she yanked herself back into where she was, who she was. Duncan's wife. His daughter's mom. "Scrambled eggs and toast today?" With a sleepy nod from her baby, Susie gave her a hug and absorbed herself into the everyday things she enjoyed that she did still have. Her baby. Making breakfast. Her kitchen. Her friends. She had enough. She was fine.

A knock on her door as they finished breakfast made her hesitate. She didn't want him there. Maybe it wasn't him. Nella ran to answer. "Danielle, don't open that."

"I looking. See?" She pulled up her little step ladder and pressed her face against the peep hole. "*G'andpa.* I open it now. Yes."

"Yes, go ahead."

Nella hugged his legs until he picked her up. "Hey pumpkin, you're not dressed yet. Ready to go?"

Susie took a sip of coffee and settled on the couch. "Go where?"

"You forgot. I should have called." He carried Danielle in and set her on his lap. "The circus. I promised to take her. Ben's downstairs gathering Keith."

"*Yes!* Mummy, G'pa taking me to see *aminals* at the circus!"

"Animals, you mean."

"Yes." She jumped down. "I ready fast."

"Don't run in the house." Susie wasn't sure why she bothered to keep telling her when it never did any good.

Her dad studied her face. "Do you feel all right, sweetheart?"

"Yes. Tired. I didn't sleep well." And she'd kissed her best friend.

"Well then go back to bed when we leave. You'll have a couple of hours or so. I'll take her to lunch afterward."

"Dad..."

"Don't worry. It won't be anywhere people will pay any attention to who she is. And I have a new hat for her in the car. Found it in St. Louis."

"When were you in St. Louis?"

He raised his eyebrows. "That's where I just came from. Big new system just went in."

"Oh. Sorry. It gets kind of hard to keep up." She swallowed lukewarm coffee. "Want some while you wait?" She went to pour another cup and refreshed her own.

He followed. "What are your plans for today?"

"I don't have any. I don't know."

"Suse." He moved closer. "You need to do more. If the band doesn't keep you busy enough, start giving lessons again. Or go back to school. Something."

"I can't. I can't have students here anymore because of the band, because it's impossible to keep fanatics out who only want to see them. I can't go anywhere without someone recognizing me and I hate the sympathy. I don't, I mean I don't hate that they're sympathetic. I hate hearing it."

"You should consider moving. Maybe go back to Glenn Heights and stay with Diane. She'd love to have you."

"No."

"Temporarily. There's no reason not to. Give yourself a break. You can work at the studio there. I know they'd love to have you back. She asks me about you every time I see her." He grasped her fingers. "Sweetheart, you have to have something of your own. You can't sit around here with nothing to do. It'll drive you insane."

"I'm still Raucous's manager. I go to practices. Sometimes."

"But that's not for you. It was never for you. It was to help Evan, then it was ... for Duncan, but it was never for you. It will be better for you to move somewhere you can continue dancing. Get back into your own life."

"I can't."

"Why can't you?"

"This." She motioned around her apartment. "This is mine. This is ours. I've already... I've agreed to rent out the house that I should be living in by now. But I can't leave this. I can't lose everything."

"You will never lose everything, Suse. You have Danielle. Me. Evan. Diane. Duncan's family. You will never lose everything. Don't let yourself think you could. We will never allow it."

"I can't move."

After a pause and deep breath, he nodded. "Okay. But find a way to get back to your own work. Hire security during classes if you need to do that. But get back to work, Suse. It's time."

Time. He meant she'd let herself mourn long enough. It was time to move on. Like she'd told Evan. But it was different.

Nella returned in an outfit she chose herself, completely unmatched. Susie shook her head and set her coffee down to take her daughter back to her room to try again. While there, she heard another knock on the door, voices. Evan. No. She didn't want to see him. "Go get me the hairbrush and let me fix your hair before you go."

"No. I do it." Nella ran to the bathroom and came back with the brush and a pony holder that didn't match.

"Honey, get the purple one. You can't wear orange with this."

"But I like it my mummy. I want this one."

"Only if you change your clothes again."

"Noooo." She shook her head hard.

"Come here." With some coaxing, Susie claimed the hairbrush and pulled the plain, black band out of her own ponytail. Her dad said he had a hat for her. So she gave Nella a neat braid down her back and bound it with the plain band. The child's hair was growing fast. Since she'd trimmed it not long before, it was again well past her shoulders, shining its reddish tint in the light from the window. At least it was bright today, not cloudy. Danielle would enjoy herself at the circus with her grandpa. Susie didn't know how the child would cope if not for her grandpa being able to take her out like any other kid since Susie couldn't.

"Okay, tell Grandpa you're ready, but make sure you take your big coat. It's cold. Give me a hug."

Danielle nearly jumped on top of her as she wrapped her arms around her neck and squeezed tight. And she kissed her nose.

"Silly girl." Susie kissed her nose in return, getting a giggle. "Be good for Grandpa and remember, use your play name, okay? I love you, my Nella."

"Love you, my mummy." With another squeeze, the child bounded off toward the living room.

Susie sat a minute, then went into her room, bending a leg in front of her on the bed. It made her nervous to let her baby go out there when she wasn't with her to make sure everything was okay. Of course her dad would never let anything happen. Susie knew that without a doubt. Anything within his control.

"We're heading out."

She looked up at her dad's voice in her doorway and nodded.

"Evan's here."

"I heard. Will you tell him I'm going back to bed?"

"I have a feeling he wanted to talk to you."

"Not now." She dropped her eyes to the floor.

"Are you fighting again?"

"No."

"Want me to send him back here?"

"No." She raised her eyes. "Please, just ask him to go. I want to lie down."

"What's going on, sweetheart?"

"I don't want to talk about it. I can't. I don't have the energy."

"Should I stay? I'll take Danielle another time."

"No. She's been looking forward to it and there's no reason. I just want to lie down." He wasn't buying it. "I'm not sick. We're not fighting. I'm just tired. The storm kept me up, two nights in a row."

Coming in closer, he touched one side of her head and kissed the other. "Okay. I'll bring you lunch. Anything you're interested in especially?"

"No. I don't care."

He gave her a hug and she reminded him to make Danielle wear her big coat, although she didn't like it. And she lay down, scrunched on her side. She heard muffled voices and then the door close. She was truly glad Evan gave in and left as she asked. She wasn't at all sure he would. He was so completely stubborn at times. So annoyingly stubborn. One of his many annoying qualities, as he would say. Stubborn. Facetious. There were others. Even if she couldn't think of them now.

"Now you're going to refuse to see me?"

She sat up at his voice. Standing in her bedroom doorway. So annoyingly calm. That was another. He was always way too damned calm. It irritated her to no end. "I'm resting."

He nodded lightly. "You couldn't tell me that yourself?"

"Go away, Evan." She lay down again, faced away from him.

Silence invaded. She knew he wasn't leaving. She knew he was standing there, waiting for ... for what? She wasn't going to talk to him. She felt like an idiot. So stupid. Anything but calm and rational and ... and like any of his strengths, like any of his good qualities. She didn't have any of them. She couldn't imagine why he even wasted his time with her.

Movement at her back told her he was sitting on her bed, not quite touching her, but watching, staring at the back of her head.

"Go."

"No."

Fine, then she would ignore him. Eventually, he would get tired of being ignored and leave. Mad, maybe, but that was his own fault. He shouldn't have come to her last night. He should have gone back home when her dad told him to. He could be mad if he wanted. It wasn't her responsibility.

"Don't make this a big deal, Suse. It isn't."

She wouldn't answer. He wouldn't goad her into talking to him.

"And it changes nothing."

Maybe for him it didn't.

He set a hand on her shoulder. "It was nice, though. Better than the last two."

Pivoting, she stared at him. "Nice? It was stupid. You know it was stupid, so don't pander to me. Don't be so damned nice about this. It was stupid to try to take advantage and you know it was and ... I'm sorry."

He grinned. "I'm not."

"Not what?"

"Not sorry. And it was nice. I'm actually rather jealous of Duncan now because it was very nice. He was a lucky man to be kissed like that. Or better than that since you actually meant it with him."

Actually meant it. He was making it too easy. Playing it off. Like ... like the friends they were. "You've had better kisses than that. Don't tell me you haven't."

"No. More intense, yes. Better?" He shook his head. "I'm still waiting to get both together."

"What?"

"Both. Intense. And nice. It's hard to find both together."

"Is it?"

He grinned and stood, reached for her hand. "Come on. Nella said you didn't eat with her. I'll make you breakfast and then you can come back and rest."

"I don't want to eat."

He sat again, leaned in, and stroked her hair. "I know you don't. And I haven't said anything but you've lost weight again and that has to stop. Don't bother to argue. Come eat. Or I'll go down and tell Stu you kissed me a hell of a lot better than you kissed him."

"You would not."

He stood, started to leave.

"I'm getting up." Ignoring his victorious gloating, she pushed herself to her feet and ran fingers through her hair, paused to grab a pony holder to replace the one she gave Nella, and then held him and snuggled her face into his neck. Yes, he was stubborn and facetious and annoying to no end. But no one on earth had been there for her the way he had. He was her rock. Always. And he was right. The kiss had been nice.

10 December

"No, you don't need to tell him. I'll try another time." Susie heard

the agreement at the other end of the line at the McGuire residence and
hung up with a sigh. Laura was at school. Susie knew she would be. But
she thought Danny might be home.

Cooking school. Laura enjoyed cooking, but only now and then.
Susie didn't imagine she would stay with cooking school very long, but
she supposed it filled her time.

The apartment was quiet. She could go down to practice, where
Nella was since Evan took her with him. She wasn't sure she wanted to
go. Instead, she skimmed through her albums and pulled out *Chicago
VI*. She held it a bit as she decided whether she could deal with hearing
it, then put it on the record player and moved the needle to the second
song. She might as well plunge in.

As she listened to their song, she went to the most open part of her
living room and did light ballet moves with it. She didn't have much
space, but it felt good to allow her body to do as it wished, within her
small space. If she moved into the Victorian, she'd have plenty of room
to move around.

But she agreed to rent it to Doug.

And she didn't want to move in without Duncan, without ...
without the baby they were supposed to adopt. It was insane to miss
the child she didn't even know yet she would get, Susie supposed, but
she did.

As the song ended, she went to move the needle to the beginning
of the album. The phone interrupted. She waited for the machine to tell
her who it was before she picked it up. "Hey, I'm here."

"What's up, Sis? They said y' just tried t' call. Everything alright?"

"Yes. I also told them you didn't need to call back."

"Yea' and they told me. How are y' today?"

"I'm ... well, good enough, I guess. How many girlfriends do you
have by now? Can you still count them?"

He laughed. She loved to hear him laugh. "I am back with Amy.
And y' should try to reach me there. I am only stoppin' through
tonight. Thought I would use Gene's phone bill instead o' my own
since I am here."

She chuckled. "I can call back so it'll be on mine."

"Nae this is fine."

"Is it? You have time to talk or did I interrupt? If you have to go..."

"I 'ave as much time as y' want. Amy doesnae bitch abou' things like that. No' that she doesnae bitch, bu' about lesser things than about if I am home in the middle of the night or not. Odd lass. Y' might like her once y' get t' know her more."

"I liked her fine so far. So you're living with her again?"

"Aye for now. We will see 'ow it goes, right? Her parents still donae approve so much, bu' more than they did since I 'ave worked steady for ... however long it has been by now."

Susie pushed him to talk more about Amy, her parents, and his job, then Laura's school which he agreed she wouldn't stick with, and a few family updates. Gene interrupted when he found she was on the phone, talked for a few minutes, then told Danny to take his time. They sounded civil. More than civil. It sounded actually friendly. It was good. It would be nice for both of them to connect better. Gene would gladly take Danny as his son if Danny would let him. At twenty-six, he didn't technically need a father, still...

Still. She was twenty-four and couldn't imagine not having hers. The thought of Danielle having to do without rushed in and she shoved it back out. Not fast enough. Danny asked what was wrong.

"No. Nothing. Sorry."

"It has been quiet at your end. Where is li'l Nella bird?"

"At practice. Evan took her because she was driving me crazy."

"Aye and then why are y' nae down at practice, as well?"

"I don't know."

A pause. "He would want y' to go, t' stay involved, since it means so much t' you."

"Yeah. I suppose."

"Y' donae have t' suppose. I know he would. Go on down and be with your friends. They are lookin' after y' well, yes? I havenae talked t' Stu recently."

"They are, but I can take care of myself. I'm a big girl." She teased.

"Aye right. Y' arenae all too big. I am surprised my brother didnae hurt y' as whole-hearted as he does ... did anything he enjoyed."

She couldn't help but laugh, despite how inappropriate the comment. "Yes well, I'm not all that fragile, either, despite what people think."

Another pause. "And I am glad t' know I was wrong abou' tha' as well, Sis. Still..." His tone lightened again. "Y' might consider that when y' decide y' want another mate. At some point. And make sure the bloke knows we are still your family an' will be watchin'."

"Don't worry. I don't plan to ever give you up." And she had to change the subject but couldn't figure out how through the silence.

"Laura 'as come in and is going t' clobber me if I donae let her talk t' you, so I will go on back to Amy now. Go t' practice, Suse. Keep them in line well and keep them working. Tell Stu I said hello."

She talked to Laura a good half an hour. By that time, it was too late to bother going downstairs. Instead, she rifled through her cabinets and started dinner. It was half done by the time Evan knocked. But it wasn't Evan.

Stu sniffed the air. "Wow that smells good. What are you making? I brought your kid back, by the way, since Evan has plans and she didn't want to stop building her *Sco'ish castle*, so she called it."

Nella talked about how big it was as she ran into the kitchen saying she was hungry. Susie started to follow, but Doug and Ali showed up at the door before she got it closed. "Come on in." She chased her daughter. "Nella, get out of that. Dinner's almost ready."

"I hungry my mummy. I want 'nana."

"Not now. Go wash." At the girl's argument, Doug picked her up and took her to the living room.

Ali handed Susie an envelope. "I wanted to give you this. Of course you don't have to come and I'd understand if you don't. It's going to be bigger than I wanted. My parents have invited everyone they've ever known like it's a big deal."

"It is a big deal." Doug set an arm around her as he came back. "You've worked hard for this."

An invitation to Alison's graduation party.

"Anyway, I wanted to invite you but don't feel obligated to be there. I know how you feel about crowds and you deal with it enough..."

"Of course I'll be there. Doug's right. Thank you for wanting me there."

"Oh Suse, other than Doug and my family, you're the closest friend I've ever had. Of course I'll be delighted if you come, but like I said, there will be a lot of people..."

"That's okay. I wouldn't dare miss it." She gave Ali a hug. "I'll hang out with Stu and he can deal with the crowd for me."

"Sounds good to me. Hey, does that make you my date?" Stu taste tested the soup and put the lid back on the pot. "Wow that's as good as it smells."

"You're welcome to stay for dinner. Any of you."

Ali grinned. "Thanks. Mom's expecting us."

"I'll stay and mooch. I'm not proud." Stu nudged up to her side.

Susie chuckled. "Maybe ask next door, too. I did make plenty."

"Yeah they have plans, like I said. Double date."

Double date. He hadn't said that. Evan was dating?

"Kelly's bringing a friend. I've met her. So has Evan. She's not a blind date. Super hot, though. Majorly stacked and..."

Ali shoved him as Nella came back.

Super hot. Susie hoped she had a decent personality to go along with it. Maybe she'd be the one to give Evan that kiss he wanted: both nice and intense.

"So anyway." Ali rubbed Nella's head. "Bring her, too. There will be plenty of kids. Mike and Keith already accepted. And I'm so glad you'll be there."

"I'm so proud of you for this, you know, for doing this around the restaurant and his schedule. You'll be an incredible teacher."

Ali blushed. "Oh, well it's not just me. Doug's been so understanding about it. I can't imagine how I would have, otherwise."

"Of course he is. He's darn lucky to have you and he's smart enough to know it." She gave Doug a grin and told Nella to entertain Stu until dinner, somewhere other than in the kitchen.

As Doug and Ali left, Stu asked if she wanted the record playing since the stereo was turned on. She told him he could turn it back on if he wanted, or change it, and gathered the tomatoes to slice to go along with the hamburger and vegetable soup which Nella would fuss about.

Really stacked. Nice. Why did she have to know that?

The knife she pulled out was too dull so she rinsed it and grabbed a different one.

Hot. Not a blind date. He'd met her. When? At a show maybe? But they'd only had a couple recently and Susie had been to both, and when he wasn't on stage he was with her. Although she'd told him not to be. She told him to go socialize. To date. She told him to date.

He actually listened to her. She was surprised.

That one was dull, also. Too hard to cut tomatoes with a dull blade.

Or he only ... needed a date.

The third knife was just as bad and she slammed it on the counter. Maybe she needed a date, too. No. She didn't. And she didn't want one.

"What's wrong, Suse?"

"Nothing. Trying to find one of these sharp enough to work right."

Stu moved in. Looked at the several knives on the counter. "They will sharpen, you know."

"Yeah, but I hate doing it. Duncan always did it for me because I hate the sound and the feel of it." And their song was on.

"Where do you keep the sharpener?" He opened drawers and found it before she could tell him.

"You don't need to do that. I will."

"I don't mind. It doesn't bother me."

"Oh, but I..."

Stu paused and met her eyes. "I'm glad to take over stuff like this, or Evan would if you asked."

"I don't need to be babied. I can do it."

"Hey, it's a small thing in return for all the meals I mooch. I could cook for myself if I wanted, too, but I'd rather sharpen your knives." He set it down for a moment and hugged her. "It's okay to let us help." Backing up, he told Nella to set the game up and he'd be there in a minute. "Besides, the sharper I make these, the faster you can cut stuff up so food's ready and I can get out of playing *Candyland*." He rolled his eyes with a grin.

13 December

Evan was glad to see her dancing. The other guys would be down for practice any minute but for now, he stood back and left her alone. Genesis, their newest. The first song of the first side, which means she'd barely started. He hated that they'd interrupt. Maybe he could hold them off a while as long as no one had plans for after practice.

Her strength was coming back, her flexibility, her control. She extended into an arabesque, modernized, straight out instead of angled, held it still, released slowly. Beautiful. The girl was such a beautiful dancer; it was a shame to keep it hidden. John asked him to help encourage her to go back to teaching. Evan figured he'd do one better than that, when it was time. She needed to do more with it than teach. He would push her that direction. When she had enough of her strength back. There was no reason for her not to, now that she had the only child she could have and he didn't see her tying herself to anyone in a hell of a long time. She might as well get back on her own path. He could work his schedule around her, around supporting her.

The next song was slow, emotional, and she changed from modern style mixed with ballet to ballet touched with her own style and the feel of the music. *Undertow.* She could relate. Too well. And it showed in her movements, her expressions.

He startled at a touch to his shoulder. Mike. He didn't bother to speak, only gave him a look as though he understood, and watched with him. By the time the song ended, Stu and Doug were there. They decided they should let her know they were intruding on her privacy.

Stu jogged over and joined her until she gave up and took the needle from the record.

"Don't stop." Evan moved closer. "We can wait."

"No, it's okay. I was only stretching out, trying to get my blood moving."

"You haven't even broken a sweat. Go ahead, Suse." She gave in when the others agreed and started it on *Snowbound*, with a quick glance at him. After the song, she turned it off again, grabbed her sweatshirt ... Duncan's sweatshirt, and pulled it over her head.

They went ahead with practice and she jumped back in, using their music, just to keep moving, easy, light. And she sang to some of the lyrics as she danced. Mike tried to pull her up to sing with him. She refused. Nella and Keith came down with Kate ... and Kelly and Mary Ellen. Evan stopped, held up the band, although Nella had joined her mom and was dancing with her. Susie hadn't seen Mike's girlfriend yet, or his own date. Why in the hell was she there?

Kate explained. She'd heard the knock on the door and let them in, said she was about to go downstairs, and invited them. Without anyone's permission. Mike greeted Kelly with a kiss and told her to have a seat. He introduced Susie and Mary Ellen. Evan made himself greet the girl, but with no kiss involved. He echoed his friend's invitation to stay and listen, not by choice. Kate was having far too much fun over his discomfort.

As they got back to practice, Nella begged her mom to keep dancing with her and Susie gave in. It was only simple movement with the beat and showing Nella a couple of steps she picked up easily, then she pulled Keith out. The boy flushed and tried to pull away but his mom came over and insisted. It didn't take Kate and Nella long to get Keith to relax and smile as he bopped along with the music. Evan figured it was more Nella than Kate; she was good for his shyness because she refused to acknowledge it.

Susie let them at it and backed away, stood by herself watching the kids and the band, enjoying the music even with its glitches. Evan noticed Mary Ellen look over at her, a curious expression on her face, then say something to Kelly. Kelly shrugged it off. Mary Ellen kept watching her. When Mike insisted they do their newest, the one Stu had begged Evan to do lyrics for, then begged him to sing it, Susie moved closer.

It made him nervous, her attention so rapt on his singing, on his words. He did a bad job of it and stopped, talked to Stu about a spot he didn't like, started again.

She smiled at him as it ended. "That was beautiful. It's yours, right? Your words?"

He gave her a nod and Stu jumped in to explain how he had to nearly twist his arm off to get him to do it.

"It's nice, Evan. Really. That has to be on the next album."

The guys agreed and pushed him to try it again. And she danced to it. Along the side away from the other girls. But it was beautiful. His eyes stayed on her the whole time.

Susie wiped her forehead and wondered if Evan was satisfied since she'd more than broken a sweat. Figuring she better be polite to the women she didn't want there, she pulled a chair beside Kate, at the far end from Mary Ellen. Kelly told her she looked great, she was such a good dancer, which she'd heard from Mike but it was nice to finally see. The woman beside her echoed the same thoughts but it was fake. As was the smile. Stu was right; she was stacked and curvy, but her face had a sharp edge to it and her blouse was too tight. She went on about her first date with Evan and that she planned to get even farther this time even if he was a gentleman, at which Kelly tried to hush her and Kate chuckled. Susie went to play with the kids.

When they took a break, he came to her first, complimented her on how well she was coming back, on how strong she was starting to look again. As he touched her arm and turned to go talk to his date, she supposed, Susie stopped him. "She's not close to good enough, either. Try again."

He raised his eyebrows but didn't comment. He also didn't accept when Mary Ellen tried to get him to go somewhere with her when he was done.

Get farther ... it meant he didn't sleep with her although she'd tried. Susie was glad for that. The woman wasn't close to good enough. Maybe Kate was right; maybe she'd never think anyone would be, but this one wasn't close.

Susie stayed through the end of practice, although it was running into dinner time and she was hungry and Nella was getting fidgety. She wanted to be there, to hear what she'd missed by only coming now and then and leaving early. They were set to do short tours starting in January, a few days here and there just to get out again, to show some album support. Evan wanted her to go. They all wanted her to go. She should, as management, but she hadn't decided yet if she could.

As he crouched to talk with Nella, Susie turned the album over and put it on the last song: *Follow You, Follow Me.* She'd been following him since she was seventeen and she would have sooner than that if she'd been allowed. The song reminded her of him, always. And of course she would go.

She went over and asked him to dance, in between Mary Ellen trying again to get him to go out with her.

He accepted and set his arms around her waist. She rested hers over his shoulders. The song wasn't fully appropriate; it was about a couple, but it was close enough. Wherever either of their roads led, the other would be there, also. In some way. Always.

He held her in as it ended.

15 December

Susie did her best to stay at the sidelines at Ali's graduation party. Stu's mom kept drawing her in, though, and attracted too much attention by asking if she needed anything or talking with Danielle, bringing people over to talk with her any time she happened to escape for a few moments. One of Ali's cousins kept hitting on her until Stu noticed and backed him away.

Mainly, she stayed with Evan or Mike. Mike's girlfriend hadn't come with him, although Kate was there and took some of his attention. She left Keith with him most of the time. It worked well. Nella and Keith entertained each other and played with the other kids while Susie and Mike hung out and kept an eye on them. Doug's sister spent a lot of time with Evan, since she'd gathered more nerve than she had the last time they'd been around each other, at a New Year's Eve party a couple of years earlier. She was still single. Apparently, Doug's family went into marriage rather cautiously. His parents had mentioned they were nearly thirty when they married.

Susie was still the only one who knew of Doug's plans for Ali's graduation gift. She looked forward to it nearly as much as if it would be her getting the proposal, with the memory of her proposal still so keen in her thoughts. A deep breath pushed it back further.

"Can I get you anything?" Doug touched her shoulder.

"No, of course not. You have guests. Don't worry about me."

"Ali has guests."

"Yes well, it's pretty much the same thing by now, isn't it?"

"Soon. I hope."

"Are you nervous?"

He glanced over at where Ali laughed with Stu's brother. "Yes. I'm thinking I may change my mind and wait until we're not surrounded."

"Then I won't get to see it, and I've really looked forward to this. Maybe I shouldn't tell you that."

"To seeing me act like a stammering fool in front of both of our families and most of our friends?"

"You won't. And I mean to her reaction. It seems like only..." She stopped. It wasn't fair to bring her own into it.

He leaned in. "It was only. But someday, when you've had time to heal, this will happen for you again."

"No." She shook her head. "No, I ... I can't even..."

He gave her a hug. "I know you can't yet. But you're young, Suse. Don't mourn forever. I have to tell you, you and Duncan are what pushed me to this faster than I expected. I'd planned to wait until the band was doing less, winding down, so it would be more fair to her. But..."

"Don't waste the time while you have it." She felt her eyes water, but she wouldn't let them overflow. Not on Ali's day.

"Right." He touched her face. "Eventually, I may tell you the same thing."

"So you don't think we pushed too fast? Barely knowing each other?" She was teasing. He was the only one who had never suggested they were back when their four month acquaintance became a proposal.

"Apparently not. It sure worked well. And it would have..."

"He's over there flirting with Susie."

They both turned at Stu's voice in the near distance. Ali grinned at them, hushed Stu, and asked if she could borrow her boyfriend a while. She wanted him there for the gift opening. Doug leaned in to finish his thought. "It would have kept working beaufully. The two of you were an inspiration to all of us. You should know that. You chose well, Suse. And you will again."

Susie couldn't argue with Doug when he insisted she come up farther with him. She did stop outside the inner circle of their families. She wouldn't cross that far. Finding herself beside Stu, she nodded when he asked if she was okay.

Ali was a certified teacher with plans to teach first grade or as close to that as she could get. Some of the gifts were funny things such as chalk and erasers and a big wooden paddle. Stu commented now and then into Susie's ear; she chuckled and told him to behave. Susie had given her a big gift basket full of things to help her relax at the end of a noisy day: herb tea, soft music, candles, a couple of bottles of wine, and an inscribed wine glass that said *Teacher's Aid.*

Doug saved his for last by hiding it in another room until she thought she had finished. Then Evan brought it out. It was a big box, wrapped all in white with a green ribbon, Ali's favorite color. Getting it open, she pulled out tissue paper piece by piece, laughing at him for making her dig through the box. She asked if a box full of tissue was supposed to be the gift or a hint that she might need them. He told her to keep looking. She got to the bottom, held frozen a moment, and pulled out a small jewelry box.

Doug took it from her as Evan pulled the box out of the way. "Alison, I'm so very proud of the way you fought to get here, for what you want, through everything, even while you put so many others first, through staying up until all hours to finish what needed to have done so you could still be there for those who needed you, which includes me. You've always been there when I needed you. And you did all of it with grace and class and elegance. I'm proud to be part of your life." He lowered to one knee. "I want to always be part of your life, to be at your side as you begin your new career. I will help you succeed in any way I can, as you've done for me. I will always cherish you. I will always respect and honor you. I will do my best to always show you how much I love you." He kissed her fingers. "Ali, will you do me the honor of being my wife?"

Her hands shook, tears falling. "Yes. Of course, yes."

Susie had to wipe her own eyes as he slid the ring onto her finger and Ali grabbed him in a hug. She felt Stu's hand on her back and his body close in more. Maybe he knew, also. He didn't seem surprised. They stayed back while the families gave their hugs and congratulations. Ali's parents loudly welcomed him to the family and said they couldn't be more pleased with her choice. Doug's parents were more quiet about it, accepting but not gushing. Susie couldn't imagine they had ever, at any time in their lives, gushed about anything, maybe not even about their own proposal. She found it sad.

Of course, Stu's mom gushed all over Doug and Ali, then let Stu know it should be his turn soon.

He laughed, raising his eyebrows at Susie. "Yeah, can you just see that? Me? Trying to convince any girl she should actually tie herself to me forever? Nah, I don't see it happening."

His mom patted his arm but looked at Susie. "Tell him he'll change his mind some day. He needs a girl to help take care of him."

"Yes, I'm sure he will some day." She grinned at Stu. "Any time soon, I can't see."

"No damn kidding it won't be any time soon if it happens. Hey, the bride-to-be is free, or close enough." He dashed between a couple of people to envelop Ali in a big hug, until Doug backed him off.

Susie had to congratulate Doug first. "I'm so happy for you."

"Thank you." He caught her eyes only a moment before Ali showed her the ring and accepted a hug. And Susie moved back into the background, letting Evan and Mike move in, shuffling farther away toward the crowd's edge, with the excuse of finding Danielle and Keith.

She sat on a folding chair nearby and watched them build a fort with Lincoln Logs, using Little People from Fisher Price buildings to populate their village. Blissfully unaware of what the adults were doing. Lost in their own little imaginative world.

Stu's brother came to talk and invited her to stay with them in New

Hampshire if she ever wanted an escape. Susie looked up at Evan as he joined them. "Thank you. Maybe some day. I've heard how quiet it is, and how pretty."

He acknowledged Evan's presence. "You're both welcome."

"We'll keep that in mind." Susie hadn't meant to answer for them both. She had no business answering for Evan. But she couldn't imagine going up there without him, if she ever decided to escape to New Hampshire. Or anywhere else.

Stu's brother excused himself. She was glad to be alone with Evan as they sat and watched the kids, talking a bit and staying silent together. And she was more than ready when he asked if she wanted to go home.

16 December

Five months.

She needed to go down to practice. She told Evan she would. But she had trouble making her feet move. He'd been away for five months. "Duncan, come home already." She clenched her eyes and tried to feel him, tried to hear him answer. It had been too long since she felt his presence, since he assured her he'd be back.

She smoothed the pillow case she'd just put back on the bed. It had taken her too long to make herself wash his with the rest of the sheets. But it didn't smell of him anymore and she wanted it fresh for when...

Crumpling down onto his side of the bed, Susie lay there and held his pillow. She'd washed it off, the part of him that was still there. But it wasn't. Now it truly wasn't. It smelled like fresh laundry.

She had to do it; she *had* to. Just like she'd had to wash his T-shirts that she'd been wearing. They couldn't stay dirty. They'd held their scent for some time, through several washings. Now they didn't, either.

Her insides burned with frustration, anger, with ... sorrow. She'd allowed it too far in, allowed herself to start thinking she was wrong, he wasn't coming home as they all said he wasn't. It hurt as much as it had that first day, the burning aching all-consuming pain through every inch of her body. "Duncan. Please. You said you would. I need you home. I can't do this anymore." Her tears fell on his pillow. She didn't care.

Kate knocked. No answer. Evan said she was coming down but it had been an hour and she was concerned. Especially because of the date. Trying the door, it opened and she called Susie's name as she went into what used to be the apartment they shared. No sign of her.

"Suse?" She moved slowly down the hall, somewhat afraid to find her, to find that she'd decided she couldn't ... just couldn't. Susie was far too unstable these days. Kate was never sure what she might do. Good thing she had Nella. Kate was fully sure she'd put Nella first, before...

She was on her bed, on Duncan's side, cuddled up with his pillow in her arms. "Are you awake?" Susie ducked her face farther into his pillow and Kate sat next to her. "Hey, come on. Come downstairs with me. The guys want your opinion..."

Sobs shook her body.

"Oh Suse, come on, sweetie." Kate stroked her hair, pulled it from her face. "You still have so much. You have a beautiful little girl who adores you and you have so many of us who love you and we're right here to help. Evan's worried. He said you were coming down. So come on now. It's good to let it out. You did that. Come clean your face and come downstairs. I'll sit with you. We'll bring tissue, as much as you need." Kate tried to coerce her up. "Come on, Suse." There was an advantage to being stronger, largely from her exercise with Mike through the past few years, private and playful exercise. She'd yet to find a man who could live up to that.

She imagined Susie had one, though. As she pulled her friend into her arms and cuddled her, Kate decided to tease her out of it, like Stu did, but girl-style. Best girl friend style. "I know what it really is, you know. You have all kinds of friends, people to talk to and hang out with, so it has to be his body, right? You were lying there wishing it was his hard firm really sexy body you were holding onto."

Susie grabbed at more tissue and wiped her nose.

"Yeah, it's gotta be tough to have that in your bed every night and then not have it. Although it's gotta be tough for those who never get to have that, too. Kinda why I keep going back to Mike, because damn he's hard to replace. At least that way, he is. The moody shit I can find anywhere. But you think his voice is sexy? That's nothing compared to..."

"Kate." She sniffed.

"Come on, Suse. It's girl talk. Girls do it, you know. It's normal and healthy and all that jazz. So, you could tell me now. If he's up there listening, he won't mind. Might even get a laugh out of it, right? Was he as good as he looked like he would be?"

She shook her head, but she chuckled. Through her tears.

"No? Are you telling me he wasn't? I have a hard time believing that."

"Stop."

"No, come on. He really won't care. He told me once you liked to be forceful, and if he can say that, you can..."

"No he didn't."

"Yeah, he did. Honest. Not that I believed him. It was a joke. I know it was a joke. Still, he wouldn't care. Just a hint?"

She shook her head again.

"Fine, but I'm going to keep trying." Kate stood and grasped her hand. "And it's really okay to admit you miss all the incredible sex. Not like I don't know."

"Do you ever think of anything else?"

"Nah. Well, now and then. You know, if I'm dealing with slobby ugly men you don't really want to have to look at, then I think about anything else in the world, like ... strawberry ice cream."

"You hate strawberry ice cream."

"Yeah, I do, but not as much as I hate jiggling slobby ugly men. Really, they could have some self-respect."

"That's mean, Kate."

"Yeah well, I never said I wasn't. And I'd rather eat strawberry ice cream by the gallon than to have to be leered at by those things when you just *know* what they're thinking and you know you'd vomit if you even considered doing it with them..."

"You're horrible." She wiped her nose.

"Yeah but you know, I work hard to look like this. Why should I bother with anyone who doesn't just because they don't want to bother but still want what I work for? Not gonna happen." She tugged on Susie's hand until she got her to her feet. "So let's go on down and leer at some kinda sexy guys who do kinda take care of themselves and have to let us leer since they're working and stuck with us watching."

"Kinda sexy?"

"Well, you know, some more than others. Stu's kinda cute but not sexy. And Doug .... well, he could be but he's stuffy and that interferes."

"He's not stuffy. He's quiet."

"Whatever. Kinda the same."

"That's why you call Evan stuffy? Because he's quiet?"

"No, I call Evan stuffy because he is. Still, he's kinda sexy, too. Gotta admit it. Yeah?"

Susie swallowed hard and wiped at her eyes. "I washed his pillow case."

"What? Evan's? Why? He can't do his own?"

"No. Duncan's. I washed it. It was... It's been..."

"Well I would sure as hell hope you did. Damn Suse, you mean just today? I hope you're kidding."

"It was barely used. And ... it smelled like him. Now it ... smells like fresh laundry."

Kate pulled her in again. "Yeah, fresh laundry smell isn't near as sexy as sweaty man in your bed smell."

She chuckled. Her shoulders shook. And she kept laughing until her body engulfed itself in deep gasping breaths. At least Kate thought it was laughter. Maybe not. Maybe a mix.

"Alright. Go wash your face. I bet we can find some sweaty man smell pretty easy. Not quite the same as it being in your bed, but it's a start."

Kate was taking her friend out of the apartment. The girl needed to get out and about again, the crowd be damned. They could take a couple of guards and shop. Susie needed a girl's shopping day. Maybe she could get her to flirt or to at least look.

17 December

Why had she agreed to go shopping with Kate? It was too soon. But still, why couldn't she just go shopping and not be ... be accused of...

Susie pushed her hand against her head and asked Nella to please quiet down. She wanted to hear about Nella's day at Doug's house, never mind it wasn't really Doug's house, it was her house, but still, it was nice of them to let Nella and Keith run around the house while they were setting it up, getting ready to move in. They wouldn't until after they were married. Ali wouldn't. Not that she wouldn't be spending plenty of time there, usually alone with Doug. Kate's comment about a sexy man in your bed popped in her head and made it throb worse.

"Nella, I hear you. Don't yell."

At a knock on the door, Susie sighed and checked. She let Evan in. "That was fast. We just walked in the door."

"Beau said you're not feeling well. Another headache?"

"Nice of him to let you know." Susie wasn't sure if she meant it sincerely or sarcastically. Evan seemed not to be sure, either, but he didn't mention it.

He stayed with her through the evening, made an easy dinner, entertained Nella, and once the girl was in bed, he got Susie to tell him about her day, about how some woman had bumped into her, hard, called her a bitch, and explained to someone with her who Susie was and how she was never good enough for him and now refused anyone else to share in her memory because she was cold-hearted and already sleeping with two other *friends* in the band or maybe all of them, and ... how Kate jumped in to yell, called the woman not only a stupid bitch but also an ignorant ass and whatever else Susie blocked out. Security came, along with Beau who stood with Susie as Kate fended for herself quite well. By the time they got out of the mall to the parking lot, some reporter was there with a camera.

"I just wanted a regular day, you know. I'm trying hard to just get through the days and Kate thought this would be nice and I suppose it would have been, but... Why can't they leave me alone? I can't deal with this now." She gripped his shirt.

"I know, Angel. You shouldn't have to, and I have to say I'm glad Kate came back at her."

"Are you really? How is that going to look for the band?"

"She's not part of the band. Mike's dating Kelly and that's well known by now. What she does is on her, not us. So yes, I'm glad she did. And even if she was actually with Mike and more connected with the band, I would be glad she did and I wouldn't expect her to do otherwise. You've done enough for her. It's time she stepped up to be your friend."

Susie allowed herself to sink into him and close her eyes. *Cold-hearted.* If she wasn't so tired, she would laugh. It would be so much easier if she was cold-hearted.

20 December

"Suse, I am so sorry. It's me she's trying to get to..."

"Don't worry about it, Lee." Susie cringed when her daughter tried to dive as Robin showed her and instead belly-flopped. She gave Nella credit, though. The girl only rubbed her stomach and frowned and got up to try again. Adam had pushed them to have the meeting at his place and invited them to unwind in the pool afterward. It was nice, Susie had to admit, to sit around a table on the deck with the humid warmth surrounding them, along with the frosted from steam windows that barely allowed a view of the trees along the property.

Robin entertained Nella and Keith while Adam ran the meeting. Susie half considered joining the swimmers instead...

She realized they were still talking about Mary Ellen and how she'd told whoever would listen how rude Susie was not to speak to her, how distant she was, with everyone but Evan who she'd hung all over. When led to it, the woman said yes, she figured the rumors of the two of them were true, from what she saw.

There was talk of countering it. Again. For what purpose, Susie couldn't imagine. What more was at stake? The adoption was cancelled. Her husband was ... was maybe with someone easier on his nerves by now. With Raucous not doing much, any talk of them for whatever purpose would be better than nothing. Why did it matter what she did?

"Angel?"

"What?" She forced herself to look at him instead of the kids.

Stu laughed that they'd called her name and she didn't even hear it, but she sure enough heard when Evan called her by her nickname.

"I can easily enough say she's only upset that I stopped dating her. And I'll rebut the rumors..."

"Why?" She continued with his questioning gaze. "Seriously, Evan, how would you argue with her? She's right; well, except for the rumors, she's right. I was rude. I did avoid her. And I did hang all over you in front of her, if that's the way she wants to look at it. I don't like her and I did want to help discourage her. It would be hard to deny. Why should we bother?"

Stu laughed. "Right. Tell it the way it is. I didn't like her, either. But she is majorly stacked. I didn't mind looking at her. You coulda kept her around just a while longer, Ev."

Susie shrugged. Stu was trying to get to her. It wasn't going to work. "Yes, he could have. I could have kept ignoring and given her even more reason to call me rude."

"Kelly feels bad for bringing her." Mike tapped Adam's pencil on the table. "She told her off, not that it matters now. But she didn't expect this and she told me to let you know she's sorry and if you don't want her around..."

"That's ridiculous. She's your girlfriend. It's your right to have her around."

"Well, we did tell Stu not to bring his girls to the apartment because it was causing trouble. I can't very well refuse to do the same."

"It's not the same. Girls and girlfriends are different. And you know, I don't care how many girls Stu brings to his place. It's his right and ... we probably never should have asked him not to." Susie set her hand on Stu's arm. "I'm sorry. It was unfair..."

"Hell. No, you're right. It is different. I like Kelly, too. Keep bringing her around. She's also not bad to look at..."

Susie smacked his arm. "Don't be a pig. I like her."

He laughed. Mike said it was a good thing she did, so she was still allowed.

"And you, don't be an ass. I just said it wasn't fair to say who could or couldn't come to the building. It was ... the adoption. It had me too much on edge. You shouldn't have let it interfere with everything. But it doesn't matter now..."

"It still matters." Evan leaned forward, his arms crossed on the table. "Suse, it still matters. And I think we need to counter this."

"Why? Hell, Evan, maybe we should just do it and get it over with so at least they have reason to talk about us."

Stu nearly choked. Mike dropped his jaw. Doug was amused. Adam lowered his face and scratched his nose. Evan... Evan looked far too serious.

"I'm kidding. It was a joke. Like countering rumors, you know? It's a joke because it doesn't work and... It was a joke."

"Maybe it shouldn't be." Mike eyed them both.

"Right. Because I would ever do something like that just because of what people are saying." Susie tried not to see whatever Evan was thinking. She supposed she shouldn't have joked about it.

"I agree with her." Doug leaned back in his chair. "I think you should say nothing. Ignore it the way..."

"The way Duncan always did." Susie finished it for him.

"Yes. Answering it looks like you're bothered by it. Ignoring it says you're not concerned what they think."

"Or it looks like we can't deny it." Evan was now staring at the table between his arms.

Maybe he was right. Susie didn't care for herself. As Stu told her some time back, maybe people would leave her alone after they pulled her from whatever pedestal they thought she was on. But she didn't want to pull Evan down with her. "You know what? Let me. That'll look better. I'll handle it."

He met her eyes. "Handle it how?"

"Trust me."

"Angel..."

"You know I have your best interest at heart, right? Like Adam does. I'm assistant manager. It's my job. Trust me to do it."

"I trust you completely to look after the band's interest. You know I do." He unwrapped his arms and took her hand. "I'm just not sure I trust that you won't sacrifice yourself for us, and I don't want that."

"What more can they do, Lee? What more can I lose? They can't take my daughter away just because of..."

"That won't happen." His back straightened.

She gave him a grin. "No, I know. And I know you'll be here." Susie heard the guys chime in that they would be, also, but she kept attention on him. "Sacrifice what?"

"Okay, a question then. What happens ... when, eventually you get remarried? And I figure you will somewhere down the line. You're not going to try to adopt again? You don't think what happens now might affect that?"

Married again. She felt her head shake. "No. I have no plans to get married again and if I do, it would be ... so far down the line that... No, I don't think anything that happens now will matter by then." She wouldn't need to get remarried. Duncan would be home. They were already on the list once; they'd have to put them back on it. Or they wouldn't. She couldn't let that one thought run her life any longer. She shouldn't have for as long as she did. It had been unfair to her husband. A mistake. But she would learn from it. Duncan was right. It didn't matter what people thought. If they had to, they'd use their influence, their name, their ... their money, to pull influence. Why not? All of that was causing the problem in the first place. If any of this happened to anyone else, no one would pay attention. They were being slammed only because of the band's popularity. Why shouldn't they use it to their advantage, also?

Evan nodded, a thoughtful nod but unconvinced. "Well, what you say about it is up to you. But think about it first. It won't hurt us either way. Fair or not, your reputation, as a woman, will bother people more than ours does. That's changing, I realize, but still..."

Susie leaned in and kissed the side of his face. "Thank you for worrying. But don't. I'm a big girl. I'll handle whatever gets thrown at me, or duck from it, whichever I'd rather at the time. Either way, you need to stop worrying." She leaned back. "But, maybe be more choosy about your dates so I don't have to be so rude to them."

"Or don't bring them to the building." Stu got a smirk from Evan and leaned closer to her. "Hey, if you wanna get the rumors away from the two of you, I'm still free and open and willing and all. Just a reminder. I'll even let you say we are when we're not. But you know..."

"Thank you. Stop there."

Adam routed the conversation to other business. Show dates. Venue info. Specifically whether she planned to go with them. With a glance at Evan, she nodded. "It's my job, right?"

Evan tried to get her to swim after the meeting. She nearly gave in. But she backed away and sat with Adam. As she watched the boys and kids play, Susie couldn't help think about Kate's sexy, sweaty men comments. And she was wrong about Stu. He was sexy: not knock out sexy, but he was in good shape and had some muscle to him. And he was adorable. Adorable was always sexy, as far as she was concerned.

Doug and Mike both had very nice builds. Doug was a bit stockier along with his extra height but Mike was sleek and obviously worked more on his abs. Kate's doing, maybe. That was a must for her.

Evan, though... Kate's "kinda sexy" comment didn't come close. Evan was knock out sexy. The most muscular, the broadest, the most perfectly formed legs and arms... definitely the sexiest of the group. At least now he was, and maybe he was anyway. Duncan had fit her so much better; he wasn't so severely bigger than she was, but...

He caught her looking at him. Susie decided to play it off and signed: *it wouldn't be too terribly horrible* – one of Kate's phrases for guys she wouldn't mind doing. And she winked. He laughed and told Mike to never mind when he asked what she said.

Keith came to sit with her, his large beach towel draped over his little shoulders and held closed with a little hand.

"Do you want to go change, honey?" When he nodded, she told him to go ahead, he knew where the changing room was. Adam had one connected to both the pool and the house, a walk through. Keith tilted his head down and raised his eyes. "Want me to walk with you?" At another nod, Susie got up and took his hand. Mike said he could go by himself, but she shrugged and said she needed to get up and move a bit anyway. Nella followed. She was done, too. Robin took her to the girls' side as Susie waited outside the door for Keith.

"The boy wouldn't even change in the same room with us." Mike rolled his eyes as he came over. "A four year old shouldn't be worried about that, should he?"

"Oh I don't know. I hear I was that shy that soon."

"Yeah, not surprised on that, but ... you know, most men aren't. I guess some are, but..."

"He's not a man. He's four, barely."

"Right, so why would he be uptight already?"

She studied his face; he was actually concerned. "Why does it bother you?"

"Well." Mike shoved wet hair back from his face. His skin dripped water around his feet. "I guess with ... the way he's growing up, and Kate's penchant for... well..."

"For sex?" She grinned at his raised eyebrows. "Not like I don't know. Probably more than you wish I knew."

"Ah well, can't say I'm surprised. I know she talks and I've told you she does." He shrugged. "No guilty conscience in that department. She can say what she wants. But, I do worry about her lifestyle scarring him. I keep thinking I need to ... I don't know, settle and give him a steadier base, away from whatever she's doing."

"She doesn't when he's there. That much, I know. If she has plans and you're busy, I get him. I think it's fine. He's just geared that way. There's no harm in it. And honestly, I'd be less worried about that than I am about Nella's complete lack of fear."

"Her father's kid. He did okay."

"Right but..."

"Understood. But she has good sense along with it, like he did. I can see that already. She'll be fine, Suse. And you think Keith is okay and it's just ... innate?"

"I would guess so. He doesn't shy away from affection or anything."

"He does with Kate. Unless she goes to him for a hug. He won't try anymore."

Susie grabbed a deep breath. "Well, I can't blame him for that. It's easier not to try than to try and be rejected. Yes, I've seen her do that. But you make up for it..."

"So do you. And I appreciate it."

"I just adore him, and Kate's an idiot at times, about some things. But I think Keith will be fine. He has good sense, too. He knows who to trust, who to look up to. He's smart enough to make that judgment from what he sees."

Mike gave her a quick hug. "Hope you're right. I think I'll go check on the boy whether or not he wants me to." He pushed the door open, but let it shut again and stepped closer. "She does brag about me, right? I mean, if she's being honest, she can say what she wants, but if she's not..."

"I don't let her brag as much as she tries. Too much information."

He gave her a sly grin. "Good to know." He disappeared as Nella and Robin came out.

"I hungry, my mummy. My Keith hungry, too. Yes."

Robin insisted on keeping Nella, waited on Keith, and took them both in for a snack. Mike tried to convince Susie to swim with them. She still refused, but she stayed there when Adam joined Robin inside. Leering at her band, in Kate's words. Not leering. Appreciating. She especially appreciated when Mike asked her advice about Keith. The personal openness was new, and maybe a test of sorts, but it was nice also. She was glad he realized he could be open with her, that maybe she wasn't quite as stuffy as he used to think.

But then, he used to be right. Things changed.

22 December

With Nella and Keith at Kate's to decorate cookies, since Kate liked to roll them out and bake them but hated to mess with frosting, Susie dragged Evan down to help her work out. She promised she wouldn't be bitchy. He laughed it off.

They worked with weights until she had enough and by then Stu had joined them, so Susie left the guys to spot each other, forcing herself not to think about the fact that it used to be Duncan working out with Evan, and slipped into her toe shoes. She changed the music to Billy Joel, Kate's album, on side two since her favorite was on that side, and pushed herself to advance her routine, to get the details right, the landings neat and precise, her frame more elongated and more controlled. By the time *She's Always A Woman* came on, Susie was getting tired and took it easier and softer. She didn't realize until the end of the song they'd given up on the weights and were watching.

When she sat to stretch and untie her shoes, Evan came over and sat next to her. "Very nice, Angel. That song looked like it was made for you."

She gave him a grin but didn't answer. He smelled like ... like sweaty male: sexy sweaty male, not acrid sweaty male. She wondered about her own scent. Did Duncan still remember her scent? Did it matter to him like it did to her? He'd told her once she didn't need perfume, so maybe it did. Or maybe by now, someone else's scent mattered to him.

He was still... He was. So if he hadn't bothered to come home...

Susie pushed to her feet and went to stop the music. She would go shower quick and then join Kate and the kids with the cookies. Nella was still with her. If he came back, Nella was still hers. Susie had stayed. Whoever he found and wherever he decided to be, Danielle was hers. She would not back down on that, if it ever came up. Never.

23 December

The sand tickled her toes as it sifted between them. Wet, cold sand. She dug her feet into it as she sat just far enough up on the beach the water wouldn't reach the rest of her. Only her toes. They were cold. It was too cold to swim. The water was frigid enough it sent a shock through her system when the wave brushed up to her toes.

"Come in, my luv."

She shook her head at him. Goose bumps covered his chest and his arms and yet he stood in the cold water beckoning to her. He handled cold better. She would freeze.

"I will keep y' warm, y' ken." He grinned and the blue eyes sparkled in a tease.

"How will you keep me warm when you're cold?"

"Aye and y' are right. I am cold ou' here on my own. Bu' I willnae be when y' are at my side. Come." He reached a hand to her.

She stood, brushed sand off her legs, off her arms ... how did it get on her arms when she was sitting up the whole time? ... off her stomach. She was in her black bikini, the one he loved. And she was cold. If she was cold anyway, she might as well join him. Creeping forward, the water splashed up onto her legs. She moved back. Too cold. Goose bumps covered her body. Still, he beckoned. She tried again, got as far in as her calves, nearly to her knees, but it splashed her stomach and ... and hurt. It was so cold, it hurt her skin. She backed out, shook her head. "I can't."

"Come, my luv. We will be warm together. Come and warm me." He moved backward, deeper into the water, until it was up to his chest.

"No. Duncan, no. Come back. It's too cold."

"Come to me."

"I can't. It's... I can't."

He slipped farther away, up to his chin. She was too frozen to move, too frozen to yell at him to stop, to come back. It was up to his nose.

"No." She headed into the water. Shivered. Shook head to toe. She saw only the top of his head and lunged toward him. Something pulled her back.

"It's too cold. You can't go in." The voice was soothing, but the strong arms held her back.

She couldn't see him, could only see a ripple where he'd been. "Come back. *No*, you *can't* go alone. Come back. Come *back*." She shook. Cold. Frightened. Alone on the beach. Sand between her toes. Wet, cold sand. It hurt her feet, like glass shards pricking at her.

Then he was next to her, behind her, warm; his arms held her and his heat seeped through her skin. "Stay ou' of the water, my luv. Stay warm and safe. I will be here with you. Only with you. Forever."

She turned to him. Nothing. No one was there.

"No. Come back." Her voice was a whisper. And she was cold

again.

"I here, my mummy. Yes." A soft hand touched her face.

Susie jumped. It was dark. She wasn't on the beach. Her room. The clock shined 5:00 am at her.

"Bad dream only." Nella stroked her hair the way Susie did to her after a nightmare. "I tell dream fairy no bad dreams for my mummy. Yes."

She remembered. Duncan had told Nella that after a nightmare. Susie cuddled her baby in against her and kissed her cheek. How did she remember that? He'd said it a few times. But it was ... nearly half a year ago and she was so young. "Want to stay here with me until time to get up?"

Nella nodded her sleepy little head. Coaxing her under the blanket, Susie felt guilty that she'd waken her daughter. Too cold. He was cold and asked for her and she didn't go. She didn't go. She should have.

Was it too late now? Could she have found him if she'd tried sooner?

Biting back the tears so Nella wouldn't see, Susie felt a cringe through her whole body. She'd failed him. She said no. She let herself be stopped.

Maybe she didn't deserve to have him back. But her daughter did.

Kate teased her son about getting coal in his stocking and then had to assure him she was only teasing. The kid was too sensitive, far more Susie's kid than hers. Nella, however ... Kate could claim Nella with as fiery as she was. Not that it would be a good idea, as Susie had said. Probably best her own kid was calm. But the sensitive shit drove her crazy.

And speaking of, in the middle of everyone decorating the tree beside the main door in front of the window, with far too many lights for her own taste, Susie went and sat by herself on the steps. She'd hardly said a word all day. Now she just sat and watched.

Not if Kate could help it. She went over and sat next to her. "It's not done yet."

"They're doing fine."

"Not the point. Come on." Kate stood and grasped her friend's hand. Susie pulled it away and she sat again. "Feel okay?" She got a nod. "Yeah then what's wrong?"

"I'm fine."

"No you're not. What happened?"

Susie's chest rose high and fell hard. "I think you were right."

"About?"

"Doesn't matter. Go. Keith's enjoying your company. Go do this with him."

"I will if you will."

Susie stared at the tree, the lights, some steady some flashing, at the decorations going up, the guys joking with each other, Ali pushing Stu away when he flirted. Everything was festive but her.

"What was I right about?"

"I can't talk about it now."

"Okay, then get your ass up and let's do this and when it's done, we can go talk at my place and leave the kids with Mike and Evan..."

"I can't just leave her with Evan when I decide. He's not her father."

"He wants to be, and I bet you can."

Susie pushed herself up and went to Nella, crouched to talk to her. The girl hugged her neck. At least Kate got her up and moving. She'd do better later.

Evan told Kate he expected it was because this was the first Christmas without him. She was fine the day before, had teased him the past few days. It had to be the group decorating and that Doug, Ali, and Stu would head up to New Hampshire as soon as they finished. They'd planned to go the next morning but with snow predicted overnight, they pushed it up. Susie wouldn't go to Pennsylvania, so they would celebrate at Doc's. She didn't seem enthused about that, either.

She was far more than unenthused today, though. Kate was right. He gladly offered to keep Nella and Keith after they said their goodbyes to the New Hampshire-bound part of the group. Mike had plans with Kelly. Evan told him he should have asked her over for the decorating party, but for Keith's sake, he decided to just be as much family as possible with Kate and their son.

As soon as Evan sat down, Nella crawled up on his lap. He smoothed her hair and she rested her head against his chest. "Are you tired, little one?"

She nodded.

Evan felt her forehead. It was normal. "Do you feel all right? No pain in your ear?"

"No. My mummy nae happy 'day. No. Bad, bad dream at night. I seep with her make her feel be'er."

He had to grin at the accent. A bad dream? And Nella noticed? He kissed her head. "I'm sure your mom was glad you slept with her. Did she feel better then?"

Nella nodded again and gripped his fingers. She played with them as her little body grew heavier against his and he waited until sure she was asleep to move her to the couch. Keith pulled a blanket over her. Evan gave him a smile and asked if he wanted to help start dinner. He would do lasagna tonight. It had been a while. And maybe a dessert of some kind chock full of sugar. He didn't have to eat it.

"So spill."

Susie shoved a hand through her hair and accepted the glass of wine as she slumped back into Kate's easy chair. "You remember ... back when we were still dating. Me and Duncan. When..." She bit her lip and took a swallow. "You were asking me about Evan and if I really..."

"You're falling for him again."

"What? No."

"No?"

"Kate..." She shook her head and took another swallow. "No. I... I still miss my husband so much I can hardly breathe at times. But..."

"But Evan has caught your eye recently." Kate swirled her wine glass with a cat-eating-the-canary grin. "You did say the other day he was kinda sexy."

"No. You did."

"I did?" She scrunched her mouth. "Oh, guess I did. Did it get to you? You're starting to see it again?"

"I've always seen it."

Kate smiled through a sip of wine.

"Forget it." Susie forced herself up.

"No, come on." Kate caught her before she got far. "Isn't that where this is going? Just trying to make it easier on you. You're bothered because you don't want it to go there. Am I right?"

Her head shook again. Susie felt it. She felt Kate pull her back and nudge her into the chair. Felt the cool sweet wine on her tongue, trickle down her throat. "You said you were worried about Duncan, because of me, that maybe I ... I shouldn't ... because I would hurt him..."

"Oh Suse, wow your memory is too good. Why are you bringing that up now? Just to say I told you so?"

"No. Maybe you were right." Her friend stared. Silent. Susie sipped more wine and set it down. "Kate, I should have looked for him. And I didn't. And I think ... maybe it's too late and I failed him, and I don't ... I don't deserve him to..."

"What? Are you insane? Does your wine have something in it mine doesn't?"

"I'm being serious."

"Then you are insane. Really, Suse, your dad may be right."

"Thank you." She got up again.

Kate stopped her again, eyeing her like ... like she thought Susie had lost it. Fully.

"I dreamed of him. In the water, frigid water, calling me to join him. And I didn't. Then he was gone, and..."

"It was just a nightmare. Don't make it more than that."

"It is more than that. I know it is. I..." How did she make Kate understand?

"No it's not. Suse, it's not. You just won't let yourself accept it and it's your own mind haunting you. Nothing more. It's nothing more than that. You have to let go."

"I still feel him."

"Of course you do, because you still love him. You will always feel him, but Suse, really, you have to tell yourself it's wishful thinking, that it's only your own mind telling you not to let go. Nothing more. You have to come out of this."

Her own mind. Was it? She felt her head try to shake again, felt cold shivers crawl up her spine. Was she doing it to herself? Either way, Kate was right. She couldn't do it to her daughter. She'd caught Nella eyeing her all morning, confused, or worried. What could she do now anyway?

With Kate's prompting, she sat again, picked up her glass, put it down and said she just wanted water. She had to clear her head. Kate told her to keep the rest of the wine and she'd get her water to go with it. As her friend went to the kitchen, Susie curled up into the chair and closed her eyes.

In the cold water beckoning to her. Evan wasn't sure Kate should have told him about the dream but she was worried. Nella mentioned her mom's dream that woke her up early this morning. Evan had tried to decide whether to ask Susie.

When he and the kids walked down to Kate's to see if they were ready to come up and eat, Susie had been asleep. For an hour, Kate said. He hated to wake her but he wanted her to eat with them. She'd wrapped her arms around his neck as she awoke. Held tight. Would she tell him about the dream if he asked? It spooked him already. *Beckoning to her.* Out in the cold water. He wasn't about to leave her alone overnight, not until he was convinced it was safe.

"I really need to get to bed." Susie sat up from where she'd been leaning against his shoulder. He didn't move. "Evan?"

"Yes. You should."

She chuckled. "Are you going home so I can?"

"I don't know."

"Lee, what is it? You've been quiet all night."

He nodded lightly. "You know ... you made me promise a long time ago that I would be here for you whenever you need."

Her stomach twisted. "Yes. Do you want out of that promise? Am I making it too hard? Is there ... somewhere else you want to be? You're not leaving the band...?"

He took her face in his hands and leaned close. "Shh, relax. No. To all of that. I don't want out of the promise. Not at all. I just think I neglected to ask the same of you. Maybe I only expected it. Maybe I've taken for granted you know I want the same. But I think I have to ask." His thumb caressed her cheek. "Suse, I know you're still struggling with this. All of it. And ... maybe it's unfair to ask you now, but ... no matter how mad you get at me, and I know you will again, probably often, but even so, I want you to promise the same, that you'll always be around. Not ... I'm not asking you to stay where I am or to stay here. I want you to do what you need, or go where you need, but ... just be around. Promise me."

Be around? Was he kidding? She felt herself nod. "You are my anchor, you know. You always have been. If you ever need that from me, I will do my best. I promise."

His eyes moistened. "Oh Angel, you think you aren't already? You are. Remember that. Whatever happens, and whatever ... just ... remember that. I need you here. At least close enough to talk, to hear your voice."

"Lee." She moved in and held him. "Don't worry. I'm not going anywhere, never far enough I can't find you."

25 December

Susie slid Danielle's now opened Christmas gifts under the tree so she could find them again in the morning and gathered bits of torn paper. She looked over at a soft knock on the door. After nine-thirty. It had to be Evan. Her dad had left not long ago. Dumping the paper in the garbage, she went and checked first, although she knew she didn't need to check.

"You weren't getting ready for bed?"

"No, cleaning up. Come in." She left him to close the door and continued to gather garbage and clutter until satisfied it was good enough for the night and sank onto the love seat.

Evan sat adjacent to her on the couch. "I have something for you."

"You already gave me something: something incredible by the way. I told you that, right? That it's incredible?" He'd given her a copy of Chicago's newest LP, *Hot Streets*, signed by several band members. With Adam's help, he said.

"You did, and I'm glad you like it. That was for Christmas. This is just ... because you need to have it. I've been debating whether or not I should give it to you today but since today's nearly over..." He handed her a 45. It had Adam's studio label on it and was printed with a song title: *Intervolve (July 1978), E. Scott/D. McGuire.* "You said you wanted it so we recorded it for you. He meant to give it to you after he mastered it, but since he didn't get that far, I asked Ken."

The duet. The one Evan had written, with Duncan's help on the music, that they sang together. She'd forgotten. It was so beautiful. She'd been so struck by it that it brought her to tears the first time she listened. It did again as she remembered.

"Maybe I shouldn't have done this today."

Susie went to his side and hugged him close. "Thank you. Yes. This

... this is incredible. You made my whole day. It's been hard, without ... watching Nella..." She held him a while longer then got up to put it in the stereo. She had to hear it, even if it made her cry all the way through.

> *In between my skin and your breath*
> *a chasm quakes, and aches to be*
> *relieved. Are we*
> *couriers only, or does the message belong to us;*
> *trapped within doubts and sighs.*
> *Our lives belie*
> *their thoughts, beliefs that we*
> *must not intervolve, must wait, must tie*
> *the strings too tight to move, to grow.*
> *They can not know what we are, what is true;*
> *how we wind around what is us*
> *Separate, yet entwined still*
> *We will...*

When it ended, she put it back in its paper jacket and returned to him, leaned against his arm, dried her eyes. "You should write more often. It is incredible, Lee. You should keep writing."

He kissed the side of her head and asked if she wanted to find something to watch until bed time. She settled beside him with *It's A Wonderful Life*.

27 December

Her in-laws would be there soon. Stu, Doug, and Ali would be home the following evening. Mike and Kate were wrestling the kids in the back yard, in the snow, with Beau and Clemens at watch. Susie was at a loss as to what to do with herself. She'd thought about playing in the snow with the kids but she wasn't sure a virus wasn't trying to start and she didn't want to risk it. Probably she was only tired. She and Evan had worked out the day before and she pushed too much. It was only achiness from the strain.

And she was restless. She supposed she could answer more fan mail or at least sort more of it, but she didn't have much interest. Adam told her it was still Christmas break and she should take it, also. A break from what, she'd asked? They weren't doing much. Neither was she. It was starting to drive her crazy.

As she wandered the apartment, she thought of things she could do: pull curtains down to wash, wash Nella's walls again or straighten her drawers again, clear out old clothes she hadn't worn in ages to donate, file her own paperwork that sat in a plastic box until she decided to do it. None of the thoughts appealed to her in the slightest. Finding herself in the guest room/music room, she rubbed her fingers down the Mustang's strings. She should ask Evan to tune it again, to play it a bit, so it didn't just sit there. Or she could. Maybe she could. Evan had taught her some time back. But she didn't dare. The Strat, maybe, or the Telecaster. She could try with those. If she snapped a string, she'd just have Evan fix it. Not with the Mustang. She didn't dare. The most she dared was to keep it dusted for him.

The old acoustic Evan used to play also rested against its stand. He'd left it for her to play with if she wanted, or for her to let Nella play with. He'd never played it often; the sound wasn't good enough or at least right enough for his own taste.

Susie picked it up and sat on the edge of the bed, pulled a leg up to support it. The thing felt huge to her. It fit him. It was normal size for an acoustic, but she wasn't particularly normal sized. He'd said they could get a 3/4 size student guitar. Maybe she would, for Nella. It would be easier for her daughter to play with.

Trying to adjust it to the right position, she strummed a pick over the strings. It was way off. She grabbed the tuner.

It didn't take long to get frustrated and she set it aside, then picked it up again and went over to Evan's. Susie didn't bother to knock and then thought she should have, in case he had company, but she didn't think he was dating. He was on the couch, a book in hand, one leg crossed atop the other. "Interrupting?"

He put the bookmark in and closed it. "Nothing that won't wait."

"Want to tune this for me? I know, you've showed me how and I tried but I think I made it worse."

With a grin, he accepted it and grabbed his own tuner. He made it look easy and she supposed it should be. He said it was largely a matter of patience. That would explain it, Susie guessed. She didn't have any today. He played part of one of their songs to check it, adjusted again, and repeated the phrases. And handed it back.

"Thank you, although I don't know why I bother. I mess with it once and let it sit until it needs to be tuned again."

"So try messing with it just a little more often."

"I'm not doing anything but..."

"Keeping your hands busy. I know." He moved a pillow so she could sit next to him.

"Well, my brain, anyway." She set it beside her propped against the couch. "Actually ... you're sure I'm not interrupting?"

"I'm sure. Did you want me to help you learn more chords?"

"No. Maybe. Not... Lee, have you ever ... felt something inside so deeply that you knew was right, really right, so much so that it consumes every part of you and affects everything you do, everything you think, and ... still think you could be wrong? I mean, you don't think you're wrong but ... others say you are and you know better but maybe you are wrong and you just can't accept it because it feels too real, too ... too right. Am I making sense?"

"Yes." He took her hand.

"Really? Have you?"

His eyes held hers, softly, seriously. "Yes." His voice was also soft. He wasn't laughing at her, doubting her.

"So ... did you just let it go? Because I ... I can't and yet ... I guess I'm not sure I'm not ... that Dad isn't right and I don't have a true grasp of..."

"Angel." He slid a hand aside her face. "Your dad is only worried you'll do what he did, that you'll let yourself keep hurting as long as he did, and he doesn't want you to do that. But you know what? You're stronger than that."

She snickered. "Right."

"You are. And I know you won't. I know part of you will hurt forever and part of you will never let go of ... that thing that feels so deeply right to you. Or maybe you will eventually. But until then, you are going to go on and do what you need to do and let it out when you need to let it out, which you should, and between those times, you'll learn to be happy again, to feel actual joy again."

She felt her head shake.

"You will, Suse. I know you don't now, even when you look to others as though you're fine, I know. And it's okay. Your dad ... he never let it out. I don't think he has yet. Some day he'll have to. Maybe when he meets the right woman and feels more secure again..."

"Secure? Dad has always felt secure. He's..."

"No, he doesn't. There are too many things he thinks he did wrong and he won't let himself get over it. That's why he's so protective of you. He looks like he is and he means to look like he is, but generally, those who always look together are the least fully together."

"Oh, but... You do. You're always ... you always look together."

He dropped his eyes, and his head.

"Lee." Susie raised his face with her fingers. He hadn't shaved. She felt the stubble prick her skin, similar to the cold wet sand on her feet that had felt like glass, pricking at her. She pulled herself out of the dream, as she had so many times since. "What did you do about the thing of yours? The one you felt so deeply?"

He grasped her hand and pulled it away from his face, then kissed her fingers. "It's still there, Suse. My guess is it always will be, and that's all right, because I'd rather have it than ... to not have it."

Have what? She tried to decide if she should ask. "Is it worth it? If it turns out you find you were wrong, will it have been worth it?"

His eyes moistened but he held her gaze. "Yes. But someday, I might make myself let it go, if I decide it's not worth it. It can't be up to anyone else. You're the only one who can decide when it's time to let go. You have good instincts, Suse. Trust them."

Did she? At the moment, her instinct was to hold him in, make him tell her what he felt so deeply he couldn't let go. And kiss him. His lips pulled at her. And his warm, hard, sturdy body. He pulled at her. No, her instincts weren't all that good, apparently, because she still believed Duncan was coming home. She did. It was too deep inside not to believe it. And yet Evan pulled at her.

She slid her hand around to the back of his neck and held him. "Do you want to tell me? About that thing you can't let go?"

He caressed her back. "No. Maybe someday I will. Not now."

"Lee, you know you don't always have to be together for me, right?"

He pulled back and gave her a grin. "And I haven't been."

Damn, he wanted to tell her. But he knew what hers was. Duncan coming home. He knew she was still fighting against the thought that he wouldn't. When she gave up that fight, it would be time to tell her.

Instead, he grabbed the guitar and played a couple of phrases from one of their easier songs, a four chord song, and showed her how.

31 December

Susie and Laura laughed at Stu and Danny as they competed with each other on the weight bench. Mike's youngest sister, Rosemary, who preferred to go by Rose, had come back from New Hampshire with Stu in the guise of seeing her nephew since Mike refused to go up there. She'd spent very little time with Keith that Evan had seen. Even now, she was gawking at Stu, cheering him on, although it was obvious he couldn't match Danny's strength. Danny was closing in on his brother's strength as he got older and likely worked at it. Amy was there, also. She spent more time with Laura than with Danny.

Stu kept avoiding Rosemary's advances although Mike teased him that he shouldn't bother to avoid her.

Doug's family had come and Ali's family was there. Doug's sister had sought Evan out much of the day so far. Stu said he was just as glad his family wasn't there, since he'd had enough of them over Christmas, and New Year's was a friends holiday, not a family holiday. Evan had to inwardly argue that one. John and Valerie were there and his mom and Doc. They had a good crowd, largely family.

The band had booked a local hotel to accommodate all of their visitors so no one would have to drive after midnight. They had a banquet room but also wandered between the adjacent pool and weight room. It was far nicer than their usual routine of spending New Year's Eve in their basement.

Susie wouldn't swim. Still. She let Nella get in with whoever volunteered to stay with her, often Mike and Kelly, and she kept an eye on her. Evan didn't have much interest in swimming with such a crowd around, either. He convinced himself that was her reason, that she wouldn't completely give it up only because it was such an intimate thing she shared with Duncan.

After a buffet dinner when the alcohol started to flow, they put the pool off limits to themselves and let the hotel management know it was open for other guests and they'd be in their banquet room. They had few guards there and their guards had been invited to bring their dates.

Adam and Robin stopped in for dinner and to give their greetings to everyone and left for other commitments. Chief Carr and his wife stopped in after dinner. He didn't like to be out on New Year's, he said, because of all the drunk drivers he knew very well would be out there and stopped by his men. He'd made an exception but wouldn't stay long, with a quick thanks for having the brains to book rooms for their guests to make it easier on his officers.

John and Valerie and Evan's mom and Doc weren't staying at the hotel overnight, but John wasn't drinking so he would drive them all home. Evan knew he would have a small glass of Champaign at midnight and be more than happy with that.

Susie, however, was allowing herself to bypass her wine in favor of rum and Coke. She only sipped at it, still fully on mom duty, but Evan half hoped he'd get to see her even close to as "charming" as Stu and Ali both said she was when she drank more than normal. He would help watch over Nella, not that everyone in the room wasn't watching over both kids.

"No, Danny, I've had enough." Susie tried to keep him from adding more rum to her glass.

"It is a party, Sis. Relax and enjoy yourself."

"I have to watch Nella."

"Nae you donae. Your father is doing that well enough, aye? I think he is showin' off for his new girlfriend. She is nice, yes? Y' like her alright?"

"Yes, I like her well enough." Susie sipped at the drink and nearly coughed. Too much rum. Not enough cola.

Danny eyed her and sat close, close enough Susie had to nudge over. "Y' arenae sure you do?"

"Oh, yes she's fine. Dad's happy and from what I've seen, she treats him well. It's fine."

"Y' donae like tha' he is dating?"

"No, I'm glad he is. Really."

"Wha' is it then? I see something is botherin' you."

"She's a psychologist."

"Yea' and so?"

"So ... I guess I'm not sure if... It makes me wary of what I say or do around her."

Danny laughed and wrapped an arm over her shoulder. "Ach, y' worry too much, y' ken. She thinks y' are a pure beau'iful soul from wha' she was sayin' to me." He squeezed lightly. "And she woul' be right. So stop your worryin' and le' it be as it is. Look a' your mate over there." He nodded to where Stu danced with Rosemary. "He woul' shag the barber's flair."

"The what? And no he won't, not with her."

"Nae? She is..."

"Yes, but he won't. And what was the rest of that? Shagging, I know..."

Danny nearly spit out the swallow of his rum.

"That's not what I meant."

Between his laughing, he nodded. "Right, bu' it fuckin' brilliant."

"Okay, thank you. Never mind." She started to get up.

"Nae, come Sis. I am only playin'. It means he isnae particular an' any type will do."

"Oh. But ... what is a barber's flair?"

He raised his eyebrows. "The flair in a barber's shop, aye, and wha' else woul' it be?"

"Danny, okay, but what it is a flair?"

He laughed again and sniffed at her glass. "I 'ave gi'en y' too much, aye? A flair, luv. Flair, as y' walk on." He tapped his foot on the floor.

"Floor?"

"Aye, a flair, as I said."

"Okay, I officially feel like an idiot." Susie rolled her eyes and took another sip of her drink. "And that's a disgusting analogy."

He laughed again. "We 'ave more work t' do t' turn y' into a true Scot, I see. Are y' goin' t' come over an' give us the chance?"

"So my daughter will learn to talk like that?"

"Aye and of course. She is a true bonny Sco'ish lassie. An' so she should, y' ken." He nudged her arm. "Donae worry, Sis. Laurie understands it well, bu' she doesnae use it 'erself. She is far more upstandin' than I 'ave been ever, and so Nella bird will be. I donae talk so in front o' her." He nodded back at Stu. "She isnae like any of the others I 'ave met or heard of. It is all I meant."

"No, and she's not his type. She's like Mike except his snippiness sounds more bitchy from her. Otherwise, she seems okay, but he's only giving her a nice New Year's Eve since she's here. Nothing more."

"Y' are sure?"

"Yes. She's Mike's sister. She's off limits."

"Right, and does Evan 'ave the same code?"

Evan? "Why?"

"I am only wonderin'."

Susie found where Evan was. Talking with Marilyn again, Doug's sister. She'd been on top of him all night. "He's not interested in her." Even if she was blonde. And smart. Quiet. Probably easy to deal with. She set a hand on Danny's back and got up. It was time to reclaim her friend for a while. Marilyn could talk to someone else.

Evan smiled at her approach. He couldn't resist. She looked like she was on a mission. She asked Marilyn if she was enjoying the party and talked about Doug's engagement and how happy she was for him and as she talked, she sipped at her drink and edged closer to Evan.

Marilyn wanted her to leave again. He could see it. But Evan didn't. Susie had spent more time talking with everyone else than with him. Of course he was always around. It was fair enough, as Duncan would say. Still, it was New Year's Eve and he wanted to spend at least part of it with her.

As she looked like she might give in and walk away, he set a hand on her back. "Danny is taking care of you, I see."

She rolled her eyes. "Too much. And he made this too strong. Want to share?"

He didn't, but he couldn't resist the offer. He cringed at the sweetness.

"Oh. I'm sorry. It's rum, not whiskey. I forgot." She reclaimed it.

"And it's strong."

"Yeah. When I get it low enough, I'll add more cola."

"Dump it, Suse."

"No, I don't want to waste it. It's..."

He reclaimed the glass and took a couple of good swallows. "Now there's room for Coke."

She chuckled and Marilyn excused herself. She didn't drink At all. She'd made sure to tell him how she disapproved of it. He figured she might as well know it wouldn't work to convince him he shouldn't drink.

"Exactly the right way to handle her, Evan." Doug stepped up beside him. "Wondered if I should rescue you, but you took care of it fine. Did she give you the alcohol lecture?"

"To an extent. Not a big deal." He explained about Danny's version of Rum and Coke.

Doug laughed. "Yes, he bought me a drink, as well. He's brought Stu several. Life of the party tonight, your brother in law."

"And I bet he'll feel it tomorrow." Susie shook her head. "Let me go fix this."

"I'll get it." Doug took it from her. "You had the nerve to rescue him sooner than I did since I've had a few drinks tonight and she knows it. Least I can do."

As he left, Susie took Evan's hand. "Want to dance since we're both free for the moment?"

"Of course." He walked with her to where there was empty space. One of their guards doubled as a deejay, a side job he did, so he said, and he had good taste in music, or someone guided his taste. He focused heavily on the current year's music, to include several songs from *Grease* plus The Cars, Eddie Money, Leif Garrett, Queen, Tom Petty, Styx, Lynyrd Skynyrd, Van Halen, even Randy Newman's *Short People*, The Village People's *Macho Man* and Steve Martin's *King Tut*, all of which Nella and Keith just loved. Currently it was Cheap Trick's *Surrender*. And she sang a bit of it.

Evan figured Danny's drinks were getting to her. She was relaxed against him, her arms against his side with her hands up around the backs of his shoulders. She was charming; even without help she was charming. He was glad she was in his arms, even if only for a dance. And he enjoyed the way she looked at him, different than the way she looked at anyone else in the world, more open, trusting. Not that she wasn't open and trusting with others, with a very few others, but still, it was different.

"What?" A touch of amusement lit her face.

"Nothing."

"No, come on. You're thinking about something pretty hard. Tell me. You know I'll badger you until you give in."

He grinned, stalling, teasing, enjoying the sparkle in her eyes that wasn't often there anymore. "You don't want me to tell you."

"Hm. I think I do, since you look so pleased with yourself."

"Do I?"

She tilted her head, eyebrows raised.

"Okay, but don't say I didn't warn you. I was just thinking how beautiful you look tonight. Of course you always do, but tonight there's ... something more. I can't say what it is..."

"Too much rum."

He chuckled. "Oh I don't know. I think you're fine. And you're surrounded by friends so it's safe."

"I always know I'm safe when I'm with you." She held his gaze, asking if he remembered. Back before she started to date Duncan, at the club, where she bailed Kate out of a potential jam by putting herself in the line of fire. When he complained that she did, she told him she knew she was always safe when he was around.

He gave her a nod. "Always. And I'm glad I get to be one of the very few you can feel so safe with. Also, you seem..." He wasn't sure how to put it without bringing up anything to change her mood. He shrugged. "I'm enjoying being with you, as always. And you are terribly beautiful tonight." He glanced down at the shimmery gray top over her black pants, soft flowing pants that accented her graceful movements. "Danny may be the life of the party, but you're the shining star of it."

She started to answer and then stopped.

"I did say you didn't want me to tell you."

She gave him a grin, then moved closer. "Tell me you'll be here every New Year's Eve. This is kind of our holiday, isn't it? Considering everything? If ... for some reason in the future we aren't still living so close together, tell me you'll at least come back for New Year's or let me visit you. I can't imagine starting the year without you. I'm not sure how I'd manage."

He wanted to kiss her. Suddenly and passionately, he wanted to kiss her. He wouldn't. That couldn't happen.

"Lee?" Her eyes searched his.

"Yes." He allowed his thumb to caress her back. "Every year."

She set her head against his chest and shoulder. He had to be careful. His feelings were too intense. He couldn't allow them in his expression for anyone to see. *Our holiday*. She hadn't forgotten the kiss a couple of years before on New Year's Eve that had been only a dare but felt like more, that her husband had laughed about as though it was nothing. Because it was. To Susie, it was ... friendship, safety. To him it was more. But it couldn't be. Her husband wasn't concerned about it because he trusted her. He trusted them both. Even if he was gone, he was still her husband. Still Evan's best friend other than Susie. He would look after her, for the sake of Duncan's friendship, as he'd asked, and be her best friend, as she needed. And he would be her dance partner when she wanted. But she was Duncan's wife.

It sunk in that the song had changed. Exile. *Kiss You All Over.* About the last thing they should be dancing to, he figured.

"I think it's my turn." Doug set a hand on his arm. "Mind switching?"

"Not at all." Evan released Susie to Doug and accepted Ali's hand.

Kate leaned over Susie's shoulder with a hug. "Hey, I made it." With a quick greeting to her dad and Susie's dad and Diane and Doc and Gene and Linda, Kate asked if Susie would follow her.

"Where?"

"Just over here. I brought my date..."

"So bring him over. I just sat down and..."

"Um, I brought a date for you, also. Still want me to bring them over here?"

A date? "No. Keep them to yourself if you don't mind." Susie turned back and sipped her drink. "Your son is over there, by the way."

"Already talked to him. Come on, Suse, this guy is really cute and it's New Year's. You should have a date."

"I don't want a date. I told you."

A very tall very muscular man pressed in beside Kate and extended a hand. "I'm Max Revere, no relation to Paul that I know of. And you're Susie McGuire. It's nice to finally meet you."

Forward guy for someone Kate was only dating at the moment, but he fully looked her type. Very fit. Handsome. Well dressed. When Kate nudged her, Susie accepted the handshake. "And you. Have you two been dating long?" It was a hint and her friend would know it was.

"No, we're not dating." The guy smiled as though it was a joke. "Her date is a friend of mine." He nodded several feet away. That one Susie somewhat recognized. "I hope it's all right, but I invited myself when I heard where their next stop would be. I've wanted to meet you for some time."

Kate shrugged. "He's the one I mentioned, Suse." She introduced Max to the table of parents.

Susie got up and walked away. Or she tried. Kate caught her. With Max on her heels. When she stood, the guy's height was even more emphasized. She didn't even reach his shoulder. He was built like ... like a skyscraper. And he was intruding.

Journey came on. *Anytime.* The one she and Duncan danced to the night before he left. She realized she'd left her drink on the table and walked away from whatever the guy was saying to grab it, then she veered toward Evan. Sipping it on the way over, she interrupted his conversation with Laura and Amy. "I need you to be my date tonight since I'm *supposed to* have one."

He set a hand on her back. "What's wrong, Suse?"

She told him, pointed the guy out.

Laura's jaw dropped. "If you donae want him, I will take him."

"Want to say hello?" Susie took another swallow, for courage. "Come on. He can be your date. Kate says he's very sweet, well-mannered, smart, has a good job. Believe me, I've heard all about it."

"Gud enough for me. Y' are sure y' donae want t' at least dance with him? Give 'im a chance?"

"I'm sure I don't." And they were surrounded by friends and family. Laura would be safe enough talking to skyscraper Max. She didn't have to ask Evan to walk over with them. He followed. So did Amy, which brought Danny over. Susie introduced them all as she ignored Kate's glare.

The song was half over. She turned to Evan. "Dance with me. This is ... it's..."

He nodded, took her glass to set on a nearby table, and led her away from Mr. Skyscraper.

She felt part numb. Relaxed. Even through being thoroughly pissed off at Kate. As *Anytime* faded into *Time For Me To Fly*, Susie pressed closer to Evan and sang with it. She loved the song. She loved the whole album by REO Speedwagon. Screw Kate. She was dancing with her best friend to some of her favorite music. It didn't matter what Kate did.

Evan grinned at her when she stopped singing and told her to keep going. She did. And she realized others were closing in on them. Listening. It didn't matter. She loved the song.

Laura was dancing with Max. Kate had her date out there. Others were around. It didn't matter. She sang to Evan, as she used to, before any of the others even knew her. He was there. He was still there.

Evan held her well enough to keep her from stumbling. She was nearly out of it. Her body drooped against his.

Max whatever-his-name-was had switched with Stu and now danced with Mike's sister. Evan thought it was a better match, although the guy kept looking at Susie. She paid no attention to him. He finally let himself be captivated by his dance partner and they stole over to the bar. Stu looked relieved. Laura looked annoyed, but only until Stu joked her out of it.

When the first strains of Meatloaf's *Paradise By The Dashboard Light* started, Stu pulled Laura over and insisted on switching partners. Susie hesitated as she gripped Evan's shirt.

"Hey come on, I know you know the words to the girl's part on this. My turn. I've left you alone most of the night." Stu pulled at her.

She gave in. The way she moved, maybe she wasn't that out of it. Stu sang it to her. Evan was happy to dance with Laura beside them, to listen, to keep an eye on Susie. Danny and Amy moved beside them, also, amused by Stu's singing, or by the song. Evan knew it well enough to know the female lead's part was incredible. He had to wonder if Susie would actually do it. Normally, she wouldn't, but normally, she also wouldn't have sung the whole REO song to him, or not to him, exactly, but because he asked.

Stu urged her on as it came up. *"Let's sleep on it, I'll give you my answer in the morning..."*

She sang it. He and Laura stopped dancing to listen. So did Danny and Amy, and a few others moved closer. Exquisite. Even though she was looking at Stu, teasing, flirting, Evan was ... too fully turned on.

Until Gene took his side, with Linda. "It has been a long time since we heard her sing." His voice was soft.

Evan nodded but he couldn't take his eyes from her. She caught him staring and smiled between flirting with Stu. As the song faded, Gene tapped him on the shoulder, still quiet. "It is early still, bu' when the time comes, we will nae disapprove. Be careful for a time yet." With a nod, Gene took his wife in his arms to dance. *Dance With Me.* Evan couldn't remember the singer's name. But he reclaimed Susie, brought her back into his arms.

They wouldn't disapprove. If Duncan's parents wouldn't, it didn't matter much who would.

As it closed in on midnight, Susie wished to go up to her room away from the crowd, get Nella in bed, and sit and watch the festivities on television. Alone. Since she didn't have her husband there. She couldn't do it to his family, to the guys, so she focused on Danielle and Keith and talked to whoever approached her, and tried not to dread the stroke of midnight when she wouldn't have that New Year's kiss. Her mind wouldn't quit replaying the last four years when she'd been in her husband's arms and felt his lips, always starting before midnight, always so wrapped in each other she barely heard the catcalls that came with the end of the countdown.

Her head was starting to clear. She'd switched to ginger ale after her dance/duet with Stu. Skyscraper Max was content enough with the Kean girl – why couldn't Susie think of her name? – and had left her alone. She'd been rude, of course, and there was every chance the guy would tell others she was, but it didn't matter. That was a whole heck of a lot better than if she'd given in to the "date" and then he'd talked about it. She'd rather he say how badly she snubbed him.

She tried to pay no attention to Kate and her date or Mike and his, and kept Keith away from wherever they were and distracted him. Her dad told her to go on and have a good time and he'd keep up with the kids. Susie told him she'd had enough of a good time and it was his turn. She told Valerie to get him out to dance.

"Hey." Stu pushed up against her. "Do I get a kiss at New Year's?"

"No. And I'm not taking dares, either, so don't bother."

He laughed, gave her a hug and told her Happy New Year early. And some girl pulled him away. One who'd been working in their room earlier? Susie wouldn't be surprised.

She had Danielle and would give her daughter a kiss to celebrate the new year she didn't feel much like celebrating. Nineteen seventy-nine. The last year of the decade. It made her start to feel her age since it would be the fourth decade she'd seen. Not that she remembered anything of the fifties, being born in the middle of it, but the sixties were a time of living at Diane's house, losing her mom, rarely seeing her dad because of his job, and losing Jeremy. Not a wonderful decade for her. The Seventies had brought more promise, more adventure, her marriage and her daughter, the band's rise ... and a bigger loss than she ever could have imagined. The Eighties. She didn't want to even guess what would arise in the Eighties.

Music was changing so fast. Disco had taken over and she liked some of it okay, but Raucous could have trouble if it kept going that direction, especially if they didn't pick up speed again. They could already be on the wane, which would also be a devastating loss. It would happen, of course, but she had hoped for several years, several really good years of headlining. She believed the short-lived punk era was already on the decline, and that was okay with her. It was too negative, as she and Duncan talked about, although she understood the underlying intentions. They'd taken a good idea and driven it into the ground. It would leave its effect though, as did all new genres.

"It's nearly midnight." Evan handed Nella and Keith small plastic cups of what she figured was sparkling cider. And he handed Susie a small glass of wine. The kids were both nearly asleep. *Auld Lang Syne* began. Nella crawled onto her lap as Susie steadied the little cup and Evan picked Keith up onto his. He sat close to her. And he offered to keep Nella in his room since Keith would be there anyway, so Susie could sleep in past whenever the girl would wake up. They had adjoining rooms. Evan had arranged it that way.

Susie refused the offer with thanks. "I don't want to be quite that alone tonight."

"You aren't."

"Oh. I mean... I know. Thank you." With her attention on the countdown, she waited ... just for it to be over with so she could go to bed.

At twelve, she gave her baby a hug and kiss and the four of them toasted each other with light bumps of their glasses. She leaned in to give Keith a hug and kiss, as well. Then she watched the couples and families celebrate with each other, the toasts and hugs and smiles and cheers. She'd never seen it all before. She'd been busy with her own celebration. It was nice, she supposed.

"Happy New Year, Angel." Evan leaned in to kiss the side of her head. She accepted a hug around the kids. And met his lips. Briefly. Only as she had the other year for the dare. He didn't look quite as surprised as she expected and she held on with her head against his shoulder. Yes, it was their holiday. He was still there with her. He deserved to know just how much she appreciated it.

Evan tapped on the door that adjoined their rooms. Keith had fallen right to sleep, nearly as soon as his little head hit the pillow, and Mike thanked Evan for letting him stay as he led Kelly out to their room. Evan could easily see Mike and Kelly as a permanent thing.

Susie gave him a questioning look as she opened the door. She was already changed into her T-shirt and short leggings.

"Just wanted to check to see if Nella went to bed for you all right."

"Yes. She's out. Didn't take long."

"Good." Evan wanted to say more but he wasn't sure what he wanted to say that he could let himself say. "Sleep well, Angel. If she's up too early, send her over to me."

"Evan..." She held the door with one hand, as he was doing with his, and gave him a soft hug. "You have a good year ahead, okay?"

"Are you telling me that for a reason? You're not going anywhere?"

"No." She raised her head, but stayed close. "I only mean ... Nella and I will be fine. We are fine. I want you to make this a good year, as far as ... putting yourself first. Next year on the 31st, you should have a real date, someone who could maybe give you everything you deserve to have. Don't let us interfere with that."

Interfere? He allowed a deep breath to give him time to think how to respond. "I have a feeling it could work out that way."

She bit her lip and released it. "You're ready?"

"Pretty close to ready." He wanted to kiss her, to give her a hint as to how he expected it might work out.

"Good." She set a hand on his chest. "Just make sure I approve or at least that I can get along with her, because..."

"Because it matters."

"Yes."

"Yes." He kissed the side of her face. Slowly. Lingering. "Don't ever worry about that. I'll be here."

She nodded. "Good night, Lee."

He told her the same and she stepped back to let the door start to close and then stopped and held it open. Bit her lip again. "Here. Hold on." Evan motioned for her to hold his door and grabbed a chair to prop the thing open, then went into her room and did the same with her door. "Just so you don't feel too alone tonight. Shut yours for privacy if you'd rather. I'll leave mine open."

She wrapped her arms over his shoulders with a hand on the back of his neck. She stood on her toes to reach better. Why Kate brought six-foot-something Max-someone as her date, Evan couldn't fathom. Susie would never date anyone a foot taller than she was. It would feel intimidating to her, even if he was the gentlest man on the planet. She wouldn't do it. Her best girlfriend should know her better.

Evan knew he was distracting himself from the way her body pressed against his, the way she cuddled in so close, the way she smelled like ... a new perfume he didn't recognize. It was nice. Light. Barely there. Not floral. Not citrus. Sensual; it had a more sensual essence than most of what she wore. Or it was his own mood that made him think so. He wanted to kiss her, fully, on the lips, the way she had that night of the storm. He wanted to move his hands to her small waist, up her sides, feel her dancer's curves. She had such beautiful curves.

And yet, she'd told him she wouldn't interfere, to go out and find someone. He would. Temporarily. To distract himself. But only until she was ready for him.

The way she held him, the way she'd kissed him during the storm, the way she always sought him out for comfort regardless of how many others were around she trusted, the way she teased and occasionally touched his eyes with her soft gaze ... he knew. She would be ready for him.

They'd been writing the stanzas of their song for years. Soon it would be time for the chorus.

A Laugh Away From A Tear
Phillip Hartsock

When your emotions… stir in the wind
Like the cold hard rain… comin' down again
They call you in the night… like a long lost friend
When you've been… through it all
Heaven and Hell… the Hangman's ball
You can feel it…when your back's against the wall

Chorus

If you're a laugh away… from a tear
A step away… from the edge of the clear
Get yourself straight… or you just might lose it all
Don't look back… over your shoulder
Look in the mirror and see that you're older
You can do this… bring it on… one and all

Harmonica lead

I'm a laugh away… from a tear
A step away… from my darkest fear
But there's a blue sky up ahead… I can see it all
Whatever you do… don't get in my way
Cause if you do… there'll be hell to pay
My day 's comin'… I can see it all

Chorus

About The Author

LK Hunsaker is the author of a string of intertwined novels centered around the arts and societal issues, combined with strong romantic elements. Spouse of a career soldier, she has traveled widely, moved several times, raised two children, and earned degrees in psychology and art. Her short stories, poems, articles, and book reviews have been published in literary ezines and print magazines. She is now settled in western Pennsylvania.

LKHunsaker.com

www.ingramcontent.com/pod-product-compliance
Lightning Source LLC
Chambersburg PA
CBHW020512110726
47899CB00004B/1087